DANGEROUS FIND

The darkness absorbed all but a sliver of light from their flashlights. Fish swirled around them and up along the underwater ravine's walls.

A pillar of rock loomed in their path. Tanner played his beam over it, saw nothing unusual, and kept going. He stopped suddenly, backpedaled, and finned closer to the rock. Something was there, a dull glint in the stone. Using his knife, he chiseled at the rock until he'd cleared away a patch.

Heart pounding, he waved Cahil over and gestured for him to hover beside the rock. *What for?* Bear mouthed.

Scale. Just do it.

Tanner backpedaled and looked again. There was no mistake.

This was no rock.

It was a propeller.

THE END OF ENEMIES

Grant Blackwood

BERKLEY BOOKS, NEW YORK

THE END OF ENEMIES

A Berkley Book / published by arrangement with the author

PRINTING HISTORY
Berkley edition / May 2001

All rights reserved.
Copyright © 2001 by Grant Blackwood

This book, or parts thereof, may not be reproduced in any form without permission.
For information address: The Berkley Publishing Group,
a division of Penguin Putnam Inc.,
375 Hudson Street, New York, New York 10014.

The Penguin Putnam Inc. World Wide Web site address is
http://www.penguinputnam.com

ISBN: 0-425-17956-7

BERKLEY®
Berkley Books are published by The Berkley Publishing Group,
a division of Penguin Putnam Inc.,
375 Hudson Street, New York, New York 10014.
BERKLEY and the "B" design
are trademarks belonging to Penguin Putnam Inc.

PRINTED IN THE UNITED STATES OF AMERICA

10 9 8 7 6 5 4 3 2 1

This book is dedicated to the one who was always there. Thanks for not only believing in me, but also for always finding a way to keep me going.

ACKNOWLEDGMENTS

While writing is by nature a solitary endeavor, no book comes fully to life without help from others.

My heartfelt thanks to the following people:

My parents, Robert Perry Blackwood and Kathryn Irene Blackwood. Without them none of this would be possible.

My sister, Roberta, for being first to say, "You know, you should be a . . ." and for her unconditional love and support.

Julie, for being the woman I thought I would never find, but did. I'm so glad you're in my life. Dick and Jackie Robinson for taking me into their lives and hearts. You've helped make me a better person.

All my friends who never doubted. It's been said that a true friend celebrates your successes as heartily as they do their own.

Nancy Beckes and Elizabeth Katzman, for their compassion and perspective.

Clive Cussler, whose novels helped create the spark.

J. C., who pointed me in the right direction.

And finally, to the people who were instrumental in making this long-held dream come true:

Jonathon Lazear, Christi Cardenas (for her saintly patience, humor, and unwavering optimism), Neil Ross, and all the folks at The Lazear Agency, who worked so hard on my behalf. You were worth the wait. I'm glad you're on my team!

Tom Colgan, my editor at Penguin Putnam Inc./Berkley. You, too, were worth the wait. A finer editorial deity does not exist.

Thanks also to all the folks at Penguin Putnam Inc./Berkley who helped make this book the best it can be—from the copyeditors, to the typesetters, to the art department, and everyone in between.

PROLOGUE

STONEFISH WAS ONE DAY NORTH OF THE VOLCANO ISLANDS WHEN Captain Hugh Carpen paged his new executive officer to the conning tower. Having only been aboard a week, Ensign William Myers was still adjusting to life aboard the sub, so it was ten minutes before he appeared, breathless and flustered, in the con. Carpen waved him over to the chart table.

"Sorry, Skipper. I got turned around. You wouldn't think that—"

"Don't worry about it. Takes some getting used to."

"Yes, sir."

"New orders, Billy." Carpen tapped the chart. "That's our first way point. I'll give out the rest when we get there. Till then, it stays between you and me."

Myers peered at the chart. "Jesus, Skipper, that's—"

"Yep. Listen, rumors are going to start. I expect you to keep 'em under control. I don't like keeping the boys in the dark, but that's the deal."

"Aye, sir."

"Two more things. Put the word out: We're bypassing all targets this patrol. Log 'em, run a firing plan, but steer clear of them. Second, our guest—"

"The fella in forward torp?"

"Right. He'll be staying there for the duration. From now on, it's off-limits to everyone. That means *everyone,* got it?"

Myers simply nodded. As XO, it was his job to make the skipper's word law, but Myers felt far out of his depth. Less than a week aboard *Stonefish* and here he was, headed into God knew what. But then again, he consoled himself, this is what he signed up for, wasn't it? "Yes, sir," he said.

TWO DAYS LATER, CARPEN GATHERED *STONEFISH*'S OFFICERS IN the wardroom. Taped to one of the tables was a square of butcher paper; beneath it Myers could see the outline of a chart. Though he knew what was hidden there, thinking of it filled his belly with butterflies.

Once the doors were locked, Carpen began. "Gentlemen, it's time to let the cat out of the bag. While I can't give you the *why* of our mission, I can give you the *where*." Carpen ripped off the butcher paper. There were ten seconds of silence.

"Oh, holy Moses," whispered the weapons officer.

"You got that right, brother," said another.

Stonefish was fifteen miles off the coast of Shikoku, Japan.

"Four Marine Raiders died getting the details you see on this chart," Carpen said. "Here's the deal: In two hours we'll penetrate their antisubmarine nets . . . right here. Once inside, we'll navigate by chart and stopwatch through this minefield and, if all goes as planned, slip through undetected. If we manage that, we'll be about four hundred yards offshore, so make sure to tell your people to keep their voices down."

There was nervous laughter.

"From there, we'll head northeast until we reach the mouth of the Inland Sea between Shikoku and Honshu. This is the Japs' main sortie channel, so we can expect a lot of traffic."

"How much?" asked Myers.

"Anywhere from four to eight tin cans patrolling the gap."

"Oh, boy," the chief engineer muttered.

"Supposing we get that far," said the weapons officer, "then what?"

"Don't worry about that," replied Carpen. "Once we finish what we've come to do, we'll turn south and cut between the opposite shoreline and the minefield. At Tanabe Point . . . here . . . we'll make our exit, go deep, and head home."

Carpen looked around. "Questions?"

"How long do we have?" asked the navigator.

"From net penetration to the channel, six hours."

"MINE, PORT BOW, CLOSING," CALLED THE NAVIGATOR. "THEY'RE thick out there, sir."

"Time to turn?" asked Carpen.

"Thirty seconds."

The control room went silent as the time ticked away.

"Mark," called the navigator.

"Helmsman, left fifteen degrees rudder, make your course zero-two-seven, speed six knots."

"Zero-two-seven, speed six, aye sir."

No one moved now, no one spoke. Myers stood beside the chart table, eyes on Carpen. The skipper looked completely at ease, and it made Myers all the more nervous. If either their navigation or a mine's position were off by so much as a foot . . . they might hear the metallic scrape of the mine's horn, and then . . .

The navigator called: "On track, sir. Mines on both beams, opening."

"How long until we're clear?" asked Carpen.

"Fourteen minutes."

"MINE PASSING THE PORT BEAM, SKIPPER. LAST ONE COMING UP on starboard bow."

"Aye," said Carpen.

"Bottom rising, Skipper. Fifty feet in the past minute. Depth two-fifty."

"Navigator?"

"Ten seconds to turn . . . three . . . two . . . one . . . mark!"

"Helm, come left to zero-nine-zero. Planesman, make your depth one hundred. Prepare for PD."

Stonefish began her ascent to periscope depth. The bottom sloped up to meet her until only fifty feet lay between the seafloor and the keel.

"Depth one-fifty."

"Up twenty-five," ordered Carpen.

"Depth one-ten."

"Up another twenty."

"Up twenty, aye sir."

"Coming clear," called the navigator. "Last mine opening the port quarter."

"Bottom leveling at ninety feet," called Sonar.

"Engines all stop," Carpen ordered. "Diving Officer, give me zero bubble."

"Zero bubble, aye." At the control board, the diving officer turned a series of levers controlling the hydraulic manifolds, which in turn displaced *Stonefish*'s ballast. "Zero bubble, Skipper. Floating like a balloon."

Stonefish was now hovering some thirty feet from the sand.

"Sonar, Conn," called Carpen. "We're at PD, Chief. Got anything?"

"Negative contact, sir."

"Conn, aye. Up scope." The periscope ascended from the well, and Carpen caught the handgrips. "Hold. Billy?"

Myers stepped to the opposite eyepiece and pressed his forehead to the plastic. The lens was still submerged. After a few seconds he could distinguish moonlight filtering through the black water. No shadows, no lights . . .

Carpen called, "Up twelve inches . . . *slow.*"

The quartermaster complied. The hydraulics hissed. The tube ascended. The moonlight grew stronger.

"Almost there," said Carpen. "Up six. Up two . . . easy . . . There."

Myers' first view of the world in three days was breathtaking. Half awash, the periscope displayed a clear, star-sprinkled sky. A thin mist clung to the surface, and through it Myers could see the winking of navigation buoys.

Carpen said, "Okay, here we go, Billy. Look sharp.

Myers focused on the bearing viewer. Arms dangling

over the grips, Carpen began duckwalking the scope. The sea skimmed past the lens until the shoreline appeared. The trees and fishing huts stood out clearly under the moon. Myers's heart pounded. *Damn, we're close. . . .*

"Mark on Mugi Point coming up. . . . Mark."

"Bearing zero-zero-five," recited Myers.

The navigator plotted it. "Got it. Match, Skipper. We're on course."

As Carpen swung the scope past due west, Myers caught a glimpse of something in the mist, a shadow. "Hold," he called. "Back, Skipper."

"Yeah, I see it."

Sitting low in the water and shrouded in fog, the silhouette was almost invisible but unmistakable nonetheless: sleek hull, single slanted stack, deck guns. . . . It looked just like the flash cards from sub school, Myers thought. A Naichi-class destroyer. *Bad boy.*

Carpen snapped up the grips and stepped back; the periscope slid down. "Sonar, Conn. You get anything on the SJ?"

"Land to the north, faint contact bearing zero-nine-five."

"Mark her target one, Naichi-class destroyer." Carpen pointed at Myers. "Good eye, Billy. Where there's one, there's more."

FOUR MILES FROM THE MOUTH OF THE INLAND SEA, SONAR CALLED out.

"Conn, Sonar, multiple surface contacts. Screw count makes it four—no, five—bad guys. Target one bears zero-nine-zero, range two miles—"

"The Naichi," Carpen muttered to Myers. "Where's he going, Chief?"

"Listening. . . . Doppler's down. He's heading away. Shaft rotation for six knots."

"Back into the channel," Carpen whispered. "And the others, Chief?"

"Same bearing, range four miles. They're really pounding the hell out of the main channel, Skipper."

Far off, Myers could hear the wailing gong of the enemy sonar.

"Twenty seconds to new course," reported the navigator. "New course zero-eight-four."

Carpen turned to Myers: "Recommendation, Billy?"

God almighty, he's asking me? Myers could feel sweat rolling down his back. He forced calm into his voice. "Heck, we've got the Naichi heading into the channel. Might as well hitch a ride."

Carpen nodded. If they got into the destroyer's baffles, not only would its sonar be useless, but its screw cavitation would cover their own. "Good call."

"Mark, skipper."

"Helm, come right to new course zero-eight-four," Carpen ordered. "All ahead one-third for twelve knots."

INVISIBLE IN THE DESTROYER'S WAKE, *STONEFISH* WAS TWO MILES from the channel and three miles from their destination when the depth charge attack started.

"Conn, Sonar! Depth charge in the water, close aboard!"

"All hands brace for shock!"

Stonefish was rocked to port. Men were thrown from their stations into bulkheads, then back again as a second, then a third depth charge exploded. Carpen and Myers gripped the overhead pipes, their legs swinging free. The tower went black. The red battle lamps flickered. Gauge faces shattered and steam pipes burst, hissing wildly in the darkness.

"Planesman, forty degrees down! Helm, come right twenty degrees!"

Depth charges exploding around her, *Stonefish* spiraled downward. Then, as quickly as it had started, the attack stopped.

"Bottom coming up, Skipper."

"Level her off."

"They're turning around for another run," Myers said.

"Good for them," Carpen said. "We won't be here. Sonar, Conn, where is he?"

"Zero-eight-nine, range eleven hundred. Bearing shift . . . he's turning."

"Speed?"

"Sixteen knots."

"Helm, steer course zero-eight-nine, all ahead flank."

Myers did the mental calculation and said, "Skipper, what—"

"At flank speed we make fifteen knots. Add that to the Naichi's sixteen, and we're closing her at thirty-one. They're fast, but their turn radius ain't for shit. We'll be under and behind her in three minutes."

"Will that work?"

"We'll know soon enough. The question is, has he called for help?"

CARPEN'S GAMBIT WORKED. FOR WHATEVER REASON, THE FOUR warships in the channel did not come to the aid of the Naichi. Their luck was short-lived, however. Five minutes after sliding behind the destroyer, a screech echoed through the boat.

"What the . . ." Carpen muttered. "All stop, zero bubble."

"All stop, zero bubble."

The whine ceased.

"What is it?" asked Myers.

"Conn, Engine Room."

"Go ahead," replied Carpen.

"That last depth charge must've got us in the ass, Skipper. Shaft's bent. The seal's okay, so we ain't gonna drown, and we can limp home, but anything over three knots, and she'll start screaming again."

Carpen and Myers studied the chart. Their destination, marked as a red triangle, was three miles away, deep inside the Inland Sea.

"What d'you think, Billy?"

"The current in the channel is four knots at least," Myers said. "With the time we've got left, we'd have to do at least eight knots to get there. And with the shaft the way it is . . ."

"We'd be ringing the dinner bell," Carpen finished. "They'd sink us before we got within a mile of it." He paused, thought for moment. "What's that saying about discretion being the better part of valor, Billy?"

Myers felt a flood of relief. "So how do we get out?"

"As planned. It just might take us a little longer to get there."

"And the mission?"

"My boat, my call. If they don't like it, they can fire me. Conn, Sonar, report."

"Four surface contacts dead on the bow, bearing zero-eight-five. Bearing shift is changing . . . turning. . . . They're headed deeper into the channel, Skipper."

"And the Naichi?"

"He's astern of us and moving away."

"Conn, aye." Carpen said, then to Myers: "Time to make like a ghost. Helm: Come right to new course zero-nine-one, speed two knots."

"Zero-nine-one, two knots, aye, sir."

Carpen tilted his cap back on his head and grinned. "So what d'you think of the tour so far, Billy?"

Myers shrugged. "Interesting?"

"Nice way of putting it." Carpen clapped him on the shoulder. "You did good. Before you know it, we'll be back in the Volcanos drinking beer."

"Sounds good to me."

As *Stonefish* turned east and began limping through the water, neither Myers nor Carpen realized the terrible mistake they'd just made or the price it would exact over half a century later.

1

Shiono Misaki, Japan

AN HOUR BEFORE HE WOULD WITNESS THE MURDER OF A COMPLETE stranger, Briggs Tanner was floating thirty feet beneath the surface of the Pacific Ocean, watching the last rays of sunlight fade from above. He floated like that, unmoving, until he felt a slight burning in his lungs. Time to surface. He glanced at his watch: nearly four minutes. Not bad. Not as good as when he was twenty-two, of course, but not bad for forty. He righted himself, then finned upward, blowing a stream of bubbles as he went.

When he broke the surface, he was pleased to see he'd come up a hundred yards from his entry point. A mile up the shore, he could see the lights of the hotel. To the south, just across the Inland Sea, lay Shikoku, the smallest of Japan's four major islands.

He swam to shore, plodded out, and sat down on the still-warm sand, his arms and legs tingling with the exertion. A full night's sleep—a rarity as of late—would come easy that night, and he was glad for it. He'd never much cared for Kazakhstan, and the past two weeks had cemented the feeling. Left to him, the city of Karaganda would never again be on his itinerary.

He lay back on his elbows and watched the sun's lower rim hover above the ocean. How long had it been since he'd done this, sat and watched a sunset? Just sat and did nothing? Too long.

He sensed movement behind him and turned to see a Japanese boy of perhaps seven years old kneeling a few feet away. Tanner assumed he was from the fishing village up the beach, a collection of surprisingly primitive huts

made of rough planking and thatch. "Quaint" was the word
the *Fodor's* guide had used.

"*Kombanwa,*" Tanner said, using one of the three dozen
Japanese phrases he'd managed to master. *Good Evening.*

"How do you do, sir."

"Your English is very good."

The boy beamed. "I am learning at school."

"My name is Briggs."

"I am Mitsu." Introductions made, the boy scampered
over and plopped down. He eyed Tanner's swim fins.
"What are those?"

"Fins."

What were you doing in the water?"

"Diving."

"For pearls?"

"For fun."

Mitsu considered this. "Are you hungry?"

"Well, I—"

Without waiting for an answer, the boy sprinted off, gesturing for Tanner to follow. Tanner shrugged. *Why not?* He
got up, stuffed his gear into his rucksack, and followed.

DINNER CONSISTED OF BRAISED FISH, VEGETABLES, AND RICE.
Mitsu's mother, younger brother, and sister—both under
four years old—spoke no English but did their best to make
Tanner feel welcome, as though having a complete stranger
join them for dinner was a perfectly routine event.

They sat on the hut's porch, which was back a few yards
into the tree line. A pair of sputtering kerosene lanterns
hung from the eaves. In the distance Tanner could hear the
hiss of the waves.

Once the dishes were cleared away, the mother served
tea while the younger boy fanned the hibachi smoke to keep
the insects at bay. Tanner asked Mitsu where his father was.

"He went out one night. In our boat. The boat came back
the next morning. He did not."

Tanner glanced at the mother, who merely smiled at him.
Up to this point, Mitsu had been translating their conver-

sation, but he had stopped at this last exchange.

"How long ago?"

"Six months. It was after the ship stopped coming."

"What ship?"

"Every few nights for almost a month, a ship came. Over there." He pointed off the beach. "It would stay for a few hours, then sail again."

"Do you know what she—it—was doing?"

"No."

"What did the police say about your father?"

Mitsu shrugged, and Tanner realized the police hadn't been notified. It was a village matter, he guessed. He wondered why Mitsu had mentioned the ship. Was it simply the boy's way of marking his father's disappearance or something more?

Tanner stood up and bowed. With both hands he returned the teacup to the mother. *"Domo arigato, Kombanwa."*

The mother returned his bow. *"Do-ita-shimashi-te."*

Tanner tousled Mitsu's hair, shouldered his rucksack, walked down the steps, and headed down the beach.

"He went out one night. The boat came back the next morning. He did not." What happened to him? Tanner wondered. A man goes out in a boat, then disappears.

BACK AT THE HOTEL TANNER STOOD UNDER A HOT SHOWER, THEN toweled off, slipped on a pair of rough khaki shorts, a navy blue tropical knit shirt, and sandals, then headed downstairs to the hotel bar, the Tiki Lounge. He still had trouble speaking the name without laughing, but it certainly did fit the general motif of the Royal Palms Resort.

What the designers had lacked in originality they recouped in lavishness. Seemingly transplanted from the shores of Tahiti, the hotel was a man-made tropical paradise on an island with plenty of its own. The crescent-shaped hotel was bordered on one side by the beaches of Cape Shiono and a forest of evergreen and bamboo on the other. Nestled between the concave sides of the hotel was the requisite kidney-shaped swimming pool, cabana bar, and

artificial waterfall. And palms. Large and small, fake and
real, they sprouted from every corner, with or without the
aid of soil. Hidden in the foliage came the muted squawks
of parrots. Tanner had yet to see a live bird, but to the
hotel's credit, neither had he spotted the loudspeakers.

He strolled through the Tiki's doors, took a stool at the
bar, and ordered a Kirin beer. It was a quiet night, with
only a half-dozen patrons seated at the tables. His beer arrived, and he took a sip.

Then he sensed someone standing behind him.

"Do you ever get the feeling you're in the wrong place?"
the voice said.

He turned.

She had lustrous, shoulder-length black hair and a deli-
cately curved neck that could only be called elegant. Her
skin was flawless and tanned. She was stunning, Tanner
thought.

As do most men, Briggs did his best to convince himself
he was in control of his reactions to women, and like most
men, he was wrong. Happy he hadn't fallen off his stool,
he smiled and said, "Pardon me?"

She gestured to the nearby tables. He looked and suddenly realized the rest of the Tiki's patrons were couples—
all newlyweds, he guessed.

"It seems we're surrounded," he said.

"May I?"

"Please do."

"My name is Camille."

He shook her extended hand and felt an ineffable tingle;
her accent was Eastern European, perhaps Slavic. She
smelled like plumeria. Or was it hibiscus?

"I'm Briggs."

"Interesting name."

"A long story. An ancestral name my father took a liking
to."

"I like long stories. Tell me."

Tanner shrugged. "Okay. Let's go outside. It's too nice
a night to waste."

They ordered two more drinks, then stepped onto the

pool deck and wound their way through the umbrella-covered tables and sat down at the edge of the pool. The aerators gurgled softly, and the underwater lamps glowed amber. Camille took off her sandals and dangled her legs in the water.

"So," she said. "Your story."

"You're sure you want to hear this?"

"Yes."

"Do you want the unabridged version or the *Reader's Digest* condensed?"

"Unabridged."

"Okay. . . ." Tanner said. "According to my father, it began back in 1774. . . ."

BY THE TIME HE FINISHED THE STORY, CAMILLE WAS LAUGHING SO hard she was doubled over, tears streaming down her face. He caught her arm and gently pulled her upright. A few wisps of her hair had dipped into the pool, and she brushed them away.

"You made that up." she said.

"Every word is true."

"So you're named after a . . . a . . . what is the word? A pirate—"

"Back then they were called privateers."

"Is there a difference?"

"Not much." He took her glass and stood up. "I'll go freshen our—"

Beyond the fence came the squealing of tires. An engine roared, brakes screeched, followed by a crash and shattering glass.

"That sounds close," Camille said, jumping up.

Tanner ran toward the fence. He was ten paces from it when he noticed a figure scrambling over it. The man reached the top, teetered, then tumbled headfirst into the shrubbery. Dragging his left leg, he lurched onto the patio.

Tanner caught him as he fell. "I've got you, slow down—"

"American!" the man sputtered. "You're American?"

"Yes. What—?"

The man glanced over his shoulder. "They're coming!" Tanner looked but saw no one. "Help me! *Please!*"

On an impulse that would be his first of two that evening, Tanner nodded and helped the man to his feet. "Okay, come on."

They were turning toward the Tiki when Briggs saw movement out of the corner of his eye. He glanced back. A pair of arms were reaching over the top of the fence. Then a head appeared. Tanner caught a glint, moonlight on metal. Instinctively he knew what it was.

"Gun!" he yelled and shoved Camille to the ground. "Down!"

The *crack* came a second later.

The slug entered the man's upper back and exited the hollow above his collarbone. Off balance, Tanner felt the man slipping from his arms and tried to compensate by stepping backward. His foot plunged into the pool, followed by his leg.

The man was lying on his side, head resting on the concrete. He was alive, Tanner realized, but not for long. Dark blood was pumping from the wound. *Subclavian vein,* he thought. Without help, he'd be dead in less than a minute.

The man reached toward Tanner. "Please . . ."

"Hold on, don't move!"

"Briggs!" Camille called.

"Stay down!"

Tanner pulled himself out of the pool, crawled over to the man, rolled him onto his back, and ripped open his shirt. Tanner wiped the wound clear and shoved his index finger and thumb into the hole, searching for the vein. The bullet had destroyed everything in its path—veins, bone, muscle, ligaments—all gone.

The man gripped Tanner's hand. "Help me, please . . ."

"I'm trying, I'm trying, stay with me."

"God, it hurts. . . ."

Tanner stopped working and looked into the man's eyes. They were bulging with pain, but there was something else: aloneness. He was dying among strangers, and he knew it.

Tanner would never remember hearing the second shot.

The man's forehead seemed to split open before Tanner's eyes. The eyes and nose disappeared in a gout of blood. Tanner felt it splatter him. What little remained of the man's head lolled backward onto the concrete. The body spasmed twice, once more, then went still.

Lying a few feet away, Camille said, "Briggs, are you—"

He wiped the blood from his face. "I'm okay," he replied. He looked to the fence line. There was nothing. "You?"

"Uh-huh."

One of the dead man's fists had unfurled, revealing a small key; he'd been clutching it so hard it left an impression in the flesh. On yet another impulse, Tanner pocketed it.

In the distance came the wail of sirens. Then, from the lobby turnaround, an engine revved, followed by the screeching of tires. Headlamps pierced the fence. Tanner jumped to his feet.

"Briggs!" Camille called. "What're you doing?"

Hunched over, Tanner sprinted to the fence and scrambled over in time to see a pickup truck accelerate around the curve. In seconds the taillights disappeared.

Ignoring the chattering guests loitering in the lobby entrance, Tanner walked across to the man's car—a red four-door Nissan with an Avis sticker in the back window—which lay crumpled against a tree. Both doors were dented, as was the rear bumper. The trunk was riddled with pencil-sized holes, all in skillet-sized patterns. *Shotgun,* Tanner decided.

The sirens grew closer. Tanner reached through the window, opened the glove compartment, and found a sheaf of papers. It was a rental agreement: name: Umako Ohira . . . address, credit card number . . . In a blaze of flashing lights, three police cars screeched to a halt beside the wreck. Headlights blinded Tanner.

"Ya me te! Ya me te!"

Though his Japanese was limited, he guessed he was being ordered away from the car. The *clack-clack* of several

pump shotguns convinced him of it. He raised his hands
and walked toward the headlights. From out of the glare,
three figures charged forward and tackled him to the
ground.

IT TOOK CAMILLE AND THE ROYAL PALMS'S MANAGER TEN MINUTES
to convince the Kagoshima Prefectural Police (*Todo-Fuken
Keisatsu*) he was in fact a guest of the resort and an innocent bystander.

Under the watchful eye of one the officers, he was escorted to the bathroom to wash up. There was a small cut
on his right cheek. *Bone fragment,* he thought dully. He
plucked it from the wound and watched it swirl down the
drain. He splashed water through his hair and did his best
to ignore the bits of flesh dropping into the bowl. His hands
were still shaking. Adrenaline.

He'd seen death before, but it was something to which
he'd never become immune. He preferred it that way. Once
it became easy, you had a problem. He'd learned to put his
feelings on hold, but at best that only delayed the inevita-
ble. If you didn't deal with them, such feelings began to
eat you from the inside out.

The officer escorted him back to the pool, where the
body was being loaded onto the coroner's stretcher. The
concrete was stained with blood. Some of it had trickled
into the pool's aerator, and thin black tendrils of it floated
on the surface like seaweed.

Camille was standing beside one of the tables. A few
feet away, a plainclothes police officer was talking to the
resort's manager. Tanner walked over to Camille. "Are you
okay?"

"I think so. Why did they shoot him, Briggs?" she whispered.

"I don't know."

"Mr. Tanner?" The inspector walked over.

"Yes."

"I am Ishu Tanaka, homicide investigator for the Kagoshima Prefect."

Camille was still staring at the puddle. Tanner put his arm around her and walked her away. "I'm sure he felt no pain," Tanaka said, sitting down. "How are you feeling, then? No injuries to you or Miss . . ."

"Sereva," Camille replied. "I'm fine."

"Glad to hear it. I'll take as little of your time as possible." Tanaka opened his steno pad. "First, your full names, please."

"Briggs Tanner."

"From the United States, I assume. Vacationing?"

"Yes," said Tanner. He was in no mood for talking.

"Ms. Sereva?"

"I am Ukranian. Vacationing also."

"Now, please, in you own words, tell me what you saw tonight."

Tanner did so, leaving out mention of the key. Unsure if Camille had seen it, Tanner half expected her to interject, but she said nothing.

"Witnesses said there were two shots," Tanaka said. "Where did they strike, can you tell me?"

"As far as I can tell, one entered his upper back, the other the top of his skull."

"The shots came from the fence?"

"That's correct."

"You were hunched over the body when the second shot came. Why is that?"

"I was trying to stop the bleeding. I thought if I could—"

"Are you a doctor?"

"No."

"A bold move, jumping over that fence."

"I didn't really think about it."

"Mr. Tanner, why were you near the car when we arrived?"

"I was looking for anyone else who might have been injured."

"Had you ever seen this man before tonight?"

"No."

"Did he speak to you?"

"Nothing that made any sense. He was panicked, scared."

"And you, Ms. Sereva?"

Camille shrugged. "I didn't see much. I'm sorry."

Inspector Tanaka nodded. "Mr. Tanner, you told the responding officers you saw the truck carrying the gunman. Can you tell me anything else?"

"As I reached the top of the fence, they were pulling away. It was black or dark blue, no license plate. There was a driver and the gunman—"

"You saw the gun?"

Tanner nodded. "A rifle, bolt action, medium length, with a scope."

"Please go on."

"The gunman and another man were in the back," Tanner replied, then thought: *How long from the time the truck left to when the police arrived? Thirty seconds, a minute? Surely they had to have passed the truck.*

As if reading Tanner's mind, Tanaka said, "We found some fresh tire tracks just inside the woods about a hundred yards down the drive. We believe the truck pulled off, doused his lights, and let us pass." Tanaka stood up. "This was an unfortunate incident. You and Ms. Sereva may rest assured we will get to the bottom of it. You are both certain you are not injured?"

"We're fine, thank you," Tanner replied.

"Then I'll say good night. You will be staying a few days, in case we need to ask more questions?"

Tanner and Camille nodded.

"Very good." Tanaka stood, shook both their hands, and left.

AFTER SEEING CAMILLE SAFELY TO HER ROOM, WHICH WAS DIrectly one floor below his, Tanner took a shower. He stood under the spray for twenty minutes, then got out, toweled off, poured himself a vodka, and stepped onto the balcony. The moon was high and the sky clear.

So much for a quiet vacation, he thought.

It had been a professional killing, that much was certain. The gunman—whoever he was—was not a paper target shooter. If the first shot had been a few inches to the right, it would have struck at the base of the skull. Even so, the first shot had been fatal. Why the second shot, then? Insurance?

This was no murder, Tanner decided. It was an execution.

And now, because of a stupid impulse—no, two impulses—he was involved. *Not very smart, Briggs.* There was something about the man named Umako Ohira, though. . . . He'd been desperate for help, as would have anyone, but he'd seemed especially glad Tanner was American. Why? And the key . . . Of all the things to be carrying, why that?

He took a sip of vodka, felt it warming in his belly, and leaned on the railing. Below him, Camille stood on her own balcony. He was about to call down when he saw movement in the trees below. It moved again: a figure in dark clothing. After a moment, it slipped back into the shadows and disappeared.

Tanner looked again for Camille, but she'd gone inside.

2

Beirut, Lebanon

THE MAN KNOWN AS MARCUS STUMBLED OVER A DISCARDED TIRE
and fell, gashing his shin. He cursed. God, what he
wouldn't give for a working streetlight! But in Beirut—
especially in Muslim West Beirut—they were as rare as
mortar attacks were common. He could feel the cuts and
bruises on his hands and face. His clothes were shredded.
He'd lost count of the number of times in the past hour
he'd fallen.

He sat down to catch his breath. At the end of the alley
he could see a gutted apartment building, half its facade
crumbled and blocking the adjoining street. Here and there,
rifles cracked and he could hear the faint *crump* of grenades. The Shia and the Phalange were fighting again,
somewhere near the airport shantytowns.

Suddenly an engine revved. Marcus froze.

He strained to listen. *Where are they?* The engine faded,
went silent. A dog barked. Silence. Maybe he'd lost them.
In the past half hour he'd done so several times, but still
they managed to catch up. They knew the city at least as
well as he did, perhaps better.

He patted his coat pocket and realized the pieces of colored chalk were still there. He emptied his pockets. He
couldn't afford to be caught with them. His pursuers were
simple men but not stupid. They would make the connection.

Behind him an engine growled. Headlights swept over
him. *Run!* He climbed to his feet and half limped, half ran
down the alley and into the street.

He was pinned by spotlights. Behind the glare, he could

make out the outline of a pickup truck. Half a dozen men stood alongside it, their weapons leveled at him. Behind him, a car skidded to a stop; doors opened. Footsteps pounded toward him.

Marcus turned, looking for an exit. Left . . . right . . . Nothing, nowhere to go.

Allah be merciful, he thought. *I'm caught.*

TWO HOURS LATER, WHEN MARCUS STILL HADN'T APPEARED FOR their meeting, the old Armenian named Salah knew something was wrong. Marcus had never been late without giving a . . . What did he call it? A wave-off. He had checked all four drops and found no markings, but still no Marcus.

Salah was old enough that the various factions in the Muslim Quarter paid him little attention. Tonight, three patrols had stopped him at their *hajez,* or checkpoints—in each case a pair of burned out cars sitting diagonally across the particular street they governed. In each case he had been waved on.

At last he reached Marcus's neighborhood. The street was quiet. Rats skittered in the shadows. This was a good neighborhood by Beirut standards; aside from a few bullet scars, most buildings were undamaged. Here a building wasn't considered uninhabitable until it had collapsed. Beirutis had a sixth sense about the many dangers of their city, structural integrity being only one of them.

Salah turned the corner, then stopped, ducked back.

A car sat in front of Marcus's apartment building. A pair of men, both armed with AK-47s, stood at the curb. Through the curtains of Marcus's apartment Salah could see shadows moving. The light clicked off.

Moments later, four men trotted down the building's front steps. The lookouts waved an all clear, and the group came forward, pushing a man between them.

Marcus! They shoved him inside the trunk and slammed it shut. The group piled into the car, and it pulled away.

*   *   *

FORTY-FIVE MILES EAST OF BEIRUT IN THE FOOTHILLS OF THE ANTI-Lebanese Mountains near the village of Ma'rubun, Abu Azhar sat before the glowing fireplace in his cottage, flipping through a cracked leather photo album.

The album was ordered chronologically, so many of the older photos were tinted sepia, but the newer ones, the images that should have evoked in him stronger memories, seemed as distant as the older ones. Photos of his mother and father; of brothers and sisters; of the now-abandoned An Nabatiyah refugee camp north of the Litani River; of a group of young men huddled around a table, smiling and drinking.

Without realizing it, Azhar smiled, a reflex. The images meant nothing to him. He turned the page.

Here the photos were of a young girl of perhaps two years old surrounded by balloons and streamers, her friends in the background, laughing and blowing noisemakers. A woman bent over the girl's shoulder, their smiling faces pressed together for the camera.

Azhar turned to the next page and he felt his heart fill his throat.

The headline was from *Al Quds*, an Israeli-Arab newspaper:

YOUNG GIRL DEAD: AUTHORITIES SUSPECT ABUSE

Tel Aviv—Authorities today charged a young Levanda couple in the negligent death of their seven-year-old daughter. Though the names of the girl and her family have not yet been disclosed, sources say the cause of death appears to be . . .

The next page, another headline, this one from the *Jerusalem Post*:

COUPLE SUSPECTED OF
CHILD ABUSE FOUND SLAIN

Tel Aviv—The bodies of Helena and Ira Ya-
kov, who were acquitted last month of the negligent death of their adopted daughter, were
found murdered in their apartment yesterday
morning. Details of the murder have not been
disclosed, but police investigators state the Ya-
kovs both died of single bullet wounds to the
head. As yet, neither motives nor suspects have
been found. . . .

"Abu, why do you do this to yourself?"

Azhar turned to see his wife sitting in the doorway. She
jostled the wheels of her chair and pushed herself into the
room. A petite woman of fifty, Elia Azhar would have
been beautiful if not for the worry lines creasing her face.
Allah, how he loved her. For all she had been through, she
never felt sorry for herself but was instead a quiet rock for
him.

"Why aren't you in bed?" he asked her.

"You cried out."

"Oh. I'm sorry."

"Husband, you are killing yourself. It was so long ago. . . .
Please let it be."

"I cannot."

"You must!" She lashed out, knocking the album to the
floor. "Please—"

"Stop it, Elia." He gripped her hands. "Stop it."

She leaned forward into his lap and began sobbing.

"It is not over, Elia," he said. "She was ours. Ours! And
you . . . you are . . ." *Sweet wife . . . so forgiving,* Azhar
thought.

"Barren," she finished. "You should find another wife
who can give you sons. I will take care of the house and
you can—"

"No," he replied. "No. Allah be witness, I will not bring
another child into this world."

After a while, he carried her back to bed and lay beside her until she fell asleep, then returned to the fire. On the floor, the album had flipped open to a photograph he hadn't seen in years.

It showed him and another man, a Westerner with coffee-brown hair and laugh-lined, ocean-blue eyes, at a dinner table. Their arms were draped around one another's shoulders, and they were smiling. The man wore one of those silly hats with the flat top and the tassel . . . What was it called? Such a ridiculous hat. The scene seemed so familiar, yet so distant, as though he were enjoying someone else's well-told story. Who was he? Why couldn't he remember this? *Why?*

Azhar closed the album and laid it aside. It didn't matter. None of it. Only one thing mattered anymore, and before long, that, too, would be over.

HE WAS AWAKENED BY A TAPPING ON THE DOOR. HE PICKED UP the Makarov pistol from the table and crept to the door. "Yes?"

"It is Mustafa."

Azhar opened the door a crack, saw the man was alone, and let him enter.

Mustafa al-Baz had been Azhar's closest friend and ally for four years. A dedicated soldier, al-Baz wore many hats as Azhar's second-in-command: operations officer, intelligence officer, and chief enforcer.

"Shu fi?" asked Azhar. What's going on?

"He was watching the building in Basta,"said al-Baz. "We caught him near *al-Mataf.* He was trying to slip across."

"Going where?"

"We don't know. We searched his apartment but found nothing of use."

"Where is he now?"

"We took him to the warehouse."

"Good. We must vacate Basta—"

"I've already ordered it."

"Have you gotten his name yet?"

"We've just started on him. He claims his name is Marcus." Al-baz hesitated. "Abu, I think he's American."

"American!"

"Or their agent. Also, after we started questioning him, he mentioned a ship."

Azhar bolted forward. His teacup clattered to the floor. "What!"

"We could not get any more; he lost consciousness."

"Find out what he knows—quickly. We must know before the final phase."

"We may get what we need from him, and we may not. He may have only a small view of his operation. This is common; it is what the Westerners call 'compartmentalization.' "

"Then we may need to go to the source."

"My thinking as well. For that, I have a thought."

"Tell me."

Al-Baz did so, briefly outlining his idea.

Azhar was silent for several minutes. "It is risky."

"So is going ahead with the operation blindly. When I was in Khartoum last year, I saw a training transcript from a former KGB officer who specialized in this kind of operation. He is retired but does contract work, I believe. And from what I have heard, he is in Damascus."

"And the man on the ground? Who do you have in mind?"

Al-Baz told him.

"The timing would be difficult," said Azhar.

"Perhaps," al-Baz said. "But the information we require is simple. Either they know, or they do not. We, too, can play the compartmentalization game. Once we know why this Marcus has come here, we can make the decision. Better to know now, while we can stop it. Once the operation has reached a certain point, it cannot—"

"Yes, yes, I know."

"Besides, I grow tired of being the target. Always *Al-mu ammara!* Always it is American agents, Mossad—they all think Lebanon is their playground. Perhaps it is time to play our own games."

Azhar nodded, sharing his deputy's feelings. *Al-mu ammara* was a distinctly Lebanese term meaning "the conspiracy." For decades Lebanon had been the world's chosen surrogate battlefield. Superpowers played their spy games, tested their weapons, exercised their tactics and strategies, and Lebanon paid in blood and ruination. But truth be told, Azhar was also using Lebanon. But this was different, he told himself. What they were doing was for the good of all. Strife always preceded change. The coming months would either ruin Lebanon or save it.

Mustafa was right, Azhar decided. They would take the initiative. "I will contact the general. You find the other man and arrange a meeting. Before we go ahead, I want to know if this is feasible."

"And Marcus, the agent?"

"Work on him. But for the time being, he stays alive."

Israel

IN HIS TEL AVIV APARTMENT, ART STUCKY, THE CIA'S NEAR EAST division chief, awoke to the ringing of his phone. He groaned and reached across the nightstand, knocking over an empty bottle of gin. "Fuck . . ." He fumbled the receiver, found it. "Yeah."

"Sir, this is the embassy communications center. We have traffic for you."

Stucky looked at the clock: 5:00 A.M. His head pounded. "What kind?"

"Pardon me?"

"I said what kind!" The voice on the other end sounded young. These college punks were worthless, but they were easy to fluster, which was always fun. "You call me at five in the morning, and you don't know what kind? What's your name?"

"Peterson, sir."

"Well, I'm waiting, Peterson, what kind of message?"

"Uh . . . uh . . ." Paper rustling. "Landline, sir. It was a SYMMETRY—"

"What!"

"SYMMETRY. Alternate three, off protocol."

Shit, thought Stucky. One of SYMMETRY's agents had panicked about something—probably lost his goddamned camel or turban or something—and made contact. In covert operations the terms *protocol* and *off protocol* indicated whether the method of contact followed ComSec (communication security) guidelines. In short, whoever this "alternate" was, he'd fucked up.

"What'd you tell him?" Stucky asked.

"To call back in an hour on a scrubbed line That's in . . . another forty minutes."

"Jesus, why didn't you call me earlier!"

"We did, sir. You didn't answer. And your pager is off."

"Huh." Stucky smiled. *Really tied one on, Art. Didn't even hear the phone.* "Okay, I'm on my way."

Stucky hung up and lit a cigarette. His mouth tasted like wool. He downed the last dribble of gin from the bottle, swirled it around his mouth, swallowed, then forced himself upright and began looking for his pants.

THIRTY MINUTES LATER, HE WALKED THROUGH THE EMBASSY'S gate, flashed his ID at the Marine sentry, then took the elevator up two floors to his cubicle, passing the CIA station chief's office as he went. "Let me know as soon as you hear something, Art?" called the station chief.

Fucking Peterson. "Sure, boss," he muttered. The current chief—working under the same diplomatic cover as Stucky, Office of Economic Liaison—was another bureaucrat in a long line of lifers who knew nothing about operational intelligence. And as far as Stucky was concerned, the guy didn't know a dead letter drop from his asshole.

For that kind of discernment he relied on case officers like Stucky, the backbone of the Operations Directorate. *Spy* and *agent* are widely misused terms, as both refer to controlled intelligence sources, not the people like Stucky who did the controlling. In the intelligence community there is no greater insult than calling a case officer an agent.

After finding himself ousted from the Army just three months short of his twenty years, Stucky was hired by the CIA for paramilitary operations, but when they started steering away from "active field measures," instead of finding himself terminated, Stucky was promoted. His superiors found he had a knack for controlling people in hairy situations.

Over the years Stucky made the conversion from knuckle dragger to case officer, to Near East (NE) operations deputy, then to NE division chief. He was a natural at office politics and had good instincts about how far and with whom he could push. Around superiors who held a more tolerant view of homosexuality, Stucky was careful to avoid using phrases such as *ass bandit* or *rump ranger*. In the company of women, especially since the introduction of stricter harassment rules, Stucky did not discuss their anatomy or in what fashion he wished to fondle it. It was all about knowing where—and how elastic—the line was.

As a soldier, the routine and regimen of army life suited Stucky. His lackluster people skills notwithstanding, he earned a reputation for ramrodding tough jobs. Subordinates followed him not out of respect but out of fear. They were simply too afraid to go against him.

Stucky knew he'd found his home when he stepped through the doors of the south Detroit army recruiting office at the age of eighteen. He'd been a bully in high school, and he was a bully in boot camp. Surrounded by young men frightened by the harshness of basic training, Stucky thrived. Even at that early age, he knew that when you're at your lowest, it feels good to belong to a group and to make others feel worse than you.

His first tour in the highlands of Vietnam proved two things: One, Stucky was cool under fire; and two, Stucky liked hurting people. The first quality made him a perfect sergeant, and the last quality was largely overlooked. In the middle of a firefight, when your biggest concern was being overrun, a creature like Stucky improved the odds dramatically.

Though Stucky's moderate success with the CIA would later have the Personnel Directorate scratching its collective head, he was in fact currently running SYMMETRY, one of the CIA's two most critical ongoing operations.

He plopped down in his chair, searched his drawer for a bottle of aspirin, and downed four of them dry. The secure phone rang. He snatched it up. "Stucky."

"Uh, Peterson here, sir. He's called back—on protocol, this time. I'll hang up, there'll be a series of tone bursts, then—"

"Yeah, yeah. Put it through."

As advertised, Stucky heard a tone burst as the call went through the electronic scrubbers. Then a voice: "Hello? Hello?"

Stucky checked his watch; duration for landline calls was ninety seconds. "Three, this is Limestone. You have a report?"

"Yes, yes. I—" There was the crackle of automatic weapons in the background. "Marcus is gone, Limestone. They took him."

"Who took him? When?"

"It was last night—no, this morning, about three hours ago. He missed our meet, so I went to find him."

"Goddamn it!"

"Yes, I know, but I was worried. I went to his apartment. They put him in a car and drove away."

"Give me details." The man did so. "Do you know this group?" asked Stucky.

"No. What should I do? I'm afraid. Should I—"

"Don't do anything, you understand? Nothing! If you have any meetings set, wave them off. Pretend none of it exists. You understand?"

"Yes, but what do I do?"

"You're not listening!" Stucky glanced at his watch: twenty seconds to go. "Go about your business. Whatever you normally do during the day, do that. Got it?"

"Yes."

"Where you're calling from . . . Is it safe?"

"In this city? It is as good a place as any."

"Fine. Call back at this time two days from now. I'll be waiting."

"Two days from now, this time. Understood."

Stucky hung up, thought for a moment, then redialed. "Peterson, get me the DDO on the secure line."

3

DIRECTOR OF CENTRAL INTELLIGENCE DICK MASON FORCED A SMILE
on his face and waited for the chairman of the Senate Intelligence Committee to finish his question. *Not much of a
question,* Mason thought. Senator Herbert J. Smith did not
ask questions; Senator Herbert J. Smith made speeches that
just happened to have question marks tacked to their tails.

"And so, Mr. Director, my question to you is: What tangible progress in your so-called war on state-sponsored terrorism can you show this committee?"

Mason held his smile but didn't answer, knowing
Smith—the master of "porcupine power" on the Hill—
wasn't quite done. Smith didn't seem to realize this was a
closed hearing; there were no media to impress.

"We all know about the supposed Tehran/Damascus/
Khartoum/Tripoli connection, and these governments' support of terrorism. What we don't know is what exactly the
CIA, under your leadership, and at the direction of the president, has done about it. On behalf of the citizens of this
country, I would like to know what we have gotten for the
hundreds of millions of dollars you've spent."

Mason cleared his throat. "That is your question, Senator?"

"Indeed it is."

"In general terms—"

"I'm not interested in general terms, Mr. Mason. You—"

"As I understand it, sir, my deputy of operations is
scheduled to appear here tomorrow. He'll be able to provide
you with more specific details about the scope of our op-

erations. That's not why I'm here today. My answer to your last question, then, is quite simple: money."

"Money?"

"Yes, sir. We've a better grasp of how funds are transferred from sponsor governments to the command structures of terrorist groups. Money is the key. We can't dampen a terrorist's fervor; we can't cut off their source of training; and we can't hope diplomatic measures will curtail covert support of these groups."

Mason paused to take a sip of water. God, he hated these things. He sounded like a goddamned sound bite from C-SPAN.

"What we can do, however, is attack their pocketbook. As the U.S. and other Western nations strengthen their defenses against terrorism, terrorists have to work that much harder. They can't do this—not at sustained levels—without capital.

"While the four biggest sponsors are not necessarily dependent on foreign trade and inclusion in world economic communities, all are beginning to feel the pinch of living on the fringes. They may talk about neither wanting nor needing any part of Western progress and values, but the story on the street is quite different."

Smith said, "Are you telling us, Mr. Director, these countries *care* what the rest of the world thinks, that their feelings are hurt because they don't get to play with the big kids?"

"No, sir, I'm not. I'll give you an example. In the past three years alone, while Syria has balked at the peace process and has continued to support terrorism—especially in Lebanon—the United States, along with Canada and the United Kingdom, have all but stopped buying Syrian products such as manganese, chrome, and phosphates. This alone has cost Syria hundreds of millions of dollars—money President Assad doesn't have to spend keeping his country militarized.

"So, I ask you, Senator: What's your guess as to what President Assad is feeling? The big kids have stopped playing with him, and his power base—his very ability to remain in power—is being eroded."

Smith put his hand over the microphone and whispered to his vice chairman, Senator Dean. Smith was good at rhetoric, Mason knew, but rarely did his homework, and in this case he was so intent on punching holes in one of the president's pet projects, he didn't bother to find out what the hell he was talking about. Even so, Smith wielded power on the Hill. Though a confirmed womanizer and a borderline drunk, he won countless battles by simply wearing down his opponents. Victory by forfeiture was still victory.

"That's a start, Mr. Director. Now you've caught on to what I'm talking about: *tangible* progress. But is your example an isolated one, or is it representative?"

"It is becoming more the rule rather than exception, Senator." *But we've got a long, long, way to go,* Mason didn't add. Destitute or flush, state-sponsored terrorist groups would never quit altogether.

Smith considered this and nodded. "Very well, Mr. Director, we appreciate your time. We may call on you again."

"Of course."

Mason nodded as the committee filed out of the hearing room. Once they were gone, he let out a long breath.

CIA Headquarters, Langley, Virginia

HE WAS BACK IN HIS OFFICE AN HOUR LATER.

"Morning, Mr. Director," said his secretary.

"Morning, Ginny." Mason had stopped trying to get Ginny to call him anything but "Mr. Director."

"The world still in one piece?"

"You tell me. You're the one who faced the beast this morning."

"And got away only slightly scathed."

"Mr. Coates and Ms. Albrecht are in your conference room."

"Okay." Mason walked into his office, checked his inbox and voice messages, then opened his door to the adjoining conference room. George Coates, his deputy director, Operations (DDO) and Sylvia Albrecht, his deputy director, Intelligence (DDI) were waiting. Coates and Albrect headed the two main directorates at the CIA, the "doers" and the "thinkers," as Mason called them.

Dick Mason had been appointed by the previous administration and then asked to stay on by its successor. From day one, Mason dedicated himself to revamping the CIA and had never wavered in that pursuit. Among the many problems he tackled, the biggest had been rivalry: in-house rivalry between his directorates and outside rivalry between the CIA and other agencies such as the FBI and NSA. He handled the former by first doing some housecleaning that included cutting the position of DDCI, or deputy director of Central Intelligence, and becoming his own number-two man; and then by simply converting other agency heads through the sheer force of his personality.

Within a month of his appointment, Mason fired the incumbent DDO and DDI, both career bureaucrats. To their replacements he gave the simple warning, "Work together, or I'll fire you." They didn't, so he did.

Mason then appointed George Coates and Sylvia Albrecht, gave them the same warning, and got very different results. For the first time in years, Operations and Intelligence began working hand in hand. The DI got quality raw product from the field, and in return the DO got unvarnished analysis. Most importantly, the agency's output was unslanted and immune to the vagaries of political winds. This, Mason felt, was the CIA's primary job.

"Why the long faces?" he asked as he took a seat.

In reply, Coates slid a buff-colored folder across the table. On the diagonal red stripe across the cover was the annotation, NOFORN/TS/EYES ONLY/SYMMETRY. Mason mentally translated the spookese to plain English: No Foreign Dissemination/Top Secret/No Unauthorized Electronic Reproduction or Conveyance. The last word, SYMMETRY, was the computer-generated name for their Beirut operation.

"We lost Marcus, Dick," said Coates. "The report's on top."

Mason opened the folder and scanned Art Stucky's message. He sighed. "Anybody claiming credit for it?"

Coates shook his head. "No. Too early anyway." Like Mason, the DDO was hoping this was simply a random kidnapping. In Beirut, it was possible.

"What did Stucky do?"

"He told the agent to lay low and make contact again in two days. That should give us time to make decisions."

"Okay, you and Sylvia put your heads together. I want all the SYMMETRY product sifted, and I want rough conclusions by tomorrow. Focus on whatever Marcus had going the last few weeks. Maybe he struck a nerve somewhere, and we missed it. Next, I want OpSec checked inside and out, and I want a plan to cauterize this thing if we have to. Questions?"

Both deputies shook their heads.

"This is not good news," Mason said. "Aside from the fact we've lost a good agent and maybe a whole network, there's a political side. I just got done with Smith over at the IOC—by the way, George, you best put on your hip waders before you go over tomorrow."

"That, bad?"

"He's got an agenda, that's for certain."

"What about SYMMETRY?"

"Not a word. Right now, there's nothing to tell. My call—I'll take the flak.

"Bottom line: SYMMETRY is our flagship on our 'war on terrorism' as Smith put it. The president is dedicated to making a dent in terrorism, and everybody knows it—especially on the Hill. Plenty of people are looking for anything they can use to sink him. Being able to label a major policy a failure would be just the kind of ammunition they need. And as much as I'd like to think we're above politics, that's just not the case."

Mason leaned forward to make sure he had their attention. "This is what they call a career decider, people. Whatever it takes, we fix SYMMETRY, and if it can't be fixed, we find a way to turn it into a win. Understood?"

What Mason had essentially told Coates and Albrect was, *I think it stinks, but if we don't make this thing right, we're all out of jobs.*

Quantico, Virginia

WHEN CHARLIE LATHAM'S BOSS FIRST APPROACHED HIM WITH THE idea of teaching a few seminars at the FBI academy, Latham balked. He wasn't a teacher, he argued. As usual, his wife Bonnie had simplified it for him: "Crap." Whether he was in the field teaching by example or in a classroom teaching by lecture, it was the same thing. Now, two years later, Latham had to admit he enjoyed it.

Today's topic was the fall of the Soviet Union and its effect on espionage operations in Europe and Asia. Though a decade had passed, the U.S.S.R.'s dissolution was still an idea backdrop for the kind of lessons fledgling agents needed to learn.

To the trainees Latham was something of a legend, perhaps the greatest CE/I (counterespionage and intelligence) and spy hunter in FBI history. Now he was working counterterrorism.

". . . it's important we don't get tunnel vision when assessing threats," he said. "The former Soviet intelligence community hasn't vanished. And there are other organizations out there that deserve our attention. Think about the old Cold War term the Soviets used for its bloc countries: *satellites.* Initially, they were designed to insulate the U.S.S.R. against invasion, but it didn't take long for the Kremlin to see the opportunity. These satellites could be molded in Russia's image, could carry out its clandestine dictates. In other words, surrogate covert warfare. Why do the dirty work when you can get someone else to do it for you?

"So, when you get into the field—and if you are so blessed as to find yourself in CE and I—" Latham paused as there was general laughter. "—ask yourself this: All that infrastructure, all those agents, all those controllers . . .

Where did they go and what are they doing now?"

A young trainee raised his hand. "Hold on a second, sir. Can anybody today mount operations with the same sophistication of the Soviets?"

"The French, the Germans—"

"But those are our—"

"Allies? No such thing, not when it comes to espionage. It goes on everywhere, all the time. Allies simply aren't as likely to act as vigorously against one another, that's all. Sophistication is nothing more than training, creativity, and resources. Those things don't go away. There'll always be someone with a need, and someone willing to supply it."

"You're talking about freelance espionage, aren't you?"

"Could be. Look at all the weapons scientists that found themselves out of work after the Soviet Union collapsed. We were—still are, in fact—trying to figure what they're doing. Same deal with all those KGB boys and their Czech and Bulgarian counterparts. Some are working in factories making shoelaces. Some aren't."

Another trainee raised his hand. "Sir, I know this is off the subject, but I was wondering if you might . . . I mean, we'd be interested to hear about the Vorsalov case."

That caught Latham by surprise. He hadn't thought about that for . . . How long? A whole week? He paused, took a sip of water. "Maybe next time. You're right, though, it's a good, uh . . . case study." *On just how quick a rookie agent can die, right, Charlie?*

Suddenly he felt like a hypocrite, standing there as a supposed expert when just a decade ago an agent not much older than these kids died in his arms. And it had been his fault. What could he tell them? *Even if you run a flawless op, track down and corner Russia's most dangerous KGB illegal, you can still lose.*

He hadn't expected the Russian to bolt, and he certainly hadn't expected him to kill to get away. It just wasn't done—or so the rules went. *That was crap then, and it's crap now,* thought Latham. He should have known better.

He glanced at his watch. "I want you to think about something for next time. On the robbery side, banks can be held up only a certain number of ways; serial killers usually stick to predicted profiles. But CE and I is a fluid business. The threat never goes away. It might mutate—tactics or allegiances or goals might change—but it's always there. Where there are secrets, there'll be people who want them and will do anything to get them. Okay, see you next time."

Latham watched the students file out, then walked to the window and looked out. "Demons, Charlie," he muttered.

Kingston, Jamaica

IN A BUNGALOW OVERLOOKING THE ISLAND'S SOUTHERN SHORE, THE man resealed the false bottom of the suitcase and carefully repacked the clothes. He could hear her in the bathroom, humming as she finished putting on her makeup. Once satisfied the case was ready, he returned it to the bed and sat down beside it. He closed his eyes and took a deep breath.

She came out of the bathroom, placed her kit in the bag, then closed it. She leaned over and kissed him. "I wish you could come," she said.

"As do I. As soon as I finish my business, I will join you." He traced the line of her jaw with his fingertip. "I think I'll have a hard time waiting."

She giggled. "Hard? Did you say hard?"

He kissed her again. "Don't tempt me. You'll miss your flight."

She was a pretty woman, if slightly overweight, and he'd had no trouble orchestrating their whirlwind romance. To his practiced eye, she was the perfect target: Just the right mix of low self-esteem and neediness. All it had taken was some attention and well-rehearsed passion.

There had been a surprise with this one, however. In the past he'd been able to use the skills with a certain detachment, not unlike the skill a golfer uses to assess a putting green. But this time . . . He couldn't put his finger on it. He wrote if off to weariness. He needed rest.

The woman stroked his shirtfront. "We have time. . . ."

"When I'm with you, there is never enough time. Now go, before I lose control."

She beamed. "All right. You'll call me with your flight number?"

"Of course."

He hefted the green checkered suitcase off the bed, guided her to the front door, and opened it. A yellow taxi waited at the end of the path.

They embraced again. Her eyes were wet, and he dabbed them with his handkerchief. Abruptly, the feeling returned. *What is this?* he thought. *She is nothing. A tool, nothing more. Get on with it!*

He walked her to the cab, put her bag in the trunk, and closed the car door behind her. "I already miss you," she murmured.

"Travel safe." He patted the taxi's roof, and it pulled away.

Beirut

BOUND AND BLINDFOLDED, MARCUS FELT HIMSELF SHOVED FROM behind. He fell to his knees. The floor was made of stone, damp and cold. He could feel the chill seeping into his bare feet.

They led him down some steps, then turned left at the bottom. Now he could hear water lapping. He caught the smell of tar and rotting wood. *Docks,* he thought. Where, though? It could be anywhere in the city—anywhere in the country, for that matter. His heart sank. How were they going to rescue him if they didn't know where he was?

Another turn. Down another corridor, this one longer. He heard a crackling noise to the left. It sounded like a welder's torch. An acrid stench filled the air. A man's scream echoed down the corridor. *Oh, God, oh God . . .*

He was jerked to a stop. He felt cold steel at his throat. The blade paused, then ripped downward, cutting away his shirt and pants. The blindfold was torn away, and he was shoved forward. The door slammed behind him.

Marcus blinked his eyes clear and found himself standing in a windowless stone cell.

4

Shiono Misaki, Japan

TANNER SHOWERED, ORDERED COFFEE FROM ROOM SERVICE, AND sat on his balcony. The day was sunny and warm with a slight breeze. He had half an hour before breakfast with Camille, and there was a lot to think about.

Lying in bed the night before, images of the shooting kept playing in his mind. *Umako Ohira.* Irrational as it was, Tanner couldn't help feeling he'd failed the man. In those brief seconds before the fatal shot had come, could he have done something different?

The figure below his window was also a curiosity. It could have been anyone—hotel staff, a guest—but long ago he'd developed a healthy suspicion of coincidence. This counted, he felt.

Though now a civilian, Tanner had spent almost a third of his life in the U.S. military. After graduating from the University of Colorado, he enrolled in Navy Officer Candidate School, after which came four years in the Naval Special Warfare community, followed by four more years with SEAL Team Six, the Navy's counterterrorist group, and a final four attached to a multiservice hybrid experiment called the Intelligence Support Activity Group, or ISAG.

In the inner circles of the Pentagon, ISAG members had been called "the new breed of elite warrior/spies," the world's elite special operators. Their training made them unsurpassed in unconventional warfare and covert intelligence gathering deep inside contested territory, in myriad cultures, environments, and situations. Two years after Tanner left ISAG, it was disbanded, a victim of a budgetary turf war between the Pentagon and the CIA. He'd been one of only sixty graduates.

After resigning his commission, Tanner forced himself to take a sabbatical. He'd forgotten what it felt like to simply do nothing—to just *be*. No training, no midnight planes bound for cold waters or humid jungles. It took him most of that year to realize he would never be happy in a nine-to-five job. Luckily, it never came to that.

Tanner's mentor, former ISAG instructor, chief tormentor, and friend, Master Chief Boatswain's Mate Ned Billings, made him an offer he couldn't refuse, and again he found himself part of an experimental group. The group's official designator was NSCD ("Knee-sid") 1202, named for the National Security Council Directive from which it was born. The plaque on the door to the group's Chesapeake Bay office read Holystone, Shiverick.

In the tradecraft jargon, Holystone was a "fix-it company." It worked outside normal channels, silent, unacknowledged, and answerable only to the Oval Office. Where the CIA was a shovel, Holystone was a pair of tweezers. Most importantly, Holystone provided the president plausible deniability. In other words, Holystone and its people did not exist. It was called working on the raw. No cover, no backup.

Holystone had unrestricted access to the U.S. intelligence loop without the accompanying squabbles and political infighting. Its budget—a fraction of the size of the CIA's annual cafeteria allotment—came directly from the president's covert ops fund and was therefore off-limits to both the General Accounting Office and congressional oversight.

How long had he been with Holystone? Tanner thought. Six years. Cliché or not, time did, in fact, fly. In that time, he'd found a home with Holystone and its people. He'd also lost his wife on a mountain in Colorado and his mentor Ned Billings during a project in the Caribbean—the very same ordeal that had reunited him with his finest friend, Ian Cahil.

And now this. A simple vacation turned murder mystery. *So what?* he thought. He was witness to a murder. He'd picked up a key Ohira had carried in his hand. It was an impulse—an unwise one at that—but he could turn it in to the police and be done with it.

But try as he might, Tanner couldn't shake the image of Ohira's panic-stricken face. And then the shot . . . the head exploding . . . Who was Ohira, and why was he worth murdering?

It was one of his many failings, he knew. As a child, the surest way to get Briggs to take on a challenge was to tell him it was either impossible or the answer was a mystery. This same character quirk had pushed him toward the SEALs, where only one in four candidates graduate, then to the ISAG, where the attrition rate exceeded 90 percent. Now, that same quirk—though tempered with hard-earned wisdom—was pushing him toward the mystery of why a man was executed before his very eyes.

CAMILLE SAW BRIGGS WALKING ACROSS THE POOL PATIO. SHE FELT her heart skip. *Stop it, Camille.* He was handsome, yes, but it was more than that. Approaching him last night was so unlike her, but she'd felt lonely and out of place. And then, as if on cue, he'd appeared.

Tanner stood about two inches over six feet, 185 pounds. He carried himself with a sureness, an economy of motion. He was comfortable in his own skin. His hair was coffee brown, his face well tanned—probably from more time spent out-of-doors than in—and his smile was easy. His eyes were ocean-blue, their corners laugh-lined. *The eyes,* she thought. Yes, they were warm, but there was something else there, a hardness. It was as if they were constantly dissecting and categorizing everything they took in.

She hadn't slept well the night before. The incident had shaken her, but more than that, she was troubled by the way Briggs had reacted to the shooting. She'd seen such reactions before—usually in soldiers—but in other kinds of men as well, and that's what worried her. And what about the key? He had palmed and pocketed it smoothly, without hesitation. Was he somehow involved in what had happened?

"Sorry I'm late," he said, taking a seat under the umbrella. "Have you ordered?"

"Not yet."

The waiter appeared. They both ordered a fruit salad, wheat toast, and coffee.

"How did you sleep?" Tanner asked.

Camille shrugged. "You?"

"The same."

A bellman approached the table and offered Tanner a small tray with a receipt and bill. "The item you requested, sir. The concierge is holding it."

"Thank you," Tanner signed the slip and handed the man a tip.

"What's that about?" asked Camille.

"A gift for a friend I met yesterday."

Breakfast came, and they ate in silence, enjoying the sun. A pair of finches landed beside their table, and Camille dropped them some bread crumbs.

"So," said Camille. "I never asked. Are you on vacation or business?"

"Vacation. And you?"

"The same. Though last night, it didn't seem like much of one. May I ask you a question?"

"Go ahead."

"Why did you do it? Jump over the fence, I mean. They had guns, yes? How did you know you wouldn't get shot yourself?"

"I didn't. It was stupid."

Perhaps, thought Camille, *but probably more considered than the average person's impulse*. "Well, I'll tell you this, Mr. Tanner: If this thing between us is to go any further, it just wouldn't do to get yourself killed."

"This thing?" he said with a smile. "What makes you think there will be anything between us?"

"Women know. It's in your eyes."

"Really."

"Oh yes. It's a gift we have. So, your curiosity: What

did it get you?" she asked. "What great mystery did you find in the car?"

"No mystery. I was mostly concerned about other passengers. Now you: What kind of work do you do?"

"I'm an attorney—immigration law. In fact, I do a lot of work in America."

"I didn't realize that many Ukrainians wanted to emigrate."

"Quite a few, really, but also to Israel, Canada, Great Britain. Camille sipped her coffee. "I'm sunbathing this morning, I think. Will you join me?"

"Maybe later. I'm going to take a run, do some diving."

"Diving where, for what?"

"Up the coast a bit . . . for fun."

"You have a strange idea of vacation, I think, running and swimming."

"So I've been told."

"You'll be careful?"

"Always. I'd hate to miss our dinner date tonight."

Camille smiled. "How do you know we're having dinner tonight?"

"Men know. It's a gift."

Camille laughed. "I accept. On two conditions. One, we make it tomorrow night. I must take the shuttle to Tokyo tonight for a meeting. I'll be back in the morning. And two, over dinner you tell me your life story."

Tanner stood and pushed in his chair. "Conditions accepted. Tomorrow night, seven o'clock?"

As Tanner walked away, Camille thought, *What in God's name are you doing?* It was silly; nothing could come of it. She shrugged, deciding she didn't give a damn.

Tanner took the two-mile run slowly, but with the twenty-five-pound bag of rice over one shoulder and his rucksack over the other, it turned out to be a fair workout. The time passed quickly as he thought of Camille.

Though she'd covered it well, she'd been probing him. Was it simple curiosity? Or perhaps she was wary of him, thinking he wasn't what *he* claimed to be—which he wasn't, of course. Whatever her reasons, a part of his brain was telling him to tread carefully. Another part, however, was hoping she was exactly what she seemed. *Careful, Briggs,* he told himself.

He found Mitsu sitting on the front steps of the family's hut. The boy was engrossed with a quarter-sized beetle that was crawling up his forearm.

"Good morning," Tanner said.

Mitsu looked up and smiled. "Oh, hello."

"Who's your friend?"

"He lives under the house."

"A good place for him. Is your mother home?"

Mitsu nodded, ran into the hut, and returned with his mother.

Tanner laid the bag of rice on the porch. "Mitsu, please tell your mother I enjoyed dinner very much, and I would be honored if she would accept this gift."

Mitsu translated, and the mother smiled and bowed several times. Tanner asked Mitsu, "How would you like to take a short trip with me?"

"I would like that very much."

With Mother's blessing, they climbed into the family skiff and began rowing into the breakers. Mitsu would have made a fine addition to any crewing team; his stroke was steady and strong, and within minutes they were a quarter mile off the beach. "Here," Mitsu said, handing Tanner a small oilskin bag with a cork stopper.

"What's this?"

"Air. When you run out on the bottom, you breathe."

"Good idea. I'll be back in five minutes."

Briggs adjusted his mask, slipped on his fins, and rolled over the side.

He hung motionless in the cloud of bubbles for a moment, then turned over, finned to the bottom, and started swimming. He wound his way around and through the coral outcrops and sea grass, watching fish and crabs and even an occasional octopus dart along the bottom. Here and there he stopped to drop a shell into his bag.

After three minutes, his lungs began to burn, so he stopped and took a lungful of air from the bag. He swam for another three minutes, then headed for the surface. He climbed aboard the skiff.

"Did the bag work for you?" Mitsu asked.

"Like a charm. You're a smart man, Mitsu-san. You know these waters well?"

"Oh, yes."

"I found a warm spot yesterday, but I couldn't find it today. . . ."

"The oyster beds. Over that way," Mitsu said. "Do you want to go?"

"No, I was just curious."

"We can go if you like."

"No, that's okay—"

Something caught Tanner's eye. On the beach, hidden among the trees, he saw a glimmer, like sun on glass. The breeze shifted the limbs, and he saw it again.

"How about tomorrow?" Tanner said.

"Okay."

"Mitsu, does anyone in your village have a car?"

"An automobile? Oh, no."

"Okay, let's go back."

As they neared the shore, Tanner was able to make out a front fender, but as if on cue, the vehicle began creeping back into the trees. When only the windshield was again visible, it stopped.

The skiff's hull scraped the sand, and they climbed out, pulled the skiff ashore, and tied it to a nearby palm. Tanner pulled a shell from his bag and handed it to Mitsu. "For your rowing skills."

"Thank you! We go again tomorrow?"

"We'll see. Go on home now."

Mitsu nodded and ran off.

Tanner loaded his gear into his rucksack, hefted it over his shoulder, and started jogging back toward the hotel. After a hundred yards, he dropped the rucksack, veered into the tree line, and turned again, circling back. After fifty yards he stopped, crouched down.

Thirty feet across a dirt track he could see the vehicle's rear bumper jutting from the foliage. He crawled ahead until he was within arm's reach of it, only then realizing it was a dark blue pickup truck, almost identical to the one Ohira's killers had used the night before. The license plate was missing.

The driver's side door opened. Tanner froze. Footsteps crunched through the undergrowth, moving toward the front of the truck. Tanner peeked over the tailgate. One man sat in the passenger seat, and through the windshield Briggs could see the driver standing near the tree line, scanning the beach with a pair of binoculars.

Looking for me? Briggs wondered. *If so, why?* Because of what he'd seen, or because of the key? Or was it something he hadn't yet considered?

The footsteps were returning.

Tanner risked another glance over the tailgate. The driver was Japanese, a bull of a man with a thick neck, square face, and heavy brows. Tanner committed the face to memory, then ducked down and crawled out of sight.

The truck's engine growled to life. After a moment it backed out, turned onto the road, and drove off, disappearing into the trees. Tanner watched it go, thinking hard.

By the time the taxi dropped him off in Tanabe and he found a phone booth, it was almost two P.M.—almost midnight in Washington. He was about to wake somebody from a sound sleep, but it couldn't be helped.

It took only moments for the overseas operator to route the call to the U.S., but once there, he waited through twenty seconds of clicks as the call was sent to the National Security Agency in Fort Meade, Maryland, where it was electronically scrubbed, bounced off a FLTSATCOM (fleet communication satellite), then transmitted to a secure trunk line to the Holystone office.

Finally, the sleepy voice of Walter Oaken answered. "Hello."

"Morning, Oaks."

"Briggs . . . ? What time is it?"

"Depends on where you are."

"How's the vacation?" Oaken asked.

"Never a dull moment. Can you conference me with Leland?"

"Sure, hang on."

More clicks. Leland Dutcher's voice came on the line. "Morning, Briggs."

"Sorry to wake you both."

"Don't worry about it. What've you got?"

For the next five minutes, Tanner related what had happened, from the shooting of Umako Ohira to his spotting of the truck.

"And you think this was more than a simple murder?" Dutcher asked.

"Pretty sure."

"You have the key with you?"

"Yes."

"Bad impulse, son."

A forty-year veteran of the intelligence community, Leland Dutcher had plenty of experience with on-the-spot judgment calls. He'd made his own fair share of them— good and bad.

If ever a man embodied the "walk softly but carry a big stick" image, it was Leland Dutcher. He was soft-spoken but direct, a man of quiet authority. His appearance was a spymaster's dream: average, medium, and unremarkable, except for a pair of hard brown eyes. In the tradecraft jargon, Dutcher was a "gray man," and it was this lack of distinction that made him one of the CIA's best controllers during the Cold War as he slipped in and out of the Soviet bloc under the noses of the KGB and the East German *Stasi*.

When it came to his people, however, Leland Dutcher was anything but gray. He was protective to a fault. People were his most valuable resource, especially in this business, and the ends *did not* always justify the means.

It was, in fact, this protective nature that had caused Dutcher's decline at the CIA. While substituting for a hospitalized DDO during a counterinsurgency operation in Peru, Dutcher weighed the risk to the team unwarranted and ordered it out. Lives were saved, but the DDO, a political appointee from a university think tank, lashed out. Outcome notwithstanding, he argued, Dutcher had overstepped his authority. The rift was widened further as the rescued team was debriefed and it became clear the order had not only saved lives but had also saved the network.

For Dutcher, it didn't require much analysis to know bullets directed at supposedly covert assets indicated a rapidly deteriorating *overt* situation. He said as much to both the DCI and the Senate and House Intelligence Oversight Committees, both of whom secretly agreed. Neither, however, was willing to cross swords with the DDO, who had powerful backing in the private sector.

The subsequent intra-agency feud began to erode Dutcher's ability to protect his people, which in turn began to taint the product. Knowing the DDO's grudge would eventually gut the directorate, Dutcher resigned. Politics had no business in the intelligence trade, he felt. It was too dangerous for the country and too dangerous for the people who were asked to do its secret bidding.

Six months later, newly elected President Reagan invited Dutcher for a weekend at Camp David to "shoot the breeze." There in a cabin in the Catoctin Mountains of Maryland, Reagan outlined the idea of a detached intelligence organization, chartered by NSC directive and controlled by the executive branch. By the end of the weekend, Dutcher was sold. In trademark Reagan-esque fashion, the president simply shook Dutcher's hand and said, "I'll give you what you need. You make it work."

In the years that followed, Dutcher did just that. He and his people had fixed more "unfixable" problems than the American public ever knew, or would know, existed. Now Dutcher was wondering where this latest problem would take them.

"Tell me about the key," he said to Tanner. "We'll do some digging."

Tanner described the key in detail.

Dutcher asked, "Walt, what's the embassy's role in something like this?"

In addition to keeping all the gears at Holystone turning,

Walter Oaken was their resident encyclopedia. The running joke at the office was that the game show *Jeopardy!* had settled out of court to keep him off their show lest he break the bank. For all his knowledge, though, Oaken was unpretentious and keenly aware that people, not information, made the world go 'round.

"By now, the Prefectural Police will have already contacted the legal attaché. It's standard procedure."

"Then what?"

"Not much. At most, a routine message to State."

"Good," said Dutcher. "Do we have any in-country assets we can tap?"

"Maybe," Oaken said. I'll make some calls.

Dutcher said, "Briggs, tell me about this woman you met."

Tanner told them what he knew about Camille.

"We'd best check her, too. How about these folks following you?"

"Right now it looks like simple curiosity. I'm okay."

"Stay that way. Whoever they are, don't give them any more reason to be interested in you."

THE CIA'S NATIONAL PHOTOGRAPHIC INTERPRETATION CENTER (NPIC) is a nondescript concrete building with tinted windows surrounded by a barbed-wire fence at the intersection of First and M Streets. Inside, two thousand analysts and technicians go about the business of making sense of the thousands of radar, thermal, and visual images produced by satellites with names like *Keyhole, Lacrosse*, and *Vortex*. Despite such James Bondian technology that includes computers costing more than the average citizen makes in a lifetime, most of the NPIC's analysts are devotees of the plain old eyeball.

This was the case with Rudy Grayson, the chief interpreter on duty when the latest KH-14 images from the Golan Heights came off the printer.

He aligned the strips vertically on his light table, then scanned them with a magnifying glass. He liked to get a feel for what he was seeing before moving on to a complex dissection, using the computer to manipulate the millions of pixels that comprised the image.

Pixels are individual cells of varying grayscale contrast, each carrying dark and light values ranging from 1 to 10,000, each of which a computer can adjust to highlight selected features. While the human eye cannot detect the difference between, say, a value of 12 and 14, a computer can, making millions of such adjustments until an image reaches optimal resolution.

Today, as he had been for the past four months, Grayson's job was to confirm that both Israeli and Syrian troop strengths on the Golan matched the agreed limits.

The nearer the date for the UN-managed buffer expansion on the Golan came, the more skittish the involved parties became. UN troops on the Golan was not a new idea, but this expansion was to begin a disengagement of both Israeli and Syrian forces that would eventually demilitarize this greatly contested chunk of land.

The theory behind the plan was two-pronged: As long as Israel occupied the Golan, Syria would not engage in the peace process, and as long as Syria planned to militarize a repatriated Golan, Israel would not give it back. Israel remembered too well the years of Katyusha bombardment its northern kibbutzes suffered from Syrian positions before the Golan was captured during the '67 war.

Grayson was scanning the last strip when something near the border caught his eye. It was not on the Golan, but to its north and east, in the deserts of Syria.

What the hell is that?

He turned to his computer, double-clicked a file, then ran his finger down the screen. He frowned and picked up the phone. "Hey Linda, is Jerry around? I've got something he should take a look at."

Japan

AT DUSK TANNER TOOK A TAXI INTO TANABE AND FOUND A SE-cluded *shokudo*, or neighborhood restaurant. At the front door he was greeted by a smiling hostess who bowed, offered him a pair of cloth slippers, and led him to a table overlooking a small garden. Paper lanterns lined the roof's overhang.

He started with *ocha,* or green tea, then had an appetizer of *chawan-mushi,* a dish of vegetables and steamed shrimp. For the main course he ordered tempura and *mizu-taki,* a dish of chicken, leeks, and vermicelli boiled in a fish stock. It took all his willpower not to order a second course and simply settle for a pot of hot saki.

He was savoring his second cup when the hostess approached and handed him a small white card:

SATO IEYASU
Inspector, (retired)
Criminal Investigative Bureau

Tanner looked up at the hostess, who merely smiled.

Interesting. The CIB was the Japanese equivalent of the FBI. He shrugged. "Ask the inspector to join me, please."

She returned with a Japanese man in his early sixties. "Mr. Tanner?"

"Inspector Ieyasu."

Ieyasu nodded and bowed. He was a short man with thinning salt-and-pepper hair. "Thank you for seeing me."

"What can I do for you?" Tanner asked, gesturing for him to sit.

"It is not what you can do for me, but what I can do for you."

"You've lost me."

"We have a mutual friend: Walter Oaken. He thought I might be of some help. As I understand it, you found yourself in a bit of trouble last night."

"I see. At the risk of sounding paranoid—"

Ieyasu raised his hand. "I understand. Call him if you wish. I will wait here."

Tanner went to the lobby and borrowed the house phone. He waited through two minutes of clicks before Oaken answered.

"Oaks, its me."

"Funny you should call," Oaken said.

"I'll bet. Guess who I'm having dinner with?"

"Sato. Sorry I didn't have time to warn you."

"No harm done. Describe him."

Oaken did so, and Tanner said, "That's him."

"If there's anybody who might have some answers, it's him. Talk to him, then call me. One piece of advice, though: Don't get into a saki drinking contest with him. He's dangerous."

Tanner laughed. "Okay."

He hung up and returned to the table.

"Well?" Ieyasu asked.

"Oaks told me not to drink with you."

For the first time, Inspector Ieyasu smiled. "A wise man, Walter."

AFTER A SECOND POT OF TEA, IEYASU CAME TO BUSINESS. "WHAT did Walter tell you about me?"

"Aside from the fact that I can trust you, nothing."

"It's important you understand that I do not work for your government."

"I do."

"Walter and I have a long-standing relationship. In matters of mutual interest we have been known to share information. So. Why don't you start by telling me about the incident."

Tanner did so, giving Ieyasu the same details he gave Dutcher, and finishing with his second sighting of the pickup truck.

"The night of the murder, you saw none of the men's faces?"

"No."

"The victim, Umako Ohira, had you ever seen him before?"

"Never."

"I don't suppose Inspector Tanaka told you he was assaulted three days ago?"

"Again, no."

"I'm unsurprised. You see, I know Tanaka. He lives beyond his means, if you understand me. Ohira was very specific about his description of his attackers; he even picked one out of a photo file."

"For a retiree you certainly have solid information."

"I have many friends. The man Ohira identified is named Tange Noboru. Your description of the driver at the beach matches him perfectly. Noboru is a former *yakuza*—what you call the Mafia—enforcer. He now works for one of our largest industrialists—some say for the richest man in Nippon—Hiromasa Takagi."

"Of Takagi Industries?"

"The same."

Tanner's interest was piqued. Takagi Industries was a multinational conglomerate with holdings in everything from textiles to nuclear energy. That alone made Hiromasa Takagi influential, but it was his alleged connection with the Black Ocean Society that most concerned Western intelligence agencies. Though never proven, Black Ocean is said to consist of Japan's richest men, a group whose clout not only dictated the direction of Japanese industry but also the policies of the Japanese government.

"This man that was murdered last night," Ieyasu continued, "was an employee of Takagi's, in his maritime division. He worked as an engineer at the shipyard south of Anan."

"Let me see if I understand this," Tanner said. "First Ohira is mugged by Takagi's chief of security, then three days later he's shot dead, and the police have missed the connection?"

"I doubt anyone has missed the connection. Certainly not Inspector Tanaka. As you Americans say, he knows where his bread is buttered."

"I see."

"I don't think you do. Over the past year, eight Takagi employees have either gone missing or have died in accidents."

"Takagi employees probably number in the thousands, many doing hazardous work," Tanner countered. "Besides, most conglomerates have skeletons in their closets. Takagi is probably no different."

"That might be true if there weren't more to it. Do you remember the Tokyo subway gas attack a few years ago?"

"Of course."

"I was still with the CIB then. I was assigned to the task force. Eventually, we found an informant who claimed the cult was simply a front. You see, the components used were more sophisticated than the government allowed. This informant alleged a connection between the cult, the Japanese Red Army, and Takagi Industries."

"What connection?"

"The JRA supplied the material—most of which was very hard to obtain—to make the gas bombs, who was in turn supplied by contacts at Takagi Chemical. I pursued this but was told to stop. I refused, so I was . . . invited to retire."

"And you think Ohira's murder is somehow connected to that?" said Tanner.

"Not necessarily, but his makes nine mysterious deaths of Takagi employees in the last year. Perhaps it is my background, but I have never been a believer in coincidence."

Tanner smiled; he liked this man. "That makes two of us. You said the previous eight employees either disappeared or had not-so-accidental accidents?"

"That's correct."

"So by simply murdering Ohira they broke tradition. I wonder why."

"That, Mr. Tanner, is a very good question."

6

THE PRESIDENT, DCI DICK MASON, AND NATIONAL SECURITY AD-
viser James Talbot sat in the Oval Office reviewing the
president's daily brief. Classified top secret and tightly restricted, the PDB offers the president a condensation of
what's new in the world. Over the years, presidents have
varied in how they got the PDB's information. The current
president liked to read the PDB personally and in an informal setting. Shirtsleeves, coffee, and bagels were usually
the order of the day.

Dick Mason watched the president put down his bagel.
He knew which section his boss was reading: a transcript
of the Iranian prime minister's most recent speech to a
group of senior *Pasdaran* officers. The *Pasdaran*, also
known as the Islamic Revolutionary Guards, was one of
Iran's deadliest terrorist exports.

The CIA had long believed the prime minister was being
influenced by the current ayatollah, which in itself was unremarkable, but the content of this particular speech con-
tradicted the call for reconciliation he'd been spouting for
the past eight months. In Mason's eyes, this meant that
while Iran's goals remained unchanged, their methods were
leaning more toward the covert.

"This is an accurate translation, Dick?" the president
asked, running his finger along the text. " 'At every turn
we lure the Great Satan into our traps, and then crush him
under our heel like a squirming beetle. We have countless
allies, more than there are stars in the heavens, and when
the sky rains fire, our enemies will be pushed into the
sea.' " The president looked up.

"It's accurate, sir. But to be fair, we couldn't expect him to talk nice about us in front of a group of fanatical *Pasdaran* officers."

"How much is just talk and how much is real?"

"Not an easy question, Mr. President. Islam is more than religion for them; it influences every aspect of their lives, including government. The U.S., along with the rest of the nonbelievers, are evil incarnate. Failing to set us straight jeopardizes their own souls. For them, that's serious business. The only change we can likely expect is a heavier reliance on covert action. Same goes for Syria and Sudan."

"Define *covert*," said James Talbot.

"Increased use of surrogates, front groups, political interference. In short, deniable operations."

The president was silent for a few moments. "Okay. Next topic."

"Still Iran," said Mason. "Latest estimates have their oil exports down four percent in the last six months, but production itself hasn't changed. Same with the peripheral industries."

"Where's it going?"

"Into diesel production, then storage. This could mean a lot of things, but the clearest analogy we have is the Iran-Iraq war; we saw this same trend in the years prior to it. Iran was stockpiling for tanks and trucks and the like."

"Are you telling me something, Dick?"

"Not necessarily, sir. As I said, there could be any number of reasons. We know next month they're conducting an army exercise outside Hamadan. They've done it at this time every year, four years running."

"Did they stockpile for previous exercises?" asked Talbot.

"No. The point is, though, we've got nothing to suggest they're on the warpath. It does bear watching, and we're doing that."

"Jim," the president said to his national security adviser, "OPEC's meeting in Bahrain next week. Talk to State, see if the Saudis will do a little probing."

"Yes, sir."

"Okay, Dick, what's next?"

"Syria."

"Good news or bad news?"

"Good news and undecided news, sir. Routine ELINT shows the Golan is still stable, no changes. But yesterday the NPIC caught a side-lobe image of what looks like a group of Syrian APCs, tanks, and even a few companies of airborne troops making a drop a couple hundred miles south and east of the Bekka."

"An exercise?"

"It appears so. It's an odd mix of forces: elements from the First Armored Division and the Seventh and Ninth Mechanized, which will probably be replacing their counterparts in the Bekka in a couple months. It's a routine rotation, but we've never seen them exercise this close to a changeover period. The other elements are remnants from the downsized Golan Task Group—the Third Armored and Tenth and Eleventh Mechanized. On the upside, the Dar'a Task Group isn't involved; all its units are accounted for."

"Pretty big exercise," said Talbot. "They moving in any particular direction?"

"It's early yet, but it doesn't look like it. We have no idea about the mission or duration, but it matches previous exercise profiles, if a little larger. The other interesting thing is the commander in charge: General Issam al-Khatib."

"How do you know he's in charge?"

"He was at the site."

"So?"

"We photographed him."

Both the president and Talbot glanced up in amazement.

"Khatib was formerly in charge of the Saraya and Difa Defense Companies, about twenty-five thousand special forces soldiers, until it was re-formed into Unit five sixty-nine, ostensibly a regular armored and mechanized group," Mason said. "He's also part of Assad's inner circle, fanatically loyal, and an Alawite to boot."

"Alawite?" said Talbot.

"Assad's religious sect," Mason explained. "It's a Muslim minority group, but it has key members in positions of power in both the government and the military. After Khatib left the defense companies, we lost track of him for a year. There were rumors he was attached to Air Force intelligence, which handles terrorist liaison: recruitment, training, supply, that sort of thing."

"Is that significant?" asked the president.

"Maybe, if it's true. Like his father, Bashar Assad has always placed someone from his inner circle in those kinds of roles. It could have been nothing more than a career builder. At any rate, wherever Khatib *was,* he's in the desert now."

The president said, "So, bottom line?"

Mason paused. His boss wanted a prediction. Like most laypeople, the president didn't recognize the difference between capabilities and intentions. In the intelligence community the rule was: Never talk about intentions; talk about capabilities. Talk about what the enemy can do *if* he decides to do it. Intentions were, after all, products of the human brain, which is an unpredictable organ at best.

Mason smiled, spread his hands. "Syria is conducting a military exercise."

The president smiled. "Okay. Jim, any statements from Syria?"

"No, Mr. President."

"Let's let 'em know we're curious. Have State handle it, and do it quick, before the Israelis get nervous. Dick, your boys will be paying close attention, I assume?"

"We've retasked the bird to include the exercise area in the Golan sweep."

"Good. Anything else?"

"One thing, sir. SYMMETRY."

"The Beirut operation."

"Yes." Mason briefly explained their loss of Marcus.

"Damn it! How in hell does something like this happen!"

"It just does, sir. Not often, but it does happen. Especially in Beirut."

"So I've heard. What are we doing?"

"We've ordered the network to go quiet, and we're working the product. Maybe Marcus was onto something we missed. Also, we're checking OpSec—"

"OpSec?" asked Talbot.

"Operational security. That includes all the communication and cover procedures we had in place: dead letter drops, safe-call locations. As far as who took him, we're stumped. No ransom, no body . . . nothing. No one is taking credit for it, either. That worries me. Usually, they can't wait to let the world know they've snatched someone."

"Suppose this isn't a routine kidnapping. Suppose somebody took him for a reason," Talbot said. "What then?"

"If they've got him, he *will* talk. How long he holds out is the only question."

"And the network?"

"We'd have to assume it's blown."

The president took off his glasses and rubbed the bridge of his nose. "Dick, we've got a lot riding on this thing—on that whole damned region—and SYMMETRY is part of the big picture. You know that."

"Yes, Mr. President."

"Then fix it, Dick. Whatever it takes, fix it."

7

La Guardia Airport, New York

IF POLLED, ANY PILOT, MILITARY OR CIVILIAN, WOULD RANK TAKEOFF and landing as the worst times for an in-flight emergency. These are times when the plane and its crew are performing their most complex functions, from braking to throttle adjustments to glide-path trimming. It's also the time when aircraft is most vulnerable, those moments when it's poised between being a 125-ton aircraft and a lumbering 125-ton bus with wings.

A former Thud driver in Vietnam, Carl Hotchkins was a seventeen-year veteran of the airline industry, the last five of which he'd spent in aircraft just like this 737. Today he was carrying 104 passengers, most returning from vacation in Kingston, Jamaica, and Orlando, Florida.

Crossing the runway threshold at 120 feet, Hotchkins was easing back on the throttle when the explosion came. In the cockpit it sounded like a dull *crump,* but Hotchkins instinctively knew what it was.

The blast had ripped a hole in the aluminum fuselage just below and aft of the port wing. Fire and shrapnel tore into the passenger cabin, most of it directed upward, but some of it engulfing the passengers on the right side of the aisle. Those opposite them tumbled, still buckled into their seats, through the gaping hole. At the wing root, shrapnel ripped open a pair of fluid lines, both of which immediately began gushing.

Hotchkins reacted instantly. Even as the 737 heeled over, he throttled down and punched a button that immediately sealed the fuel system. With his airspeed dropping rapidly, the landing gear down, and less than sixty feet of air between them and the Tarmac, his first concern was leveling the aircraft. If he could do that, the 737 could almost drop out of the sky, and they'd still have a fair chance of survival.

"Tower, this is Delta nineteen alpha declaring emergency," Hotchkins radioed.

"Roger, Delta, we see you. Emergency crews rolling. Luck."

Hotchkins switched to intercom. "Flight crew, prepare for emergency landing."

"Fuel leak, Carl, port side system," called the copilot. "Hydraulic malfunction, port side system. The wing took most of it."

"Yeah," Hotchkins grunted, struggling with the yoke. "Altitude?"

"Fifty feet . . . coming level."

"More flap. Landing gear?"

"Starboard and nose are down and locked. . . . Shit! Port side's shows half."

"Right," Hotchkins said, and thought: *Gotta assume we're streaming fuel. One spark and we're gone.* And they *were* going to spark when that gear collapsed.

The Tarmac loomed before the windshield. Forty feet, Hotchkins judged—ten seconds. Out the side window, he glimpsed fire trucks racing down the opposite runway, their lights flashing and sirens warbling.

"We're still losing fuel," said the copilot.

That decided it. Their best chance was to lay the wing into the grassy median; if the gear held, good, but if not, the ploy might just keep the wing off the concrete.

"Tower, nineteen, be advised, I've got a fuel leak. I'm putting her down in the grass."

"Roj, Delta," was the reply.

"Help me, Chuck. . . ." called Hotchkins.

Altitude dropping through 30 feet, Hotchkins forced the 160-foot, 125-ton Boeing laterally through the air toward the median. Hotchkins eyed the blue border lights as they whipped under the wing. Almost there . . . steady . . . steady . . . Now!

Hotchkins cut power and flared the jet, lifting the nose slightly as the starboard gear thumped down with a screech. The port gear followed a moment later. Hotchkins held his breath. The gear trembled, then held. The plane shuddered as the wheels plowed through the grass. With a rhythmic *ca-chunk, ca-chunk*, the wingtip sheared off the border lights. Hotchkins could hear screaming from the cabin.

"Speed?" he called.

"Eighty . . . seventy-five . . ."

"Braking . . . reverse thrust . . . ! Help me . . . step on 'em!"

At that moment, the port gear snapped.

The 737 lurched sideways. Hotchkins was slammed against the window. He pulled himself upright, hands white around the yoke, the veins in his neck bulging. He scanned the gauges. Sixty knots . . . 300 feet of runway left. Past the end of the Tarmac stood a row of maintenance sheds. In the middle of the runway a lone Cessna was desperately trying to taxi clear.

"Come on, come on," Hotchkins chanted. "Stop, baby. . . ."

Slowly, the 737 began slowing, yawing to port as the wingtip plowed through the grass, bulldozing soil before it. Hotchkins fought to keep the nosewheel out of the ditch. He watched, transfixed, as the speed gauge wound down through thirty knots, then twenty-five, then at last to ten. Zero.

The aircraft shuddered to a stop.

Hotchkins exhaled. *Down safe.*

Outside, emergency trucks were pulling alongside. Workers raced toward the plane as the firefighters began laying hoses.

Hotchkins took a moment to force some spit into his mouth, then switched on the intercom. "Ladies and gentlemen, this is the captain. We are on the ground and safe, but as a precaution, we'll be deplaning rapidly. Stay calm and follow the flight attendant's instructions. Flight crew, proceed with emergency egress."

He switched off the intercom and laid his head back

against the seat. He cast a wan smile at the copilot and navigator. They were both pasty white.

Wonder what the hell I look like, Hotchkins thought.

TWO HOURS LATER, THE CRIPPLED BOEING WAS SITTING IN A HANgar at the east end of the airport, illuminated by the overhead fluorescent lights. Fire-suppression foam dripped from the wings and struck the ground with fat *plops*.

The oblong blast hole measured ten feet and extended from under the wing mount to just below the cabin windows. Through the hole, the passenger cabin and baggage compartment were plainly visible.

Despite the bustling activity, the hangar was eerily quiet. Outside, Port Authority Police held back the already-assembling media. Each time the door opened to admit a worker, flashbulbs popped and reporters shouted questions.

Beside the plane stood a Delta Airlines vice president, a regional VP from Boeing, La Guardia's airport manager, and the maintenance manager. An inspector from the National Transportation Safety Board stood staring into the hole.

"Hey," he called to one of the workers, "nobody touches any baggage. Got it? Leave everything." He turned and walked over to the group. "Gentlemen, can I assume you agree this damage was not caused by a routine malfunction?"

"Well, Jesus!" said the airport manager, "what the hell do you think!"

The NTSB man smiled. The question did sound idiotic. Everyone knew what had made that hole. Still, procedure was procedure. Somebody had to make it official. "Please understand: My initial finding will determine where this investigation goes. It's awful hard to unring a bell."

With that, everyone looked to the maintenance manager. The man removed his ball cap and scratched his head. "Ain't too tough a call. Nothing that was *supposed* to be aboard that bird could have done that."

The NTSB man nodded. "Okay, gentlemen, I have some

calls to make. Stick around. In a few hours, this place is going to be a full-fledged circus."

TWO HOURS LATER, THE HANGAR'S POPULATION HAD TRIPLED. NOW reinforcing the rapid-response NTSB team was a full investigative team made up of two dozen men and women. Next came a smaller team from the ATF, or Alcohol, Tobacco & Firearms, followed by representatives from the governor's office, as well as the state attorney general's office. And finally came the FBI, represented by Harry Owen, the SPAIC of the New York Field Office, and Charlie Latham.

Owen and Latham sat in the maintenance office overlooking the hangar. They watched in silence as dozens of figures crawled under, over, and through the crippled Boeing. There was a lot to do, Latham knew, and it had only just begun.

There was luggage to be checked for additional devices; debris to be collected and sorted; samples to be taken, the most important of which would likely come from blast residue, and hopefully, from the bag that held the device—and better still, from the device itself. Considering the nature of the blast, Latham considered this unlikely. It could have been much worse. If the plane had been at altitude, that much explosive would have been overkill. The pilot had done a hell of a job.

Carl Hotchkins had already been debriefed, as had the flight crew and passengers. Their statements would be combined with those of the tower personnel, then checked against the 737's black box recorder. According to the FAA's snapshot report, there was no indication of malfunctions, no weather problems, no air control or approach miscues, and no pilot error.

That left one possibility: Somebody got a bomb aboard the 737 and blew a big hole in it.

Latham was guessing the device had malfunctioned. Though landings and takeoffs were vulnerable times for an aircraft, nothing was surer to kill one than violent depressurization while flying 500 miles an hour at 35,000 feet. Pan Am 103 was proof of that.

But instead of hundreds dead, this one had cost only five lives.

Only, thought Latham.

The dead had already been tentatively identified from the plane's manifest. Visual identification was going to be impossible, since the bodies had skidded along the concrete for more than a quarter mile. There wasn't much left to look at. Of the other 175 passengers, only 7 were injured.

"So tell me again," Latham said to Owen. "Why'd you call me? Hasn't your office got its own—"

"C'mon, Charlie, it was headed for your desk anyway. I just speeded things up," Owen replied. "To the regular guy on the street, this is the kind of thing that happens in Europe or the Middle East. It happens here, it's different. Once the media gets its teeth into it, it's going to turn into a big, ugly circus." Owen grinned. *"Your* circus, pal."

"Thanks a bunch."

Among its many other responsibilities, the Criminal Investigations Division was tasked with all of the Bureau's counterterrorism efforts, and Latham was the best they had. CT work was not that different from CE and I, and with Latham, the FBI had the best of both worlds.

Short, wiry, and bald save a fringe of salt-and-pepper hair, Latham was patient and tenacious and flexible—all qualities that made him not only a great spy hunter, but an even better hunter of terrorists.

Latham started out in CI eighteen years before as a brick agent from the academy and immediately fell in love with spy hunting. Playing cat and mouse with superbly trained KGB and GRU officers was hugely satisfying, and through the years he'd been involved in some of the biggest cases: Pollard, Walker, Koecher . . . and Vorsalov. KGB Colonel Yuri Vorsalov.

In the beginning, Vorsalov had been just another "legal" assigned to the Russian embassy, but four years after being arrested and "persona-non-grata-ed" from the country for attempting to recruit a Raytheon employee, he returned to the U.S. as an "illegal"—a spy working without diplomatic cover. This was the most dangerous kind of agent, for if caught, they face prison rather than deportation.

Latham knew all this, but it hit home one night in Rock Creek Park when the ambush they'd set for Vorsalov went bad. To everyone's shock, the Russian had bolted and run straight into the arms of one of Latham's agents.

The memory was still vivid for Latham: sitting in the rain, cradling the agent as he stared at the oozing puncture in his sternum. He'd never had a chance. Vorsalov had been good with the ice pick, a KGB favorite, and it had taken only a split second.

Though an inquiry said otherwise, Latham knew the agent was dead because of something he'd missed, a detail he'd overlooked, and he'd spent the last ten years trying to figure out what it was.

The door opened and Latham's partner, Paul Randal, entered with a clear plastic bag; inside was a piece of charred suitcase material.

"That it?" asked Latham.

"Yep. Plus a few pieces of what looks like a device."

"What kind?"

"Hard to tell, but it's complex . . . not an egg timer and dynamite, that's for sure."

"What about explosive?"

Randal opened the evidence bag and held it in front of Latham's nose.

"Plastique," said Latham. The odor was distinctive. Now the trick was to determine its kind and origin. He was betting it was Czech Semtex, a favorite of terrorists.

"And the owner of the luggage?"

"Should have that within a couple hours."

Owen said, "Good news, bad news."

"Yeah."

Latham was both relieved and frightened. Frightened because it took a fair amount of sophistication to not only design such a device but also get it aboard an aircraft. Relieved because that same sophistication would narrow their list of possible suspects.

* * *

Langley

DDO George Coates stepped off the elevator and into Mason's outer office. Ginny looked up. "He's on the phone, Mr. Coates. He should be done in a couple minutes."

"Okay." Coates sat down.

On his lap Coates cradled a file labeled DORSAL. Containing all the nuts-and-bolts details of an ongoing operation, it was what case officers called "the book." So restricted is a book's information that it is traditionally off-limits to everyone but the case officer, his division chief, and perhaps a handful of others. This restriction extends even to the DCI and his deputies. However, the summons from Mason had been unambiguous: "Get the book on DORSAL and come on up." Next to SYMMETRY, DORSAL was his directorate's most important ongoing operation.

Ginny said, "Okay, Mr. Coates, you can go in."

Mason waved Coates to the seat in front of his desk. The television was tuned to a CNN report of the crash in New York. Coates watched for a moment. "How bad?"

"Five dead, seven injured."

"Accident?"

"Don't know yet. I've got a call in to the FBI director. I meant to ask: How was your heart-to-heart with Smith and the IOC?"

"Manageable," replied Coates. "He's a prick, but there's not much to him. I think he gets a thrill out of seeing himself as part of the spy business."

"That was my impression, too." Mason muted the TV. "Does the name Umako Ohira mean anything to you?"

"Not offhand."

"Check."

Coates opened the DORSAL file to the bio section. There was only one agent, the primary: *"Code name, Kingfisher. Identity, Umako Ohira."* Coates turned the file for Mason to see.

Mason nodded. "Ohira was murdered two days ago outside Osaka."

"What?"

"A shooting. The report just landed on the embassy LegAt's desk. Aside from the fact that an American saw the whole thing, it didn't mean anything to him or the station chief."

"No, it wouldn't." Kingfisher—Ohira—had been working alone, with no controller. "That's where we got it, the LegAt?"

"No. Blessing or curse, the witness is—or used to be—an operator."

"Used to be?"

"I'll explain later. He's one of Dutcher's people."

Coates noded. "I know Dutch. Good man. You've lost me though. How—"

"Dutcher's man claims there's more to it. The car Ohira had been driving was shot up, and the next day Dutcher's man—"

"What's his name?"

"Tanner. The next day he was followed by the same kind of truck used in the shooting."

"That's a problem."

"Understatement of the year. In a span of forty-eight hours, two of our biggest ops have been gutted."

"You think they're connected?"

"Doubtful, but we can't rule it out till we know more. I want you and Sylvia to dissect this thing from top to bottom, just like we're doing with SYMMETRY. All the product, all the OpSec." Mason pushed a file across the table. "Dutcher's report."

Coates scanned it, then said, "We're worse off here than with SYMMETRY. Ohira ran the network. We don't know much about it—next to nothing, in fact."

Mason heard the self-reproach in his deputy's voice. "It was the only way, George. Running an op on Japanese soil is about as dicey as it gets. It was either let him run it or get nothing. Besides, we may have a trump: Tanner. He's on the ground. He might be able to—"

"Dutcher's guy? I don't know—"

"It's a possibility."

"Not unless I sign off on it, it isn't."

Mason wasn't offended. In all things operational, Coates was king unless Mason decided to overrule him, and that wasn't his style. You didn't give your people the authority unless you trusted them, and trust was not something you awarded and withdrew capriciously.

"Understood," Mason said. "Before we take that route, you'll know everything you need to know about him."

Tunis, Tunisia

IN THE CITY'S OLD QUARTER, IBRAHIM FAYYAD STOOD ON HIS VEranda at the Hotel M'Rabet and watched the bustle of the souk market below. Here, not five miles from the heart of Tunis proper, few tourists ventured into the mazelike medina without a guide. He did not blame them.

For thousands of years, Roman, Turk, and Arab conquerors had built and rebuilt the streets and alleys of the medina, each hoping not only to memorialize their supremacy but also to thwart invaders. The result was Old Tunis, the epitome of ancient Arabism.

Fayyad enjoyed Tunis not only for the anonymity it provided him but also for the irony. Here he was, hiding just a few miles from the one-time headquarters of *al-Fatah*, where Arafat himself had signed Fayyad's death warrant. Back then, as the PLO was growing cozier with the Israelis, certain activities and individuals—like Fayyad—became unpopular, and *al-Fatah* decided his execution would make a wonderful sign of goodwill.

Fayyad turned away from the window. On the television, CNN was repeating the top story of the day. He turned down the volume and watched the images of the crippled plane sitting on the Tarmac.

The bomb had malfunctioned. The engineer had come highly recommended, a well-trained former Egyptian soldier. Apparently his reputation was ill-deserved. No matter, Fayyad thought. He'd done his part; he was safe. She would not remember his face as clearly as she would remember her feelings for him. It would confuse her, this fuzziness.

Fayyad knew the female mind: Once in love, a woman's emotions color everything. Appearance becomes subjective. It would all become random bits of memory: the way he smiled, the sparkle of his eyes, his way of making love to her.

Yes, he was safe.

Still, something bothered him. He stared at the TV. Five dead, seven injured. Suddenly, from nowhere, the thought came: Was she one of the dead?

"Stop," he muttered.

Why was he thinking about her? And then another unbidden thought: If alive, what must she be feeling now? Betrayed . . . heartbroken?

Enough. He stood up, turned off the TV.

A knock came at the door.

From the nightstand drawer, Fayyad removed a Browning nine millimeter, palmed it behind his back, and crept to the door. "Yes?"

"A message, *effendi,* for a Mr. al-Kabar." A boy's voice.

Fayyad opened the door a crack; the boy was alone. "Give it to me."

The boy handed him the note. Fayyad gave him a dinar and closed the door.

The note instructed him to go to the Café Afrique on Bourquiba Avenue. There would be a public phone that would ring in precisely two hours. Fayyad knew the cafe, and such a time limit would not have been chosen by the authorities; it gave him too much time to reconnoiter. Who, then?

AN HOUR LATER HE WAS SITTING IN A CAFÉ ACROSS THE STREET from the Afrique. The table he'd chosen was perfect, casting him in shadow.

Fayyad, a Jordanian, was just shy of fifty years old but looked fifteen years younger. He had smooth olive skin and chiseled features offset by an easy smile. More often than not, he was mistaken for being Italian, which suited him perfectly.

For the next hour, he drank tea and watched the Afrique, searching for repeat customers; customers who lingered too long over their cups. He saw nothing. Cars and motor scooters came and went, none routinely.

He checked his watch. *Almost time.* He paid the bill and walked across the street. As he drew even with the booth, the phone rang. He lifted the receiver. "Yes."

"Do you recognize my voice? We met four months ago in Sidi Darnah."

Fayyad remembered. "Yes."

"Are you free to travel?"

"That depends."

"It will be worth your time. Meet me in Khartoum. You know the old berber's café on the Street of Canals?"

"Yes."

"Good. Two days' time, at noon."

Washington, D.C.

DR. MARSHA BURNS'S HEART ACHED FOR THE WOMAN SEATED across from her. A marital abuse survivor herself, Burns understood what she was going through. At last her patient was beginning to question some of the false beliefs that were imprisoning her.

This woman's case was different than most, not because of the celebrity of her spouse but because of how thoroughly she'd convinced herself she must remain in the union. As far as Burns knew, the abuse had not become physical, but the husband certainly sounded capable of it.

The woman accepted a tissue from Burns and dabbed her eyes. "He tells me I'm ugly," she said. "I try hard to look good, especially when we go out, but he always finds something."

"Judith, he's wrong. You're beautiful."

Burns meant it. Judith was in her early fifties, with flowing, frosted silver hair, delicate features, and flawless skin. She dressed stylishly and carried herself with poise. Burns bet the woman drew plenty of admiring stares.

"He says those things out of his own weakness. It's his own lacking, not yours. In his heart, he's afraid you *are* too good for him. By doing what he does, he keeps you inferior to him."

"I know, I know. It's just . . ."

"Hard to listen to the man you once loved say those things?"

"Yes."

"You're asking yourself, 'How can he do this to me? Doesn't he love me?' "

"Yes."

"Judith, the hard truth is, he doesn't love you. He probably never did. Not really, anyway. It's not about you; it's because he doesn't know *how* to love. Look at his life outside of you. He has no real friends, only colleagues. He uses intimidation to get what he wants. What you need—what you deserve—from him is something that isn't even in his dictionary."

Burns went silent as Judith digested this. They'd discussed the idea before, but only recently had Burns felt Judith was absorbing the concept. "Have you considered what we talked about last week?" Burns asked.

"About leaving him? I . . . I don't know."

"Does it frighten you?"

"Yes."

"Good. That means you're thinking about it. Listen, I'm not telling you to leave your husband. That's your decision to make. I just want you to remember: You are *not* stuck. Your life is *not* over. You deserve happiness, and it's out there."

Judith laughed, embarrassed. "I'm fifty-two years old. Who would want—"

"Judith, if you were available, you'd have more men than you'd know what to do with. Hell, you'd have more *sex* than you'd know what to do with."

"Marsha!" Judith gasped, but Burns saw the hint of a smile, too.

"It's true!" Burns glanced at the clock. "Okay, until next week, just think about what we've talked about. You don't have to make any decisions—just think. Okay?"

"Okay."

*   *   *

New York

AS THE REMNANTS OF THE DEVICE AND THE RESIDUE SAMPLES were on their way to the FBI Laboratory Division at Quantico, Latham and Randal had identified the owner of the luggage.

A twenty-four-year-old American citizen, an honor graduate of Princeton and a former candy-striper and Meals-on-Wheels volunteer, Cynthia Hostetler was about as likely a terrorist as was Mother Teresa.

"I've saved the best for last," Randal said. "It also seems Ms. Hostetler is the only daughter of one Delaware congressman, Stanley Hostetler."

"Oh, shit," muttered Latham."

"Yep."

"What's out?"

"Nothing except she was aboard and injured. She's at Bellevue. Doctors say she's okay: broken femur in five places, crushed an artery, but she'll recover. She's coming out of surgery now."

"Let's go."

THEY WERE HALFWAY THERE WHEN LATHAM'S CELL PHONE RANG. It was his boss, the assistant director of investigations. "Where are you, Charlie?"

"Heading to Bellevue. We've got the bag and its owner."

"Good. Listen, there's something you should—"

"I heard. Congressman Hostetler."

"How did you—"

"It's his daughter we're going to interview."

"Shit."

"My words exactly. We'll know more in a couple hours, but my guess is she's not involved. She was probably just a mule."

"That's the upside, then. Hostetler is already breathing down the director's neck, and when he finds this out, it's going to get ugly."

"I know."

"Then get hot, Charlie. This goes to the top of your list, got it?"

After Latham hung up, Randal asked, "Too late to request vacation, partner?"

Latham laughed. " 'Fraid so."

TWENTY MINUTES LATER THEY WERE STANDING OUTSIDE CYNTHIA Hostetler's room. The congressman had not yet arrived. "We've repaired the damage," said the doctor, "but her recovery will be tough. Considering the alternative, she's one lucky girl."

"Can we see her?" asked Latham.

"For a few minutes. The anesthesia hasn't worn off entirely, but she's fairly lucid. If you don't mind, I'll stand by."

The room was lit only by a small table lamp in the corner. Already there were a half-dozen flower baskets on the window credenza. Cynthia was pretty, slightly plump, but Latham bet that bothered her more than anyone else.

"Ms. Hostetler, my name is Charlie Latham, and this is Paul Randal. We're with the FBI. How are you feeling?"

"Okay," she said fuzzily. "Where's Daddy?"

"He's on his way. Do you feel up to talking to us?"

"Uh-huh."

"Do you remember anything about the accident?"

Cynthia shook her head. "We were almost on the ground, then there was a loud boom, and I looked over, y'know, across the aisle, and there it was."

"What?"

"The hole, and the ground going by really fast. There was a flash, too, and then heat." She bit her lip and her eyes welled with tears. "Those people, they . . . they were just gone, their seats and everything." She started crying. "Are they dead?"

"Yes."

"What was it, what happened?"

"A bomb."

Latham wasn't sure how to proceed. He had a guess

about where his questions would lead; if he were right, it would mean more pain for her. On the other hand, once her father arrived, their access to her might disappear.

"Cynthia, I want you to listen to me: You haven't done anything wrong, okay? You're not in trouble. Do you understand?"

"Yes. . . ."

"We think the bomb came from your bag."

She stared at him. "What? No, no . . . that can't be. . . ."

"We need to know—"

"I didn't . . ." She broke into tears again. "Where's Daddy?"

"Cynthia, your bag was leather, right, green-checkered leather?"

"Y-y-yes. It was new."

"Where did you get it?"

"It was a gift."

"From who?" Latham steeled himself.

"From a friend. A man I met on vacation, in Jamaica."

Son of a bitch. "What was his name?"

"Ricardo."

"Ricardo what?"

"I don't . . . I can't remember. He was Italian. He's coming to visit me in a few days."

"Describe him for me."

She did so, but the image was vague. Latham was unsurprised; these people knew how to pick their targets.

"I don't get it," she said. "What's going on? What are you saying?"

"Cynthia, I'm sorry. We think it came from him."

"What?"

"The bomb. We believe he may have planted it."

"No, no, he wouldn't. He said he loved me. He . . . Oh, God."

She curled herself into a ball and began sobbing. Latham squeezed her arm and pulled the doctor toward the door. "You have someone who can stay with her?" Latham whispered.

"You think she might hurt herself?"

Latham shrugged. *What the hell do you think, Doc?* he thought. *The man of her dreams lied to her, betrayed her, then used her to kill five people. Yes, I think she might want to hurt herself.*

Latham said, "She's going to need help, Doctor. Lots of it."

8

Japan

FOLLOWING DUTCHER'S ORDERS, TANNER LOITERED ABOUT, SUN-
bathing and drinking Alcapulcos, neither of which he
minded, but he quickly grew restless. He wanted to either
jump into the mystery of Ohira's murder or be done with
it.

The previous night Camille had left him a message saying her business in Tokyo was taking longer than she anticipated, but she would be returning in a day or so. She
was looking forward to dinner. In spite of himself, Tanner
was, too.

Lurking in the back of his mind, however, was a hesi-
tancy to get involved with her or with anyone else for that
matter. It was a familiar feeling, one with which he had
made a shaky truce after Elle's death. There had been other
women since her, but nothing of any permanence. He'd
never been a fan of the "better to have loved and lost than
to have never loved at all" theory. As far as he was concerned, the jury was still out.

He'd been at Holystone a year when Elle died. Dutcher
had pushed him to go see a counselor. Tanner balked, so
Dutcher made it easy. "Go. You're on vacation until you
sort out what's going on in your head."

To Tanner's surprise, the half-dozen visits to the counselor had helped. He hadn't talked to anyone about the accident, or his feelings, or that hollow ache he carried around in
his chest. "You're going to find it hard to trust again," the
psychologist had warned him. "No matter what your head
says, subconsciously you believe anything is better than
going through this again. It's a kind of self-preservation

mechanism . . . and given the business you're in, that mechanism is pretty damned strong. Problem is, left unchecked, it'll do more damage than good."

Even before he heard the words, Tanner knew they were true. Time had dulled the mechanism, but at times—like right now—it still talked to him.

He picked up his jogging pace and turned away from the tide line, digging his heels into the softer sand. A quarter mile ahead, a figure sat on a driftwood log. Tanner stopped and sat down.

"You did not have to run, Mr. Tanner," said Sato Ieyasu. "But I admire your desire to be punctual."

Tanner laughed. "Exercise, Inspector."

"Ah, I see. I admire your discipline. Thank you for meeting me."

"My social calendar is uncluttered at the moment."

"I brought something for you." Ieyasu handed him a photograph. "Tange Noboru, Takagi's chief of security."

"That's him. He was the one driving."

"At the murder."

"No, here."

"Well, if he's watching you, you can be sure it's on direct orders from Takagi himself. Have you seen him again?"

"No."

"That is best," Ieyasu said. "You don't want Noboru interested in you."

Too late, Tanner thought. *Now I'm interested in him.*

Chesapeake Bay, Maryland

IT WAS MIDEVENING, AND WALTER OAKEN WAS STILL AT THE HOlystone office. As Dutcher's deputy, most of the routine administrative tasks fell to Oaken, but unlike most men, he thrived on detail work. In his world there was a place for everything, and everything had its place. A dedicated indoorsman, Oaken preferred the neatness of the office. So strong was this idiosyncrasy that Tanner had long since given up trying to lure Oaken on a camping or hiking trip.

"No chance," was Oaken's standard reply. "I like my adventure predictable, preferably on the pages of a magazine."

"Planned spontaneity?"

"Exactly. You'll be happy to hear, however, I just renewed my subscription to *National Geographic*."

"I'm proud of you."

Oaken smiled at the memory. Though opposites in many ways, he and Tanner counterbalanced one another, and their friendship was stronger for it. He wondered what Briggs's love of the unknown had gotten him into this time.

A voracious reader and an information pack rat, Oaken loved reports, forms, cereal boxes; if it had print on it, he read it. His wife Beverly fought an ongoing battle to keep his "gonna get to 'em soon" magazine stacks below three feet tall, lest one of their daughters bump one of the monoliths and be crushed by an avalanche of *U.S. News & World Report*. Whether at his home office or at work, a television was always tuned to CNN, and whenever Bev came in to clean, her opening of the door stirred up a blizzard of newspaper clippings that took hours to settle—or so she joked.

At forty-eight years old, Oaken had assimilated enough knowledge about the world—past and present, scientific and cultural, obscure and pertinent—to speak authoritatively on almost any subject. That which he didn't know, he learned.

Standing six and a half feet tall, his chronically rumpled suits hung from his shoulders like lab coats, and he lacked any modicum of fashion sense. He looked every bit the absentminded professor.

The phone rang. "Holystone, Shiverick."

"Walter, it's Leland."

"You just caught me. I was about to head home."

"I'm sure Bev will enjoy the change. I'm landing at Andrews in a few minutes."

"What's up?"

"Not sure. Just in case, call Ian and get him ready to travel."

"Okay." *Japan,* Oaken thought. "I'll get things rolling."

* * *

Japan

IT WAS SHORTLY BEFORE NOON WHEN TANNER RETURNED TO THE hotel. He found Camille at the pool, reclining in a chaise lounge in a black one-piece bathing suit, wide-brimmed beachcomber hat, and horn-rimmed sunglasses. She looked every bit the 1950s Hollywood starlet.

"Hello, sailor," she said, lifting her sunglasses. "Running again, are we? Dinner is still on, I assume?"

"Of course."

"I was worried you would give up on me."

"Not a chance."

Tanner sat down and ordered lunch: seafood salad, kiwi, and iced tea. "Care to join me?"

"I've already eaten, thanks. When you're done, there are a few spots I couldn't reach with the lotion."

Tanner smiled. Camille had the unique ability to sound mischievous, sexy, and innocent all at once. "My pleasure," he said.

As he ate, they chatted easily, and it felt like they'd known each other for years rather than days. She asked him about diving, the kinds of fish he saw, and whether there were any sharks. Sharks scared her, she said.

"They're more frightened of us than we are of them. Most attacks are cases of mistaken identity."

"Where did you learn so much about the ocean?"

Tanner decided a half-truth was the best answer. "My family lived in Maine for a while. I earned extra money working a fishing charter."

Finished eating, Tanner sat on the edge of her chaise and unscrewed the cap of the suntan lotion. Camille rolled onto her stomach. He slid the suit's straps off her shoulders and began smoothing lotion on her back.

"That feels good," she murmured. "You have good hands."

Lying at his feet Tanner saw Camille's towel and the card key to her room—the same number as before she left, one floor below his own. He picked up the card and slipped it in his sock.

When he finished with the lotion, Camille was almost asleep. "I'm going to wash my hands," he said. "Be right back."

"Mm-mmm."

Tanner walked into the lobby and laid Camille's card on the counter. "Any messages for me?"

The attendant glanced at the number, retrieved a message from Camille's box, and handed it to Tanner. He memorized the message—Stephan Karotovic, U.S. area code 212—then switched Camille's card with his own.

"Excuse me, this is for room four oh eight; I'm five oh eight."

"My apologies, sir." He returned Camille's message to her box and checked Tanner's. "No messages, sir."

"Thank you."

Langley

LELAND DUTCHER WAS MET IN THE LOBBY BY AN OFFICE OF SEcurity escort, who took him up to the seventh floor. As the elevator doors parted, a man pushed his way inside. It took a moment for Dutcher to recognize Art Stucky.

"Hello, Art."

Stucky stared at him for a few seconds. "Leland. What brings you here?"

"Just visiting."

Stucky smiled, but there was no humor in it. "Hmm."

They faced one another in silence. Finally Dutcher smiled and stepped off the elevator. As the doors closed behind them, the escort gave Dutcher an oblique glance.

"Old friends," Dutcher explained.

"Yes, sir."

Dutcher hadn't taken two steps into the DCI's outer office when Ginny was out of her chair and running to hug him. However formal she was with Mason, she had a soft spot for Dutcher.

"Leland, how are you!"

"Fine, Ginny, and you?"

"You've made my day!" She leaned in and whispered, "I wish you'd never left. It just isn't the same."

Dutcher smiled. "Oh? Dick's a slave driver, is he?"

"No, it's not that. It's just not the same."

-"Thanks, Ginny."

"You'd better go in. Director Mason is waiting for you."

"Something big? Do I have time to skulk out the back?"

Ginny laughed. "Go."

Mason was standing at the window. "Dutch. Thanks for coming. Coffee?"

"Sure."

They sat in a pair of captain's chairs around a low coffee table. Mason filled two mugs from the pot and passed one to Dutcher.

"I saw Art Stucky in the hall," Dutcher said. "Where have you got him?"

"Near East Division. He just got back from Tel Aviv. I didn't know you two knew each other."

"Years ago. The Peru thing. He was Army, a Green Beret top sergeant. Counterinsurgency work."

"Interesting. I don't know much about him. What's your take?"

Warning bells went off in Dutcher's head. *They don't know,* he thought. *How could they not?* But then again, outside of the Army, only he, Briggs Tanner, and Bud Grenson of ISAG knew what Art Stucky had done in Peru. Briggs had been the only one to witness it firsthand.

Dutcher was careful with his answer. "Dick, it's not my place."

The response had the desired effect. "Something I should know?"

"If I were in your place?"

"Yes."

Dutcher nodded.

"Okay. Let's get down to business. You know why you're here?"

"I have a guess," said Dutcher.

"The man Tanner saw murdered was an agent of ours."

"Industrial target?"

"Yes. Takagi Industries."

"You're getting bold in your old age, Dick."

"The stakes were worth it. You think Tanner is up to doing some legwork?"

"Tell me the story."

"I'll give you the condensed version. Back during the Gulf War, about a week into the air campaign, a Navy Prowler brought back some data on a couple of Baghdad's SAM sites that CENTCOM was having a tough time killing.

"CENTCOM sent in an SAS team, which toasted one of the batteries and grabbed some of the hardware. CENT-COM looked at it but couldn't make much of it, so they sent it to the DIA, who didn't get anywhere, either. Finally the NSA took a stab. It turns out this site, along with the five others, were using a new kind of frequency agile radar. It was way beyond anything we had, beating our frequency skip rates by eighty percent or more. There wasn't a missile in our arsenal that could keep up with it."

Dutcher was stunned. If widely distributed, that kind of technology would require U.S. forces to first develop effective countermeasures, then play catch-up as weapons systems were refitted. It would take years and billions of dollars, not to mention the huge window of vulnerability it created.

"Lucky for us, the Iraqis didn't have many of them," Mason continued. "The one we got gave us some good countermeasure stuff. Better still, we were able to track down the manufacturer."

"Takagi Industries," said Dutcher.

"Yep. Through several front companies, that is. The following year, we started DORSAL. At first it didn't generate much; then along came Umako Ohira."

"Straight recruitment?"

"A walk-in—with bona fides."

"No kidding?"

"No kidding. Believe me, we put that man under the microscope. He was the real thing, and his product proved it."

A walk-in differs from a recruited agent in that the former presents himself to an agency and volunteers to spy for them, while the latter must be courted into doing the same work. Generally, walk-ins generate better product, but they are rare beasts and rarer still are they genuine. Nine times out of ten, walk-ins are planted by an enemy agency to spread disinformation.

"He was an engineer," Mason continued. "He worked on the hardware we pulled out of those fire control radars. He thought they were headed for the Japanese Maritime Self-Defense Forces, and when he found out Takagi was selling them to Saddam, he couldn't stomach it."

"That's it?" asked Dutcher. "A good conscience?"

"Yep. His product was stellar, Leland. And now that he's been murdered . . ."

"His bona fides are all the more solid," Dutcher finished.

"Right."

"How was the network set up?"

"No cutouts, no controller," replied Mason. "Ohira ran the whole thing. It was a tough choice, but given the territory, that's the call we made. The cultural barrier alone was hard enough, but Takagi's physical security and information protection is top notch. With Ohira, we had the perfect conduit, and his job gave him almost unlimited access."

Dutcher considered this. "What do you want from us?"

"Just a circuit check. We just want to know if the network is viable. If so, we'll start figuring out how to restart it."

Dutcher nodded; it seemed straightforward enough. "Usual terms?"

"Yes."

For Tanner, that meant he was on his own. He would be disavowed if caught and ignored if imprisoned, a private citizen breaking Japanese law.

"Support?" asked Dutcher.

"We can give you equipment and information, but you'll have to work out the logistics."

"When?"

"As soon as George signs off. Give me a couple days."

Mason looked hard at Dutcher. "This is big for us, Dutch. I'd consider it a personal favor."

Dutcher had discretion over which projects Holystone undertook. He weighed the pros and cons and decided Mason was right: This was big. If Takagi Industries was dabbling in the underground weapons market, the U.S. would have to deal with it sooner or later. Sooner would be better.

"Let me see the file," said Dutcher.

Syrian/Lebanese Border

SIX THOUSAND MILES AWAY, ABU AZHAR AND GENERAL ISSAM al-Khatib stood on a rocky outcrop overlooking the Syrian desert. Every few seconds, the horizon bloomed with bursts of orange; even at this distance al-Khatib could feel the accompanying explosions in his belly.

Azhar raised his binoculars. "Artillery?" he asked.

"And tanks. Integrated warfare: armor, infantry, artillery, and aircraft working together."

"It is impressive, but is such a large force necessary?"

"We must not only get their attention but keep it as well." General al-Khatib smiled. "Abu, yours is the difficult job. Your men are ready?"

"Of course."

"Good. I know how you feel about this, but I think you should consider—"

"We've already discussed this. The answer is—"

"You've chosen your target well, but we gain more leverage if—"

"No! No children! That was my only condition. You knew that from the start."

General al-Khatib nodded and clapped Azhar on the shoulder. "Yes, of course. We won't discuss it again. So, what was so urgent you needed to see me?"

"We have captured a spy."

"What? When?"

"Last week. He's working for the Americans, that much he has already admitted. Otherwise, he is resisting well."

"Give him to me," General al-Khatib said. "I will—"

"No, we will keep him. My concern is the operation. This close to the final phase, I am worried the Americans may know something."

"Impossible."

"Improbable, but not impossible. We need to be sure before we're committed."

"What do you propose?"

Azhar explained. "Mustafa has already contacted the Jordanian. We have the funds and the target, and the logistics are fairly simple once we're in-country. What we need is a man who has experience in this area."

"For participation?"

"No. Consultation," said Azhar. "Mustafa tells me you know a man, a former KGB officer."

General al-Khatib hesitated. The operation Azhar was proposing was one of unprecedented daring. His first instinct was to forbid it, but al-Khatib heard the resolve in Azhar's voice. He'd heard it many times before.

In the years after the loss of Azhar's child, he'd provided Azhar with refuge and friendship. He'd also grown to love him like a brother, all the while seeing the hidden potential. Azhar was a brilliant planner, a fierce soldier, and a charismatic leader.

Were Azhar's worries justified? al-Khatib wondered. Could this tangent of his jeopardize the operation? No, he decided, compromise was unlikely; they were well insulated. The most important part of that insulation was Azhar himself. In fact, without him the heart of the plan would collapse. Perhaps appeasement was the wisest course. Besides, this new venture might provide necessary distraction.

"Very well," al-Khatib said. "I'll send him. Where?"

"Khartoum."

"His price will be high."

"We will pay it," Azhar said. "The price of failure for us is even higher."

Japan

THE POOL PATIO WAS NEARLY DESERTED. THEIR TABLE WAS LIT BY a hurricane lantern. Candle rafts drifted on the surface of the pool. The dinner Tanner had arranged was simple but delicious. They started with fresh shrimp cocktail and fruit salad, followed by braised albacore fillets and baby asparagus with hollandaise sauce.

"So," Camille said, sipping her wine. "You were telling me about the Navy."

"Was I?"

"Yes."

"I seem to be doing all the talking."

"Not so," she said. "You know I am Ukranian, you've heard the woes of my childhood: strict, religious parents, our small backward village. . . ." Camille smiled suddenly. "Would you like to hear about my first lover? I was nineteen," she said. "He was a sailor . . . like you."

Tanner laughed. "Like me because he was a sailor, or like me because we're alike?"

"You are nothing like him. You are genuine and warm and have a wonderful heart, though you try to hide it sometimes."

Be careful with this one, Tanner thought. "You're very insightful, Ms. Sereva."

"Yes, but am I very correct?"

"So, this sailor . . ."

"I loved him, and he loved sleeping with me. I was a naive little girl."

"Gender has little to do with naïveté."

"So you've been in love and made a fool of yourself?"

"More times than I care to admit."

She leaned forward. "I want to hear about it."

"You've steered the conversation away from yourself again."

"Have I?" Camille said. "By what miracle are you not married?"

Tanner paused and took a sip of coffee. "I was."

"Was?"

"It was a long time ago. She died in an avalanche in Colorado. We were skiing. Some teenagers had stolen the boundary markers as a prank, and we ended up where we shouldn't have been."

After the avalanche he'd tried to get to her, but he couldn't. The snow was so dense, so heavy; it was nearly impossible to dig. For a while he thought he heard her voice, and he called to her but heard nothing. With two ribs cracked and his collarbone shattered, he clawed at the snow, every move agony, his mind slipping in and out of consciousness, everything white and cold and dank.

After twelve hours, the rescuers found him. He was within four feet of where they eventually found Elle's body. As they'd loaded him on the stretcher, he stared at her still lying in the snow, her face blue, eyes open. . . .

That had been four years ago last month. He'd sensed its passing but hadn't actively noted it. Elle had always loathed what she called "morbid anniversaries," like the day Kennedy was shot, or Pearl Harbor Day, or the day you buried a loved one's body in the ground. She thought it better to dwell on the time someone was here, not on the single day on which they left.

When he remembered her, it was the peculiarities that stood out, the bits of memory that defined her in his mind: Elle demanded all their houseplants have names; Elle cried at happily-ever-after films, giggled at horror movies; Elle loved to fish, refused to bait the hook. Elle was unique and irreplaceable, and her death had been pivotal in his life.

Afterward, there had been times of drinking, of staring at the walls, and of listening to the phone ring but not answering because he knew it was a well-wisher, and he no longer had the strength to muster another "I'm fine, thanks."

He sometimes wondered—though not too often lest he give it real consideration—whether any woman would feel right again. This, he realized later, would have bothered Elle most of all.

But getting to that realization had taken many months. He didn't like the person he saw in the mirror. It was the face of someone who'd stopped trying. She was gone. It was done. He could stay in limbo or choose to live. He chose the latter. Later, he realized Elle had given him something else: her ability to live each day as it came. Moments were important, each one a sliver of time you could only experience once, each one a building block of a life.

"You blame yourself," Camille said.

"Some."

"A lot, I think. I'm sorry, Briggs. What was her name?"

"Elle . . . Susan Ellise."

They sipped their coffee in silence. Inside the Tiki Lounge, a Frank Sinatra tune was playing on the jukebox. "What is that?" Camille asked.

" 'Summer Wind' by Frank Sinatra."

"Aren't you a bit young to be a Sinatra fan?"

"I grew up listening to him and Henry Mancini and old Herb Alpert stuff. Hated it back then. Now . . . I guess it sort of grew on me."

The waiter approached their table. "Mr. Tanner, a message for you."

"Thank you."

Tanner opened the slip and read: "Meet me, Mandarin Oriental, Hong Kong. Dutch." At the bottom there was a postscript. "Regarding your new business partner, still checking references." Feeling mildly guilty, Tanner had forwarded the name Stephan Karotovic to Oaken.

"Bad news?" Camille asked.

"Just business. I have to go out of town for a couple days."

"When? Not tonight, I hope."

"In the morning."

"Good. I'm due to leave day after tomorrow. I may not be here when you return." She paused. "Unless, of course . . ."

"Yes?"

"Unless you pleaded for me to stay until you get back."

Tanner smiled. "My pleading skills are a tad rusty."

"Ask, then."

"All right. Will you stay until I get back?"

"Well, since you asked . . ."

* * *

THEY STROLLED ARM-IN-ARM ON THE BEACH, WATCHING THE TIDE curl around their ankles and talking until almost midnight. When they reached the door to her room, she leaned against the jamb as he opened it for her.

"Good night, Camille."

She put her arms around his neck and drew him against her. She turned her mouth upward, waiting for his.

Their first kiss was unhurried as their tongues touched, withdrew, and touched again. Briggs pressed his hands into the small of her back and drew her hips against his. She gasped and arched herself. "Please, Briggs, take me to the bed."

"Camille—"

"I want you. Please ... What?" she breathed. "What is it?"

"I have to go," Tanner said, then thought, *What are you doing?*

"Don't you want me?"

"Yes, very much."

"Then—"

He put a finger to her lips. "We have time, Camille. There's no hurry."

Her expression softened into a smile. "You're sure about this?"

He chuckled. "Not entirely. I'll find you when I get back." He pulled away.

Slowly, reluctantly, Camille swung the door closed. Just before it clicked shut, she poked her head out. "I'll tell you this, Briggs Tanner, if you die in a plane crash or from food poisoning or anything else, I'll never forgive you."

Tanner smiled. "That would make two of us."

9

Hong Kong

TANNER LOVED HONG KONG, ITS VITALITY AND ITS MYSTERIOUS blend of Old and New Worlds. While many things had changed here since China took over from Great Britain, few of them were visible to the tourist. One thing that would never change, Tanner guessed, was the taxis.

He clutched the taxi's door handle tighter as his driver weaved from lane to lane, shouting Mandarin curses out the window and flailing his arms. To their right lay Victoria Harbor, teeming with hundreds of junks, and through the windshield he could see Victoria Peak, its upper reaches cloaked in mist.

The driver veered left off Connaught Road, then again onto Charter before screeching to a halt in front of the Mandarin Oriental Hotel. "We here," he announced.

"And then some."

"Eh?"

"Nothing," Tanner replied, handing him the fare.

Tanner stepped onto the curb. The driver retrieved his bag from the trunk and deposited it on the curb, where a bellman smiled, took Tanner's passport, then scurried into the lobby. In all, the operation had taken four seconds.

"Gotta love Hong Kong," Tanner murmured.

"Eh?" asked the driver.

"Nothing."

The Mandarin Oriental Hotel combines British Old World taste with Oriental opulence. Two of the city's finest restaurants, the Pierrot and the Man Wah, share the top floor, while on the ground floor guests can choose from the Mandarin Grill, the Clipper Lounge, and the Captain's Bar.

By the time Tanner reached the main desk, his bag was
already en route to his room and the register ready for his
signature. Two minutes later, the bellman was escorting
him to his room.

He had a half hour before he was to meet Dutcher, so
he unpacked and took a long shower, then dressed and
headed downstairs to the Chinnery.

Beside the bar's double oak doors was a brass plaque
that read, Men Only. Sexism nothwithstanding, this, too,
was part of the Mandarin's Old World charm, Tanner admitted. Inside, the pub was all polished walnut and teak
and brass lanterns. Nautical paintings and memorabilia
dominated the shelves and display cases. At the bar, patrons
hefted imitation pewter tankards.

Tanner spotted Dutcher in a corner booth.

"How was your flight?" Dutcher asked, rising to shake
Briggs's hand.

"Good. And yours?"

"Uneventful."

The waiter appeared and took their orders. After their
drinks arrived, Tanner and Dutcher reminisced about Hong
Kong. Their memories were from different perspectives;
Dutcher's mostly from his days there as a CIA station chief
during the seventies, Tanner's mostly from his time there
with his family.

For the better part of his first twelve years, Tanner's family followed his father from one history teaching assign-
ment to the next. Before he was ten, Briggs had lived in a
dozen cities and countries including Paris, Geneva, Kenya,
Beirut, Venice, and Hong Kong. He'd never missed what
others would call a normal childhood. Traveling had
opened the world to him.

When it was time for Briggs to enter middle school, they
returned to Maine, where the Tanner clan had lived for 160
years, and settled into a more routine life as Briggs entered
the world of high school, coed dances, football games, and
girlfriends. He'd always admired his parents' wisdom: They
hadn't forgotten what it was like to be an adolescent. While
youngster Briggs delighted in the travel, teenager Briggs

needed home and stability. The two lifestyles had made him well-rounded and self-assured. In that respect, he was the perfect amalgam of his mother and father.

"What happened to your face?" asked Dutcher.

Tanner touched his cheek. "Bone sliver."

Dutcher nodded and was silent for a few moments. "Was it bad?"

"Pretty bad."

"Anything more on your watchers?"

"No sign. I seem to have lost my popularity."

"Good. You up to a little legwork?"

Tanner smiled into his drink. "So now I'm the Man Who Saw Too Much?"

" 'Fraid so."

"I was getting bored, anyway."

"Finish your drink," Dutcher said. "Have you ever been to Luk Yu's?"

LUK YU'S IS A HONG KONG LANDMARK THAT DATES BACK TO THE early 1900s. Inside, past an authentic-looking Sikh doorman, Tanner found a polished marble foyer and humming ceiling fans. Booths were separated by stained glass panels. According to the brass plaque beside the grand staircase, the second floor contained a sitting room where British governors and aristocrats had once debated Hong Kong's future.

Though the service and the meal—Szechuan was their mutual choice—were mediocre, Tanner decided Luk Yu's decor made up for it.

After dinner they walked through the gardens surrounding The Peak Tram Station. "Umako Ohira was working for us," Dutcher told Tanner. "CIA."

"Agent or case officer?"

"Agent . . . a walk-in."

Dutcher recounted the briefing he'd received from Mason. Tanner asked many of the same questions Dutcher had. "What was Mason's take on Ieyasu's suspicions about Takagi and the JRA?" Briggs asked.

"He didn't have one."

"Doesn't that strike you as odd?"

"A bit, but the chemical angle is thin. What they found in the Iraqi SAM radars was tangible."

"And that's all they want from us—to check the network, nothing else?"

"In their eyes, Ohira was a tool. The network is all that counts now."

Tanner didn't like that mind-set but said nothing, knowing Dutcher felt the same way. That kind of brutal pragmatism made it too easy to use people, then dispose of them. Besides, remembering those few seconds he'd stared into Umako Ohira's eyes made it impossible for Tanner to see the man as a tool.

"Do we know what Ohira was doing the night he died?" asked Tanner.

"According to his last report, a few weeks ago, he'd been approached by someone wanting to buy information about Takagi Industries. They were supposed to meet that night, but he didn't say where or when. His impression was they were trying to false-flag him."

False flag is an agent recruitment method where an enemy agent pretends to work for a friendly, or at least neutral, service. False flag recruits often go years without knowing the true identity of his paymasters, if ever.

"Did he make the meet?" asked Tanner.

"We don't know."

"I'll need to see the details of the network."

"I have a loaded laptop for you. Walter's included a brief on Takagi Industries. You'll find it interesting reading."

"From what I gather, he's probably the most powerful industrialist in Japan."

"No doubt about it. One of the ten richest men in the world, in fact. If there's any truth behind the Black Ocean connection, he's probably pulling a lot of strings in the government."

"Are they on friendly terms?"

"Not as friendly as Takagi would like," Dutcher replied. "The current prime minister is a tough SOB. We think

Black Ocean isn't getting its way on a lot of policies, and they don't like it."

"What kind of support is Mason giving?" Tanner asked.

"The usual. I'm sending Ian over in a couple days; he'll have light cover for status."

Tanner understood the decision: They would be moving fast, and a fully backstopped cover for either of them was impossible. Either way, Briggs was glad to have Cahil along. As friends, they were as close as brothers, and as colleagues, their teamwork was uncannily empathetic, having been forged during their years in Special Warfare and ISAG. Early in training, Cahil's gregarious nature earned him the nickname "Mama Bear" from his fellow candidates. Bear was genuine, fiercely loyal, and as reliable as the setting sun.

"The key you picked up from Ohira matches a locker at the Sannomiya Railway Station in Kobe," said Dutcher. "Now, as far as this woman at the hotel, Camille . . ."

"Sereva."

"Nothing turned up on her, either. The name Stephan Karotovic is real. He's an immigration attorney in New York. She looks legitimate." Dutcher saw Tanner's half-smile and asked, "Something I should know about?"

"Not if she's clear."

"She is."

"Then no."

"One more thing," Dutcher said, stopping. "Ieyasu's story about all the dead and missing Takagi employees is true. In fact, one of them was in Ohira's network."

Tanner thought about this for a moment. "It seems our Mr. Takagi takes his downsizing seriously."

Khartoum, Sudan

IN THE OLD BERBER'S CAFÉ ON THE STREET OF CANALS, FAYYAD watched Mustafa al-Baz approach the table. Two steps behind him was a European with pasty skin and flat, blue eyes. *Dangerous,* Fayyad thought.

"Ibrahim, this is Sergei," said al-Baz.

The two men shook hands. "Hello," said Sergei.
Russian.

"He is here as an adviser," said al-Baz. "He is trustworthy."

"Very well."

After tea was ordered, al-Baz got down to business. "We have a job for you, Ibrahim. Your specialty."

"Where and who?"

"The where is America—"

"Pardon me?" The United States was the last place he wanted to be right then.

"You will know the who when you accept."

"When and for how long?"

"It would begin in a week. We will handle the logistics. As for duration, we're estimating three to four weeks."

In the back of Fayyad's mind, he was hearing *No, no, no.* "And my fee?"

"Three hundred thousand dollars, in an account of your choosing."

Fayyad's teacup froze halfway to his mouth. "Three hundred thousand?"

"That is correct."

With that kind of money, Fayyad would be free. If handled wisely, he could leave this business forever, find a plain, simple-minded wife, and settle down. Three hundred thousand! Whatever the risk, it was worth it.

"I accept," he said. "Now: Who is the target?"

"Once you are committed, there can be no—"

"I understand. Who is it?"

Al-Baz told him.

"You can't be serious."

"We are very serious." Al-Baz slid a photograph across the table along with a sheaf of papers. "Can you do it?"

"I can do it." Fayyad turned to Sergei. "This is your area of expertise?"

"One of them."

"Is it feasible?"

"As I told Mustafa, yes. The woman fits the profile, but the target may or may not have the information you seek.

If he has access to it, it will be through secondary sources. His inquiries may draw attention. Also, the timetable is too ambitious. You'll have to move fast and put great pressure on the target."

Fayyad asked al-Baz, "Is all this true?"

"We think Sergei is being overly cautious."

The Russian said nothing, his face blank.

"Are you still willing?" asked al-Baz.

Fayyad had no choice. Between the lure of the money and the consequences for backing out now, he was committed. He nodded. "I will do it."

ACROSS THE STREET, HIDDEN BEHIND A PAIR OF CRACKED SHUT-ters, a man watched the trio as they talked. Every few seconds, as one of them turned or inclined his head suitably, the man raised a Nikon camera and took a photograph. He was careful with his selections, occasionally changing positions as necessary. After taking two rolls of photos, he packed his case and slipped out into the alleyway.

Now would come the tricky part, the man told himself. Who would pay the best price? If his guess about the men's identities was correct, he knew of at least three potential customers. It would take delicacy, for these customers were unforgiving. But that didn't worry him.

It should have.

In addition to being a master at surveillance and a savvy entrepreneur, the man was greedy and naive—naive to think he could play stringer agent to not only the Israeli Mossad, but the Russian Foreign Intelligence Service and the PLO as well without eventually getting burned. None of this entered his mind, however.

He hurried down the alley, already calculating his profits.

Washington, D.C.

CHARLIE LATHAM SCANNED THE REPORT OF THE SAMPLES COL-lected from the La Guardia crash site. His phone rang. "Charlie Latham."

"Charlie, Jed. Step over for a minute, will you?"

"On my way."

Report in hand, Latham started down the hall. He passed a man wearing a visitor's badge. The man stopped. "Agent Latham?"

"Yes?"

"Stanley Hostetler," the man said, extending his hand. "I understand you're handling the Delta bombing for the bureau."

"That's right, Congressman."

"Where do we stand?"

"I assume you've just spoken with my boss."

"I have, but—"

"He's got the same information I have, Senator." *Most of it, at least,* Latham added, conscious of the report in his hand. "It's still early into the investigation, sir, but it's coming along."

"I'm glad to hear that."

"How is your daughter?" asked Latham.

"Physically she'll be fine, but that's only part of it." Hostetler hesitated. "You interviewed her. . . . You know what I mean."

"Yes, sir."

"When I think what that son of a bitch did to her . . ."

As a father, Latham understood Hostetler's rage. Someone had defiled, used, and then tried to murder his little girl.

"At any rate," said Hostetler, "I told your boss I have every confidence in you and the bureau."

"I appreciate that."

"And I'm sure you understand the need for decisive results, Agent Latham?"

"Clearly, Congressman."

"Good. I look forward to hearing more from you." With that, Hostetler strode toward the elevator.

Latham walked into his boss's office. "I just got button-holed in the hall."

"Don't worry about it," said the assistant director. "We'll

handle Hostetler, you concentrate on the case. Where are we?"

Charlie Latham liked his boss. The man wasn't an investigator by nature and made no pretense about being one. He was a superior administrator who had enough sense to let his people work and stay out of their way.

Latham handed him the report. "Just got it. Pretty sophisticated device. A pound of Semtex molded into the lining of the suitcase. The steel toe rivets had been wired to act as a circuit for the detonator."

"What kind of actuator?"

"A combination barometer-timer. That's where it went wrong."

"Let me guess: single-route circuit?"

"You got it." They'd seen this before.

A single-route barometric detonator measures air pressure—thus altitude—and is designed to trigger the bomb when a preset limit is reached. A double-route circuit, however, must reach two of these limits for detonation. A combination barometric/timer detonator is designed to work in two, and sometimes three stages. Stage one occurs when a timer activates the first barometer; once its limit is reached, it in turn activates yet another barometer, which finally detonates the bomb. Such a trigger lets the bomber set the device to explode far from its point of origin, oftentimes well into other countries and after several landings and takeoffs.

In this case, the lab found the bomb's engineer had miswired the timer, so instead of sending the detonation signal when the plane reached cruising altitude, the barometer had to settle for the next best thing, which was the plane's landing at La Guardia.

"That tells us they've got access to sophisticated equipment, but they screwed it up," said Latham. "The irony is, if they'd gotten it right, we'd have a better idea of the engineer."

"And we'd have a hundred eighty dead instead of five."

"Yeah. Unfortunately, the device isn't going to lead us anywhere. But this guy Cynthia Hostetler described rings a

bell. It's a textbook honey trap. Hostetler matches the profile to a tee: single woman traveling alone, swept off her
feet by a stranger; a romance ensues; plans are made to
have the man return home with her, but he's delayed at the
last minute; he asks her to take a package with her as he
can't fit it in his suitcase; she gets on the plane, and—"

"Boom."

"Right. Israel's *Shin Bet* thinks the technique was per-
fected by Ahmed Jabril and the PFLP general command.
Whether this incident is theirs or not. . . ."

"You recognize Hostetler's mystery man?"

"Maybe. We sent a sketch artist over to the hospital, and
she gave us a few more details. Her description matches
others. But the kicker is the name and nationality he used:
Ricardo, Italian. He's used it before. Sometimes it's Ricardo, sometimes Paolo or Antonio, but always Italian."

"Bad habit for a terrorist. So where do we go now?"

"I have a friend in *Shin Bet*," said Latham. "I want to
call him, see if he can point us in a direction. But I'm
betting Liaison is going to scream bloody murder."

"Make the call. I'll handle the bullshit," said the assistant
director.

White House

"WE'RE BEHIND THE GAME ON THIS ONE, GENTLEMEN," NATIONAL
Security Adviser James Talbot told the members of the National Security Council. "The administration has yet to state
its policy, and it's starting to show. The president needs
options."

Sitting at the table were the secretaries of defense and
state, Chairman of the Joint Chiefs General Chuck Cathermeier, and Dick Mason.

Mason heard Talbot's words but was having a hard time
concentrating. Between both DORSAL and SYMMETRY,
his plate was becoming increasingly crowded. He'd aver-
aged four hours of sleep a night for the past month, and
judging from the tone of this meeting, that average was

about to plummet. Someone had pushed the near-panic button at the White House.

The NSC, which met at least once a week—more often as events dictated—was only one of the dozens of committees on which Mason sat, including the NFIB (National Foreign Intelligence Board) and the PFIAB (President's Foreign Intelligence Advisory Board). Often, however, their agendas overlapped, and Mason found himself rehashing the same topics. It was maddening.

DORSAL and SYMMETRY. Two separate operations, 5,000 miles apart, yet they had one thing in common: Both their primary agents were gone, one dead, the other kidnapped. Movie portrayals aside, the loss of an agent was not a common occurrence. Was there a connection? If there was, they had yet to find it. Worse, they still had no idea what had gone wrong.

Today the NSC's agenda dealt with Syria, Iraq, and Iran. The Syrian military exercise was gaining momentum, and Assad's government was stonewalling; all back-channel inquiries through the State Department had been politely brushed off.

Next door to Syria, Iraq was reacting to Iran's military exercise by beefing up its own maneuvers along the border. Caught in the middle was CENTCOM, forced to play watchdog. The commanding officer of CENTCOM was frying the phone lines to the Joint Chiefs, warning this was a perfect excuse for Saddam to mobilize. If that happened without the U.S. having a strategy to deal with it, escalation would surely follow. Mason agreed, clearly remembering those dangerous months back in 1990 when the U.S. had been forced to play catch-up with the Iraqi Army.

Soon after his appointment as DCI, Dick Mason began studying Middle Eastern history, culture, and politics. He quickly realized why the word *byzantine* was so often used to describe the region. It was a millennia-old quagmire of imperialism, tribal squabbles, and religious discord. And nothing epitomized this better than the relationship between Syria, Iraq, and Iran.

Syria was perhaps the most Machiavellian of the players.

As a member of the country's minority Alawite sect, President Bashar Assad's power base lay in his ability to keep the country militarized and enmeshed in conflict, whether in Lebanon, in Iraq, or covertly against Israel.

The examples of such serpentine agendas were countless: Iran making back-channel overtures to Israel during the Gulf War while supporting *Hezbollah* terrorists in Lebanon; Syria temporarily lowering its anti-Zionist banner and joining the Gulf War coalition against Iraq; Lebanese Muslims, fearing Syrian Alawite rule more than Israeli intervention, tacitly aligned with Israel during its 1982 invasion of Lebanon; Saddam Hussein harboring exiled Ayatollah Khomeini from Iran while murdering his own Shiite population.

In the Mideast, Mason knew, rarely could you take events at face value.

"So is Iraq the only wild card here?" asked NSA Talbot.

"Not necessarily," said Mason. "All we know for sure is what Syria and Iran *appear* to be doing, and that's conducting exercises. Syria is being tight-lipped, which is nothing new, but Iran has been pretty open about it."

"It all appears routine," added General Cathermeier. "If there's anything more to it, we'll have to wait for further indications. Iraq we know all about. Saddam is his old duplicitous self. This mix-up is just what he's always looking for."

"That's what we need to focus on," said the secretary of defense. "Iraq can bear the burden of whatever response we choose, and if we choose correctly, Syria and Iran are sure to get the message."

This got nods, but Mason was apprehensive. The policy of oblique message sending had never proven effective in the Mideast, but it was popular in Washington as it was an easily renounced position. If you don't commit, you don't get burned.

"So what are we talking about?" said Talbot. "Statements, UN resolutions—"

"Forget that," said the secretary of state. "We need something tangible. Syria almost never responds to diplomatic pressure, and we sure as hell can't tell the Iranians to stop their goddamned exercise because we don't like the timing of it."

"I agree," said the sec def. "Better we act before the Israelis get jumpy. A reaction from them is bound to draw more fire than one from us. Besides, everybody expects us to rattle the saber a bit. We have an image to consider here."

Everyone chuckled.

They were now talking about a military response, Mason realized. Though it would likely be a simple showing of the flag, it was a decision not to be reached hastily, especially where the Mideast was concerned. The lessons of the hostage crisis, the Marines in Beirut, and the Gulf War were not far from any of their minds.

"Any ideas, General?" James Talbot asked the JCS chairman.

"We've got the *Independence* battle group off Italy on exercises. They're due to wrap up in three days. And the *Enterprise* group is on the Indian Ocean. Both are just coming off a refit cycle. Get them in position, increase CENTCOM overflights, and we'll have their attention."

"And if we need more than that?" asked Talbot.

"It would depend on the situation, but it would give us increased firepower."

Talbot considered this; he looked around the table. "Any problems with this?"

No one spoke. Mason looked down at his notes. He'd expressed his opinion to both the president and Talbot, but it was clear the course had been chosen. "How long to draw up an op plan, General?" Talbot asked.

"Five days."

"Do it. I'll brief the president."

10

Japan

TANNER TOOK THE AFTERNOON FLIGHT FROM HONG KONG TO Osaka and arrived back at the Royal Palms at dusk. He was stepping from the shower when a knock came at his door. It was a bellman.

"Mr. Tanner, your party is waiting for you in the restaurant."

"My party?"

"Yes, sir."

Camille, Tanner thought and smiled. "Please tell her I'll be down shortly."

Ten minutes later, he walked into the restaurant. He was two steps through the doors when he saw her in the corner booth.

Even at this distance her black hair shimmered in the candlelight and her eyes shone as they returned his gaze. Her dress was simple, low-cut black silk with a single strand of pearls dipping into her cleavage.

He stared for a moment longer and then walked over.

"Welcome home," she said.

"Hello." He stared.

She smiled. "Do you want to sit down, or are you going to eat standing up?"

They shared a bottle of wine, then ordered dinner, which Briggs barely tasted. The conversation was effortless, and again he was surprised how natural it seemed between them. Even so, he felt an undercurrent of electricity, pleasant, yet slightly unnerving

Camille said, "It was a long two days."

"For me, too."

Suddenly she became demure; she toyed with the rim of her wineglass. For a moment Tanner wondered, disappointed, if this was an affectation, but he decided it wasn't. There was a duality to Camille that he found irresistible. She was sexy and chaste, bold and uncertain, strong and submissive.

"So," she said. "Shall we sit for a while, or we can walk on the beach—"

He stood up and extended his hand. "Come with me."

"Where—"

"Just come."

She took his hand.

Two minutes later they were at her room. Without a word, Camille opened the door, and Briggs followed her inside. He shut the door. The room was dark except for the moonlight filtering through the balcony door; a breeze billowed the curtains.

Camille leaned against the wall. "Don't leave me this time, Briggs."

"I promise."

Then they were together, kissing, her arms around his neck. She arched her back against the wall, pushing her hips and breasts against him. Tanner drew down the zipper at her back. Her dress slid away. She wore no bra. He grazed his fingertips over the upper swell of her breasts, then gently cupped them and traced his thumbs over her nipples. She sucked in her breath and leaned her head back.

"Oh, God. Hurry, Briggs; I don't want to wait."

In one smooth motion, Tanner lifted her off the ground. She wrapped her legs around his waist and began unbuttoning his shirt as he carried her to the bed. As they fell together, she curled her hands around his neck and drew him down on top of her.

AFTERWARD, THEY SAT ON THE BALCONY WRAPPED TOGETHER IN a blanket, watching the ocean. Camille traced her finger along the corner of Tanner's eye. "What's this scar?"

"I got careless with a razor." *A razor that happened to*

be in the hands of a Korean soldier at the time, Tanner didn't add. "Nicked myself."

"And this one?" Camille touched under his right armpit.

"You wouldn't believe me if I told you."

"Try me."

"I fell on some broken glass."

"Mmm. You should be more careful."

After a while, she whispered, "Briggs, I have to leave in the morning."

"What? I thought it wasn't until the day after."

"So did I. Something from work came up. I'm sorry I didn't tell you. I didn't want it spoiling our evening."

Tanner smiled. "Never argue with a woman's wisdom."

"Pardon?"

"Something my dad once told me."

"A wise man, your father."

Her tone was light, but Tanner knew she was thinking the same thing as he: Whatever they had now would probably end tomorrow. He wasn't sure which feeling dominated his heart: sadness or relief. He was torn, and he hated it.

"I hate this," Camille murmured.

"Me, too."

"I don't know how to . . ." A tear ran from Camille's eye and fell on his chest. "What do we do, Briggs?"

Tanner wrapped his arms around her. "In the morning we'll have breakfast, I'll take you to the airport, we'll promise to meet again, and then we'll say good-bye."

She looked up at him. "Just that easy?"

"No, not easy. Not easy at all."

Camille kissed him, then lifted her leg over the chair and straddled him. She pulled the blanket around them and smiled. "Well, we still have time."

She shed her robe and moved against him until they were both ready, then rose up and lowered herself onto him. She stayed that way, unmoving except for a gentle circling of her hips. They made love slowly, almost lazily, until she climaxed. She made no sound save a small gasp, then curled up against his chest.

They dozed and talked until the first tinge of sunlight appeared on the horizon.

"Almost dawn," Tanner murmured.

"Take me back to bed, Briggs."

A FEW HOURS LATER, AFTER SHE FINISHED DRESSING, TANNER TOOK her luggage to the lobby, called for a taxi, and sat down to wait.

After sunrise they'd shared breakfast on the balcony. Camille's mood was cheery and playful, but it was forced as she dawdled about the room, combing her hair, packing and repacking, avoiding the clock. When Tanner finally told her they had to leave, she simply nodded and asked him to take her bag downstairs.

Suddenly the lobby doors burst open and in strode a genuine cowboy, complete with snakeskin boots, a silver and turquoise belt buckle, bolo tie, and a ten-gallon Stetson. Tottering his wake was a single bellman, his arms piled with luggage.

The cowboy stood about five eight and tipped the scales at a solid 220 pounds. His close-cropped beard and mustache were light brown.

The check-in process for the cowboy was swift, and within minutes he and his bellman were headed for the elevators. As he passed Tanner, Ian "Bear" Cahil tipped his hat at him, gave him a "Pardner," then disappeared into the elevator.

The cavalry has arrived, Tanner thought with a smile. *What was it Dutcher had said? Light cover for status?* Briggs suspected Bear had chosen his own. It would do the job, though; the Pecos Bill act would be what people remembered; out of costume, Cahil would be almost invisible.

A moment later the elevator opened and Camille stepped out.

"Ready?" Tanner asked.

"Yes."

*   *   *

AN HOUR LATER, THEY WERE STANDING AT HER PLANE'S BOARDING
gate. The attendant announced the last call for her flight.
She cast an irritated glance at the jet way.

"Damn it." She pressed a finger beneath her eye, trying
to keep it from brimming. "This is silly. After all, this was
just a vacation romance, wasn't it?"

He took her in his arms. "No."

She looked into his eyes. "No, I guess not." She kissed
him, then pushed herself away and picked up her carry-on.
"I should go. I'll miss my plane."

"Good-bye, Camille."

"Good-bye, Briggs." She placed a tentative hand on his
chest, then turned and walked onto the jet way.

TANNER ASKED THE CABBIE TO DRIVE FOR A WHILE, NOT CARING
where, then returned to the Royal Palms. He walked up to
Cahil's room and knocked.

"Hold yer horses!" Tanner heard.

The door opened. "Sheriff," Briggs drawled and walked
in.

"You like it? I'm kind of enjoying it. They love cowboys
here."

"So I've heard."

Cahil frowned at him. "You okay?"

"Yeah."

"She make her flight?"

Tanner nodded.

"You want to talk about it?"

"No."

Cahil ordered coffee and sandwiches from room service,
and they spent the afternoon fleshing out their game plan.
First they would check the locker at Sannomiya Station,
which Tanner felt could be important for two reasons: One,
instead of having secreted it somewhere, Umako was carrying the key when he died; and two, he hadn't told the CIA
about it.

Next they would check DORSAL's series of dead-letter drops. Following that, assuming they got no response from the drops, would be to get clearance from the CIA to restart Ohira's network, beginning with the one and only agent the CIA knew about, an engineer at Takagi Maritime. All this would take some finesse. Ohira's contacts had probably heard of his murder, and a sudden reactivation might send them running.

"What about equipment?" asked Tanner.

"We should have it by tomorrow. When do you want to check the locker?"

"Tonight."

Cahil nodded and downed the last of his coffee. "Then get the hell out of here and let me sleep. My body's still on Washington time."

11

Langley

ONE OF THE BY-PRODUCTS OF THE END OF THE COLD WAR AND the U.S.S.R.'s subsequent demise was a spirit of renewed cooperation between the U.S. and Russian intelligence communities. As the struggling commonwealth's primary source of subsidy, the U.S. had demanded and received many concessions, one of which involved Russia's former links to state-sponsored terrorism. In the years following the breakup, the KGB's successor, the Foreign Intelligence Service, had aided the CIA's war on terrorism by serving as an information clearinghouse. To facilitate this conduit the DCI and his deputies were linked to their Russian counterparts via encrypted phones.

The phone's distinct double buzz caught DDO George Coates by surprise. He opened the drawer and lifted the receiver. He heard several clicks, then a muted tone burst, which told him the encryption and recording units were functioning.

"George Coates."

"Hello, George."

"Pyotor, this is a surprise." Pyotor Kolokov, his opposite number in the FIS, used the "bat phone" sparingly.

"A pleasant one, I trust."

"Of course. How is Karina?"

"She is well. Thank you for asking. George, I am sending you something in the diplomatic pouch. It concerns a former friend of ours, someone you've expressed an interest in."

Coates had a guess what this meant. Most often, information passed by the FIS regarded the CIA's hit parade, an informal list of assorted bad guys they were tracking. The upper ranks of the DO's current hit parade were filled almost exclusively by Islamic terrorists the KGB had once nurtured.

"How much interest?" asked Coates.

"For you, some. But for your sister, quite a lot, I think."

"I see." The CIA's "sister" was the FBI.

"Once you've had a chance to digest the material, call me."

Coates laughed. "After-the-sale customer service, Pyotor? That's not like you."

"I am in an expansive mood. Good-bye, George."

Coates hung up and redialed. "Marie, George Coates here. I'm expecting a package from the Russian embassy. Bring it up as soon as it's clear, will you?"

Dulles International Airport, Washington, D.C.

IBRAHIM FAYYAD STOOD IN THE CUSTOMS LINE READING A COPY of *La Republica*. The line inched forward, and he picked up his bag, stepped ahead, then set it down again. Behind him, a woman did the same.

"Don't you just hate lines?" she asked him.

Fayyad turned. *"Mi scusi?"*

"These lines," she repeated. "Don't you just hate them?"

"Oh. *Si.*"

"You're Italian, aren't you?"

"Yes, I am."

She was a midthirties platinum blond with vacuous eyes and too much eyeliner. Her figure was gorgeous, however, and Fayyad let his eyes settle on her generous cleavage. Her smile broadened.

"You know, I just love Italian men," she cooed.

And very often, I suspect, Fayyad thought. *"Grazie."*

For a moment he considered the invitation. The physical release would be welcome, and this woman was just what he needed—a receptacle. She made no pretenses otherwise.

She said, "Say, would you like to have a drink or—"

"I'm sorry, I am late for an appointment. Thank you, though."

"Another time, maybe?"

"Possibly, yes."

She jotted her number on the back of his newspaper. Her name was Candi. The "i" was dotted with a heart. "Call me."

He gave her a smile and slipped it into his pocket. "Candi. *Bello.*"

"*Bello?* What's that?"

"It means beautiful."

Fayyad was next in line. The customs agent nodded and took his passport as his bag was searched. "Your name, sir?"

"Vesuchi. Paolo Vesuchi."

"Do you have anything to declare?"

"No."

"And the purpose of your visit, sir?"

"Business."

The agent stamped his passport and handed it back. "Have a nice stay."

FBI Headquarters

CHARLIE LATHAM'S HEBREW WAS JUST GOOD ENOUGH TO TELL THE switchboard operator at *Shin Bet* headquarters who he was looking for. A moment later, Avi Haron's booming voice came on the line. "Charlie Latham!"

"Hello, Avi."

"They told Avi it was an American calling, and of course I knew it was you." One of Haron's most endearing quirks was speaking of himself in the third person. "To what do I owe this honor?"

"You've heard about the Delta bombing?"

"Ah, yes. Bad business, that. I wondered if you were involved. Where does it stand?"

"That depends on you. You remember your trouble with the PFLP a few years ago . . . the honey trap business?"

"Do I remember? Of course. You don't think—"

"The woman in question met a man on vacation, had a romance, etcetera. . . . The whole thing fits the profile. So does his description and the name he used."

"I see. Give me the details," Haron said, and Latham did so. "So who is your guess, Charlie?"

"Ibrahim Fayyad."

"Ah! This is bad, Charlie. These are not nice people. But Fayyad is freelance now. Unless you have more for me, there is no way of knowing who hired him."

"I know, Avi. I'm looking for a direction before this thing stalls on me."

"Perhaps I can help. But we are out of channels, are we not? Aren't your liaison people going to get testy? You know me, I am a stickler for protocol."

Latham laughed. "Since when? If you want, I can send it up the line, but this is information I need now, not a year from now."

"Am I hearing that the wheels at the FBI turn slowly? Charlie, I will help you. One friend to another. Give me a day. If we are lucky, and Fayyad sticks to his routine, he may return to one of his favorite haunts for some rest and relaxation."

"Thanks, Avi. You have my home number. Call me day or night."

"I will be in touch, my friend. And Charlie?"

"Yes?"

"How many died?"

"Five."

"And the woman?"

"She made it."

"Good. A bit of justice in that, perhaps."

"Not enough, Avi," said Latham. "Not nearly enough."

Langley

"ALL RIGHT, LET'S WRAP IT UP," SAID FRANK RHODES, THE CIA'S counterintelligence director. "We need a recommendation for the boss."

At the direction of George Coates, Rhodes had drawn

together this working group to determine if SYMMETRY's op sec—or lack thereof—had contributed to the loss of Marcus.

As far as Art Stucky was concerned, the reason was clear: The man had gotten careless. Stucky knew Rhodes was anxious to submit his report before the Intelligence Directorate had a chance to point the ugly stick at ops. Being blamed for this mess was bad enough without getting it from that Albrect bitch. How she had landed the DDI slot in the first place was a mystery to Stucky. Women had no business in the spy business.

"Let's go around the table," said Rhodes. "Julie?"

"All the other SYMMETRY contacts are untouched. Same with the safe-call locations. Either Marcus is dead, or he hasn't given them anything."

"Yet," said Stucky. "Once they put his nuts in the vice, he'll start singing."

Julie ignored him and continued. "I think we can rule out communication procedures as a weak link."

"Ditto for personnel compromise," said another analyst. "Nobody but the alternate who reported the snatch knew Marcus personally. The rest were handled via drops only."

"Any word on ransom demands or credit?" asked Rhodes.

"Nothing," said Julie. "We tapped all our sources, official and unofficial. Whoever took him isn't bragging about it. If they killed him, they did a good job disposing of the body."

"So the bottom line is, Marcus was taken by persons unknown, for reasons unknown."

"I'll tell you why the raghead got caught," Stucky said. "He fucked up, that's why. SYMMETRY was wired tight. Marcus screwed up and got himself killed, period."

The other analysts at the table stared at Stucky with a mixture of distaste and amazement. "Jesus, Art," said Julie.

"I'm just saying what everyone's thinking."

"Well, you don't speak for me."

"Well, no shit—"

"Okay, people, enough," Rhodes said. "Art may be right.

This could be a case of operator error. Unfortunately, we may never know. Okay, I'm meeting with DDO this afternoon. Our report will indicate no compromise on our side of the house, with the recommendation that SYMMETRY be shut down to preserve the network until it can be reactivated. Any disagreement?" No one spoke. "Okay, that's all. Thanks."

Everyone filed out of the conference room except for Rhodes and Stucky, who reclined in his chair and lit a cigarette, ignoring the No Smoking sign above his head. "Christ, that Julie is one bleeding-heart bitch, ain't she?"

"Maybe," Rhodes said, "but you might want to ease up a little bit—"

"My guess is she just needs some."

"Some what?"

Stucky laughed. "Good one. Okay, let's get this thing filed so I can get back to Tel Aviv."

"I would have thought you'd want to stay here," said Rhodes.

"What the hell for?"

"Exposure. It'd do your career some good."

Stay here and rub elbows with management cocksuckers? Stucky thought. *No thank you.* Field operatives were the backbone of the CIA, not assholes who sat around deciding the cafeteria lunch menu. All their good manners and college degrees made him sick.

His encounter with Dutcher last week was proof of that. Wasn't it enough that Dutcher—and Briggs Tanner, *especially him*—had trashed his Army career? Twenty years down the toilet over some little Spic girl. He'd done what was necessary, what guys like Tanner didn't have the balls to do. And now Dutcher wouldn't even give him the time of day when they passed one another on a goddamned elevator.

People like them eventually got what they deserved, of that Stucky was sure. And if there was any justice in this world, he'd would be there to see it. He would pay money for that. He smiled at the thought.

"What's so funny?" asked Rhodes.

"Forget it." Stucky stood up and crushed out his cigarette. "Listen, Frank, just make sure you get it straight in your report, okay? I ain't gonna get bent over because some raghead got himself snatched."

Tel Aviv

HAYEM SHERABI, DIRECTOR OF THE ISRAELI MOSSAD, STUDIED THE NAKA report before him. All Mossad case officers—known as *katsas*—submitted operational reports in this standardized format. No variation was allowed, and NAKA training constituted several weeks of a Mossad recruit's training.

This particular report was correct in all respects, but its source concerned him. There were those in Mossad that believed friendship had no place in the intelligence business, but Sherabi thought this naive. This particular *katsa* was a friend—or more accurately, the child of a long-dead friend. How to balance loyalty, discipline, and the security of Israel was a question with which Sherabi often wrestled.

Known formally as *Ha Mossad, le Modiyn ve le Tafkidim Mayuhadim* (the Institute for Intelligence and Operations) and informally as The Institute, Mossad is a small agency by U.S. standards, fielding less than fifty *katsas* worldwide. Despite this, Mossad is considered one of the most effective agencies in the world and certainly one of the most ruthless. Surrounded by a sea of neighbors who have sworn to destroy its mother country, Mossad lives by a brutally pragmatic motto: "By way of deception, thou shalt do war."

There was a knock on Sherabi's door. "Come."

His guest entered and stood at attention before his desk. He studied her. A fine *katsa* and a beautiful woman, Sherabi thought, but to him Camille Sereva would always be the little girl of a dear friend.

Since Amil Sereva's death ten years ago, Sherabi had kept his promise to watch over Camille. Of Amil's three children, Camille was the only one still living, the rest having been taken by forty years of war. Her two brothers had died while stalling the Syrian advance on the Golan in

'73 as 1,200 Syrian tanks were defeated by 175 Israeli Shermans. It had been a glorious but costly victory: 6,000 dead in less than three weeks of fighting.

Sherabi stifled the impulse to embrace Camille. "Sit."

She did so.

"I've read your report. The murder of your contact was unfortunate."

"Yes, sir."

"But your interlude with this man, this American . . . Who authorized it, can you tell me that?"

"No one, sir."

"And yet you did it. Why?"

Camille hesitated.

"Answer me!"

"It . . . it was a . . ." She trailed off

A mistake? Sherabi thought. Interesting she couldn't— or wouldn't—say the word. He'd never seen Camille at a loss for words. Nor did she say anything she didn't mean. She was stubborn like her mother.

"Why did you include it in your report?"

"Because it happened . . . it happened during an operation. The guidelines are quite clear regarding—"

"I know the regulations. I also know that regulations cannot cover every circumstance a *katsa* may encounter." Sherabi closed the file. "Since you did not attempt to hide it, we're going to treat this as a lesson learned."

"Thank you, sir."

"Learn it well, though. Here, you do not get many second chances."

"Yes, sir."

"Your impressions of the man were correct." Sherabi opened another file. "Briggs Tanner is a retired Navy commander, attached to the Navy Special Warfare Group and Special Operations Command, but it appears he no longer has any links to either the government or military. Aside from an interesting background and his behavior at the murder scene, we found nothing unusual about him. You, however, attracted some interest."

"What?" Camille asked.

"The Karotovic cover was probed. It held up, of course, but all the same, we are shutting it down for the time being. Now: new business.

"We've received reports of an increased Iranian *Pasdaran* presence in Beirut. We believe the Syrian *Mucharabat* and Air Force Intelligence are providing secret base camps and training."

"In the city proper?" Camille asked, surprised. Most Iranian activity was confined to Baalbek and areas south of the Litani River.

"Yes."

"For what reason?"

"We don't know. It may be nothing, it may be something. Who can know the Arab mind? At any rate, we are considering options. One them would involve reactivating some of the Lebanon networks."

"Yes, sir."

"The decision hasn't been made yet. For now, I want you to take some time."

"Why? I am—"

Sherabi raised his hand. "This is not a punitive measure, Camille. You are due some time off. Take it; relax. Consider it an order, if it helps." Sherabi came around the desk to sit beside her. "Enough business. How is your mother?"

Camille smiled. "Fine. She asks about you."

"I haven't seen her in some time."

"She said that, too. She said you should be ashamed."

Sherabi chuckled. "The most direct woman I know." Sherabi took her hand and patted it. "Camille, you are a fine *katsa*. You are young, though. This thing with the American—"

Camille raised her chin. "Are we talking as family now, Uncle Hayem?"

"Yes."

"Then it is none of your business."

Again Sherabi chuckled. "Stubborn like your mother and direct like your father. Do you know what we called him in the Haganah?"

"No."

"We called him Badger. Small, tenacious, and fierce in battle. Camille, listen, as a friend . . . as the voice of your father . . . I tell you this: There are those that feel a *katsa* is not entitled to a personal life. Everything you do is in the service of Israel . . . even who you love."

"They are wrong."

"Perhaps so. Tread carefully, though. I will not always be here. I overlooked this liaison of yours. Others would not."

Camille was silent.

"Never ignore your heart," Sherabi continued, "but God help you if you are forced to choose between your heart and your duty."

"Have you ever faced such a choice?"

"Once."

"Did you choose correctly?"

"I think so."

"Which did you follow . . . your heart or your duty?"

Sherabi smiled. "Who are you to ask me such questions? Impudent child!" Sherabi kissed her forehead and stood up. "Now run off before I become angry."

Camille laughed and headed for the door.

"By the way, Camille . . . ?"

She turned. "Yes?"

"Welcome home."

CAMILLE OPENED THE DOOR TO HER APARTMENT AND STEPPED OVER the pile of mail beneath the slot. She set her bag on the kitchen table and looked around. Nothing had changed. Had she expected otherwise? Had she expected someone to be waiting at the door to greet her?

The apartment was empty, aside from a small love seat and a battered wing chair. There were a few paintings and tapestries, but these lay on the floor, still in their packing boxes. What few plants she owned had withered in her absence.

She opened the refrigerator and saw a bottle of wine, a tupperware container filled with God knew what, and a rotten head of lettuce. She grabbed the wine, poured herself a glass, and found a box of crackers in the cupboard.

She paced the floor, watered the plants, thumbed through the mail, stared into the refrigerator again.

Nothing felt right. This was her home, but it felt foreign. She took a gulp of wine. Why couldn't she stop thinking about him? Probably for the same reason she hadn't been able to use the word *mistake* in Uncle Hayem's office. Why couldn't she make sense of what was going on in her head?

"God help you if you are forced to choose between your heart and your duty." Wasn't that what Hayem said? Duty was something she understood. Of the two—heart and duty—only one could exist for her right now.

Camille raised her glass and toasted the bare walls. "To duty, then."

12

Japan

TANNER TOOK A TAXI TO THE UNDERGROUND UMEDA STATION IN Osaka, where he bought a one-way ticket and boarded the Tokaido Line train. Thirty minutes later he arrived at Sannomiya Station

The terminal was a three-story structure with marble concourses, a central atrium, and domed skylights. The upper levels containing the lockers were reached by spiraling ramps at the north and south ends of the train platform.

Tanner found the platform almost deserted, with only a few late-night commuters milling about. Ian Cahil, sans Stetson and wearing a conservative blue suit, sat on a bench at the opposite end of the concourse, reading a newspaper. Without a glance in Tanner's direction, he stood, folded the newspaper under his left arm, and started up the south ramp.

All clear, no surveillance, Tanner thought. Had Cahil folded the newspaper under his right arm, it would have been a wave-off: *Go away, don't look back.*

No matter how many times Tanner went through the tradecraft, he had to remind himself it was all necessary. You never trusted luck alone unless you had no choice.

He waited exactly three minutes before starting up the north ramp. Above him, Cahil stood at the railing with a disposable coffee cup in his right hand.

Tanner kept going.

The third level was all but empty. Aside from Cahil, who now sat on a stool in the Sannomiya's *kissaten,* or coffee shop, there were three other people visible: two standing at the shop's counter and the attendant at the tourist kiosk.

Footsteps echoing, Tanner strode past the *kissaten*. As he did so, Cahil opened his suitcase, removed a magazine, laid it facedown on the stool beside him.

Tanner walked to the bank of lockers, found 312, opened it, removed the leather valise he found inside, shoved it under his arm, closed the door, and walked down the south ramp.

Three minutes later, he boarded the Shinkansen Line back to Osaka.

HE RODE FOR TWENTY MINUTES AND THEN DISEMBARKED AT SHIN-kansen and walked across the concourse to the Tokaido platform. According to the schedule, the next train was due in five minutes.

It was nearly midnight. Except for a lone janitor sweeping the platform, the station was quiet. Briggs found a bench and sat down. Moments later, he heard the clomp of footsteps coming down the stairwell behind him. He turned.

First down the stairs came a hard-looking Japanese man wearing a loose-fitting gray suit. With a thick neck and heavy brows, he could have been a clone of Tange Noboru. He stopped at the bottom of the steps, clasped his hands in front of him, and stared at Tanner. A moment later, three younger men appeared behind him, each wearing a black leather jacket, jeans, and combat boots. The taller of the three whispered to the suited man and got a nod in return.

Tanner glanced around. The janitor had disappeared.

It was then that Tanner recognized the thugs. They'd been aboard his train at Umeda but had disembarked two stops before Sannomiya. Instead of setting the ambush at the more public Sannomiya, they'd gambled he would return on the same line. *Stupid mistake, Briggs.*

There were only two exits nearby, one of which was blocked by these four men, and a second one a hundred yards away. *Too far,* he decided.

The three thugs swaggered forward. The leader shoved his hand into his pocket. If the trio was armed with anything more than knives, this one had it. Clutching the valise to his chest, Tanner stood up, glanced around, then turned and began walking toward the far exit. The thugs followed, fanning out behind him. Tanner stumbled, regained his balance, and picked up his pace.

As Tanner drew even with one of the platform's pillars, he stopped and turned. "What do you want?" he stuttered. "Leave me alone."

The leader stepped forward. "Give wallet and case."

"My wallet?" Tanner said. "Why?"

"Give!"

Tanner glanced around, eyes wide. "Please. *Please,* I don't—"

One of the other thugs muttered something. The other laughed. The leader took another step forward. "Give case *now!*"

"Oh, God," Tanner sputtered. "Please . . ."

The leader pulled his hand from his pocket. With an audible click, the knife's blade shot open. He reversed it, blade backward, parallel to his forearm—the classic grip of an experienced knife fighter. "I said, give case!"

There would be no more talking, Tanner knew. *Wait for it. . . .* "Please, I—"

The leader lunged forward, knife slashing diagonally toward Tanner's face.

Simultaneously ducking under the blade and stepping forward, Briggs dropped the valise, seized the leader's arm at the wrist and elbow, then sidekicked, sweeping the man's right leg from under him. As he fell, Tanner spun on his heel and slammed the man face first into the concrete pillar. From the corner of his eye, Tanner saw the other two closing in, but slowly, confused by their target's sudden transformation. It was typical wolf pack mentality, Tanner knew, and the solution was simple: Pick the leader and wreck him.

Still gripping the leader's wrist, Tanner heaved the man to his feet, then wrenched forward and down. With an audible pop, the man's radius bone snapped. He screamed, and his knees buckled. Tanner shoved him into the other two. They stood frozen.

Down the concourse came several shouts. *"Ya me te! Ya me te!"* Stop!

Eyes locked on the thugs, Tanner bent down and picked up the valise. One of the thugs suddenly regained his courage. He flicked open his switchblade and charged. Tanner met the thrust with the valise. The blade plunged into the leather. Tanner took a step backward, drawing the man along, then toe-kicked him in the kneecap, shattering it. The man fell hard, groaning.

Footsteps pounded down the concourse. *"Ya me te!"*

The third man turned and ran. Tanner looked for the Noboru clone, but he was gone.

THE TWO OFFICERS SPOKE LITTLE ENGLISH, SO TANNER WAS ES-corted to prefecture headquarters, where he was questioned through an interpreter.

A few minutes later, Inspector Tanaka arrived. He nodded at Tanner, scanned the report, then took a chair. As he had at the hotel, Tanner took an immediate dislike to Tanaka; it was partly gut reaction and partly trust in Ieyasu's insinuation that Tanaka was dirty.

"You are having an eventful stay in Japan, Mr. Tanner."

"Not by choice, Inspector. How is it you got this case?"

"Homicide and Violent Crimes are part of the same division. I was on duty, and I recognized your name. I thought I might help."

"Thanks, but no harm done."

"Except to the two men you put in the hospital."

"Are you more concerned for them, Inspector, or for tourists who get mugged in your subways?"

"For our tourists, of course. These men were severely injured, however. I am wondering where you learned to—"

"Call it dumb luck."

"But these were experienced street hoodlums. I just find it curious that—"

"Inspector, am I being charged with something?"

"No. The circumstances are quite clear here."

"Then let's finish. It's been a long night."

"Very well. We just need a statement, and then we'll return you to your hotel."

Tanner stated he left his hotel and took the train into Kobe, where he boarded the Portliner monorail for Port Island, a thirty-minute round trip.

"And the reason for this trip?" asked Tanaka

"Sightseeing."

"At this hour?"

"I don't sleep well."

"May I see the ticket?"

"I threw it away."

"Please continue."

From the Portliner he returned to Sannomiya and boarded the Tokaido to Shinkassen, where he was attacked. He described both the confrontation and his attackers but mentioned nothing of the Noboru clone.

"What did they ask for?"

"My wallet."

"Not the valise?" Tanaka asked, pointing to the the case in Tanner's lap.

"No. In fact, I offered it to them, but they didn't want it."

"May I?"

Tanner didn't bat an eye. "Go ahead."

Tanaka dug through the case for a few moments, then handed it back. "Well, Mr. Tanner, we will file a report and continue the search for the third attacker. I'll have an officer return you to your hotel."

Tanner stood. "Thank you."

"One piece of advice, however," Tanaka said. "This is your second incident in our country. You might be wise to be more cautious in the future."

"You're afraid my string of bad luck might continue?"

Tanaka smiled greasily. "I certainly hope not, but who can say?"

"I'll keep that in mind, Inspector."

*　　*　　*

AN HOUR LATER, BACK IN CAHIL'S HOTEL ROOM, BEAR HELD UP the valise and wiggled his finger through the knife hole. "Made some friends, I see."

Tanner poured them a pair of scotch rocks, handed one to Cahil, then dropped into a chair. "Three of them."

"You okay?"

Tanner nodded. *Good ol' Mama Bear.* It was good to have him along. "One got away," he said. "A Noboru look-alike was there, too, but he disappeared."

"Slowing in your old age, Briggs."

"Tell me about it. Let's see what they wanted so badly."

Cahil opened the valise. There were only two items: a nautical chart and a day-planner organizer. Cahil unfolded the former on the bed. It was a coastal chart of southern Honshu Island, the Inland Sea, and Shikoku Island. Written in along the border were the words "Toshogu" and "Tsu-mago" and "Anan, Secure Dock 12—???"

"Takagi's shipyard?" Cahil asked.

Tanner nodded. "It's just south of Anan, over on Shi-koku. One of Ohira's contacts worked there. Here, what do you make of these?"

A series of asterisks and fractional numbers—all with three-digit numerators and four-digit denominators—had been scribbled on the chart. Four of the asterisks lay within miles of the Royal Palms. A pair of red dots—one just inside the mouth of the Inland Sea and the other a few miles off Shiono Misaki—were linked by a dotted line.

"Interesting," said Cahil. "Wonder what it means."

"Let's see the day planner."

The contents appeared unremarkable, except for several pages on which they found handwritten geometric symbols: squares, triangles and diamonds, each in different se-quences and each followed by four numbers.

"Military time," said Tanner. "It's symbol code—prob-ably listings of Ohira's contact locations and wave-off meets." He retrieved the laptop computer, powered it up, typed in his password, and opened a file. "Here we go. . . . Check the night he was killed."

Cahil flipped pages. "Busy boy. Three meets: eight, ten, then eleven."

"He was killed at about nine-thirty, so he was probably on his way to the second meet. Anything written down?"

"No, just the time."

"Could be his false flag. So, let's assume he made the first meet. . . ." Tanner said, checking the laptop's screen. "Here: A bar outside Tokoshima. It was his shipyard contact, the enginneer. Why all the interest in the shipyard, I wonder? The fire-control chips were supposedly made by Takagi's electronics division."

"Most of Takagi's contract work for the JDF is handled by the Maritime Division."

"True, but still . . ."

Cahil squinted at him. "Let me guess: You see a late-night visit to the shipyard in our future."

"It might be a good idea. Okay, how about Ohira's last meet?"

Bear checked the day planner and found Ohira's eleven o'clock appointment had been set at the Nintoku Mausoleum in Osaka. "Wow," he said. "The contact's a lawyer in Takagi's Office of Counsel. Big fish."

"No kidding. Okay, that was the primary meet. How about the secondary?"

"Ten o'clock at Sorakuen Garden in Kobe. Day after tomorrow."

"Good," said Tanner. "Now let's just hope his contact hasn't gone to ground."

SOUTH OF NAGOYA, IN HIS HILLTOP MANSION OVERLOOKING AT-sumi Bay, Hiromasa Takagi steepled his fingers and stared at the black-and-white photograph lying in the center of his desk blotter. "This is the man who helped Ohira?" he asked.

Tange Noboru nodded. *"Hai."*

"The same man you followed to the village?"

"Hai."

"Is he working alone?"

"We think so. After leaving the hotel he boarded the train

at Umeda, but he was lost when he switched to the Shin-kansen. He returned by the same route, this time carrying a briefcase. An attempt was made to intercept him." Noboru cast a reproachful glance at the gray-suited man standing behind him. "It failed."

"Explain."

Noboru barked at the gray-suited man, who stepped forward and recounted the confrontation with Tanner. *"Gomen nasai,"* he murmured. Please forgive me.

For a full minute, Takagi stared at the man, who stood bowed at the waist. In feudal Japan this was a posture of submission, the symbolic offering of one's head as atonement for wrongdoing. Today, according to the code of conduct of the Black Ocean Society and its subculture, the *yakuzza,* atonement was not as final, but it was harsh nonetheless. A sign of renewed fealty was required.

Takagi spoke. The phrase was idiomatic and roughly translated as, "By the blade, you are cleansed."

The man nodded. *"Hai."*

He walked to the low coffee table against the wall and knelt beside it. On the table lay a small oak cutting board. In deliberate, almost ritualistic fashion, the man wound a silk handkerchief around the base of his pinky finger and then drew the handkerchief into a knot. Immediately the finger began to swell purple. From his jacket pocket he withdrew a *kento* knife and laid it beside his splayed finger.

He looked at Takagi. Takagi nodded.

The man jammed the tip of the knife into the wood beside his little finger, and rocked it sideways.

There was a sharp *crunch-pop* and blood gushed from the severed stump. The man let out a stifled cry. On shaking legs, he rose to his feet, swayed slightly, then picked up the cutting board and placed it on Takagi's desk blotter.

Takagi nodded. "Go." The man turned and left the room.

Takagi considered the situation. He knew little about Tanner aside from his military background and current employer, an exporter/importer in the United States. There was nothing to suggest he was anything more than an ordinary vacationer. Nothing, that is, except his actions at the hotel.

Was it all coincidence? Perhaps, perhaps not. Takagi was tempted to settle the matter, but another murder—especially of an American—would raise too much suspicion. Ohira's murder had been necessary. It had left many unanswered questions. Who had he been working for, if anyone? Could there be a compromise?

Takagi dismissed this. Like so many men of wealth and power, he considered himself untouchable, and in Japan this was the virtual truth. *No,* he decided, there was no compromise. The ship would depart soon, and once the facility was destroyed there would be no trail left to follow. He was safe.

"Watch him," Takagi said to Noboru. "As long as he remains a simple vacationer, he is to be left alone. If his interests change, however, I expect you to handle it personally. Do you understand?"

Tange Noboru nodded. *"Hai."*

FOR A LONG TIME AFTER NOBORU LEFT, TAKAGI STARED OUT THE window and considered his decision. Was there a connection beyond Ohira's chance encounter with Tanner? Had he overlooked—

Stop this! he commanded himself. Doubt? Hiromasa Takagi, doubting himself? He jabbed the intercom button on his desk. "Susiko! Come in here!"

The door opened and a young girl entered. She was sixteen years old, beautiful and delicate, with short black hair framing her face. Her eyes were liquid brown, doelike. Susiko had been fourteen when Takagi purchased her from a courtesan in Kyoto. Then, as now, she was perfect. A child-woman.

I am in control, Takagi thought, staring at her. "Disrobe," he commanded.

Eyes downcast, Susiko shed her robe. Her breasts were pert and just budding. In accordance with Takagi's instructions, she was smooth-shaven.

"Come here."

Susiko walked around the desk and stood before him. He

reached up and fondled her right breast. The girl trembled but made no sound. She was frightened. He relished it. He felt himself hardening. He caressed her nipple between his thumb and index finger, paused, then pinched down. She cried out and collapsed to his feet.

"Tell me what you want," Takagi murmured.

Shoulders trembling, she stared at the floor. "Please, I—"

"Tell me what you want!"

"You," she choked. "I want you."

He gently cupped her chin and lifted her face. He slapped her; a red welt appeared on her cheek. "Tell me what you want."

"I want you."

Takagi smiled and nodded. "Very good."

13

"FOR CHRIST'S SAKE, JUDITH, HOW MANY TIMES DO I HAVE TO tell you: Your ass is too big for that dress!" Herb Smith yelled from the bathroom. "You're not a goddamned supermodel, you know."

Judith Smith bit her lip. "Well, I just . . . I just thought—"

"Put on something else, and hurry up. The car will be here in five minutes."

Judith nodded, blinking away the tears. "Okay, Herb."

She went into the bathroom, careful not to slam the door lest it draw another bark. She snatched tissues from the counter dispenser and dabbed her eyes. *My eyeliner . . . I can't ruin my . . .* "Your ass is too big. You're not a goddamned supermodel." How would Marsha tell her to handle that? Maybe she wasn't a model, but she was certainly attractive, wasn't she? But Herb said—

"Stop it," she said, staring at her reflection. "Stop it. You deserve better—"

"Judith, quit talking to yourself and get ready. I will *not* be late because you can't fit your ass into a five-hundred-dollar dress!"

"Okay, Herb, I'm coming."

She stared into the mirror. The woman she saw was so different from the one of twenty-five years ago. Young Judith had been bright and confident and madly in love with a promising Georgia state senator who had won her heart on their first date. Less than a year later they were married, and that's when everything changed. She soon realized Herb had campaigned for her just as he campaigned for office: with ruthless pragmatism. She was simply window dressing, and he'd chosen her as he would choose a pair of shoes.

As the years went by and she worked at the marriage, certain that her dedication would change him, Judith made a fatal mistake: She began to believe it was her fault. She wasn't trying hard enough. She wasn't attentive enough. She wasn't this, she wasn't that. She tried harder. And thus the cycle began. Smith grew more abusive; she took the blame. He controlled, she submitted.

What had it felt like to be that younger woman? Was she gone? Judith wondered. Was *this* who she was? Marsha Burns didn't think so, and neither did her friends—her real friends, that was, not the Washington gossips. She'd overheard the conversations: *"She's damaged goods. Even if she managed to find the courage to leave that drunken, philandering husband of hers, who would have her?"* Judith knew about the drinking, the affairs, all the hushed-up gropings of young staffers. She even knew about the bimbo he had tucked away in that studio apartment in Georgetown. Despite all that, it terrified Judith to think of herself as anything but Mrs. Senator Herbert Smith.

"Judith, if you're not down here in one minute, I'm leaving without you!"

"Okay, Herb, almost ready."

Judith peeled off her dress and selected another from the closet. It was her least favorite, but he approved of it. It presented the right image, he said. She smoothed it over her hips, took one last look at her makeup, and hurried downstairs.

DOWN THE BLOCK FROM THE SMITH HOME, IBRAHIM FAYYAD watched the couple climb into the limousine. He checked the photo folder on his lap. There was no mistaking Herb Smith: the paunch, the ruddy skin, the thinning hair idiotically combed over his balding pate. The man was a pig. His wife, however, was another story. She was a handsome woman.

He watched the limo pull out of the driveway and disappear down the street. He pressed the Talk button on his portable radio. "Ibn, you have them?"

"We have them. We are following."

Fayyad nodded to Hasim in the driver's seat. "Let's go."

THE SMITHS' BACKYARD WAS INVITINGLY DARK WITH THE NEAREST neighbor a hundred yards away behind a tall fence. It took Fayyad less than a minute to pick the lock to the back door and another thirty seconds to bypass the alarm system. Once inside, he stood still, letting his eyes adjust. The house was dark except for a small bulb over the stove.

Fayyad told Hasim to wait in the kitchen.

He walked through the dining room and into the living room. The decor was predominantly feminine. All her choices, Fayyad suspected. The senator could not be bothered. As long as the correct image was portrayed, he would not care. Fayyad touched nothing but closely studied the photographs and paintings. Each one told him something about her. All the paintings were impressionist, most of them Monets. No pictures of children. According to al-Baz's brief, the marriage was childless. *Why?* he wondered. *And what effect did that have on her?*

Ibrahim Fayyad knew the opposite sex. He knew their bodies, but that was simply a matter of mechanics. A woman's heart was captured with more than good looks, charm, and bedroom skills. What a woman wants more than anything is to have her soul laid bare before her lover and have him cherish her without reservation. You must know a woman's heart, her dreams, her fears. Once you understand these, you play them in concert; need and hope and fear all swirling together until they blossomed into love.

Those with low self-esteem were the most vulnerable, as were abuse sufferers, whose need for validation was immense. This would be the case with Judith Smith. The challenge would be to overcome her resistance. She had probably gotten good at quashing her feelings, and Fayyad would have to break through that wall. Behind it, he knew, would be a torrent of emotion.

He walked upstairs. At the top of the landing, he stopped and closed his eyes. He could smell her perfume. He turned right, used his foot to push open the door, and stepped into to the master bedroom. It was decorated in country-style powder blue. The bedspread was adorned with tiny yellow daisies. He grazed his fingertips over it.

He pulled on a pair of latex gloves and went to work.

HE EXAMINED EVERYTHING OF HERS, FROM HER DRESSES AND HER jewelry to her undergarments. Judith was full-figured, he saw, only slightly plump, her hips still trim from not having given birth. Her bras and panties were white cotton. No lace, no color. Nor did she own any lingerie. Her robe was a simple white terry cloth; it smelled of soap and sandlewood lotion. Fayyad wondered if the Smiths still had sex. Probably, he decided, but only when the senator needed release or when he felt the need to reassert his ownership of her.

In her nightstand drawer he found a small cedar box. He picked the lock. Inside was a cloth-bound diary filled with Judith's neat, flowing script. The last entry was two days ago. He pocketed the diary, closed the box, and broke the lock. The senator would be blamed.

Also in the drawer was a scrapbook containing news-paper clippings and brochures about the Washington art community: gallery openings, shows, reviews, fund-raisers. Judith sat on several committees, one of the articles reported. Fayyad quickly scanned the rest, including one that included a short biography of her interests and tastes.

Next to the scrapbook was a day planner. She was meticulous. Every lunch date, appointment and social event was noted. He examined every page for the past three months, as well as the upcoming three, taking careful notes as he went.

He returned the scrapbook to the drawer, scanned the bedroom for anything out of place, then smoothed the bedspread and pulled the bathroom door closed to its original position. He was turning to leave, but he stopped.

He walked to the senator's side of the bed and opened his nightstand drawer. Inside were a pair of bifocals, a pulp detective novel, and a bottle of nasal spray. Near the back he found a neatly folded handkerchief. Fayyad opened it.

What he found surprised him. He slipped the item in his jacket pocket and then headed downstairs.

Langley

JUDITH WAS EXCITED. SHE'D NEVER BEEN TO CIA HEADQUARTERS and, like most civilians, she expected an aura of intrigue to be wafting through its corridors. She was slightly disappointed to find the glass-enclosed lobby fairly ordinary except for the memorial wall and an imposing bronze statue of Wild Bill Donovan.

According to Herb, this dinner was given every year by the CIA for select members of the intelligence community and Senate IOC. As chairman, Smith was the guest of honor. Having listened to enough of her husband's anti-CIA diatribes, however, Judith suspected Dick Mason would rather punch Herb than socialize with him.

With practiced ease, Judith followed the senator through the crowd, exchanging greetings and smiling. She knew most of the faces, and she disliked half of them. Even so, she laughed and mingled, the perfect actress. Sometimes she hated that part of herself, wondering if her own act made her as two-faced as the rest.

"Judith!"

She turned. "Bonnie! Oh, I'm so glad you're here." Bonnie Latham was one of her few genuine friends. They had met a year ago at a gallery opening. "Is Charlie here?"

"Yes, somewhere . . . There he is." Bonnie pointed across the room to where Herb Smith and the FBI agent were talking. "He hates these things."

"I don't blame him. Herb's probably grilling him about the Delta bombing."

"He's going to have to get in line."

"That bad?" Judith asked, accepting a glass of wine from a waiter.

"You didn't read the story in the *Post*? Congressman Hostetler's daughter was on the plane."

"Oh, my God. Is she okay?"

"From what I understand, she'll recover. So, how are you?"

"Wonderful. How're your kids—"

"You don't sound wonderful."

Judith shrugged. "Just the usual. Nothing to worry—"

Bonnie placed her hand on Judith's forearm. "Do you want to talk?"

"No, I'm fine, really."

"That's what you always say. We're having lunch this week, no arguments."

"Okay," Judith agreed gratefully. "Thank you, Bon."

"Sure. Now let's go find a quiet corner."

ACROSS THE ROOM, DICK MASON, GEORGE COATES, AND THEIR wives stood at the head of the receiving line. "Judith Smith looks lovely," said Mason's wife.

"Too lovely," Coates's wife replied good-naturedly.

"I concur," Coates added and got a poke in the ribs.

"Hard to believe he won her," said Mrs. Mason.

"Harder still to believe he kept her," Mrs. Coates muttered.

Herb Smith's unsavory lifestyle was one of the best kept nonsecrets in Washington. If not for his power, Smith would long ago have been railroaded out of town. Mason would have gladly shoveled coal into the firebox. Ironically, the widespread animus for Smith was countered by a widespread fondness for his wife. Depending on who you asked, Judith's devotion marked her as either a saint or an idiot.

"Ladies, no gossiping," said Mason.

"Richard, this is *not* gossiping," replied his wife. "We like Judith."

An aide approached. "Mr. Coates, the item you were expecting has arrived."

"Thank you."

"Kolokov's mystery package?" asked Mason.

"Yep."

"Let's go take a look. Ladies, if you'll excuse us—"

"Dick, you promised no shop talk."

"Ten minutes, no more."

IN THE ELEVATOR, MASON ASKED COATES, "ANY WORD ON DOR-SAL?"

"Last report I got, Dutch's people were—"

"People? I thought it was just Tanner."

"Dutch sent him some help. Cahil, Ian Cahil," Coates said, then noticed Mason's smile. "You know him?"

"You remember the Tromaka Islands thing last year?"

"Yeah. . . . That was them?" Coates asked, astonished. He'd read the postmortem on SAILMAKER. If not for Tanner and Cahil, the defection of Yurgani Pakov would have never come off, 300 sailors would be dead, and a billion-dollar destroyer would be lying at the bottom of the ocean. "No kidding."

"No kidding," said Mason. "You were saying . . ."

"Depending on what they find in the locker, they'll service the drops and see if they get any response. If not, they'll have to go hunting for this engineer of Ohira's," Coates said. "By the way, how was it with the boss yesterday?"

The day before, Mason, General Cathermeier, and National Security Adviser Talbot had briefed the president on the Mideast situation.

In Syria, the army exercise now involved five divisions of armor, two of mechanized and standard infantry, and two squadrons of strike aircraft. Assad's government was still mute, having ignored requests for additional information. In Israel, where outspoken members of the Knesset were accusing Syria of tyring to upset the peace process, Israeli defense forces along the Golan Heights and in the Northern

Military District were on heightened alert, and the IAF was increasing its overflights of the border.

As expected, the wild card was Saddam Hussein. Elements from four Iraqi Army divisions were moving toward the Iranian border. This move would have three effects. One, Saddam, ever paranoid of his arch-rival Syria, would likely redistribute army units toward the Syrian border; two, since some Republican Guard and Baghdad units—Saddam's personal guard—would likely be involved in such a move, the nagging question of whether the Iraqi president was fully in control of the army would finally be settled; and three, U.S. Central Command and regional U.S. forces would have to respond lest they be forced to play catch-up.

The president's decision, based largely on the advice of Talbot, the secretary of state, and the prime ministers of Britain and Israel, was weak, in Mason's opinion.

The *Independence* battle group would be positioned off the coast of Northern Israel, while the *Enterprise* group, including a Marine Expeditionary Force, or MAU, would be routed to the Persian Gulf to bolster CENTCOM forces.

From the start, both Mason and General Cathermeier advised the president to clarify their objectives before dispatching the groups. In failing to do so, they were ignoring what had kept the U.S. out of a quagmire in the Gulf War, namely the Powell Doctrine. Named after then Chairman of the Joint Chiefs Colin Powell who, like many of his contemporaries, had watched the U.S. military flail about in Vietnam, the doctrine demanded three conditions before military force was applied: the objectives must be clearly defined, the force must be overwhelming and decisive, and the achievement of the objectives must be virtually guaranteed.

The secretary of state argued that such "machinations" sounded too much like a call to war and that while Iraq certainly had a history of aggression, it was flanked by two neighbors who had shown equal if not greater aggression in the past. Saddam's response was clearly defensive in nature, he said.

The president agreed—but conditionally. "Fine. Just as long as we make it clear that any offensive action on Iraq's part will result in immediate retribution. Nor will they be allowed to maintain their new positions once the Syrian and Iranian exercises are finished. Clear?"

"Yes, Mr. President," said the sec state.

We're giving the bastard the proverbial inch, Mason thought. To the Arab mind, such a toothless response was tantamount to victory. As far as Mason was concerned, the only appropriate response was the same kind George Bush had given in August of 1990: Get back where you belong, or we'll put you there.

But that wasn't going to happen. In response to Coates's question, Mason simply said, "We're moving a pair of battle groups into the area. The president's making the announcement tomorrow."

The elevator doors parted, and they entered Coates's office. Lying on his desk was a Manila folder. Attached to it was a receipt—"Cleared, CIA Office of Security"—and the initials of Security Directorate Deputy Marie Calavos.

Coates opened it and withdrew an eight-by-ten photo and a note:

> *My dearest George,*
>   *This was taken in Khartoum. Though the source of this photo is losing favor with us, we feel it is genuine. This man (the European) is wanted by us as well, but I believe you would find more use for him. Good hunting.*

"If they know him," Mason said, "why not mention him by name?"

Coates grinned, shook his head. "Pyotor's sense of humor."

"Do you recognize him?"

"No, but I know somebody who might. He's got to be Russian, and the other two are obviously Arab. . . ." Coates picked up the phone. "Art, come on up for a minute, will you?"

"Wonder what that means: 'quickly losing favor with us'?" Mason said.

"Some of the third-party stuff we've been getting from the FIS looks like this. Like the photographer is being selective with his shots. See right there. . . . It's daylight with no shadows to speak of. At that angle, he could've gotten a clear shot of all their faces."

"But he only gets the one. The other two are just fuzzy enough to make a solid ID impossible."

"Right. The theory is, this photo and the others like it come from a stringer who's double-dealing with several agencies."

Mason smiled grimly. "Same house, different paint."

"Exactly," Coates added.

Art Stucky knocked on the door, and Coates waved him in. "Art, what do you make of this?"

Stucky studied the photo. "Holy cow!"

"Somebody you know?" asked Mason.

"You could say that. Yuri Vorsalov."

"You sure?"

"Yep. We knew he had a falling-out with the Russians, but he went to ground about two years ago. Is this recent?"

Coates nodded. "We think so." To Mason, he said, "Last we heard he was doing some consulting in the Mideast."

"Can we get him?" said Stucky.

"We don't know, Art. Thanks for coming up."

"Okay, boss." Stucky turned at the door. "You know, the FBI has the real expert on this guy. Charlie Latham was on him years ago."

"Thanks, Art."

"What's this about Latham?" Mason asked when Stucky was gone.

Coates told him the story. "He took the kid's death pretty hard."

"You think we should give him a look at this?"

"Definitely. Nobody knows Vorsalov better than Latham."

"Okay. He's downstairs; talk to him. If we can get Vorsalov, I want him. If we're right about his Mideast connections, he's a potential gold mine." Mason tapped the photo. "Also, see what we can find on these other two. They were meeting for a reason. I want to know why."

DOWNSTAIRS, BONNIE LATHAM HELD JUDITH'S HAND AS SHE talked. Judith was near tears, and Bonnie knew why; the woman had put up with Herb Smith for twenty-five years, and his abuse tonight had been just more of the same. Usually, Judith suffered such episodes gamely and made light of them, but tonight she seemed almost . . . resolute. Bonnie wondered if her friend had reached a turning point.

"What does your therapist say?" Bonnie asked.

"The same thing you do," Judith replied. "That I deserve better."

"She's right."

"I just wish I could believe that."

"Judith, when you come in a room, heads turn. For Christ's sake, even Dick Mason, battle-hardened cold warrior that he is, fawns over you."

"Oh, Bonnie, please—"

"Judith, you're bright and sexy, and you're one of the most intelligent women I know. That's why you make me so damned mad!"

"What?"

"You're ignoring the obvious. I tell you—and everybody who's a real friend tells you—how wonderful you are. Listen, I want you to start thinking about something, okay?"

"What?"

"Just start to think that maybe, just maybe, we're right and you're wrong."

Judith smiled. "Marsha said that, too."

"Good! You don't have to convince yourself overnight, you know. Just think that maybe Herb is the one who's screwed up. That doesn't sound so farfetched does it?"

"Not when you put it like that."

"Good. Now, let's go get another drink."

*   *   *

FAYYAD'S TEAM CONSISTED OF FOUR OTHER ARABS, ONLY ONE OF which he knew. Ibn, a former *As-Sa'iqa* freedom fighter, and he had fought together in the PFLP-GC during the '82 invasion of Lebanon. Ibn and the other three had rented a house in rural Greenbelt, while Fayyad had chosen a condo in the Glen Echo area.

Ibn assured him the others were reliable. They were sleepers, he said, three of hundreds of men and women stationed throughout the world—usually as full-fledged citizens—to lend help on such missions. As citizens, it was easier for them to find housing and vehicles. Two of the men even had wives and children.

From the beginning, Fayyad suspected the operation was being backed by the Syrians, but that was a question best left unasked. If these men were in fact sleepers, they were the first Fayyad had heard of in America. Al-Baz's group had committed substantial resources to the mission. *Why?* Fayyad wondered. *What could be so crucial?*

The operation was proceeding well. While he and Hasim were in the Smith home, Ibn and his team followed them to CIA Headquarters in Langley. It was a social function, Ibn reported, with hundreds of guests. After three hours, the senator and his wife left separately, she home in a taxi, and he in the limousine to an apartment in Georgetown, where they found he was keeping a mistress, an early-twenties blond named Suzie Donovan.

Fayyad was unsurprised at the senator's indiscretion. Simply keeping a mistress wasn't enough for Smith's ego; he had to flaunt it; he had to show he could do it with impunity. How humiliating that must be to Judith. But then again, Fayyad thought, that, too, could be useful.

Fayyad returned to Judith's diary. He was beginning to understand her. She fit the profile perfectly. His approach would be textbook. Like all women, she was emotionally complex, but her basic needs would be simple, whetted by twenty-five years of the senator's neglect and abuse.

For me, Fayyad thought, *she will open like a flower.*

14

DESPITE A THROBBING HEADACHE, CHARLIE LATHAM WAS IN HIS office by seven. It was only after three glasses of wine at the CIA reception the night before that he remembered he had no tolerance for the stuff. Bonnie had smiled indulgently, called him a dummy, then got him some aspirin.

Yuri Vorsalov. My God. Even if the photo was recent and even if Vorsalov was still in Khartoum, it didn't matter. Sudan and the U.S. weren't exactly on good terms, so capture was out of the question, as was extradition.

His phone rang, setting off waves of pain in his temples. "Charlie Latham."

"Charlie, Avi Haron here. You don't sound so well."

"I'm fine, Avi. How about yourself?"

"Avi is wonderful. Listen, our friend Fayyad is traveling. If he returns to one of his hideaways . . . Who knows?"

"Don't take too long. I've got a U.S. congressman breathing down my neck."

Congressman Hostetler was a prominent figure on the AIPAC (American Israel Public Affairs Committee) as well as a powerhouse on the Appropriations Committee, which influenced how and where U.S. dollars were spent, including foreign-assistance subsidies. Hostetler was strongly opposed to further support for Israel since Rabin's assassination, stating that the current leadership wasn't dedicated to the peace process.

Haron was silent for a moment. "I don't understand."

"Hostetler's daughter was on that plane, Avi."

"Oh my."

"What I'm saying is, Hostetler's got his teeth into this case. Eventually, he'll hear about our conversation. He's already growling, Avi. Just think what he'll do if he thinks you're withholding."

"I see. Will you be in your office?"

"I can be."

"I'll get back to you."

The call came fifty minutes later.

"We have a photo, Charlie. It appears your man was in Northern Africa last week with two others. We don't know why nor do we have their identities."

"Where exactly?"

"Khartoum."

"Describe the photo." Haron did so, and Latham asked, "One Arab, one European?"

"Yes, that's right. What—"

"Where is Fayyad now?"

"We are not sure. He left the same day but by a different route, via Cyprus. If he follows routine, he may return to this area, but it will be to one of our tougher neighborhoods."

Lebanon, Latham thought. "Can you confirm that?"

"Perhaps. I've passed this information along, of course, and I expect it will draw some interest," said Haron.

Latham knew the Israeli's method of obtaining confirmation would probably come from a cross-border raid by one the IDF special forces groups. Such a mission could only be authorized by the chief of staff.

"If I hear anything more, I will call," said Haron.

"Thanks, Avi." Latham hung up and redialed. "George? Charlie Latham. That Vorsalov photo you've got . . . describe it to me."

The DDO did so.

Latham asked, "One is Vorsalov, the other two unidentified Arabs?"

"That's right. What's going on, Charlie?"

"We'd better meet. I think we're working on the same puzzle."

*   *   *

AN HOUR LATER, LATHAM WAS IN MASON'S OFFICE PITCHING HIS Vorsalov/Fayyad theory to George Coates, Sylvia Albrecht, and the director of the FBI. Obviously the two photos sold to the FIS and *Shin Bet* came from the same source, he said. Whoever the stringer was, he was either gutsy or stupid. Double-dealing two of the world's most ruthless intelligence agencies was not the road to a long, happy life.

Fayyad was the prime suspect in the Delta bombing, and Vorsalov was a known freelancer. That they were meeting in Khartoum just days after the bombing was compelling; either they were connected by the bombing or by an impending operation. Latham suspected the latter, since freelance terrorists rarely bothered with postmortem briefs on their operations. Plus, it was unlikely Vorsalov would be consulted on a simple bombing; it wasn't the Russian's forte. The identity of the third man in the photo was still unknown, but Latham hoped by pooling the CIA's and FBI's resources they could not only identify him but uncover the reason behind the Khartoum meeting.

"Find one and we find the other," Latham said. "Find them both and we find out what they've got cooking."

By the end of the meeting, Mason ordered an interagency working group be set up. It would consist of Latham, his partner Paul Randal, and selected members of Art Stucky's Near East Division.

Fayyad's and Vorsalov's lives were to be dissected, examined, then plugged into a time line that would trace their movements over the past three years. There would be gaps, of course, but their careers had never been examined side by side. It was a logical place to start.

Washington, D.C.

JUDITH SMITH LEFT HER PSYCHOLOGIST'S OFFICE AND WALKED TWO blocks to Bistro Francais. It was sunny and warm, and squirrels darted from tree to tree along the sidewalk. A popular nightspot overlooking the C & O Canal, Bistro

Francais was usually uncrowded during the day. Coming here was a ritual for Judith, quiet time to mull over what she and Marsha had talked about.

There was only one other patron on the terrace, a broad-shouldered man in his midthirties. He was engrossed in the lunch menu, so she couldn't see much of his face, but he looked Italian—and handsome. He wore twill olive trousers, a collarless cream shirt, and a light blazer. As she took her seat, he looked up and smiled. Judith glanced away. He *was* handsome.

Despite herself, she watched him out of the corner of her eye. *Oh stop it, Judith,* she thought. She was acting like a little girl.

"Pardon me, *signora.*"

Judith's breath caught in her throat. She looked up. She suddenly realized how long it had been since she looked into a man's eyes. "I'm sorry?"

"For intruding. I apologize."

"Oh . . . ah . . . you're not."

"I am wondering. Can you help me with a . . . *il menu?*"

"I can try. What do you—" Judith stopped, seeing the brochure in his hand.

"You know this place? The Coco . . ."

She smiled; he pronounced it "cocoa." "The Cocoran Gallery. Yes. In fact, I'm on its fund-raising committee."

"Yes?"

"Have you been there?"

He smiled; his teeth were flawless and white. "It is where I was going this morning. I got lost. Silly, yes?"

"Washington can be confusing."

"I have discovered that. Perhaps you can tell me? Is it far from here?"

"No, not at all," Judith said. "Take the Metro to Seventeenth, then five blocks south on New York."

"*Grazie.*" He held her eyes for several moments. "I'm sure you are waiting for someone. I will leave you to your lunch." He turned to go.

Judith's mind raced. *Let him go. He just needed help, that's all.* But there was another voice, suddenly powerful:

He's interested, the voice said. They way he smiled and held her eyes . . . Besides, there was no harm in lunch, was there?

Before she realized it, her mouth was opening. "You know, you might want to wait until Thursday to go to the Cocoran."

He turned. "Oh?"

"They're debuting some new Kramer pieces."

"Kathleen Kramer?"

"Yes," she said, then hesitated. *Leap, Judith!* "Would you . . . I mean, would you like to join me for lunch?"

"I would not be imposing?"

"Oh, no. We could . . . talk about art."

He smiled and extended his hand. "I am Paolo."

Judith took his hand. He turned it, grasping just her fingers, European style. Ever so briefly he grazed his thumb over the back of her hand.

"And your name?" he asked.

"Judith. My name is Judith."

Before she realized it, three hours had passed. Paolo was an engaging listener, asking her about her taste in art and books and theater. His eyes rarely left her face as she talked, straying away only to refill their wineglasses. It was a childishly simple thing, but it felt wonderful, nonetheless. This stranger had paid her more attention in the last few hours than Herb had in two years.

She realized she knew nothing about him. She said so.

"With respect, Judith, I refuse. You are much more interesting. Please tell me more about—"

"No, I want to know about you. Where do you come from?"

He lived in Tuscany, he said, and was here doing research for his doctoral thesis in art history. His family owned a ski resort in the Italian Alps, which he had managed until two years ago. His heart was not in business. Art was his love. Upon hearing this, his father had virtually ostracized him from the family.

"And so, Judith, you see, I am passionate. I sometimes wonder if that is a good thing. Without it, I would be a rich businessman. With it . . ." He smiled, shrugged. "Well, I am here, having a wonderful lunch with you."

"It has been nice."

"So what is your opinion?"

"About?"

"Passion. Can it be not such a good thing?"

Judith folded her napkin, then refolded it. "Well, I don't know. I've never given it much thought."

"No? You appear to me as a passionate woman. The way you talk about art, your eyes shine."

"Really?"

"Truly." He leaned forward conspiratorially. "Judith, I have a belief. Would you like to hear it?"

"Please."

"I believe passion is a matter of finding what makes you feel alive and following it. We are alike, I think. For the first thirty-four years of my life, I suppressed my passion. I ignored what made me feel alive, but it waited patiently until I could no longer ignore it. It is the same for everyone. Whether we know it or not, our hearts know the right way. Some people listen; some do not."

Judith was uncomfortable. Passion had no place in her life. Everything she did and thought and felt was ruled by Herb. Passion? She'd forgotten what it felt like.

Listening to Paolo, however, her mind cleared, and she suddenly heard what he was saying. The words combined with the voices of Bonnie Latham and Dr. Burns and bolstered that little, quiet voice in the back of her mind. She suddenly felt free and vastly confused at the same time.

"I am sorry," Paolo said. "I have become too personal with you. Please accept my apology."

"No. You don't have to apologize. I just . . ." She hesitated. "It's just hard to . . ."

"You think it's too late."

"Yes, I do."

Paolo stood up and pushed in his chair. He took her hand and kissed it. The gesture seemed more respectful than romantic. "Judith, it is never too late. Of that I am sure. I have enjoyed meeting you. Perhaps I will see you at the

Cocoran show. If not, I wish you happiness."

Judith could only nod as he turned and walked away.

Japan

TANNER AND CAHIL TOOK SEPARATE ROUTES INTO KOBE. THE meeting place, Sorakuen Garden, was near Sannomiya Station in the foothills of Mount Rokko.

The morning after Tanner's near mugging in Shinkansen Station, Sato Ieyasu had called. The body of a young man matching the description of the third attacker had been found in Osaka Harbor early that morning, he reported. Tanner assumed he'd been executed to insure his silence. If the other two attackers were not already dead, they soon would be.

Later that day, they received a Federal Express package containing their equipment dump, which consisted of nothing more than a pair of ordinary-looking cellular phones and an equally ordinary 3.5" diskette for their laptop computer.

The phones were Motorolas adapted by the CIA's Science & Tech Directorate. Each was equipped with twenty-four encode chips, one designed to control pulse repetition rate, the other to manage automatic frequency selection. Together they gave the user tens of thousands of secure channels on which to transmit data to a dedicated MilStar satellite.

Any significant data would be passed via the phone's condenser/burst function, which could record a five-minute message and condense it into a three-second digital burst. The software on the 3.5" diskette, whose twin Oaken had at the Holystone office, would unstuff and decode the transmissions into clear text on their laptop computers.

Once the phones were operational, Tanner sent a report describing the contents of Ohira's locker and asking Oaken to research the words *Toshugu* and *Tsumago,* as well as the Takagi shipyard secure dock area. For whatever reasons, the facility had been important to Ohira, and Tanner wanted to know why.

The remainder of that evening and part of the next morning, he and Cahil separately toured Osaka, servicing the dead-letter drops. Each of DORSAL's three agents had been allocated three drops. Traditionally, drops are preceded by message-waiting signals, usually in the form of marks left in specific locations. Ohira had quickly realized this wouldn't work, however, given the maddening efficiency of the city cleaning crews. It took him almost three weeks to realize his marks were disappearing before agents saw them and then devise another system.

All nine drops were empty. According to Mason's orders, they could go no further without approval. But as Tanner had guessed, Mason was unsatisfied with this and approved the Sorakuen meet.

The rest of the afternoon they spent reconnoitering the shipyard. Though naturally inclined toward a water-borne penetration, Tanner didn't want to discard the land approach. If security were lax enough, it might simply be a matter of scaling a fence. It was not to be, however.

Tange Noboru knew his business. The shipyard was run with militaristic efficiency, with armed patrols (both on foot and in four-by-four trucks) guard dogs, floodlights, and electric fencing. Though these measures were not insurmountable, they made the seaward approach all the more inviting.

Tanner disembarked the Tokkaido at Sannomiya Station and started walking. The night was balmy with a slight breeze. He turned right on Tor Road, walked north two blocks, then turned left toward the garden. Down the block he glimpsed Cahil standing in front of a shop window, studying bonsai trees.

The Sorakuen was an amalgamation of English and Oriental styles with labyrinth hedgerows, tall cedars, and colored accent lights lining the walkways. He walked through the entrance and onto a small footbridge spanning a brook. He reached the center fountain courtyard and sat down on the southernmost bench.

He glanced at his watch: twenty minutes to go. Hidden

somewhere nearby, Cahil would be watching. One less thing to worry about. Now he waited.

FORTY-FIVE MINUTES LATER, HE WAS ABOUT TO LEAVE WHEN A lone woman appeared on the path. She stopped at the fountain. Heart pounding, Tanner watched. *Come on, come on.* . . . She sat down on the fountain's rim, took off her left shoe, shook out a pebble, then put it back on.

I'll be damned.

Tanner removed his coat and laid it across his left knee.

She walked over to him. *"Gomen nasai, e-ki wa do ko desu ka?"* Excuse me, where is the train station?

Now came the test. Tanner replied, *"Massugu mae yu-binkyoku. Taka sugimasu."* Straight ahead in front of the post office. It's very expensive, though. Tanner watched her carefully; she was agitated but standing her ground.

"Yoyaku shimashita," she said. I have a reservation.

"Do you understand English?"

"Yes."

"Please sit down."

"Who are you?" she whispered.

"Sit down."

"No. I know Umako is dead. Tell me—"

Tanner could see little of her face, but she looked young. "If I meant you harm, we wouldn't be talking. Sit down."

She hesitated, then sat down. "Who are you?"

"A friend of Ohira's."

"How can I believe you?"

"How did I know about this meeting?"

"Perhaps you tortured him."

"You know that's not true. I was with him when it happened. He gave me a key to a locker—"

"You're lying! He told me he used some kind of code."

"He did . . . *we* did. We need to talk. Is there a place we can—"

Abruptly, she stood up. "I don't know you. You could be the police."

"I know you're scared," Tanner said. "I don't blame you.

I can help you. It's your choice, though. If you decide to go, I won't stop you."

She paused, thinking. "How well do you know Kobe?"

"Enough to get around."

"I know a place. I will give you directions."

HER DIRECTIONS TOOK TANNER AND CAHIL TO A SMALL *SHOKUDO*, or neighborhood restaurant, in an old residential neighborhood. It was after midnight, and the streets were deserted. The cobblestones glistened under the streetlights.

Even before they knocked on the paper-paned door, it opened. A teenage boy waved them inside, then led them through the kitchen and into the alley, where they climbed a wooden stairway. At the top was a door. The boy knocked, and it opened, revealing the woman. She let them inside, whispered something to the boy, then shut the door.

"He has nothing to do with this," she said. "I don't want him involved."

"He won't be," Tanner said.

"I've made tea."

Tanner smiled; even now, Japanese politeness asserted itself.

She poured and they sat on tatami mats around a low table.

"Now tell me what happened to Umako."

Tanner did so, leaving nothing out. As he finished, the woman began sobbing.

Tanner and Cahil exchanged glances. She and Ohira had been lovers, he suddenly realized. What in God's name had Ohira been thinking? Had the affair been genuine or simply his way of turning her? If so, what did she know that was important enough to risk such an entanglement?

"What's your name?" he asked softly.

She brushed the tears away. "Sumiko Fujita."

"I'm very sorry, Sumiko. How long had you and Umako been . . ."

"Lovers. You can say the word. I am not ashamed. Almost a year."

"What kind of help were you giving him?"

"No. Not until I know who and what you are."

Tanner was torn. He looked to Bear and got a shrug: *Your call, bud.* Tanner decided to trust his instincts. He told Sumiko their names. "As far as what we are . . . How much do you know about Umako's work?"

"He was spying on Takagi."

"Do you know why?"

"Something about illegal arms dealing."

"He told you that?"

"Yes."

"Did he tell you who he was working for?"

"I'm not stupid, Mr. Tanner. As soon as I saw you, I knew."

"How do you feel about that?" asked Cahil.

"I knew Umako. He was a good man. I also know Hiromasa Takagi. He is not a good man. I am a lawyer in Takagi's Office of Counsel. I have seen enough. You still haven't told me why you are here," Sumiko said. "But, to be honest, I'm not sure I care. Will you find who killed Umako?"

"If we can," Tanner replied.

"If you want my help, you must promise to get them."

Cahil said, "That might be easier said than done."

"But not impossible."

"No, not impossible."

"Umako died in your arms, Mr. Tanner. He was working for you."

Tanner nodded.

"Then you must make this right. You must do the honorable thing."

Tanner had already thought the same thing. Ohira had put himself in harm's way doing what he thought was right. For him, integrity had transcended all else, and Briggs respected that. "We'll find the man," he said.

"Good. Now tell me what you want to know."

* * *

FOR THE NEXT TWO HOURS, THEY QUESTIONED HER. SHE HELD
nothing back. She had a near-photographic memory and a
razor-sharp mind. "Lately, Umako had been especially interested in the Tokushima Shipyard," she said at last.

"Why?" asked Tanner.

"I don't know. When we first started, he was concentrating on the electronics division: patent information, pur-
chasing contracts, end-user certificates."

This made sense. Patent information and purchase agree-
ments were logical places to start, and end-user certificates
are designed to identify the buyers of restricted technology
and weapons systems, who, in theory must be recognized
governments. In reality, however, they were easy to circum-
vent.

"When did he start asking about Takagi Maritime?"
asked Cahil.

"Two months ago. He wanted details on shipbuilding,
insurance subsidiaries, underwriting . . . and whether Takagi handled contract salvage jobs."

Suddenly Tanner remembered Ohira's chart and the
hunch he needed to pursue. "Do they?" he asked.

"Salvage work? Not that I know of. They do build on
contract, but I'm not sure what exactly. I had just started
getting some of the things Umako wanted when he . . .
when they killed him."

"Where is that information now?" asked Tanner.

Sumiko stood up, walked to the wall, removed a section
of baseboard, and withdrew an accordion folder. She
handed it to Tanner, "Recently Umako felt sure he was
under suspicion, so he asked me to hide this."

"Could anyone have connected the two of you?"

"No. He was very cautious. We both were. We met only
here." She smiled. "Umako would come at night and we
would have dinner and talk. This was our place; it's in my
grandparents' name. I keep another apartment downtown."

"Good. We need to talk about how this is going to
work," Tanner said. "We'll use you as little as possible. It's
safer if you—"

"I don't care about safety. I want you to get men who killed Umako."

"I know you do, but it's going to get complicated. The less you're involved, the better. If we need to reach you, what's the best way?"

"Call here and leave a message; I will get it. We should agree on a phrase, shouldn't we, so I'll know it is really you?"

They discussed it for a few minutes and agreed on a recognition code.

"How can I reach you?"

Briggs had already worked this out. He laid a small map of the Kobe area on the table. Each numbered red dot represented a telephone booth, he explained. To request a contact, Sumiko would first choose a booth then add the number four. She would then call the hotel and leave a message for Tanner such as, "Unable to make our 12:30 lunch." By subtracting and multiplying by the variable, Tanner would know to call booth number eight in two hours.

Tanner had her repeat the system to him, which she did flawlessly.

"One last question," Tanner said. "Do the words Toshugu and Tsumago mean anything to you?"

Sumiko frowned. "Strange you ask. Umako asked about them, too. He thought they were ships, but I didn't find anything," she said. "If they are, they don't exist on paper."

15

DESPITE THE HURRIED TIME LINE WITH WHICH HE'D BEEN SADDLED, Fayyad was pleased. The chance encounter had gone well. Regardless of age and status, women react similarly to attraction stimulus, and it was no different with Judith Smith, though her stimulus was more emotional than physical. Her diary had told him that much, and their meeting had confirmed it.

Accordingly, he had been attentive and gracious and reserved—and above all, nonsexual. Her defenses would not be breached simply because she needed a roll in the hay. With her, it would be the emotional that sparked the physical.

By now she would be comparing their brief lunch to the two decades of marriage to the senator. When was the last time Smith asked her about her dreams? Or why she preferred Monet to Degas, or why Winslow's work made her melancholy? Thinking of their time together, she would want more.

He smiled, anticipating the seduction. She was a beautiful woman. Mature women were generally better in bed, he found, less concerned with putting on a show and quite open to new experiences.

He glanced at his watch. Almost time.

He showered, shaved, and dressed with care, choosing an Italian-cut double-breasted olive suit.

He could feel himself falling into character. You could not play a woman's ideal lover without at least partially losing yourself in the role. But that had its price, didn't it? To convince a woman he had fallen in love with her, Fayyad oftentimes did just that—if only for a brief time. In recent years, however, he'd been finding it increasingly difficult to slough off the masks he chose.

The affair in Kingston had been the hardest yet. Listening to her stories about her fears and longings, Fayyad had ached for her. She was so trusting, so innocent. All she had wanted was someone to love her, and now she was—

Stop! He gripped the bathroom counter and glared at his reflection. *Enough!*

Kingston had been a mistake. He'd let down his guard. This would be a simple seduction, an exercise in mechanics. He would do what was necessary, then leave.

AT THE COCORAN, JUDITH GLANCED AT HER WATCH FOR THE TENTH time in as many minutes and took a sip of wine. Was he coming?

The gallery was filled nearly to capacity. Spaced along the gallery walls were the eight new Kramers, each a square of vivid red, blue, and yellow on the stark white walls. Just as Kramer's pieces were always uniform in color and form, they were always uniformly hated or loved as well, and this exhibit was no different, causing brisk debate among critics. Judith barely heard any of it.

Where *was* he? How could she even be considering this?

She'd taken special care dressing that evening, doing and redoing her makeup, then dabbing perfume behind her ears, between her breasts, and then, impulsively, on her belly. She kept telling herself she only wanted another chance to talk with him about art. After all, he was an art student. What could be more natural?

It was a lie, and she knew it. He had sparked something in her. She remembered the way his eyes stared into hers and how easily he laughed and smiled. But it was the way he *listened* to her that affected her most. It had been as though she were the only person alive. Lying in bed before Herb came home, she was surprised to feel her nipples hardening. She hadn't felt this way in . . . God, she couldn't remember when.

By the time Herb arrived, she was burning with desire. On an impulse, she drew him to bed and let him take her. As always, Herb's erection needed coaxing, and once inside her, his thrusts were robotic and painfully hard. He kneaded her breasts, grunting until he climaxed a minute later. Without a word, he rolled off her and went to sleep. She went to the shower, lathered herself clean, then stood under the spray, crying.

She lay awake all night. Near dawn, she made her decision. She would go to the show and hope he came.

And now he isn't. Perhaps it was best this way. The Cocoran was in the heart of the capital. Any rendezvous would certainly draw attention. What was she thinking? This wasn't like her. . . . She was acting—

Then, there he was, standing in the doorway.

He saw her, smiled, and walked over. Her heart pounded so hard the wine in her glass rippled.

"Judith, I'm so glad you are here," he said.

Be casual, Judith. "I was hoping you'd come." They were just friends, an innocent encounter in a public place, nothing more. "I'm glad you did."

Paolo accepted a glass from a waiter. "Oh?"

"Yes. I enjoyed our lunch the other day. You gave me a lot to think about."

"I'm glad. Are you with anyone tonight?"

"No, my . . . No, I came alone."

"Then would you be my guide?"

"I'd love to."

As had their lunch, the evening sped by. Paolo was a complete gentlemen, discreet and reserved. When he smiled at her, though, his eyes crinkled with humor. *He's enjoying this,* she thought. It was like a secret between them, an interlude yet not an interlude.

By ten o'clock, most of the patrons were gone, and when the lights dimmed at closing time, they found themselves alone.

She turned to Paolo. "Well, thank you . . ."

He was smiling at her.

"What?" she asked.

He tilted his head. "You are nervous."

"No . . . no, not at all."

"Do you have someplace to be?"

"No."

"Will you walk with me? I have not yet been to the Tidal Basin. I'd like to see the apple blossoms."

She laughed. "Cherry blossoms. But they aren't in bloom."

"Too bad. Walk with me anyway?"

Judith looked into his eyes and saw something different this time. The invitation was unmistakable. *Leap, Judith!* "I'd love to," she heard herself say.

AFTER WALKING THE PATH AROUND THE BASIN, THEY STOOD ON Kutz Bridge, looking at the reflecting pool. In the distance they could see the White House illuminated by spotlights. He took off his coat and draped it over her shoulders.

"Paolo, you know I'm married," Judith whispered.

"I know."

"Do you . . . doesn't that—"

"No, Judith. At first, yes, but after our lunch I couldn't stop thinking about you. I even planned to stay away tonight, but I couldn't. You are not happy with him, are you?"

"No."

"How long have you been married?"

"Twenty-five years."

"Were you ever happy?"

"In the beginning," Judith replied. "For the first few years."

Paolo nodded, but without judgment. She liked that. Most men would have asked why she stayed. "Judith, tell me: Italian men, we have a . . . reputation, no?"

Judith laughed. "Oh my, yes."

"You may not believe this, but I have been with only three women in my life."

"Just three?" she asked, astonished.

"*Si.* I tell you this so you will not think I . . . So you

won't think I seduce women for sport. Even as a younger man, I was never this way. My friends found it quite humorous."

"I can imagine."

"So, whatever happens between us, even if we never see one another again, you must know how . . . You are . . ." He threw up his hands. *"Mi dispiace,* I am not making sense!"

"No, go on, please."

"For me, beauty is more. You are bright like the sun. In the way you talk, the way your eyes shine. I want to listen to you, to watch you. . . . Ahhh . . . I sound silly!"

My God, no you don't. "No, Paolo, it's not silly at all."

"Even if we cannot be lovers, I want to be with you. How, I do not know, but that is what I want. Is that possible, Judith? Am I asking too much?"

All she could do was shake her head. She wanted him so badly her legs were trembling. This man standing before her was everything Herb was not. "Oh, Paolo, no, you're not asking too much. I want you, too. I don't care how or for how long! Please, let's go somewhere. Right now."

He wrapped her in his arms, and she melted into him. As their lips met and his tongue touched hers, she hesitated. She'd never been kissed this way. It felt wonderful and new. She parted her lips and took his tongue into her mouth.

"When, Judith?" he whispered.

"Now."

He shook his head. "I want you, Judith, please know that. But I want it to be perfect, and I want you to be sure."

"I am, Paolo. I'm sure—"

He put a finger to his lips. "You must decide this with a clear heart, Judith. When you come to me, I want it to be completely and without reservation." He kissed her again. "Do you understand?"

"I—"

Paolo placed his palm over her heart. *"This* is from where your decision must come. The heart . . . *Il cuore.* Not from lust. I want all of you, not just your body. Now do you understand?"

Judith nodded dumbly. *"I want all of you. . . ."* Moments ago she would have given her body wantonly, right here on the bridge. But he wanted *her!*

She knew her decision was made.

Japan

SITTING IN A CLUSTER OF TREES NEAR THE SHORELINE, TANNER had a perfect view of the shipyard, which sat nestled in a cove a mile away.

Earlier, just after sunset, he'd left the hotel and taken a shuttle north to Wakayama to catch the ferry across the Inland Sea to Tokushima. From there it was a half-hour taxi ride to Anan, where he continued on foot through the forest.

He'd been watching the shipyard steadily for two hours.

The security on the seaward side was as stringent as that of the land approaches. A twelve-foot electric fence encircled the cove and followed it inland to the yard's outlying buildings. Spaced at intervals along the fence stood spotlight-equipped guard towers.

The real surprise came when he focused on the patrol boats and the sea gate through which they came and went. The fence appeared to be made of heavy steel links. Tanner was betting it was fixed to the seabed as well. The gate itself, which served as a bridge between the two pontoon guard shacks, sat at the mouth of the cove.

What would warrant this kind of security? Tanner wondered. The answer, he hoped, lay with a pair of ships inside Secure Dock 12.

Behind him, he heard the double hoot of an owl. "Come on in, Bear," Tanner whispered.

Cahil walked forward and stooped beside Tanner.

"Barn owl?" Briggs asked.

"Great horned. I brought supper: pastrami on rye."

"Thanks." Tanner unwrapped the sandwich and took a bite. "Anything from Leland?" Along with their report on the Sorakuen Garden meet, they'd requested Mason give them the name of Ohira's shipyard contact.

"Not yet."

So far, Oaken's research had confirmed Sumiko's conclusion about Ohira's mystery ships: If in fact *Toshogu* and *Tsumago* existed, neither were documented, either by Takagi Maritime, Lloyds of London Shipping Index, or the UN International Maritime Bureau.

"So how's it look?" asked Cahil. "Easier than the land approach?"

"No, but it's still our best bet." He handed Cahil the binoculars. "Watch the patrol boats."

Within a few minutes, a pair of boats exited the gate, then fanned out along the fence, one to either side of the guard shacks. Moving at two knots, they trolled along, shining their spotlights into the water.

Tanner said, "See the flashing red lights on the fence pontoons?"

"Yeah. . . . Antiswimmer mines?"

"That's my guess."

"They're pretty damned serious about something. Okay, I see Dock 12. How many are there?"

"Four." Each were secured by giant hangar doors, and judging from their size, Tanner guessed each could house a couple of 500-foot-plus ships.

"How regular are the boat patrols?" Cahil asked.

"Every forty minutes, like clockwork."

Cahil grinned. "Gotta love routine."

ONE HOUR AND TWO ROLLS OF FILM LATER, THEY WERE PREPARING to leave when the doors of Dock 12 groaned to life and began rolling upward. Even a mile across the water, the whine of the motors was audible. Inside the cavernous interior Tanner could see yellow flashing lights and figures scurrying about on a pier. Soon a tugboat appeared at the entrance and began churning forward. Moments later a bow appeared out of the darkness, followed by the rest of the ship.

She measured 400 feet and displaced a solid 12,000 tons, Tanner estimated. On the afterdeck stood four massive derricks and a raised central combing half the size of a football field.

"It's a moon-pool," Cahil muttered. "She's a salvage ship. You get the feeling Ohira was on to something?"

"Starting to. If she's one of his, we'd best get a look at her sister before she sails."

BACK AT THE HOTEL, THEY SAT ON THE BALCONY AS TANNER FIN-ished laying out his theory for Cahil. "How sure are you about this?" Bear said.

"Not very, but it doesn't feel like a coincidence."

The idea had gelled as Briggs recalled Mitsu's story about the ship appearing in the waters off his village. It forced him to look at Ohira's chart with new eyes. Each of the six numbered asterisks on the chart was a navigational fix, he theorized. The numerator was a bearing, the denominator a distance. Using a compass and dividers, he'd calculated the fixes. With remarkable precision, all six points triangulated on a single spot on the chart: precisely where Ohira's red-dotted line ended, and almost exactly where Mitsu claimed the ship had anchored each night.

"So we've got Ohira interested in this spot, plus a non-existent Takagi salvage ship nosing around," Cahil said. "What the hell could be out there?"

"Don't know. Maybe they lost something; maybe they found something. Whatever it is, it makes me wonder why Noboru followed me to the village. Was it me, or the location?"

"*That* is a good question," Cahil said with a grin. "So when do we go?"

16

FAYYAD CHECKED THE CHICKEN ALFREDO TO MAKE SURE IT WAS simmering properly, then went into the living room and turned on the stereo. He selected a CD—Vivaldi's *Four Seasons*—and hit Play. Strains of music filled the apartment. He scanned the dining table to make sure everything was ready for her arrival.

She had called the day before. "Are you at home?" he asked.

"No, no, darling, I'm at a pay phone."

Good girl. "I'm glad you called."

"How could I not? You're all I can think about. When can I see you?"

"Tomorrow night. I will cook for you."

"That sounds wonderful."

Fayyad gave her directions and hung up. It rang again immediately.

"Is Heloise home?" said the voice.

"Who?"

"I'm sorry, I think I have the wrong number. I was dialing five four two eight."

"No, sorry, wrong number."

Fayyad frowned. Why were they contacting him now? It wasn't scheduled for another four days. From a compartment in the jamb of his bedroom door, Fayyad retrieved a sheet of paper and matched 5428 to a safe-call location.

He drove to the phone booth, dialed, and waited as the overseas operator connected him. The number's prefix told himit was Larnaca, Cyprus. A minute later, Mustafa al-Baz's voice came on the line.

"Give me a report," al-Baz said.

Fayyad said, "The next contact wasn't due until—"

"I am aware of the schedule. Give me a report."

Fayyad did so, then mentioned his dinner with Judith the next evening.

"Judith, now, is it? Enjoying our work, I see."

Fayyad clenched the phone. "Why have you called me?"

"Things are not moving quickly enough."

"Not quickly enough? What—"

"You are taking too long. Bed the whore and get on with it."

Fayyad felt his face flush. *Motherless bastard! She is not a . . .* What in Allah's name was he doing? *Focus . . . think! Al-Baz was clearly agitated. Why? What was their hurry?*

Fayyad had run dozens of honey traps, and this one was proceeding with amazing speed. Soon he would move to the next phase. The senator was likely to react badly, he knew, but how badly? And how fast could he get results? If not fast enough, Fayyad asked himself, what were the consequences for al-Baz—and for him? There were three options, he decided. Either they would abandon the operation, allow him to continue at his own discretion, or demand drastic measures.

"I will move forward in a few days," Fayyad said. "I don't dare go any faster."

"Just do it, Ibrahim," al-Baz ordered. "Quickly."

Fayyad forced the call from his mind, checked to ensure the bedroom was prepared, then returned to the kitchen and opened the wine.

JUDITH'S HANDS SHOOK ON THE STEERING WHEEL AS SHE PULLED beside the condo, an expensive ranch-style fronted by hibiscus hedges and plumeria-draped eaves.

Arranging the evening had been easy. Herb was working late on some committee finding, which really meant he was at his little bimbo's apartment. Though Judith had long ago ceased being jealous, the humiliation still stung. Acquaintances no longer spoke her name without preceding it with "poor" or "too bad about."

Well, not anymore, she thought.

She tingled with anticipation. It couldn't be wrong, she told herself, not the way it felt. She took a deep breath— *Leap, Judith!*—then checked her makeup in the rearview mirror, took one last look at her dress—a black strapless Givenchy—got out, and walked up the path.

She rang the bell. The door opened. Paolo stood there, staring at her, not smiling. *Oh no,* she thought, *what—*

"Judith . . . My lord, Judith, you look stunning." He extended his hand, drew her into the foyer, and shut the door.

"Is that Vivaldi?" she asked.

"Yes."

"I love Vivaldi."

"I thought you might."

She melted into his arms and pressed her face against his chest and inhaled his musk. "Oh, I'm glad I came."

OVER DINNER THEY TALKED VERY LITTLE, SIMPLY WATCHING ONE another in the flickering candlelight. Afterward, they sat together on the couch, sipping wine and listening to Mendelssohn's *A Midsummer Night's Dream.* It was a fitting choice, Judith thought. This felt like a dream. She felt her inhibitions slipping away. She wondered what they would feel like together.

After a time, he put on some Mancini and asked her to dance. As they moved, everywhere their bodies touched, she tingled. God, the way he held her . . . moved his hips against hers, his hand pressed into the small of her back, eyes fixed on hers, his lips at her throat . . .

She was breathing faster now, pressing against him, feeling his hardness pressing back. "Paolo, I . . . it's been so long for me, I don't . . ."

"Shhh, Judith. Don't say a word."

*　　*　　*

ONCE IN THE BEDROOM, HE TOOK GENTLE COMMAND OF HER.
They stood kissing for a time, and then, turning her, he lifted her hair and kissed the nape of her neck, one hand resting on her stomach, the other unzipping the dress and letting it slide away. She wore a black lace bra and matching panties, both newly purchased. He turned her again. Judith watched his eyes wander up and down her body and was suddenly embarrassed. He gently lifted her chin and grazed his fingertips along her jawline, down to her shoulders. His touch left gooseflesh.

Judith leaned her head back and closed her eyes.

His hands glided over the slope of her breasts and down her flanks to her hips.

Judith moaned. "Oh, God . . ." Never had a man done this before . . . taken such care and time.

He undid the front clasp of her bra, and her breasts fell free, heavy and flushed. He did not touch them, instead kneeling at her feet and carefully removing her panties, kissing her belly as he did so. He stood again and gently cupped her breasts—adoringly, she thought—his thumbs grazing and circling, grazing and circling. Very slowly, he leaned down and touched his tongue to her left nipple.

"Ohhh!"

A shiver of electricity shot through her. She cradled his head as he took the other nipple in his mouth and bit ever so gently. Judith's knees buckled beneath her. He caught her and swept her into the air.

ONCE SHE WAS LAID OUT ON THE BED, HE STOOD BESIDE IT AND undressed. Judith watched him, transfixed. When he was fully naked, she couldn't help but stare. "Oh, my. Is that for me?"

He smiled. "*Si*, Judith. All for you."

HE LAY DOWN WITH HER. SHE COULD FEEL HIS HARDNESS PRESSING against her belly. She parted her legs, ready for him, wanting him, and was surprised at what he did next. He kissed her breasts, then trailed his tongue down to her belly, her thighs. And then inward. *Oh, my God, he's not going to . . . down there?* She had read about this in Harold Robbins novels, but certainly it wasn't something real people did.

She was about to tell him to stop, when he placed his hands under her buttocks, lifted her hips off the bed, and put his mouth on her.

HE WAS EXPERT AND GENTLE, BRINGING HER TO THREE SHUDDERING climaxes in fifteen minutes, until she lay breathless and dizzy. "Please, darling, please," she murmured. "I want you inside me."

Gently lowering his weight on her, he cradled her head and in one fluid motion slid himself into her. She groaned and lifted her knees. He lay still on her, stroking her face. She panicked. Why wasn't he moving? By now Herb would have been rutting away. And then she realized: He was waiting for her, waiting until she was ready.

Oh sweet God, this was how it was supposed to be. . . .

They made love three more times that evening, and she found herself doing and saying and feeling things she never imagined possible. He was a perfect lover, strong, gentle, and patient.

After the last time, they lay quietly together. She felt a thousand things at once: glowing, satiated, sexy . . . but most of all, *woman.* She basked in it. She felt the tears welling in her eyes.

FAYYAD COULD FEEL HER TEARS TRICKLING ONTO HIS CHEST. THIS often happened, tears following lovemaking, and for him it had always meant one thing: She was his.

This time, however, he felt an unsettling mix of fear and contentment. Judith felt wonderful in his arms. This one was different from the others.

He kissed her forehead. "Judith? Have I hurt you?"

"Oh, no, darling, God no. I've never been happier."

"I'm glad," he said. *Oh, Allah, what have I done?*

Lebanon

"WHAT ARE YOU SAYING?" AZHAR ASKED. "YOU DON'T BELIEVE he can do the job?"

Al-Baz considered his answer. He knew Fayyad's ways. In the pursuit of his goal he became the perfect lover, and in so doing fell in love himself. Perhaps this was the case with the Smith woman. No, he decided, there had been genuine rage in the man's voice.

"Perhaps," answered al-Baz. "At best, he is growing soft."

"Then we must increase the pressure. No, better still, put someone else in command."

"Who, though? Who could . . ." The answer suddenly occurred to al-Baz; one glance at Azhar told him they were thinking alike. "Shall I make the arrangements?"

Azhar nodded. "Quickly."

17

Japan

TWO HOURS AFTER MIDNIGHT, TANNER AND CAHIL LAY HIDDEN IN the undergrowth watching the shipyard through binoculars. Earlier, dark clouds had rolled over the Inland Sea, and now a cold rain was falling. Fog horns drifted across the water.

That morning, they had rented the dive gear and old skiff from a Mugi shop owner. Just after sunset, they left the shop, drove up the coast to the Anan peninsula, where they parked on a deserted fire road. From there they carried the skiff to the opposite shore and waited for nightfall.

Ideally, their minimum equipment loadout for this kind of penetration would have included an SDV (swimmer delivery vehicle), night-vision equipment, H&K MP-5 assault rifles, and a pair of LAR V bubbleless rebreather tanks. But they had neither the time nor the resources for such a wish list. Tanner's greatest concern was their bubble trail, but the rain would take care of that, cloaking their approach and rendering the patrol boat's searchlights almost useless.

The weather also brought a downside. The water temperature was sixty-five degrees, not numbingly cold, but still thirty-three degrees below their core body temperatures. Barring any glitches, they would be in the water less than three hours, but even in full wet suits, the cold would immediately begin to sap their bodies of heat and energy.

To reduce this risk, they planned to take the skiff part of the way, cutting the distance to the sea fence by two miles—or about an hour's swim in the crosscurrent. Once at the gate, they could remain submerged for an hour before having to turn back.

Tanner watched the patrol boats finish their tour of the

fence and return back through the gate. "Okay, they're through."

Cahil nodded and set the bezel on his watch. "Shall we?"

"Let's get wet."

AN HOUR AND TEN MINUTES LATER, TANNER CHECKED HIS WATCH and wrist compass, then gave the buddy line two jerks. Cahil swam out of the darkness to join him. Twenty-five feet above, the water's surface bubbled with rain.

They put their masks together for a face check. In the green glow of their watches, Bear was grinning broadly; Briggs felt the same. This is what they did best. Despite the absolute blackness, the water felt safe. It was a world without edges, where up/down/left/right could become meaningless unless you kept a grip on your mind. Tanner had seen otherwise hard, unflappable veterans panic in such conditions. Without its everyday reference points, the human mind begins to feed on itself, magnifying fears and sowing doubts. Until they were moving again, he and Bear would stay in constant physical contact.

You okay? Tanner mouthed.

Cahil nodded and gave a thumbs-up. *You?*

Tanner nodded back. He gestured ahead, made a clam-shell with his hands, then pointed to himself: *Checking the sea fence.* He returned in thirty seconds and gave a thumbs-up. They were in position.

Now they waited.

IT WASN'T LONG BEFORE THEY HEARD THE MUFFLED WHINE OF PRO-pellers approaching the sea gate. The sound faded and was replaced by the chugging of engines. Garbled voices called to one another, followed by a metallic *clank* as the latches were released. A moment later, Tanner felt a surge as the gate swung outward.

Knowing it would remain open only long enough to let the boats through, he and Cahil had decided against trying to dash through. That left piggybacking. A trip to a local glazier had provided the necessary tools.

Once the boats exited the gate and peeled away to their respective fence lines, spotlights came to life, knifing through the water and illuminating the boat's hulls. With Cahil following, Tanner finned toward the nearest boat.

Each armed with a pair of glazier's tongs—dual suction cups on U-shaped handles—they swam hard until they were alongside the hull. Tanner mounted his tongs along the keel line, while at his feet, Cahil did the same, then scooted forward, locking Tanner's legs against the hull. The illuminated fence skimmed by Tanner's head.

After another five minutes, the boat turned back and headed for the gate. Tanner heard the latches clank open, followed by the groan of steel. The boat surged forward, then stopped. Flashlight beams tracked along the waterline, then clicked off, and the boat started forward again.

THREE HUNDRED YARDS INTO THE COVE, TANNER FELT A SQUEEZE on his calf. Ian was disengaging. Tanner waited a few seconds, then dropped away. They joined up, and Tanner checked the compass: Dock 12 was about a quarter mile away, bearing 282. They started swimming.

THE HANGAR DOOR LOOMED BEFORE THEM. TANNER TOUCHED IT: heavy-gauge steel. He jerked his thumb downward. They finned to the seabed, clicked on their penlights, and groped until they found the door's lower lip. Here Tanner found the break he'd been betting on: The shipyard's designers had failed to seat the hangar doors on a concrete foundation.

Using garden trowels, they started digging.

When the hole was large enough, Tanner wriggled under the door, then turned left and swam until his fingers touched concrete. He finned upward and broke the surface under the pier. Cahil came up a moment later.

The dock was cavernous, measuring some 700 feet deep,

200 feet wide, and 300 feet to the vaulted ceiling. The waterway was bordered by a pair of concrete piers on which sat forklifts, cranes, and equipment sheds. Along the walls, stretching into the distance like runway markers, were dim yellow spotlights.

Looming over them was a ship's bow. A pontoon scaffolding floated beside the half-painted hull, and tarps and electrical lines drooped over the edge of the forecastle.

Cahil whispered, "Your choice, bud,"

"You take the ship, I'll search the rest of the dock," Tanner said. "We'll meet on the bridge in twenty minutes."

AT THE REAR OF THE DOCK, TANNER FOUND A RAISED BOOTH CONtaining radio equipment and controls for the ventilation, lighting, and the main doors. In the corner was a locked filing cabinet, which he picked open. Inside he found a spiral notebook. Its contents were written in Kanji. It was obviously a log, but aside from a few headings such as Dock Number, Date, Time, and Destination, it was beyond his translation skills. Two words caught his eye, however: *Toshogu* and *Tsumago*. Which had they seen leave the other night? He flipped pages until he came to the correct entry: Departure Time, 0100—*Toshogu*.

He photographed entries for the past six months, returned the log to the cabinet, and left.

THE SHIP TANNER NOW KNEW TO BE CALLED *TSUMAGO* MEASURED 350 feet from bow to stern and 60 feet from beam to beam. As ships went, she was a fireplug. Her two-story superstructure housed a glass-enclosed bridge and overhanging wings. Between the pilothouse and smokestacks stood a mainmast, much of its latticework covered in tarpaulins.

He took the easiest, if least covert way aboard by trotting up the midship gangplank. He found Bear on the bridge, studying the wave guide, the vertical conduit containing the intestines of the ship's radar system.

"Anybody aboard?"

"No," Cahil said. "I tell you this, bud, this ain't your ordinary cargo ship."

"How so?"

"This, for one thing. It belongs on a battleship, not a banana hauler. Hell, there's enough conduit here to handle power for both air and surface search."

"Civilian?"

"Military. OPS-eighteen or twenty-eight at least. Here, look at this."

Cahil pulled aside a curtain on the aft bulkhead, revealing a small alcove containing two radar scopes and what looked like an ESM (electronic surveillance measures) console.

"Serious hardware," Tanner said. "How about the main-mast?"

"Climbed it. There's nothing under the tarp. Here's something else."

Cahil walked to the hatch and pointed to exposed bulk-head lining. "Kevlar, an inch thick."

Kevlar was a DuPont product famous for its bullet-resistent characteristics. A quarter inch of it could stop a .44 Magnum round. Despite outward appearances, *Tsumago* was not a run-of-the-mill cargo ship. She was a floating tank.

"Look at this hatch," Tanner said. "The hinges are mounted on the inside; impossible to pop from the outside. Christ, she's siege proof."

"My thoughts exactly."

"Have you checked the rest of the ship?"

"And let you miss out on the fun? No way."

Tanner smiled. "You take engineering, I'll cover the rest."

They met back in the pilothouse armed with sketches and two rolls of film between them. Cahil opened his mouth to speak, but Tanner shook his head and pointed out the win-dow. On the pier, a pair of security guards stopped at the gangplank and started up, their flashlights playing over the superstructure.

"Time to go," Tanner whispered.

They made their way down to the forecastle and shimmied down the mooring line to the pier, where they slipped back into the water. Once back in their dive gear, they ducked under, squeezed back under the hangar door, and finned to the surface.

The shipyard was quiet. In the distance, the spotlights on the guard shack reflected off the water. The rain and wind had picked up.

"How long before our ride?" Cahil asked.

Tanner checked his watch. "Twenty-five minutes." They were both tired and cold, but if they kept moving, they would be okay. He glanced at Cahil, got a broad *I'm with you* grin in return, and reminded himself how lucky he was to have him along. There was no one better in a storm.

"Last one to the gate buys Irish coffee?" Tanner asked.

"Deal."

THEY REACHED THE HOTEL JUST BEFORE SUNRISE. TANNER STOPPED at the main desk to check messages. There were none. "But a woman has been waiting for you, sir."

"Where?" he asked.

"On the pool patio. She insisted on waiting."

He found Sumiko asleep in a patio chair. His first instinct was to turn around and sever all contact with her. Takagi had them under surveillance, and while they had so far managed to shake the watchers, Sumiko was a different matter. Takagi had already killed one person and possibly dozens more. What was another?

Sumiko opened her eyes. "Briggs?"

"What is it, Sumiko? Is everything all right?"

"The engineer you were asking about . . . He's disappeared."

"When was he last seen?"

"Four nights ago. No one has seen him since, either at work or home."

Four nights ago, Tanner thought. *The same night* Toshogu *sailed.*

18

SENATOR HERB SMITH WAS NURSING A RAGING HANGOVER WHEN his secretary poked her head in the door. "Morning!"

"Who the hell says?"

Heidi frowned, puzzled. She wasn't the sharpest knife in the drawer, Smith knew, and she couldn't type to save her life, but she had a great pair of tits, so it was a fair trade.

"Did Senator Dean reach you?" Heidi asked. "He wants—"

"I know," Smith said.

"He really needs the report on—"

"I heard you, Heidi. Get me a cup of coffee."

"Sure," Heidi chirped.

His hangover was only partially responsible for his foul mood. He'd spent the previous evening at Suzie's apartment, listening to her commiserate with the characters of *Melrose Place*. As the end credits rolled, he slid his hand up her thigh. "Uh-uh, honey," she said. "My friend is visiting."

"Your friend? What the hell does that mean?"

"You know . . . that time of the month. I feel awful."

"Well, Jesus, you could have told me that before I came over!"

"Well, I thought we could, you know, cuddle."

"Cuddle? You've got to be kidding."

Suzie pouted. "Herb, sometimes I think you only want me because I let you fuck me."

"*Let me?*" he roared. "Is that what you said? *Let me!*"

"I'm sorry," she stammered. "I—"

"Would that be anything like me *letting* you live here rent free?"

"I'm sorry, I didn't mean it. I just don't feel good, Herb. Can't we just sit and talk? You know, have some quality time?"

"Been watching *Oprah* again, I see. Okay, forget it." He lay back on the couch. "Just give me a blow job, then."

"Herb! I told you I don't feel good!"

"Oh, for God's sake!" He picked up his coat and stormed out.

At home, Judith was sitting in bed reading. He climbed in beside her and pressed himself against her hip. To his amazement, she said, "Not tonight, Herb," rolled over, and turned out the light. Just like that—as though *she* were in charge.

In fact, thinking back, she'd been acting strangely for the past week. *Bubbly*—that was the word for it. She was downright *bubbly*. She hummed in the shower, flitted about the bedroom, fussed with her makeup as she prepared for one of her meetings or openings or whatever the hell she did. What was going on?

Then it hit him: She'd started acting this way after he'd come home the other night and she was all hot and bothered. Had he been that good? Sure, he decided, why not? Then what about last night? Smith thought, rubbing his temples. Maybe she had been tired. Tonight maybe he'd try again, give her another chance.

Heidi's voice came over the intercom. "Senator, it's a Dr. Burns's office on line one."

"Who?"

"Dr. Burns. Regarding your wife."

"What. . . . okay, send it through." His phone rang. "Senator Smith, here. Listen Doctor, I've got a busy schedule, so—"

"You'll want to make time for me, Senator." The voice was male.

"Who the hell is this?"

"You can call me Antonio. I apologize for the ruse, but I needed to get your attention."

"Well, you've lost my attention. Good-bye—"

"Hang up and your life is over, Senator."

"What the hell does that mean?"

"I have information regarding your wife. It is a delicate matter."

"Listen, you dirtbag, if you're playing some kind of game, I'll wreck you! I'm the last guy in the world you want to mess with! Do you know who I am?"

"I know precisely who you are, Senator. Tonight at ten o'clock. Meet on Bison Bridge in Rock Creek Park. You will come alone; you will not alert the police."

"Not gonna happen, my friend. I'm busy."

"With Miss Donovan, I presume."

Smith's breath caught in his throat. "Hey, asshole, if this is about money—"

"This is not about money, Senator."

"What, then?"

"Tonight, ten o'clock, Bison Bridge."

Smith hesitated. Whoever this guy was, he'd done his homework, and he sounded very serious. "Listen . . . Antonio, right? You've got my attention, but without knowing more, I can't—"

"You can, and you will," the man said firmly. "And Senator?"

"What?"

"If you mention this to anyone, your world will come crashing down around you. Do you understand me?"

Suddenly Smith did understand: He was in trouble. "Yeah, I understand."

The phone went dead.

Langley

DICK MASON FINISHED READING TANNER'S REPORT AND LOOKED across the desk at Dutcher and Oaken. "Dutch, where exactly did your boys get the okay to penetrate Takagi's shipyard?"

"I gave it to them."

It was true—for the most part. He had approved the mission, albeit after the fact, but Mason didn't need to know that. Dutcher trusted Tanner's instincts; that was enough for him. Plus, they'd pulled it off. Nothing succeeds like success.

So now they had new information but also more questions. For whatever reason, Ohira had been interested in Takagi's shipyard and a pair of ships named *Toshogu* and *Tsumago*. Tanner called them mystery ships. It was an apt term. *Toshogu*, the salvage ship, had skulked out of port in the dead of night, and *Tsumago* was locked away in a secure dock undergoing a refit worthy of a destroyer.

"Dick, time was short," Dutcher continued. "One of the ships had already sailed, and they wanted to catch the other one before she did the same."

Mason considered this. "Fair enough. What do we know about them?"

"Not much," Oaken replied. "We're looking for a paper trail on them, but so far nothing. Same with the product from the Fujita woman. Lots of info, just nothing on these ships."

"When can we expect some conclusions?"

"A week."

"Good. Dutch, I have to tell you, I'm thinking about pulling the plug."

"Why?"

"The last few months—about the time Tanner says Ohira got interested in Takagi Maritime—a lot of his product had a doctored feel about it. Everything was a little too pat. It didn't have the jigsaw look to it, like pure field stuff."

"You think he was being fed?"

"Hard to say. Either way, he was on a tangent, and aside from an interesting mystery, we've got nothing to show for it.

"That I can deal with," Mason continued. "What bothers me is the body count. Ohira's dead; another's missing and presumed dead; another was sharing a bed with Ohira; Tanner was attacked in a subway. The harder we work to keep DORSAL alive, the greater the chance Takagi will bury his connections to the arms market. It might be better to roll over and play dead, then take a look again in a few months. In the meantime, we'll pick apart what we've got, see where it takes us."

Dutcher was inclined to agree, but Tanner and Cahil were the ones on the ground, and they thought this new angle was worth pursuing. Briggs especially would be reluctant to give up—not as long as there was any chance of seeing it through.

"I agree with you," said Dutcher. "But—"

"But you'd like to give them a little more time," Mason said. "Why doesn't that surprise me? Okay. One week, then they're out."

Rock Creek Park

SMITH ARRIVED AT BISON BRIDGE A FEW MINUTES EARLY AND waited, growing angrier by the minute, until 10:30, when he gave up. He looked down the adjoining paths and saw no one. "Screw this," he muttered.

He was turning to leave when footsteps clicked on the wood behind him.

"Good evening, Senator."

Smith turned. The man was of medium height with broad shoulders, slim hips, and black wavy hair. "Who are you?" Smith said.

The man extended his hand. "Antonio."

"Fuck you. You're late."

"I've been here for an hour. I wanted to make sure you were alone."

"Well, aren't we the little spymaster. What do you want?"

The man gestured to the bench. "Shall we?" Without waiting, the man sat down and waited until Smith did the same. "Thank you for coming, Senator."

"You're lucky; I almost didn't. Now talk."

The man shrugged, pulled a manila envelope from his pocket, removed a five-by-seven photograph, and handed it to Smith.

Smith gaped at the photo. "Oh, good God."

The photo showed a nude Antonio sitting on the edge of a bed. Kneeling at his feet with his penis in her mouth was Judith Smith.

"Oh, God."

"Senator, I want you to listen carefully. This is how our relationship will work. I will give you orders, and you will obey them without hesitation. If you do not, or if you contact the police or speak to anyone about this, I will destroy you. Is that clear?"

Smith was still staring at the photo. "Uh-huh."

"I know everything about you, Senator. I know where you go, I know what you do. I know you are a drunk and a womanizer. I've been in your home—"

"You *what!*"

"And most important of all, Senator, I own your wife."

Smith felt like he'd been punched in the stomach. "I don't believe you."

"No?" The man gestured to the photo. "Has she ever done that for you? Or this?" The man produced another picture, this one showing Judith on her hands and knees, her face pressed into the pillow as the man took her from behind. "She especially enjoys this position."

"This can't be Judith," Smith whispered. "It can't be."

"She is a lovely woman, Senator, and quite open to experimentation."

"What do you want?"

"First of all: These photos were taken from a videocassette. If you fail me, copies of the video will be sent to the *New York Times*, the *Washington Post*, the *Los Angeles Times*, the four major news networks, a few of those trendy tabloid magazines, and finally to the FBI.

"Within days, three things will happen. One, I will disappear. Two, America will know that Senator Herb Smith is not man enough to keep his wife. And three, the FBI will begin asking questions about your relationship with your wife's lover, a man who will eventually be linked to several European terrorist groups."

"Don't do that," Smith whispered. "Don't. Tell me what you want."

"Information. Once you provide it, you get all originals and copies of the videos and photos, and you'll never be bothered again."

"How can I trust you?"

"If you cooperate, I'll keep my word. The sooner you deliver what I want, the sooner this will be over."

Smith considered the alternatives. He could go to the FBI. He had dozens of contacts, people who owed him favors. But how could he be sure the news wouldn't leak? He also had plenty of enemies. He could imagine the gossip: If Smith doesn't have the power over his wife, how can he possibly hold a seat in the United States Senate? He would be emasculated. He would be the laughingstock of the country!

And if he cooperated? All the man wanted was information. That was the real currency of power in Washington, after all. Trading information was something Smith understood. It was how things got done. Plus, after this nightmare was over, there would be plenty of time for payback. And she *would* pay. *Stupid bitch.*

He turned to the man. "Tell me what you want."

19

Chesapeake Bay

WALTER OAKEN STARED BLEARY-EYED AT THE STACKS OF REPORTS and computer printouts on his desk. Had he been able to tell Beverly about the project, she would have accused him of obsessing. He couldn't shake the feeling he'd missed something. What was it? There had to be good reason why Ohira had switched his attention to Takagi Maritime.

For Oaken, research was an adventure full of hidden facts, buried leads, and dead ends. As far as he was concerned, the Loch Ness Monster and Bigfoot were nothing compared to a fact that didn't want to be found.

The more he dug into Takagi's operations, the more he realized *Toshogu* and *Tsumago* were aberrations. Takagi had delivered on hundreds of contracts, and each one had been handled identically, from purchase agreement and blueprint design to owner's acceptance trials. Until now.

He'd started with maritime insurance. With *Toshogu* and *Tsumago*'s price tags in the millions of dollars, he felt certain Takagi would have underwritten them against loss or damage. He found nothing.

Next he turned to customers. *Tsumago*'s warshiplike characteristics made the Japanese MSDF the most likely buyer, but Oaken could find no open marine contracts between Takagi and the Japanese government.

That left two options: One, *Toshogu* and *Tsumago* were not only Takagi-built, but Takagi-owned as well, which probably meant Takagi had either bonded them or underwritten them with Lloyd's of London.

This theory also went nowhere. He found no listing in Lloyd's Shipping Index, and none of Sumiko's information indicated Takagi Industries was itself carrying the financial burden.

The second possibility was the ships had been commissioned for a foreign company, which again meant they would be bonded by the purchaser or underwritten by Lloyd's. Another dead end.

And then, out of the blue, he got his break.

He ran across two entries in Lloyd's Shipping Index, the first of which described a Belgian shipbuilder who, after conducting sea trials for a South African client, had delivered the ship to Capetown, at which point the client—a subsidiary of the Belgian shipbuilder—took possession. This was a simple and perfectly legal cost-saving device, in which the builder and purchaser—in truth the same entity—split the cost of underwriting the vessel. Could this be what Takagi had done?

The second Lloyd's entry described an oil tanker, but gave only the company's name, a synopsis of the contract, the vessel's dimensions, and the method of delivery. There was no mention of the builder's name. Oaken scanned for similar entries and found dozens.

This gave him a trail to follow. In less than an hour he found what he wanted.

Like most industrialists, Takagi had his fingers in hundreds of businesses around the world, either as a shareholder, an investor, or a board member. His interests ranged from textiles and mining to entertainment and auto parts. Most of these ventures were well-documented, but some were not. Among the dozens of boards on which Takagi secretly sat, Oaken found one, a Norwegian company named Skulafjord Limited, that dealt exclusively in marine salvage and mining.

Now in the tenth hour of his hunt, he logged onto to the Lloyd's Shipping Index and the United Nations International Maritime Bureau's databases, then ran a keyword search using the word *Skulafjord*. The response came back in less than a minute:

```
SKULAFJORD LIMITED
   (BUYER)
DATE OF BID
   ACCEPTANCE:        10/10/98
DATE OF PURCHASE
   AGREEMENT:         12/1/98
DATE KEEL LAID:       2/9/99
VESSEL OF RECORD:     UNNAMED ICEBREAKER,
                      MARINE SALVAGE; 410 FEET/
                      55 FEET/GWD 12,500 TONS
```

The dimensions seemed to match those of *Toshogu*. Oaken kept scrolling:

```
PROPOSED METHOD       AT-SEA BUILDER'S TRIALS;
   OF DELIVERY:       BUYER REP ABOARD;
                      VESSEL DELIVERED TO
                      BUYER-DESIGNATED POINT.
```

"Come on. . . ." Oaken muttered, scrolling. "Gimme the delivery date. . . . Gotcha!" He glanced at the wall calendar, then back at the screen. "What the hell . . . ?"

Japan

"SO YOU LOST THEM," HIROMASA TAKAGI SAID.

"Yes, sir," said Noboru.

Takagi now knew Tanner was more than a simple tourist. Nor was he working alone. Despite this, Noboru's men could not pin down their activities, let alone maintain surveillance. The pair was wandering about Honshu and Shikoku, and no one could tell him what they were doing. That wasn't quite true, though. While their activities were a mystery, the identity of one of their contacts was not. That would be settled soon enough.

"What did they do after leaving the ferry?" Takagi asked.

"We know they went south—"

Takagi shot forward in his chair. "Toward Anan? Toward the shipyard?"

"Yes, but past it, south toward Mugi. We lost them on the coast road."

Takagi grunted. "Did they return the same way?"

"No. We're not sure how, but they returned to the hotel just before sunrise."

"And this is where Tanner met her?"

"Yes, sir. She had been waiting for him."

His watchers recorded the name of the taxi company she'd used, Noboru explained. The rest had been simple. From the hotel she was taken to a neighborhood in Kobe and dropped off outside a *shokudo* owned by an elderly couple named Yokeisha, the maternal grandparents of one Sumiko Fujita.

This answered many questions for Takagi, first of which was: What had sparked Ohira's interest in the shipyard? In her position, she certainly had access to the right kind of information, but thankfully, not enough to derail the transaction.

What should be done about Ms. Fujita and her partners in crime? Takagi wondered. They were the only remaining loose ends. So close to *Tsumago*'s departure, could he afford the complication? The Arabs were already skittish. Any hint of trouble, and they might pull out. He could not allow that. He had invested too much, and the stakes were too high.

"Where is *Toshogu* now?" Takagi asked

"She should be nearing the Bering Strait."

"Who did you send?"

"Yamora."

"Good. From this point on, you will handle everything personally. You will see that *Tsumago* safely reaches the facility, you will make sure the transfer goes smoothly, and you will make sure all the loose ends are tied up."

"And the woman?"

Takagi shrugged. "She is a traitor. See that she gets a traitor's reward."

*   *   *

Bering Strait, Alaska

FORTY-SIX MILES SOUTH OF THE ARCTIC CIRCLE, *TOSHOGU* SLICED through the waves. Forty miles off the port beam lay the east coast of Siberia; to starboard, Alaska.

Skulafjord Limited's representative, Hallvard Sogne, stood on *Toshogu*'s bridge wing, bundled in foul weather gear, and stared at the water hissing down the hull. God, even in his native Norway he'd never felt cold like this before. If not for the spectacular view of the night sky, he would never leave his cabin.

For the hundredth time Sogne cursed his luck. He was a marine engineer, not a sailor. But evidently Skulafjord thought he was the best man for the job. Three weeks at sea! The plan was to put the ship through its paces as it sailed west through the Arctic Circle, along Russia's northern coast, into the Barents Sea, and finally to Skulafjord's docks on Svalbard Island.

So far *Toshogu*'s captain and crew had been very accommodating, and the ship was performing as designed, which was fine with Sogne. Perhaps if they finished early, his boss would send a helicopter to pick him up.

The bridge hatch opened, and a seaman poked out his head. "Mr. Sogne, the captain asks if you would step inside."

Sogne ducked inside.

The pilothouse was warm and illuminated only by the green-lighted helm console.

"Ah, Mr. Sogne," said the captain. "Would you care for some hot chocolate?"

"Not tea?" These Japanese were fanatical about their tea.

Namura laughed. "For you, we have hot chocolate."

"Thank you. Or should I say *domo arigato.*"

"Ah! *Do itashimashite.* Your Japanese is improving."

"I hope so. You know, Captain, I'm amazed at how little crew *Toshogu* requires. Eight men aboard, correct?"

"That is correct. She is quite self-sufficient. Most of her functions are computer-controlled. Your company is receiving a fine vessel."

"Indeed. Tell me, are the maneuvering trials still on for the morning?"

"Yes." Namura checked his watch. "In fact, you would be wise to get some sleep. It promises to be a long day."

"Good idea. In the morning, then."

FOUR HOURS LATER, *TOSHOGU* WAS THIRTY MILES NORTH OF THE Arctic Circle in the Chuckchi Sea. Hallvard Sogne lay wide awake in his private cabin, listening to the ocean lap against the ship's hull. Too late he remembered hot chocolate had caffeine, something he'd given up at his wife Ilga's insistence. Perhaps a walk would do the trick.

Five minutes later, he was out the door. The passageway was deserted and lit only by those eerie red lamps all ships seemed equipped with. Why was that? Why not some nice, bright lighting? He looked down the passageway, hoping to see a crewman. He didn't know the ship very well. He saw no one. Which way, then? The after hold area, he decided. That was one place they hadn't yet shown him.

He headed to the nearest ladder and took it down. As he reached the next deck, he felt the ship's motion change, rocking from side to side. The hum of the engines faded. They were slowing. Why? The fan blowers cut out. Sogne stood in the darkness, feeling dizzy. He had gotten so used to the ship's motion and sounds, the sudden change was unnerving.

From below, there came a shout.

"Iye . . . Iye! Onegai shimas—"

The voice was cut off. Silence. Outside, the sea lapped at the hull. The ship's rocking was more pronounced now. What was happening?

He leaned over the ladder rail. "Hello down there?"

Silence.

"Hello, is anybody down there?"

Sogne started down the ladder until he reached Sub-3, the lowermost level of the after hold area, a large, cavernlike space lined with catwalks and storage bays. He stepped through the hatch.

"Hello?"

Down the catwalk Sogne spotted a pile of twisted metal, half of which had spilled over onto the deck below. Walking closer, he saw it was debris of some sort, most of it covered in rust and algae. Sogne knelt down and picked up a few pieces, causing a small avalanche.

"What *is* this?" he whispered.

Behind him came a *click-click* sound. He spun around.

A shadowed figure stood on the catwalk.

"Oh, thank God!" Sogne said. "I'm glad you—" He stopped and peered closer at the man's face. "Who are you? I haven't seen you before."

20

FOR THE THIRD TIME IN AS MANY WEEKS, GEORGE COATES FOUND himself before the Intelligence Oversight Committee. Aside from Coates, the CIA's chief legal counsel, and the IOC panel, the hearing room was empty. Their amplified voices echoed off the walls.

This hearing was unavoidable, Coates knew. The decision to shut down SYMMETRY had ensured that. Just as the CIA was obligated to inform the IOC of all ongoing operations, it was bound to disclose failures as well.

Thinking of SYMMETRY and Marcus—a man he'd never met—Coates found himself almost hoping the man was dead. It would be far better than spending months—perhaps years—chained in a Beirut basement while his captors decided how to best dispose of him.

With that image in his mind, Coates had a hard time finishing the rather clinical statement his staff had drafted. ". . . and so, given the agent's capture, and fearing he would be forced to disclose operational details of the network, we've suspended operations pending future review."

"Pending future review," Smith repeated. " 'Future review' certainly can't help your captured agent, can it."

"I disagree. If his captors manage to extract information from him, it'll lead them nowhere. SYMMETRY is a dead conduit. Finding nothing of interest, they may choose to release him."

Smith barked out a laugh. "How very naive of you, Mr. Coates."

Coates was opening his mouth to reply when the chief counsel laid a hand on his forearm. Coates took a breath.

Don't give him the satisfaction. "You might think it naive, Senator. I like to call it solution-oriented thinking. We already know SYMMETRY has failed. Dwelling on that fact won't get us anywhere."

"No sale, Mr. Coates. Who do you think you're talking to? You think you can hide the fact that the CIA has not only wasted over four million dollars of taxpayers' money, but it has also got an agent murdered?"

"We don't know that, Senator. Marcus may still—"

Smith banged his fist on the table. "Stop trying to paint a happy face on this thing! You screwed up, and we've got nothing to show for it! Nothing!"

"You're wrong, sir. Before his capture, Marcus had been forwarding valuable product, which we are currently—"

"What kind of product?"

"Pardon me?"

"You heard me, Mr. Coates. I said, what had Marcus been delivering? In fact, I think we'd be wise to hear a lot more about SYMMETRY."

"Such as?"

"Anything that might help us understand what went wrong. For example, what exactly was Marcus's task in Lebanon? What type of information was he gathering? Had he penetrated any terrorist operations, and if so, which ones?"

"Senator, I don't—"

"I know you don't want to answer, Mr. Coates. I know the CIA wants to protect its ass. Well, the time for dodging is over."

Coates was stunned. Several members of the panel glanced nervously at Smith. The IOC vice chairman, Senator Dean, leaned toward Smith, only to be waved off.

Smith had just crossed a very big line in the CIA-IOC relationship. In his four years as DDO, Coates had never been asked such questions. The premise behind the IOC could be found in its very name: oversight. The CIA was not expected to divulge tradecraft particulars such as raw product or op sec measures. It just wasn't done.

"The question stands, Mr. Coates," Smith said.

What was Smith up to? Coates wondered. Was he simply flexing his muscles, looking for ammunition? If so, he might be appeased with some juicy yet insubstantial answers. He leaned over and put the question to the chief counsel.

"Fine, but not today. Don't talk off the top of your head."

"We're waiting, Mr. Coates."

"Senator, I did not come prepared with the information you're looking for."

"I'm unsurprised."

"If we can reschedule for another day, I can—"

"No, Mr. Coates, I will not—"

Smith was cut off as Senator Dean put a hand over the microphone. They whispered for several minutes, then Smith said, "Fine, Mr. Coates, we'll reconvene in three days. But be advised: Bring answers."

COATES WAS WALKING DOWN OUT OF THE ROOM WHEN SENATOR Dean stopped him. "Got a minute, George?"

"Depends. On or off the record?"

"Off."

"Then sure," Coates said. He and Dean had a solid relationship.

"It's Smith. His questions were news to the rest of us. In fact, he and I had discussed the format yesterday. This wasn't part of it."

"So he's got a burr under his saddle. What's new?"

"What I'm saying is, whatever his agenda, he's keeping it to himself."

"It'll be a cold day in hell when I give him what he wants, Harry. What he's asking for is need-to-know stuff, details even the DCI doesn't have. And if Dick Mason doesn't need to have them, Smith sure as hell doesn't."

"I agree. Take my advice, George: Next time we meet, give him a few details . . . minor stuff. Chances are it'll satisfy him. You know Smith, if he's not pissed off, he's not happy. Whatever witch hunt he's on, he'll get tired and move on to something else."

"He'd better, Harry, because he's on thin ice."

Glen Echo

NEAR DUSK, JUDITH SMITH AND FAYYAD LAY TOGETHER IN BED. She propped herself up on an elbow. "I stopped by earlier. I missed you."

"Oh? What time?"

"About four. I thought I'd surprise you."

"I went for a drive."

"Where?"

"Up to Harper's Ferry. It was beautiful; we should go." In truth, Fayyad had met Smith and collected his notes from the hearing. Fayyad had yet to review them.

Judith played with his chest hair. "I hear they have wonderful B and Bs in Harper's Ferry."

"B and Bs?"

"Bed-and-breakfasts. The emphasis being on the former, of course."

He smiled. "Of course."

Fayyad was pleased with the relationship. They made love often and in every imaginable way, which was to be expected. What he hadn't expected was his reaction to her. She was a remarkable woman: intelligent, bright, and warm, and he found himself responding to her. He found himself torn between his two selves. Which was real? he found himself wondering.

"What are you thinking about?" Judith asked.

"Pardon me?"

"You look so far away. Were you thinking of something?"

Fayyad smiled. "Yes. You."

The bedside phone rang, and Fayyad reached for it. "Hello."

"Is Heloise home?" said the voice.

Fayyad felt his heart skip. *Damn them!* "I'm sorry, I think you have the wrong number."

"This is not six seven two four?"

"No, sorry, wrong number." Fayyad hung up.

"What is it, darling?" asked Judith.

"Nothing, wrong number." He checked his watch. "It's late. We must get you home."

"I don't want to go home," she said.

"Are things bad?"

"No more than usual. He's drinking more, and he's nastier, but it's nothing I haven't seen before."

"Do you think he suspects anything?"

"He's oblivious to anything but work, scotch, and his little bimbo." She looked at him. "You're very curious about him all of the sudden."

"I know he hurts you. I want to understand."

"It feels good to have someone worry about me."

"Is this increased drinking of his unusual? Or the meanness?"

"Whenever he's under stress he gets that way. I'm first in the pecking order. Can we stop talking about this? I don't want to ruin our time together."

"I'm sorry. Speaking of time—"

"I know," she said, slipping her hand beneath the covers. "Just a few more minutes . . . ?"

"You are a beast, Judith."

She smiled and rolled on top him. "Blame yourself, lover."

ONCE ALONE, FAYYAD DROVE TO THE PHONE BOOTH AND DIALED. Al-Baz answered. "What took you so long?"

"She was with me."

"More film for the library? When this is over, I think I would like to see—"

"Is this why you contacted me, to exchange entendres?"

"Exchange what?"

"Never mind. What do you want?"

"We are considering a change."

"What kind of change?" Fayyad asked.

Al-Baz explained. "In fact, we've already sent for him."

"Mustafa, I know this man's methods. He'll ruin what we've accomplished."

"Accomplished? What have you accomplished? The bedding of a middle-aged slut?"

"Damn you! I—"

"You have lost your objectivity. Whether you approve or not is irrelevant. The only question is whether we can count on you. I trust we can."

Fayyad read between the lines. He leaned his head against the booth's glass and forced himself to think. Al-Baz said they were *considering* a change. What did that mean? Were they having trouble convincing the Russian? He was wanted by the FBI; perhaps he was reluctant. Fayyad hoped so. Once in charge, the Russian would ratchet the pressure on Smith, either directly or indirectly, and that would mean using either the mistress or Judith. *Oh, lord, what if he wants to take her?*

"And if I refuse?" Fayyad whispered.

"You are not listening, Ibrahim. You have no choice."

Langley

"HE ASKED FOR *WHAT*?" MASON ASKED.

"Operational details," George Coates replied. "Nuts and bolts stuff."

"Give me the whole thing, from start to finish."

Coates recounted his testimony and ended with his conversation with Senator Dean.

Sylvia Albrecht said, "Witch hunt or not, it's absurd. Smith has to know that. Obviously he's got another agenda."

"My thinking, too," said Coates. "He wants another meeting the day after tomorrow."

What is Smith's game? Mason wondered. He knew the senator had long-term designs on the Oval Office—if not for himself, at least for his party—and was looking for leverage against the current administration. Or was this in fact just another Herb Smith tirade? Either way, Mason didn't like the feel of it.

"We've done our part," he said. "A postmortem is all we're required to give."

Coates said, "Dick, if we clam up, we'll be handing him a banner. Look, we give him a few scraps—just enough to placate him—and he goes away."

Mason looked at his DDI. "Sylvia?"

"Might be the best course."

"Okay. George, put something together. But this time, he's coming to us. Let's find out what's on the good senator's mind."

Japan

TANNER FINISHED DECODING OAKEN'S LAST MESSAGE ON THE LAPtop.

"Good news or bad?" Bear asked.

"A little of both. We have a week before they pull the plug."

"No surprise there. And the good?"

"The verdict is still out on our haul from the shipyard, but Oaks has figured out the *Toshogu* angle. Takagi sold her—and I use that word loosely—to a Norwegian company called Skulafjord Limited on whose board he just happens to have a secret seat."

"What's their business?"

"Salvage and mining. Apparently *Toshogu*'s destination is a Skulafjord station on Svalbard Island."

"So it's a dead end."

"Not necessarily. Oaks wants to put a satellite track on her."

"Good luck. Even if Leland gets the tasking order, it'll be like looking for a snowflake on a bedsheet. Besides, why go to all the trouble?"

"You mean besides the fact Leland trusts our uncanny instincts?"

"Yeah, besides that," said Cahil.

"Oaks also found *Toshogu* was supposed to have been delivered four months ago," Tanner said. "Takagi Maritime blamed the delay on defects in the rudder post. Supposedly, it was just fixed last week."

"I don't buy it."

"Me neither. Takagi went to a lot of trouble to run interference for her. I'd like to know why."

"Speaking of Oaks, did he find anything on our other request?"

"Nothing. No wrecks in the last forty years." One of Tanner's theories regarding *Toshogu*'s visits to the waters off the village was that somebody had lost a ship in the area, and Takagi had salvaged it for reasons unknown. "On paper, it's a dead end."

Cahil eyeballed his friend; he knew the look on Briggs's face. Tanner was not about to let a lack of solid evidence throw him off track—not yet.

"But you still want to take a look," Cahil said.

Tanner smiled. "How'd you guess?"

21

Washington, D.C.

TO HIS OWN AMUSEMENT, CHARLIE LATHAM LOVED GROCERY SHOPping. It had started when their children were old enough to baby-sit themselves for an hour or two, and he and Bonnie needed time alone. Even now, though the kids had moved away, they still practiced the ritual, pushing the cart up and down the aisles, pricing toilet paper and debating the quality of off-brand canned peaches.

Bonnie walked up to the meat case where Charlie was scrutinizing a package.

"This is a good deal, huh?" he asked.

"Charlie, that's rump."

"So?"

"We're making stew. We need stew meat."

"Oh."

Latham's cell phone buzzed; he mouthed *Sorry* to Bonnie and answered. "Charlie Latham."

"Charlie, it's Paul. Your *Shin Bet* guy just called. He wants you to call him on a secure line. He sounded pretty excited."

"Okay. You'll have to come pick me up . . . the Fresh-Rite on Burton." He hung up and handed Bonnie the car keys. She frowned at him. "Sorry, hon. I'll be home as soon as I can."

"I've heard that before. I'll keep the stew warm."

LATHAM WENT STRAIGHT TO HIS OFFICE AND DIALED AVI HARON'S number in Tel Aviv. He glanced at his watch: almost ten at night in Israel.

"Avi, it's Charlie. What's up?"

"You remember the three men in the Khartoum photo?"

"Of course."

"We've tracked the European. He's moving."

Latham was momentarily confused at Haron's phrase, "the European," then he remembered the Israeli's photo only clearly showed Fayyad; to them, Vorsalov was an unknown. The third man, the other Arab, was still a mystery to everyone.

"You could've told me you were tracking them," Latham said.

"Be thankful I'm calling you at all."

"Yeah, you're right. Sorry. What about the other Arab?"

"No luck there."

"Where's the European going?"

"Larnaca, Cyprus. He's booked on the noon flight from Aswan."

Latham jotted down the particulars. "What's your stake here, Avi? I mean—"

"Do we plan to intercept him? I doubt it. This is Institute information; if they hadn't wanted it passed along, I would have never heard about it."

That made sense, but it wasn't like Mossad to be magnanimous. What was their agenda? "But you are tracking him."

"I don't know."

"You don't know, or you can't say?"

"I don't know, Charlie," said Haron. "I'm surprised they gave us even this."

"Me too. I owe you, Avi, thanks."

Langley

WITHIN TWO HOURS, LATHAM, COATES, SYLVIA ALBRECHT, AND Art Stucky were sitting in Dick Mason's office.

Haron's news was big. The primary question was, what to do with it? It was quickly agreed they must tag Vorsalov in Cyprus and keep him under surveillance for as long as possible. If they were lucky, he would lead them to Fayyad.

To this end, Coates proposed an unorthodox plan.

"I'm pretty sure the FIS will go along," he said. "They gave us the Vorsalov tip in the first place."

"We have no assets in place that could handle it?" Mason asked.

"Not by tomorrow," said Coates. "But I'm sure the Russians do. If not directly, then through some locals. Cyprus was one the KGB's favorites for years."

Mason looked at Latham. "Charlie?"

"If we're right about Vorsalov and Fayyad's connection, we can't afford to miss the chance. He's moving, and we know where he's going. That's an advantage we don't usually get."

"Ain't that the truth. Okay, I'll make the call. In the meantime, let's get the ball rolling. George, get the op center staffed. If we're able to tag Vorsalov, we'd better be ready to track him."

FORTUNATELY FOR MASON, THE DIRECTOR OF THE RUSSIAN FIS was an early riser. It was not quite dawn in Moscow when the call went through.

Now, after twenty minutes of sparring, Valerei Ryazan was leaning Mason's way. "What you ask, Richard . . . It is a difficult thing."

"But not impossible, Valerei."

"We have no assets in Cyprus."

"But you have connections."

The Russian chuckled. "Perhaps. What would you have us do?"

"Just trail him, find out who he's meeting, where he's headed. We're looking for a possible link."

"To what?"

"The Delta bombing."

"I see. I assume you know we want him as well. It would be much easier for us to simply take him."

"I'm aware of that," said Mason.

"We could pass along any information we get from him—"

"No good, Valerei. If you take him out of the loop, the rest of the operation—whatever he's got brewing—would collapse."

"*Da,* that is possible. Tell me, Richard, if you were in my place . . . if you had the chance to capture Vorsalov, you would not hesitate."

"No. He's wanted for murder here. He's still on the FBI's hit parade."

"Oh, yes, the young agent," Ryazan murmured. "A terrible thing."

"Add that to the bombing, and Vorsalov's body count for U.S. citizens is six."

"I can count, Richard." Ryazan was silent for a few moments. "And in return for our cooperation?"

"You would have my thanks."

"I will require more."

"Such as?"

"If you come to possess Colonel Vorsalov, he will be returned to us in a timely fashion."

"Define *timely.*"

"Five years."

"Valerei, he'd get life in prison for the agent's murder alone. Besides, I don't have the authority to—"

"Oh, Richard. You have the authority. Just as I have the authority to do this highly irregular favor for you."

Checkmate, thought Mason. By first tipping them off to Vorsalov's Khartoum meeting and then by ignoring a chance to capture him, Ryazan was taking a big risk. Though the name had changed, the FIS was no less vengeful than its predecessor when it came to dealing with traitors, especially ones like Vorsalov, whose many clients included guerillas in Chechniya and Kazikstan.

Mason considered the deal. Either way he went, they lost something. Justice for a decade-old murder or capturing those responsible for the Delta bombing?

"Deal," Mason said.

22

KEMAL AND PANOS WERE UNLIKELY PARTNERS. KEMAL, A TURKISH Cypriot, and Panos, a Greek Cypriot, had once been enemies and had in fact anonymously exchanged Molotov cocktails across Nicosia's Attila Line in 1981, six years after the failed Colonels Coup sundered the country.

While burdensome for the average Turk or Greek, this decades-old conflict makes Cyprus a paradise for terrorists and criminals, both of whom find life easy as the military and the police are focused on the ever-present threat of civil war.

Each mistaking the other for a compatriot, Kemal and Panos met in a Nicosia pub and by the time they discovered they were enemies, they were both thoroughly drunk and had realized they shared a passion stronger than their hatred.

And so, almost ten years after their first meeting, they were still in business, having graduated from pickpocketing to robbery and murder. Unknown to them, one of their frequent employers in the early eighties was the KGB. Sometimes it was a burglary, sometimes a murder, and sometimes, like today, they were simply to follow the man and gather information.

After spotting the target at the Larnaca airport, they followed him into the city proper. When the taxi took its third turn in as many minutes—this time toward the Acropolis—Kemal pushed their rickety yellow Renault to maintain the 200-yard gap.

"No ordinary tourist, this one," said Panos. "He's acting like he knows he's being followed."

"The driver is conning him," said Kemal. "Taking him for a ride."

"We'll see." Though neither of them were NASA material, Panos was the sharper of the two, Kemal the tougher.

The taxi wound its way through Larnaca for another twenty minutes before swinging back onto Grigoris. "He's heading for the marina," said Panos.

As the taxi turned right past the Swedish Consulate, Panos said, "Keep going, keep going! We'll catch him coming the other way."

Kemal frowned, confused. "But—"

"Just do as I say! Go around the post office."

Three quick right turns brought them to the waterfront. They pulled to the curb just as the man was paying off the taxi.

Panos studied the man. Something about the face bothered him. The eyes. That was it. They were a flat, expressionless blue. Panos had seen such eyes in other men, and they were usually men best left alone.

The man walked into the green-bricked ferry office.

"Wait here," said Panos, climbing from the car. He returned five minutes later. "He bought a ticket for the Beirut ferry."

"Beirut?" Kemal said. "Stephan said nothing about Beirut. What do we do?"

"We follow him."

"To Beirut? Stephan said nothing about Beirut. Why are we—"

"Kemal, just do as I ask. If we don't follow him, we don't get paid. Go park the car, and I'll get the tickets."

PANOS AND KEMAL BOARDED JUST BEFORE DEPARTURE, FOUND THE man sitting on the bow deck, then climbed to the upper deck where they could watch him. Panos took the first shift and sent Kemal down to the car deck to wait.

Two hours after leaving Larnaca, the man still hadn't moved. He sat reading a magazine and watching the ocean.

Panos was about to slip away to the bathroom when another man came strolling along the deck.

This one was an Arab, with a handlebar moustache and a newspaper tucked under one arm. He lit a cigarette, then turned and gestured to the bench. The man shrugged, and the Arab sat. After a few minutes, the Arab laid the newspaper on the bench, tossed his cigarette, and left.

Panos kept his eyes on the target. Finally the man stood up, slipped the newspaper under his arm, and walked aft.

AS THE SUN DIPPED TOWARD THE HORIZON, BEIRUT'S SKYLINE ROSE from the horizon. Panos could see the city's artillery-scarred buildings jutting from the landscape like denuded trees on a battlefield.

He'd followed the man to the rest room, where he entered a stall, remained inside for five minutes, then emerged without the newspaper. Panos found it behind the toilet stool; a section had been torn from an inside page.

Panos met Kemal where they could watch the passengers disembark. "Are we going to follow them into the city?" Kemal asked.

"No." Stephan could not pay them enough for that. "There is one more ferry going back tonight; we'll follow if he takes it."

As night fell, the ferry nudged alongside the pier. The mooring lines were secured to the bollards, and the gangway was lowered. Under the glare of spotlights, Lebanese Forces jeeps patrolled the marina, and at the head of the quay stood a roadblock of armored personnel carriers.

Panos could see lights winking in the foothills, followed seconds later by a *crump crump crump. Artillery,* he thought. The fighting could be between any of the dozens of factions in the city. What a horrible place. The skirmishes along Cyprus's Attila Line could be fierce, but never like this. In Nicosia it was Turk against Greek; Greek against Turk. Here it was everyone against everyone.

"There, is that him?" Kemal asked.

Panos looked. The Arab was among the first off the

gangway and into the customs building. He came out the other side, walked through the blockade, and climbed into a waiting blue Volvo.

The target followed ten minutes later. A second Volvo, this one gray, was waiting for him at the head of the quay. As he approached, an Arab climbed from the front seat and held open the door.

"Bodyguards," Panos murmured.

The Volvo sped away and disappeared into the night.

Beirut

YURI VORSALOV HATED LEBANON. HE HATED ITS SMELL, ITS sounds, the grime it left on his skin. But most of all, he hated its ceaseless violence.

His twenty-two years in the KGB had taught him the value of violence. But, like any tool, violence is best applied with discipline. With its ancient hatreds, ridiculous factions, and never-ending wars, Beirut was a cesspool of base savagery. Any idiot can throw a grenade. It takes vision to apply violence as a means to an end.

Early in his career Vorsalov had urged Moscow to take a more active role in the Mideast. The average Arab nation was too entrenched in tribalism and internecine warfare to understand, let alone formulate, cohesive long-term strategies, he'd argued. Pan-Arabism was a pipe dream. Alas, his assessments were overtaken by history as the fifties saw the United States rallying behind Israel. Domination, the Kremlin decided, would best be achieved through the slow and steady spread of communism. Patience, they said. America hadn't the stomach for a protracted nuclear stalemate. *A good joke*, Vorsalov thought. *Now, instead of ruling the world, Mother Russia struggled to feed her people.*

And I am a hired gun. Vorsalov knew why he'd been summoned, of course. Al-Baz's little project was going badly. Vorsalov was unsurprised. The entire operation was ill-advised lunacy.

The Arab in the passenger seat handed him a hood. "Put this on."

"Why?"

"You must not see where we are going."

"Then I won't watch," Vorsalov said with a smile.

The car screeched to a halt. "You will put this on. Now."

Vorsalov sighed. "God-cursed theatrics." He took the hood and slipped it over his head.

He felt the car lurch from side to side as the driver negotiated the rubble-strewn streets. Whether they were trying to disorient him or were simply avoiding craters, he did not know, but after another five minutes, they pulled to a stop.

His door opened. He was helped out and led down some steps. The air smelled damp and musty. He heard the squeal of rats. He was led up another flight of steps, then right. They stopped. He was guided to a chair. Through the hood's weave he could see flickering candlelight.

"You may remove the hood."

Vorsalov did so. Against the far wall stood a guard armed with an AK-47. Seated across from him was Mustafa al-Baz and a hooded man in battle fatigues. This was the leader, Vorsalov assumed, one of Khatib's sleepers. Probably aged fifty to sixty, average height and weight, physically unremarkable. This was always the case with the best terrorists. They were, in CIA franca lingua, gray men.

Sitting on the table were a pitcher of water and a bowl of bean curd. The hooded man gestured. "Please eat and drink if you would like."

Vorsalov poured a glass of water, took a sip, and set it aside. He was ravenously thirsty, but he knew this was a test. The Arabs enjoyed tests of character. They knew he was disoriented and thirsty, and how he conducted himself even in the simple act of drinking was telling.

He folded his hands on the table and waited.

After a long five seconds, the hooded man said, "Your trip was safe, I trust? Our precautions did not inconvenience you?"

"Such measures are often necessary. I would expect nothing less from a man such as yourself."

"What do you know of me?"

"Nothing aside from the general's praise."

"I see."

"The general thought I might be of assistance to you."

"Yes."

"In what fashion?"

The hooded man gestured to al-Baz, who said, "We are having complications. The matter we discussed in Khartoum."

Of course you are, you idiots, Vorsalov thought.

"We feel our man on the scene may be . . . unreliable."

"Explain." Al-Baz did so, and Vorsalov said, "You believe he has genuine feelings for this woman?"

"Who can say? It's almost certain he doesn't have the stomach to do what is necessary."

Vorsalov understood. They wanted to increase the pressure on the target, and Fayyad was balking. "A difficult situation," he agreed. "But I'm not sure what I can do for you."

"We want you to go to Washington and take command."

"What?" Vorsalov blurted before he could catch himself. "That's impossible."

"How so?" asked the hooded man.

"I'm known there. Their federal police want me."

"That is not my concern. The general has guaranteed your cooperation."

"I don't believe that. He knows I am a face there. He would never—"

"As I understand it, you are under contractual obligation, are you not?"

"Yes, but—"

"General al-Khatib has loaned you to us."

"I am not some piece of livestock—"

"Enough!" the hooded man barked. "You will help us. You will go to Washington. You will take command of our operation. And you will get us the information we need."

"And if I refuse?"

The hooded man's eyes blinked once. "That would be unwise."

He means it, Vorsalov thought. If he failed to cooperate, any number of fates awaited him: extradition to Russia,

imprisonment, death. At best, he could never return to the
Mideast, and with most of the major intelligence agencies
hunting for him, the world would become a very small
place indeed. What in God's name was driving this operation of theirs?

"For your cooperation," the hooded man continued, "you
will receive compensation in two forms: One, your obligation to General al-Khatib will be fulfilled. And two, a
bonus of five hundred thousand dollars will be posted to
your account at Bank Grunewald in Vienna." He slid a
piece of paper across the table. "This is the account number,
yes?"

Five hundred thousand! Vorsalov forced himself to remain calm. "Yes, it is correct. But the amount is—"

"Nonnegotiable. Can I assume you accept?"

"It seems I have little choice."

"None at all." The hooded man stood up. "Mustafa will
provide you with the details." He walked to the door, then
turned. "One more thing."

"Yes?"

"If you fail, you will receive no money, and you will
find yourself without friends. Do you understand my meaning?"

"I understand," said Vorsalov. "Now you must understand something: The target you've chosen is a prominent
figure. To get the information you seek might require . . .
harsh methods."

"That does not concern us. Do what you have to do. Get
us the information."

23

Beirut

FOUR HOURS AFTER THEIR TARGET BOARDED THE LAST FERRY FOR Larnaca, Panos and Kemal stood on the uppermost deck to decide their next move. The wind whipped around them and fluttered the pennants on the buntline.

"He's in the café drinking coffee," Kemal argued. "He'll have to piss sometime. The only bathroom is on the car deck. It's dark, and no one is around."

"I don't know, Kemal."

"You said if we don't find out his destination, we don't get paid."

"I know. I'm not sure about this one. Something about him bothers me."

"What?"

"I don't know. He feels . . . dangerous."

Kemal grinned cockily. "More dangerous than us? He is old, we are young. We'll surprise him. Come on, we've done this a hundred times."

Panos thought it over. Kemal was right. There *were* two of them, and this is what they did best. "Okay. But no killing. We will tie him up in the back of one of the cars. By the time he's found, the ferry will be docked, and we'll be gone."

WHATEVER KEMAL LACKED IN SHEER INTELLIGENCE, HIS ESTIMATE of their target's bladder capacity was keen. After two more cups of coffee, the man exited the salon, took the stairwell down to the car deck, and entered the bathroom. Kemal and Panos met in the corridor outside. Panos reached up and unscrewed the single lightbulb, casting the corridor in shadow.

They positioned themselves on both sides of the door. A moment later, the toilet flushed. The door swung open. Kemal stepped in front of the man and flicked open his switchblade

"Don't move. No sound."

The man reacted as expected. He took a step back. His expression never wavered, however. Panos saw no fear in his eyes.

"I have very little money," the man said, "but you may have it."

He's Russian, Panos thought.

"Empty your pockets," Kemal barked.

The man nodded, smiling slightly. "Certainly."

"This funny to you?" Kemal growled. "What is funny?"

"Nothing." One by one, the man began pulling items from his pockets. "I have breath mints, would you care for a breath mint?"

"What?" Kemal said. He shoved the man.

"Kemal, don't—"

"You think we are joking, mister? I will cut you!"

"I believe you would."

"Then hurry up!"

Panos's heart pounded; nothing about this felt right. "Empty your jacket pockets," he ordered. "Now!"

The man reached inside his jacket and handed over his wallet; Panos rifled through it, pocketed the money inside, dropped it. "The rest of it." He took the man's passport and a plain white envelope. It was too dark to read. He backed into the light, flipped open the passport, scanned the contents, tossed it aside. The envelope contained an airline ticket. Panos squinted, trying to decipher the details.

The man looked Kemal up and down. "You are a Turk, yes?"

"How do you know that?"

The man chuckled. "Why do you think I offered you a breath mint?"

"Fucker!"

"Kemal, no!"

The man parried Kemal's knife thrust, pulled him in, and lashed out with his left hand. There was a soft crunch. With a grunt, Kemal clutched his throat and fell. Panos instinctively knew his friend was dead.

"Drop the envelope, boy," the Russian said. "Drop it and run while you can."

"I'm sorry, mister, I—"

"I said leave it and go! You're trying my patience."

Panos stooped, placed the airline ticket on the ground, then turned and ran.

Langley

FOR THE PAST TWENTY HOURS, THE OP CENTER HAD BEEN RUNNING fully staffed, augmented by the periodic presence of Coates, Stucky, Sylvia Albrect, and Latham, all of whom came and went as their schedules dictated. The waiting was hardest for Latham.

What would he do if he found himself face-to-face with Vorsalov? Countless times he'd relived that night, and always it came out the same. *Not this time. This time, you son of a bitch, if you come here . . . What was taking so long?*

Dick Mason strode into the conference room, shut the door, and snatched up the phone. "Okay, Ginny, patch it through."

There was a series of clicks. FIS Director of Operations Pyotor Kolokov's voice came through the speaker "Hello?"

"Yes, Mr. Kolokov," Mason said. "This is Director Mason. You're on speakerphone. Present are my DDO, DDI, Near East Division chief, and a special agent of the FBI."

"This is a secure line, I presume? And you are recording?"

"Yes to both."

"We have the information you requested. Whether you will consider it favorable or not, I do not know."

"Whatever you've got, we appreciate the effort."

"First you must know: Our mutual friend made our surveillance team; one of them was killed."

"I'm very sorry."

"The price of business. The target stayed in Beirut for approximately two hours. We do not know who he met. He is traveling under a passport issued to a Yan Karnovsky, a Belorus citizen working as an industrial chemical buyer. We will fax you the particulars."

"And his destination?"

"According to the surviving member of the Larnaca team, Vorsalov was carrying an airline ticket. If he follows the route, his flight will take him first to Rome, then London for another connection. That is the interesting part."

"How so?"asked Mason.

"His last connection is bound for New York."

Washington, D.C.

"SO YOU HAVE NO NEW INFORMATION," FAYYAD SAID.

"Christ, I've already told you!" Smith snapped, glancing around. The footpath leading to and from their bench was deserted. "I'm going to Langley tomorrow." Smith flicked a fern branch from his face. "This is idiotic!"

"You're not a lover of nature, Senator?"

"Fuck nature."

As planned, Fayyad's choice of the United States Botanic Garden as a meeting place was causing the Senator fits. Just a stone's throw from Capitol Hill, the garden was a favorite of tourists but was rarely frequented by politicians. Though Smith did not realize it, the chance of their being observed was slim.

"This trip to CIA headquarters . . . Was it your idea or theirs?" asked Fayyad.

"Theirs," Smith said.

"Isn't that unusual?"

"Given what I'm asking for, no. You've got no idea how unusual these damned questions of yours are. You just don't ask the CIA for these kinds of details."

"So you told me."

"You've got no idea what you're doing."

"I think I do, Senator. I know all about you. You've made quite a reputation for yourself. The king of porcupine power, they call you. You berate and belittle your opponents until they surrender. It will be the same with this. You will bully them until—"

"This is different, damn it! This is the fucking CIA—"

"Just like you bully your wife—"

"My wife? Listen, pal, just because you're fucking her doesn't mean you know shit about our marriage. Judith is perfectly happy."

"She is not happy—" Fayyad caught himself, took a breath. "Senator, your wife and your marriage are not my concern. All I care about is the information, and your time is running out."

"What's that mean?"

"I will be frank. Believe me or not, I want nothing more than to get this information and leave. Once I'm gone, your involvement will be over. You will be able to resume your life as before."

"Suits me fine."

"The problem is, I'm no longer in control. The people I work for are not so patient. They are insisting on more . . . stern methods."

"Are you threatening me?"

"I am being honest with you. If they knew I was telling you this—"

"Bullshit. This is the good cop/bad cop routine. You watch too much TV."

"Senator, for once in your life, stop and listen! Another man is on his way here. He is a professional. His job will be to get results, whatever it takes. Do you understand?"

Smith stared at Fayyad. His face went pale. "You're serious, aren't you?"

"Yes."

"Who is he?"

"That doesn't matter. I know him. I know what he is capable of."

"Jesus, I'm trying to get it! Don't they know that?"

"I've told them."

"I'm doing my best! Can't they give me a little more time?"

"He is already on his way."

"Oh, God . . ."

"We still have a few more days, Senator. If you can get me the information before then . . ."

"Sure, sure. The meeting's tomorrow. I can get it tomorrow."

"Good."

"If I do, you can stop this, right? I mean—"

"Yes. You understand, then? To protect you, I must have the information. Otherwise I have no control over what happens."

"Yeah, sure, I can see that. I can get it."

Though having seen it many times before, Fayyad was amazed at Smith's transformation. The threat of violence, combined with the oblique offer of friendship had worked its magic. There were drawbacks, though. The fear would begin to gnaw at Smith, make him careless.

"I want you to go home and get some sleep," said Fayyad. "Try to relax."

"Right. Good idea. Okay, so I get this information, and there's no reason for this guy to bother me, right?"

Fayyad nodded. "You have my word."

24

PLEASANTRIES EXCHANGED AND COFFEE POURED, DICK MASON said, "Senator, George tells me you have some questions regarding SYMMETRY."

"Ever the diplomat, your Mr. Coates," Smith replied. "Grave reservations would be the more appropriate phrase. And I'll tell you this, Director Mason: Before we're through here, I'll have answers."

The other attendees, Coates, Sylvia Albrecht, and Senator Dean, shifted nervously in their chairs as Mason and Smith faced one another across the table.

Though Mason had never considered Smith a handsome man by any stretch of the imagination, today the senator had underdone himself; red-eyed, hair askew, and jacket rumpled, he looked like he had just come off a three-day binge, which, Mason reminded himself, was a distinct possibility.

"You've reviewed our report, I assume?" Mason said.

"And found it lacking. I'm looking for the truth, not rhetoric."

"What else do you want to know?"

Smith flipped open his legal pad and read off a list of questions: names of terrorist groups Marcus's network had penetrated, particularly those in Lebanon; the network's communication protocols; what, if any, side-lobe product had been uncovered by the network. . . .

George was right, Mason thought. Smith was far out of bounds. Such details were beyond even the DCI's purview.

Mason's first instinct was to be suspicious, but regardless of his personal dislike for the man, Smith's handling of IOC matters had thus far been beyond reproach. Herb Smith a traitor? Mason didn't buy it. The man was a grade-A son of a bitch, but he wouldn't sell out his country. So what, then? Mason wondered.

"How long have you been chairman of the IOC, Senator?" Mason asked.

"You know very well how long. Four years."

"In all that time have we ever given you these kinds of operational details?"

"Damn it, don't patronize me! Your agency's history of withholding information is well-documented. You don't like us shining the light on you and your pet projects; it makes you scurry for the corners."

"I'm sorry you feel—"

"You're perfectly happy keeping your secrets and playing your games. You've wasted millions of dollars and a man's life on this fiasco, and I'm going to get to the bottom of it."

"Senator, there are reasons for withholding certain details—"

"To cover your collective asses. Yes, I—"

"It's called compartmentalization and need-to-know. The theory behind—"

"I don't need a lecture, Mason."

"I think you do. Operations are compartmentalized so damage to one part doesn't spread. And need-to-know is just that: If you don't need access to classified information, you don't get it. Period. Even I'm not privy to the particulars of all ongoing ops."

"Including SYMMETRY?"

"Including SYMMETRY."

Smith grinned, shook his head. "Looks like I just found one of the problems. Do you even know what's going on in your own agency, Mason? Maybe this fiasco is just the tip of the iceberg. I wonder what else I might find with some digging?"

"You haven't been listening, Senator."

"Oh, I've been listening—maybe too well, and it's got you worried. All of a sudden you're finding yourself up against somebody who doesn't buy your spook-speak bullshit!"

Senator Dean laid a hand on Smith's forearm. "Herb, why don't we—"

"No! No, goddamn it! I've listened to this double-talk for too long." He jutted his finger across the table. "I've watched you people dance in the dark and play your games long enough. The president has given you people too much power, and this SYMMETRY disaster proves it. You haven't got the slightest idea of the concept of account-ability to the public you serve. Well, guess what? That's about to change. Starting now. Starting with you answering my questions!"

Smith's left eye twitched. He dabbed his forehead with a handkerchief.

"Are you feeling all right, Senator?" asked Sylvia Al-brecht.

"I'm fine! I'm waiting, Mason."

"Senator, since you've been so frank with us, I feel obliged to do the same. I don't care—even remotely—about your impressions of this agency. I'm proud of our accomplishments, and I stand behind every project we've undertaken during my tenure."

"That's very moving, but you still haven't answered my questions."

"And I don't intend to. Everything you need to know is in that briefing folder."

"That's not good enough. I want—"

"Senator, I don't pretend to understand politics, and I have no desire to. I'm not sure where this agenda of yours is coming from, but I suggest you drop it. You're playing a dangerous game."

Smith blanched. "You can't talk to me like that."

"I just did. Now, if that's all—"

Smith pounded the table. "No, that's not all, you son of a bitch!"

Senator Dean blurted, "Jesus, Herb!—"

"Shut up! Mason, you—"

The DCI stood up. "This meeting is over. George, Senator Smith is leaving; let's get him an escort. Senator Dean, it's been a pleasure."

Smith bolted up. "I'm not going anywhere! You can't . . . can't . . ." His face flushed. He plopped down in his seat, gasping.

"Senator?" Mason asked.

Smith waved him away. "I'm fine . . ." he croaked.

Mason said, "George, call Medical."

SEVEN FLOORS BELOW MASON'S OFFICE, LATHAM HUNG UP THE phone and turned to the other team members. "He just deplaned in Heathrow. They've got him."

Vorsalov was now under the watchful eyes of MI-5, the British counterpart to the FBI. If the world's intelligence services were to hold Olympic contests, Latham was convinced MI-5 would come out the undisputed champion of mobile ground surveillance. Vorsalov wouldn't be able to use the toilet without eyes on him.

"How long before his connection?" asked Randal.

"Forty minutes."

"Plenty of time for something to go wrong," muttered Art Stucky.

"Nothing will go wrong," Latham said. He hadn't liked Stucky upon their first meeting four years ago and liked him even less now. He was a narrow-minded bigot and generally an asshole. Latham had encountered enough sociopaths to recognize their aura, and Stucky was steeped in it.

"You *hope* nothing goes wrong," Stucky replied.

"He's not going anywhere."

"Always the bright side, eh, Charlie?"

Paul Randal asked, "Did he come in on the Karnovsky passport?"

"Yep."

"Surprised he hasn't switched."

"Me, too. If he's going to do it, Heathrow's his last chance."

"Does MI-5 know that?" Stucky asked.

"They wrote the book on this, Art," Latham said.

"Right. Nobody tighter-assed than the Limeys."

Latham began reviewing his mental checklist. They had eight hours from the time Vorsalov boarded at Heathrow until he touched down in New York. As of two hours ago, Harry Owen and the New York FO were putting the finishing touches on the surveillance net. The machinery was in place. Now they waited.

Why had the Russian come back? he wondered. The man knew how badly they wanted him, so what could be worth it? Whatever it was, Latham wasn't about to question his good fortune.

Aside from the details of Vorsalov's itinerary, the most interesting piece of information from the FIS's Larnaca team was their description of his contact aboard the ferry. Though far from a positive match, it sounded like the unidentified Arab from Khartoum. Latham played the scenario in his head: The Arab, based in Beirut, hires Vorsalov and Fayyad in Khartoum; Vorsalov's travel is related to the job. But in what way? And where was Fayyad now? The most obvious answer was also the most frightening: the United States. Again, Latham found himself asking the same question: What had drawn Fayyad here only weeks after the Delta bombing?

"COME ON. . . ." LATHAM CHANTED, STARING AT THE PHONE. "Come on. . . ."

Only minutes before, he'd gotten the call: Somewhere in the expanse of Heathrow airport MI-5 had lost Vorsalov. "Quite embarrassing, Charlie," the contact said, "but it seems we've mislaid your package."

"You what?"

"Not to worry, he'll turn up."

"Damn it, Roger, how—"

"Oh, he's slick, that one. Did a bit of dry cleaning in a lift. A quick turn to loose our close-in boys, then a slip out the back door of a gift shop. No worry. He won't get away again. . . ."

Latham checked his watch: ten minutes before Vorsa-lov's flight boarded.

The secure phone trilled. Latham grabbed it. "Latham here."

It was Roger. "You're back in the game, Charlie. He's smart and fast, your boy. Made it all the way to another concourse before we spotted him. He'd done a quick change in a bathroom: heel lift, doffed his coat, picked up a cap. He's first rate. Professional, I assume. Ivan?"

"Yes. Semiretired."

"It shows. Anyway, he's boarded a BA flight with a different passport. I'll fax the details straightaway."

"Where's he headed?"

"Montreal. He touches down in seven hours."

Somehow Latham had known Vorsalov wasn't going to make it easy. Rule 26 in the professional spy's handbook was: "Always assume you're under surveillance and behave accordingly. Change your route, change your destination, do whatever it takes to shake up the opposition."

Now they had seven hours to regroup, get the Canadians into the loop, and organize a net that would not only track Vorsalov but also hand him off at the border without so much as a hiccup.

"Apologies for the scare," said Roger. "Anything else we can do for you?"

"No. Thanks, Roger, I owe you." Latham hung up and turned to Stucky. "Art, you'd best get your boss down here. Paul, get on the horn to the RCMP in Quebec."

25

TANNER DOUSED THE RANGE ROVER'S HEADLIGHTS AND COASTED to a stop in the tree line. He and Cahil sat still, waiting for their eyes to adjust and listening to the jungle's symphony of squawks and buzzes.

"Gotta love the jungle," Cahil whispered, slapping a mosquito.

"Amen." Like the water, jungle was darkness; jungle was cover.

They got out, shouldered their rucksacks, and started down the trail. In a few minutes, they reached the outskirts of Mitsu's village. In the distance, a dog barked, then went silent. As if on cue, Mitsu appeared on the trail before them.

"You are late," he whispered, smiling.

Cahil mussed his hair. "You're early, scout."

"You have the boat?" Tanner asked.

"Yes. Come."

After a few hundred yards, the boy stopped at the crest of an embankment; through the foliage came the sound of gurgling water. Tanner's flashlight beam illuminated the nose of a skiff.

Mitsu said, "Shall I come with you?"

"No, wait here. We need you to hold the fort." Mitsu frowned, confused. "Keep this place safe while we're gone," Tanner added.

Mitsu smiled. "I will hold the fort."

"If anyone comes around, stay out of sight. I'll want a report when I get back."

Mitsu nodded solemnly and saluted.

Tanner half-expected company tonight. Earlier that afternoon, Cahil had returned to the dive shop to exchange a defective regulator. When he came out, one of Takagi's security trucks was sitting across the street. They followed him, but he was able to shake them on the way back to the hotel.

"So they know we've got dive gear," Tanner said.

"Sorry, bud. I screwed up."

"Forget it. It was bound to happen sooner or later."

"Now what?"

"Now it gets interesting. They'll probably assume we're going for the shipyard."

"Or Ohira's mystery X-mark off the village. If there's anything to it, that is."

The previous few days had dragged by as they waited for the weather to improve. It gave Briggs plenty of time to ponder the strange course DORSAL had taken.

Truth be told, he was surprised Mason had given them the week. Ohira's investigation appeared to be a tangent: a pair of mystery ships, one of which had skulked away into the night, "sold" to a company on whose board Takagi secretly sat; the other a floating fortress packed with advanced electronics gear. And what of the mysterious X-marks-the-spot chart with which Ohira had seemed obsessed? Was it all connected, and if so, how? Tanner couldn't shake the feeling there were larger, unseen forces at work.

He'd experienced the same sensation before and had come to trust it. In special ops this was called the k-check, or kinesthetic check. It was intuition, plain and simple, and he was a believer, not only because he'd seen it work but because he'd seen the effects of ignoring it.

With DORSAL, he felt as though invisible pieces of the puzzle were falling into place. He suspected Mason was withholding something. For Ohira to be working so far outside DORSAL's mission without their knowledge seemed impossible.

None of that mattered, he decided. He would see this through to the end. Unprofessional though it was, he felt his hatred for Hiromasa Takagi growing. Takagi had Ohira executed, tried to do the same to him, and was likely up to his neck in black-market arms dealing. Those things alone made him easy to loathe.

They loaded the skiff and began pushing their way through the mangrove roots. Above their heads, the canopy shook and squawked with night birds. Soon they heard the roar of waves and the jungle thinned. When the water reached their chest, they climbed aboard, and Cahil began rowing.

"Once more unto the breech," Bear murmured, working at the oars.

Cahil was, in Tanner's opinion, the most unlikely Shakespeare aficionado on earth. "We few, we happy few, we band of brothers," Briggs countered.

WITH CAHIL FOLLOWING HIS STEERING ORDERS, TANNER MATCHED fixes from Ohira's chart against landmarks onshore until he felt they were in position. He called a halt and tossed out the anchor. "We should be right on top."

"The question being, of what?" Cahil said, shrugging on his scuba tank.

WITH BRIGGS IN THE LEAD, THEY FOLLOWED THE ANCHOR ROPE TO the bottom.

Their flashlights cut narrow arcs through the black water. When Tanner's fingers finally touched the sand, his depth gauge read forty-two feet. To their right, lost in the darkness, lay the hundred-meter curve where the seabed dropped away into the depths. Divers called it the "deep black." He felt that familiar prickle of anticipation and fear.

Cahil stopped beside him. They inspected one another's gear, exchanged thumbs-up signs, hooked themselves to the twenty-foot buddy line, and started out.

THE CURRENT WAS NEGLIGIBLE SO THEY MOVED QUICKLY, SKIMMING over coral and rock formations teeming with fish. Here and

there crabs skittered over the sand. Momentarily caught in
Tanner's beam, a moray eel stared at them with its doll's
eyes, then snaked back into its cave.

They reached the end of the first 100-meter leg. Tanner
set himself and signaled Bear to make the swing north.

Now the terrain began to change. Open sand gave way
to low ridges blanketed with sea grass. Briggs felt an almost
immediate increase in the water temperature as well, then
remembered the same warm current from his previous dive.
It came from the oyster beds, Mitsu had said. They must
be close by.

He was skimming low over a ridge when he dropped his
flashlight. It bounced off a clump of coral and dropped into
a crevice. He signaled Cahil to stop and went after it.

Sea grass billowed over the opening, partially obscuring
the beam. He reached for it, fell short, and reached again.
Suddenly the rocks crumbled and he fell headfirst into the
hole. The edge of his mask struck a rock. Water gushed
into his eyes. He fell into the blackness.

The line went taut. He jerked to a stop. He swung free
for a moment, then cleared his mask, groped around, and
pulled himself to the ledge. He felt two rapid tugs on the
line: Cahil questioning. Tanner tugged back the *okay* signal.
The flashlight lay a few feet away. He retrieved it and
looked about.

This was no crevice, he realized, not even a cave in the
strict sense. The sea grass had formed a canopy over what
appeared to be a ravine. Rising above him, the rock lip
disappeared in a forest of sea grass.

He gave the line three short jerks, and a few seconds
later, Cahil dropped through the canopy and hovered beside
him. *What?* he mouthed.

Tanner pointed. Ahead, the ravine sloped into the darkness.

Cahil nodded, and they started forward.

THE DARKNESS ABSORBED ALL BUT A SLIVER OF LIGHT FROM THEIR
flashlights. Fish swirled around them and up along the ravine's walls.

A pillar of rock loomed in their path. Tanner played his beam over it, saw nothing unusual, and kept going. He stopped suddenly, backpedaled, and finned closer to the rock. Something was there, a dull glint in the stone. Using his knife, he chiseled at the rock until he'd cleared away a patch.

Heart pounding, he waved Cahil over and gestured for him to hover beside the rock. *What for?* Bear mouthed.

Scale. Just do it.

Tanner backpedaled and looked again. There was no mistake.

This was no rock. It was a propeller.

THEY HAD TRAVELED FIFTY FEET WHEN BRIGGS NOTICED THE WALLS widening. His depth gauge read seventy-six feet, thirty feet below the seabed proper. He checked his watch: thirteen minutes of air left. If they went much deeper, they would have to make a decompression stop.

Ahead, Cahil was shining his flashlight along the curve of the hull where it met the sand. However it had come to be here, the vessel's hull was tightly wedged in the ravine, with only a couple feet of clearance between it and the rock walls.

Cahil finned up along the hull and disappeared. Tanner followed. He found Cahil standing on a steel platform. He gestured with his flashlight: *Look!*

Tanner saw the three vertical, polelike structures behind him, but the shapes didn't register. He shrugged. *What?*

Cahil tapped two fingers on his face mask: *Look closely!*

Bear traced his light along the curve of the railing, then up the three poles. Now Briggs was seeing it. He backed up, looked again. Suddenly everything snapped into focus: the vessel's narrow beam, the cigar-shaped hull, the tapered screw blade . . .

Cahil was standing on the bridge of a submarine.

26

BRITISH AIRWAYS FLIGHT 9701 WAS FOUR MINUTES FROM TOUCH-down at Montreal's Mirabel International Airport.

We're ready, Latham told himself. They'd done everything they could. Still, the practical pessimist in his head was prattling away. *Something would go wrong.* No matter how exhaustive its design, some piece of the plan, whether significant, trivial, or something in between, would go awry. All they could do was to be ready.

"Agent Latham, we're patched into the RCMP command van at the airport. We'll hear exactly what they're hearing from the field units."

"About damned time," Art Stucky muttered, crushing out his cigarette.

"Put it on speaker," said Latham.

"All units, this is Command, the flight is on final approach," a voice from the RCMP command van said. "Radio check by section."

"Gate team in place."

"Concourse team in place."

"Mobile teams in place."

"Roger. Gate, you'll start us off; notify us as soon as the subject disembarks."

"Six teams?" Stucky asked Latham.

Latham nodded. "Three in the airport and three mobile. Almost forty Mounties in all, plus Mirabel Security. They'll have a dozen cameras on him."

"If this guy can give the slip to the Brits, he sure won't have any trouble—"

"All units, this is Gate, the subject is on the ground."

"Here we go," said Latham.

As Vorsalov stepped off the jet way, he was invisibly surrounded by a fluid cordon of RCMP watchers who shadowed him through Immigration and down to the baggage claim area. As the concourse team—which consisted of almost a dozen officers, none of which Vorsalov would see twice in his passage through the airport—took over, the radio reports became increasingly brief.

"Concourse Three, this is Two. Subject descending escalator east two."

"Got him."

Latham and the others studied a map of Mirabel Airport. "There he is," Latham said. "There are three more levels below this one: the taxi stand, garage, and car rental desks."

They didn't know whether Vorsalov had any baggage to claim; in the commotion at Heathrow, MI-5 had missed that detail. He had several transportation options available, all of them problematic; whichever he chose, the RCMP would have to scramble to catch up before he escaped the airport grounds.

"Command, this is Concourse Two. Subject is off the escalator. Stand by." There were thirty seconds of silence. "Command, he's got baggage . . . single piece, a brown suitcase. . . . East escalator now, descending. Concourse Four, he's yours."

"Roger, got him."

Two minutes passed.

"Come on," Stucky muttered. "Where is he?"

"Wait," said Latham.

"Command, Four. Subject is descending again. Five, he's coming your way."

Going for a taxi, Latham thought.

Sixty seconds of silence. Heart thudding, Latham stared at the speaker.

"Five, this is Command. Report."

"Stand by. . . . I think we've lost him. . . ."

"God*damn it!*" Stucky roared.

"Shut up, Art,"

"I knew it! Shit, I knew—"

"Command this is Five, he's done a U-turn. . . . Going back up the escalator. Four, have you got him?"

"We see him." Long pause. "Command, subject is at Avis counter."

"Understood. Mobile Units converge. Subject is on rental car level."

Latham turned to Randal. "Paul, have the Mounties fax us his rental receipt. I want to see that credit card."

VORSALOV DROVE HIS RENTED LUMINA DIRECTLY TO THE RAMADA Inn Parc Olympique. To the surprise of the Mounties, he made no U-turns or quick backs. In fact, his driving was so sedate the mobile units had to adjust their pace to avoid overtaking one another. Vorsalov pulled under the hotel's awning, tipped the valet, and walked into the lobby.

"All units, Command. Subject is inside. All units take secondary positions."

Randal walked into the conference room and handed the fax to Latham.

"What is it?" said Stucky.

"He's still traveling under the Karnovsky alias."

"So?"

"If he was going to switch, Mirabel was the perfect place; he could've hit the ground clean."

"That's good for us."

"His paper trail is too long. It's out of character for him."

"What the hell does that mean?"

Latham shook his head. "I don't know."

Montreal

IN ADDITION TO BEING THE YOUNGEST MEMBER OF THE SURVEIL-lance team, Corporal Jean-Paul Lemond was a walking recruiting poster for the Royal Canadian Mounted Police. Clean-shaven and lantern-jawed, he stood six foot three inches and had a face that seemed both stern and boyish. He also had an uncanny eye for detail.

Lemond could look at a picture of a suspect at age eight

and pick him from a lineup as a middle-aged man; from a crowd of hundreds he could single out a blond-haired, clean-shaven man who had once been a black-haired, bearded felon. On one occasion he even fingered a Quebec Separatist who had undergone extensive cosmetic surgery. The giveaway, Lemond later explained, had been his ear-lobes.

Had anyone told Lemond this unusual talent would save the Vorsalov operation from disaster and make the day of an FBI agent he'd never met, he would have laughed at them.

Ten minutes after Vorsalov entered the lobby, Lemond walked into the hotel's parking garage and jogged up the ramp until he came to the valet section. A red-coated attendant walked by. Lemond stopped him and flashed his badge. "The green Lumina that just came in. Where is it parked?"

"Uh . . . over there, by the red Puegot."

"Anyone else on this level?"

"No."

"The stairwell and elevator are the only ways up here?"

"Yeah."

"I want you to wait by the elevator. If anyone comes up, make some noise. I need to inspect this car. Can you do that?"

"Uh, sure, I guess so."

It took Lemond only a minute to slip inside the Lumina, search it, and plant the transmitter under the bumper. He gave the valet a wave and started back down the ramp.

Suddenly, from below, he heard a door slam shut. He waited for the wail of an exit alarm, but none came. He stopped, listened. Rapid footsteps echoed on concrete. Lemond walked to the railing just in time to see a figure exit the ramp and turn onto the sidewalk. He got only a glimpse of a black fedora and a khaki trench coat before the figure disappeared beneath an elm, but it was enough. Something in the figure's stride, the tilt of his head as he turned to look for coming traffic . . .

He pulled out his radio and started running. "Command, this is Lemond. . . ."

AS THE SURVEILLANCE COMMANDER WAS SCRAMBLING TO RESPOND to Lemond's report, Lemond himself was jogging up to the corner Vorsalov had just turned. "Command, subject just passed Sherbrook and Ontario."

"Roger, stand by, hold position."

Lemond peeked around the corner. A block away, a La Salle taxi swerved to the curb beside Vorsalov. "Command, I need instructions. We're going to loose him."

"Stand by. . . ."

Lemond hesitated. *No time, no time . . .* He holstered his radio. The problem with a surveillance net this big was it took time to adjust. And the problem with following a subject without backup was he could find himself in trouble very fast. He'd read the KGB man's file; better to not be caught alone with him.

He took a deep breath, then turned the corner at a stroll. Ahead, the taxi was pulling away from the curb. Lemond waited until it turned the corner, spun, and raised his hand for a cab. "Command, subject is in a La Salle, number 4201, heading south on Iberville. I am following."

"Negative, negative, wait for backup."

"Negative, Command, he'll be gone by then. I'll contact you." He climbed inside and flashed his badge to the driver, a turbaned Pakastani. "Did you see that La Salle that just turned the corner?"

"Yes."

"Follow it."

"Certainly you are not serious, Officer?"

"Certainly I am. Move!"

HOWEVER TENUOUS THE CABBIE'S GRASP OF ENGLISH, HE WAS A good driver. They had closed to within fifty meters of the La Salle. "What's your name?" Lemond asked.

"Punjab."

"Stay with him, Punjab."

"Certainly I will, Officer."

Ahead, the La Salle took a sharp left.

"He's turning!"

"Indeed he is," Punjab replied, going straight ahead.

"Follow him!"

"Oh no, he will be coming out ahead of us. Three blocks, you will see."

"How do you know?"

"I am a taxi driver for twelve years now. They can only go east from there. All one-way streets, you see. Also, I know that driver. Only airport runs for Henri. The hotel district to Dorval Airport only. You will see."

"I hope you're right."

True to Punjab's prediction, the La Salle appeared ahead of them and turned back onto Iberville. Through the La-Salle's rear window Lemond could see a black fedora.

"There is Henri," Punjab said. "Dorval Airport, you see."

Lemond noticed a black duffel bag lying on the front seat. "Is that yours?"

"Yes."

"What's it for?"

"Athletic attire. I play squash."

"May I borrow it?"

"My bag? It contains my lucky racket. Why must you have it?"

"Police business."

Punjab grinned. "Oh, I see. Yes, very good."

"Thanks. Give me one of those airport maps, too."

Why Dorval? Lemond thought. Dorval handled only domestic flights.

TWENTY MINUTES LATER, THEY PULLED UNDER THE TERMINAL'S awning. Ahead of them, the La Salle pulled away from the curb. Vorsalov was gone.

With Punjab's bag in one hand and the airport map in the other, Lemond climbed from the cab. "I'll contact you about your bag."

"Before tonight, I am hoping," said Punjab "You see, it contains my—"

"Your lucky racket, I know. Thanks."

Lemond made a show of studying the map as he walked down the sidewalk. He spotted a security guard. "Excuse me, can you help me?"

"Certainly, sir."

"RCMP," Lemond whispered, unfolding the map to reveal his badge. "Take me to the security office immediately."

AS LATHAM WAS GETTING THE BAD NEWS AND THE MOUNTIES were converging on Dorval, Lemond was standing before a bank of camera monitors. *Where are you?* These next few minutes might well decide his future with the RCMP—and whether he had one at all. He could imagine the charges: disobeying orders, misappropriating civilian property, endangering the welfare of the public.

Where in the hell is the man?

"You can thank terrorism," said the security director.

"What?"

"Up until five years ago, we only had three cameras in the whole terminal. Terrorists have the government scared of its own shadow, so here we are . . . more cameras, more guards, more everything."

"What have you told your people, Mr. Director?"

"To look for a man matching your description but not to interfere with him. The gate attendants and the security guards are watching for him."

"Good. When is the next flight due to leave?"

The director consulted a sheet. "Five minutes, gate seven. That screen, there."

"We can transfer images to that big screen, also," said the operator.

"And we can see all of the gates?" Lemond asked.

"Plus the waiting areas."

"Put gate seven on the big monitor, please." Lemond

leaned closer, studying the gate's waiting area. "Can you pan?"

"Sure," said the operator.

The camera scanned the lounge from corner to corner, but Lemond saw no sign of the Russian. "How many guards are assigned to that area?"

"Two," replied the director.

"Have them walk through. And for God's sake, if they see him, tell them to stay clear."

As the director relayed the orders via radio, Lemond studied the other cameras. Twelve gates, twelve waiting areas . . . lots of territory. "Wait! Gate ten."

"You see him?" asked the director.

Lemond peered closer, shook his head. "No, the height is wrong."

Gate seven announced its final boarding. The attendants began closing the jet way doors.

"Well, so much for that one," said the security director. "Next we've got two flights leaving at the same time. Gates one and four. Bring them up, Jorge."

As the operator reached for the switch, Lemond saw a flash of movement at the corner of the monitor. "Hold it! Pull back and pan right."

"What is it?" asked the security director.

The camera moved just quickly enough. On the monitor, a trench coat–clad figure handed his boarding pass to the attendant and slipped through the door.

Lemond grinned. "That's him," he said. "That's him! Where's he going?"

The director consulted the schedule. "Yarmouth, Nova Scotia."

27

SEEING THE WRECK WITH FRESH EYES, TANNER RECOGNIZED IT IM-
mediately as a World War II U.S. fleet submarine. A dozen
questions filled his mind, chief among them: What was it
doing here, less than 400 yards off the mainland?

Tanner finned up to join Cahil on the bridge. Both periscopes were snapped off at their midpoint, but the masts
for the surface- and air-search radars were intact. Below
them, the foredeck sloped into the darkness, casting everything forward of the escape trunk in shadows. *Had the trunk
been used?* Briggs wondered. *Had there been any survivors
left alive to use it?* There was only one way to find out, he
knew, but the trick would be getting inside. With a nod
from Bear, he finned over the rail.

Beneath the bridge they found a gash in the hull. Tanner
tried to recall what he knew about a fleet sub's layout. As
a child he'd been fascinated by submarines and spent many
hours poring over artists' diagrams. They had to be somewhere near the forward battery compartment, he decided.

Working together, he and Bear dug through the rubble
until the gash was wide enough to accommodate them. Tanner shined his flashlight inside. The beam revealed nothing
but darkness and swirling silt. His heart was pounding. He
forced himself to take a deep breath. It was likely that no
human had seen the inside of the submarine for better than
fifty years. How many of the crew were still trapped inside?
He looked at Bear's face and his own emotions reflected
there: anticipation and fear.

He checked his watch, then signaled, *Ten minutes left.*
Bear nodded.

Tanner turned sideways, wriggled through the hole, then waited for Cahil to join him. They were in the main pump room, Tanner realized, looking around. Above them would be the control room, diving station, and conning tower.

They swam aft through the hatch to the fresh water tank, into the radio room, then through to the galley and crew's mess. Pots and pans littered the deck and flotsam swirled in their flashlight beams. A cabinet door wafted open and shut with a muffled banging sound. Tanner found an escape trunk hatch, rubbed the grime from the porthole, and peered inside; it was flooded. *From damage or use?*

They swam aft into the crew's quarters. The bunks were empty, mattresses long ago rotted to pulp that billowed with their passage. There were no skeletal remains, which surprised Tanner. Had all of the crew gotten out? He hoped so. The only other option was grim: The boat had sunk so quickly that everyone had died at their battle stations.

The door to the washroom stood open, revealing a toilet fuzzy with algae. Tanner saw a light wink at him from the darkness, and his heart skipped. It was his own reflection in the bathroom mirror.

They continued into the forward engine room, found it empty, and continued into the after engine room. On either side of the catwalk lay the boat's two Fairbanks-Morse 1600-horsepower engines. They were in the heart of the sub now, and this is where Tanner hoped they might find a clue to its identity.

With Cahil's help, he pried open the catwalk hatch, slipped feetfirst past the barrel-like generator, and rolled over onto his belly. On elbows and knees, air tank banging on the catwalk above, he wriggled forward, shining his flashlight along the engine casing. Silt swirled in the light beam. He could feel the press of tons of steel hanging over him; he forced it from his mind.

There! Stamped in the engine casing were a series of numbers. He rubbed away some of the algae and peered closer. 5-4-7-9-1-1-2-3-6. He committed the serial number to memory, then wriggled backward and let Cahil pull him back up.

Well? Bear mouthed.

Tanner gave him a thumbs-up, then checked his watch: four minutes of air left. With their reserves, they had just enough time to explore the rest of the boat.

THEY FOUND THE FIRST SKELETON IN THE OFFICER'S WARDROOM.

It lay faceup on the deck, both arms crossed over the chest cavity. Nearby lay a cap, dissolved save the plastic brim and a badly corroded steel emblem. It was an officer's insignia: a lieutenant junior grade. Tanner shined his light over the skull and caught a glint of something inside the eye socket. Using his hand, he fanned away the silt and looked closer.

In the center of the forehead was a perfectly round hole. Gently, Tanner turned the skull until he found a matching hole at the back, this one larger and more jagged. Out of it dropped a lump of metal. He picked it up. It was badly corroded and partially squashed but unmistakably a bullet.

SWIMMING THROUGH THE AFTER TORPEDO, THEY FOUND THEIR SEC-ond skeleton. Here also was the cause of the sub's demise. The skeleton lay at the edge of a gaping shell hole in the deck, which began above their heads, arced through the compartment, and exited below their feet. Tanner shined his light up through the hole and could see the rocky edges of the rift. Amazing the torpedoes hadn't detonated, he thought, running a hand over the blunt nose of one of them. The shell had probably been a dud. If not, the bow would have been blown off.

He turned back to the skeleton. It lay sprawled beside the torpedo rack, one wrist chained to a stanchion, the other to a rotted leather briefcase. Gently, Tanner opened the case's lid. Inside was a manila folder and a small automatic pistol, a .25 caliber Beretta. As he touched the folder, it dissolved into a cloud of pulp. He slipped the gun into his rucksack.

Cahil tapped him on the shoulder. He pointed at the skel-

eton's lower legs. Half covered in silt were a pair of stainless steel braces, the leather straps still encircling both tibias
at the knee and ankle. These, too, Tanner slipped into the
rucksack.

Cahil tapped his watch.

Tanner nodded and pushed off the deck into the shell
hole. Bear followed. Once on the foredeck, Tanner finned
toward the canopy of sea grass. He cast a glance over his
shoulder. Bear was gone. He could see a flashlight beam
moving inside the shell hole. He swam back.

Cahil gestured him closer, then pointed to the edges of
the hole.

They were smooth and freshly blackened by a blowtorch.

WHEN THEY GOT BACK TO THE THE RANGE ROVER, MITSU WAS
waiting.

"Did we have any company?" Tanner asked.

"No."

Tanner squeezed his shoulder. "Thanks, scout. You did
good. Run on home."

Mitsu ran off into the darkness.

As Tanner started the engine, Cahil said, "So tell me:
Aside from the obvious, what the hell did we just find down
there?"

It was a good question. Tanner had felt certain Ohira's
markings on the chart had meant something, but now he
wasn't so sure. What did they have, really? A sunken
World War II submarine, and a dead man's insinuation that
a nonexistent Takagi salvage ship had been lurking in the
same area.

"I don't know, Bear," Tanner replied. "I don't know."

BACK AT THE HOTEL, TANNER STOPPED AT THE FRONT DESK FOR
messages. "Yes, sir," the receptionist said. "One. From a
woman. She did not leave her name."

Tanner read: "Must postpone our date; called to office
for urgent meeting."

Inexplicably, Tanner felt a chill. How unusual was it for Sumiko to get a late-night summons to Takagi headquarters?

"What is it?" Cahil asked.

"Maybe nothing."

Briggs walked into the deserted Tiki Lounge, flipped open his cell phone, and dialed Sumiko's office number. He let it ring a dozen times and was about to hang up when the line clicked open.

"Hello?" Tanner said in Japanese.

Silence. Breathing in the mouthpiece.

"Hello?"

The line clicked dead.

HIS NEXT CALL WENT TO INSPECTOR IEYASU. HE EXPLAINED AN acquaintance of his might be missing. They'd already checked her apartment and could get no information from the Takagi corporate office. As Tanner expected, Ieyasu only half bought the story but immediately agreed to look into it. He knew several officers in the prefect. He would have them drive by Takagi Headquarters.

IEYASU CALLED BACK AN HOUR LATER. "NOBORU AND HIS SECURITY people were already there in force," he said. "They tried to bar the police from entering, but they finally gave in."

"And?"

"This friend of yours was a woman?"

"Yes."

"What is her name?"

"Sumiko Fujita."

"I'm sorry, Briggs. I'm so sorry. She was found dead in the parking lot."

28

Bar Harbor, Maine

UPON HEARING OF LEMOND'S IMPROMPTU TAILING OF VORSALOV, Latham promised to buy the Mountie a steak dinner. Upon further hearing Lemond had requested the Yarmouth constabulary canvass Nova Scotia's only two departure points to the U.S. (the local airport and a ferry terminal) for any sign of the Russian, he upped the ante to a case of scotch. As it turned out, their luck was holding: Vorsalov had chosen the ferry.

Now, almost eight hours after Vorsalov had left Montreal, and with just an hour to spare, Latham and his thirty-agent team had arrived in this quaint town of 5,000 people and, with the help of the local police, quietly hijacked the marina area.

Latham sat inside his command van, watching the ferry terminal and listening to the radio chatter as the agents got into position. Through his binoculars he could see the *Bluenose* ferry edging past the breakwater. Beside him, Randal was donning his customs uniform. "Ready?" Latham asked.

"Ready."

THE CHURNING IN YURI VORSALOV'S STOMACH HAD WORSENED with each passing mile and now, as the ferry's bow slipped past the breakwater and into the harbor, he began to sweat. A gust of cold wind whipped across the deck and cooled his face.

How had this happened? he asked himself. What was he doing back here?

It was simple, of course. It was the lesser of three evils.

Either come here and salvage this operation for the Arabs, live the rest of his life in a cave, or die.

Since going freelance Vorsalov had found it relatively easy to stay hidden in the underworlds of the Mideast, Africa, and the Mediterranean, but if he failed here, he would find himself persona non grata in those areas as well. That was, of course, providing he managed to stay alive at all.

Like it or not, this was his best course. Besides, how many times had he beaten the Americans at this game? He'd done it before and would do so again. He allowed himself a smile. He would be done and gone before they realized he was here.

LATHAM KEPT HIS EYES FIXED ON THE TWO IMMIGRATION CHECK-points, each a small whitewashed shack through which the ferry's passengers were funneled. He scanned each passenger's face, then moved to the next. "Come on, where are you?"

There!

The Russian had aged, but there was no mistaking him. His hair had thinned, his face was more worn, but the eyes were the same flat, cold blue.

Latham keyed his radio. "Paul, I've got him: Gray trench, black garment bag."

"Roger."

On the dock, Randal began strolling that way. At the head of the quay, a second agent, Jim Stephans, moved to join him.

VORSALOV STEPPED FORWARD IN LINE. THIS WAS THE TIME HE hated most. Getting past customs was virtually the last hurdle. Movie portrayals aside, most spies are not captured in a wild shoot-out or car chase but rather as they enter a target country. If it was going to happen, now would be the time. But from where? Where would they—

From the corner of his eye he glimpsed a customs agent turn in his direction. Alarms went off in Vorsalov's head.

He scanned the crowds, searching for telltale signs of surveillance: shielded radios, averted eyes, movements out of sync with the crowds. If this was a trap, other agents would be converging.

Across the quay, the customs agent kept coming.

Vorsalov clutched his bag tighter.

LATHAM SAW VORSALOV'S BODY LANGUAGE CHANGE. "JIM, BREAK off," he called. "He's eyeballing you."

On the quay, Stephans stopped, consulted his clipboard, then turned toward the other shack. Latham watched Vorsalov. After a full minute, the Russian's posture eased, and he picked up his bag and stepped forward.

Latham exhaled. "All units, ease up. Our boy's on a hair trigger."

AS VORSALOV CLEARED CUSTOMS AND WALKED INTO THE TOURIST center, the FBI watchers began their ballet. What happened in these next few minutes would decide a lot. As at Mirabel, Vorsalov had several transportation choices—taxi, shuttle bus, or rental car—all of which would require adjustments on their part.

"Command, subject is inside," radioed Pearson, the agent in the tourist center.

Three minutes passed. Everything now hinged on the single word from Pearson. It came a minute later: "Command, Pearson. Rental."

Thank God, Latham thought.

This was a break for which they'd been hoping. Doubting the Russian planned on staying in Bar Harbor, they'd posted an agent at the terminal's only rental car desk.

"Command, subject is heading for the parking lot."

Latham turned his binoculars to the hedge-lined rental lot and picked out the blue Ford Taurus. He froze. On the ground below the bumper was a square black box.

"Paul, where are you?"

"The east lot."

"The transmitter has—" Latham broke off. Vorsalov was exiting the tourist center and starting toward the Taurus. "The transmitter's dropped off, Paul. Stand by. Command to Pearson."

"Go ahead."

"Catch the subject, stall him!"

"Roger."

"Paul, get moving—"

"On my way."

Latham kept his attention divided between Vorsalov, who was being hailed from behind by Pearson, and the Taurus. Behind it, crawling through the hedges, came Paul Randal. Pearson was offering Vorsalov a brochure. Latham changed channels on his radio so he could listen.

". . . I'm sorry, sir, I'm sort of new at this. I forgot to offer you supplemental insurance on your vehicle—"

"I'm not interested," Vorsalov replied. "I must go now."

"One more thing, sir."

Vorsalov turned back. "What?"

"The state of Maine requires all drivers be insured, so if you'll just sign here. . . ."

"What is this?"

"A waiver, sir, stating that . . ."

Latham switched channels. "Talk to me, Paul."

"It's back on."

Latham looked through the binoculars: Vorsalov was walking toward the car.

Latham exhaled and got on the radio. "Mobile units, get rolling."

ASIDE FROM TWO STOPS FOR FUEL, ONE MEAL BREAK AT A MC-Donald's in Boston, and several U-turns, which Latham and his team assumed were routine attempts at countersurveillance, Vorsalov had been driving steadily south for nine hours. They were approaching Philadelphia. The transmitter, which had a range of fifteen miles, was working flawlessly. Latham could hear its steady beep through the van's speakers.

The mobile teams—comprised of twelve cars and a helicopter disguised with changeable hospital and charter service markings—were working in four-hour shifts. The armada ranged from minivans to beat-up VW bugs. The agents were disguised as yuppie couples complete with Baby on Board stickers; gray-haired spinsters in Buicks; and even a bearded agent on a Harley.

It was a painstaking process, but it was paying off. The Russian was giving no indication he was aware of the surveillance. Even if he were, it would do him little good, Latham felt. His team was first rate, the majority of them having cut their teeth chasing dedicated KGB and GRU agents during the Cold War. More importantly, he'd been up against Vorsalov before. He knew the man's methods . . . he hoped.

"Almost two A.M.," Paul Randal said. "You think he'd stop to sleep."

"Old habits," Latham replied.

The van's speaker's came to life. "Command, this is Mobile Lead."

"Go ahead."

"Subject's pulling into the Days Inn on Island Avenue."

Randall consulted the map. "Right by the airport, Charlie."

Latham nodded. "Lead, once he's settled in, let's put a tight lid on him. We've got an airport close by,"

"Roger."

"Paul, you got your wish. Get some sleep."

"Okay." Randal yawned. "I guess you know we're running out of cities."

Latham nodded. "Yep."

The farther south Vorsalov drove, the stronger Charlie's hunch grew. They'd passed Boston and New York. Washington was looming. Vorsalov could be headed anywhere, but he couldn't shake his gut feeling.

Same city, same players. But what were the stakes this time?

29

Japan

TANNER'S REPORT OF SUMIKO'S DEATH GOT AN IMMEDIATE REAC-
tion from Dick Mason, who ordered them out. "We've done
all we can, Briggs," Dutcher told them. "Come on home."

He and Cahil had anticipated the order and agreed to
withhold their discovery of the submarine. The more they
discussed it, the more they doubted its significance; men-
tioning it would be the proverbial last straw. As it turned
out, Sumiko's murder fulfilled that role itself.

According to Ieyasu, the police were calling her death a
robbery gone bad. Her empty purse had been found a few
blocks from the Takagi headquarters. The coroner's report
was expected to support what Ieyasu's contacts reported:
Sumiko's throat had been slit. So severe was the wound
that her larynx had been severed, as had the carotid artery
and jugular vein. It wasn't the signature of a strong-arm
robber, Tanner thought. Cutting a throat is neither easy nor
clean. She'd either been ambushed from behind or been
subdued while the attacker worked on her.

The police, led by none other than Inspector Tanaka,
were not able to explain how the alleged assailants eluded
Takagi's security force or why a mugger would go to such
lengths when easier targets were walking the streets of
Kobe. Not that it mattered; Tanner knew who was responsible.

This felt more personal than ever. He'd gotten Sumiko
killed. He was in dangerous water, he knew, but he refused
to quit until Takagi and Noboru answered for what they
had done. First, however, he had to deal with Mason's order.

"Leland, I don't—"

"I know you don't, Briggs. But look at this from his perspective," Dutcher said. "He's got one dead agent, a dead stringer he was sleeping with, another missing from the shipyard, and a gutted network. This is the CIA's show. It's their call."

"What about Sumiko's last delivery? From the looks of it, Takagi has his hands in dozens more conglomerates, including several in the Mideast."

"It'll be analyzed. Listen: Don't let this get personal. This is what we get paid for. We go in, we do the job, we get out. Unless you've got some angle we haven't considered, we're done."

Tanner recognized his boss's tone of voice: You don't have to like it, but accept it and move on. . . . *Unless you've got some angle we haven't considered.* But there would be a proviso: They would have to produce results, and quickly. Dutcher could run interference for them for a few days at most.

"The salvage ship," Tanner replied. "She doesn't exist on paper; a Takagi engineer who worked on her is gone; and until she skulked out of port, she was hidden away next to a ship that was more destroyer than freighter. If that doesn't interest Mason, okay, but what's to stop us from checking it out?"

"Better question is, why bother?" Dutcher asked.

"Why sell her to a company on whose board you hold a secret majority? Why murder a man because he's nosing around her? It stinks, Leland, from top to bottom, and I want to know why."

"This sounds a lot like a pitch I got from Walt last week."

"Oh?"

"You have any idea what you're asking for? Do you know what it takes to retask a satellite for that kind of search?"

"As a matter of fact, I do. But I doubt there'd be much retasking involved."

"Explain."

"The Russians are scrapping some of their boomers at Pavek. I'm sure we've got some eyes on them."

"And the Eastern Siberian Sea is right next door."

"Worst case, we get some side-lobe images. It's a place to start."

Dutcher was silent for a few moments. "Okay, you two sit tight and stay low. I'll turn Walter loose on *Toshogu*."

National Photographic Interpretation Center, Washington, D.C.

OAKEN SETTLED INTO ONE OF THE THEATER-STYLE SEATS AND opened his notepad. Aside from him and the AV technician sitting at the control podium near the back, the theater was deserted. Oaken rolled down his sleeves against the chill.

"What's your name, by the way?" he called over his shoulder.

"Skip, sir."

"Why the deep freeze in here, Skip?"

"Computers. We've got a couple Crays running for image enhancement. Okay, sir, where to?"

Good question, Oaken thought. Finding a ship of *Toshogu*'s dimensions in the expanse of the Arctic Ocean was a daunting task.

The real work had started back at Holystone as he first checked with the Coast Guard for sightings that might correspond to *Toshogu*. He was amazed at the number of distress reports they had on file. As cold and forbidding as the Arctic Ocean was, it saw a brisk traffic, and in any given month a good 10 percent of them radioed Guard stations for help.

Oaken knew the Arctic Ocean held a special place in the nightmares of seamen since the first keel was laid centuries ago. Once submerged in those waters, the average human life expectancy was less than ten minutes, the last six of them spent unconscious as the body's systems were overwhelmed by the numbing cold.

No thanks, Oaken decided. If he wanted that kind of adventure, he'd watch The Discovery Channel.

It had taken him half the night to sort through the list provided by the Coast Guard and determine none of the sightings matched *Toshogu*. That left two possibilities: Either she hadn't been spotted, or she had taken an altogether different route to her destination.

"What have you got watching the Arctic?" Oaken asked.

"Two satellites. A Keyhole over the Kamchatka Peninsula watching Ivan dismantle some SLBMs, and a commercial LandSat bird doing topography for Exxon in the Chukchi Sea."

"A LandSat? How'd we get access to that?"

"Don't ask."

"Oh. Okay, let's see what the Keyhole's got." Based on *Toshogu*'s cruising speed and the weather conditions, Oaken recited the general coordinates where he felt she might be found. "Let's start there."

Five seconds later, the screen was filled with a black-and-white image of the eastern shore of Siberia and a portion of the Arctic Ocean. Oaken watched, fascinated, as the image moved ever so slowly as the Keyhole orbited the earth.

"This is real time," said Skip. "Given the area and time frame, this is about as good as it's going to get."

"Okay. Can you freeze it and put a grid on it?"

"Sure." Skip typed a command, and a moment later the computer superimposed an alphanumeric grid over the image. "Just call out the coordinates. The Cray will do the rest."

For the next two hours, they checked each and every square of ocean. They found forty-three possible targets, twenty-two of which the computer decided were icebergs. That left twenty-one. After another hour, Oaken determined none of them matched *Toshogu*.

"How close are the computer's size estimates?" asked Oaken.

"Give or take a meter, I guess. What now, sir?"

"Let's see the LandSat."

"Thermal or standard?"

"Standard."

The LandSat images showed more of the Chukchi, Siberian, and Alaskan peninsulas. As with the Keyhole image, there were dozens of shiplike dots on the ocean's surface. Of these, eighteen turned out to be ships, but after two more hours, the Cray eliminated all of them as possible matches.

Where is she? Oaken wondered. Given her speed, range, and the prevailing weather conditions, she could have only gone so far. "Well, we might as well take a look at the LandSat's thermal pics," Oaken said.

"I wouldn't recommend it, sir. It's like watching grass grow. The computer's got to convert the digital pixels into the visible spectrum. Looking at them now would be like trying to make sense of a bad Jackson Pollack painting."

"How long?"

"Five, six hours. Leave me your number. I'll call you when they're ready."

TRUE TO HIS WORD, SKIP CALLED THE MOMENT THE COMPUTERS finished. Oaken got dressed, whispered an explanation to Bev, and drove to the NPIC.

It was even colder than before in the amphitheater. "AC still works, I see."

Skip laughed. "Yep."

"Don't you have a home? I hate to think there's a wife out there cursing me."

"She's the understanding type. Take a look. I think you're going to like this."

An image appeared on the screen. The background was uniformly black but was speckled with dozens of white, blue, and red dots.

"Each of the dots represents a surface anomaly . . . icebergs, ships, whatever," said Skip. "While you were on your way over, I matched this plate against the Keyhole pics and eliminated ships we'd already checked. This is what I got."

One by one, the computer began erasing dots until all that remained were a dozen white blobs and one tiny blue dot.

"The white ones are icebergs," Skip said. "The blue one is—"

"A ship," Oaken finished.

"You got it. Same dimensions as our target, too. Its temperature signature is just a couple degrees above the bergs. That's why we missed it on the Keyhole pictures."

"I'll be damned. Her decks must be iced over, the engines shut down."

"That's my guess. At that latitude, if you haven't got crews working constantly, you can get some serious buildup real quick."

"So how do we know it's the one we're looking for?"

"I backtracked her using the six previous hours of LandSat shots. Up until hour four—when she started drifting—her course matched the one you gave me."

"Skip, you're a miracle worker. Bring up the rest of the shots."

"That's the problem. This is the last one. The LandSat's out of angle now."

Oaken stared at the blue dot. "How old is this image?"

"Nine hours."

"Damn," Oaken muttered. "Plenty of time for her to capsize under all that ice."

30

Point Hope, Alaska

NINE HOURS AFTER LEAVING JAPAN, TANNER AND CAHIL WERE nearing their destination.

Tired, sore, and anxious to be away from the constant hum of the Cessna's engines, Tanner stared out the window at the barren shoreline jutting into the Chukchi Sea. They were 130 miles north of the Arctic Circle and 150 miles from mainland Russia. The water was a startling royal blue. In another month it would be a solid sheet of ice; already the surface looked slushy. Briggs could almost feel the cold in his bones.

"Reminds me of home," Cahil shouted over the engines. Bear was a born-and-raised Monhegan Island fisherman.

"Glad you like it. Say, what's the temp on the ground?"

"Midtwenties," replied the pilot. "With windchill, five or ten degrees."

Tanner grunted. "This is the last time I let Oaks plan my vacations."

It had taken Oaken only a few hours to compute the wind and sea currents around *Toshogu*'s last known position and come up with a target area that stretched between Point Hope and Cape Lisbourne—almost 100 miles of desolate coastline.

Oaken said the Coast Guard had reported no distress calls from the area, which seemed to suggest *Toshogu* had not been in peril. So why had the crew allowed such a dangerous buildup of ice on the decks? Tanner wondered. One thing was certain: Rare was the disaster that could sink a ship so fast she couldn't send a distress signal.

"Hold tight," the pilot called. "We're going in."

They lined up over Point Hope's single runway and touched down in a cross wind that whistled through the cabin and rattled the windows. They taxied toward a small Quonset hut. Hanging above its door a sign read, Point Hope International Airport—Hub to Nowhere.

"Enjoy, gentlemen," the pilot said.

"Thanks." Tanner said.

They climbed out amid swirling snow. The cold ripped the air from Tanner's lungs. In all directions, all he could see was white. He slipped on his sunglasses.

"Hear that?" Cahil called.

"What?"

Cahil walked a quick circle. His boots crunched in the snow. "That. That's how you know when it's really cold."

"Thanks, Bear, that's handy information."

The door of the hut cracked open, and an arm jutted out, waving them over.

Inside they found a bar, several pinball machines, and a short-order kitchen. The bartender/cook, who sat on a stool watching *Wheel of Fortune*, never looked up as they entered. The person attached to the waving arm was a bearded man in granny glasses. "Simon Braithwaite. Been expecting you."

Tanner made the introductions. "How much did Walt tell you?"

"No more than I need to know. Come on, I've got somebody I want you to meet. I did some digging around."

TIGARA TIM'S BAR WAS A SQUAT LOG BUILDING SITTING AT THE head of Point Hope's docks. Through the swirling snow Tanner saw several fishing boats rocking at their moorings, and he caught the scent of tar and sea salt.

The bar was warm and dimly lit. Like a bad Western movie, all activity froze when they walked in. They followed Braithwaite to a corner booth. Several dozen eyes tracked them.

"I take it you don't get many visitors," Tanner said.

"Not many aside from the occasional cargo barge from

Seattle. We're early. They should be here in a bit."

"Who?" Cahil asked.

"Shageluk. He and his two sons fish the coast. They're Inupiaqs . . . Eskimos. They ran into something yesterday that might interest you."

"Any luck with transportation?" Tanner asked.

"I think so. Can either of you fly?"

Tanner nodded. "I'd feel better if the weather lifted, though."

"I'll check the forecast. Here they are."

Shageluk, dressed in jeans and a yellow anorak, nodded at Braithwaite then said something to his two sons, who took a table across the room. Simon slid over to make room for Shageluk, who sat down and nodded to Tanner and Cahil.

"You're looking for a ship," Shageluk said.

"That's right."

"Simon says you can be trusted. No one can know we talked."

Tanner looked at Braithwaite. "What are we missing here?"

"There are only five registered fishing boats in Point Hope. If you don't register, you don't fish. Problem is, the fees run almost a quarter of an outfit's annual net. Shageluk doesn't have a permit, but he's got a family to feed."

"I understand," Tanner said, then to Shageluk, "You have our word."

Shageluk looked at Braithwaite, who nodded. Shageluk shrugged. "It was yesterday morning, about forty miles north of here. The fog was bad, and my radar was not working so good. We almost ran into her, she was so close. We saw her through the fog for a few minutes before we turned away."

Tanner pulled a map from his pocket and spread it on the table. "Show me."

Shageluk pointed. "Here."

"How big was she?"

"About four hundred feet, wide in the beam."

"Was she under way? Any sign of life?"

"I don't think so. We didn't want to be seen, though; we turned away quickly."

"Running lights?" asked Tanner

"No. And no distress lights. We listened on the radio also. Nothing."

For the next few hours, Shageluk explained, they kept getting sporadic radar contact on the ship, which seemed to be drifting toward the coast. Then, as they turned and headed for home, they saw her once more, this time ten miles from shore.

He pointed to the spot on the map about thirty-five miles north of Point Hope. "There. Very close to the coast."

"You said this was yesterday. What time exactly?" Tanner asked.

"About eleven in the morning."

He and Cahil exchanged glances. *Too long,* Briggs thought.

THOUGH THE BELL KOA HELICOPTER'S HEATER WAS BLOWING FULL blast, the cabin temperature hovered around forty degrees. Tanner scanned the ground as it swept below the windshield. Aside from the occasional patch of evergreen, the land was uniformly gray tundra sprinkled with glacial scree.

"How're we doing on gas?" Tanner asked.

"About ten minutes till turnaround," Bear said.

Fuel was their main concern. Braithwaite had only been able to secure enough fuel for twelve hours' flying time. Such was life in the Arctic Circle. Almost everything came at a premium . . . even light. This time of year, days and nights were equally divided, but with each passing week, Point Hope lost about an hour of daylight. By early December, they would have none at all until February.

According to their map, the coastline between Point Hope to Cape Lisbourne was pocked with hundreds of coves and inlets, any one of which could hide *Toshogu.* The likelihood of her running aground on a straight stretch of shoreline seemed slim. In three hours they'd found two grounded shipwrecks, both derelict trollers.

"You were up here last year, weren't you?" Cahil said. "The pipeline thing."

"Yep. Nearer Fairbanks, though. By comparison this is the dark side of the moon. Not exactly on Oaks's vacation list."

Cahil chuckled and tapped the gas gauge. "Time, bud."

Bear swung the Koa around, dropped the nose, and headed south.

Tanner raised the binoculars. "We better get lucky soon, or we'll be spending the winter up here."

THEIR LUCK CHANGED WHEN THEY RETURNED TO THEIR MOTEL, THE Starlight Inn. Their room was an aqua and gold nightmare. The pillows smelled like Lysol, and the bedspreads were emblazoned with the words, Starlight Inn: Comfort at a Discount. It was warm inside, though, which went a long way to balance the scales.

Tanner was taking off his boots when there was a knock at the door. Cahil opened it to find Abe, the motel's owner/manager/janitor/maid.

"Somebody called for you!" Abe was excited; Abe didn't see many patrons.

"Yeah?"

"Yeah. Here. I didn't read it." Abe peered into the room. "You boys need anything? Towels? soap? More shampoo—"

"No, thanks, Abe. We're doing great," Tanner said.

Cahil said, "Maybe some coffee?"

"Surely! I'll be back."

Cahil shut the door and read the note. "Walt's got something."

"DON'T THANK ME," OAKEN SAID. "THANK SKIP."

"I'll do that," Tanner said. "Who's Skip?"

"NPIC. He worked some overlay magic with the thermal images. From there, I punched in the current and weather data, and *voilà*."

"How about ice? The water's getting thick up here."

"All in the numbers."

"Oaks, you're the best," Tanner said, putting another mental check on his number-of-times-Oaks-has-saved-the-day list.

"Thanks. Hook up; I've got an image for you."

Tanner attached his cell phone to their laptop computer. "Okay."

"Go to channel four, then get back to me."

Tanner switched channels, and moments later, the laptop's screen was filled with an image of the coastline. Tanner switched back to Oaken. "Got it. What're we looking for?"

"See the red dot about fifty miles north of you? Unless my numbers are skewed, that's were she should be, give or take. That is, if she didn't sink before she got there."

FORTY-EIGHT MILES NORTH OF POINT HOPE, CAHIL LIFTED THE KOA through the fog and swept over a ridge of evergreens. Through the mist Tanner caught a glimpse of a cove so small they'd almost passed it when something caught his eye: an elongated shape, straight lines against the cliff face.

"Swing her around, Bear, I think we've got something."

Cahil banked hard and reversed course. As the cove again came into view, he stopped in a hover. Tanner opened the door, braced himself on the cabin frame, and leaned out. "Bear, are you seeing what I'm seeing?" he shouted.

"Damned right I do!"

The ship lay half-grounded on the beach, her bow on the sand, her stern still afloat in the cove. She was awash to her gunwales and listing a few degrees to port, with only the deck railing and the pilothouse visible. Wave after wave had washed over the decks, leaving an ever-thickening coat of ice.

"Size looks right," Cahil said. "Superstructure, too."

"There's a moon pool on the afterdeck. Looks good."

"Where do you want me to put her down?"

"Try the cliff. We can rope down."

*   *   *

THEY SECURED ONE END OF THE ROPE TO THE HELICOPTER'S LAND-
ing strut, then tossed the other end over the edge. Tanner
peeked over and saw the rope dangling into a three-foot
gap between *Toshogu* and the cliff. The ship groaned and
shifted, grating against the face. Ice popped, each as loud
as a gunshot.

"She ain't long for this world," said Cahil.

High tide was less than twenty minutes away. Once it
came, she would likely float free and capsize under the
weight of the ice.

Tanner lowered himself over the cliff and rappelled to
the bottom, where he swung out and hooked his foot over
the encrusted railing. Ice snapped off and crashed to the
deck below. He tied off the rope and belayed Cahil as he
came down.

Every inch of exposed deck was thick with ice—a skat-
ing rink broken only by the derricks and J-shaped ventila-
tors. The ice sparkled dully in the gray light.

Slipping and clutching for handholds, they left the railing
and began picking their way across the canted deck. "Watch
yourself, Briggs. If we fall in . . ."

"I know." *Three or four minutes to live*, Tanner thought.
"Check aft; I'll go forward."

Five minutes later, they met back on the forecastle. All
entrances to the pilothouse were as good as welded shut.
Even with blowtorches, it would take an hour to break
through. They continued forward, scrambling and clawing
until they reached the bow railing. Four feet below them,
waves licked at the hull. Tanner shuffled forward, peered
over the edge, then pulled back.

"Do you hear that?"

"What?" said Cahil

"Some kind of echo. Here, hold on to me."

With Cahil clutching his belt, Tanner leaned farther over
the railing. After a moment, he pulled himself back up.
"There's a hole about the size of a VW in the hull. The
water's filling it, but I think if we time it right . . ."

Cahil groaned. "Oh boy. We're gonna get wet doing it. And you complain about Oaks planning bad excursions. So who goes first?"

"Me. It's my bad idea."

31

North of McLean, Virginia

AFTER LEAVING PHILADELPHIA, VORSALOV STOPPED BRIEFLY FOR breakfast at an IHOP, then got on Highway 95 and headed south in the predawn darkness. Three hours later, he was approaching the outskirts of Washington, D.C.

Following ten miles behind, Latham was anxious.

He wanted to be on the front lines, but he knew it was impossible. Vorsalov knew his face too well. Even with the van's bank of monitors that allowed him to see everything the cars saw, it was maddening being so far removed from the action. The feeling worsened as they neared the city.

"Command, this is Mobile Lead."

Latham picked up the handset. "Go ahead, Paul."

"Subject is turning, heading southeast on Old Dominion."

"Roger."

Sixty seconds later: "Another turn . . . onto Dolly Madison, heading north. Subject is turning into a Denny's. Okay, units four and five spread out, give me a wide perimeter."

Denny's? Something didn't add up for Latham. Vorsalov had eaten breakfast two hours before and made a bathroom stop in Essex outside Baltimore. Was this simply a coffee break? "Paul, stay sharp. I got a weird feeling about this."

RANDAL TOOK UP POSITION A HUNDRED YARDS UP THE ROAD FROM the restaurant. Through his binoculars, he watched the hostess seat Vorsalov at a window booth, then take his order. She returned a minute later with coffee.

Ten minutes passed. The Russian sipped his coffee and read a newspaper.

"What's he doing?" Randal's driver asked.

"Drinking coffee, looks like."

"Why's the boss getting hinky about that?"

"He's out of pattern. Why drive this far off the interstate for coffee?"

After a second cup of coffee, Vorsalov paid his bill and walked outside.

"All units, this is lead. Subject is moving. Get ready to roll."

As Randal spoke, another car—a black Oldsmobile—pulled into the lot and parked beside Vorsalov's Taurus. The driver, a woman in a blue blazer, got out. Vorsalov waved to her. Randal focused his binoculars on the sticker in the Olds's rear window: Avis

"Shit! He's switching cars, he's switching goddamned cars!"

LATHAM HEARD RANDAL'S REPORT, BUT EVEN AS VORSALOV WAS transferring his bags from the Taurus to the Olds, his mind was elsewhere: Vorsalov was switching. Fine, he's dry-cleaning. But why here? Why not at an Avis office?

In addition to a laptop and a satellite communications console, the command van was equipped with a library of maps that would've done *National Geographic* proud. Latham found one of the Georgetown Pike area and flipped it open. It took him less than a minute to see it.

"Mobile Lead, this is Command," he called.

"Go ahead."

"Paul, have you got a car to the east of the parking lot?"

"Negative. That's a one-way street. He can't . . ." Then Randal understood. "Lead to Four, head east to where the one-way dumps out. Move!"

"Roger, we're rolling."

Randal said, "I screwed up, Charlie. Sorry."

"Forget it. Hold your breath."

Latham cursed himself. He should have seen this the mo-

ment Vorsalov pulled into the lot. The road to the north
was a two-lane, one-way street. If Vorsalov had chosen this
Denny's for a reason other than its superior coffee, it was
because it was the perfect spot to lay one of the oldest
countersurveillance traps in the game.

VORSALOV WAVED GOOD-BYE TO THE RENTAL AGENT, GOT INTO THE
Olds, then pulled up to the exit, his blinker signaling a right
turn. A dozen cars flew by. The speed limit was fifty miles
per hour, but no one was doing less than sixty.

Randal called, "Four, this is Lead, are you in place?"

"Not yet. Almost there. . . ."

"Push it."

There was a lull in traffic. Vorsalov pulled out. Abruptly,
he veered left, up the one-way, and sped around the corner.

"Go, go, go!" Randal yelled to his driver. "All units, this
is Lead. Subject is running, I say again, subject is running.
Four, are you in place?"

"Negative."

Randal pounded the dashboard. *Damn!* Vorsalov had
been a lamb all the way down the coast; now this. They'd
gotten comfortable, and he'd nailed them.

AS OFTEN AS NOT, SPIES WHO SUSPECT THEY ARE UNDER SUR-
veillance do not try to shake their watchers; they try to
expose them. In doing so, the roles are reversed and the
watchers must work twice as hard to not only remain invisible but to maintain contact. If Vorsalov could lure
someone down the one-way street, he would gain the upper
hand. The trick for Latham's team would be to reestablish
contact without letting the Russian see them. That was now
in the hands of the team's only woman agent, Janet Paschel
in Mobile Four.

"Command to Four," Latham called.

"Go ahead."

"Janet, this is Charlie. He won't go more than two
blocks. Any farther, and he risks attracting the cops. Just

get in place and look sharp. If he gets even a whiff, we're finished. Just slide in behind him and stay there. We'll catch up."

"Roger." Janet's voice was tight.

Paul Randal called, "All units copy that?"

The units checked in one by one. The net went silent, waiting.

Sixty seconds passed.

Ninety seconds.

Finally: "Command, this is Four. I've got him."

THE NEXT TWO HOURS STRETCHED LATHAM'S TEAM TO THE BREAK- ing point. After leaving the one-way, Vorsalov headed southwest on Kirby Road, away from the city and back toward McLean. With Paschel in the lead, Latham juggled units until they were paralleling Vorsalov on side streets, invisibly boxing him in.

The Russian hadn't forgotten the terrain. He was taking them on a grand tour of the city: Rock Creek Park, The Mall, Union Station, Arlington National Cemetery, Dupont Circle. He made unsignaled turns and U-turns, parked suddenly and ducked inside cafés, only to reappear sixty seconds later. At one point, he parked his car and took a taxi two blocks to the Reflecting Pool, where he sat on a bench and watched the Olds for ten minutes before walking back and driving away.

Randal reported in: Vorsalov was pulling into a convenience store on Georgia Avenue outside Howard University.

What's he doing now? Latham wondered, then caught on: Howard University had 12,000 students, the majority of them African-American. It was a smart move. Gambling that any surveillance team would be predominantly white, Vorsalov had chosen a place where they would stand out.

"Paul, has Tommy been up front recently?" Tommy was one of the six black agents on the team.

"Not since Philly. No way he's been made."

"Have him pull into the store and get something to drink. I want to know what our boy's doing."

"I copy that," Tommy answered.

Seven minutes later, they had their answer. While Tommy was deciding between a blueberry slushy and a Coke, Vorsalov used the pay phone, then left.

"Secure that phone," Charlie ordered. "Be discreet, but nobody uses it."

"Command, he's turning northeast on Rhode Island."

Latham consulted a directory, then dialed his cell phone. He got the main switchboard at Bell Telephone. He identified himself then said, "I need to speak to a supervisor. It's urgent."

"One moment, sir."

A woman came on the line. "Agent Latham, my name is Marie Johnson. What can I do for you?"

"Ms. Johnson, I need some information." Latham gave her the number of the pay phone. "There was a call made there about four minutes ago. I need to know to where."

"No problem. Hold for a minute." It took four. "The call went to a bank of phones on the corner of California and Kalorama. It's a sequenced bank."

"Okay, hold on." Latham got on the radio. "Paul, it's California and Kalorama. Get somebody moving."

"On our way."

"Ms. Johnson, what's that mean, a sequenced bank?"

"Calls to and from that bank are routed on a single trunk line. They don't go to individual phones until they reach the bank."

"You've lost me."

"We can't tell exactly which phone the call went to, and all six have been pretty busy in the last few minutes. Roughly twenty-six incoming and outgoing calls."

"Smart sons of bitches."

"Pardon me?"

"Nothing. Can you narrow that down, give us phones with incoming only?"

"Yes, but, it'll take some time. Ten, fifteen minutes."

"I'd be grateful." He gave her his cell phone number.

*   *   *

VORSALOV CONTINUED HEADING SOUTHEAST. THE CAR RANDAL
sent to California and Kalorama reported nothing unusual
at the phone booths.

After ten minutes of random driving, Vorsalov turned
onto fifteenth, then swung west on Constitution into the
heart of Capitol Hill.

"Passing Virginia Avenue," Randal reported.

Latham checked his watch. *Come on. . . .*

"Coming up on Roosevelt Bridge. . . . We're over the
bridge, heading north to the George Parkway."

Latham traced the route on his map. Vorsalov was taking
the bridge over the Potomac and to Teddy Roosevelt Island.
Roosevelt Island . . . Latham thought, reviewing what he
knew about it. *Good place for a meeting; plenty of trails.
An easy place to spot surveillance.*

"I see him," Randal called. "All units keep driving, nobody pull in. Command, he's pulling into the Roosevelt
Island parking lot. The only exit is northbound, so we're
setting up down the parkway. The median is blocked by a
barrier. No way he can get across."

"Roger," said Latham. There were only two ways to
reach Roosevelt Island, one from the parking lot, the other
a pedestrian bridge crossing from Rosslyn Station. "Don't
forget Rosslyn, Paul."

"It's covered. We're also collecting plate numbers from
the lot."

Now to find out who the Russian was meeting.

VORSALOV CLIMBED OUT AND STRETCHED HIS LEGS. HIS MUSCLES
were sore. It felt good to be out of the car. He looked
around. Most of the cars in the parking lot were from other
states. Tourists with children. That would make it hard for
watchers. Good. He started across the footbridge.

The last few hours had been gruelling but satisfying. Just
like the old days. His hands shook with excess adrenaline.
God, how he missed this. He was safe, he decided. Even

if by chance he'd been intercepted, he'd long since lost them. He knew the city too well and had played this game too long to be trapped.

He turned his attention to the island, picking out landmarks and trails from the guidebook. A ninety-acre game preserve, the guide said, named after Theodore Roosevelt. He skimmed his fingertip along the map until he found the trail he wanted.

He turned off the bridge and east onto the path. Time was critical now. He picked up his pace.

ONE MILE SOUTH OF THE ISLAND, LATHAM'S COMMAND VAN SAT in the visitor parking lot of Arlington National Cemetery. Ten minutes had passed since Vorsalov had parked. Latham's cell phone buzzed. "Latham here."

"Agent Latham, Marie Johnson here, from Bell—"

"Yes, ma'am."

"I've got the information you requested. There were only three incoming calls to that bank of phones. One wasn't answered, the other was a busy signal. The third was picked up. The call lasted just over a minute."

"Great," Latham said. "Was that phone used—"

"I thought you'd ask that. About fifty seconds after the first call came in, the phone was used again, this time for two minutes." She gave him the number, a 202 area code, 333 prefix. Inside the city.

"Where—"

"The number is registered to Brown's Boat Rental at Virginia and Rock Creek."

Latham froze. He knew Brown's. It lay on the east bank of the Potomac, not three hundred yards from Roosevelt Island.

Jesus. Vorsalov wasn't meeting anyone. He was still dry-cleaning.

"Thanks, Ms. Johnson, you've been great." Latham hung up and keyed the radio. "Command to Mobile One."

"Go ahead."

"Paul, get somebody back across the bridge. I want one

car in the parking lot of Brown's Boat Rental and two patrolling north and south on Rock Creek."

"What's going on?"

"Our boy's making a run."

VORSALOV'S PLOY WAS A MASTERSTROKE, LATHAM WOULD LATER admit.

Vorsalov calls a partner at the booth on California and Kalorama, who then calls Johnson's to confirm a boat is reserved and waiting on the island, a common request during tourist season. Meanwhile, Vorsalov crosses the bridge to Roosevelt, maneuvering any pursuers into a perfect bottleneck that would trap them on the west side of the Potomac with no quick way to get back across during noon rush hour.

Latham did the calculations: Six or seven minutes for Paul to reach Rock Creek Parkway, another two minutes to reach Brown's. Add to that the ten minutes head start Vorsalov had, plus four minutes for him to paddle across the river . . .

It would be close.

TWENTY MINUTES LATER, THEY HAD THEIR ANSWER.

Randal reported finding an abandoned canoe on a beach just south of the boat center. "Are we sure it was him?" Latham asked.

"Pretty much. One of the attendants saw him ditch the canoe and take off toward the GWU Metrorail stop. The description matches."

Latham stared into space. He was numb. They'd worked so hard. . . .

"Charlie, are you there? Should we—"

"No," Latham said. "Forget it. He's gone."

32

Alaska

THE TIDE WAS ALREADY BEGINNING TO LIFT THE STERN, BANGING it against the cliff face and breaking free chunks of ice that shattered on the deck. Tanner looked aft and saw waves lapping at the midships rail. Soon the entire afterdeck would be submerged.

Bear tied off the rope, set himself, and lowered Briggs over the side until he was perched against the hull. Below his feet, waves rushed through the hole with an explosive sucking sound. The billowing mist froze almost immediately into clouds of vapor. Tanner peered into the hole but could see nothing of the interior.

"Ready, Bear?" he called.

"Ready!"

Briggs watched the waves surge, timing them. *One one thousand, two one thousand . . .* He eyed the hole's ragged edges; if he timed it wrong, he'd be gutted like a fish.

Tanner pushed off the hull, swinging out and down. Jagged metal flashed past. He plunged into the water and he felt like he'd been hit with an electric current. Then he was up again, gasping for breath. A wave broke through the hole and blotted out the sky. His ears squealed with the pressure change.

He looked around. He was submerged up to his waist; already he could feel his legs growing numb. Above him was a horizontal steel railing. He grabbed it, pulled himself up, and rolled himself onto the catwalk.

He was in the anchor windlass room, a small compartment containing the winch that raised and lowered the anchor. A few feet away, a ladder ascended into the darkness.

"Briggs," Cahil called. "Hey, Briggs—"

"I'm okay, Bear," Tanner shouted. He untied himself and tossed the rope through the hole. "There's a catwalk a few feet inside the hull. Once you get through, reach out. I'll grab you."

With a banzai cry and a splash, Cahil swung through the hole. Tanner caught his hand and pulled him onto the catwalk. "Welcome aboard," Tanner said.

"God, that's cold."

"I noticed." Briggs shined his flashlight over the blackened edges of the hole. "Shaped charge," he said. "They tried to scuttle her."

"Just one's not enough to sink her," Bear said. "There's gotta be others."

"Yep. Let's get moving."

THEY CLIMBED THE LADDER TO THE NEXT DECK. THE TIDE HAD NOT yet reached this high, but they could hear it below them, sloshing and echoing. They headed aft, passing several machinery rooms and the galley, all of which were deserted. In a crew's lounge they found a magazine lying open on a couch; a paperback novel spine-up on a coffee table; a mug, half full of tea. There were no signs of disorder. It was as though the crew had just walked away.

Cahil picked up the magazine; it was written in Kanji.

In the crew's quarters they found several lockers containing clothes. "Here," Tanner called to Cahil, tossing him a towel. They both stripped, toweled off until the color returned to their arms and legs, then found a couple pair of coveralls that fit.

"This feels creepy," said Cahil, slipping into one.

Tanner nodded. "Like borrowing clothes from ghosts."

THEY MADE THEIR WAY TO THE PILOTHOUSE. THE WINDOWS WERE rimmed with ice, and rainbowed sunlight danced on the bulkheads. Like the crew's quarters, the bridge was a pic-

ture of orderliness. Tanner found the helm controls set at
All Stop.

They made a quick search. "No logs, records . . . nothing," Briggs said. ·

"Same with charts. Everything's gone."

Under their feet, the deck groaned and leaned farther to
starboard.

THEY DESCENDED TWO DECKS BUT WERE STOPPED BY RISING WA-
ter at the entrance to a machinery room. The hatch was
open, however, and Tanner shimmied down the railing and
shined his flashlight inside.

"There's another hole," he called. "About the same size
as the one at the bow. Its filling up quick."

"Just time for one more stop, then," Bear said.

IN THE ENGINE ROOM, THE SEA HAD FLOODED ALL BUT THE UPPER-
most catwalk on which they stood, and Tanner could hear
gurgling *whooshes* as air pockets were forced ever upward
by the tide. They trotted through the next hatch and down
a ladder.

The after cargo hold. Water lapped at the edges of the
catwalk beneath their feet and up the bulkhead, leaving an
ever-thickening sheet of ice. Tanner could feel the chill on
him.

"Briggs, you better get over here."

Tanner walked to where Cahil was kneeling.

The bodies were lying faceup and side by side against
the port bulkhead. All but one of them were chained to the
railing, and all were submerged up to their chests, their
faces crusted with ice. Several of the corpses' wrists were
rubbed raw, some clear to the bone. Tanner tried to picture
it: chained here as the scuttling charges exploded . . . flailing in the rising water, screaming for help, but no one coming.

What a god-awful way to die.

The only body not chained had met a different fate than
had the others. Aside from being the only non-Oriental, this

man, a Caucasian with thinning blond hair, had been shot once in the forehead.

One by one, Tanner shined his flashlight over each face. At the fourth face, he stopped. "Bear, recognize him?"

"Yeah."

It was the missing engineer from the Takagi Shipyard.

CAHIL TOOK SOME QUICK PHOTOS, THEN FOLLOWED TANNER DOWN the catwalk to where it widened into a small alcove. Here, beneath the catwalk, they found an undetonated scuttling charge attached to the port bulkhead.

"Sealed bowl charge," Cahil said. "Half pound of RDX, looks like. See the funnel at the bottom of the bowl?"

"That's not good," Briggs whispered.

The charge was armed with a hydrostatic trigger, essentially a funnel at the bottom of which sat a detonator designed to fire when water poured in and caused a short circuit.

Tanner looked down. Water was lapping at the catwalk. "We're out of time, Bear."

THEY WERE CLIMBING THE LADDER WHEN THE DECK LURCHED UNDER their feet, then leaned sharply to starboard. The ship started wallowing. Instinctively, Tanner knew what was happening: the tide had floated the ship's stern. They had only minutes before the bow followed.

"Go, Bear. Run!"

Chasing the beams of their flashlights, they charged up the ladder, through the engine room, and out the opposite hatch.

They heard a groan of steel. The deck rolled beneath their feet. They crashed against the bulkhead. Cahil's flashlight clattered to the deck and rolled away, the beam casting jumbled shadows against the bulkheads. They stood up, braced themselves, kept moving. The list was passing fifty degrees now.

"Ever see *The Poseidon Adventure*?" Cahil called.

"As a kid. It scared the hell out of me."

"Me, too. I think we lost our exit, bud." The hole in the bow was now either submerged or buried in silt.

"Let's go for the one in the MR," Tanner said.

It took them sixty seconds to reach the ladder to the machinery room. They shimmied down the rail and slipped into the icy water. Water was boiling through the hatch. *Too fast,* Briggs thought. As the ship was rolling over, the trapped water was cascading from port to starboard, gaining speed like a self-contained tidal wave.

The water reached their waists, swirling higher and faster.

"Gonna be a tough swim!" Cahil shouted.

"We'll wait till the hatch fills! The current will lose some speed. There should be an air pocket below the hole."

"Should be?"

"Will be!"

Tanner felt the fear swell in his chest. He quashed it. The water reached his chin, the cold like a vise around his chest. He raised himself onto his toes. With a final *swoosh* of escaping air, the hatch disappeared beneath the foam.

Tanner nodded to Cahil, then took a breath and dove.

Inside the machinery room they found a jumble of inverted catwalks and ladders. Above their heads, the gash in the hull was open. Tanner could see murky daylight. They headed for the nearest ladder and started up.

Three feet below the hole, they broke into an air pocket. Outside, Tanner could see the face of the cliff. Waves and spume broke against it and rushed into the hole. He stretched his arm, caught the edge, and pulled. "Gimme a shove," he yelled. Cahil hunched his shoulders and Tanner pushed off. He pulled himself out, rolled onto the hull, grabbed Cahil's hand, and lifted him up.

Toshogu lay prone on her starboard side, her decks perpendicular to the water. Behind them, the stern rolled and crashed against the cliff face. With a deafening grating of steel on gravel, the bow began sliding off the beach.

"Now *there's* something you don't see every day," Cahil yelled.

Tanner followed his outstretched finger. His heart filled his throat.

Jutting over the edge of the cliff was the helicopter's tail rotor. The rope, taut as a piano wire, ran from the strut to the ship's railing where they'd tied it off.

Toshugu rolled again. The helicopter skidded toward the edge.

Tanner pointed to the cliff face. "Think you can make that ledge?"

"Yep."

"Do it. I'm going for the rope."

"Wait, Briggs—"

"If we lose the helo, we'll die out here."

Tanner took off running, arms outstretched for balance as he sprinted along the hull. He slipped, fell hard, scrambled for a grip. He pulled himself up and kept going. Behind him, he heard a muffled explosion. *Scuttling charge,* he thought absently. He kept his eyes fixed on the rope; it trembled with the strain. The helicopter lurched closer to the edge.

"Jump, Briggs!" Cahil called. "She's going over!"

Ten feet from the rope, Tanner leapt. Even as his feet left the hull, he felt it sliding away beneath him. He caught the line in both hands, pulled his dive knife from its sheath, and sliced the rope below his knees.

Then he was swinging, the wind rushing around him. The cliff face loomed before him. With a teeth-rattling jolt, he hit the rock and bounced off. He reached out, found a handhold, and pulled himself to a ledge.

He caught his breath and looked over his shoulder.

Toshugu was gone. Only her port railing was still visible above the waves, and as Tanner watched, transfixed, that, too, slipped beneath the waves and disappeared in a cloud of bubbles.

"Briggs! You there?"

He leaned out and saw Cahil perched on the ledge, grinning like a maniac. *Alive!* Tanner felt it, too. "I'm here! You okay?"

"Yeah, but all things being equal, I'd rather be back at the Starlight!"

33

THIRTEEN SLEEPLESS HOURS LATER, A TAXI DROPPED THEM BACK at the Royal Palms Hotel. There was a message waiting for Tanner. He handed it to Cahil.

"Wonder what the good inspector Ieyasu wants," Bear said.

"I'll call and arrange a meeting."

Cahil yawned. "Make it a couple hours, huh?"

BEFORE LEAVING TO MEET IEYASU, TANNER CALLED HOLYSTONE TO check in, the first time since discovering *Toshogu*. Oaken listened while Tanner told the story.

"Good God. So are you thawed out?" Oaken asked.

"I am, but the tips of Bear's toes are still blue."

Cahil said, "Better that than my—"

"I get the picture," said Oaken. "So bottom line is we have a scuttled ship with a murdered crew. Is she reachable?"

"I doubt it," said Tanner. "She probably stayed afloat long enough to get washed out past the shelf. We're talking about some deep water."

"How deep?"

"Five, maybe six thousand feet."

"Then no salvage operation. My guess is Leland is going to call this the end of the road. We've got nothing else solid to follow. Unless . . ."

"What?"

"I'm working on something. Can you lay low for a day or so? That'll give me a chance to finish this; if it pans out, we might have something."

Tanner almost asked why Oaken was going to such trouble, but he knew the answer. Oaken loved a mystery as much as anyone, though his detecting was more the armchair variety. "Thanks, Oaks."

"You bet. I'll get back to you."

IEYASU STOOD NEAR THE TIDE LINE, TOSSING STONES INTO THE surf. Tanner introduced Cahil. "And you are a tourist as well?" Ieyasu asked.

Cahil smiled. "What can I say? I've heard good things about your country."

"My country would be better without people like Hiromasa Takagi."

"Agreed."

Tanner led them to a log, and they sat down. "Inspector, it's time for some truth between us. You know we're not tourists, and you know Ohira and Sumiko were more than just employees of Takagi Industries."

"Yes."

"The U.S. government believes Takagi Industries is involved in illegal arms dealing. Ohira had been trying to help us put a stop to it."

Again Ieyasu simply nodded, saying nothing.

"Takagi's involved, that much we know. What we don't know is, with whom and how. My question to you is, will you continue to help us? Can we trust you?"

Tanner felt naive asking such a question, but the success of espionage ops often came down to the solidity of personal relationships. In a word, trust.

Ieyasu was silent for a minute. "I've seen too much to think the world is black and white, and that good and evil obey national borders. I am a patriot, but I am not a fool. So, the answer to your question is, yes, you can trust me. Tell me what you need."

Tanner briefly outlined Ohira's interest in *Toshogu* and their subsequent search for her. He opened his laptop, called up the file into which they had downloaded the digital photos from Alaska, and turned the computer toward Ieyasu.

"There were eleven bodies. This one we know; he's an engineer who disappeared a few days before *Toshogu* sailed. According to the records, she sailed with seven crew and a representative from Skulafjord. That's nine, leaving two unaccounted for . . . these two here, we believe. I'm hoping you can use some of your contacts to identify them."

"That is not necessary," said Ieyasu. "I know these men."

"From where?"

"In the CIB we had a list similar to your FBI's Most Wanted. Both of these men are still on that list. They are *Rengo Sekigun*, Japanese Red Army. Both are wanted in connection to the subway gas attacks. Back then, I was certain they had served as go-betweens for Takagi. Until now, no one had seen them for over eight months. How were they killed?"

Tanner told him.

"Oh, my. Your theory about Takagi is more plausible now. The JRA has strong links to Mideast groups; these two men were well-traveled: Lebanon, Syria, Iran."

They talked for a few more minutes before Ieyasu stood up. "One more thing I thought you would like to know: Ms. Fujika's funeral is tomorrow in Totsukawa. As I understand it, Hiromasa Takagi will be attending." Ieyasu shrugged. "Whatever it is worth."

Tanner nodded. "Thanks."

"I will be in touch." Ieyasu left.

Finally Cahil said, "Don't tell me you're thinking about it."

"I am."

"Not a good idea, bud."

"A bad idea, in fact. But I think it's time we met Hiromasa Takagi face-to-face."

*   *   *

Holystone Office

THAT SOMETHING THAT HAD BEEN NAGGING OAKEN WAS A TINY voice shouting, "You missed something!" The answer popped into his head while he was shaving in the Holystone bathroom. He stopped, razor poised on his cheek. "That's it."

He wiped his face, ran to his desk and thumbed a stack of folders. It took him only moments to locate the photo he wanted. He grabbed a magnifying glass from the drawer and peered at the corner of the photo. "Bingo."

DUTCHER ACCEPTED A CUP OF COFFEE FROM OAKEN AND PULLED up a chair in front of his desk. "I know that look," Dutcher said. "It's your *ahha* face."

"First, Briggs and Ian called." In fact, Tanner had called a second time to report Ieyasu's ID of the two JRA soldiers.

Dutcher raised his eyebrows. "So they found her."

"Yep." Oaken related the story. "Eleven bodies, three of them identified; the rest was probably the crew. I'm running the JRA names now."

"Good. Without the ship, though, we're spinning our wheels. Does Briggs have any idea why she was scuttled?"

"Not really, aside from it being a very permanent way to dispose of witnesses."

"And evidence, whatever the hell that might be. We still have no idea what Takagi's up to."

"True, but we may be able to find what *Tsumago*'s been up to. Remember the deck log from the shipyard Briggs photographed? It listed her as having made eight trips in the last six months, each about five days long."

"Shakedown cruises?"

"Maybe, but I doubt it." Oaken handed Dutcher one of the photographs. "That's her helm console. I knew I'd seen the design before. I saw an article on it in *Jane's* last year."

"I assume there's something special about it."

Oaken nodded. "It's going to tell us where she's been going."

*   *   *

Japan

SUMIKO'S HOME VILLAGE LAY IN THE MOUNTAINS, AN HOUR'S DRIVE
from Osaka. In a steadily falling rain Tanner and Cahil
parked in what appeared to be the village's central square
and got out. Tanner asked directions from a passing
woman, and they began walking.

They found the Fujika ancestral shrine sat at the edge of
a spruce forest.

A dozen or so mourners surrounded the shrine, which
was decorated with small wooden plaques called *ema,* each
a memorial from a family member. Tanner knew many Japanese practiced a blend of both Shinto and Buddhism; this
seemed the case with Sumiko's family, for while the shrine
was Shinto, the presiding priest was Buddhist.

"Tell me what's wrong with this picture," Cahil whispered.

"I see him."

Standing a dozen paces away from Sumiko's family, was
Hiromasa Takagi. Tange Noboru stood by his side, shel-
tering him with an umbrella.

The priest recited a prayer, wafted an incense stick over
the shrine, then turned and nodded to the mourners. It was
over.

"Some would question your judgment in coming here,"
a voice whispered.

Tanner turned and saw Inspector Tanaka standing behind
them. Tanner felt rage flood his chest. Tanaka had helped
cover up both Ohira's and Sumiko's murders, and now here
he was at her funeral. As far as Tanner was concerned, he
was as guilty as Noboru and Takagi. He took a deep breath
and turned his back on the man.

Near the shrine, the mourners were dispersing, except for
Takagi, who was speaking quietly to Sumiko's grand-
mother. After a moment, she began weeping.

"Inspector, why don't you introduce us to Mr. Takagi?"
Tanner said.

Tanaka laughed softly. "I don't think that would be
wise."

"Introduce us, or I will."

Tanaka shrugged. "Very well."

Flanked by Noboru, Takagi stopped in front of them. Up close, Noboru was even more imposing, a bull of a man with huge shoulders and a thick neck. Deadpan, he stared at a spot in the middle of Tanner's forehead.

Standing this close to Hiromasa Takagi, Briggs could feel the man's power radiating outward, like a palpable force. He suddenly realized just how dangerous Takagi was. This was a man who could do exactly as he wanted, to whomever he wanted, with near impunity.

Tanaka made the introductions. Takagi bowed stiffly. Briggs countered with an inclination of his head. Takagi accepted the insult with a thin smile. *We're gnats to him.* So far, they'd been simply annoying. That was about to change.

"Inspector Tanaka tells me you knew Ms. Fujiko," Takagi said.

"She was kind enough to show us around Osaka," Tanner replied.

"And now that you've seen my country, what do you think of it?"

"Aside from the crime, it's beautiful."

Takagi frowned. "Ah, yes, I see. Mr. Ohira. Terrible thing. Interesting that both the Takagi employees you've met have died under mysterious circumstances. Some might call you bad luck."

"There's little mystery involved," Tanner replied. "Ohira was executed by a sniper who escaped in a truck very similar to those you use at your shipyard, and Ms. Fujika was butchered in the parking lot of your headquarters. It's been three, by the way."

"Three what?"

"Three Takagi employees I'm aquatinted with. The third was an engineer in your maritime division."

Takagi's eyes darted toward Noboru. "And has your bad luck affected him, too?"

"If you call being chained inside a sinking ship and dying of hypothermia bad luck, then I'd say yes."

Takagi's face went red. Noboru growled and took a step toward Tanner. Cahil blocked him and shook his head: *Bad idea.*

"The job was botched," said Tanner. "She didn't go down right away. Not to worry, though: The water's at least a mile deep where she sank. No one will ever reach her, and no one will ever know . . . except for us, that is."

Takagi balled his fists. "What are you after, Mr. Tanner?"

"You, Mr. Takagi."

"A lot of men have tried that."

Tanner gave a hard smile. "I love a challenge. Plus, I think you'll find I do business a little differently than you're used to."

"We will see."

"At last something we agree on." Tanner leaned forward and stared into Takagi's eyes. "Make no mistake, though," he whispered. "Whatever it takes, however far I have to go, I'm coming for you."

"Enough!" Takagi barked. "I suggest you leave Japan, Mr. Tanner!"

Takagi stalked away, drawing Noboru and Tanaka in his wake.

Cahil clapped Tanner on the shoulder. "And yet another Christmas card you won't be hanging over your mantel."

Tanner let himself exhale, then smiled. "So many friends, so little mantel."

34

TANNER KNEW TAKAGI HAD NO INTENTION OF LETTING THEM LEAVE
Japan alive. That left only one alternative: Get out before
he could trap them. Tanner hated the idea of running, but
cliché or not, here discretion was in fact the better part of
valor. Staying would get them nowhere.

It was dark by the time they returned to the Royal Palms.
The lobby was empty except for the receptionist standing
behind the front desk. Tanner recognized the young man.
"Evening, Kenzo. Any messages?"

Eyes on the counter, Kenzo shook his head. "No, sir."

"Can you check anyway, please?"

"Oh, sorry, just a moment." He walked over, checked
Tanner's box, and returned. "No messages."

Tanner stared at Kenzo until he looked up.

"Everything okay?" Briggs asked.

"Oh, yes, fine."

Tanner joined Cahil at the elevators.

"What's up?" Bear asked.

"Kenzo's not his usual gregarious self. He wouldn't even
look me in the eye."

"You know him well enough to—"

"I've never seen him without an ear-to-ear grin."

The elevator's doors parted. Tanner glanced back at the
counter. Kenzo was nowhere to be seen. "I'm getting a bad
feeling, Bear. Come on."

The kitchen was closed for the night, so they walked
through the grill area to the exit. Written on the door in
both English and Kanji were the words Emergency Exit:
Alarm Will Sound.

"Bear, I need a—"

"Hang on."

Cahil rummaged through a nearby drawer until he found a steel spatula. Tanner wedged it between the jamb and the door's bolt, then pushed the crash bar. Cahil held the spatula in place as Tanner slipped into the alley. He returned a minute later. "There's a Takagi security truck on the road behind the trees."

"That didn't take long. Do we have anything in the room we need?"

"The laptop's in the Rover; so's most of our gear. I've got the cell phone and my passport."

"Me, too." Cahil shrugged and smiled. "What say we check out."

After making sure Kenzo was still absent, they walked through the lobby and into the parking lot. They were halfway to the Range Rover when Tanner saw a figure—another Noboru clone—crouched beside the rear bumper.

Briggs gestured for Bear to circle through the trees, gave him a minute to get into position, then walked toward the Rover. When he was ten feet away, the man looked up.

His eyes went wide. He reached inside his jacket. He was fast; his gun was already clear when Cahil slipped from the bushes behind him and palm-butted him at the base of the skull. He crumpled. Tanner walked over, kicked the gun away, and checked his pulse. He was dead.

Tanner looked around; the lot was empty. "Grab his feet."

They loaded the body into the rear of the Rover, covered it with a tarp, climbed in, and drove away.

WITH NOWHERE ELSE TO GO, THEY DROVE INTO THE FOREST NORTH of Mitsu's village. Once well into the trees, Tanner doused the headlights and coasted to a stop. They carried the body to the mangrove creek, found a large rock, tied the body to it, and rolled it into the water.

They hiked deeper into the forest until they found a small clearing. Here and there, fireflies winked, and the trees were filled with the occasional clicks of cicadas. Tanner plopped down on his duffel bag, pulled out the cell phone, and dialed.

Ieyasu picked up on the third ring. "Briggs. Where are you?"

"Don't ask.

"Did you go to the funeral? Are you okay?"

"Yes and yes. We're leaving, though. Forget you met us and lay low."

"Briggs—"

"If Takagi finds out you've helped us, you're dead."

Some might call you bad luck, Takagi had said. It had struck a nerve, Tanner admitted. Though not true of Ohira, Sumiko had died because of her involvement with them. "You've been a great help and a good friend, Sato, but promise me you'll leave it alone."

"I promise. You take care of yourselves, both of you. You will contact me if—"

"You have my word."

Tanner hung up and checked his watch: early morning in Washington. He dialed Holystone, listened to it ring, then heard a double-click as the call was routed to Oaken's home.

"Hello?"

"Did I wake you?" Tanner asked.

"No. Where are you?"

"Camping. How soon can you and Leland be at the office?"

"I was on my way there; so is Leland. We were getting ready to call you."

"Good timing, then. Call us when you get there."

"What's this business about camping?" Dutcher asked an hour later.

"We're persona non grata at the hotel," Tanner said, then explained.

"I told you to lay low. I wouldn't call going to this woman's funeral and throwing rocks at Takagi laying low. What were you thinking?"

Tanner didn't know what to say. Leland was right; he

was wrong. "It was a bad idea, I know. Takagi sits back, orders the execution of dozens of people—that we know of—then has the balls to go to Sumiko's funeral. I wanted to look him in the eye. I just wanted to see for myself."

Dutcher sighed. "Well, it's done with. Two things: We checked on the names of those two JRA soldiers. Ieyasu was right. They were hard-core members, active in the Mideast. They even did some mule work in Israel a few years ago. You remember the bombing in at the Hagana Museum in Tel Aviv?"

"I remember."

"Word is, one of these boys carried the explosives across the border. Whatever they were doing for Takagi, it was dirty."

"And second?" Tanner asked.

"Walter's got an idea about *Tsumago*. I'll let him explain."

Oaken asked, "How do you guys feel about another tour of Takagi's shipyard?"

Cahil groaned. "Oh, boy."

"What have you got in mind?" asked Tanner.

"You remember her computerized helm console? I'm betting it logs the ship's projected courses and speeds. Unless the crew is unusually meticulous, they probably didn't clear the computer's buffer after each trip."

"How big's the buffer?"

"Just guessing, I'd say a gigabyte. Plenty of space to record her last dozen voyages. In the last six months, she's made eight of them."

"Oaks, you're the best," said Tanner. "Leland, are we paying him enough?"

"Not enough money in the world."

"Okay, okay," Oaken said. "Can you do it? Can you get back into the dock?"

"We'll get in. Tell me how we download the data."

Oaken explained the procedure. "Once you've got the laptop plugged in, it'll load the data onto the hard drive. Any questions?"

"None," said Tanner. "Leland, we're gonna have to move

fast. As soon as Takagi realizes we're gone, he'll start making calls: police, Immigration, the works."

"We'll handle that. You worry about getting into the shipyard . . . and back out."

THEY LOADED THEIR GEAR INTO A SINGLE DUFFEL, WALKED TO THE main road, and found a bus that took them to Wakayama, where they found an open rental car agency and used one of Tanner's sanitized credit cards to rent an Accord. From there they took the ferry across to Shikoku and drove south to Mugi. The dive shop was closed, but it took them all of five minutes to break in, collect what they needed, and leave a generous bundle of *yen* on the counter.

Thirty minutes later, they were crouching in a cluster of trees across from the shipyard. Cahil was sorting through their gear as Tanner scanned the sea fence one last time. He lowered the binoculars. "Ready for round two, Bear?"

Cahil dipped his hand in the water. "Warmer this time, I think."

HOVERING MOTIONLESS IN THE WATER, TANNER COULD SEE THE green glow of Cahil's chem-light beside him. Briggs peered ahead but was unable to see the fence. He checked his watch and compass. Perfect. Now it was just a matter of time.

In the distance, he heard a faint grinding sound, like metal scraping concrete. He signaled Cahil to wait, then finned up to the surface and popped his mask above the water. He focused his binoculars on Dock 12.

The hangar door was open, and the interior was dark except for several flashing yellow lights. A tugboat sat at the mouth of the dock. He tapped twice on his tank and Cahil surfaced beside him. "We're too late," Tanner whispered and passed him the binoculars.

"They're rigging the tow lines. I count three . . . no, four crew on the forecastle. Can't see the bridge. They've got it pretty damned dark in there."

"All the better to skulk away. How long before she's at the gate?"

"Twenty minutes at most," Cahil said. "Unless you want to hitch a ride . . ."

"I know. Let's go."

SWIMMING HARD AGAINST A CROSSCURRENT, THEY REACHED THE shore eighteen minutes later and climbed out just as *Tsumago* was reaching the fence. Once through the gate, the tugboat disengaged its towlines and peeled away. Almost immediately, *Tsumago*'s wake broadened, white against the dark water.

"She's moving fast," Cahil said.

Tanner nodded. "How long since you've done a five-minute mile?"

"Oh, shit."

"Once she makes the turn around the headland, we'll lose her. We have to know which direction she's headed."

"I'm right behind you."

IT WAS ALMOST TWO MILES TO THE END OF THE PENINSULA. FOR the first mile, Tanner caught glimpses of *Tsumago* as she steered for open water, but soon the forest thickened and they lost sight of her.

The path they chose was a hiker's trail, and they made good time despite falling several times in the darkness. By the time they reached the headland, their shins were bruised and bloody. Panting hard, they scrambled up the rocks at the water's edge.

"You see her?" Tanner asked.

"No. Wait . . . there." Cahil pointed at a pair of lights in the distance.

"Give me a fix."

Cahil pulled out their map, picked out a couple landmarks, and did a quick calculation. "She's at one-five-zero."

"I see green running lights."

"That makes her starboard side to us. She's heading south; make it one-eight-five."

Across the cove they heard the thumping of the helicopter rotors, followed a moment later by a strobe light streaking across the water. Five minutes later, the strobe merged with the *Tsumago*'s outline and blinked out.

"BAD NEWS," TANNER TOLD OAKEN AN HOUR LATER, THEN EX- plained.

"You're sure she was heading south?"

"Yes."

"Okay, I might have something. It's not gonna be as accurate as data from the helm, but I've got a guess where she's headed."

"Oaks, I'm certainly not one to complain, but it would've been nice if you'd thought of this a few hours ago," said Cahil.

"I know, sorry. There's just so much information—"

"I'm kidding, Walt."

Tanner asked, "How long until you can give us a guess?"

"Tomorrow. In the meantime, we're getting you out. Got a map?"

"Yep. Go ahead."

"There's a small airstrip outside Iyo on Shikoku's north- western shore."

"I see it."

"Go there. A charter will be waiting."

35

Washington, D.C.

VORSALOV WAS GONE. LATHAM AND HIS TEAM WERE ANGRY AND demoralized. He did his best to rally them, but in his heart he wasn't hopeful. The odds were against them and getting worse with each passing hour.

The repercussions of Vorsalov's escape would not be long in coming. This operation was under scrutiny by not only the FBI and the CIA, but by Senator Hostetler and his allies on Capitol Hill as well. Hostetler wanted the man who'd almost killed his little girl, and the nation—when and if it found out about this operation—would want the man who'd visited terror on its shores. Once the ax started falling, Latham knew his head would be on the short list.

He forced himself to focus on their next step. There was only one, really: interviewing and canvassing. So while his agents discreetly beat the bushes, Latham waited.

SIXTEEN HOURS AFTER VORSALOV ESCAPED, THEY STRUCK GOLD IN the form of a xenophobic deli owner.

According to Paul Randal, the deli owner claimed to have seen a pair of "Eye-rabs" parked in a minivan two blocks from Brown's Boat Center around the time of Vorsalov's escape. Suspicious of Middle Easterners and their well-known fondness of wanton destruction, the deli owner not only remembered the license plate but also the movements of the occupants, one of whom left the van for ten minutes, then returned. This in itself was not significant until Randal questioned an employee at Brown's, who confirmed that Vorsalov's canoe had been reserved and paid for by an Arab. The time frame fit, as did the general description.

"Why didn't they just rent it over the phone?" Latham asked Randal.

"They tried, probably. Last year during homecoming a bunch of high school kids reserved a dozen paddle boats by phone, then took them out and played a little demolition derby. Since then, they only take reservations face-to-face . . . credit card, waivers, all that."

"What else?"

"This is where it gets good. The deli guy says the van sat there for about twenty minutes. Just sitting there. He's getting nervous; the Arabs look nervous. Then all of a sudden a white guy, walking fast from the direction of Brown's, climbs in, and they pull away."

"I'll be damned. And the van?"

Randall handed him the report. "Rented by a Henry Awad, a naturalized citizen. He's a cook at a diner in Hyattsville. Wife, no children. The van goes for three hundred a week. He pulls down four."

"Henry must really love minivans," Latham said. "Okay, put him under the microscope."

WITHIN TWENTY-FOUR HOURS THEY KNEW MORE ABOUT HENRY Awad than did his closest neighbors. Most of the information was trivial, but several things caught Latham's eye.

According to INS, Awad had come to the U.S. from Egypt six years before. Ever the skeptic, Latham called in a favor from the FBI's Linguistics Department and had a Near East expert visit the diner for lunch. While eating her cheeseburger and fries, she listened closely to the voice in the kitchen.

"Wherever he's from," she later told Latham, "it isn't Egypt." Her best guess was Syria or Iraq. Latham knew this proved nothing, but it piqued his interest.

The second curiosity was that the Awad family's Windstar—the one costing Henry three-quarters of his weekly income—was nowhere to be seen. Awad drove a brown

Dodge Aries K, and his wife never left the house aside from walking trips to the grocery store.

During the second day of surveillance, Randal called Latham. Charlie could hear the excitement in his partner's voice. "Remember that load of groceries Henry's wife bought yesterday?"

"Yeah."

"He's loading them into the trunk of his car."

"Picnic, maybe?"

"Doubt it. It's just him, no basket, no blanket . . . just him."

LATHAM HAD WORKED ENOUGH CASES TO KNOW THE MAJORITY OF them are exercises in tedium, broken by occasional moments of excitement. Seemingly dead cases can turn 180 degrees in a matter of hours. This is exactly what happened when Randal tailed Henry Awad.

Without so much as a glance over his shoulder, Awad drove straight to a strip mall in Greenbelt and parked. Five minutes later, the blue Windstar pulled up beside him.

"Charlie, you're not going to believe this."

"Try me."

"Henry's loading groceries into our wayward minivan. He's being helped by a pair of Arabs that look a whole lot like the ones our deli owner described."

"Okay, forget Henry for now. Stay on the van. We pin them down, we're back in the game. I'm sending backup. Stick with them."

AN HOUR AFTER SUNSET, LATHAM PARKED IN A CLEARING OF PINES in rural Greenbelt, old horse country about five miles off Highway I-95. He got out and walked up a path leading into the trees. He was met by Janet Paschel.

"How's it look?" he asked.

"Good. The HRU boys are already here."

Following his call, it had taken the Bureau's Hostage Rescue Unit only thirty minutes to get mobilized. HRU was perhaps the best hostage team in the U.S., military or civilian.

Paschel led him to a ranch-style house fronted by a long porch. Latham found Randal and Stan Wilson, the HRU commander, standing in the darkened living room before a bay window that overlooked a meadow.

Latham shook hands with Wilson. "Thanks for getting here so quick, Stan."

"Sure. This is Hank Reeves, my second-in-command."

"Good to meet you, Hank." To Randal: "Nice digs. Whose is it?"

"Belongs to the Taub family. They own the stables and corral, too. They're in Kentucky for a month or so. We ran into a caretaker who gave us their number. Seems Mr. Taub is an ex-DEA agent. He said—and I'm quoting here—as long as we don't bring in any hookers and promise to clean up after ourselves, we can have the run of the place."

Latham laughed. "I think we can manage that. Stan, how's it look?"

"Depends on what you want."

"Let's see the layout."

Wilson handed him a pair of binoculars. In the distance he could see a two-story, whitewashed farmhouse. Several windows were lit, but Latham saw no activity. A narrow access road led from the house, around the edge of the meadow, and out to the main road.

"Can't see it from here, but there's a garage to the right," Wilson said. "Van's parked in front of it."

They had chosen a good hidey-hole, Latham decided. There were only three ways to approach the farmhouse: the road, through the pine trees surrounding the house, or across the meadow.

"Have we got blueprints?" Latham asked.

Randal handed them over. "Care to guess who's listed as the renter?"

"Good ol' Henry Awad?"

"You got it."

"Stan, how thick are the trees?"

"A good mile in all directions."

"How close to the farmhouse?"

"About a hundred feet of clearance on all sides. The meadow grass is maybe six inches tall," Wilson added. "No cover there."

"Okay, this is what I need: Bore mikes on each major room, plus the upstairs if possible, an eyeball map of the grounds, pictures of the occupants, and a wire tap."

"Can do. You'll handle the warrants?"

"Yep." Latham called Janet Paschel over, pulled out his cell phone, and dialed the U.S. Attorney's Office. "Janet, start driving. They'll be ready when you get there."

IF THERE WAS ANY SILVER LINING TO THE WORLD TRADE CENTER and Oklahoma City bombings, it was the legislative and judicial system's increased support of the FBI's antiterrorist efforts. As Latham stood in the Taub house in rural Greenbelt, the FBI's power to pursue terrorists was greater than it had been since the days of J. Edgar Hoover. Within two hours of sending Paschel to fetch the warrants, Latham was listening to the radio as the HRU team moved into position around the farmhouse.

It was cold outside, in the low fifties, and from where Latham sat, he could see dew glistening on the meadow grass. In the distance came the occasional whinny of a horse. Randal sat beside an audio tech at the coffee table.

Wilson's voice came over the radio. "Eyeball, give me a report."

"I count three tangos in the kitchen. All windows clear. No other lights."

"Roger, move in."

Latham peered through the infrared scope and could barely make out two of Wilson's men crawling from the trees and merging with the shadows along the farmhouse wall.

Thirty minutes later, it was done. His hair soaked with sweat, Wilson walked into the living room. "Any problems?" Latham asked.

"Couldn't get to the upstairs. Maybe if they leave, but

not while they're home. We've got mikes on all the ground-floor rooms, plus a wiretap on the phone, a map, and some good pics of the inside."

"Great job, Stan; thanks. How about the two we're looking for?"

"Didn't see them."

Short of canvassing area hotels for Vorsalov, Latham had no choice but to hope these Arabs would lead him to the Vorsalov and Fayyad—if in fact the Jordanian was part of the operation.

He turned to the audio technician. "How about it?" he asked.

"Perfect. It's like we're sitting in the same room."

Latham nodded. "Start the tapes and pray they're talkative."

BORN FROM A COMBINATION OF ARROGANCE AND A FIRM BELIEF in hiding in plain sight, Vorsalov took a room at the Marriott Key Bridge at the bend of the Potomac, a stone's throw from Roosevelt Island and Brown's Boat Center.

After showering and calling room service for a seafood quiche and a bottle of white Coutet, he took a chair by the window and read Fayyad's report. He was impressed by the Jordanian's progress. The seduction had been swift and complete. Fayyad had read her perfectly.

The turning of the senator had also gone smoothly, though Fayyad was a bit too congenial for Vorsalov's taste. Fayyad reported Smith was compliant, frightened, and slightly desperate—a powerful combination. But would it be enough? And what of the ridiculously short time line? Would these Arabs never learn? Yet another case of zealotry-induced blindness.

He finished the report and set it aside. Ill-advised as it might be, tightening the vise on Smith was their only recourse. Vorsalov scanned the report again until he reached the page he sought. He read the passage twice more before the germ of a plan began to form. It was workable, he decided, but very dangerous.

But this was America, he reminded himself. Security
here was a sieve, and their police were restricted by rules
and regulations and other such niceties. Yes, he decided, it
could be done.

36

Philippine Sea, 30° 28' N 140° 18' E

THOUGH THE END OF THE WAR WAS STILL A YEAR AWAY, BY THE
early summer of 1944, America's island-hopping campaign
had already obliterated Japan's forward bases and the Al-
lied forces were steadily tightening the noose on the Japanese Empire. Destroyed or bypassed were the island
fortresses of Guadalcanal, Tarawa, Rabaul, and dozens of
other atolls standing between the U.S. advance and the Japanese mainland.

By mid-June, two months after Truk's airfields and lagoon were decimated by the Hellcats of Task Force 58,
Vice Admiral Kelly Turner's amphibious landing forces
were swinging north. Blocking their way were the Marianas
and Saipan, the headquarters of Japan's Central Pacific
Fleet.

Unlike Truk, however, the Marianas could not be bypassed. Doing so would leave Nimitz's flanks exposed and
deprive the allies of Saipan's airfields, which they needed
to launch B-29 bombing raids on the mainland. Conse-
quently, the Japanese high command knew Saipan and the
Marianas would bear the full fury of U.S. forces, and they
had been preparing for it since February of that year. Cling-
ing to what had become their standard of battle, they chose
to fortify not only Saipan but every island, atoll, and rock
they had captured since 1941.

One such island, Parece Kito, situated roughly 350 miles
northwest of Saipan, had begun its fortification in March
of 1944. Here, as before, Japan had not learned from its
previous battles with the U.S. American commanders had
no interest in forward naval bases. They wanted homes for

their bombers, and Parece Kito's four square miles of jungle and mangrove swamps did not fit the bill. Even if Nimitz had hand-delivered this information to Tokyo, however, it would not have mattered, for the empire's defense strategy was based as much on stubbornness as it was on sound military planning. Not a scrap of ground was to be yielded. Not a palm tree, not a spit of sand.

And so by June of 1944, Parece Kito was home to a regiment of Japanese Marines, a sprawling underground bunker complex, and an interwoven system of eight-inch gun batteries designed to decimate any landing force trying to enter its lagoon.

Alas, the guns never fired a shot in anger.

They and the troops remained on Parece Kito, unused and ignored until the end of the war thirteen months later, when the island's commander received word of the Empire's surrender. The closest it had come to seeing an invasion force were three overflights by U.S. Navy PBYs, whose photos convinced Nimitz to bypass the island and let it wither on the vine.

Six weeks after the bombing of Hiroshima and Nagasaki, a dozen ships arrived at Parece Kito, took aboard the demoralized Japanese troops, and transported them back to internment camps in Japan. The guns were destroyed in place, and the bunker complex was sealed, an overnight ghost town.

It was to this island, over fifty years later, that Walter Oaken was sending Briggs Tanner and Ian Cahil on the trail of *Tsumago*.

After reaching the airstrip outside Iyo, they had boarded the charter plane awaiting them, and three hours later, they touched down at a rural airstrip on Okinawa. They were cleared through customs without incident, and Tanner assumed that either Takagi had not yet contacted the Okinawan authorities or Oaken had pulled some of his own strings. They found a secluded phone booth and called Oaken.

"I wish we had *Tsumago*'s helm data to confirm it, but this is about as close as we're going to get," Oaken began.

"The log listed *Tsumago* as sailing eight times in the last six months, average duration three days, give or take twelve hours."

Armed with the ship's cruising speed of twenty knots and the longest time she'd been gone (eighty-five hours), Oaken had multiplied the two figures and halved the answer, leaving a maximum one-way range of 950 miles. With the shipyard at its center, the arc encompassed eastern China, Korea, Taiwan, all of Japan, and a good-sized chunk of the Pacific Ocean, including thousands of tiny, uninhabited islands.

Oaken checked all the major ports in Korea, China, and Japan for record of *Tsumago*'s docking. He found nothing. Like her sister ship *Toshogu, Tsumago* was a ghost. So why, he asked, wouldn't Takagi use similar methods to hide her existence and destination? It was the right question.

Like *Toshogu*, which had been purchased by Skulafjord Limited, a secret subsidiary of Takagi Industries, *Tsumago* had been purchased by yet another secret Takagi holding called Caraman Exports, among whose many offshoots was a company called Daito Properties. Daito openly owned real estate in Taipai, Malaysia, and Sumatra. It was one of Daito's buried holdings that interested Oaken, however, namely a small 100-acre island in the Philippine Sea called Parece Kito.

"It has no real value," Oaken explained. "No mineral deposits, no tourist attraction . . . nothing. But it does fall into the nine hundred-mile arc, and it's in the middle of nowhere."

"How much trouble did Takagi go to keep this place secret?" Tanner asked.

"Lots. If I hadn't been looking for something specific, I wouldn't have found it."

Tanner looked at Cahil, who said, "We either check it or go home."

Briggs didn't feel like going home. "How do we get there, Oaks?"

*   *   *

OAKEN'S ITINERARY SENT THEM ON A FLIGHT FROM OKINAWA TO
the Bonin Islands and finally to Asuncion Island in the Marianas, where he'd arranged a charter boat for the final 300-
mile leg. It had taken a tripled fee and a substantial deposit
to convince the owner of the company, Mr. Privari, to let
them captain the boat themselves.

At dusk, fully fueled, supplied, and seventeen hours behind *Tsumago*, they sailed out of Asuncion's harbor and
turned northeast. The weather was hot and sunny, with a
mild easterly breeze. Tanner breathed in the salt air and
was suddenly glad to be at sea. The past few weeks had
taken its toll, and he hadn't noticed how tightly he was
wound. It felt good to be in the middle of the wide-open
nowhere.

Standing at the helm, he accepted a bottle of beer from
Cahil.

"So what do we know about this rock?" Bear asked. "Are
we talking Club Med or Guadalcanal?"

"You didn't catch Mr. Privari's lecture on Parece Kito's
delights?"

"Uh-uh. What'd he say?"

"In the water, razor sharp coral, sharks, and poisonous
fish; ashore, dysentery, malaria, saber grass, vines as strong
as steel cable, snakes, and giant lizards."

Cahil froze with his beer bottle halfway to his mouth.
"You're kidding me."

"Nope. And I quote: 'Don't drink the water, don't eat
anything that grows on the land, and don't breathe the air
too deeply.' "

"Takagi's own little tropical getaway. Suits his personality."

Tanner smiled. "How long till we get there?"

Cahil checked the chart, made some calculations. "At this
speed, fifteen hours give or take."

CAHIL'S ESTIMATE WAS NEAR-PERFECT. EARLY AFTERNOON THE FOL-
lowing day, they spotted Parece Kito on the horizon, a
hump of green rain forest surrounded by the churned white

line of the reef. They circled to the opposite side of the island and followed the shore until the lagoon came into view.

"Big," Cahil muttered, peering through the binoculars. "Great natural harbor."

"Any sign of her?"

"Nope. Looks deserted. The beach is pristine. Doesn't look like anybody's walked on it since the war."

Tanner took the binoculars and scanned the island. According to Oaken, the Japanese forces had razed most of the jungle in preparation for the invasion, but it had returned with a vengeance. So dense was the canopy that he found it hard to distinguish individual trees. It would be dark as night inside. If Takagi was hiding something, this was the right place.

"Hop on the prow, Bear."

With Cahil leaning over the water and calling out hazards, Tanner steered through the outer reef, turned parallel to shore, and began circling the island. Soon the beach tapered to a ribbon about three feet wide. Trees dangled over the water and scraped the hull. After ten minutes, Cahil called out, "Port bow, Briggs. We've got ourselves a back door."

Tanner saw it: a creek, about twenty-five feet wide, almost overgrown by jungle. It looked more like a tunnel than the mouth of a river. He throttled back and nosed the bow toward the opening. Cahil signaled a halt and lowered a sinker into the water. "Fifteen feet," he whispered to Tanner. Something about a jungle, Briggs thought, that encouraged whispering. "Plenty of draft."

Tanner eased them forward. Within seconds, the jungle swallowed them.

AFTER HALF A MILE, THE CREEK WIDENED INTO A SMALL LAGOON. Tanner cut the engines and let the boat glide on its own momentum. Cahil crawled back into the cabin and held a finger to his lips. He pointed through the windshield. What little sunlight found its way through the canopy was no brighter than moonlight, but the object of Bear's attention was unmistakable: an L-shaped pier, made of rough planking and bamboo pilings. Not more than two years old, Tanner thought.

He realized his heart was pounding. "Grab the boat hook," he whispered. "We'll push our way in."

As quietly as possible, they eased the boat to the bank and secured the bow to a tree. With Tanner in the lead, they jumped ashore, found a narrow game trail, and started walking.

NOT FAR FROM THE PIER THEY FOUND A TRAIL LEADING INTO THE forest. The foliage at the path's edge was freshly trimmed.

"Here, Briggs," Cahil called, crouched a few feet away. Tanner joined him. "Pretty heavy foot traffic."

There were dozens of overlapping footprints; beside them were parallel ruts in the dirt. "A cart of some kind," Tanner said.

Cahil grinned. "Natives taking their bananas to market?"

"Doubt it."

They started down the trail. Traveling in the open was against Tanner's better judgment, but hacking their way through the jungle would be not only noisy, but it would consume precious time.

Cahil was walking point when the trail abruptly opened into a clearing. He ducked down. Tanner scuttled forward and peeked through the foliage. Sitting in the middle of the clearing was a helicopter.

"Sikorsky UH-60," Cahil whispered. The 60 could carry eleven men.

"Let's take a look around," said Tanner. "I'll meet you back here."

Five minutes later, they were again crouched on the trail. With a cat-and-canary grin, Bear showed Tanner a pair of .45 pistols. "Found them under the pilot's seat."

Tanner hefted one of the guns, glad for it. Several times in the past weeks he'd wished for a weapon, but in the real world, spying and guns were a bad mix. "I found another path across the clearing," he said. "Looks like a lot of recent traffic heading inland."

"Let's go," said Bear.

Almost immediately, the new path took a sharp turn to the right. Tanner stopped, halting Cahil in midstride. Tanner turned, studying the edge of the trail. *Something there . . .* Suddenly it snapped into focus: They were standing beside a low concrete wall, its facade overgrown with foliage. He mouthed *bunker* to Cahil, and they backtracked until they found a path that led them to a clearing.

The bunker was enormous, roughly the size of a football field. Its exterior was so interwoven with vines that only patches of stonework were visible. Spaced at intervals along the walls were huge gun ports; between these, machine gun slits. Briggs tried to imagine what the Marines would have faced here and found himself applauding the Allies' decision to bypass Parece Kito.

They settled into the underbrush and watched. The jungle squawked and buzzed around them. After fifteen minutes, nothing had moved.

"Shall we?" Bear finally asked.

Tanner nodded. "Let's go find out what Mr. Takagi's hiding."

37

Greenbelt, Maryland

AFTER ALMOST TWO DECADES OF CHASING SPIES AND TERRORISTS, Latham had learned plenty of lessons, but one topped the list: Regardless of how well-trained, dedicated, or disciplined a bad guy may be, he *will* make a mistake. It may be a harmless mistake, or it may *be* something that puts him away. The most common error—especially among terrorists—was the tendency to assume a safe house was just that: a sanctuary where you can let down your guard. Standing in the Taub home staring across the meadow, he knew this is exactly what had happened here.

In the past twenty-four hours, the Arabs had made half a dozen phone calls. All but two turned out to be benign. These were the two that led Latham's team to a stylish condo in Glen Echo, which, according to the real estate office, had been rented by a Ricardo Pamono at approximately the same time Henry Awad rented the Greenbelt house.

A team had been watching the condo since the previous morning, but so far, the occupant had neither shown himself nor made any phone calls.

Randal walked into the living room. "Anything?"

Latham shook his head. "The condo?"

"Quiet. Whoever this guy is, he's a homebody."

Glen Echo

JUST PAST SUNSET, THE CAMERAMAN IN THE STAKEOUT VAN watched a Diamond Cab pull to a stop down the street and a woman get out. She was in her early fifties, stylishly dressed, wearing a head scarf and Jackie O. sunglasses.

"Talk about conspicuously inconspicuous," he said. "Looks like our boy might get a visitor."

"You get the car number?"

"No, the angle's wrong. Okay, yep, she's going up the walkway."

"I'll call Charlie, see if we can get some help from the cab company."

AS A PAIR OF HASTILY RECRUITED DCPD OFFICERS WERE RECORD-ing license tags from the 200-plus cars in the parking lot from which Diamond had picked up the woman, Judith Smith and Fayyad had just finished making love. She lay with her head on his chest, her hand tracing circles on his belly.

"You're angry," she whispered. "I should have called."

Yes, I'm angry, Fayyad thought. The further he kept her from this, the better chance she had of staying alive. Even that was not certain, however. What was Vorsalov planning? When would he move?

"No, Judith, I am not angry. How could I be anything but pleased to see you?"

"You mean that?"

"Of course." *God help me, I do.* "We must be careful, though. How are things at home?"

"Better than normal. He's a lamb when he's not feeling well."

"I don't understand."

"He's been home since yesterday. From what I heard, he nearly fainted during a meeting. He hadn't eaten anything that day and hadn't been sleeping well, so—"

Fayyad's heart lurched. "Is he all right?"

"He's fine. The doctor said it was just stress, bad diet, that sort of thing."

Her words were so indifferent, as though she were describing an ailing houseplant. Her bond to the senator was quickly unraveling. The professional in Fayyad was pleased; inside, he was unnerved. "So he's not ill?" he asked.

"No. Since when do you care so much about Herb?"

"I don't, but like it or not, he's a part of your life. If it affects you, I care."

She kissed him playfully. "My hero."

Fayyad glanced at his watch. "Darling, I'm sorry, but I have to go."

"Where?"

"I have a meeting with a professor at school. I'll call you a cab."

FIVE MINUTES AFTER THE CAB LEFT, THE CONDO'S FRONT DOOR opened. In the FBI van, the cameraman was already recording "Ah, at last, he appears."

"What's he doing?" said his partner.

"Heading to the garage. Door's up. . . ."

"Shit."

"Car's coming out. License, four hundred twenty-one-romeo-zulu-november. Looks like a brown Toyota Camry . . . nope, make it an Avalon. How're we doing at the lot?"

"The cops got called away; they only got about half the plates. Charlie's trying to break somebody free to tail her. Gonna be close, though."

"Well, our boy's moving. Get Charlie on the horn."

LATHAM HAD KNOWN IT WOULD HAPPEN SOONER OR LATER. TOO few agents, too much territory. Something had to give. "Stay on him," he ordered. "We'll have to give up the woman. Janet and Chuck are heading to the lot. I'll divert them your way. Stay on this channel, let them know where you're headed. As soon as they're in position, head back to the condo."

"You got it, boss."

"Did you get a look at him and the woman?"

"Not really. We've got some good film, though."

"Transmit it over here, will you?"

While one agent drove and the other transmitted the camera's digital images, Fayyad led them north on River Road, then south on 495. Ten minutes later, Fayyad veered off the highway onto Leesburg Pike. "We're heading into Falls Church," the driver called. "South on the pike."

"I copy," Latham said. "Stay with him. Janet's ten minutes away."

Latham was surprised. If in fact this was Fayyad, he was showing much more caution than were the other Arabs.

"Take a look, Charlie. Randal was standing over the technician's shoulder. One by one, the thumbnail photos appeared on the computer screen.

Latham walked over. "Can you enlarge 'em?"

"You bet. Which one?"

"The woman . . . number six." The tech did so.

"Something, Charlie?" asked Randal.

"No." Latham shook his head. "No, I guess not. How about the man?"

The tech called up the thumbnails.

"How about that one, where he's walking by the porch light," said Latham. The tech punched a series of keys, and the image expanded. "Tighten on the face."

The image contracted on the face, then swam into focus. Latham stared at it.

"It's him. It's Fayyad."

AFTER TURNING ONTO THE LEESBURG, FAYYAD MADE A U-TURN and backtracked to Lee Highway. There the surveillance van passed him off to Janet Paschel. At the Key Bridge, Fayyad turned off and pulled under the awning of the Marriott.

Janet drove down a block, parked, and picked up the radio.

VORSALOV GESTURED FAYYAD TO A CHAIR BESIDE THE BALCONY doors and poured them both a cup of coffee.

As before, Fayyad was struck by the Russian's presence.

Though of medium height and build, Vorsalov was solidly built. And his eyes . . . *Like staring at a corpse,* he thought. He imagined those eyes on Judith and shuddered.

"You were not followed?" Vorsalov asked him.

"No. If I had been, they would be crashing through the door."

"Perhaps, perhaps not." Vorsalov shrugged. "You don't approve of my involvement, do you? You don't like my methods."

"Whether I approve or not is irrelevant. I simply think it's unnecessary."

Vorsalov shrugged. "Believe it or not, I agree. I've read your reports. You've made amazing progress in a short time. This woman—Judith, is it?—is in love with you?"

"Yes."

"Too bad it may go to waste."

"I don't understand."

"Her husband was the wrong target for this operation. He's not in a position—"

"I wouldn't know. I'm simply doing my job."

"And now you want to know what I have planned."

"Yes."

"We have no choice but to take her."

Fayyad felt his heart thud, but he kept his face impassive. "The wife?"

"No. Her disappearance would cause too much commotion. The mistress. She's a nobody. She won't be missed until we're done."

"I see," said Fayyad. "And when we have her? Then what?"

"Whatever is necessary."

"I don't think Smith can take the strain," Fayyad said. He told Vorsalov about Smith's fainting at the CIA meeting. "He is near the breaking point."

"As long as he's under our control, such a break could be useful."

"I'm not so sure. I've come to understand him. He's—"

"It's already been decided."

"I think it's a mistake."

"As you said earlier, whether you approve or not is irrelevant. However, I assumed you would feel this way, so I have arranged confirmation from your superiors."

"I don't understand."

Vorsalov handed him a slip of paper. "Memorize it, then burn it. Tonight at eleven you will receive the call."

"At home? That's not—"

"Follow the script. Nothing can be gleaned from it. The call will be short. Tomorrow morning, call me at this number." Vorsalov recited a number and had Fayyad repeat it twice. "I'll explain the rest then."

JANET PASCHEL WATCHED FAYYAD TIP THE VALET, GET IN HIS CAR, and drive off. Latham, who had joined them a few minutes before, said, "Let him go. Radio Glen Echo and tell them he's coming back."

Janet relayed the orders, then got out, walked across the street, and entered the lobby. She returned in ten minutes. "I had the night manager check the log for the night Vorsalov would have checked in," she said. "None of the names rang a bell."

"Damn."

"But," Janet said, smiling. "The night he would have arrived there was only one bellman on duty."

"Fancy place like this, I'll bet nobody carries their own bags. Can we talk to him?"

"If you don't mind driving to Fairmont Heights."

THE BELLMAN, A YOUNG BLACK COLLEGE STUDENT, OPENED HIS front door and peeked out. "FBI? What for?"

"We just need your help."

"Uh-huh. What for?"

"Listen—it's Parnell, right? Parnell, you're not in trouble, okay?"

He considered this, then shrugged. "What's up?"

Latham handed him a photo of Vorsalov. "You were on

duty at the Key Bridge day before yesterday. You remember seeing this man?"

Parnell studied the photo. His face lit up. "Shit, yeah, I remember."

"You're sure?"

"Uh-huh. Pasty-faced guy, some kind of accent, too. Bad tipper. Room four-twelve."

38

Parece Kito

THEY FOUND AN OPENING IN THE VINES AND CRAWLED THROUGH one of the gun ports. They crouched against the inner wall, listening, waiting for their eyes to adjust to the cavelike interior.

Spaced evenly down the bunker's axis were three spiral ladders. Tanner peered down one and saw nothing but blackness. Somewhere he heard water dripping. The floor, walls, and ceiling were splotched with mold. Behind them, something moved. They spun. Caught in their flashlight beams, a lizard skittered across the floor and disappeared into a crack in the wall.

Tanner tested the handrail, found it sturdy, and they started downward. Briggs counted steps, and by the time they reached the bottom they were twenty-five feet underground. Ahead lay a dark passage.

Tanner raised the .45, clicked on the flashlight, and shined it down the passage. Ten feet away lay a stainless steel door. They walked closer. The door's edges were bordered by a thick rubber gasket, and its handle was a lever type like those used on industrial refrigerators.

Cahil pressed his ear against the steel, then shook his head. "Maybe Takagi's hoarding rump roast," he whispered.

"He strikes me more of a veal man. Higher brutality factor."

They checked the door for alarms or sensors and found nothing. Tanner grasped the handle and lifted gently until he heard a soft *click-click*. A puff of air escaped. That meant air-conditioning, which in turn meant electricity.

Tanner opened the door the rest of the way, and they stepped through.

Two things struck him simultaneously: the coolness of air, which after the jungle heat felt like an arctic blast, and the feeling they'd stepped into a high-tech laboratory.

Instead of stone, the walls, floor, and ceiling were made of gray Lexan plastic. So well-seamed were the walls that Tanner had a hard time telling where they ended and the floor began. There were no corners, no right angles. He felt momentarily dizzy.

"Briggs, take a look."

Cahil pointed to a stack of shelves containing plastic gowns, hair caps, and booties. "Whatever they're up to, its delicate," he said.

Tanner nodded. "No symbology on the walls." Sanitary, anonymous.

The corridor ended at a T-turn. Tanner looked left, then right. More pressure doors. "You have a preference?" he asked.

"Let's try right."

Cahil led the way to the door, eased it open, waited for the escaping air to dissipate, then slipped through. Here the walls were not made of Lexan but of concrete. Judging from its decayed state, Tanner assumed it was the original structure. Darkened lightbulbs hung from the ceiling.

They clicked on their flashlights. The passage before them was fifty feet long. Spaced along the left side were two doors.

Inside the first room they found half a dozen bunk beds and a washroom. Cahil opened a locker to reveal neatly folded clothes. Tanner picked up a Sidney Sheldon paperback from one of the bunks. It was written in Kanji.

"Looks like they left in a hurry."

The second room was a small kitchen, its steel counters spotted with rust. Several cabinets contained canned food, loaves of bread, and bags of rice. Tanner poked the bread; it felt fresh. He opened the refrigerator and found it well-stocked.

"Briggs."

Cahil was standing in front of a pantry door. He pointed at the floor. It took a moment for Tanner's brain to register the brownish red rivulets for what they were. Heart pounding, he stepped back, raised the .45, and nodded. Cahil opened the door.

"Sweet Jesus," he murmured.

The pile of bodies almost touched the ceiling. Arms and legs and heads lay jumbled together. The stench of blood and feces filled Briggs's nostrils.

"There must be a dozen of them," Cahil whispered.

From the pile there came a moan.

"Somebody's alive!" Bear said.

Together they began pulling at bodies, checking for signs of life. While most of the corpses were riddled with bullet wounds, three of them, dressed in gray coveralls, had been shot once, execution-style, in the back of the head. At the eighth body, Tanner found a pulse. The man, a Japanese, was ghostly white, his chest barely rising. His shirt and pants were blood-soaked. They carried him out and laid him on the floor. Cahil ripped off his shirt.

There was a single bullet hole under his left nipple; they rolled him over and found the exit wound was just below his shoulder blade. Tanner found a dishcloth in a drawer and pressed it against the wound as Cahil pulled a roll of duct tape from his pack and bound the dressing.

"I don't see anything else," Cahil said. "Lucky boy."

"He's lost a lot of blood, but his heart's strong. Breathing's regular."

The man's eyes fluttered; he gripped Tanner's hand. The man opened his mouth, but only a croak came out. Tanner said, "You're safe. What happened here?"

"Dead . . . They're all dead."

What happened?"

"Have they . . . have they gone?"

"Who?" Tanner asked.

"Noboru. He was here. He . . . he . . ."

Tanner leaned closer. "Where is he?"

"In the work section."

"Why did they do this?" Cahil asked.

In answer, the man feebly raised his arm and pointed to the ceiling. Strapped to one of the support beams was a black box. Cahil jumped onto a counter for a closer look. "Bomb," he said. "Signal detonated. I don't dare touch it. Briggs, if they've rigged more of these, this whole place will come down on itself."

Tanner paused, thinking. "Okay, get him out of here."

"But—"

"Take him and go. He's our only witness."

"You'll get buried," Bear said.

"I'll run fast. Can you handle him?"

"Stubborn son of a . . . Yeah, I've got him."

With Tanner on his heels, Cahil swung the man onto his shoulder, headed for the pressure door, and pushed through. "Target!" Cahil called.

He ducked, and Tanner raised the .45 just in time to see a man down the hall raising his own Ingram machine pistol. Tanner fired twice, and the man went down.

"Go, Bear!"

"See you up top."

They separated at the T-turn, Cahil going left, Tanner ahead to the next door. Passing the dead man, Tanner noticed his gray coveralls. The three in the pantry had been Noboru's.

Tanner burst through the door.

This corridor, like the others, was lined with Lexan. To his right was a sliding glass door. He clicked on his flashlight and slipped through.

To his left stood a Plexiglas-enclosed room. Opposite that, to his front, was a second. *Clean rooms,* he thought immediately. Between them ran an alleyway, ten feet wide and bordered by handrails. Set into the floor at its head was a hatch. Through it Tanner could hear the hum of machinery.

He shined his flashlight into the first clean room and saw a long, stainless steel worktable and a bank of cabinets. He was about to turn back when something caught his eye. Lying on the floor in the corner were three more bodies.

He checked the second room. This one contained several

pieces of machinery, one of which looked like a precision
lathe. Wired to its leg was what looked like a soda can.
Tanner looked closer and realized what he was seeing: a
MK 8 white phosphorous grenade. He scanned the rest of
the room. He counted eight more grenades; with each burning at 5,000 degrees, they could turn this room—this whole
level, for that matter—to molten rock in less than a minute.

Where's Noboru?

From the open hatch came a metallic clang. Tanner froze.
He checked the .45's magazine: Five rounds left.

Walking on cat feet, he kneeled beside the hatch and
peeked inside. A short ladder led downward. The humming
sound was louder. He slipped feetfirst into the hatch and
crept down.

The room was narrow, no wider than the alleyway above,
and generators and transformers lined the walls. Near the
back wall Tanner saw the glow of a lightbulb. Hunched
beneath it was a figure. The squarish head was unmistakable: Noboru.

Tanner ducked behind the nearest transformer, crawled
around a generator, and stopped. Noboru was twenty feet
away, still hunched over, intent on his work. Tanner had a
fair guess what that was.

Now what? Between them lay nothing but open floor.
Could he get close enough before Noboru spotted him? He
crawled around the generator, paused, then wriggled forward.

Fifteen feet to go.

Tanner would never know why, but at that moment
Tange Noboru looked up. Their eyes met. Even as Tanner
raised his .45, Noboru snatched his gun from the floor and
ducked left. They fired simultaneously. Tanner's shot struck
the wall beside Noboru's head. Something buzzed by
Briggs's ear and *thunked* into the generator.

Silence.

Tanner went still. Noboru would be doing the same, he
knew, each waiting for the other to make a mistake. *Patience, Briggs. Make him move.* That Noboru hadn't yet
used the detonator suggested one of three things: either the

devices were not ready; Noboru had no wish to die; or he wanted to first kill Tanner, up close and personal. Whichever it was, Briggs didn't care. He still had time.

One minute turned into two. The generator hummed.

Tanner saw a shadow of movement against the far wall. He laid his face on the ground and saw a booted foot resting beside the generator's leg. The foot shifted, paused, then slipped forward.

Tanner didn't hesitate. He took aim and fired.

The .45 slug struck Noboru just below the ankle, blowing off his heel. As he screamed and toppled over, Tanner was up and running.

He found Noboru lying on the floor, groaning and clutching his ankle. Blood gushed from the stump. Tanner kicked his pistol away. Grimacing, Noboru pushed himself upright and kneeled on his good leg, swaying slightly.

"You are too late," he said.

It was then Tanner noticed a loaf-sized package tucked against the generator. The charge was at least four pounds of plastic explosive. Whatever secret this place held, Takagi was making sure it died here. Lying beside the bomb was what looked like a transistor radio. On its face, in red letters, were two numerals: 26. As Tanner watched, the display clicked to 25.

"You will not make it out," Noboru said.

Tanner swallowed the bile rising in his throat. "Did you kill Ohira?"

Noboru nodded. "Good shot, yes? I should have killed you, too. It would have been easy."

"Lucky for me your judgment isn't worth a damn. What about the crew of *Toshogu?* That was you, too?"

"Hai."

Twenty seconds . . .

"And the woman? Sumiko?"

"Hai. She fought, that one. Perhaps if you hadn't brought her into this—"

"One more thing: You did all this on Takagi's orders?"

"It was my honor to—"

"That's all I needed to know."

Tanner raised the .45 and took aim. In that last second, Noboru's eyes went wide as he realized what was happening. *He's surprised,* Tanner thought. *The stupid son of a bitch is surprised. He thought he was going to have it his way.*

Briggs shot him once in the chest. Amazingly, Noboru took the slug and managed to stay upright. Dumbfounded, he looked down at the oozing wound, back up at Tanner, then toppled onto his side.

The timer clicked past thirteen seconds. Tanner turned and ran.

He scrambled up the ladder, through the hatch, and was almost at the sliding door when the first charge exploded. The floor heaved beneath his feet. He stumbled and fell. Behind him, a gout of flame shot from the hatch. When it cleared, the floor of the alley was gone, a gaping hole in its place.

Almost simultaneously, blinding white flames erupted in both the clean rooms. The Plexiglas began bubbling. Tanner watched in amazement as the machinery first glowed red, then white, and then began melting like hot clay.

He stumbled to the door. A wave of heat washed over him. His pack burst into flames. He shrugged it off and kept going. He felt a stab of pain in his calf, turned, saw a chunk of flaming Plexiglas plastered to his pants. *Knife . . . knife!* He unsheathed it and began hacking at the material, slicing skin and cloth until the pant leg fell away. He crawled through the door and rolled into the hall. Even here, the heat was intense. The Lexan walls were sloughing away, revealing the stone beneath.

He pushed through the pressure door, turned right at the T-turn, and ran for the main door. Behind him came another explosion. He looked back. The ceiling was gone, and through it came an avalanche of rubble and dust and smoke.

He groped for the door handle, heaved back, and charged into the passage. He ran forward until he collided with the ladder. He mounted it and began climbing hand over hand. At the top, he pulled his upper body onto the floor.

At the far end of the bunker, the ceiling was plunging

into the crater below. A car-sized chunk of concrete crashed
to the floor beside him. With a shriek of steel, the ladder
tore free and dropped into the darkness. His legs swung
free, and he started to slide back. He scrambled for a handhold, found one, and pulled himself up.

All around him, jagged cracks were opening on the floor.
He tried to stand, but collapsed. The pain in his leg was
nearly blinding. He began hopping one-legged toward the
nearest gunport, eyes fixed on the sunlight peeking through
the vines. It seemed miles away. *Keep moving,* a voice in
the back of his head said. The floor was crumbling now,
falling away behind him. Five feet from the gunport, he
tripped and fell. Pain burst behind his eyes. He began dragging himself forward. *Not gonna make it,* he thought
numbly. *Not gonna—*

And then a hand thrust through the vines and reached
for him.

He grabbed it.

39

Washington, D.C.

LATHAM AND RANDAL WERE REVIEWING THE PREVIOUS NIGHT'S stakeout reports from Greenbelt, Glen Echo, and the Marriott Key Bridge. "Looks like Vorsalov went to bed early," said Randal. "The Arabs stayed up late playing cards and watching *I Love Lucy* reruns. How about Fayyad?"

"Straight home from the Marriott. No visitors, no outgoing calls. How about his mystery woman?"

"No luck. We only got half the license tags. We're running them now."

"Hmmpf . . . What's this?" Latham said, turning a page. "The call into Fayyad's place? Late last night, lasted fifty seconds. Here, listen to this. . . . 'Caller: You met with our friend? Fayyad: Yes. You approve of his plans? Caller: I do. You will assist him, I assume? Fayyad: If it is what you want.' " Latham looked up at Randal. "What do you make of that?"

"Don't know."

Latham turned to the report's conclusion. " 'Voice analysis of caller indicates a Middle Eastern man, approximately fifty to sixty years of age, well-educated. Caller in position of authority. VA suggests significant stress. No significant background noise. Call traced to public telephone exchange in Nicosia, Cyprus.' "

"So what then?" asked Randal. "Vorsalov has taken over from Fayyad?"

"And Fayyad doesn't like it. Something's changed, Paul."

"Like what?"

"Think about it: What's Vorsalov do best? He runs agents."

"Right. And Fayyad is a terrorist. So, what are they doing together?"

"They hired Vorsalov and Fayyad at the same time. Maybe Yuri started off as a consultant, and now he's here, running the show. They wouldn't bring him in for a simple terrorist op."

"Not likely."

"So maybe he's here as a controller. If so, that means sooner or later he'll have to start having some face-to-face meetings."

LATHAM'S PREDICTION TURNED OUT TO BE PROPHETIC. THAT NIGHT he was sitting down to dinner with Bonnie when the phone rang. It was Randal. "You may have called it, Charlie. He's moving."

"Which one?"

"Clyde." For brevity's sake, they'd given Fayyad, the Arabs, and Vorsalov code names. Vorsalov was "Clyde."

"Are we set up?

"For now. If he starts dry-cleaning, we might need more bodies."

"I'm on my way." Latham hung up, took a gulp of milk, and smiled at Bonnie. "Sorry, gotta go."

"So I gather. More bad guys?"

"More bad guys."

FOR THE NEXT HOUR, AS LATHAM WAITED AT HEADQUARTERS AND listened to the radio traffic, Vorsalov led them on yet another tour of Washington and its environs.

At 9:30 he left the Georgetown Pike, pulled into Great Falls Park, and parked beneath a giant oak. The park, though usually closed, was open for a Boy Scout night hike. The lot was full, 80 to a 100 cars.

"Smart boy," Randal said. "Hiding in plain sight."

"You said the park's usually closed," Latham said. "How do you know?"

"Charlie, I have a teenage girl. When I found out this place is a prime makeout spot, I did my research."

"Ah, the joys of fatherhood. You're on scene, Paul. What do you think?"

"If we mingle in, we might just get it covered."

"Do it. I'm on my way."

AN HOUR LATER LATHAM WAS SITTING WITH RANDAL ON A FIRE road at the park's edge. The surveillance teams reported Vorsalov was still in his car. "How's our coverage?" asked Latham.

"Could be better. We can see cars coming in but not where they park."

"Can we put anybody on the pike?"

"Too open."

Another twenty minutes passed. Twenty-four cars entered the lot; sixteen left.

One of the surveillance teams called in: "Another car pulling in."

Then a moment later: "Command, Clyde has just flashed his headlights."

"This is it," Latham said.

"Clyde is out of his car. Second subject is approaching."

"Description," Latham said.

"White male, midfifties. Medium height and build. They're talking now."

"Command, we've got another vehicle pulling to the shoulder on the pike."

"Make and model?"

"Minivan, Chevy, looks like. Whoa! Both subjects are moving to it."

"Shit!" Latham said. "Paul, get a car moving!"

"Command, they're getting in . . . van is pulling away, moving fast."

"License plate!"

"Negative, negative, can't see it."

Latham smacked the dashboard. "Goddamn it!" He should have expected Vorsalov would layer the meeting. Nothing the Russian did was one-dimensional.

"We might still catch up," Randal said.

"No, they're gone." A mile down the pike there were dozens of offshoot roads.

"He's good. I'll give him that. Now what?"

"Search Vorsalov's car, start taking plates, and hope we get lucky."

ON AN ISOLATED DIRT TRACK OFF LEIGH MILL ROAD, VORSALOV ordered the driver to pull over and take a walk, then joined Smith in the backseat. Smith's face was pale, and his eyes darted wildly.

Vorsalov smiled blandly at him but said nothing.

Smith blurted, "What do you want? Why did we come out here? To kill me? Is that it? Well, I—"

"Why would I want to kill you, Senator?"

"He told me about you, how you do things. I'm warning you—"

"I have no intention of harming you, Senator. You have my word."

"Then what do you want? I tried to get the information, I really did."

"Perhaps you lack adequate motivation."

"What's that mean?"

Vorsalov handed Smith a slip of paper. "Does this address look familiar?"

Smith studied it. His mouth dropped open.

"Who does it belong to?" Vorsalov asked.

"A woman I know . . . a friend."

"Your mistress. Her name is Suzie Donovan."

"Kidnapping her won't do you any good, you son of a—"

"Shut up." Vorsalov produced a cell phone, dialed, then said, "Put her on. Miss Donovan? Have my men told you what to say? Good. Go ahead." Vorsalov handed the phone to Smith, who listened for few seconds, then handed it back. Vorsalov hung up.

"She . . . she means nothing to me. You won't get anything this way."

"I think we will," Vorsalov said. "She may mean nothing to you, and your wife may mean nothing to you, but your career, I think, means a great deal to you."

"What are you talking about?"

"Senator, in the top left-hand drawer of your nightstand you keep a pistol, a thirty-eight-caliber Smith and Wesson, serial number 129475. It's registered in your name. Have you seen it lately?"

"Oh God."

"I thought not."

"Oh, Jesus."

Vorsalov leaned forward. "This is how it will work. You will provide us the information we require in three days, or your mistress will be found shot to death . . . killed by your gun. You will not have an alibi. You will be prosecuted and then sent to prison. Quite simply, Senator, your life will be over."

FBI Headquarters

LATHAM AND HIS TEAM LEADERS WERE REVIEWING THE NIGHT'S activity. The mood in the room was bleak. Once again, Vorsalov had bested them. It was only luck that had kept them in the game.

The Russian had returned to his hotel at 11:30; Fayyad had not left his condo since their meeting; and the Arabs were tucked away in the Greenbelt house.

"Unless anybody's got anything else, that's it," Latham concluded. "We stay sharp and keep watching. Vorsalov's had one meet; there'll be a second."

He dismissed them. Randal walked into the room. "Got a printout of the plates from tonight. Ninety-eight of them."

Latham scanned the list, which showed the plate number, make, and the registered owner's last name and initials. He was about to set it aside when he stopped suddenly.

"What is it, Charlie?"

"Smith," Latham muttered. "H. B. J. Smith. Paul, is the library still open?"

"Yeah."

"Go grab a *Washington Who's Who*."

Randal was back in five minutes. Latham rifled through the book, set it aside, then began paging through the Glen Echo surveillance log. He pulled out a photo and stared at it.

"Charlie, what is going on? What—"

"That's her. Good God, that's her. I thought she looked familiar, but—"

"Who?"

"Judith Smith. That's Judith Smith!"

LATHAM WAS OUT OF HIS DEPTH, AND HE KNEW IT. BY SIX IN THE morning, they were in the director's office. Present were Latham's boss, the director of the FBI, the U.S. attorney, and the attorney general.

It took him thirty minutes to present the case, starting with the Delta bombing and ending with the previous night's surveillance. When he laid out the final item, there was absolute silence in the room.

Finally, the director said, "So, in short, we've got a U.S. senator and his wife involved with a former KGB officer and a terrorist suspected of an aircraft bombing, both of whom appear to be sponsored by a Mideast terrorist group. Is that about it, Agent Latham?"

"Roughly, sir.

"How sure are you about this?"

"It all fits. I wish it didn't, but it does."

"Do we know what Vorsalov is asking for?" asked the attorney general.

"No, but we do know Smith's been holding some fairly intensive IOC hearings."

"How intensive?"

"We'd have to ask Langley, but rumor is he's been

pushing hard. Plus, we know Vorsalov's operation is running at a pretty fast pace."

"Have you got enough to make a case right now?" asked Latham's boss.

"No. We need to connect Fayyad and Vorsalov to the extortion of Smith. We need it on tape. So far, all we've got is Judith Smith having an affair with a bad guy and the senator keeping rotten company."

"Any attorney Smith hires would sink that like the *Titanic*," said the AG.

"What do you need to put this together, Charlie?"

Latham thought it over. "Two things. First, there's no two ways about it: This is gonna get nasty. I need the backing to see it through to the end."

The director smiled. "You don't want to find yourself alone when the shit starts rolling downhill, is that it?"

"To be frank, yes, sir."

"You'll have my full support, whatever comes. And second?"

Before Latham could answer, Randal's cell phone buzzed. Randal listened, then whispered to Latham.

"Gentlemen, it seems the decision has been made for us," Latham said.

"What is it?" asked the director.

"Last night, when I stumbled onto the Smith angle, I asked the DCPD and the Alexandria Sheriffs to contact us if they got a call involving the senator or his wife. Paul just got word they're responding to the Smiths' home."

THE DRIVEWAY WAS BLOCKED BY TWO DCPD PATROL CARS AND an ambulance. Latham flashed his badge to the officer at the door and walked inside.

On the steps above the landing, a paramedic was working on Judith Smith. Her eye was blackened and dried blood caked her chin. She saw him. "Oh, Charlie . . ."

"Are you all right, Judith?"

"I . . . I . . ." She began crying.

Latham looked at the paramedic and got a positive nod.

Randal called, "Charlie."

Latham walked into the living room. Herb Smith was sitting in a recliner with a tumbler of scotch in his hand. His eyes were red and wild. "Who the fuck are you?" he slurred.

Latham showed his badge.

"Good for you. Now get the hell out. This is none of your business."

"I'm afraid it is, Senator," said Latham. "I think it's time you and I had a talk."

40

Agana, Guam

TWELVE HOURS AFTER HE PULLED TANNER FROM THE BUNKER, Cahil wheeled him down the hallway of Agana's main hospital. "Bear, where are we going? And why the wheelchair? I'm fine."

"Hospital rules. You don't want to piss off Nurse Ratchet."

"They have a Nurse Ratchet?"

"Every hospital has a Nurse Ratchet. Besides, I doubt that deep-fried leg of yours would take much weight."

"Speaking of that, have I thanked you yet?"

"A couple times."

"Good. So tell me again: What happened after you pulled me out?"

"Figuring Takagi wouldn't mind if we borrowed it, I loaded you aboard the helo, said good-bye to Fantasy Island, and set a course for the nearest land. Guam had the best chance of having a hospital worth a damn, so here we are."

"I wish I could remember it."

"You might have if I hadn't shot you full of morphine. You're gonna have a dandy-looking scar."

"Where did you land, on the hospital lawn?"

"Of course not! I set her down in a field a couple miles out of town and traded it to a farmer for a ride here."

Tanner started laughing and suddenly found himself unable to stop. It felt damned good to be alive.

"What?" Cahil said. "He can sell it. The damn thing's worth more than he'll earn in a lifetime."

"Anybody ever tell you you're rabidly practical?"

"Only you. Now, as for where we're going . . . Somebody wants to see you."

Cahil turned into a room. On the bed lay the Japanese man they'd rescued from the bunker. Behind the oxygen mask he smiled feebly and waved to them.

"How is he?" Briggs whispered.

"Two of his ribs are broken, and he lost a lot of blood, but it could be worse."

"What's his name?"

"Ezoe. He was the cook."

Ezoe was reaching toward Tanner. Cahil wheeled him closer, and Tanner took the hand. *"Domo arigato,"* Ezoe said. *"Domo."*

"You're welcome. Do you speak English?"

Ezoe nodded.

"Good, because my Japanese is terrible. Ezoe, do you remember what happened at the island?"

"I remember."

"Would you be willing to talk to us about it?"

"Yes."

"First, though, we have a problem. I think it would be a bad idea for you to go home right now. If you'd like, you can come with us. We can't force you, but—"

Ezoe's eyes lit up. "To America?"

"Yes."

"When do we leave?"

Lebanon

ABU AZHAR SEATED GENERAL AL-KHATIB AND THEIR GUEST NEAR the fireplace and pulled the drapes shut. Outside, the temperature hovered around freezing; the peaks of the Anti-Lebanese Mountains were capped in snow.

Azhar sat down and studied his visitor. "You are *Pasdaran*?" he asked.

"Yes," the man replied proudly.

Indeed, Azhar thought, *he has the eyes of a fanatic.* Tough, well-trained, and only too ready to die for Islam, the *Pasdaran* were Iran's elite revolutionary guard corps.

This man's presence spoke volumes of al-Khatib's influence. Their role was the linchpin of the operation.

"How many men under your command?" Azhar asked.

"Thirty."

"Have you been briefed on your mission?"

"No. Whatever it is, we will succeed, *inshallah.*" God willing.

Azhar handed the man a sheet of paper. "We want these men killed."

The *Pasdaran* officer studied the list. "If it pleases Allah. When—"

"Listen to me," Azhar said. "Do you understand who these men are? They are important and well-guarded. When I ask you if you can kill them, I want an answer, not a fanatical platitude. Do you understand?"

"Yes," the man stammered. "Yes, I understand. I know who these men are. We can do this for you. We will succeed or die in the attempt."

"Succeed first. What you do afterward is not my concern. All the deaths must occur within twenty-four hours of one another, two to three weeks from now. We will give you the precise schedule."

"It will be done."

Azhar handed him a file. "You'll want to conduct your own surveillance.

"Of course."

Azhar stood. "May Allah guide you."

Once the man was gone, al-Khatib smiled and said, "You were hard on the young pup. Are you satisfied?"

"Not until it's done."

"Ever the cynic, Abu. Tell me, how goes your Washington operation?"

"I expect to have the information within a few days. Time enough to adjust our plans, if necessary. What about the ship?"

"She sailed two days ago."

Azhar nodded and stared vacantly out the window. "Now it is all timing."

Tel Aviv, Israel

"OH, SAUL, THERE IT IS!" BERNICE WEINMAN CALLED. "THERE!"

They'd chosen this spot in Charles Clora Park in hopes
of seeing the ship sail into port. Saul Weinman could just
make out her white superstructure beyond the breakwater.
"I see her, Bernice. She's beautiful."

"Tell me again, what is she called?"

"The *Valverde*. She's named after one of the Canary Islands."

"Are we going there? Is that one of the stops?"

"Yes, Bernice," Saul replied with a laugh, delighted at
her excitement. "There and other places, too: Spain, Portugal, Casablanca—"

"Like the movie? Oh, how wonderful!"

After thirty-two years of private medical practice in Tel
Aviv, Saul Weinman had retired the previous month. This
cruise was to be their first trip alone together since their
honeymoon. Bernice had waited so long for this—as had
he. This would be the start of the most wonderful years of
their life.

"Oh, Saul! What do you think our stateroom will be like?
Will it be big? Do you think they'll serve those drinks with
the umbrellas? Or dancing! Do you think there will be
dancing?"

"They'll have everything. It's going to be wonderful."

"I wish we were going today, right now."

"Patience, Bern. Day after tomorrow."

Andrews Air Force Base, Maryland

WITHIN MINUTES OF RECEIVING TANNER'S CALL FROM GUAM, A
relieved Leland Dutcher and Walter Oaken set to work getting them home. Two hours and a few phone calls later, a
VC-20 lifted off from the U.S. air base at Misawa bound
for Guam, where it picked up the trio, then headed east.

Now, some 7,000 miles later, Dutcher and Oaken stood
on the Tarmac watching the VC-20 taxi to a stop. Aided
by a cane, Tanner came down the ladder, followed by

Cahil, who turned to help Ezoe down. Oaken ran forward to help.

Dutcher shook Tanner's hand. "How's the leg?"

"Sore, but working."

"And our guest?"

"Better than he looks. Considering what he saw, he's doing great."

With Cahil and Oaken under each arm, Ezoe walked past them toward the car.

"How many dead?" asked Dutcher.

"Twelve that I could count. How did Mason react when he found out we hadn't pulled out?"

"What could he say? I fell on my sword, told him DOR-SAL wasn't as dead as we thought, and gave him the news. That bunker complex has all the markings of a chemical or biological facility. Trust me, they love you."

"Glad to hear it. Leland, there's something I didn't tell you. On the plane we had a little chat with Ezoe. Three days before we got to the island, a ship arrived. From his description, I'm pretty sure it was *Tsumago*. That night, Noboru and his men loaded something aboard her. Ezoe didn't know what. The next day, about two hours before the shooting started, a Chinook helicopter landed carrying about a dozen men. After they were aboard the ship, she sailed." Tanner paused. "He says he got a good look at them. They were Arabs."

Langley

THEY WERE MET IN THE LOBBY BY AN ESCORT FROM THE OFFICE of Security and escorted up to the DCI's conference room. Mason, Coates, and Sylvia Albrecht were waiting for them, as was a sumptuous lunch buffet. Ezoe shook hands absently and eyeballed the food.

"I understand you've been through a lot," Mason said to him. "You must be hungry. Let's eat before we talk."

Ezoe needed no encouragement. Tanner couldn't help but smile at the scene. This man, this simple cook, who'd not only witnessed the execution of eight of his friends but had also been buried alive under their corpses and possibly held the secret to Takagi's Parece Kito complex, sat before the CIA's top spymaster shoveling meat loaf into his mouth. As for Mason, Tanner was impressed; however important Ezoe's information might be, Mason was going to let the man eat first.

Finally, Ezoe folded his napkin and let out a satisfied sigh. He looked up, saw that everyone had finished long ago, and grinned sheepishly. "Thank you for lunch."

"You're very welcome," said Mason. "Can we get you anything else?"

"No, thank you."

"I'm sure you're tired, but would you be up to answering some questions for us?"

"I will try."

"Why don't you start at the beginning. How did you get involved?"

Ezoe's story was short. Five months ago, while working as a cook at the Anan shipyard, he was approached by Tange Noboru, who asked if he would be interested in a special job. A fifteen-year veteran of Takagi Industries, Ezo had come to consider it home, so he proudly accepted. A week later, he was flown to Parece Kito.

Over the next four months, Ezoe saw no one else aside from the complex's other maintenance and housekeeping personnel. Only a few workers were allowed on the "other side," as he called the clean room area. He described the basic routine of the complex, who came and went, and how often *Tsumago* visited.

He ended his story with *Tsumago*'s final visit. "It was almost midnight when it started. They just walked into the kitchen and started shooting. They never said a word. I fell down, and I felt . . ." Ezoe touched his chest. Tears seeped from the corner of his eyes. Sylvia Albrecht handed him a tissue.

"It's hard, I know," Mason said. "You're a lucky man."

Ezoe nodded at Tanner and Cahil. "Not luck . . . them."

For the next hour Mason, Albrecht, and Coates questioned him. This was just the first round, Tanner knew.

Later would come the full debrief. "One more thing," Mason said. "How certain are you about the men in the helicopter? You said they were Arabs. How can you be sure?"

"They looked like Arabs and they spoke their language. And their leader was carrying one of their books . . . umm, like your Bible?"

"A Koran?" Oaken offered.

"Yes, Koran. I was looking at it; he got very mad."

"Do you think you could help us put a sketch together of this man?"

"I'm not a good drawer."

"That's all right. The computer will do it for you. Sylvia, will you take our guest down to OTS?"

Once they were gone, Mason turned to Tanner and Cahil. "Gentlemen, I'm not used to having my orders disobeyed, but in this case, I'm glad you did. Dutch told me you had good instincts. I'm convinced." He turned to Oaken. "You uncovered Parece Kito. How solid is the link between it and Takagi?"

"Are you asking if we have enough to nail him?"

"Yes."

"No, he's insulated himself too well. Even the executions would be hard to link to him. Legally, at least. Ezoe never spoke with Takagi, only Noboru, who's now dead. If push came to shove, Takagi could paint Noboru as the bad guy."

"What about evidence from the complex itself? Mr. Tanner, you say it's destroyed. Are you sure there's nothing left that could help us?"

"I'm sure. Noboru knew what he was doing. Whatever wasn't crushed to dust is probably still burning from the phosphorus. I counted at least a dozen grenades, each one hot enough to melt rock. Whatever was there, it's gone."

ALBRECHT RETURNED CARRYING A FILE, WHICH SHE HANDED TO Mason. Inside was a composite portrait of Ezoe's Arab. He had jet black hair, black eyes, and a bushy handlebar mustache. "What's the probability of error?" he asked.

"Minus three. Arab bone structure, eye offset, and skin tint are pretty uniform."

Cahil asked, "Minus three . . . What's that mean?"

"It means there's a ninety-seven percent chance if somebody handed us a photo of this guy, it would look identical to this composite. We're running it through our database now. It'll take a few hours."

Mason handed the composite to Coates. "George, take this down to Near East, see if it rings any bells."

"Sure." Coates got as far as the door. He turned back, his mouth agape.

"What is it, George?"

"You don't recognize him?" He held up the composite. "The Khartoum meeting between Fayyad and Vorsalov . . . This is the third man."

41

COATES'S REVELATION COMPLETED A CIRCLE WHOSE EXISTENCE NO
one had suspected. Hiromasa Takagi, Yuri Vorsalov, Ibrahim Fayyad, Senator Smith, and Parece Kito were all in-
tertwined. But how and why?

Mason wasted no time drawing together the people he
hoped would fill in the blanks: Dutcher, Oaken, Tanner,
and Cahil for their work on DORSAL and discovery of
Parece Kito; Art Stucky for his Mideast experience; George
Coates and Sylvia Albrecht, who would provide the necessary resources; and Charlie Latham for his knowledge of
the Fayyad/Vorsalov/Smith triangle.

"Thanks for coming, all of you," Mason began. "I think
everyone knows National Security Adviser James Talbot."

"Mr. Talbot will be briefing the president later today.
I've asked George to put together a summary of what we
know. What we discuss here today is classified top secret.
None of the details are to be discussed outside this room.
George?"

Coates walked to the podium. "The scenario I'm going
to lay out is by no means flawless, but most of the pieces
seem to fit."

For the next thirty minutes, Coates laid out what they
knew and how the pieces fit into the larger picture. "Eventually," he concluded, "Vorsalov led Latham and his people
to a team of Arabs in a house in Greenbelt, then to Fayyad,
and then, finally, to a prominent U.S. senator, who we believe is the target of an extortion operation."

"What's their leverage on this senator?" asked Talbot.

"His wife," Mason replied. "We believe Fayyad seduced

her, then used the affair to turn the senator."

"What are they after?"

"We don't know yet. Agent Latham, will you fill in the blanks?"

"We believe Vorsalov was brought in to crank up the pressure on the senator," Latham said. "Problem is, Vorsalov pushed too far, and the man snapped. He and his wife are in protective custody. This morning, Vorsalov contacted Smith and set up a meeting for tomorrow night. We plan on being there. We'll also be hitting the Greenbelt house and Fayyad's condo."

"Is this senator cooperating?" asked Stucky.

"Reluctantly, but I expect that to change this afternoon."

"Why?"

Latham smiled. "I'm going to make him an offer he can't refuse."

There was general laughter.

"Who exactly are we talking about?"

Coates looked at Mason and got a nod. "Senator Herb Smith, chairman of the Intelligence Oversight Committee."

There were several moans around the room.

Mason said, "Glad to see we're all familiar with the dynamic Senator Smith."

More laughter.

"Now for the punch line," Coates continued. "Two days ago, we received some disturbing information from Tanner and Cahil. In the course of their work on DORSAL, they found an informant who described a meeting between Hiromasa Takagi's chief of security and an Arab man. A composite of this man was made. We've identified him as the third unidentified man from the Khartoum meeting."

There was silence in the room as the attendees tried to absorb the implications. Tanner and Cahil exchanged glances: The DDO had left out any mention of Parece Kito and *Tsumago*. Why? Tanner looked over at Mason, who gave him a barely perceptible nod.

Oaken said, "There's one thing that bothers me: Fayyad's approach. The standard time line on a honey trap is four months, minimum. They've done it in three weeks. Why the hurry?"

"That's one of the questions we need to answer," said Mason. "But we think we know what put it in motion. Go ahead, George."

Coates picked it up: "Three weeks ago, we lost an agent in Beirut. Within a week of his kidnapping, Vorsalov and Fayyad were meeting in Khartoum. A week after that, Vorsalov was summoned to Beirut, then he came straight here. More importantly, the information Smith was fishing for was related to the Beirut op."

"So, something this group squeezed from Marcus made them nervous," said Cahil.

"Exactly. Problem is, we don't know what set them off, and we don't know what they've got cooking."

"But its something that involves Takagi Industries," said Oaken.

Mason nodded. "And that's the piece we need to find. What's the connection, who's running the op, and what is it?" He stood up. "So, while we wait for the result of Agent Latham's roundup, we start working the puzzle. Any questions?"

There were none.

As the group dispersed, Mason said to Dutcher, "Dutch, will you and your people stay behind a minute?"

Once the room was empty, Mason shut the door. "First, I know we glossed over Parece Kito and the ship. I'll explain why in a minute. Second, the brief you just heard was classified top secret. What I'm about to tell you goes beyond that. Aside from the people in this room, only George, Sylvia, and Jim Talbot know about Parece Kito and *Tsumago*. For now, it stays that way. Understood?"

There were nods all around.

"Dutch, when this started, I told you about a link between Iraqi fire control systems and Takagi Industries. That's all true. The part I left out is what's got us worried.

"Of all the Scuds fired during the war, we got a good salvage on only one of them. It was a conventional missile but stripped down for different payload. Actually, it was a reconversion: a Scud that started as conventional was converted into a bio/chem carrier, then back to conventional.

They fell short on quality control, though. Part of a telemetry package contained an actuator system designed to control an airburst release."

"Oh, boy," Cahil muttered.

Dutcher said, "Dick, are you telling me you sent my people into this thing knowing they could be dealing with chemical or biological weapons?"

Mason nodded. "That's one of the reasons I finally pulled the plug. As long as they were simply checking DORSAL's network, they were safe. Briggs, Ian, I ordered you out for two reasons: One, we wanted to be able to restart DORSAL in the future; and two, I didn't want you flying blind. I hope you understand."

"We're big boys," Cahil said.

"Ohira's product lead you to the bio/chem angle?" Tanner asked Mason.

"Yes. About a month before he was killed. We weren't sure what to think when you two uncovered Ohira's interest in Takagi Maritime. To us, it felt like a goose chase. To you guys, it felt solid, and you were right. Ohira's tangent scared Takagi enough that he had him killed."

"Along with a lot of others," Tanner said. "So far, he's murdered almost thirty people to keep his secret." *Including Sumiko,* Tanner thought. *But he missed one, didn't he? He missed Ezoe, and now it was going to cost him.*

Dutcher said, "So, bottom line, Dick: You think Takagi was hired by this Beirut group to deliver a chemical or biological weapon, then Marcus turns up, stumbles onto something he shouldn't have, so they grab him and mount the Smith op."

"Exactly."

"And now, whatever the hell it is, it's aboard *Tsumago* headed for . . . Where?"

"That's the million-dollar question," Mason said. "Either it's going to be stored for future use, or it's going to be used immediately. If that's the case, we feel the two most likely targets are the United States or Israel."

*   *   *

Mediterranean Sea

ACCOMPANIED BY FIREBOATS SPOUTING GEYSERS OF WATER AND blaring their horns, *Valverde* had left Tel Aviv two days before. Standing on the deck, Saul and Bernice Weinman gazed at the distant island of Crete, *Valverde*'s first port of call. A warm wind fluttered the pennants over their heads. Bernice had not stopped smiling since they boarded, and now she leaned over and kissed Saul on the cheek.

"What's that for?" he asked.

"Just thank you. We've waited so long. It's wonderful."

After a brief layover in Crete, *Valverde* would weigh anchor and head west for stops in Greece and Sicily before sailing through the Strait of Gibraltar and into the Atlantic Ocean.

Syria

AS NIGHT DESCENDED ON *VALVERDE*, EIGHT HUNDRED MILES TO the east, a helicopter landed in the lee of a sand dune and General Issam al-Khatib climbed out. He ducked under the whirling blades and walked to an outcrop of rock over-looking a *wadi*.

Parked bumper-to-bumper in the dry riverbed were two miles of empty semi truck transports. Hundreds of soldiers hurried about, rigging lines and pulling camoflauge tarpau-lins into place.

Al-Khatib checked his watch: Almost time.

Far to the southeast, the exercise continued. If it were daylight, al-Khatib might have been able to see the dust storm raised by the tanks and APCs. *All that power,* he thought with a smile. *Just waiting*. He felt the surge in his blood.

To the west and south, also too far to see, were two U.S. Navy battle groups, one off the coast of Lebanon, the other patrolling the Gulf. And Israel, rattling its saber, posturing and threatening action. *The game continues. But not for much longer*.

He looked up at the black sky. Somewhere up there an

American spy satellite was racing in its orbit toward them. He checked his watch again. They would make it.

In the *wadi*, the troops kept working.

Rappahannock River, Virginia

PRIOR TO JOINING HOLYSTONE, TANNER AND ELLE MOVED TO THE Chesapeake Bay area and rented a house in Hills Point not far from Annapolis, where his father taught at the U.S. Naval Academy.

For the first month, Briggs had fished, camped, spent time with Elle and his parents, and generally did a lot of nothing which, after twelve years in spec war, was a novel experience.

After joining Holystone, they started looking for a permanent home and stumbled on the lighthouse in a backwater cove of the Rappahannock River. They immediately fell in love with it. The two-story cabin-style house and attached light tower had been abandoned for forty years. With the blessing of the Virginia Historical Commission, they bought it, moved in, and Briggs had been working on its upkeep ever since. Surrounded by forest on three sides and the cove on the fourth, it was secluded and quiet. And after six weeks away, it was a welcome sight for Tanner.

He dropped his bags on the kitchen table and opened the fridge. It was empty save a tupperware container filled with something fuzzy and green; he tossed it in the garbage. That left a shrunken apple and a beer. Tanner tossed the former and opened the latter.

On the counter, his answering machine blinked at him. Half the messages would be from his parents. He hadn't called them since the start of DORSAL, and there would be hell to pay with his mom. He decided he could use a little motherly nagging.

AN HOUR LATER, HE WAS SHAVED AND SHOWERED AND SITTING IN the living room in front of the stone-hearth fireplace. The decor was simple, consisting of wood paneling, a couple rattan pieces, a sectional sofa, and a modest collection of Winslow Homer prints on the walls under track lighting. Outside, the wind was picking up, and Tanner could see a rain squall on the horizon. The hanging plants on the deck swung wildly.

Unexpectedly, Camille's face popped into his head. He missed her, he realized. *Think about something else*, he commanded. On the coffee table sat the box he'd brought back from Japan. He reached for the phone and dialed.

When the line clicked open, he said, "Mrs. Tanner, have you got room at the table for your wayward son?"

HENRY AND IRENE TANNER NOW OWNED A SMALL COLONIAL IN Bay Ridge. Regardless of where they'd lived while Briggs was growing up—whether Switzerland or Kenya or points in between—their homes had always been warm and smelled of cinnamon and freshly baked bread. It was the magic of Mom, Briggs supposed.

He was halfway up the walkway when Irene burst from the front door and ran to him. After a long embrace, she pulled back and squinted at him. "You look tired."

"I am tired. It's good to be home."

"What's in the folder?"

"Something for Dad. A mystery."

"Oh, he'll love that." She put on her stern face. "Where have you been? Oh, never mind. I should know better than to ask. Come in."

Henry shook Briggs's hand, then gave him a hug. As usual, his father wore an old, loose cardigan and equally old leather moccasins. Perched on his nose were a pair of half-glasses. He tilted his head back and studied his son. "Starting to get a little worried about you."

"I know. I should have called."

"No matter. You're here now."

"Dinner's almost ready," Irene called.

Henry took his son's arm. "You better be hungry."

*   *   *

AFTER DINNER, TANNER AND HIS FATHER SAT OVER COFFEE. "DAD, are you working on anything right now?" Tanner asked. Henry was an avid amateur historian, and it was rare for him to not be absorbed in some obscure research project. World War II was his specialty, and much of its intrigue had rubbed off on Tanner.

"No, as of late, your mother's got me weeding the garden. Why?"

"I've got something that might interest you."

"Shoot."

"During the war, how many U.S. fleet subs were lost off the coast of Japan?"

"Depends on how you define *coast*. How close do you mean?"

"Three, four hundred yards."

"I've never heard of anything like that."

"What would you say if I told you I found one a stone's throw off Honshu?"

"Is that what you're telling me?"

"Yes."

"How did you find it?"

"Recreational diving," said Tanner.

"Uh-huh. Did you get a sail number?"

"Tanner shook his head."

"Hmm," said Henry. "That is a mystery. You check with the local guides?"

"Nothing. No wrecks within two miles of the area."

"Did you get inside?"

"That's where it gets good."

Tanner recounted their discovery of the two skeletons, one in the wardroom with a bullet hole in the forehead, and the other in the forward torpedo room with one wrist chained to a stanchion.

"And this one was wearing leg braces?" Henry asked.

"Yes. I'm thinking polio. He couldn't be one of the crew."

"Curiouser and curiouser. You want me to do a little digging?"

"I thought we could work on it together. I've got some free time."

"I'd like that." Henry peered at him over his glasses. "So tell me: Is all this just a matter of personal interest?"

"Why?"

"First of all, my boy, I know that look in your eye; it's the same one you got as a kid when you fixed your sights on something. Like the time you got the Evel Knievel bug and set about jumping your bike over everything in sight. You remember?"

Tanner laughed. "I remember."

"Plus, you're back in town less than a day, and you bring this to me."

Henry had a point. He wasn't sure how to answer. Looking at Ohira's chart three weeks ago, he'd felt certain the spot off Shiono Misaki had been significant. But now? Perhaps Ohira had been a recreational diver, and the sub had been a favorite spot of his. Hell, maybe he and Bear had misread the chart altogether. There could be any number of explanations. Why then, wouldn't that nagging voice in the back of his head go away?

"For now, let's just call it personal interest," he said.

"Fair enough. Now, without a name, we—"

"Would engine serial numbers do?"

Henry grinned. "Damn right they will. Let's see them."

42

LATHAM, RANDAL, STAN WILSON OF HRU, AND JANET PASCHEL met in Latham's office to finalize details of the sting that evening.

"Janet, you'll be heading the Glen Echo team. Paul, you and Stan will take the Greenbelt house, and I'll handle Rock Creek. Once we take Vorsalov, that'll be the signal for the other teams to go. Timing will be critical. We'll all be moving at nearly the same time. Stay on the radio. The last thing we need is a firefight.

"Tomorrow night is do or die for Vorsalov and his people. If they don't get the information from Smith, or if Smith fails to show up, chances are they'll either run or go violent.

"There's also another complication," Latham said and held up a copy of the *Washington Post*. The headline said, "Senator Smith AWOL?" "This is an advance of what they're running Thursday. We're not sure how they got the story, but it reports Smith has taken an 'unplanned vacation.' If Vorsalov or Fayyad see this, we're sunk."

"Speaking of the senator, how'd you get him to cooperate?" asked Wilson.

"I talked his language."

Latham knew the U.S. attorney was not as interested in nailing Smith as they were in catching Vorsalov and Fayyad. Smith was a would-be traitor, but they were murderers. In return for his cooperation and agreement to immediate retirement without pension, Smith would avoid prosecution.

Still half drunk from the previous night, Smith laughed

at the proposal. "You've got nothing that ties me to either of these assholes, or whatever the hell you think they're doing."

Smith's lawyer said, "Herb—"

"Shut up, Harmon."

Latham leaned forward. "Senator, I'm going to give it to you straight, so listen closely: The two men you've been dealing with are killers, and I'm going to get them. If I have to ruin you to do it, I will. The Russian murdered an FBI agent ten years ago, and the other man is a terrorist. You know about the Delta bombing, I assume. That's his work. Five people killed, seven injured, including the only daughter of Congressman Hostetler. I wonder how he would react if he knew you refused to cooperate. Do you think your career would survive it?"

Smith's mouth was hanging open. "You can't do—"

"You bet I can. This is your last chance. Turn it down, and in a month's time you'll be the most miserable son of a bitch in Washington."

"You can't talk to me—"

Smith's lawyer gripped Smith's arm. "Herb, shut up. As your attorney, I'm telling you: Take this offer."

And it was done.

Rock Creek Park

TWO HOURS BEFORE THE MEETING, LATHAM AND HANK REEVES sat inside the command van on the outskirts of the park, listening to the radio chatter as the team got into position. Since dusk, heavy rain clouds had been rolling in from the east, and now they blanketed the capital. Leaves skittered across the van's roof.

"Pray the rain holds off," said Reeves.

"Amen." Latham had a dozen agents in the park, most disguised as evening strollers, a cover that would become untenable in the rain.

"Charlie, this plan of yours . . . I'm not so sure it's—"

"I know, but I don't see any other way."

"It's too damned risky—"

Over the radio came Paul Randal's voice. "Command, this is Greenbelt."

"Go ahead, Greenbelt."

"We're in position and ready."

"Copy that. What about our stray?" Thirty minutes earlier, one of the Arabs had driven off in the Windstar. Latham let him go and stayed focused on the house.

"Still no sign. The other three are inside."

"Roger. Glen Echo, how about you?"

"Ready to roll," reported Janet Paschel. "Subject is inside."

"Key Bridge, how about the guest of honor?"

"Clyde's still in his room. He just ordered supper."

"Okay everybody, make yourselves comfortable."

AT NINE P.M. the Key Bridge team reported Vorsalov leaving. Twenty minutes after that, the Windstar returned to the Greenbelt house and pulled into the garage, returning the count inside to four. Randall reported a brief argument, which ended in a channel change from *I Love Lucy* to *Wheel of Fortune*. At Glen Echo, Paschel reported Fayyad still in front of his own television set.

"All units, this is Command," called Latham. "Clyde is on the move."

If Vorsalov held true to form, he'd drive through the capital, do some dry-cleaning, then head for Rock Creek, where he would sit and watch.

FAYYAD STARED AT THE TELEVISION, NOT REALLY SEEING IT.

Whatever happened, tonight it was over. Vorsalov had ordered the mistress killed, no matter the outcome. Fayyad felt sorry for her. An empty-headed girl, really. Stupid that she had to die because she had bad taste in men.

Vorsalov had been explicit in his instructions: If he failed to call, it would mean something had gone wrong, and they were to kill the girl, leave the capital, and scatter. If the meeting went as planned, they were to kill the girl and then stagger their departures over the next three days.

And what of Judith? Fayyad wondered. He had no choice, really. He couldn't stay. There was no chance for them. There had never been a chance, not from the start.

Rock Creek Park

AT 9:20, THE PARK'S OUTER SURVEILLANCE TEAM REPORTED VORsalov's car pulling into the east lot. The Russian parked, shut off the engine, and sat in the darkness.

"That's it, Yuri. . . ." Latham whispered. "Keep watching."

A light rain began to fall.

AT 9:40, AS THE GLEN ECHO AND GREENBELT TEAMS BEGAN MOVing to their staging positions, Latham ordered Smith's car brought up. "Use the north lot," he said. "We've got to force Vorsalov to come to the fountain."

FIVE MINUTES LATER, THE OUTER TEAM CALLED. "COMMAND, HE'S leaving. Say again, Clyde is leaving."

"Give me a direction."

"He's pulling out, turning onto the frontage road . . . heading for Riggs."

What are you doing, Yuri? Latham wondered. *Wait. . . .* What panics a surveillance team more than a subject bolting? Vorsalov was shaking the tree. "Let him go," Latham ordered. "All units, say put."

Reeves asked, "What about Smith's car?"

"Keep it coming."

EYES GLUED TO THE REARVIEW MIRROR, VORSALOV TOOK A LEFT onto Riggs Road and headed east, accelerating rapidly. He drove a quarter mile, stopped suddenly, backed into a driveway, and shut off his lights. Ten minutes passed. The road was empty.

He flipped on the headlights and pulled back onto the road.

* * *

BY THE TIME THE OUTER RING REPORTED VORSALOV'S RETURN, THE rain was falling heavily. Throughout the park, Latham's strollers opened their umbrellas and kept walking. "This isn't going to work, Hank," said Latham. "Pull them back. Pull back into the trees and have 'em hunker down."

Reeves gave the order, then said, "We still go as planned?"

"Yep."

VORSALOV PULLED HIS HAT LOWER ON HIS HEAD AND FLIPPED UP his collar. His breath steamed in the air. Rain pattered the leaves beside the trail. Down the path he could see the old-fashioned gaslights that encircled the fountain.

An elderly couple walked by arm-in-arm. Vorsalov tensed.

"Evening," they said.

Vorsalov nodded and looked over his shoulder. They were hurrying toward the parking lot now, coats pulled around their heads. He exhaled and looked left, then right. Nothing moving.

Fifty feet from the fountain, he peered ahead. He couldn't see Smith. Where was he? He scanned the benches around the fountain. *There.* The senator wore a black overcoat. Rain glistened off his umbrella.

Vorsalov kept walking.

Greenbelt

AS VORSALOV NEARED THE FOUNTAIN, THE OTHER TEAMS GOT THE go-ahead signal. "Roger," said Randal, parked in a car at the end of the driveway. "All units, proceed. I say again, proceed."

Through his night scope he watched the eight members of the HRU team slip from the trees around the farmhouse and charge forward.

"Let's go," he said to his driver.

Tires squealing, they accelerated up the driveway.

Glen Echo

JANET PASCHEL SLID OPEN THE VAN'S DOOR AND JUMPED OUT, followed by three HRU members. They reached the condo door in seconds. "FBI, search warrant!"

The doorman crashed his ram into the lock, and it shattered inward, wood chips and plaster flying. Paschel charged inside, gun leveled. Behind her, the rest of the team fanned out into the condo. She spun left, then right.

"One clear!"

"Two clear!"

In the living room, Paschel stopped short and stared.

The room was empty, the TV set flickering snow.

Greenbelt

PAUL RANDAL WAS LEAPING FROM THE CAR AND RACING FOR THE front door behind Wilson when he heard Paschel call, "Greenbelt, Glen Echo, come in!"

"Go ahead!"

"Be advised: We have no target! The target is gone!"

From the rear of the house, Randal heard the crashing of glass and the rapid *pop pop pop* of gunfire. Then a *whoosh-boom* as the flashbang grenades exploded. Now shouts, a mixture of Arabic and English.

"FBI, freeze!"

"Down, everybody down!"

In one jumbled second, as Wilson crossed the threshold ahead of him, Randal realized what had happened. When the Windstar returned, it had parked in the garage. *In the garage.* They'd never done that before.

"Stan, we may have five in the house!" he yelled.

Too late. The HRU commander was through the door.

* * *

FAYYAD WAS ON HIS WAY TO THE BATHROOM WHEN THE FIRST
window shattered. He hit the floor. Behind him came a *pop,
pop, pop,* followed by a blast of bright light.

"Freeze, FBI!"

"Down, everybody down!"

In the kitchen, two of Ibn's men leapt for their guns.
Gunfire erupted, and they went down. Bullets peppered the
living room wall. The TV exploded. Plaster dust filled the
air.

"Get down! Get down!"

Fayyad began crawling. From the corner of his eye, he
saw Ibn snatch up his Ingram and run for the stairs. The
front door crashed inward. A man in black coveralls
charged through. Beside Fayyad, Tamir whipped around
and raised his gun. *Pop, pop.* Tamir's chest exploded, and
he went down.

What was Ibn doing? Fayyad thought. "Ibn!"

Ibn turned, grinning, his eyes ablaze. *"Allah akbar!"*

Then Fayyad understood: the girl! Something in his
mind snapped. *He's going to kill her . . . kill her in Allah's
name . . . an empty-headed harlot. It was insane!*

He leapt up, ran for the stairs. Ibn was five steps ahead
and moving fast.

"Freeze!" Fayyad heard from behind. *Pop, pop.* The bannister shattered under his hand. He ducked, kept running.
Ibn reached the top of the stairs and turned toward the girl's
room. Fayyad launched himself forward and hit him
squarely in the back, slamming him into the door.

THOUGH ONLY THREE SECONDS BEHIND WILSON, BY THE TIME RAN-
dal came through the door, it was nearly over. Two Arabs
were down in the kitchen, a third beside the couch. HRU
members were stalking through the kitchen and dining
room, guns raised, tracking for movement.

"Freeze!" he heard Wilson call.

Randal saw motion and turned to see a pair of men
charging up the stairs. It was Fayyad.

On the second-floor landing, Fayyad tackled the other

man and drove him into the door. Locked together, they stumbled backward. The other man whipped around, tore himself free, and raised his gun. Fayyad kicked at the barrel, missed, snagged his foot in the sling. Arms cartwheeling, Fayyad crashed through the bannister, falling. He hit the floor with a sickening crunch. Above, the man took aim on him.

Weapon already drawn and leveled, Randal beat him to it.

Rock Creek Park

VORSALOV STOPPED BEHIND THE BENCH. "EVENING, SENATOR."

Smith stood up and began to turn. Immediately Vorsalov knew something was wrong. The build was right, but there was something about the posture. He took a step back, senses alert. In his pocket he tightened his grip on the stiletto.

"EVENING, YURI," SAID CHARLIE LATHAM.

In that brief second, Latham saw in Vorsalov's eyes a mixture of fear and uncertainty. He searched for signs of recognition, but saw nothing. *He doesn't remember me.*

"I'm sorry," said Vorsalov. "You've mistaken me for someone else. Please excuse me." He turned to walk away.

"Don't bother, Yuri," Latham called. "You're done."

It was this moment ten years ago when the capture of Vorsalov had gone bad. He'd punched the arresting agent and ran. Ran into the rain, through a stand of trees, into the creek, up the bank . . . and straight into the agent stationed there. The young man never knew what hit him. The same instinct that spurred Vorsalov into action then gripped him now. He looked around, eyes darting. He spun on Latham.

"Don't even think it, Yuri. As God as my witness, this time I'll shoot you dead."

43

Washington Navy Yard

HENRY TANNER'S FIRST STEP IN PURSUING BRIGGS'S SUBMARINE was to dial directory assistance. Knowing most World War II U.S. fleet submarines had been equipped with Fairbanks-Morse engines but not whether Fairbanks-Morse was still in business, he put the question to the operator. Yes, Fairbanks-Morse still existed, but it had been taken over by Coltech Industries, headquartered in Beloit, Wisconsin.

It took four transfers from Coltech's switchboard before Henry reached an engineer who might be able to help. Explaining he was researching a book, Henry gave the man the serial number and explained his predicament. The engineer promised to get back to him by day's end.

Next Henry arranged an appointment with an old friend who was serving as an assistant curator at the Washington Navy Yard's Historical Archives.

Built in 1799 beside the Washington Canal, the yard is the Navy's oldest shore establishment and home to warehouses full of archived data on naval history, from routine operational orders and recon photos of Guadalcanal to the personal diaries of Chester Nimitz. If it exists, chances are it is secreted somewhere in one of three yard warehouses.

Henry parked his car on N Street and walked two blocks to Building 57, the home of the Operational Archives Branch. He was met at the third-floor reception desk by his friend. "Henry, how are you!"

"Good, John. Thanks for your help."

"That's what we're here for. Come on, I've got a room set aside for you."

The first thing Henry asked for was records on U.S. fleet submarines reported missing or sunk in Japanese territorial waters during World War II. It took an hour, but the master chief returned with a two-foot stack of material. "Sorry they're not organized any better. We're still working to get everything on CD. It's a big job."

"I can imagine. This'll be fine. I prefer hard copy anyway."

HENRY FOUND THIRTEEN SUBMARINES THAT MIGHT FIT THE BILL, all of whose last known locations were well-documented, right down to latitude and longitude, and many of whom who had been cross-referenced with Japanese Imperial Navy records. Out of these thirteen, he narrowed the list to three possible matches.

He then dug through the stack until he found each boat's operational orders. In each case, the sub in question was lost during a routine patrol. No secrecy, no covert mission, nothing that would account for the scrubbed sail number Briggs reported. *But then again*, Henry thought, *if the sub's mission was that secret, she wouldn't be listed in these archives.*

He'd reached his first hurdle. Pursuing the sub's identity any further would depend on Fairbanks-Morse, so he turned his attention to the civilian Briggs had found in the forward torpedo room.

Since his leg braces obviously made the man ineligible for military service, Henry had a guess for whom he might've worked. As far as he knew, the only World War II personnel to carry .25 caliber Berettas were government employees; and the only government employees who had reason to be aboard fleet subs were operatives for the Office of Strategic Services, the precursor to the CIA.

Langley

WHILE HENRY TANNER WAS CHASING FIFTY-YEAR-OLD LEADS, THE newly resurrected DORSAL working group was sorting through all of DORSAL's product, from Marcus's capture in Beirut to Tanner's discovery of Parece Kito. This last thread was being examined by Walter Oaken.

Under his direction, half a dozen analysts were digging into the secret holdings of Takagi Industries. The industrialist covered his trail well, but the CIA had cut its teeth on tougher corporate hideaways, most notably the money-laundering labyrinths of Colombia's drug cartels, so it wasn't long before they found dozens of buried links to companies specializing in chemical engineering and agricultural research.

"How hard would it have been for Takagi to keep this kind of secret?" Sylvia Albrecht asked.

"Not very," said Oaken. "You've got to understand how tough it is to track this kind of stuff. Alone, the individual chemicals are pretty benign. It's not until you combine them that you've got a weapon. Take a few pesticides, refine them correctly, and you've got a nerve agent like sarin or tabun."

"The kind used in the Tokyo subway gassing."

"Right. If the compounds are bought by front companies over a long period of time . . . Think of it like a jigsaw puzzle being assembled by a hundred different people in a hundred different locations, none of whom are talking to each other."

Not only could Takagi refine such chemicals, Oaken further explained, but given what they'd found on the salvaged Scud, he also had a workable delivery system. Add to that his connection to the JRA, whose links to Mideast groups were well-documented and . . .

"You can see the possibilities," he said.

Secondary to the pursuit of paper trails, however, was the hunt for *Tsumago*. To this end, Mason ordered the NRO to retask an additional two satellites, a Keyhole and a Lacrosse. Armed with her approximate sailing date and cruising speed, the satellites began scouring millions of square miles of ocean.

*   *   *

Bay Ridge

HENRY TANNER WAS UNDER NO ILLUSION: SEARCHING FOR A LONE OSS operative who may or may not have existed was a daunting task. During the war, the OSS was known to reconnoiter enemy territory via submarine, but such excursions were rarely documented. Finding a name would mean wading through the CIA's archives; if it came to that, he wanted to be armed with the name of the sub.

He got his wish later that afternoon. "A man from some company in Wisconsin called for you," Irene said when he got home. "Coltech, I think. He wants you to call him."

Henry did so. "I'm short on details, Mr. Tanner, but I can tell you the numbers match a pair of engines we delivered to the Charleston Yard in July of 1942."

"I appreciate your work. Have you got a name?"

"You bet." Henry heard keys clicking. "Here we go: According to our records, those engines were put aboard a boat called *Stonefish*."

Falls Church, Virginia

THE SAFE HOUSE TO WHICH VORSALOV WAS TAKEN WAS MORE A well-disguised prison than a house. Surrounded by acres of woodland in rural Falls Church and staffed by specially trained HRU guards, it was reserved for the most prized catches.

Fayyad's disappearing act notwithstanding, the simultaneous assaults on Greenbelt and Glen Echo had gone well. How Fayyad managed to slip the net was still a mystery, as were his actions in Greenbelt. None of the Arabs had survived the assault, and Fayyad was at Bethesda Naval Hospital, still unconscious from surgery to repair his shattered hip. It had not been until Randal discovered Smith's mistress in the upstairs bedroom that the Jordanian's actions made sense. But why had he done it? Latham wondered. Why try to save a woman he'd never met, a woman Smith had sent to slaughter to cover his own butt?

"That son of a bitch," Latham said when he heard. "He served her up!" The U.S. attorney was considering rescinding Smith's deal, which was dependent upon the senator's *full* cooperation. Maybe Smith and Vorsalov would end up cell mates. Doubtful, but he enjoyed the thought.

Latham stared at the Russian through the holding room's one-way glass. "Has he said anything?"

"Not a word," said Randal. "I think it's finally hit him."

"Good. Bring him to the interview room."

ONCE VORSALOV WAS SEATED AND HANDCUFFED, LATHAM SAT down opposite him.

"Hello, Yuri. It's been a while."

"Yes, it has, Charlie."

"Ten years."

"I know." Vorsalov held up his cuffed hands. "Can we please—"

"They stay on."

"Charlie, I . . . what happened with your man—"

"I don't want to hear it."

"It was a mistake, you know. It was dark, I was running, and then he was there in front of me—"

"He was twenty-three years old, Yuri. His parents have never gotten over it." *Stop it,* Latham commanded himself. "I'm not here to talk about that."

"You want to talk about Senator Smith."

"No. I'm here to give you your options. You've got two. One, you give us your full cooperation—"

"Which means?"

"Every detail of every operation you've worked since leaving the KGB. We want the who, what, when, where, and how of every group you've ever dealt with."

"And if I do this?"

"You spend the rest of your life in a federal prison."

"You'll forgive me if I'm not thrilled by your offer," said Vorsalov.

Latham shrugged. "Option two: We wash our hands of you and put you on the next plane back to Moscow."

The Russian went pale. "Charlie, you know what Moscow would do to me."

Latham said nothing.

"You are lying. You do not have the power to arrange any of this."

"The U.S. attorney does. One signature and it's done. You killed a federal agent, Yuri. That comes with an automatic life sentence."

"I've never been tried. I know your law. You can't—"

"You were convicted in absentia nine years ago; you've been a fugitive since then. Throw in your extortion of Smith, the kidnapping and attempted murder of the girl, and your link to Fayyad, who killed five people on that Delta flight . . ."

Vorsalov blinked hard, looked away.

He's afraid, Charlie thought. Probably for the first time in his miserable life. "We've got you, Yuri. You're finished. All that's left to decide is whether you go to prison here or back to your buddies in the basement of Lubyanka."

Vorsalov's shoulders slumped. The prospect of months of torture in the dungeons of Lubyanka followed by a summary execution had suddenly become an all-too-real possibility. The Russian stared at his hands.

Ten seconds passed.

Latham stood up. "Okay, have it your way." He was halfway to the door when Vorsalov called, "All right. All right! What do you want to know?"

Langley

TANNER AND CAHIL SAT THROUGH YET ANOTHER UPDATE MEETING on DORSAL. Aside from answering occasional questions—most of which they couldn't answer because of Mason's gag order—neither of them had much to contribute.

After the meeting, Tanner spent an hour with Ezoe, who was fully enjoying the CIA's hospitality, then returned to the op center, where he and Ian wandered around, listening to discussions and looking at photos.

Oaken saw them and walked over. "How's it going?"

"You mean aside from feeling like a fifth wheel?" said Tanner.

"Come on, this might interest you." Oaken led them to the audio room. "Latham and his people recorded a call between Fayyad and another man. We think it's the big boss. The call was traced to an exchange in Cyprus, but we're pretty sure it originated in Beirut."

Tanner felt his stomach tighten. *Beirut*. Some things never got easier, he thought. He and a four-man team had gone into the city, and only two came out. It had been a rude awakening for Tanner. No matter how well-trained and well-prepared you were, an operation can go catastrophically bad in a matter of seconds.

They had spent four months chained to that basement wall, listening to the sounds of Beirut: the *crump* of distant artillery, the clatter of automatic weapons, the haunting voices of muezzins calling from their mosques. And always the sound of boots clumping down the stairs, and wondering which one they were coming for.

Tanner slipped on the headphones. "How sure are we this is the boss?"

"Listen for yourself." Oaken nodded to the audio technician. "The first voice."

" 'You met with our friend?' "

" 'Yes. You approve of his plans?' "

" 'I do. You will assist him, I assume?' "

" 'If it is what you want, I will, of course.' "

Oaken said, "That's the gist of it."

Tanner was frowning. "Run it again, will you?" The technician did so. And then a third time.

"Something?" asked Cahil.

"I don't know. Is that all of it?"

"There's another thirty seconds or so, but it's small talk. We think it's just padding."

"Can I hear it all?"

From behind Tanner a voice said, "Well, well, if it ain't Briggs Tanner." Tanner turned.

"Hello, Art. I didn't know you were here."

"Near East Division. Marcus was my agent."

"Bad break," Tanner said, meaning it.

"Shit happens."

It had been over a decade since Tanner had last seen Stucky. Time had not been kind. Liquor and cigarettes had turned his complexion pasty and thick. His hair, which he still wore in a crew cut, was a yellowish gray, and his nose was lined with broken blood vessels. Despite the paunch around Stucky's middle, Tanner could see solid muscle beneath. *Still dangerous*, he thought. *Still the same cruel SOB.*

"See you around, Art." Briggs started to turn back around.

"So, did you retire?"

"Pardon me?"

"From the Navy," Stucky said. "Did you retire?"

"I resigned my commission."

"Nice to have the option. I was just shy of my twenty, you know."

Enough of this, Briggs thought. "We all make our choices, Art." Tanner turned his back on him. There was a long five seconds of silence. Briggs could feel Stucky's eyes on him.

Stucky laughed, a bark. "You know, some things never change. You were an asshole back then, and you're an asshole now." He walked away.

Once he was gone, Cahil muttered, "What the hell was that?"

"Art doesn't like me."

"So I gathered. What's the deal?"

"Later. Oaks, can I hear it again?" The tech rewound the tape, and he listened to the conversation twice more before giving up.

"You think you heard something?" Oaken pressed.

"No. . . . No, it's nothing."

44

ARMED WITH A NAME, HENRY RETURNED TO BUILDING 57 THE FOL-lowing morning. It took ten minutes for John to return with three boxes. "Gotta warn you, it ain't sorted."

"That's okay, John. Thanks."

Over the next four hours, Henry read every scrap of paper in the boxes. *Stonefish* had a long record, he found. He found lists of patrols, crew manifests, dry dock records, situation reports—everything was there. Finally, at the bottom of the last box he came across a message from COM-SUBPACFLT (Commander, Submarine Pacific Fleet) to the chief of naval operations that recounted *Stonefish*'s fate. He scanned past the header to the text:

> PBY BASED SAIPAN REPORTS USS STONEFISH (COMMANDED LT. HUGH CARPEN) SUNK BY ENEMY AIRCRAFT, 30 JULY. APPROX. POSITION 158° 12' EAST, 27° 14' NORTH. ONE SURVIVOR RECOVERED, EN ROUTE AUSTRALIA.

"What the . . ." Frowning, Henry read it again. He opened his pocket atlas and plotted the coordinates. This couldn't be right. According to the Navy, *Stonefish* was sunk not off the coast of Honshu, but almost 500 miles to the south.

Bethesda Naval Hospital

THOUGH THERE WOULD BE MONTHS OF INTERROGATION IN VOR-salov's future, the first questions Latham asked had been assembled by the DORSAL group. Vorsalov's answers sent Latham directly to Bethesda, where he found Fayyad sitting up in bed.

Latham introduced himself. "We have Vorsalov in custody. None of your friends from the safe house made it."

"They were not my friends, Agent Latham."

"So it seems. I read Agent Randal's report."

Fayyad looked at Paul. "Randal. I owe you my thanks."

"Why did you do it?" Paul asked. "Why risk your life for hers?"

"When I saw Ibn run for the stairs, I knew what he was going to do. In that moment, none of it made sense. What they do—what I have done—is no longer about a cause. It's about hate. Their Islam is not my Islam." Fayyad smiled sadly. "Perhaps I am getting soft."

Despite himself, Latham smiled back. "Well, as it stands now, the charges against you are murder, espionage, and extortion. The U.S. attorney has declined to press accessory to kidnapping charges."

"Why?"

"He also read Agent Randal's report."

"I see."

"We also know about the Delta bombing. The girl survived and—"

"Cynthia. How is she?"

"She'll recover."

"I'm glad. So what happens now?"

"That depends. If you help us, they've agreed to not push the death penalty."

Fayyad nodded, but Latham saw nothing in his eyes. *He doesn't care.*

"Tomorrow will take care of itself," Fayyad said. "Ask your questions."

WHEN THEY FINISHED, LATHAM AND RANDAL STOOD UP AND headed for the door.

"Agent Latham." Fayyad called. "A moment in private?" Latham walked over. "I know I have no right to ask, but . . . Tell me about Judith. Does she know?"

"About you? Not yet. We haven't . . . We're still sorting it out."

"When you do, please tell her I am sorry. I know she won't believe me, but I wish . . . Just tell her I am sorry."

Langley

"THERE'S TWO IMMEDIATE ISSUES WE'VE GOT TO DEAL WITH," Latham told Dick Mason. "One, Vorsalov has to contact Beirut with an update. Do we call it quits, or do we spread the net to reach the group that hired him? At most, we have four days before he's got to report."

From Mason's expression, Latham saw he'd struck a chord. *They want the whole bunch,* he thought. *But how?* Hollywood portrayals aside, it was exceedingly difficult to dash into a foreign country, scoop up the bad guys, and dash back out.

"And the second issue?" said Mason.

Latham recounted his discussions with Vorsalov and Fayyad. "Their stories match," Charlie said. "The names, the dates, the places . . . everything. On top of that, we know Vorsalov has been freelancing for them for years."

Coates said, "Even so, we can't rule out the chance he's lying."

"To what end?" said Sylvia Albrecht. "We've got him, and he knows it. If I were in his shoes, I could think of a dozen clients I'd rather betray. That's a pretty strong selling point."

Mason stared at the wall. "Charlie, before I ruin a lot of people's day, I have to be sure, so I'm putting you in the hot seat: Is he telling the truth?"

"Yes, sir, I believe his is."

"Okay." Mason nodded and pushed his intercom button. "Ginny, call the White House. Tell Jim Talbot I need to see him right away." He turned to his DDI. "Sylvia, I want everything you've got on General Issam al-Khatib."

*   *   *

Rappahannock River

WHEN TANNER GOT HOME, HE FOUND HIS FATHER SITTING ON THE deck. "Dad?"

"Nice view you've got here. You can almost see down to the bay."

"A little farther when the fog lifts. Come on in. You've got something?"

"You could say that."

Over coffee they sat down at the kitchen table. Tanner could see the glint in Henry's eye as he plopped down a stack of photocopies. "You've been busy."

"You weren't kidding, y'know," said Henry. "This is a genuine mystery."

It took fifteen minutes for Henry to recount his search. He ended with the report of *Stonefish*'s sinking. "That can't be right," Tanner said. "Five hundred miles south . . . that's near the Bonin Islands. I got the serial numbers right; I'm sure of it."

"I believe you," replied Henry. "I did some cross-checking. The report stated she was sunk by enemy aircraft. First of all, there's not a single documented case of a submarine going down with all hands after that kind of attack. If she sinks on the surface, somebody has always gotten off. Second, I couldn't find a single reference to a search-and-rescue effort."

That got Tanner's attention. Since its birth, the U.S. Navy had never given up on a missing ship until all hope was lost. "Are we talking about a cover-up?"

"Maybe. I took a copy of *Stonefish*'s crew list, and we plugged the names into the computer—"

"You *what?*" Tanner asked with a grin. The closest his father came to computer literacy was using a pocket calculator to do his taxes. "You plugged the names into a *what?*"

"Well, John did it. I watched."

"Dad, are you telling me you hacked into the Navy's mainframe?"

"I did no such thing. We checked the names against the

Bureau of Personnel's listings, then matched those against the VA. I figured if anyone had actually survived, there had to be some record of it: duty assignments, separation date, that sort of thing."

"And?"

"All but one of the crew is dead." Henry consulted his notepad. "An ensign—a captain, I should say—William Myers, retired."

Tanner smiled. "Are you telling me he's still alive?"

"Yep. And he's only a stone's throw from here: Manassas."

45

Manassas, Virginia

HAVING NO IDEA WHAT HE WOULD SAY, TANNER DECIDED AGAINST calling Captain Myers in advance. He left Rappahannock early that afternoon and arrived in Manassas by four. He stopped at a café, had a late lunch, and asked for directions to the Myers home. The waitress knew "the Captain," as did most everyone, she explained. Not only did Myers live in what had been the temporary headquarters of Stonewall Jackson during the Battle of Bull Run, but he also grew the best tomatoes in Prince William County.

The directions took Tanner to a plantation-style house surrounded by willow trees. If not for the sound of traffic on the nearby highway, he could almost imagine himself in the antebellum South. He knocked on the door and it opened, revealing an elderly woman. "Yes?"

"Good morning, ma'am. I'm looking for Captain Myers."

"Come for the tomatoes?"

"Not exactly ma'am. Are you Mrs. Myers?"

"Yes . . . Peggy."

"I'm Briggs Tanner." *Now what?* "I was in the Navy, also."

With that, Peggy Myers smiled. "Come on in, I'll take you to him."

She led him to the backyard and pointed toward a garden in the corner. "Just go on over."

"Thank you."

Captain Myers was kneeling in the dirt, tying a tomato vine.

"I didn't realize they still grew this late in the season," Tanner called.

Myers squinted up at him. "They're tough. They'll keep growing until we get a hard frost." Myers was of medium height, with stooped shoulders and brown eyes. "What can I do for you?"

Tanner didn't know what to say. He decided on the partial truth. "I'm doing a little research on the war. I was hoping you could help me."

"You military?"

"Not anymore."

"Navy?"

"Yes, sir."

"What'd you do?" Tanner told him, and Myers smiled. "Back then we called them UDT. Always thought those fellas were a different sort."

Tanner laughed. "That's a nice way of putting it."

"Come on, I'll see if Peg has some lemonade around."

MYERS'S DEN WAS A MUSEUM OF WORLD WAR II SUBMARINE history. The walls were covered with prints depicting the various battles of the Pacific war: Guadalcanal, Iwo Jima, Bella LaVella. He handed Tanner a glass of lemonade and pointed him to a chair. "Haunting aren't they?" Myers asked.

"That they are."

"Submarines played a part in all those. We were there. The silent service, y'know. It wasn't just because we were sneaky. We did what we had to do and didn't talk about it. So, how can I help you?"

Again Tanner hesitated. How do you tell a man you suspect the story behind his boat's fate is a lie? Briggs decided the direct approach was best. "I'm looking into the disappearance of *Stonefish*."

Myers pursed his lips, nodded, but said nothing.

"You were her XO when she was lost?"

"Yep."

"Can you tell me what happened?"

"Did you read the report?"

"Yes, but—"

"Then you know what happened."

"There's a few things I don't understand," Tanner said.

"Such as?"

"Such as why she was reported sunk near the Bonins."

Myers took a sip of lemonade.

Tanner pulled a sheet of paper from his file and handed it across. "According to Fairbanks-Morse, *Stonefish*'s engines were installed in July of 1942. According to the Navy, she kept those engines until her sinking."

"What's your point?"

"A few weeks ago, I pulled that same serial number off the engine of a sub I found four hundred yards off the coast of Honshu."

Myers stared at Tanner for ten seconds, "You were there?" he whispered. "You were aboard her?"

"Yes, sir."

"How'd she look?"

"A little beat up."

"You're being generous. Were they still there? The bodies, I mean?"

"One in the wardroom, the other in forward torpedo."

Myers smiled sadly and nodded.

"Can you tell me about it?" Briggs said.

"It was a long time ago. I'm the only one left. It doesn't really matter, does it?"

"I think it does. I'm betting you think so, too."

Myers went silent, studying the pictures and memorabilia around the study. Tanner guessed for his entire life Myers had been haunted by *Stonefish* and the secret he kept about her.

Finally Myers said, "You want the whole story or the abridged version?"

AS SOON AS HE STARTED TALKING, TANNER REALIZED MYERS hadn't lived a day in fifty years without thinking about *Stonefish*. His recollection was vivid, as though he were watching it on a movie screen.

"We were docked at the Volcano Islands to resupply. The

skipper pulled me aside and gave me a couple orders: First, he wanted me to offload sixteen of our fish. It was an odd request, but I was the new guy, so I did it. Second thing he said was he wanted everybody off the boat at sixteen hundred. Everybody, he said, including me and the brow watch. Well, I gave him an 'Aye, sir,' and got to work.

"Two hours later, the torpedoes were off and everyone was ashore. I was in the wardroom trying to catch up on paperwork and lost track of time. It was sixteen-fifteen, so I hurried on deck and headed for the brow. Carpen was standing on the pier. He gave me a hard stare and barked at me to get moving.

"Just then a couple trucks—two army deuce and a halfs—were pulling alongside. About a dozen GIs jumped out and posted themselves around the boat. The last thing I saw was a civilian shaking hands with the skipper. I remember that clearly. This guy was tall, ramrod straight, almost bald. He might've been dressed as a civvie, but he was military for sure. I heard his name, too, but it didn't ring any bells: John Staples. Funny kind of name, I thought.

"Later that night when everybody was back aboard, we sailed. Right away the crew knew something was up. I didn't see the guy until later, but scuttlebutt said there was a civilian holed up in the forward torpedo room. I figured it was the fella I saw on the dock. I found out later it wasn't.

"The next morning, the skipper called me to his stateroom. He told me to spread the word: Forward torp was off limits. Then he showed me the chart. Green as I was, even I could see where our course was gonna take us. Even that late in the war anything north of Nanpo was still bad news for submarines . . . and we were going *way* up north. I asked him why, but he didn't answer.

"Two days later, he sprang it on the rest of the wardroom. Up till then, nobody else knew where we were. I tell you, it was damned funny looking at their faces. I mean, three days before we're drinking beer in the Volcanos and now we're twenty miles off the Jap mainland and fixin' to get a whole lot closer.

"Round about midnight, we started out.

"Those next ten hours were the longest of my life. We slipped through a hole in the coastal net that couldn't have been much bigger than the boat, then picked our way through the minefield inside.

"Once we got through, we turned east, parallel to the shoreline. About a quarter mile from the beach, the skipper took a peek through the scope and spotted a Jap destroyer— a Naichi class—about four miles out. We took a fix, then ducked back under. Sonar got contact on four tin cans in the main channel between Honshu and Skikoku . . . sitting right in our path. We had four miles to go, and five destroyers blocking us.

"We were creeping along at three knots, quiet as a ghost, when we got a break. The Naichi turned away from us, so we dashed ahead and got in behind his baffles. The idea was to use his screw noise to mask us. We would slip into the channel, do whatever we came to do, maybe torpedo one of the tin cans, then sneak out in the confusion. Well, it didn't work out that way.

"The Naichi found us and started dropping depth charges. We must have taken a dozen near hits. Rivets were popping, steam pipes bursting, glass all over the deck . . . Seemed like it lasted hours, but it was probably only three or four minutes. The Naichi came around for another run at us. But the skipper had other ideas. That man was good . . . the best sub driver I've ever known.

"While the Naichi was circling, we kicked it into flank and slipped beneath 'em. If I hadn't been so damned scared, I would've laughed; here they were looking ahead, and we were behind them and heading for the channel.

"We would've made it, too, except one of the depth charges had landed a bit too close. A god-awful grinding sound shook the boat. Our propeller shaft was bent. It wasn't much, maybe half an inch, but that's all it takes. From then on, any speed above three knots would be like ringing the dinner bell. Problem was, the current coming out of the channel was a good four knots. We just didn't have the horsepower. The skipper decided to call it quits.

"That's when the civilian flipped his wig. Nobody had

seen him come into the control room, but there he was.

"Two things about him hit me right off: One was that briefcase he was carrying. The damn thing was chained to his wrist. Second thing was those leg braces. He got around pretty good, but you could see the brace poking out his pant leg.

"Anyway, he started shouting that we couldn't turn around, that we had to reach the 'drop-off point,' is what he called it. He looked like a ferret, the way his eyes kept darting around. Depth charge attacks have a way of doing that to your brain, I guess.

"The skipper ordered him back to forward torp, but he wouldn't go, kept saying how we had to make it, we *had* to. A couple of men tried to calm him down, but he backed away, swinging that briefcase like a wild man. Finally, me and a bunch of guys tackled him to the deck. Carpen ordered him handcuffed in forward torpedo.

"As shaken up as we were, we were damned glad to be getting out of there. From the start, the whole patrol had been odd, and it was getting worse by the minute. I mean, here we were in Tojo's front yard, Jap warships all around us, our propeller shaft bent to hell, and this guy looses his marbles right in front of us.

"So, with the four tin cans north of us and the Naichi to the west, we turned south along the coast of Honshu. By then we'd been submerged for six hours; the air was getting thick. We needed to ventilate. We went to periscope depth and took a peek. We couldn't have been more than a couple hundred yards offshore. I scanned the beach and saw a bunch of huts and a couple cooking fires. That's how close we were. Tanabe Point—our exit—was nine miles. At three knots, it would take us a few hours, so the skipper decided to come up and get some air. A fog bank had rolled in, so we figured it was okay.

"We took her up until the deck was awash, then me and Carpen climbed the bridge ladder and popped the hatch. I still remember that smell: Air. Just plain, clean air. It was the best smell in the world.

"Astern of us I could just see the running lights of the

Japs doing racetracks in the channel. I started thinking we were gonna make it. I guess I jinxed us, because that's when it started.

"The only thing I can figure is a coast-watcher spotted us. All of a sudden, three parachute flares exploded over the beach. It was almost like daylight, they were so bright. Bullets started smacking into the hull. The bastards were taking pot shots at us from the beach . . . shooting at us with goddamned rifles.

"The skipper ordered emergency dive and shoved me toward that hatch. I looked back, and there she was . . . the Naichi. She was maybe two miles behind us and blasting away with her five-incher. I was almost down the hatch when the first shell hit. It sheared off the tops of both periscopes and dropped into the water ahead of us. I heard a scream and looked up. The skipper was gone. I ran to the railing.

"He was lying on the foredeck, half underwater. His whole left arm was gone. It was just a stump. I heard another shell hit, this time just off the port side. The skipper was crawling toward the ladder, yelling, 'Take her down, Billy! Take her down!' and I just stared at him. I was frozen. Blood was gushing from his shoulder. He yelled again, 'Take her down! That's an order!'

"So I did it. I left him. God help me, I left him.

"By the time I got the hatch closed, we were angling down sharp. Just then I heard the shots, three of them—*pop, pop, pop*—right in a row. They sounded like caps. I could tell they came from the forward part of the boat, and I had a pretty good idea who was doing the shooting, but there was too much going on to worry about it.

"I ordered full dive and hard right rudder. Above us, I could hear the shells dropping. I don't remember much of what happened next, except knowing we'd taken a hit. I figured out later a shell had clipped our bow and taken off one of the planes. The boat tipped forward . . . must've been seventy degrees. We were dropping fast. Everybody was looking at me. I remember thinking, 'Christ, I'm in charge. They're waiting for me to do something.'

"I ordered 'blow all ballast,' hoping it would either level us off or bring us to the surface. I figured we'd have better luck there than sitting on the bottom, suffocating to death. We slowed a bit but kept heading down.

"It got real quiet in the tower. Nobody was saying a word. Nobody looked at anybody else. I felt helpless. There was nothing else I could do. I ordered 'all hands brace for shock.'

"It wasn't a bad landing, all things considered. After we hit, I remember hearing the hull grinding on the sand. It reminded me of fingernails on a chalkboard. We'd almost settled when she rolled hard to port and started sliding again. I thought we were going off the shelf, but after a few seconds, we stopped. It got quiet again. I could hear creaking and bubbling, but aside from that, silence.

"First thing I did was check for injuries. There were some, but nothing too serious. The sound-powered phones were out, so I sent out runners, one forward to find out about the shooting and another to the engine room to get a damage report.

"The second one came back ten minutes later. Not including the bow, we had at least two leaks: One around the shaft, and one in after battery. That got my attention. When the seawater hit the batteries, the boat was gonna fill with gas. I ordered the Momsen Lungs broken out and everybody to the escape trunks.

"The second runner came back and said the master-at-arms had been shot. He was dead, lying outside forward torp. The way I figure it, he went to check on the civilian, and the guy had a gun we didn't know about. We carried the body back to the wardroom, then I sent the runner to his escape station and went to forward torp.

"I could hear him in there, screaming, banging his handcuff against the stanchion. I pounded on the door and told him we were sinking, that we had to get out. He just kept hollering, so I undogged the hatch and peeked through. He was sitting on the floor cradling that briefcase like it was a baby. There was a watermelon-sized hole in the hull and about three feet of water on the deck.

"I called to him, and he took a shot at me. Bullet whizzed right past my ear. I slammed the hatch shut. I must've stood there for another five minutes, trying to talk to him, but it was no use.

"The boat was filling up with gas—I could smell it—so I gave up and ran to the escape trunk. Everybody else was already gone. I was so scared I could hardly work my Momsen, but I got it on, got into the trunk, flooded it, and punched out."

Tanner realized he was clenching the chair's armrests. "So what happened," he whispered. "How many made it to the surface?"

"Out of seventy-eight of us, forty died before we were fished out by the Japs. Some drowned, some were washed out to sea, some got the bends because they'd held their breath on the way up.

"After they collected us, we were shipped off to a camp outside this village called Kawanoe, I think it was. This close to the end of the war, the Japs were scared and pissed off. They were sure we were about to invade, so when we popped up—a submarine within a stone's throw of the mainland—they figured we were part of an advance landing force. They started in on us right away." Myers paused and took off his glasses; his eyes were glistening. "The things they did . . ." He took a deep breath.

"Anyway, the second day they rousted us before dawn and lined us up. This officer—I think he was military intelligence—marched down the line, tapping every fourth man until he had ten of us, including Balsted, our sonar chief, and Ensign Michaels, the weapons officer. He had them step forward and kneel on the ground." Again Myers paused; he stared at his hands. "One by one, he went down the line and shot them in the back of the head. He never said a word. Just shot 'em and left them lying in the dirt. Then they marched us back into the barracks. We were numb. I mean, we had heard stories, but you just never . . .

"They worked on us for the next five days. No food, no sleep, lying in your own mess . . . I knew we were in big

trouble. If it came at all, the invasion wouldn't be for another six months at least.

"Turned out I was wrong," Myers said. "It ended a lot
quicker than that.

"On the sixth day we were lined up for morning muster
when it happened. I'd lost track of the date, and they'd
taken my watch, but I later found out it was eight-fifteen,
August sixth.

"We were standing with the sun at our backs. Then all
the sudden there was another sun. That's exactly what it
looked like: A giant sun that had popped up over the horizon. About twenty seconds passed, then the mushroom
cloud began forming. It was red and black and boiling, and
it just kept climbing into the sky, higher and higher. The
two things that struck me was how slowly it was moving
and that there was no sound. It was spooky.

"So we just stood there, all of us—the Japs, too—staring,
until about ten minutes later when the wave hit us. It was
like a strong wind, so strong you had to lean into it to stay
upright. And the sound . . . God almighty, it was like a
freight train."

Myers paused. "It's strange. I've always felt like what
happened at Hiroshima that day happened to me, too. I
know what they went through was awful . . . Hell, I'm not
sure what I'm trying to say.

"I read somewhere the bomb we dropped was twenty
kilotons," Myers said. "That's enough TNT to fill a couple
dozen railroad cars. A lot of people have trouble imagining
that. I don't. I've seen it. A hundred thirty thousand people
died outright. Seeing it from ninety miles away . . . well,
there's no imagining what it must've been like at ground
zero. It must've been hell on earth."

46

Rappahannock River

TANNER LAY AWAKE AND LISTENED TO THE RAIN PATTER AGAINST the window. In the distance, a foghorn wailed and faded. He lay in bed for a few more minutes, then threw on his robe and went downstairs to make some coffee. Cup in hand, he poked at the logs in the fireplace until they glowed back to life, then sat down.

He knew the source of his insomnia. After weeks of following the twisted trail left by Ohira, Hiromasa Takagi, and now, unexpectedly, a Jordanian terrorist, an ex-KGB colonel, and a mysterious Arab who was at this minute sailing *Tsumago* to God knew where carrying God knew what, his brain was screaming, *Enough!*

His visit to Myers and his retelling of the story to his father had been the proverbial last straw. "That's amazing," Henry said as he finished. "Myers sounds like a heck of a guy."

"He is. In the space of a minute he went from being a nugget XO, to the captain. Hard way to grow up."

"Tell me again about their stop at the Volcano Islands," Henry said.

Tanner did so.

"And Myers didn't know the name of the civilian that came along?"

"No."

"Did he get a look inside the torpedo room?"

"Not really. He peeked inside, but got shot at for his trouble."

"Fella sounds like he was a few sandwiches shy of a

picnic," Henry said. "What about the other civilian, the one on the pier? Did Myers get a name?"

Tanner dug through his notes. "Yes. John Staples."

Henry was barely listening. "Mmm. John Staples, huh?"

The rest of the evening he had been reserved, sitting in his chair and staring at nothing. Briggs knew the look; it was what his mom called his "lost in space look."

Tanner was going for another cup of coffee when the phone rang. It was Henry. "You, too, Dad?"

"Yeah. Have you got a few minutes?"

HE ARRIVED AN HOUR LATER CARRYING AN ARMLOAD OF BOOKS, maps, and a pad full of notes. Tanner poured him a cup of coffee, and they sat down beside the fire. As Henry took a sip, Tanner noticed his hands were shaking. "The story you got from Myers . . . Do you believe him?"

"Yes. The man spent twenty-two years in the Navy, retired a captain. Decorations, letters of commendation, perfect evals . . . he was a four-o sailor all the way. Why are you asking?"

"Here, let me show you."

Henry spread out his books and began talking.

IT WAS ALMOST SUNRISE WHEN HE FINISHED. OUTSIDE, THE RAIN had stopped, and the sun was peeking through the clouds. Tanner got up from the table. "Dad, you're a great researcher; I've always thought so. But . . ."

"But it sounds crazy."

"Frankly, yes."

"I know. Listen, I've gone over this forward and backward. I've checked and cross-checked. That's what I've been doing for the last eight hours."

"But is it possible? Were there enough—"

"Plenty. That's what most people don't know."

It all made sense, Tanner decided. It bordered on the unbelievable, but there was an underlying logic to the scenario. If his father were right, Dick Mason and the CIA were headed down the wrong track.

"Dad, would you be willing to tell this again to Leland?"

"Sure." He and Dutcher were long-time fishing companions. "When?"

"Right now."

By seven a.m., Tanner and his father were sitting in Holystone's conference room. Henry had just finished recounting his theory. Like Briggs, Dutcher and Oaken were stunned into silence.

Finally Dutcher said, "Henry, I've got to tell you: This is the wrong time to be starting a wild-goose chase. Bottom line: How sure are you?"

In all their years as friends, Henry had never seen Leland's face so grim. It gave him pause, but only for a moment. "Very."

"Briggs?"

"It all fits."

That was all Dutcher needed. "Okay. I've got some calls to make."

White House

One call to Mason was all it took to get them invited to the DCI's meeting with James Talbot. When Mason asked for an explanation, Dutcher said, "It's best you hear it in person." By nine, they were walking through the White House's west entrance.

Bookworm that he was, Henry was overwhelmed. He glanced nervously at the Secret Service agents, then smoothed the front of his cardigan. He whispered to Tanner, "You know, maybe I should have changed—"

"You're fine, Dad. Just tell it the same way you told me."

"Maybe you should tell part of it."

"You know the history better than I do. You're the one who put the pieces together, not me. You'll do fine."

They were ushered into Talbot's office, which was furnished in muted gold and burgundy. Talbot walked around his desk and greeted each of them in turn. If he was surprised by their presence, he didn't show it. He shook hands with Henry last.

"Mr. Tanner, I don't think we've met. Since we've got two of the Tanner family here, do you mind if I call you Henry?"

"Not at all."

"Good. Dick here tells me you have something that might interest us. Let's get to it."

Mason started by detailing Tanner's and Cahil's discovery of *Stonefish* and its tenuous connection to the salvage ship *Toshogu*. "At that point, they had nothing linking the two except pure conjecture. Out of curiosity, he asked his father for help tracking down the sub's identity. I'll let him explain what he found."

Henry Tanner stood up, walked to the podium, and shuffled his notes. "The account I'm going to give is based on an interview with a retired Navy captain named William Myers as well as several unclassified documents.

"The submarine Briggs found off the coast of Japan was a World War II S-class fleet boat named *Stonefish*. At the time of her disappearance, she was commanded by Lieutenant Hugh Carpen.

"Navy records, which we now believe to have been falsified, indicate *Stonefish* was sunk by enemy aircraft near the Bonin Islands on July 30th, 1945. One survivor was reported found: the boat's executive officer, then Ensign William Myers. Myers has confirmed this story was contrived by the Navy. And now we think we know why."

Henry spent the next ten minutes recounting the voyage of *Stonefish*, from her penetration of the antisubmarine nets to her sinking off the coast of Honshu.

"Did Myers explain the purpose of their mission?" asked Talbot.

"No. According to him, there were only two people on board who knew that: Captain Carpen and the civilian."

"Please continue."

When *Stonefish* hit bottom, Myers realized she was badly

damaged. They were taking on water in two areas, one of which was the after battery compartment."

"Gas," Talbot said quietly.

"Exactly."

He's got them, Tanner thought. Like any good history teacher, Henry was a superb storyteller.

"Myers had another problem, however. During the surface attack, the civilian shot and killed one of the crew. Myers ordered the survivors to don their Momsen Lungs and head for the escape trunks. Once they were on their way, he went to check on the civilian. According to Myers, the man refused to leave. With no other choice, Myers put on a Momsen and made his own escape."

"So this civilian . . . he's still down there?" asked Talbot.

Briggs nodded. "Chained to the stanchion. We also found the master-at-arms lying on the wardroom deck, exactly as Myers described."

"So everybody else got out?"

"They all got out," said Henry, "but only thirty-eight survived to be picked up by the Japanese." Henry finished the story with the crew's imprisonment, torture, and subsequent release following the Japanese surrender. "After spending three weeks in the hospital, Captain Myers returned to active duty and spent the next twenty years as a submariner."

Talbot said. "This is a fascinating story, but I don't see how—"

Henry nodded. "I know. I've saved that for last."

He then retold the first part of Myers's story: the offloading of torpedoes at the Volcano Islands, the army trucks, and the mysterious "military civilian."

"As Myers was leaving the boat, he saw Carpen and this man shaking hands. Myers remembered his name: John Staples."

Both Mason and Talbot looked at him blankly.

"The name doesn't ring a bell?" asked Henry.

"No, should it?"

"John Staples was a Navy captain during World War II.

In 1945, he worked as ordnance coordination officer of the
Bomb Delivery Group at Los Alamos. In other words, gentlemen, John Staples was the man responsible for the delivery of the Hiroshima and Nagasaki bombs."

47

THE ROOM WAS COMPLETELY SILENT. THOUGH BRIGGS HAD HEARD the story twice already, he again felt a chill on his neck. *God help us if we're right about this. . . . Tsumago* could be anywhere, headed anywhere.

Finally Talbot said, "Henry, let me get this straight: Are you telling me you think an atomic bomb was loaded aboard *Stonefish* and that bomb has been salvaged and may now be in the hands of a terrorist group?"

"I don't know about the latter, but as for the former, yes I am. I'm not suggesting the device was usable as it was found. And compared to today's standards, it would be crude—probably of the gun-type variety—something designed to be ejected through the sub's torpedo tubes."

"Explain that—a gun-type bomb."

"Physics is not my strong suit. Perhaps Walter can explain it better."

Oaken said, "A gun-type bomb involves ramming a uranium bullet down a barrel into what's called a pit . . . a lump of uranium. Separated from one another, the bullet and the pit are stable, but when combined with enough force, they form the critical mass required for an explosion.

"The engineering is pretty straightforward. Anyone with the right kind of machining equipment and a rudimentary understanding of physics and explosives could make one. It's the uranium that's hard to get hold of."

"Unless you happen to find it sitting at the bottom of the ocean," Talbot muttered. "God almighty, an untraceable, deniable source of uranium."

Tanner saw Talbot glance at Mason and knew what they were thinking: Could this have been the real purpose behind

Parece Kito? The compartmentalized clean rooms, the machinery . . . Could it have all been for the disassembly of *Stonefish*'s bomb, the extraction of the uranium, and the construction of another device?

"How big would something like this be?" Talbot asked.

"Little Boy was a gun-type. It was ten feet long and weighed almost 10,000 pounds. But a lot of that weight was necessary to make it droppable from a plane; not only did it have to be aerodynamic, but it had to detonate just like a conventional bomb."

"So it's conceivable something similar could have fit aboard the *Stonefish*."

Henry answered. "Easily. Her Mark 14 torpedoes were twenty feet long and weighed 5,000 pounds."

"Okay, that was then," said Mason "How about now?"

"With current technology," replied Oaken, "the sphere enclosing the pit could be the size of a beach ball, and the attached barrel would be about the size of three soda cans stacked on top of one another."

Talbot said to Dutcher, "Leland, I haven't heard your take on this."

"Assuming we're right about *Stonefish*, I think it's a very real possibility there's a workable nuclear weapon out there somewhere."

"Holy Christ."

"How about yield?" asked Mason.

"We know *Stonefish*'s device couldn't have been a Fat Man type . . . an implosion bomb," said Oaken. "It would've been too big; it had to be similar to Little Boy. Say, twenty kilotons. With today's technology, it could go as high as thirty."

"Casualties?" Talbot asked.

"It would depend on the target, but on a population center the blast alone would probably kill 150,000."

ONCE AGAIN, SILENCE SETTLED OVER THE ROOM.

"Let's not hit the panic button quite yet," Mason finally said. "We don't *know* anything yet. First of all, how can we be sure we're talking about the same John Staples?"

"We can't," said Henry. "But I did do some digging into his activities during that time."

"Is he still alive?"

"No. He died in 1953."

"You said he was in charge of delivering the damn things," said Talbot. "When Myers claims to have seen him, wasn't he supposed to be on Tinian with the Hiroshima bomb?"

"No. In fact, his deputy, Howard Tudor, handled Little Boy. From the time Tudor left for Tinian—while the bomb was en route there aboard *Indianapolis*—until just before Fat Man was dropped, there is no account of Staples's whereabouts."

"Could he have been aboard *Indianapolis*?"

"It's possible, but I don't think so," said Henry. "My guess is we had three to five bombs at our disposal in August of '45. Truth is, back then, no one knew how powerful they were going to be. In fact, there was a pool going at Los Alamos to guess the yield. The planning committee felt it might take as many as fifty bombs to bring Japan to its knees."

"Fifty!" said Talbot.

"Or more. The military had instructed them to be ready to deliver six to seven a month until it was over. Of course, they ran tests at Trinity, but until one was dropped on a real target, there was no telling what it would do."

"All right," Talbot said. "First things first: How do we prove or disprove it?"

"First, we take a photo of Staples to Captain Myers. Next, we round up all the surviving top-level people from Los Alamos and start asking questions. And lastly, we press the Navy to open its classified archives on *Stonefish*."

Talbot nodded. "Dick, put it together. Leland, we'll need you and your people as well . . . including you, Henry."

Henry looked up, startled. "Pardon? I'm not qualified—"

"I think you are. We need your help. Will you give it?"

"Well, uh, of course."

"Good. As far as *Tsumago* goes, nothing's changed.

We've got to find her before she reaches her destination. Dick, where do were stand?"

"I've got four satellites looking for her and a team of analysts working on the feed round the clock."

Talbot pushed his intercom button. "Betty, I need to see the president immediately; have the secretary of defense and the chairman of the Joint Chiefs meet me there." He clicked off and said, "Gentlemen, once we find *Tsumago*, we'd better have options for stopping her. Mr. Tanner, Mr. Cahil, you two know her firsthand. Is a boarding feasible?"

"It's feasible," Tanner replied. "But given her cargo and construction, it would take the right kind of team and careful planning. We'd only get one shot."

"Understood. Okay, we've got a lot of work ahead of us." He stood and smiled grimly. "As this is by no means a finished race, I'll save my thank-yous for when it's over. Yes, Dick?"

"One more thing: Yesterday, Latham interviewed Vorsalov and Fayyad. The man they met in Khartoum is second-in-command of the group that contracted them. His name is Mustafa al-Baz. We know very little about him, even less about the leader, who wore a mask during his meeting with Vorsalov."

Talbot asked. "And this al-Baz is the one piloting *Tsumago*?"

"Right. Here's the interesting part: Vorsalov claims al-Baz is a deep-cover operative for the Syrian *Mucharabat* and that he works directly for General Issam al-Khatib."

"Khatib . . . Where'd that name come up recently?"

"General al-Khatib is in charge of the exercises the Syrian Army is conducting."

Talbot sat back down. "You think Syria is—"

"We don't have enough to draw that conclusion yet," Mason said. "But at first glance, it appears so."

"So, if in fact there's a bomb out there, it could be in the hands of a Syrian intelligence operative."

"That's correct."

Everything had just changed, Tanner knew. Having a rogue terrorist group holding a nuke was terrifying enough, but for Syria to have one was a nightmare come true. Syria was the wild card in any Mideast peace initiative. If in fact they had the bomb, the scales of power in the region had just collapsed.

Langley Operations Center

WALKING INTO THE OP CENTER, TANNER SAW DORSAL's STAFF of analysts had doubled in the space of hours. The murmur of voices and ringing of phones filled the room; the walls were covered with photos, maps, and flowcharts.

"The party's gotten bigger," said Cahil. "You think any of them know?"

"Doubtful. They know *something's* changed, but not what. Hell, I'm not sure I'd want to know, myself."

Cahil nodded across the room to where Art Stucky stood. "There's your buddy. You ever gonna tell me the story?"

Tanner nodded. "How about lunch? Give me an hour; I want to check something." He left Cahil and walked to the audio room. "Have you got a minute?" he asked the technician.

"Sure. What's up?"

"I'd like to listen to our mystery man again . . . the one talking to Fayyad."

"No problem. Use the first booth. I'll cue it up for you."

Tanner found the booth, sat down, and donned the headphones. The tech's voice came through. "You're all set. Just use the buttons in front of you to control it."

"Thanks."

For the next hour, Briggs played and replayed the minute-long conversation. The nagging feeling in the back of his head continued to grow until it became a conviction: He knew the man on the tape. Tanner couldn't tell from where, or when, or how, but there was no doubt.

"Who are you?" he muttered aloud.

The rational side of his brain balked at the connection: The chances were astronomical, but the intuitive side of his brain—the same one that hadn't let him quit on *Stonefish*—was saying something different.

There was a knock on the glass. It was Cahil. "Lunchtime," he mouthed.

IT WAS CHINESE BUFFET DAY IN THE CAFETERIA. THEY WENT through the line and then found a table. Bear's tray was a pyramid of egg rolls, sweet and sour pork, and crab Rangoon. "A little hungry?" Tanner said.

"I'm a growing boy."

"I've noticed. Did Maggie know that when she married you?"

Cahil nodded, his mouth full. "It was why she married me. She loves to cook."

Tanner smiled and shook his head. *Good ol' Bear*. Looking back at their years together, he knew he couldn't have asked for a better friend. How many scrapes wouldn't he have survived without Bear? In Japan alone the tally was at least four. But that went both ways, didn't it? It was part of the cement of their friendship: Both knew the other would be there when it counted.

"So," Cahil said. "Stucky."

"It was back when we were still on the teams. He and I met on an op in Peru—"

"Where was I?"

"As I recall, in the hospital with a bullet in your right ass cheek."

"Oh, yeah. Go on."

STUCKY HAD BEEN A SERGEANT IN THE GREEN BERETS, TANNER explained. Though never having met the man, he knew Stucky by reputation. "Junkyard-dog mean" was the phrase he most often heard.

Stucky had been in charge of a team training Peruvian guerillas to fight Shining Path terrorists, a Marxist group whose recruiting methods involved the torture and murder of reluctant peasants. Consistent with Reagan's vow to keep South America from falling to communists (or Marxists, both of which fell from the same ideological tree) the U.S.

Army had been supporting Peruvian anti-insurgency for years.

Stucky and his team had been in-country six weeks when the CIA's Operations Directorate—who was jointly running the op with Army Intelligence—discovered their informant had been exposed and killed. The likelihood of his talking before he died was considered high, so Stucky and his team were ordered out by then DDI Leland Dutcher. A communication glitch cut them off, however, leaving the team stranded. Ground intelligence reported three local Shining Path cells heading in their direction, so a rescue mission was ordered. As the Green Beret camp was only four miles inland, Tanner and his team of three SEALs were sent in.

After eight hours of searching the countryside, they found the Green Berets holed up in a small village called Tantara.

Stucky had already realized they'd been burned and, for reasons he never explained, was convinced the villagers at Tantara were responsible. By the time Tanner arrived, Stucky's interrogations had killed four people. He was working on his fifth—a seven-year-old girl—when Tanner walked into the hut.

By the flickering glow of a lantern, Briggs could see the girl was almost dead. She sat tied to a chair, her face pasty white. Stucky had cut off all the fingers from her left hand and was working on the right when Tanner interrupted.

"Stop right there, Stucky."

Cigarette dangling from his mouth, Stucky turned, saw Tanner, and grinned. His fingers were bloody. "Lookee here, its the cavalry."

"Move away from her."

"I'm not done yet."

"I said move away!"

"Fuck you."

Tanner shot him in the thigh. Stucky collapsed and rolled onto his side.

"You son of a bitch!" he roared. "You shot me!"

Tanner walked over and kicked the knife away. He

checked the girl's pulse; it was there, but barely. "Taylor!"

His corpsman rushed inside and knelt beside her. "God almighty . . ."

"Can you move her?" Tanner asked.

"I think so."

"Do it. Get her out of here."

"What about him?"

"Forget him. Go."

Once they were alone, Stucky said, "What's your name, dickhead?"

Tanner told him.

"Well, ain't you a pussy. Can't even stomach a little wet work."

Tanner pressed the barrel of his MP5 to Stucky's forehead.

"You gonna shoot me?" Stucky said, grinning. "Go ahead, if you've got the balls. I'm betting you don't."

"Bad gamble," Tanner said, and clicked the MP5's selector to single shot.

Tanner's exec appeared in the doorway. "Briggs, don't. He's not worth it."

"Leave, Nock."

"Don't, Briggs. Let the Army have him."

"I said get out."

"If you do this, you'll be just like him. I'm telling you, he ain't worth it."

CAHIL HAD STOPPED EATING. "OBVIOUSLY YOU DIDN'T KILL HIM."

"No." Tanner stared into his coffee cup. *I should have,* he thought. *I should have put a bullet in his head and been done with it.*

"So what happened? What did the Army do to him?"

"They discharged him short of his twenty."

"That's it?"

"That's it."

"How'd he get here?"

"I don't know. Lousy interviewer, maybe." *Or maybe*

they needed somebody like him, Tanner thought. *Someone, somewhere, would always need a Stucky.*

"And the girl?"

"She spent almost a month in the hospital, but she made it. She and her older sister still live together at a mission outside Barranca."

"Still? How do you know?"

For the first time since retelling the story, Tanner smiled. "We're pen pals. She just graduated from high school."

48

Langley

THE WORKING GROUP FOUND FOUR MANHATTAN PROJECT MEM-
bers still alive that might shed some light on *Stonefish*'s
role. While half the group tried to trace these men, the other
half sifted through five decades' worth of Navy archives.
Henry Tanner, who'd driven to Manassas to reinterview
Captain Myers, returned with the first positive news: Myers
had identified John Staples as the man he saw on the pier.

Late in the afternoon, Mason called Dutcher, Tanner, and
Cahil to his office.

"We've found *Tsumago*. She's in Luanda, Angola. We
don't know how long she's been there—can't be more than
two days—but it looks like she's refueling."

"How'd you pin her down?" asked Tanner.

With four satellites on the search, the NPIC had a steady
stream of possible matches coming in, Mason explained.
These were fed into a Dell mainframe for analysis. Those
that could not be ruled out were then rephotographed at
greater resolution.

"This one's a 97.2 percent match," Mason said, then
looked at Tanner and Cahil. "There's a reason I'm sharing
this with you. The president has approved a boarding.
We're assembling a SEAL team. We want one of you to
go along."

Neither Tanner nor Cahil were surprised by the request;
they knew *Tsumago*'s layout firsthand. "Which one of us
goes?" asked Tanner.

"We'll make that decision by tomorrow."

Strait of Gibraltar, Mediterranean Sea

WHILE BERNICE AND SAUL WEINMAN ENJOYED A DINNER OF LOB-ster bisque after a long day of shuffleboard and rumba lessons, *Valverde*'s captain, Hiram Stein, stood on the bridge and watched the sun's last rays slip beneath the horizon. *So beautiful,* he thought. Twenty-one years at sea, and he never grew tired of the sight.

A former Israeli Navy officer, Stein had taken the posting as *Valverde*'s master after retirement. With his wife dead and his children grown, the sea was his only remaining passion. Of course, managing a cruise liner was nothing like running a warship, but she was a good ship with a good crew.

On the foredeck a speck of light caught his eye. He waited for it to reappear, but saw nothing aside from the long rows of umbrella tables. Then it came again: a flashlight. It winked out. Probably someone who'd forgotten their suntan lotion, Stein thought and returned to his review of the deck log.

TEN MINUTES LATER, NIGHT HAD FULLY FALLEN. GIBRALTAR SLOWLY passed abeam of *Valverde* as she cleared the straits and entered the Atlantic Ocean. Stein peered through his binoculars, trying to catch a glimpse of the rock's massive shadow.

Outside came the clang of footsteps on the ladder, followed by a knock on the hatch. "Are we expecting someone, sir?" asked the helmsman.

"No." The bridge crew used the inside ladder, which was accessible only through a locked hatch, while the wing ladders were cordoned off with a placard reading Ship's Personnel Only. This was probably either a lost passenger or someone looking for a tour. Stein opened the hatch. "Can I help you?"

"Pardon," the man said. "Can you help, please?"

He was Arab, Stein saw. Of the 306 passengers aboard *Valverde*, 26 were Arab Christians. He noticed the flash-

light in the man's hand. "What seems to be the problem?"
said Stein.

"I believe I left my sunglasses beside the pool. I tried to
find them, but . . ."

"That's no problem. Every evening the crew checks the
pool area for lost items. Talk with the purser tomorrow
morning; your glasses will likely be there."

"Oh, thank you." The man peered inside. "This is the
pilothouse, yes?"

"Yes, sir. We call it the bridge."

"The bridge." He gave a sheepish wave to the helmsman.
"This is where you steer the ship and control her speed?"

"That's right. If you'd like a tour, we—"

"Yes, I know. I have signed up for a tour. Very exciting."

"Good," said Stein. "Unless you need help finding your
stateroom . . ."

"No, thank you, I will find my way."

Stein closed the door and turned to the helmsman.
"That's one," he said with a smile. On each cruise the
bridge crew ran a pool to guess how many passengers tried
to finagle unauthorized tours. "Fourteen more, and I'm in
the big money."

Rappahannock River

TWO NIGHTS IN A ROW, TANNER THOUGHT. HE LAY IN BED AND
stared at the ceiling for a while, then wandered into the
living room and turned on the TV. He surfed until he came
to a channel playing *The Old Man and the Sea*. If anything
could lull him to sleep, it would be listening to Spencer
Tracy's commiserations with a marlin.

In the television's glow, he noticed a figurine sitting on
the fireplace mantel. It was a carved cedar camel, no bigger
than his palm. It had been there so long he'd forgotten
about it. He smiled, remembering where—

He bolted upright in the chair. "Oh, God."

*   *   *

ONE CALL TO THE OP CENTER TOLD TANNER THE AV TECHNICIAN arrived at 7:00. Briggs was waiting outside the audio room when he walked in. "Morning," the tech said. "You're up early."

"I need a favor," Tanner said.

"You all right? You look kinda pale."

"I'm fine. I need a favor."

"Sure, what's up?"

Tanner explained. "Two conditions, though: I need it done by nine, and I need you to keep it quiet."

"Whoa, hold on—"

"If there's any flak, I'll take it."

The tech shrugged. "Okay. Can I get some breakfast first? I—"

"Tell me what you want; I'll get it for you."

THE TECH FINISHED AT 8:45. TANNER LISTENED TO THE RESULTS, thanked him, grabbed the tape, then headed upstairs to Mason's office. Dutcher was standing outside talking to Oaken and Cahil.

"Morning, Briggs," said Leland.

Cahil said, "You don't look like you got much sleep."

"I didn't. Leland, I need to talk to you."

Mason walked past. "Okay, folks, let's get started."

"After the meeting," Dutcher said.

THE MEETING LASTED AN HOUR. TO TANNER, IT FELT LIKE TEN.

So far, Mason reported, they'd had limited success with the Navy's archives, which were still in hard copy and microfiche format. After two days and 120 man-hours, the team had reviewed only about 20 percent of the relevant files.

The other avenue of research was faring better. Two top-level Manhattan Project members—one physicist and one strategic planner—had been located and were being flown in later that afternoon.

The NPIC reported *Tsumago* had left Angola and was heading north along the coast of Africa. Unless she changed course in the next two days, Mason said, her most probable destination was the Mediterranean.

After a few brief questions, the meeting ended. Once the room was empty except for Dutcher, Oaken, and Cahil, Tanner said, "I've got something you all need to see."

Mason looked at him. "The last time you had that look on your face, we found out there was a nuke floating around. Are you about to ruin my day again?"

"Depends on how you define *ruin,*" Tanner replied. He walked to the TV/VCR, inserted a tape, and hit Play.

There were a few moments of static on the screen, and then it cleared, showing what appeared to be a wedding reception beside an outdoor fountain. In the background a band played Handel's *Water Music*. The bride and groom stood at the head of the receiving line, greeting guests. The camera zoomed in on the groom's face: It was Tanner.

Mason said, "Briggs, what's this about—"

"Wait."

He let it play for a few more seconds, then hit Pause as Elle embraced a middle-aged man with salt-and-pepper hair. His face was in profile.

Mason looked at Tanner. "I don't understand what—"

"For the past couple days, something's been nagging me. I couldn't put my finger on it until last night."

"What is it?" asked Dutcher. He was concerned; Tanner looked almost ill. His eyes were distant, his voice barely a whisper.

"I think that man is the leader of the group that's got *Stonefish*'s nuke."

No one said a word.

They think I'm nuts, Briggs thought. *Maybe they're right.* What was his proof? A voice he hadn't heard in over a decade? A gut feeling?

Mason cleared his throat. "Briggs, this is—"

"I know. That's why I had the lab run a comparison." Tanner slid the report across the table. "Ninety-six percent match."

TANNER HAD MET ABU AZHAR WHEN HE WAS THIRTEEN YEARS old. He and his parents were living in Beirut, where Henry taught European history and Azhar taught Middle East politics at American University. Despite the cultural differences, the two became fast friends, Henry the academic adventurer, Azhar the opinionated but gregarious Arab who was the antithesis of everything young Briggs had seen of Middle Easterners on television. Azhar didn't carry bombs under the folds of his robe, and he didn't rant about infidels. He was kind and warm and doted on Briggs every chance he got.

Azhar and his wife spent many weekends at their home along the Corniche overlooking the Mediterranean. Briggs, on the brink of adolescence and struggling to adjust to life in Lebanon where his white skin made him a target for bullies, came to think of Azhar not only as a friendly uncle but also as a guide to the rules of his new home.

One day, Tanner came home with a black eye and a split lip. He'd been beaten up by a gang of four Shiite boys. While Irene tended his wounds, Abu whispered, "Come see me tomorrow."

For the next week, Azhar and Tanner secretly met in the gym at American University, where he taught Briggs the fundamentals of boxing—not classical boxing, per se, but rather "Beiruti boxing," as he called it. Briggs avoided the gang as best he could until Azhar pronounced him ready.

"Remember, fight only if you have to. Fight only to defend yourself or what you care about. Do you understand?"

"I think so," said Briggs.

"Not 'think'!" Azhar replied firmly. "Violence must be a last resort. If you must use violence, do so with compassion. Life is a circle, Briggs. What you give, you eventually receive. What you forget or abandon will haunt you. Now do you understand?"

"Yes."

"Good. Also, bullies are like a pack of dogs. To disperse the pack, pick the strongest one and hurt him. The others will run. Tomorrow, you will walk home from school the usual way, and you will not be afraid."

The next day, the gang cornered Briggs in an alley. Through the taunts and the tossed dirt clods he kept walking until one of the boys—the leader—shoved him from behind. Hands shaking, Briggs set down his books, turned around, and broke the boy's nose. The boy fell to the ground, crying. The others ran.

Briggs helped the boy to his feet, handed him his handkerchief, then picked up his books and walked home.

That day, Abu Azhar earned a place in Tanner's heart.

After the Tanners left Beirut, Briggs and Azhar exchanged dozens of letters, but Briggs saw him and his wife only once, at his graduation. "Uncle Abu" gave him a carved wooden camel, an Azhar family heirloom his great-great-great-grandfather had carved from the family cedar tree. "This was to be passed down to my son," Azhar said with a sad smile. "But . . . it was not to be."

Briggs later asked Henry what Abu had meant, and his father told him the Azhars could not have children.

He saw Azhar only once more, Tanner explained. At his wedding to Elle.

"That's him," Tanner murmured. "Hugging Elle."

Dick Mason stared at the screen. The man was of medium height with a slight paunch, a broad smile, and lively eyes. Hardly the portrait of a terrorist. But then, after decades of invasion and civil war, who could say what had happened to Azhar?

"So you're telling me he's a family friend?" asked Mason.

"That's exactly what I'm telling you," Tanner replied.

"Why didn't you stay in touch?"

"I was in college when Israel invaded Lebanon. I sent dozens of letters; none were answered. I assumed with the war . . ." Tanner shrugged. "Aside from going to look for him, there was nothing I could do. Eventually I got back there, but under the circumstances. . . ."

"I know. I read your file. You think Azhar is capable of this?"

"He had some strong ideas about politics, but I never saw anything militant in him. That was a long time ago, though. If we're talking about the man I knew then, I'd say no."

"Dutch?"

"If Briggs says he's the one, that's good enough for me."

"Well, I wish I could be as trusting," replied Mason, "but paranoia is part of the job. Briggs, I assume you know you've just landed in the hot seat?"

Tanner nodded. "I know."

FOR THE NEXT TEN HOURS, TANNER WAS RELENTLESSLY GRILLED by George Coates and Sylvia Albrecht. Gone were the smiles and friendly demeanor; gone also were the use of first names. This was an interrogation. They could not accept his story—or the tape, which was by now being dissected by the computer—until both had passed the toughest scrutiny.

Finally, at 11:00 P.M., he was called up to Mason's office. Dutcher, Cahil, and Oaken were already there. "Three things," Mason began. "First, we've interviewed our two Los Alamos survivors. Both were involved in bomb construction.

"There were three operational bombs: Little Boy for Hiroshima, Fat Man for Nagasaki, and a third named Baby Sally, for an undisclosed location. The Baby Sally team received specific instructions: The device had to be submersible, time-detonated, and exactly thirty inches in circumference."

"Roughly the size of *Stonefish*'s standard torpedoes," said Tanner.

"Were either of these scientists involved in targeting?" asked Cahil.

"No, but they did overhear several conversations, which tended to get loud whenever Groves was involved. The one phrase they remember hearing was *triad detonation*." Mason unrolled a map of Japan. Using a red pen, he circled Hiroshima, Nagasaki, and the mouth of the Inland Sea, then connected the circles. They formed a near-perfect triangle.

"The blast effect would have been devastating, both spiritually and materially. The precision, the timing, the targets—all would have told the Japanese government, 'We can strike whenever and wherever we want.' As it turned out, two bombs had the same effect."

Mason went on to say the search of the Navy's archives had finally turned up an unsuccessful salvage hunt for *Stonefish* in 1947. The rift in which they found her had likely masked her presence to the salvage ships, which were armed only with crude sonar. After a month, *Stonefish* was classified lost, and the matter was buried.

"Until now," said Oaken. "We have any idea how Takagi stumbled onto her?"

"No, and we probably never will. As for his motive, who knows? It could be simple greed. Last time we checked, Libya was offering a billion dollars for a ready-to-wear nuke. Syria would have no problem coming up with that much, especially with a little help from Sudan and Libya."

"That's a lot of money, even for Takagi," said Dutcher. "Enough to build the bomb, *Tsumago, Toshogu*, and still clear three-quarters of a billion in profit."

"Exactly," said Mason. "So here's the plan: We're going on the assumption *Tsumago* is carrying the device. The president has ordered us to work on two fronts: First, the boarding of *Tsumago* to recover the device. Ian, we've decided you'll be joining the SEAL team. Any problem with that?"

"No."

"You'll leave for Indian Head tonight; the team starts workups tomorrow. In five days, you'll hit the ship."

Mason turned to Tanner. "Briggs, we want to penetrate the group in Beirut. Your suspicion about Azhar was correct. He's the one. How he got where he is, we don't know, but—"

"But it doesn't matter," Tanner finished.

"Exactly. We have to put a stop to this thing, whatever it takes. Either we get the ship or we get the leadership. Given your experience and your familiarity with Azhar, you have the best chance to do that."

To do what? Tanner thought. *Talk him out of it?* If Abu was so far gone that he'd not only turned terrorist but was ready to use a nuke, there was little chance talking would do any good. Mason knew that, of course, hence his words, "Whatever it takes." *Go to Beirut and kill Abu Azhar.*

The room was silent; all eyes were on Tanner. "Can you do it?" asked Mason.

The swiftness of Briggs's answer surprised even him. "I can do it." *But God help me if I have to.*

49

Falls Church, Virginia

THE FOLLOWING MORNING, AN HOUR AFTER HE WAS MOVED FROM Bethesda to the safe house, Ibrahim Fayyad's room was buzzing with activity as the technicians readied their equipment. Fayyad's condo phone had been routed into the safe house's main switchboard, as was Vorsalov's phone at the Marriott.

"How long?" Latham asked the communication technician.

"Two minutes."

Coates walked into the room with a CIA linguist. "Ready for us, Charlie?" Coates asked, handing over Fayyad's script.

"Almost."

Latham had been expecting Mason's call the night before. Would Fayyad be willing to pass something to his superiors in Beirut? the DCI had asked. Having already raised this question with Fayyad, Latham said "Yes." *So they're sending somebody in,* he thought as he read the script. Ruthless guy, that Mason. What the DCI had planned was called the "spider and the fly."

"This oughta get their attention," he said to Coates.

"That's the idea. Dick wants you to call your guy at *Shin Bet,* see if we can work both ends at the same time."

"No problem."

"Charlie, let me ask you something: Why's Fayyad doing this?"

"Hard to say," Latham replied. "My guess is he grew a conscience."

Coates shook his head. "It's a crazy world."

The technician announced, "We're set."

Latham donned his headset and looked to Fayyad. "Ready?"

"Yes."

Latham nodded to the technician, who dialed the front number in Nicosia. When the exchange operator answered, Fayyad said, "Box one seventy-seven, please. Ricardo."

The technician disconnected. Fayyad said, "It shouldn't take long."

THE CALL CAME AN HOUR LATER. "INCOMING TO THE CONDO," SAID the technician.

"Start the recorders," Latham ordered, then nodded to Fayyad, who said, "Hello."

"Is Heloise home?"

"I'm sorry, I think you have the wrong number. What were you dialing?"

"Five four six two," the voice said.

"Sorry, wrong number."

The line went dead.

Latham consulted Fayyad's safe-call map. Five four six two was a booth at the corner of Goldsboro and Bradley, two miles from the Glen Echo condo. "Janet, call Paul and have Bell route that number to us."

"You got it."

ONCE THE BOOTH WAS PATCHED THROUGH TO THE SAFE HOUSE, Latham ordered the front number redialed. When the exchange answered, Fayyad said, "Box one seventy seven, please. Direct line. Ricardo."

Ten seconds passed; after a series of clicks, Abu Azhar's voice came on. "Yes?" he said in Arabic.

"It is me."

"Are you safe?"

"Yes," Fayyad replied, finger tracing along the script. "We've met with our suppliers. They've heard nothing about that company."

"Do you believe them? Both of you?"

"Yes."

There was long silence from Azhar, then: "Good. Anything else?"

"One item. Our supplier passed along a detail, something new. I do not know if it means anything. . . ."

"Tell me."

"They mentioned something about another supplier, a man in Luanda—"

"Where?"

"Luanda, Angola," said Fayyad. "I do not have any details yet, but there seemed to be a lot of interest in the product."

"When can you find out more?"

"Soon. We're meeting with our supplier again in two days."

"Call me immediately afterward."

The line went dead.

Fayyad looked at Latham. "Okay?"

"Perfect." Latham turned to the linguist. "Did we get enough?"

"I think so. I'll need a tape."

"Jimmy, make a copy, and give it to Mr. Coates."

Langley

AFTER THE TAPE HAD BEEN TRANSLATED AND ANALYZED, MASON sat at his desk reading the report. "Give me the gist of it," Mason said. "Is it the same man?"

"Absolutely," said the linguist.

"Did he buy it?"

"I believe so. Arabic is a complex language, but it also has a singsong flow to it. It's easy to detect awkward breaks or tone changes. Aside from one exchange, I found no significant stressors."

"Which one?"

"The part about Angola. Whatever it is, you hit a hot button."

"Good," said Mason. "Thanks for you help, Doctor. That'll be all."

"Yes, sir." At the door, the linguist turned back. "One more thing: The caller's dialect was strange. It almost sounded like a mixture of Lebanese and Iraqi Arabic. To us, it would sound like a Minnesotan using a bad Texas accent."

Once the linguist was gone, Mason said, "What next, George?"

"Depends. Are the Israelis on board?"

"They're thinking it over, but I made my position pretty clear."

"Tanner will be ready in three days. We can drop the other shoe the day after he's in-country."

"Three days," Mason muttered. Normal training time for such an operation would be eight weeks. "I hope to God we're not feeding him to the wolves."

Williamsburg, Virginia

LOCATED ON A SWAMPY THUMB OF LAND BETWEEN THE YORK AND James Rivers, Camp Perry had been a World War II Navy Seabee camp until it was seconded to the CIA in the 1950s. Known as The Farm, Perry is where CIA case officers go to learn the basics of the spy tradecraft, from cryptology and weapons handling to agent recruiting. Thanks to popular fiction, it is also the best known *secret* CIA facility in America.

Two hours after he accepted the mission, Tanner was lying on a cot in one of the camp's redbrick barracks. He got exactly three hours of sleep before being awakened, fed, then escorted to a classroom. He was the only student. His trainer was an old Mideast hand named Stan, no last name.

According to Stan, of the next seventy-two hours, Tanner would spend fifty-seven of them either in class or in one of the camp's field mock-ups. Course material would include cover story, Arabic language (which he hadn't spoken in years), surveillance and countersurveillance, communications, evasion and escape, and culture and politics.

"I understand you've already had training in these areas, but given your destination, every little bit helps. Any questions?"

Tanner had none. He was turned over to the Near East culture specialist.

SIX HOURS LATER, HE WAS SITTING DOWN TO LUNCH WHEN Dutcher appeared. "Is this seat taken?" he asked. Aside from Tanner there were only twelve trainees present. Billets to the CIA's Career Trainee Program were coveted.

Tanner smiled. "Care for some lunch? All the gruel you can eat."

"No thanks. How're things going?"

"It's pretty clear they're not happy with the time line, but they're doing their best. How's Bear doing?"

"The team's assembled. They start live-fire mock-ups tomorrow."

"When do they go?"

"It depends," replied Dutcher. "If *Tsumago* turns west within the next couple days, she's probably headed for us. That'll give them an extra forty-eight hours. If she keeps heading up the coast of Africa, they'll hit her in five days, probably somewhere off the coast of Morocco. By the way, he asked me to tell you Jurens is leading the team."

Tanner laughed. "Sconi Bob Jurens. During BUD/s he made it a point to tell everybody he was from Wisconsin . . . one of only three black men in the state, he claimed. He's a good man. With him and Bear on the team, their chances just went up a few notches."

Dutcher studied Tanner. He'd known Briggs for six years and had watched his career in the Navy and the ISAG long before that. Despite the smile, Tanner was deep inside his own head playing the what-if game.

"You want to talk about anything?" he asked. "I know you're not a big fan of Beirut, and now—"

"Beirut I can handle. Believe it or not, I have mostly good memories of it. It's just that . . . I don't know."

"You're not sure you can kill Azhar."

Tanner looked hard at his boss. "If he's part of this, if he's planning to use that thing or hand it over to Syria, I'll have no problem pulling the trigger."

"No doubts?"

"I won't lie to you: I'm having trouble believing it's him. If you'd known him like I did—"

"People change, Briggs."

"I know that. Is this why you came here, Leland?"

Dutcher shook his head. "You'll do what you have to. I know that, and so does Dick. But it doesn't mean you have to like it."

"Good, because I don't. So why the visit?"

"They've assigned you a controller. It's Stucky."

Tanner put down his spoon. "Pardon me?"

"It's his division, he was running SYMMETRY, he knows the territory. If you get a chance to rescue Marcus, Stucky's the best man to be there."

Tanner thought it over. "I guess it makes sense. How much does he know?"

"He knows about the ship and who's aboard her but not the cargo."

"How much control will he have?"

"He'll be in Tel Aviv handling communications. Once you're on the ground, you'll send reports through him." Dutcher paused. "Briggs, there's something else: I don't think Mason knows about Peru."

"I'm not surprised," said Tanner. "The Army buried it."

"I'm going to talk to him."

"No. It'll just muddy the waters. Stucky may hate me, but he's not going to fumble an entire operation to get me. Besides, even if he's inclined, what can he do? I'll be out of his reach."

Tel Aviv

HAYEM SHERABI STARED ACROSS HIS DESK AT AVI HARON. "Unusual request, wouldn't you say?"

"Very," replied Haron. "But I know Charlie Latham. If

he says the CIA will share, they'll share. Vorsalov's product alone would be—"

"Priceless, I know. Still, I don't like being in the dark. Why go to such great lengths to rescue one agent? There must be something more to it."

"Consider the downside. Say we don't cooperate. They'll probably run the operation anyway."

Sherabi considered this. Haron was right: There was more to gain by playing along. But he'd be damned if he was going to let the CIA onto his turf without knowing the whole story. Perhaps, he thought, there was a way to uncover it. "Very well. I have no objections. Who is this man they want to use?"

"An Arab, a low-level stringer," said Haron. "He's outlived his usefulness."

Khartoum

THE MAN WHOSE FATE HAD JUST BEEN SEALED BY HAYEM SHERABI finished his cup of tea at the street-side kiosk, then walked across the street to the telephone exchange building. Inside, flies buzzed on the windows and a squeaking ceiling fan churned the hot air.

"Box twelve," he told the counter attendant.

The attendant checked the box and came back with a slip of paper. On it was written, "Klaus. Urgent."

Hossein Asseal tucked the message into his pocket and smiled. Once again his talents were in demand. Generous customers, too. Things were looking up.

Holystone Office, Chesapeake Bay

IN MANY WAYS OAKEN WAS A CHILD AT HEART, A FACT HIS WIFE could and often did confirm. He was insatiably curious, tenacious, and driven to find the what and why behind everything.

In this case, he was grappling with several whats and whys at once.

If in fact Syria had the bomb, what were their plans for

it? Despite what Bashar Assad's detractors might say, like his father, the Syrian president was a careful man with a keen strategic mind. Certainly their plans for the bomb went beyond simply having a trump card. Having nuclear capability often caused more trouble than it was worth. Did that figure into their plans?

In the end it always came down to motivation, Oaken knew. It was all about understanding what a nation or group or even a person wanted. And that was the problem. Trying to read someone's mind broke one of the cardinal rules of the intell business. Talk first about what an enemy *can* do; the answer to that question will invariably lead you to what an enemy *may* do.

Walter Oaken wasn't a big fan of cardinal rules, however, so he returned to his original question: What, aside from the obvious, did Syria hope to gain from all this?

50

Camp Perry

TANNER'S DAYS BECAME A BLUR OF LECTURES AND MOCK-UPS. AS Stan put it, "Learning something is one thing. Doing it on the ground over and over until it comes naturally is another."

A series of planned exercises tested his cover story, language skills, and surveillance techniques, while others were impromptu affairs, one of them a late-night "kidnapping" that ended with a frighteningly real interrogation that took Tanner straight back to that Beirut basement. As the memories came flooding in, he found himself fighting to keep a grip on his emotions.

The afternoon of the last day, Stan pronounced Tanner "ready as you're gonna get," toasted him with a cup of coffee, then gave him an overview of what he could expect once he was in-country.

The previous few days had seen increased factional fighting in Beirut, Stan reported. Several artillery duels and dozens of skirmishes had erupted along the city's Green Line, which had officially been abolished three years before but still unofficially separated Muslim West Beirut from Christian East Beirut. Mortar attacks had been reported in several districts and the Beirut Airport, though still operating, had curtailed its flights by 20 percent, a sure sign all was not well.

In the Bekka Valley, Syrian troops appeared to be gearing up for the upcoming rotation, which was expected within ten days, depending on when the relieving force wrapped up its exercises in the desert.

"And we ain't helping much," Stan said. "The two battle

groups in the area are making everyone nervous, including Iraq, who's getting antsy about Iran playing so close to the border. But I suspect that's why Iran's doing it."

It was relatively quiet along the southern Lebanon-Israeli border and the Golan Heights, Stan continued. Relatively quiet for the Mideast, that was. "Stick to the central sections of Beirut and don't wander along the Green Line, or you're likely to find yourself being shot at," Stan concluded.

Tanner nodded. He knew all this, but hearing it again was reassuring. He felt himself slipping back into the Beirut mind-set, where chaos was a way of life and on opposite sides of any given street you can see a posh café and a demolished building.

"My best advice is to be anonymous."

"That could be difficult," Tanner replied. "I'll be short on time."

"So I gathered. Do what you gotta do, but remember: Beirut can change overnight. You go to bed on a Monday, and Tuesday morning you're at war. I've lived and breathed Lebanon for twenty years, and I'll tell you this: Right now the average Beiruti citizen is stocking up on canned peaches and water."

AFTER LEAVING PERRY, BRIGGS DROVE TO INDIAN HEAD, WHERE A phone call from the guard shack brought Cahil to meet him. Bear pulled up in a Suburban and jumped out. He was dressed in black BDUs, and his face was streaked with camouflage paint.

"Welcome to Camp Not-on-the-Map," he said as Tanner climbed in.

"It hasn't changed much," Tanner replied with a smile. Indian Head felt like home. Located a few miles north of Quantico on the Potomac, Indian Head once specialized in NBC (nuclear, biological, chemical) training. Now the 200-acre backwater base was used by SEALs and Marine Force Recon to conduct exercise assaults on oil platforms and ships.

Cahil stopped beside a pier. Anchored a hundred yards

offshore was an old, rust-streaked freighter roughly the size of *Tsumago*. Tanner could see several black-clad figures crawling over her superstructure. The muffled booms of concussion grenades and the chatter of assault rifles drifted across the water. Down the pier stood a group of trainers armed with bullhorns and stopwatches.

Tanner asked, "How many on the team?"

"A full platoon . . . sixteen. We just heard *Tsumago* is still headed north. Plan is, we're going to take her near the Canary Islands."

"Two more days, then. Will it be enough time?"

"I think so. We're working it hard." Bear laughed. "Hell, I can see the layout in my sleep."

"What've you told Maggie?" Tanner asked.

"That I'd be out of town for a few days. She's figured it out, though."

And she won't say a word, Tanner thought. It was a silly superstition he and Bear shared, and one that had rubbed off on Cahil's wife. Don't talk about the worst and it won't happen.

Tanner had already begun what he'd come to call "the narrowing." Bit by bit, his mind was discarding excess baggage and focusing on the essentials: Get in, get the job done, get out. Grocery shopping, doing laundry, friends, family . . . he could feel them all slipping away. It was a hugely selfish process but a necessary one. It was even harder for Bear and his family, Tanner knew.

A motor whaleboat pulled alongside the pier and a figure hopped out.

"Sconi Bob," Tanner said.

"The one and only," said Cahil.

Jurens jogged up to the Suburban. Tanner rolled down the window and stuck out his hand. Jurens shook it. "Briggs, how're things?"

"Good, Sconi, how about you?" Jurens was a rail-thin black man with a shaved head, a goatee, and an easy smile.

"Damned fine. Aside from having to put up with ol' Mama Bear here."

"He tells me you've got a good team."

"The best. We're ready. Two more days is just icing on the cake."

"Anyone I know?"

"Probably everyone. Slud's here, Johnson, Smitty, Wilts . . ."

Tanner nodded. He'd worked with all of them; good men. The Navy spec war community was a close-knit family, and he often missed it.

"Listen, Briggs, good to see ya. Coming, Bear?"

"In a minute."

They watched Jurens hop back into the whaleboat and head back toward the freighter. After a long silence, Cahil asked, "When do you go?"

"Tonight."

Cahil stared at the windshield. "CNN says things are heating up over there."

"So I heard."

"Listen, bud, just make sure you watch yourself. . . ."

Tanner smiled. "I will, Bear. You too. Come on, drive me back."

TANNER'S NEXT STOP WAS HIS PARENTS' HOME. PART OF HIM knew he was making the rounds, saying his good-byes, but he tried to convince himself otherwise.

Over a dinner of meat loaf and mashed potatoes, he told them he'd be gone for a while. No, nothing to worry about, just business. Yes, he'd call if he got a chance. Henry simply nodded; his mother excused herself and wandered into the kitchen.

Briggs wanted to ask his father about Azhar, but he didn't dare. Henry would make the connection, and he loved Abu as much as Briggs did. If the worst came to pass, how could Tanner ever explain what he'd done?

Finally, he said good-bye, shook his father's hand, hugged his mother, accepted a plate of leftovers, and left.

* * *

WAITING FOR HIM IN THE OPERATIONS CENTER WERE MASON, Coates, Dutcher, and Art Stucky. Coates handed Tanner his passport, wallet, and duffel bag containing clothes and toiletries, all of Canadian manufacture.

"You're backstopped as a freelance writer working on a piece for a Montreal-based travel agency," said Coates. "You already know the cover particulars and fallback stories. If you're pressed, you've got two to work with."

Tanner smiled to himself. *Pressed* was spook-speak for *interrogated*. A fallback story is designed to convince captors they have extracted the truth from their prisoner, when in fact they've simply uncovered yet another layer of the lie.

Coates continued. "You'll have two cell phones, one primary and one backup. They're similar to the ones you had in Japan. Same daily changing crypto, same rotating frequency. If you're compromised, press star zero one three; the internal software will be scrambled." Next, Coates showed Tanner how to connect the phone to a modified Palm Pilot. "You've got a dedicated MilStar satellite for the next ten days and priority access to GPS."

The Palm Pilot would perform two functions: One, it would allow Tanner to encode reports and send them via burst transmission to the MilStar, which would bounce them down to Stucky in Tel Aviv for routing to Langley; and two, it would supply tracking information from the Global Positioning System.

"Questions?" asked Coates.

"None," said Tanner.

Coates and Mason shook his hand and left. Dutcher took him aside and laid a hand on his shoulder. "Travel safe. I'll see you when you get back. Dinner's on me."

"Deal."

Dutcher nodded at Stucky, then left.

When the door shut and they were alone, Stucky said, "Small world, huh?"

"How so?"

"You working for me. Ironic."

Tanner gave him a hard stare. "Let's get something straight, Art: You don't like me; I don't like you. I can live with that. But if you can't do your job, say so now."

"I can do my goddamned job. I don't need you telling me—"

"Good. And I'll do mine, and we'll get the job done."

Stucky chuckled; his teeth were nicotine-yellow. "Suit yourself. Come on, I'll show you the comms."

AN HOUR LATER, THE CENTER WAS EMPTY EXCEPT FOR MASON, Coates, Dutcher, and a lone technician. "When does Stucky land?" Dutcher asked Coates.

"Four hours before Tanner. *Shin Bet* will meet him at Ben-Gurion. The fly arrived this morning, their time."

Dutcher looked at Mason and found himself wondering if the DCI knew about Stucky. As much as Dutcher liked Mason, he knew the DCI was grimly practical. If Stucky was the right man for the job, his past might not matter—especially given the stakes.

The phone rang. Coates snapped it up, listened for a moment, then hung up. He turned to the group. "Tanner's airborne."

51

Tel Aviv, Israel

As Tanner's plane was taking off from Heathrow, Stucky was leaving Ben-Gurion Airport in Avi Haron's car. The windows were rolled down, and a breeze blew through the interior. In the distance Stucky could see the blue expanse of the Mediterranean Sea.

"How was your flight?" Haron asked him.

"Fine." Stucky had taken an immediate dislike to Haron; he was too cheerful by half. "Why's it so damned hot?"

"It is what we call *hamseen* . . . a warm, dry wind. It is Arabic for—"

"So where do we find this guy?"

"He is waiting for us in a café just outside the West Bank."

"Waiting?"

Haron smiled. "Yes, Mr. Stucky. You see, we've done this before."

The café, which lay within shouting distance of a West Bank checkpoint, was built of rough ochre stone and cedar supports. On the front terrace, rows of wooden benches were filled with customers.

Haron's car and two Israeli Army jeeps screeched to a stop in front of the café, and a dozen soldiers leapt out. The patrons, all Arabs, hardly took notice, most continuing to drink their coffee and smoke from their *hookahs*.

"Stay here," Haron said to Stucky.

Haron got out and marched onto the terrace. He went from table to table, examining faces and asking questions until he came to Hossein Asseal, who was sitting alone. Haron asked for his identification. Asseal shook his head.

"Take him," Haron ordered.

Asseal was handcuffed, dragged to one of the jeeps, and thrown in the backseat. Haron got into the car and they pulled away. "See?" he told Stucky with a smile. "Simple."

THEY WATCHED ASSEAL THROUGH A ONE-WAY MIRROR. SEATED across from him were a pair of interrogators, one Mossad, the other *Shin Bet*. All three were smiling and joking. The room was thick with cigarette smoke.

"How long do we hold him?" asked Haron.

"Four more hours should do."

Haron nodded. "We'll be done with his things within the hour. After that, it's just a matter of satisfying appearances. Believe me, thirty minutes after we took him, half the West Bank knew." Haron grinned. "Mr. Asseal is well-known, you see. He thinks of himself as quite the businessman."

"Yeah, well, business is about to turn sour."

Haron excused himself and stepped into the cell. He dismissed the interrogators. Once alone, he shook Asseal's hand. "My old friend, how are you?"

"Better since your message, *effendi*. You said it was urgent, so here I am."

Haron slid an eight-by-ten photograph across the table. "Do you remember this?"

"Of course. Khartoum. A fine day. It was helpful to you?"

"Very. You see the man in the middle, the Arab with the mustache? His name is Mustafa al-Baz. We believe he's in Beirut. We want you to gather more information on his activities. Can you do it?"

Asseal frowned. "Of course, but Beirut it such a dangerous place. . . ."

"Five thousand. Half now, half on delivery."

"U.S. dollars?"

Haron nodded. "And a ten percent bonus if you can get the information within five days."

"Five days? That is not much time. Forty percent."

They haggled over the bonus until Haron agreed to twenty percent. "An extra thousand upon delivery."

Asseal smiled. "Done."

WITH HARON'S CAR IN THE LEAD, THE CONVOY RETURNED TO BEN-Gurion Airport via a circuitous route that took them through several Arab neighborhoods. Asseal, already mentally spending the $2,500 in his wallet, did not notice.

Others did, however.

At the terminal he was lifted bodily from the jeep, his handcuffs were removed, and his suitcase was dropped on the pavement. With a soldier on each arm, he was marched to the El Al ticket counter. Travelers in nearby lines stared momentarily, then turned away: Just another unwelcome Arab.

The soldiers released Asseal and shoved his briefcase into his chest.

"Good luck," Haron whispered to him, gave a wink, and walked away.

Falls Church, Virginia

THIS WAS TO BE THEIR SECOND AND FINAL CALL TO ABU AZHAR.

Though he wouldn't call it respect, Latham had developed a certain regard for Fayyad. Since his capture the Jordanian hadn't once tried to defend the things he'd done; he was resigned, Latham thought. Similarly, he hadn't requested anything in return for his cooperation, save one. He wanted to see Judith. Latham agreed to pass along the request but made no guarantees. This, too, Fayyad accepted without comment.

Once the recorders were running, Latham had the technician dial the Nicosia front number. The procedure was the same as last time. An hour after Fayyad's initial message, they received a call and another booth number, which they quickly cross-referenced and routed to the safe house switchboard.

Abu Azhar picked up on Fayyad's third ring.

"You recall the man from Angola we spoke of?" Fayyad said.

"Yes."

"His name is Hossein Asseal. He has worked for both American and Israeli firms. The former has asked him for a referral on one of our employees."

"He is coming here?"

"That is what we've been told."

"When?" asked Azhar.

"He's either already left Tel Aviv or will be very soon. He should be arriving evening or early morning, your time."

Beirut

As Hossein Asseal was leaving Tel Aviv, Tanner was just touching down at Beirut International Airport. Once the jet taxied to a stop, he sat staring out the window until most of the passengers collected their carry-ons, then stood up and headed toward the exit. He got a perfunctory "Enjoy Beirut, sir," from the flight attendant and started down the stairs.

Immediately the odor washed over him: the unmistakable scent of Beirut. Someone had once described it as a mixture of "cooking spices, gunpowder, dashed hopes, and barely controlled terror." It fit. It was the *tawattur*—the tension— that epitomized Lebanon.

He shouldered his duffel and joined the queue to Customs.

The terminal was a cultural smorgasbord. Shiites stood beside Christians, who bantered with Druze, who laughed with Armenian Jews. On a dark street they might be enemies; here they were neighbors. Ahead, a young Lebanese woman in denim shorts and a pink T-shirt emblazoned with Hot Stuff stood behind a Sunni muslim woman dressed in a black *aba* and veil. Amid the cacophony of voices, Tanner could hear snippets of French, Arabic, and English. *A different world.*

It took an hour to reach the desk and thirty seconds to be cleared. For whatever reason, most Lebanese love journalists, and they hold a special affinity for the Canadian variety, who they believe to be nonimperialist and therefore neutral.

Tanner bought half a dozen newspapers from the gift shop, two of them large-circulation journals, *al-Liwa* and *Monday Morning*, the other four propaganda sheets for several of Beirut's dominant factions. These, he hoped, would give him a feel for the climate of the city.

The taxi stand was bustling, so he found a bench and sat down. Several vendors and cabbies approached him with their pitch, but he declined.

Before long, a battered yellow taxi with a *Playboy* air freshener dangling from the rearview mirror screeched to the curb. A rotund Arab in a starched white *dish-dash* hopped onto the sidewalk, bartered unsuccessfully with several customers, then stopped before Tanner.

"Taxi, sir? Very clean, fair price."

Tanner shrugged. "Why not?"

Within minutes they were speeding north into Beirut proper. The road was littered with abandoned cars and the occasional armored personnel carrier. In a nearby field, children scampered over a charred T-64 tank; a hundred yards away sat a refugee camp, little more than a cluster of tents and shanties bordered by a sewage canal in which more children splashed and played.

Just north of the sports stadium, the driver pointed over a rubble-strewn berm. "Sabra. Chatila." Briggs knew the words well.

In September of 1970, Phalangist agents tipped off the Israelis that the Sabra and Chatila refugee camps were in fact PLO staging areas for *Fatah* guerillas. The Israeli army surrounded the area but refused to enter, instead allowing the Phalange Militia to round up the guerillas. What followed was a massacre that took the lives of almost 900 Palestinian civilians, many of them women and children. Soon afterward, Sabra and Chatila became a rallying cry for anti-Zionist terrorist groups.

As the taxi turned onto the Corniche Mazra, the driver said, "I was so happy to receive your call, Briggs. It is splendid to once again see you."

Tanner reached forward and squeezed Safir Nourani's shoulder. "And you, my friend. How have you been?"

"Very well."

"Your family?"

"Happy and safe."

"The city?"

"Ahhh. *Himyit.*" Roughly translated, it meant "things are getting warm." Given Safir's penchant for understatement, it meant the city was very dangerous. As proof, Safir pointed to a pair of bullet holes in his windshield. "Just yesterday."

"You can give me a rundown later," said Tanner. "First, how about one of your famous whirlwind tours?"

"Muslim side or Christian side?"

"Muslim."

"*Malesh!* Hold on!"

Without so much as a turn signal or a beep of the horn, Safir swung his taxi around a pair of cars, then screeched onto Boulevard Verdun, heading north toward the old lighthouse and the Corniche.

"I see you haven't lost your touch," Tanner said, clutching the door handle.

"Thank you, *effendi!*"

Safir Nourani was a self-proclaimed "closet Druze," living and working in the city, while still retaining ties to Druze enclaves in the Chouf Mountains. Druze were a secretive and close-knit offshoot sect of Islam, with a reputation of being fierce fighters when crossed.

Tanner and Safir (who'd been recommended to Tanner by his old mentor Ned Billings) had been friends for eight years, having met when Briggs and his team had slipped into northern Lebanon to gather intelligence on *Pasdaran* activity in Baalbek. Safir had served not only as their guide but also as their eyes and ears. If there was news worth knowing, Safir had it.

For the next hour, he took Tanner through the city while

giving a running monologue of what had changed and what
had not: Here was a supermarket gutted by a mortar attack;
there a French cultural minister was kidnapped last month;
three car bombs on this street last week; there a sniper
killed four people two days ago. Safir's account was a laundry list of terror, events most people only read about but
Beirutis lived every day.

They passed through a dozen *hajez,* or checkpoints, each
manned by teenagers carrying AK-47s, the weapon of
choice for the Beiruti *musallahheen.* So far, Tanner had
seen neither police nor soldiers. If tradition held, the authorities were holed up in their barracks, waiting for the
problems to work themselves out.

At each *hajez,* they were cleared through as Safir produced the correct password: sometimes a shouted slogan,
sometimes a bit of torn paper taken from that particular
group's propaganda sheet, and sometimes a smile and
"Keef al haal!"

At a checkpoint near the Museum Crossing, a gunman
demanded money for safe passage and reached into Tanner's jacket. Without thinking, Briggs grabbed the hand. A
dozen AKs jutted through the car's windows. After two
minutes of debate, Safir appeased the leader with a warm
Coca-Cola from the glove compartment, then drove away.

"Please excuse, *effendi,* but that was unwise of you."

"I know. Sorry. I'm still trying to acclimate."

"I understand." Safir swerved to miss a crater; the Playboy air freshener twirled. "So: Can I assume you will need
my services while you are here?"

"If you're available."

"For you, of course."

"As for—"

"No, no. Money is not discussed between friends. You
will pay me what you think is fair. We will not discuss it
again."

They followed the Corniche to American University,
then on to Hamra, Beirut's commercial center. Here there
were boutiques, shoe shops, markets: everything a western

business district had save the rubble-strewn streets and bullet-ridden walls.

"Seen enough?" asked Safir.

"Yes. I'm at the Commodore. Is it still the same?"

"The Commodore never changes, *effendi*. It is bomb-proof, that place."

He dropped Tanner at the doors and promised to return at eight.

Milling inside the lobby were a dozen or so journalists, all wearing either the thousand yard stare or the cheerful such-is-life visage that Beirut eventually foists on its visitors. A pair of saloon-style doors led to the bar, and through them Tanner could hear laughing. The birthplace for many an alcoholic, the Commodore's bar saw brisk business.

The clerk rang for the bellman, then told Tanner he must check in with the local media liaison, in this case a chain-smoking PLO man Briggs found in a small back office. Next week, Tanner knew, the liaison might be an Amal soldier or a PFLP thug. It all depended on who had the muscle.

"Passport," the PLO man said. Tanner handed it over. The man studied it for a long minute, then squinted at Tanner. "American?"

"Canadian."

"You have media pass?"

"No," Tanner said. "I was hoping you could help me with that."

"How long?"

"Five days, maybe a week."

"One week, fifty dollars. American."

Tanner counted out the money and laid a twenty on top of it. "For your help." In the Mideast it was called *bak-sheesh*—socially acceptable bribery.

Now the man was all smiles. "You need help again, you see me. Ragheb."

TANNER FOUND HIS ROOM SURPRISINGLY CLEAN, WITH A VIEW OF the Corniche from the balcony. It was a perfect Mediterranean afternoon, warm with a slight breeze blowing off the ocean.

He scanned the shoreline until he found Pigeon Rocks, then traced backward, looking for the apartment building in which he and his parents had lived. After five minutes of searching, he realized it was gone, probably the victim of a bombing or a fire.

He suddenly felt very alone.

AFTER SHOWERING AND SETTING HIS WATCH ALARM FOR SEVEN P.M., Briggs connected the cell phone to the Palm Pilot, sent an encoded message to Stucky saying he was on the ground, then switched channels to the GPS system.

After a few seconds, a map of Beirut appeared on the screen. Displayed were the six key landmarks he'd asked the CIA tech people to program into the Palm Pilot: American University, the National Museum, the airport, Tal Zaatar, the old Soviet embassy, and the junction of Tripoli Road and the Beirut River. Using these, he could navigate most of the city.

He hit the XMIT key. A red X—his current position—appeared south of American University. It was right where it should be.

"Time to see if the Israelis came through," he murmured.

He punched the RCV key. A few seconds passed, then a red square appeared near the Beirut Airport.

The fly had arrived.

52

Indian Head, Maryland

THREE HOURS BEFORE THEY WERE TO BOARD THE C-130 THAT would take them to their launching point, Sconi Bob Jurens gathered his team in the briefing room. Crowded around a scale model of the ship, he gave them the news. "We've been given the green light, gentlemen."

There were smiles and nods around the table.

"About damned time," said Ken "Slud" Sludowski, and got laughs.

"Also, it looks like we're dealing with no more than thirty bad guys."

"Two-to-one odds," said Smitty. "Hardly seems fair for them."

Jurens smiled. "We ain't about being fair. This is a straight run and gun. Anybody you see that ain't one of us gets a bullet.

"Now the bad news: Last night a P-3 did some over-flights of the target. Seems they picked up some interesting stuff. Our target isn't as toothless as we thought.

"The air- and surface-search radars we know about, but the Orion spotted a pair of suspicious-looking arrays on her superstructure. One's probably an ESM antenna . . . which means they may be able to pick up radar and radio signals. The other array could be FCR."

There were grumbles around the table. Fire control radar meant offensive weapons, which, given their plan, could put half the team in jeopardy even before it landed.

"Where'd they see these arrays?" asked Cahil.

"Aft of the bridge, port and starboard sides."

"They weren't there when she was in dock. Must be recent additions. God knows the wave guide was powerful enough for it."

"Did they have anything like a CIC?" asked Sludowski, meaning a combat information center. "Anyplace they could run FC consoles from?"

"Not that we saw. Everything looked centralized on the bridge.

"Okay, listen," said Jurens. "None of this changes anything. We're going. We've got eighteen hours to fine-tune the plan, so let's get busy."

Morocco

To the delight of Bernice Weinman, who Saul called "the greatest living Hebrew fan of Humphrey Bogart," *Valverde* had just dropped anchor in Casablanca's harbor. That the movie of the same name had actually been filmed in Hollywood did nothing to dampen Bernice's excitement.

On the bridge, the watch hardly noticed their latest port of call. Most had seen the city before, and those who hadn't were junior officers and therefore had duty that night. "Sir, if you've got a moment?" the radioman called to the officer of the watch.

The OW stepped into the radio room. "Yes?"

"Take a listen to this." The radioman clicked on the speaker, and the room filled with static and the faint murmur of voices.

"What *is* that?"

"I don't know, sir. It happened a few minutes ago and lasted about a minute. Sounds like voices, followed by a recurring pulse tone."

"Source?"

"That's the thing. It's not on any of our carrier frequencies. At first I thought we'd picked up some feedback from one of our channels, but I checked: It's internal."

"What?"

"The source is coming from *inside* the ship."

The OW thought for a moment. "I'm sure it's nothing.

Run a diagnostic, and I'll have a technician check the antenna."

Beirut

FOR NEARLY TWO MILLENNIA, THE COUNTRY KNOWN TODAY AS Lebanon has been at war with either itself or outside crusaders. As Phonecia, it was conquered by Egypt, who coveted its abundant supply of cedar trees and their resin, which the pharaohs used for the mummification process. Since then, Lebanon has been ruled by a succession of invaders: Mamluks, Turks, Assyrians, European crusaders, and Romans. Some conquered and left. Others conquered, ruled, and were themselves conquered. The faces might have changed, but the essence of Lebanon's bloody history had not. Whoever the players and whatever the era, Lebanon had always been a playground for superpowers.

Following World War I, as the Allies began dissecting the Mideast into digestible chunks, the French gave its Maronite Christian friends control of then "greater Lebanon." Prior to that, Christians and Muslims had been living in relative peace.

In 1932, all that changed. A census of the country showed Christians—especially Maronite Christians—to be in the majority, so the government was constituted accordingly, with Christians holding six parliamentary seats for every Muslim's five. The same ratio applied for every key post in the country.

Two decades later, following the influx of Palestinian refugees and the rapid emigration of rich Lebanese Christians to America and Europe, the balance of power between the two religions had shifted dramatically. By the early 1950s, Muslims had become the majority, and the Christians knew it. Bolstered by superpower sponsors and fearing for their safety from an enemy who had sworn to expel them, Christian governments refused to relinquish their tenuous hold on the country.

And so, through the years Lebanon had not only fought internally for self-control but had fought against the inter-

ventions of Syria, Iran, Israel, and the United States, as each
sought to impose its own solution to the turmoil. Syria coveted Lebanon as the linchpin to its dream of a "Greater
Syria"; Iran wanted to use Lebanon as a conduit for its
export of terrorism; Israel was wary of Lebanon's role as
a breeding ground for anti-Zionist forces; and the United
States, committed to Israel's security, knew Lebanon was
the powder keg just waiting to ignite the Mideast into war.

It was into this volatile morass that Abu Azhar and General Issam al-Khatib introduced a platoon of thirty Iranian
Pasdaran soldiers, each superbly trained and fully prepared
to lay down his life to complete his mission.

As Beirut fell into darkness, four very important men in
four separate parts of the city were finishing the day's business and preparing to leave for their homes. Consistent with
their status, each man was surrounded by an entourage of
bodyguards. Traffic was blocked off and pedestrians re-
strained; nearby windows and doorways were scanned for
possible threats. Satisfied all was clear, the bodyguards
walked their charges to their cars and drove off.

Unseen by even the neighborhood's residents, four separate *Pasdaran* teams lay hidden on nearby rooftops and in
bombed-out cellars. Once darkness had fallen and the
streets were quiet, each team slipped away with their
sketched maps, notes, and photos.

WHAT TANNER HAD ALREADY DECIDED—AND TOLD NO ONE—WAS
he had no intention of sacrificing their fly unless it was
unavoidable. He understood the pragmatism behind Mason's plan but also knew before this was over there would
be plenty of death to go around. Hossein Asseal may have
been double-dealing his clients, but the man did not deserve
to die for it.

The success of Tanner's gambit depended on four factors: one, whether the disinformation Fayyad fed Azhar
would goad him into action; two, whether the GPS would
in fact track Asseal; three, that Azhar would kidnap Asseal
instead of simply gunning him down on the street; and four,

how quickly Tanner could react. When and if Asseal was taken, Briggs had to reach the location before Azhar moved on. If he failed to do so, all was lost.

Of the four factors, the tracking system was the least fallible.

The GPS, or Global Positioning System, is a constellation of twenty-four satellites, each equipped with an atomic clock able to fix the satellite's position by measuring the time it takes signals to travel between fellow satellites and ground stations. The existence and accuracy of GPS—which is measured in mere feet—is common knowledge. Unknown to the general public, however, is the extreme sensitivity of the GPS's passive receivers.

Every chemical element on the periodic table, whether helium or cobalt or flourine, decays at a specific rate. This subatomic crumbling produces a very faint but unique radiation signature. Of all the elements, iridium produces the most readily detectible signature.

While Asseal was being held by *Shin Bet*, dozens of thumbnail-sized iridium microchips were secreted in his clothes and belongings. In all, twenty-six chips were placed in the heels of his shoes, in the lining of his belts, in the collars of his shirts, and in the waistband of his silk boxer shorts.

When he left *Shin Bet* headquarters, Asseal was a walking beacon.

This technology had its limits, however. Because of the faintness of the signature, the satellite's arrays had to be concentrated on a ten-square-mile area in and around Beirut. Any wider an area and the signal would become obscured in a sea of background radiation. Similarly, if Asseal was taken from the city, the signal would be lost. Finally, because subatomic decay is an irreversible process, Tanner had just ninety-six hours before the iridium would become too weak to detect. Past that, the fly would become just another body in a city of 1.5 million bodies.

* * *

PROMPTLY AT EIGHT, NOURANI KNOCKED ON TANNER'S DOOR. THEY
embraced, and Safir stepped back. "You look well, my
friend," he said. "After your last experience in our city, I
feared you would not return."

"Wild horses couldn't keep me away. Come on, let's sit
on the balcony."

Once they were settled, Safir handed Tanner a cigar box.
Inside was a Glock nine-millimeter pistol and five spare
magazines. Tanner laid the box aside and handed Safir a
photograph. "In the next few days, someone is going to
kidnap this man. I want to know who they are and where
they take him."

Safir smiled evilly. "Bait, eh? Brave man."

"He doesn't know."

"Poor man."

"He's staying at the Riviera. As I understand it, he likes
to gamble."

"Then that's the place for him," Safir said. "Give me an
hour."

Washington, D.C.

DICK MASON WAS ENJOYING A LUNCHEON MEETING WITH THE
president, James Talbot, and the chairman of the JCS, General Cathermeier. Halfway through his corn chowder, the
president said, "Dick, what have you brought for us?"

Mason handed the photos around the table. "These are
about four hours old," he said. "It appears the Syrians are
wrapping up their exercise."

"How do we know?" asked the president.

"We spotted the group's support units heading back
north. They wouldn't do that if they were staying much
longer."

"Makes sense," said General Cathermeier. "No fuel, no
food, no fight."

The president stared at the photo. "Damn, that's a lot of
firepower. How much did they put into this thing?"

"Troops alone, almost sixteen thousand."

"That's unprecedented," said Cathermeier. "What about the Bekka?"

"There's where we could use some help. We show everything still dug in, but there is some activity. We're assuming it's the changeover, but we could use some eyeballs to make sure."

"No problem. I'll ask the *Indy* to send a recon flight."

The president asked Mason, "Where are we with DORSAL?"

"The team is en route to Rota. They hit the ship in sixteen hours. Tanner is on the ground. Comms are up, and the GPS is tracking. Now it's just a matter of time."

"That's what worries me," said the president, setting aside his napkin. "I got a call from the Israeli prime minister this morning. He wants to know what we are doing in Lebanon. The urgency of our request wasn't lost on them. At this point I'm inclined to put him off, but if our boarding of *Tsumago* fails, I'll have no choice but to tell him what they're facing."

There was an uncomfortable silence around the table. Mason understood the president's decision, but he also knew what the Israeli response would be. Rather than let Syria have the bomb, Israel would either attempt their own boarding of *Tsumago* or sink her. Bias aside, Mason knew if a SEAL team couldn't get the job done, the chances of anyone else succeeding were slim. That left the second option—sinking—which couldn't be done quickly enough to prevent the crew from detonating the bomb.

"Mr. President," said Talbot, "I recommend delaying as long as possible. Not only could we be looking at an ecological disaster, but the Arab nations in the region will come down on Israel with everything they have."

"I know that. And so does the prime minister. Truth is, they'd rather fight it out tank to tank than have a nuke hanging over their heads. I don't blame them." Talbot started to speak, and the president shook his head. "I've made my decision. If we don't stop *Tsumago*, I will inform the prime minister."

53

Beirut

AFTER SAFIR RETURNED FROM THE RIVERIA AND CONFIRMED HOS-
sein Asseal's arrival, Tanner spent the night sitting on the
balcony, staring out over the city and periodically checking
Asseal's position on the Palm Pilot.

By sunrise the red square still had not moved.

Where is Abu Azhar? he wondered. He still couldn't accept the idea of his "uncle" as a terrorist, a man prepared
to give Syria the power to kill hundreds of thousands of
people—or worse still, a man prepared to use that power
himself. The Abu he'd once known could not be that man,
but what might time and war and death do to an otherwise
gentle person? If history had shown anything, Tanner knew,
they can turn anyone into a killer.

NOURANI ARRIVED AT SEVEN. "I HIRED TWO BOYS TO KEEP AN EYE
on Asseal," he told Tanner. "Don't worry, they are trustworthy. Ahmed and Sadiq. Both from my home village."

"I'd feel better if I handled—"

"You would stand out, Briggs. They can move about
freely."

Tanner thought it over; it made sense. "What did they
find out?"

"Asseal and his woman—"

"Woman?"

"Of the evening," Safir said. "He hired her for the week.
I don't recognize her, but others have seen her from time

to time. Her name is Lena, though I doubt it is her real name."

"Could you reach her? Would she be open to some extra income?"

"Almost certainly. Why?"

"If I'm right, Asseal will do some sightseeing today. I want to know where he goes and what he does."

"I will look into it. Anyway, Asseal gambled until about three in the morning, then went to bed . . . alone. He is still asleep."

Asseal certainly was working hard at spending the Israelis' money, Tanner thought. Hopefully, today he would start earning some of it.

BY LATE AFTERNOON, BRIGGS WAS PACING THE ROOM, AWAITING word from Nourani.

Earlier, Safir had found the woman and, after a bit of haggling, a price was agreed upon, with the proviso that whoever Nourani represented would do nothing to curtail her client's generosity.

According to Ahmed and Sadiq, Asseal awoke just after noon, had a late lunch with his companion, then took a cab into the Hamra district for a shopping spree. At two, the taxi took them south into the slums of Southwest Beirut, at which point the boys broke off and returned to Nourani.

"They say things are bad between here and the airport. Something between Amal and the Maronites. *Al'ane.*"

Tanner knew the phrase; it meant "it is being hooked or tangled." In short, someone was fighting. The reason was unimportant. "Where is he now?"

"Napping. Energetic man, this Asseal. He left a wake-up call for eight, with dinner reservations at Amici for eight-thirty. I will speak to the woman before then."

Tel Aviv

IN HIS SUITE IN THE MORIAH PLAZA, STUCKY FINISHED DECODING Tanner's latest message. On the table beside him sat a cell phone, a Palm Pilot similar to Tanner's, and a briefcase transceiver through which he could access both the MilStar and the GPS.

"Okay, let's see what you have to say, Briggs ol' buddy."

TARGET LOCATED. GPS FUNCTIONING. NEGATIVE CONTACT ON TARGET. WAITING. UPDATE SAME TIME TOMORROW.

Stucky chuckled. "No luck, huh? Ain't that a bitch."

He set aside the message and began encoding his own to Langley.

Beirut

AS HIS SECOND DAY IN THE CITY CAME TO A CLOSE, TANNER GOT his first nibble.

Following his return to the Riviera, Asseal dismissed Lena and ordered her to return later for dinner and more gambling.

She met Safir in a café on Mazzra Street. After shopping, she said, Asseal had ordered the taxi driver to take them into the Zokak al-Blat, a heavily populated Muslim neighborhood that was seeing fierce fighting between the pro-Syrian *Saiqua* guerillas and the *Hezbollah*.

Asseal made four stops, each within enclaves contested by both groups. He talked with several of the local commanders and passed around a photograph. Lena did not overhear the conversations, but judging from Asseal's mood, he'd had little luck.

On the way back to the hotel they took Damascus Road to the Green Line, at which point Asseal grew agitated, claiming they were being followed by a gray Volvo. He ordered the driver to hurry to Hamra, which he did, dropping them in the heart of the district.

"Did she see the Volvo?" Tanner asked Safir.

"No, but Asseal was clearly frightened."

"He must have thought Hamra's traffic would shield him."

"He doesn't know Beirut, then. They would kill him in front of the Vatican embassy if they really wanted him."

"How about the groups he went to see? Was it just those two?"

"No, there were others, but she didn't recognize them."

Briggs checked his watch. "Okay, Hossein's nightlife should be starting soon. Hold the fort. I'm going to take a walk around."

H E STROLLED ALONG THE CORNICHE, STARED AT PIGEON ROCKS from Lighthouse Square for a while, and then, a little before eight, headed back up the Corniche and found a restaraunt across from the Riviera.

Night had fully fallen, and down the block he could see the glare of Hamra's neon lights. The volume of strollers surprised him; either they were very brave, or they had faith in Hamra's reputation as being an unofficial haven from whatever troubles the rest of the city was experiencing. Though kidnappings and murders were still commonplace in Hamra, it rarely saw serious fighting.

The restaurant Tanner chose was run by an Armenian family, a husband and wife and their two young daughters, who served as waitresses. The husband seated him in a corner booth near the window.

"And how are you, sir?" asked the husband.

"Very well, thanks."

Tanner ordered *sanbousek,* a pastry filled with meat, spices, and pine nuts, and a glass of *kefrayek.* As one of the daughters returned with his food, Tanner smiled and thanked her in Armenian, which drew a giggle and then whisperings with her sister behind the counter.

At 8:40, Hossein Asseal stepped through the hotel's revolving door with a woman on his arm. *The lovely Lena,* Tanner assumed. Her hair was bleach blond, her dress bright red and rhinestoned. They stepped into a waiting taxi, which made a U-turn on the Corniche and sped off.

Amici restaurant was only a few blocks to the south, so Tanner paid his bill, stepped outside, and started walking.

Suddenly, from around the corner came the squeal of tires, followed by the crunch of metal. He ran to the corner in time to see Asseal's taxi stopped in the intersection, blocked on each side by a car, one of them a gray Volvo.

A dozen men encircled the taxi. Waving AK-47s at the bystanders, they yanked open the doors. The driver was dragged out and thrown aside, then Lena, screaming and kicking. Three of the kidnappers crawled into the backseat. Arms and legs flailed; the taxi rocked from side to side. They dragged Asseal out, already bound and gagged, rushed him to the Volvo, threw him in the backseat, piled inside, and sped away.

TANNER STARED AT THE EMPTY STREET, HIS HEART POUNDING. What he'd just seen had happened a hundred times before to diplomats and journalists. Fifteen seconds and you're gone. Just like that.

Down the Corniche he heard the wail of sirens. Both the taxi driver and Lena were on their feet, looking shaken but uninjured. In a flurry of flashing blue lights, the police pulled up.

Tanner turned and began jogging for the Commodore.

"JUST NOW?" SAFIR ASKED. "THEY TOOK HIM?"

"Off the Corniche," Tanner said, connecting the Palm Pilot to his cell phone.

A few seconds passed before the Palm Pilot made contact with the GPS and downloaded the information. The red square flashed on the screen. Every ten seconds it blinked, then reappeared as Asseal's position changed. They were moving north, toward the coast. Tanner pulled out his map of the city, cross-referenced it with the Palm Pilot, then circled the port area.

"The Majidiya District," he said. "Do you know it?"

Safir nodded. "Oh, yes. It's divided by the Green Line.

Heavy fighting. That is a bad neighborhood, Briggs. If that's where they're taking him . . . Allah help him."

Tanner handed him a pad and a pencil. "Draw me a map."

54

USS *Mount Whitney*, Rota, Spain

CAHIL COULD FEEL THE TENSION AROUND THE BRIEFING TABLE, AND he suddenly found himself wondering about Tanner. *What a god-awful job,* he thought. Go into a city at war and kill a man you consider a second father. *He'll make it,* Bear told himself and refocused on the task at hand.

Witney's CIC was quiet and dark except for the occasional burst of radio traffic and the orange scope faces. In addition to Jurens, Cahil, and the rest of the team, they were joined by the ship's weatherman and her tactical action officer, or TAO.

Jurens said, "Okay, gentlemen, before we walk it through, a word from the rain dancer."

The weatherman stepped forward. "By early morning you should have partly cloudy skies, a quarter moon, light surface fog, and a sea state of three or so . . . choppy, but manageable."

"How about water temperature?" asked Cahil.

"Sixty-eight, give or take."

Bear thought, *Pretty cold if we're in the water more than a few hours.* But then, if that happened, something would have already gone terribly wrong.

"Intell?" Jurens asked.

"Given the target's possible ESM capabilities, they've called off the P-3, but as of an hour ago, satellite imagery showed her on track, same course and speed. We'll get updates up until your departure. As for transport, the Pave Low is fueled and ready to fly; *Ford*'s on station, shadowing the target at two hundred miles."

"Any activity aboard?"

"Limited movement above decks and no lookouts or patrols that we can see."

Sconi glanced at Cahil. That tended to confirm what they'd hoped: Having no idea they'd been compromised, *Tsumago*'s crew was not expecting an assault.

"Radio traffic?" asked Bear.

"Zero. Best guess is they're in EMCON," said the TAO, referring to emission control status. No radio and no radar—nothing for the opposition to home in on.

Jurens thanked the two officers, and they left. Once they were gone, he unrolled *Tsumago*'s blueprint. "I ain't gonna bore you boys with the transportation details, so we'll pick it—"

Wilts said, "Uh, one thing, Skipper—"

"No, Wilts, there will *not* be an in-flight movie. No cocktails, either."

There was general laughter.

"So," Jurens continued. "Two teams: Alpha and Sierra, eight men each. Alpha, boarding by helicopter, will be led by me. Sierra, boarding by sea, will be led by Cahil.

"Bear, timing is critical. Alpha needs to hit the deck within six minutes of your boarding. Nothing happens until you say so.

"Sierra will clear the first two decks. Make sure your take-downs are quick and quiet, and be damned sure the ladders are secure, because we'll be right on your heels.

"Alpha will fast-rope onto the afterdeck, then split into two elements. One, led by Cochran, will take the signal bridge and the pilothouse. Cochran, make sure you cut their comms and anything else that looks hinky.

"The other element, led by me, will head below decks, bypass Sierra, and take the engine room."

Jurens looked around the table. "Estimated duration for the op is nine minutes, start to finish. Remember, everybody aboard is a bad guy."

Everyone understood the order: Shoot first, don't bother asking questions later.

"Any questions?"

There were none. They'd lived this mission eighteen

hours a day for the past five days. Now all that remained
was Murphy's Law of Special Ops: Be ready for something
to go wrong, because it will. What makes a successful mission is not the absence of glitches but controlling them
when they pop up.

"One last thing," Jurrens said. "We all know what *Tsumago*'s carrying; we know what could happen if we don't
get the job done." He looked each man in the eye. "There
is no prize for second place on this one, gentlemen."

Canary Islands

EIGHT HUNDRED FIFTY MILES SOUTHWEST OF ROTA, *VALVERDE* WAS
clearing the headland of Puerto del Rosario. To port, the
island's lights twinkled in the darkness.

"Clearing the peninsula, Captain," said the helmsman.

"Very well," said Stein. "Navigator, course to Fuerte-
ventura?"

"Straight along the coast, sir. Zero-eight-five. At ten
knots, we'll be there before dawn."

"Good. Helm: zero-eight-five, speed ten."

Satisfied they were on course, Stein turned over the
bridge to the officer of the deck and headed to his cabin
for a late supper.

Tsumago

FORTY MILES SOUTH OF *VALVERDE*, *TSUMAGO* STEERED A NORTH-
easterly course along the coast of Western Sahara. On the
bridge, Mustafa al-Baz studied the chart under the glow of
a small lamp.

"We're ready, sir," called the radar operator. "System is
on standby, set for sector search only."

"Good. One sweep only. Any more, and we risk detec-
tion."

"Understood."

"Proceed."

The operator reached above the panel, energized the radar system, let four seconds pass, then shut it down. "Got it," he said. "Bearing three-five-zero."

Al-Baz marked the chart and then, using a pair of dividers and a compass, projected their position ahead three hours and made a second mark. He measured the distance between the two, then did a quick calculation.

Al-Baz nodded. *Perfect . . .* "Helm, come left to course zero-three-eight."

National Military Command Center, Pentagon

SITTING AROUND THE CONFERENCE TABLE IN THE CENTER OF THE amphitheater were Dutcher, Mason, Talbot, and General Cathermeier. At nearby consoles, technicians managed radio traffic and updated the room's wide-screen monitors, each of which was capable of displaying real-time satellite and live-feed imagery.

The door opened, and the president strode in. "Where's our target, General?"

"Passing the border between Western Sahara and Morocco," said Cathermeier.

"Give me a who's who."

"We'll be hearing six call signs, Mr. President. We're designated Coaldust. Cowboy is *Ford*, the frigate trailing behind the target. Boxcar and Trolley are the team's transports, a C-130, and a Pave Low helicopter. Once the teams make their jump-off, they'll split into Alpha and Sierra."

"Where are they now?"

"Alpha is waiting aboard *Ford*; Sierra's on the Tarmac at Madeira."

"The Madeira Islands? That's Portugal. How'd we get their cooperation?"

"We didn't," replied Leland Dutcher. "During a routine training flight, Trolley developed engine trouble and had to make an emergency landing. Once we give the word, she'll make a sudden recovery."

The president grinned. "Go on, General."

"We'll be getting target updates from a Keyhole every thirty minutes. Last one showed *Tsumago*'s projected course clear of traffic. All the pieces are in place, Mr. President. We're ready."

The president was silent for a few moments, then nodded. "Okay, General, give the go-ahead."

Valverde

AT TWO A.M. Stein's cabin phone buzzed. "Captain."

"First Officer, sir. We've just received a distress call from a Tunisian cargo ship . . . the *Alameira*."

"What's the problem, Danny?"

"Some of their crew is ill, sir. They're requesting medical assistance."

"What's our position?"

"Twenty-five miles from Fuertaventura. They're forty-two miles south of us."

Stein did the calculation. *Alameira* was several hours from the nearest port. Too long if the crewmen were gravely ill. "I'm coming up."

When he reached the bridge, he took the radio handset from Danny and pressed the transmit key. "This is Captain Stein of *Valverde*. Please explain your situation."

"We have five sick crewman aboard, Captain. We don't know what to do."

"What are the symptoms?"

"They are having seizures of some sort and trouble breathing."

"Understood, *Alameira*," said Stein. "Stand by."

Stein leaned over the chart, made several measurements, then thought for a moment. He keyed the handset. "*Alameira*, we will render assistance. What's your best speed?"

"Eighteen knots."

Danny whispered, "Damned fast for a freighter."

Stein nodded. "Very well, *Alameira*. Come left to three-five-zero, best speed. We are turning south to meet you."

"Thank you, *Valverde*. Please hurry."

Stein switched off and called, "Helm, come right to one-six-five, all ahead full."

* * *

AT FLANK SPEED, *VALVERDE* COULD MAKE TWENTY-TWO KNOTS.
Combined with *Alameira*'s eighteen, Stein estimated they
would meet in approximately an hour, which was why after
only thirty-five minutes he was surprised to hear the radar
operator call, "Got her, sir. Dead on the bow."

"What?" Stein snatched up his binoculars and peered
through the window. "Danny, I thought you said she was
forty miles away."

"She was, sir. At least I thought the radar—"

"Never mind, we must have misplotted her. She's here
now."

In the rush to render assistance, Stein had just made a
terrible mistake. There could be only two reasons for the
early rendezvous: Either *Alameira*'s original position had
been in error, or the freighter was capable of making almost
double her reported top speed. Since Stein knew this to be
impossible, he assumed the former.

"Messenger, go wake the doctor and tell him to expect
patients."

AFTER BRINGING *VALVERDE* TO WITHIN A HUNDRED YARDS OF
Alameira, Stein watched through binoculars as the
freighter's launch was lowered into the water and the five
sick crewmen were helped aboard. The launch cast off and
started across the water. Stein ordered the main deck lights
turned on.

"Danny, go down and make sure they get aboard safely."

"Yes, sir."

Five minutes later, *Alameira*'s ailing crewmen were being walked up the midship's ladder and into the superstructure. Danny returned to the bridge with one of the
freighter's crew.

"The captain of *Alameira*, sir."

The man was of medium height with black hair and a
handlebar mustache. His eyes were red-rimmed. They

shook hands. "I cannot express my gratitude, Captain Stein."

"My pleasure, sir. Not to worry. Our doctor is very good."

"Of that I am certain. We were lucky you were in the area."

"Join me in my cabin? We can have some coffee while we await the doctor's diagnosis."

"You are very kind."

Stein turned the bridge over to Danny, led the way to his cabin, and seated his guest. They chatted about the weather until the bulkhead phone rang.

"Ah . . . word from the doctor," Stein said, grabbing the handset. "Captain."

"First officer, sir. Uh, sir, we have a situation."

"What is it, Danny?"

Stein heard muffled voices in the background. "Uh . . . sir, they say your guest will explain everything."

"They?" said Stein. "Danny, who—"

The phone went dead.

Stein felt the first shiver of fear. He turned around and found himself staring at the barrel of a gun. He jumped to his feet.

"Sit down, Captain," said Mustafa al-Baz.

"What is this?"

"Sit down."

"I will not. I want to know—"

"*Sit down!*" al-Baz shouted. The gun remained steady.

Stein complied. They sat in silence for thirty seconds and then from below, Stein heard the clatter of automatic weapons, followed by screaming and shouting. Then silence.

"My God, what are you doing?" Stein said. "We tried to help you—"

"Captain, if you speak again without being spoken to, I will shoot you."

A few minutes passed, then the bulkhead phone rang. Al-Baz picked it up, listened, said something in Arabic, then hung up. "Captain, your ship is under our control. The engine room, radio room, and the bridge belong to us. As we speak, your passengers are being gathered together in the main dining room. Those officers and crew not on duty have been locked inside the signal bridge. Do you have any questions?"

"Have you hurt any of my passengers or crew?"

"Not so far."

"What do you want?"

"All in good time, Captain. First, to the bridge."

Al-Baz prodded Stein from the cabin and up the ladder to the pilothouse. Danny, the helmsman, and the navigator were being held at gunpoint by a trio of men in black wet suits.

Danny said, "Captain, what—"

"It's all right. Just do as they say."

"Wise advice, Captain," said al-Baz. "However, it has been my experience that people in your situation are not so easily convinced." Al-Baz turned. "You there. Danny, is it? You are the first officer?"

"Uh, yes, sir."

"Don't," Stein whispered. *"Please,* don't. He's just a boy."

Al-Baz offered Stein a cold smile. "We were all boys once, Captain."

Al-Baz raised his pistol and shot Danny in the forehead. Danny stumbled backward two steps, teetered for a moment, then crumpled the deck.

"You bastard! You rotten bastard! There was no reason for that."

"I have your attention, do I not?"

"Yes, damn it—"

"Then it was worthwhile." He handed Stein a slip of paper. "Read this over the ship-wide intercom."

Eyes fixed on Danny's lifeless body, Stein grabbed the intercom handset. His hand was shaking; he steadied it with his opposite hand. He keyed the microphone.

"Attention passengers and crew of *Valverde*. This is the captain. I have been instructed to tell you this ship is now under the control of the Arab Liberation Command. . . ."

55

Beirut

ARMED WITH SAFIR'S MAP, TANNER SLIPPED FROM THE HOTEL AND
began walking west. Aside from a few late-night strollers,
the foot traffic was light, so he made good time and soon
reached the Omari Mosque. Its minarets towered above the
surrounding ruin, pristine white in the darkness.

At Maarad Street, a quarter mile from the Green Line,
he ducked inside a bombed-out grocery store and hunkered
down to watch the street. Several cars and pickup trucks
filled with gunmen passed by, but none more than once.
He saw only one pedestrian, an old woman carrying a bag
of potatoes.

Was it in fact Azhar who had taken Asseal, or some
group with a grudge, he wondered. He hoped it was the
former, but there was another part of him—the voice of a
thirteen-year-old boy—who was praying for the latter.

After another ten minutes, he slipped back onto the street
and started east again.

As he neared the Green Line, he could hear the chatter
of automatic weapons and the *crump* of grenades. He
sprinted across Martyr's Square, found another alley, and
kept going, heading deeper into Christian East Beirut.

He stopped beside a burnt-out Renault and rechecked the
GPS: The red square was one block north of him on Tripoli
Road.

It took another twenty minutes of moving and checking
until he found the correct building, an abandoned factory
surrounded on three sides by vacant lots. On the fourth side
stood a boarded-up building overlooking the factory. He
found a back entrance and climbed six floors until he found

an open window. He squatted beside it and peeked out.

On the street below were two vehicles: a pickup truck and a gray Volvo.

THERE WAS A GLIMMER OF LIGHT IN A THIRD-FLOOR WINDOW. Flashlight or lantern. He watched for a few more minutes, saw no lookouts, then headed downstairs.

After a quick look up and down the street, he sprinted across, slipped into the alley, and circled to the rear of the building. A long line of fire escapes stretched into the darkness. Moving slowly, his feet crunching on broken glass, he began checking them.

The first four were either so rusted or in such bad repair that his touch set them shaking. The fifth one seemed sturdier. He stepped onto the bottom rung. The scaffolding vibrated but held. He took a deep breath and started upward.

At the second floor he found some rotted boards covering the window, so he carefully pried them free, then slipped inside. He crouched down, listening and waiting for his eyes to adjust. Through the ceiling he could hear the sound of muffled voices. Silence. Shuffling footsteps. He found a stairwell and started up.

The third floor was divided by a central hallway with rooms on either side. The floor was littered with chunks of plaster, and in the dust Briggs could see a trail of footprints leading to the last room on the right.

He moved forward. The muffled voices grew louder. Three or four men, he guessed, all speaking in Arabic. He heard a sharp *slap*—flesh striking flesh—then a moan. He slipped into the adjoining room and pressed his ear to the wall.

The conversation was too rapid to follow, but he managed to catch a few words: Warehouse . . . move . . . And then another word that set his heart pounding: "Abu." "*Inform Abu. . . .*"

Did they mean Azhar? In addition to being a popular Arabic name, Abu is a common alias among terrorists, who often convert the literal translation of *father* to mean *leader*.

A door banged open. There was a brief scuffle, followed by footsteps. He pressed himself to the wall. One by one, four shadows walked past the doorway. The last two were dragging a man between them. Tanner caught a glimpse of the face: Hossein Asseal. His face was bloody and bruised. The footsteps pounded down the stairs and faded.

A minute later, a pair of engines roared to life and tires squealed.

Tanner pulled out the Palm Pilot and called for an update.

The red square was moving northwest toward the docks.

FOLLOWING CUES FROM THE PILOT, HE FOUND HIMSELF AT THE city's old wharf. According to Safir, these had long ago been abandoned in favor of the newer docks, but like so much in Beirut, they would likely remain until they crumbled into the harbor. Through binoculars he spotted the Volvo parked beside a corner warehouse.

He found a partially collapsed bait shack across the road, crawled into the basement, made himself comfortable beside the window, and called Nourani.

"I was becoming worried," Safir said. "Where are you?"

Tanner told him. "Are your boys willing to do some watching?"

"Most certainly. I'll send one immediately."

Briggs hung up and refocused the binoculars on the warehouse.

TWENTY MINUTES LATER, AHMED ARRIVED. "GOOD MORNING, effendi," he said.

"Morning. You're fast."

Ahmed beamed. "I know many shortcuts."

"I'll bet you do. See that warehouse . . . the one on the corner? After the car leaves, I'm going inside to look around. I should be back in an hour. If I don't, or something bad happens, leave and go find Safir."

"Yes, *effendi.*"

Tanner checked the sky: almost two hours until dawn.

AN **HOUR LATER, THE DOOR OF THE WAREHOUSE OPENED, AND FOUR** men came out. Asseal wasn't among them. They piled into the Volvo, pulled onto Tripoli Road, and drove off.

He patted Ahmed's shoulder and took off.

He sprinted across the road, into the ditch, crawled up the other side, and dashed across to the docks. He mounted the walkway beside the warehouse and followed it to the seaward wall, where he found a back door. He tested the knob: locked. A few feet away he found a small, tarnished window.

He wrapped the tip of his knife in his kaffiyeh and pressed it against the pane. The glass spiderwebbed. He stopped, listened. Nothing.

One by one, he began picking out the shards until the hole was large enough. He reached through, unlocked the window, opened it, and climbed inside.

The interior was empty. Moonlight pierced the overhead shutters and cast stripes on the floor. *There's nothing here.* He spotted a trapdoor in the far corner. He walked over, grabbed the iron ring, and lifted. A ladder descended into the darkness.

At the bottom he found a dimly lit passageway bordered on each side by three wooden doors, each padlocked and equipped with a viewing slit. The air was thick with the stench of stale urine. Hanging from a hook on the wall was a key ring.

He took it, walked to the first door, and peered through the slit. It was an empty stone cell, complete with shackles bolted to the wall and a wooden waste bucket in the corner. The hair on the back of Tanner's neck stood up. This place looked all too familiar. *Keep going, Briggs,* he commanded.

He found the next three cells empty as well, but inside the fifth was Hossein Asseal; he sat naked and shivering in the corner. Briggs's hand was halfway to the padlock when he stopped. *You can't.* If Asseal disappeared, they would abandon the warehouse. His stomach boiled at the idea of leaving the man behind, but there was no other way. *Goddamn it.*

The inside of the sixth cell was almost pitch black, so it took several seconds for his eyes to adjust. What he saw made him jerk back involuntarily. He fumbled with the keys, dropped them, found the right one, and slipped it into the lock.

The door swung inward.

Tanner had only seen the man's picture once, but there was no mistaking the face. Hanging from the overhead beam, his neck stretched to twice its normal length, was Jusef Khoury, the agent known as Marcus.

HE'D BEEN DEAD FOR SEVERAL DAYS. HIS EYES BULGED LIKE PING-Pong balls; flies buzzed in his nostrils and ears. Tanner stared at the feces-stained floor, the overflowing waste bucket, the shoe scuffs on the wall beside the body, and suddenly felt his stomach heave. He gulped hard. God, what a way to die. What a place to die.

He closed and locked the door, then stood against it for a moment, eyes closed. *Keep going, stay focused....* He returned the key ring to the hook, then scaled the ladder, slipped out the window, and left.

LEAVING AHMED WITH A CANTEEN OF WATER AND ORDERS TO watch the warehouse until noon, Tanner made his way back to the Commodore.

He opened the door to his room and slipped inside. The curtains were half-open, bathing the room in gray light. He stopped. Something was wrong. It was nothing apparent, nothing his senses could latch onto, but the alarm in the back of his mind was insistent. Someone was here.

He drew the Glock and stepped into the main room.

"I've been waiting for you."

The voice came from a figure sitting on the bed. Tanner saw the bleach blond hair and the gaudy red dress. *Lena.*

"Stand up slowly," Tanner ordered. "Hands out to your sides."

She hesitated.

"Do it!"

She rose from the chair and extended her arms.

"Move in front of the window."

She stepped to her left until he could see her silhouette.

"What do you want?" he said.

In answer, she reached up, pulled off the blond wig, and tossed it onto the bed.

Tanner's heart lurched into his throat.

It was Camille.

56

Aboard Trolley

CAHIL GLANCED UP AS THE RED CABIN LIGHTS FLASHED. THERE WAS a pause, then two more flashes. *Nine minutes from drop.*

The loadmasters went to work, connecting safety harnesses and pushing the team's sleds to the ramp. Bear flexed his fingers to keep the circulation going. The cabin temperature hovered around forty degrees.

The loadmaster turned and gave him a thumbs-up.

Cahil stood and signaled for final check. Each man began checking his swim buddy's personal loadout: H&K MP-5 suppressed assault rife, Magellan nav box, wet suit, radio, grenades, first aid kit, flashlight, combat knife, and chemlight sticks. Including an airfoil parachute, each man was carrying 125 pounds of gear.

The cabin lights blinked again.

Six minutes.

Cahil felt the floor angle beneath his feet as the pilot began his descent. One of the loadmasters opened the aircraft's side door. With a *whoosh*, the interior decompressed. Wind whipped through the cabin. The ramp groaned down a few inches to reveal a slice of black sky.

Smitty blew out a stream of vapor. "By the time we hit the water, it's gonna seem downright toasty," he yelled over the rush.

Cahil signaled the team to assemble.

They waddled down the ramp in a double stick—two columns of four men. The loadmasters—two for each stick—began hooking each man to his sled by a twenty-foot cable. Once done, the chief loadmaster gave Cahil the hooked-and-clear signal, then retreated to the main cabin.

The cabin lights flashed. *Two minutes.*

Cahil pulled out the Magellan and punched the keypad for a GPS update. Three rows of numbers flashed on the screen: *Tsumago*'s latitude, longitude, and course. *On track.* She was right where she was supposed to be.

With a whine, the ramp began opening. Now the real cold hit Cahil, ripping the air from his lungs. He turned the knob on his oxygen canister, heard the hiss, and took a deep breath; the air tasted metallic. He looked over his shoulder and got seven thumbs-up. *Ready.*

The ramp thudded to a stop. Cahil stared out into the blackness. Though invisible from this altitude, somewhere down there—five miles straight down—the ocean was waiting. He blinked hard, focused himself.

The lights blinked a final time: *Ten seconds.*

Cahil pulled down his goggles, gave the sled a shove, then ran after it.

National Military Command Center, Washington

NINETY SECONDS AFTER CAHIL AND HIS TEAM STEPPED INTO THE void, the latest Keyhole update on *Tsumago*'s position arrived. "Put it on the main monitor," Cathermeier ordered. The gray and black image flashed on the screen. "Tighten it up, highlight her course track."

The technician did so, and the image contracted until it encompassed 100 square miles of ocean. Running diagonally across the screen was a dotted red line. At the end of it, where the white dot representing *Tsumago* should have been, there was nothing but ocean.

"I don't see her," said the president.

Mason murmured, "Where the hell—"

"Enlarge," Dutcher ordered.

The image expanded. Northwest of *Tsumago*'s track were a pair of dots.

"Tighten on them and run a match."

The tech did so. "The southern one matches *Tsumago*."

"Distance from original course?"

"Twenty miles."

"That can't be," said Cathermeier. "Twenty miles in under a half hour . . . She had to be making—"

"Thirty-five knots," Dutcher finished. "Gentlemen, I
think we just discovered something else about our mystery
ship."

"The other ship is a cruise liner," the tech reported. "The
Valverde."

"Home port?"

"Tel Aviv, sir."

"Oh, good God," muttered James Talbot.

"General, contact your teams," the president ordered.
"Tell them to abort."

"Too late, sir," said Cathermeier. "They're already on
their way."

Southeast of the Canary Islands

GIVEN *TSUMAGO'S* RADAR CAPABILITIES, CAHIL AND JURENS HAD
decided against Sierra's using a HAHO (high altitude, high
opening) jump and opted instead to go HALO, which meant
Bear and his team would free-fall from 29,000 feet and
deploy their chutes 200 feet above the surface.

It was a wilder ride than any roller coaster in the world,
but like the rest of his team, Cahil had little time to enjoy
it. His attention was fixed on the glowing face of his altimeter. Falling this fast, his release window would be less than
a second. Open your chute too high, and you become a
radar target; open too low, and you hit the ocean like a
watermelon crashing into a sidewalk.

Ninety seconds and two miles into the fall, he took his
eyes off the altimeter and glanced below. He could see the
ocean now, a black carpet interlaced with white ripples. It
was hypnotic. *Don't watch it,* he commanded. He'd seen
three men die that way, hitting the water without even
touching their chutes.

He refocused on the altimeter. 5,000 feet . . . 4,500 . . .
*Don't forget reaction time. First the sled, then the chute,
then hard on the risers . . .*

Now!

At 240 feet, Cahil jerked the sled's release, felt it drop away, then pulled his chute release. His testicles shot into his stomach. He reached up, grabbed the risers, heaved down. He sensed the surface rushing toward him. *Feet together, deep breath* . . . The chute flared out, lifted, then everything went dark.

In pitch blackness, he unbuckled his harness, flipped over, and arched his back to clear the shroud. This was the most dangerous part. Filled with water, an airfoil weighs two tons and sticks like flypaper. He broke the surface and took a gulp of air.

Thirty feet to his right, he could see the green glow of his sled's chem-light. He sidestroked to it, detached the shield, let the weights take it down, then switched on his radio headset.

"Sierra, talk to me." One by one, the team checked in. There were no injuries, but Wilts reported the SATCOM transceiver had collided with his sled. The casing was cracked. "Weight it and drop it," said Cahil. Losing the SATCOM was bad, but they still had their tactical radios, so their link to Alpha—the most critical one—was still intact. "Okay people, my beacon's up. Form on me."

WITHIN FIVE MINUTES, THEY WERE GATHERED IN A CIRCLE. THE SEA was running about four feet and was covered with a thin surface fog. Cahil pulled out his Magellan and called for *Tsumago*'s position. He read the numbers and frowned.

"Problem, Bear?" asked Smitty.

"Don't know." He recycled the Magellan. The numbers were the same. He pulled out his laminated chart, clicked on his penlight, and plotted the coordinates. "Smitty, check yours." Smitty did so, then compared the readout to Cahil's.

"We're almost thirty miles off," Bear muttered.

"What?" asked Slud.

"*Tsumago* should be fifteen miles southwest of us. According to GPS, she's dead in the water twenty-eight miles to the east, nearer the Canaries."

"That ain't good," said Johnson. "Even if she stays put, we're three hours away."

Cahil thought it over. Without SATCOM, they couldn't call for additional orders. Time for an executive decision, then. There was too much riding on this to simply quit at the first obstacle. Unless *Tsumago*'s destination had changed—which he doubted—she'd simply made a detour. If so, sooner or later, she would resume her course. He was betting Alpha would compensate accordingly.

"What's the plan, boss?" asked Wilts.

"We head for the corner. This is straight geometry. It's in a triangle. We're on one corner and the target's on the second. If she resumes course, we'll intercept her right about . . ." He tapped the chart. "Here . . . the third corner. Twelve miles."

"And if she stays put?"

"Then we keep our eye on her, adjust as necessary, and hit her where she is."

"That's four hours in the water, Bear," said Smitty. Four hours at this temperature would put a dangerous drain on the team.

"You got anything better to do?" Cahil said. "Trust me: She'll move." *God, please make her move.* "Given their cargo, I doubt they'll loiter."

THE TEAM'S SLEDS—MARK 7 IDVs (INDIVIDUAL DELIVERY VEHI-cles)—were a marvel of compact engineering. Light, virtually noiseless, and surprisingly agile, the sled's electric motor was capable of towing a 200-pound man and his gear at eight knots for ten hours; with leg power, the top speed increased to ten knots.

After thirty minutes of travel, Cahil called a stop to check the Magellan.

"How about it, boss?" Smitty called.

"We're in business," Cahil said. "She's moving. Course is zero-eight-zero . . . straight for us."

National Military Command Center, Washington

WHAT GENERAL CATHERMEIER HAD TOLD THE PRESIDENT WAS only partially true. In fact, both teams were reachable, though not immediately: Sierra via their SATCOM unit, and Alpha via Jurens's final go/no-go check with *Ford*. Cathermeier had already sent the abort message to *Ford*. Sierra, however, was another matter. Cahil's team was still not responding.

"There are two possibilities," said Dutcher. "Either they're unable to respond or its an equipment problem. Better we assume the latter and see how it plays out." Dutcher was praying for the latter. If Ian was unable to respond, that meant something had gone fatally wrong during the HALO. At that altitude, in the dead of night . . . He leaned over the chart. "Here's Sierra's drop point," he said. "*Tsumago* and *Valverde* are here."

"Almost thirty miles between them," said Talbot. "I'd say that solves our problem. There's no way Sierra can reach the target."

"I wouldn't be so sure."

"What do you mean, Dutch?" asked the president.

"I know Cahil, sir. By now he knows they've lost SAT-COM and he knows *Tsumago*'s not where she's supposed to be. Without orders to the contrary, he'll do what it takes to reach her."

Talbot said, "It's thirty miles, for God sake!"

"Maybe not."

One of the communication technicians called: "General, we have *Ford* for you. Secure channel five."

Cathermeier took the handset. "Cowboy, this is Coaldust, over."

"Coaldust, per your request, we've been listening in on Fuertaventura's harbor channel. We've intercepted a transmission. Are your recorders running?"

"Affirmative, Cowboy, go ahead."

A new voice came over the speaker: ". . . *Valverde*, this is Fuertaventura. Say again your last transmission."

"Fuertaventura, I repeat, this is Captain Stein of *Valverde*. We have been boarded. Two of my crew are dead. They have taken hostages."

"*Valverde,* you are garbled. Understand you have been boarded. Understand you have hostages. Where are the hostages at this time?"

"I told you, man! They *took* them. They're gone!"

East of the Canary Islands

CAHIL CALLED ANOTHER HALT TO CHECK THE MAGELLAN, THEN plotted *Tsumago*'s coordinates on the chart. For the first time in his adult life, Bear was glad he'd stayed awake during high school geometry. The triangle was closing. Unless she changed course again, the third corner would be their intercept point.

"We got two miles to go," he called. "If we push hard, we'll be there in twenty-five minutes." With *Tsumago*'s top speed at twenty knots, that would leave them thirty minutes to prepare.

They beat Cahil's estimate by three minutes. Once certain they were in the right spot, he spread Sierra in a line abreast, with himself at point and Smitty at anchor. Each man was linked to the next by seven-millimeter shock cord.

Sierra would board *Tsumago* via snag-line, a method rarely used because it broke the simpler-is-better rule of special operations. Traditional assault doctrine called for a stern approach by ICRRC (improved combat rubber raiding craft) and a midships boarding. This method had its drawbacks, however, two of which influenced Bear's decision.

A stern approach would have required a HAHO jump and a boat pursuit, both problematic because of *Tsumago*'s radar. The other consideration was the ship's siege-proof construction, which could become a problem if they found themselves in a standoff. Surprise was essential. Moreover, any increase in security aboard *Tsumago* would likely come in the form of lookouts, which would spot an ICRRC a mile away. As for a bow lookout spotting them, Cahil was unworried. In this fog, they would be all but invisible.

He pulled out his binoculars, looked to the southwest, but saw nothing. "Everybody get comfortable and look sharp."

Five minutes later, Wilts called over the radio, "Target, boss. Three miles."

What? Cahil checked his watch: It was too early to be *Tsumago.*

He peered through his binoculars. In the distance, a pair of red and green running lights sat low on the water. Neither were obstructed, which meant she was headed straight for them. He checked the Magellan. The bearing and range were correct, but the timing was wrong. It was too late to second-guess, he decided.

"That's our ride, gentlemen. Tighten up the line. I'll call out steerage."

Two minutes later, Cahil could see *Tsumago*'s outline clearly. Even at this distance, he could see her bow wave curling halfway up the hull.

Smitty called, "Damn, Bear, she's moving fast."

"I know, I see it."

Thirty knots or better, Bear estimated. He did a quick calculation. *Tsumago* was bearing down on them at a rate of sixty feet per second.

"Slud, gimme a range guess," Cahil called.

"Make it thirty-five hundred."

Less than three minutes. *Decide, Bear!* Thirty knots was much too fast for a bow hook. Any miscalculation, and they'd end up red smears on the hull. But then again, they'd come this far . . .

"You boys feel like going for a ride?" he called.

"Damn straight," said Wilts.

"I was getting bored anyway, boss," called Smitty.

Cahil grinned and revved the sled's throttle. "Stick close!"

*   *   *

TSUMAGO ATE UP THE DISTANCE QUICKLY. AT FIVE HUNDRED YARDS
Cahil could feel the rumble of her screws in his belly. Four
hundred yards . . . forty seconds to go. The bow lifted and
plunged, lifted and plunged, froth hissing against the hull.

"Dump sleds," Cahil ordered.

In unison, each team member opened the ballast vents
on his IDV and let it drop away. Cahil cast a glance over
his shoulder and counted seven heads strung out behind
him.

The rush of the wave was thunderous now. He could feel
it lifting him, pushing him. He scissored his legs to stay on
the crest. The hull loomed over him. *Wait . . . wait . . . now!*

He launched himself forward and slammed the MCD
against the hull. The magnet stuck, slid a few feet, then
held. He released it, let the line slide through his fingers,
then clamped down. Water streamed over his head and into
his mouth and nose. He coughed, snatched a breath, and
pulled himself against the hull.

He felt a double pat on his shoulder: Smitty had secured
the anchor.

Cahil looked over his shoulder. One by one, seven black-
gloved hands gave the thumbs-up signal. By God, they'd
made it!

He leaned out and signaled to Slud, who braced his feet
against the hull and pulled out a rubber-coated grappling
hook. He swung it once, heaved it over the rail, then gave
it a couple of tugs and started climbing.

57

Aboard Boxcar

TWENTY-TWO MILES EAST OF *TSUMAGO,* JURENS AND HIS TEAM were awaiting Cahil's signal. Frustrated as he was, Jurens knew they were better off than Sierra. As insertion methods went, they had it easy.

At forty million dollars, the MH-53 Pave Low is the most sophisticated helicopter in the world. Manned by two pilots, a flight engineer, and two PJs, or para-jumpers who also serve as loadmasters, the Pave Low is fast, quiet, and as agile as a World War I biplane. Crammed inside a cockpit that would put a James Bond movie to shame are over 900 dials, gauges, and switches with which the pilots monitor the aircraft and its ENS, or enhanced navigation system, which includes forward looking infrared radar, LANTIRN (a low altitude nav/targeting aid) and a communication system comparable to those found on AWACS.

None of this technology improved Jurens's mood, however. Where was Sierra? The distance they had to cover to reach *Tsumago* was daunting, but if there was a way, Bear would find it.

Jurens popped his head into the darkened cockpit. "How're we doing?"

"Fine as long as the coupler stays on-line," said the pilot. "Hovering this thing manually is a real pain in the ass." To keep pace with *Tsumago,* every six minutes the pilot was disengaging the coupler and dashing ahead two miles.

"How's our juice?"

"Twenty minutes at most. Whatever we're waiting for better happen soon."

As if on cue, a light blinked on the engineer's comm

panel. "That's them!" said Jurens. "The show's on, Captain. Let's go."

"Roger. We'll be over the deck in six minutes."

"Contact Cowboy, tell them we're inbound."

Jurens went aft where PJs began assembling the fast-rope packs. One of them tapped Jurens on the shoulder and jerked his thumb to the cockpit. Jurens went forward. "What's up?"

"Cowboy gave us the abort," the pilot said.

"What?"

"It's for real. They want us to turn around."

"My people are already aboard—"

"Commander, I've got my orders—"

"I want a secure line to Coaldust." When it was set up, Jurens said into the handset, "Coaldust, this is Boxcar, over."

"Go ahead, Boxcar."

Jurens recognized Cathermeier's voice. "General, what's going on?"

"The target boarded a cruise liner. There're hostages involved."

"Sir, I've got men already aboard."

"What?" said Cathermeier. "They made it? Sierra's aboard?"

"Affirmative."

"Stand by." Cathermeier was back in twenty seconds. "Boxcar, as soon as you have Sierra on tactical, order them out. Search and rescue is en route. Coaldust out."

The channel went to static. Jurens threw down the handset. "Shit!"

Tsumago

CROUCHED IN THE SHADOWS BENEATH THE PILOTHOUSE, CAHIL LED his team aft to the first hatch. He turned the lever, peeked inside, stepped through.

The passageway was empty and dark, aside from red battle lanterns dotting the bulkheads. Spaced between the lanterns were palm-sized yellow emergency buttons. Either these folks were safety fanatics or they were planning for the worst.

"Clear right," he whispered in his headset.

"Clear left."

"Six clear." Slud, the anchor man, eased the hatch closed. The passageway was bracketed by two ladders. Forward led to the bridge; aft to below decks. "Lead moving," Cahil whispered. "Aft ladder."

He led them down. As each man took the rungs, he never stopped moving—turning, scanning, MP5 held at low-ready. At the bottom, they fanned out.

Cahil counted five hatches. *Bunk rooms and mess area. Next ladder at the end of the passageway. Last hatch leads to forward cargo.* Using hand signals, he split his team, sending Slud and two men into the bunk rooms, Smitty and three others to the cargo hold. He would disable the radio himself.

He found the radio room hatch partially open, revealing one of the crew sitting in a chair reading a magazine. On the table beside him was a Tokarev pistol. The man turned, saw Cahil, and dove for the Tokarev. Cahil fired. The three-round burst slammed into the man's side, and he crumpled to the floor.

"Boss, Slud here."

"Go ahead," whispered Cahil.

"Bunk room and mess clear. Bear, these boys were sleeping with their AKs."

"Yeah, here, too. Come aft, secure the ladder."

Cahil was starting on the radio's faceplate screws when he heard a double beep in his ear: tactical radio. He switched frequencies. "Sierra on tac two."

It was Jurens. "Sit rep, Bear."

"Second deck secured, we're heading down and forward."

"Belay that. We're aborting."

Cahil froze. "Stand by." He switched channels. "Slud, Smitty, say location."

"Third deck ladder."

"Outside the cargo hatch."

"Hold positions." Cahil switched back to Jurens. "What's up?"

"There are hostages aboard, Bear. Exfil any way you can. SAR's on the way."

Hostages? Where did they . . . Then he understood: *Tsumago*'s diversion.

His first instinct was to go for the rescue. Right now they had the advantage, but once the crew found they'd been boarded, they would button up the ship. On the other hand, Sierra's original plan was shot to hell: They had no intell and no way to evacuate hostages short of tossing them overboard.

"Roger, copy exfil," Cahil replied. He switched channels. "Sierra, backtrack to me. We're leaving."

ON *TSUMAGO*'S BRIDGE, AL-BAZ HAD NO IDEA HIS SHIP HAD BEEN penetrated. His mind was elsewhere.

In less than a day they would slip past the Strait of Gibraltar and into the Mediterranean. Once there, the crew would go to a state of constant readiness, for when news of *Valverde* got out, a boarding attempt would be imminent. This did not concern him. All attempts would either fail or come too late. He allowed himself a smile. All the planning, all the training, was now paying off.

"Sir, you're wanted in the radar room."

Al-Baz stepped into the alcove. The ESM operator sat hunched over his console. "What is it?"

"I just intercepted a signal, sir."

"What kind?"

"Radio." The operator pointed to the scope face, which showed a green spoke jutting from the center. "It's scrambled. Bearing two-zero-one, signal strength five."

That meant the source was within fifty miles. Scrambled transmissions were generally used by only military craft. Was there a unit nearby? al-Baz wondered. If so, was it merely coincidence or something more?

"Energize the radar. Give me a sector search on that bearing."

The operator did so, marked the screen with a grease pencil, and switched off the radar. There was only one blip. It was dead astern.

"It's small," said the operator. "Either a boat or an aircraft at low altitude."

An attack this soon seemed improbable. Nevertheless, here was this craft—whatever it was—shadowing them. That made no sense, though. If an attempt at surveillance, why not use a high-altitude patrol plane or a satellite?

He turned to one of the bridge crew. "Go wake Khalid and Mujad. Tell them to take lookout positions."

Boxcar

FOUR MINUTES, JURENS THOUGHT. PLENTY OF TIME FOR THEM TO get overboard. *Come on, Bear, talk to me. . . .*

A light blinked on the engineer's panel. "Alpha, this is Sierra, over,"

Jurens grabbed the handset. "Go ahead, Bear."

"Alpha, be advised, we—" The popping of gunfire filled Jurens's headphones. "—taking fire. No casualties, but things—" More gunfire. "—getting hot. Do you copy, Alpha?"

"Roger, Bear. Can you exfil?"

"Gonna be dicey. I wouldn't hold dinner. Stand by this channel. Sierra out."

"Switch me to Coaldust," Jurens told the engineer. "Coaldust, Boxcar, over."

"Go ahead, Boxcar," said Cathermeier.

Jurens explained Cahil's situation. "Request permission to assist."

"Negative; stay put. There's nothing you can do for them."

"Sir—"

"You heard me, Boxcar. Stay where you are."

Jurens ripped off his headphones. He turned to the pilot. "Captain, how's your service record?"

The pilot grinned. "As clean as new snow. It could stand a few spots."

* * *

Tsumago

CAHIL HAD BEEN LEADING THE TEAM TO THE LADDER WHEN SUD-
denly a crewman trotted down the ladder and landed ten
feet in front of them.

Ignoring the AK slung across his chest, the man lunged
for an emergency button. Cahil fired, but not fast enough.
With two rounds in his chest, the man crashed into the
button and slumped to the deck. Sirens began whooping.
The lanterns turned to strobes, casting red shadows down
the passageway.

"Move!" Cahil ordered. "I'm on point. Smitty, take rear
guard."

Cahil led them up the ladder. At the top he caught a
glimpse of movement down the passageway. He ducked
back. Bullets ripped into the bulkhead beside him. He side-
stepped, firing, as the team climbed the last few rungs and
joined him.

Ahead, a pair of heads peeked around the corner, fired,
then ducked back. Their fire discipline was good, Cahil
saw. No wild spraying, only controlled bursts. He and Slud
poured fire down the passageway. They were running out
of time. They had the edge, but that wouldn't last long.

"Talk to me, Smitty! Where are you?"

"Second deck. We got company. We're holding, but it
ain't good."

"Understood. Hold for sixty, then break off. We're leaving."

"Roger."

Using hand signals, Cahil told the team what he had
planned, then plucked a flashbang grenade off his harness.
He pulled the pin and tossed the grenade down the passageway, banking it around the corner.

"Cover!"

The team flattened against the bulkhead, eyes down and
hands over their ears.

The passageway exploded in blinding light and noise.

Cahil peeked around the corner, saw nothing, then looked down the ladder. Smitty was coming up. His collar was shiny with blood, but he grinned and gave a thumbs-up. Cahil threw open the hatch. He and Slud poured fire down the passageway. One by one, the rest of the team leapt through the hatch. Cahil shoved Slud after them, then followed.

On deck it was like daylight. Spotlights blazed down on them. Past the handrails, Cahil could see nothing but blackness. For a dizzying moment, he felt suspended in a void.

"Target, six o' clock," yelled Wilts, spinning and firing.

A trio of terrorists crouched on the afterdeck, firing through the arch. Wilts screamed, clutched his stomach, and fell. Cahil snagged his collar and dragged him back against the superstructure. The firing tapered off.

They're thinking it over, Bear thought. *Figuring out how to come at us.*

"Slud, Johnson, douse those lights!"

Pop, pop, pop. The deck went dark. From above, Cahil heard voices. He looked up in time to see a pair of AK barrels come over the rail and point toward them. Cahil fired, stitching the rail and forcing them back, but they returned a moment later. The deck sparked beneath his feet.

Cahil looked around; both Wilts and Smitty were hit.

"Ideas, boss?" Slud panted.

"We're in a funnel," Cahil said. "We gotta go forward. We're gonna need more time." The forecastle would give them more cover and better fields of fire. "We'll take rear guard while the others go overboard."

Slud nodded and relayed the plan down the line. Johnson heaved Wilts over his shoulder and nodded *ready*. With a mutual nod, Bear and Slud each tossed a flashbang, one through the aft arch, the other high onto the superstructure.

"Go, Jonce!"

As one, the team charged.

The flashbangs bought them the time they needed. By the time the explosions died away, they were on the forecastle, crouched behind the derricks and capstans. Cahil gestured Smitty and the others toward the railing, then crawled over to Slud.

Through the glare of the spotlights, Cahil saw several figures on the bridge wing. He fired. They went down. AKs started chattering. A bullet thunked into the girder beside his head.

"They're coming up the port side, Bear," Slud said.

"I see him. Just a few more seconds. Smitty's almost over the side."

Cahil counted muzzle flashes. Two . . . seven . . . twelve guns firing now. Bullets whizzed. He took aim on a spotlight and fired; it went out. He glanced over his shoulder: Everyone but Johnson was overboard.

Cahil saw movement above the signal bridge. A trio of terrorists were setting up a MG3 crew-manned machine gun. *West German,* he thought. *A thousand rounds a minute . . .*

Slud said, "Boss—"

"I see it. Okay, time to go."

Cahil started toward a nearby capstan, felt a sting in his leg, kept crawling. He looked down. His calf glistened with blood. The pain came a few seconds later, like someone had jammed a hot iron into his leg.

"Bad?" called Slud.

"Not bad enough to keep me here."

The MG3 started coughing, a deep *chug, chug, chug* mixed with the sharper cracks of the AKs. Bullets thudded into the winch drum, showering Cahil and Slud with sparks.

Smart move, Cahil thought. While the MG kept them pinned down, the rest of the crew could charge onto the forecastle and swarm them. He peeked up and saw figures running up the port weather deck.

"Get moving, Slud!"

"Uh-uh, boss. You're gimped. You'll need a head start and cover."

"No—"

"Go, Bear! By the time you hit the rail, I'll be on your heels."

"You better be! On three—"

Suddenly Cahil heard the muffled chopping of rotor

blades. He glanced over his shoulder. Materializing from the darkness behind the pilothouse came a lone Pave Low helicopter. Banking hard, muzzles flashing from the open doorway, it swooped over the signal bridge. The MG3 went silent. The terrorists on the wings scattered. Hanging from the helo's open door, Sconi Bob Jurens gave a wave as the helo disappeared into the night.

"I'm going, Slud!" Cahil yelled, and half-ran, half-limped to the rail. He slipped, crashed into the capstan, kept moving. Behind him, the MG3 started barking again. He looked back.

"Slud! Come on!"

Slud started running, turning every few feet to fire at the figures charging up the forecastle. More of the crew were scrambling down the bridge ladders. Cahil counted ten men, then twelve, then fifteen. He reached up and pulled himself to the rail.

Slud kept running. AKs flashed. He went down, struggled back to his feet. He was limping now, and Cahil could see his face twisted with pain.

"Go, Bear! I'm coming. . . . *Go!*"

Thirty feet separated them. Bear grabbed a flashbang and pulled the pin.

Twenty men were on the forecastle now, firing as they charged.

Cahil cocked his arm and threw the grenade. It landed at the feet of the lead pursuers and exploded. They scattered. Slud stumbled the last few feet and reached for Cahil's hand.

As their fingers touched, Cahil felt something slam into his chest. *Hit,* he thought numbly. *I'm hit.* Time seemed to slow. He stumbled backward, hit the rail, and tipped over into the darkness.

58

Beirut

STARING AT CAMILLE, TANNER FELT THE FINAL PIECES OF THE PUZ-
zle fall into place.

For a moment, he felt disconnected from what was happening, as though he were watching a scene from a movie.
In the next instant, he felt a rush of emotion: anger, be-
trayal, and happiness. *Get ahold of yourself*, he commanded.

Camille was staring back at him. In the dim light he
could see her eyes were wet, but there was something else
there, too: anger. He suddenly realized she was feeling the
same things as he. They had trusted but not quite trusted
one another.

He could think of nothing to say. "It wasn't you," he
finally whispered.

"Pardon me?"

"The wig. It just wasn't you."

THEY SPENT AN AWKWARD TEN MINUTES WAITING FOR ROOM SER-
vice to bring up breakfast, and then, glad to have something
to busy themselves with, they sat and ate.

To the southeast, a dozen pillars of smoke rose into the
sky, each representing a bomb or a mortar round that had
found its mark the night before. In contrast to the carnage,
the ocean was an unruffled blue, and sky clear save a few
cotton puff clouds.

Finally Tanner said, "So, how are we going to handle
this?"

"What?"

"This. Us."

She shrugged and averted her eyes.

Like a little girl whose feelings are hurt, Briggs thought. He set down his coffee cup. "Damn it, Camille, you lied—" He stopped himself. *And you lied to her.* Did he really expect her to have admitted she was a Mossad *katsa?*

"Lied to you?" she said. "Yes. Does that really surprise you?"

"Forget it."

"You're angry."

"Yes."

"Well, so am I! Briggs, you have to understand. I can't tell you—"

"I know who and what you are, Camille, and I know why you're here. We asked for your help, and you want to know why. Why you, though?"

"You think it's because of you and me?"

"I'd be stupid not to."

"The answer is no," she said. "I've been here for almost a month."

"Why?"

She waved her hand at the city. "That. We got caught unaware in eighty-two, and we learned our lesson."

"And Asseal?"

"I learned about him four days ago. Given his tastes and my cover, I was the obvious choice. I didn't know you were here until last night when I saw you on the street. My people have no idea it's you."

"But they do know about Japan."

"Yes."

Tanner went silent. He'd been wrong about her in Japan. Was now any different? He felt like a fool and couldn't decide if it was because she'd duped him or because he'd opened himself up to her. "Tell me about Japan," he said.

"I was on vacation, Briggs. They *do* allow that, you know—"

Tanner chuckled without humor. "I'll give them this: They trained you well."

"What do you want from me! We met, we had an affair,

and we parted. Briggs, I cared . . . I care . . . very much for you. Why are you doing this?"

"Okay. If this is how you want it. Do you remember Umako Ohira?"

"The man we saw killed? What about—?"

"It must've been a big surprise to see him jumping over the fence like that. And then when he was gunned down . . . I'll bet it put a real damper on your plans."

"What?"

"When you tried to recruit him, did you know he was already working for us?"

Camille blinked hard. She toyed with her napkin.

"The night he died, Ohira had two meetings," Tanner continued. "The first was at the shipyard, the second with an unidentified agent who was trying to recruit him. A false flag, in fact . . . a Mossad specialty."

"What do you want me to say?"

Good question; he had no idea. He decided it didn't matter. He had a job to do, but he couldn't simply dismiss her. As the saying went, the town wasn't big enough for the both of them.

She asked, "Briggs, aren't you wondering why I came here?"

"I assumed—"

"That I was here to find out why you're in Beirut. I could have done that by following you. Do you think I am naive enough to believe you would jump into bed with me and spill the potatoes?"

"Beans."

"What?"

"Spill the beans."

"You understand my meaning."

It was true, Tanner realized. She could have accomplished more by watching from a distance. What would Mossad do if they knew about her coming to him? "So why, then?" he said.

"I came for you," Camille replied. Her eyes glistened. "It's stupid. I think about what I'm doing . . . about what they'd do to me . . . and I don't care." Tears trickled down her cheeks. "Please, Briggs, can't we just—"

"Camille—"

"Don't you understand? None of this matters. Tell me to leave and stay away, and I will. But please, can't we . . ." She trailed off.

Suddenly Tanner realized he believed her; he believed all of it. *God help me,* he thought. He opened his arms. "Come here."

THEY MADE LOVE FOR THE BETTER PART OF THE MORNING, AND IT felt like Japan all over again. They laughed and reminisced and never said a word about what was happening outside their door. Just before ten, they got up and showered together. When they emerged, they were wrinkled and breathless with laughter.

"If every shower was like that one, I would never leave the house," Camille said. "I'm surprised the hot water lasted. Oh, I'm starving. Let's have a giant, unhealthy breakfast, then go back to bed."

He ordered a breakfast of eggs, toast, date muffins, fresh fruit, and a pot of coffee. They were about to start eating when there came a knock on the door. Tanner picked up the Glock, tucked it against his leg, and walked to the door. *"Aiwa? Shoo fi?"*

"It is I, *effendi.*"

Safir. Tanner opened the door.

"Good morning, *effendi,* I—" Safir saw Camille, then grinned at Tanner. "Oh. Oh, you scoundrel."

Briggs smiled. "What is it?"

He handed Tanner a morning newspaper. The English headline read:

SHIITE MULAH SLAIN

"Give me the gist of it," Tanner said.

"Hamdi was a leader in the Shiite community, especially in neighborhoods near the airport. Last night as he was leaving his mosque, a group of nine men ambushed his car with RPGs. He and all his bodyguards were killed."

"Has anyone claimed responsibility?"

"Three so far, but I did some checking. There were eye-witnesses who swore the attackers shouted a name: the Arab Liberation Command."

The Arab Liberation Command? The ALC was pro-Iraq. Though it wouldn't be unusual for them to attack Shiites, they hadn't been active in Lebanon for five or six years.

"Amal and some other splinter groups are swearing vengeance," Safir said.

"No surprise there." Tanner lowered his voice: "What about the warehouse?"

"Nothing. I'll have Sadiq watch until dusk; I do not think anything will happen until then."

"I agree. Can you find out more about this attack?"

"I will look into it." Safir peeked over Tanner's shoulder and grinned. "I will leave you to your breakfast."

As Briggs returned to the table, Camille asked, "A friend?"

"He's not involved, Camille."

"I was just asking," she replied with smile.

They were halfway through breakfast when Tanner's cell phone pager went off. He retrieved it, read the display, and cleared it.

Camille smiled at him over her cup.

"Business," he said.

"I didn't say a word."

THEY PARTED WAYS AND AGREED TO MEET LATER THAT AFTERNOON. Neither asked what the other had planned, but Tanner was under no illusions: The issue would have to be settled sooner or later. He had no idea how, though.

Once satisfied he wasn't being followed, he spent fifteen minutes looking for a working phone booth. When the overseas operator answered, he gave the account number of a sanitized credit card. After two minutes, the line started ringing.

"Hello," said Leland Dutcher.

"It's me. I got your page."

Whether from his distrust of Stucky or his habit of always having a backup plan, Dutcher had arranged a secure means of communication separate from that of Langley's. "Good to hear your voice," Dutcher said.

"You, too."

"Tell me how you're doing."

"I called the branch office; the phones are working fine. As for finding a manufacturer, I'm still looking, but I've found a good middleman."

Behind the padded language was the same message he had forwarded to Stucky the previous day: He hadn't yet found Azhar, but the fly had been taken, and Tanner was tracking him.

"Good," said Dutcher. "There's something else, Briggs. It's about Ian. His hiking trip. There was a storm, and he and his group got lost. They're looking, but it doesn't look good."

Tanner felt his heart lurch. He leaned his head against the booth's wall and closed his eyes.

"Briggs, you there?"

"I'm here. What happened?"

"We don't know yet. There might even be something in the papers."

Papers? What could have gone so wrong that the mission would fall into the public eye? "Have you told Maggie?" Tanner asked.

"I'm driving over this afternoon. Briggs, if it's true, you're going to have to take over his share of the business."

The message was clear: *Tsumago* was on her way. There would be no further boarding attempts. "I understand."

Tel Aviv

STUCKY HAD IN FACT RECEIVED TANNER'S LAST MESSAGE. HE'D lain awake staring at it. By dawn, he made his decision. He was considering the angles when the message from Langley arrived: The boarding had failed. Hostages were involved. *Tsumago* would enter the Mediterranean within twenty-four hours.

It was just the incentive he needed. The plan would work, he decided. And if not, he'd be covered. In a lot of ways, Stucky thought, this had been over a decade in the making. *Time to pay the piper, Briggs ol' buddy.*

He burned Tanner's message in the ashtray, flushed the remains down the toilet, then retrieved a onetime decoding pad and started working. Once done, he checked and rechecked the message until satisfied it would bear scrutiny, then picked up the phone and dialed Avi Haron's private number.

"Haron, here."

"It's Stucky. I need to see you. It's urgent."

HARON SENT HIS PRIVATE CAR, AND SOON STUCKY WAS SITTING in his office. Stucky explained the situation. The *Shin Bet* man was first astonished then alarmed. Was Stucky sure of his information? Yes. Did he realize what he was proposing? Yes again. "Listen, Avi, I don't like doing this. It makes me sick. But if the worst happens . . ."

"This is unusual, Art. I will forward the information—"

"No. I want to see Sherabi myself. This is *my* ass on the line. I want some assurances. Either I see him personally, or the deal's off."

AN HOUR AFTER HARON PLACED HIS CALL, HE AND STUCKY ARRIVED at the Mossad director's private home north of the city. The Spanish-style house was surrounded by a high stone wall. Haron and Stucky were cleared through the gate by a guard from Mossad's internal security branch, then they were met at the front door by another guard who led them into Sherabi's study.

Sherabi shook Stucky's hand and gestured him to an overstuffed leather chair. One glance at Stucky's heavily veined nose and nicotine-yellow fingers told Sherabi what the CIA man did with his leisure time. *Another Aldrich*

Ames, he thought. But then, even bullies and drunks have their uses.

"Avi tells me you have some concerns," Sherabi said. "First, tell me: Why haven't you taken this to your people?"

"I have. They won't listen. If this were any other operation, I might overlook it, but too much is at stake. I can't just sit by and let it happen."

"But you are a division chief. Certainly you have access to your DDO."

"He overruled me. The problem is, they don't see the danger. The man in question is someone I've worked with. I know him. We were even friends, once." Stucky paused and shook his head sadly. "That's what makes this so hard."

"I see. Tell me."

"I should back up and start at the beginning. You know we have an operative in Beirut who's trying to track a man . . . Hossein Asseal."

"Yes."

"What reason did my people give you?"

"To recover a missing agent."

"That's a lie," said Stucky. "Or at least a partial lie. The primary mission is to penetrate the group that took an agent of ours and identify its leadership. Through a conduit, we fed them a story that Asseal was in Beirut to locate the group's second-in-command."

"Hoping they would kidnap Asseal and lead your man to them."

"Right."

Sherabi was impressed. He hadn't thought Dick Mason capable of such ruthlessness. As he'd suspected, the CIA was not going to all this trouble to simply recover an agent. "Go on."

"As we speak, a ship is en route to your country. Aboard her is the group's second-in-command, about three dozen terrorists, and a cargo. I don't know what it is, but my government is very concerned."

"Where is this ship?"

"It'll enter the Mediterranean tonight. Three or four days after that, it should be off your coast."

Good lord, Sherabi thought. No wonder Mason was in such a hurry. But why hadn't they shared this information? Only one answer made sense: The CIA had known about the ship, failed to act, and was now scrambling to cover itself.

"And you know nothing about this cargo? Or the terrorists' intentions?"

"No."

"Why bring this to us? Why take the risk? Your people would consider it an act of treason."

"Believe me, I know that. I've watched your country fight for survival all my adult life. You're surrounded by neighbors sworn to destroy you. And now, because somebody hasn't got the balls to do the right thing, you're staring down the barrel of a gun." Stucky shook his head. "I can't sit still and let it happen."

Stucky had just verbalized the thoughts of the average Israeli citizen and soldier. The never-ending fight for survival was a heritage with which they all lived. "We're grateful you've brought this to our attention," Sherabi said. "We'll consider—"

"There might be a way to handle the situation."

"I'm listening."

"The man we sent into Beirut is familiar with the leader of the group. They're close friends, in fact . . . almost family as I understand it."

"Pardon me?"

"Langley thought it would give him an advantage. I disagreed. I thought it would cloud his judgment. I kept my mouth shut. Unfortunately, it looks like I was right. Here."

Sherabi took the slip of paper and read it.

TARGET TAKEN. UNABLE TO TRACK DUE TO GPS MALFUNCTION. WILL ATTEMPT TO TRACK BY ALTERNATIVE MEANS.

"That's his most recent transmission," Stucky said.

"And?" replied Sherabi.

"I ran a system test on the GPS link. It's working perfectly."

"You believe he is lying."

"I think it's worse than that. I think he has no intention of doing the job."

Sherabi suddenly understood where Stucky was going. The CIA man had a personal agenda. They were in very dangerous territory now, Sherabi knew. Was it worth the risk to have a CIA division chief in their pocket?

He shrugged. "I'm sorry to hear that. However, I don't see how it affects us." Sherabi saw a flicker of frustration on Stucky's face. *Anxious boy.*

"Don't you get it? We've got a golden opportunity."

"Speak plainly, Mr. Stucky. What are you suggesting?"

"He's in place; he has the access. I say we use him."

59

White House

"HOW MANY CASUALTIES?" THE PRESIDENT ASKED.

"One dead, two missing," replied General Cathermeier. "Wilts died in the water. We don't know what happened to Sludowski and Cahil."

"Cahil was your man, Dutch?"

Dutcher nodded absently. Forty years in this business and it had never gotten any easier to send people into harm's way. It didn't help that he thought of Bear as family. "Yes, sir."

"Family?"

"Wife and daughter. I've already been to see them."

"Whatever comes, we'll make sure they're taken care of. Dick, what do we know about the hijacking?"

"We think we've pieced it together," Mason replied. "*Valverde*'s captain said they received a distress call from a freighter we now know was *Tsumago*. They asked for medical help, then ferried some crewmen to *Valverde*. While Stein was occupied with the man claiming to be the freighter's captain—al-Baz, we believe—a dozen men swam across and took the ship. Al-Baz shot the first officer—"

"What? Why?"

"According to Stein, to convince him they were serious. Al-Baz then demanded a passenger manifest and began rounding up hostages, which they then ferried back to *Tsumago*."

Very smart, Dutcher thought. The hostages would not only forestall further attacks, but they would help mask

Tsumago's true purpose. Why take hostages if you held a nuclear weapon as a trump card?

Moreover, hostages would buy time. While *Tsumago* steamed ever closer to Israel, the focus would be on securing their release. Once the Israelis realized the truth, they would face a nightmare choice: Sink the ship, killing a hundred of their own citizens and triggering an explosion that would turn the Med into a radioactive cesspool, or risk the device falling into enemy hands—or worse yet, have it go off in Tel Aviv Harbor. It was the perfect lose-lose-lose scenario.

"What do we know about this group?" asked the president.

"They claimed to be the Arab Liberation Command. It's a fanatical pro-Iraq group."

"I thought al-Baz was a Syrian operative."

"He may still be. One is a ruse, the other the truth. At this point, we can't rule either of them out. Both are capable of this kind of operation."

"I need options, gentlemen. General, militarily, what can we do?"

"Another boarding is out of the question. By now *Tsumago* is buttoned up like a drum. Plus, we're blind. We don't know where the hostages are or the location of the device. What the Israelis are going to do is anybody's guess."

The president removed his glasses and rubbed the bridge of his nose. "Well, I'm afraid we're going to find out. When we're finished here, I'm calling the prime minister." Talbot began to protest, and the president waved him off. "They deserve to know what they're facing. They may already know about *Tsumago*, and I'll be damned if I'm going to withhold the rest of it."

The president turned to Dutcher. "Dutch, what about your man in Beirut? Can we pin any hope on him?"

How to answer that? Dutcher thought. If he had to gamble everything on any one person, it would be Tanner. Dutcher had done so before and never regretted it. Still,

Briggs had less than seventy-two hours to reach Azhar and put a stop to *Tsumago*.

"I think, Mr. President, we'd be wise to plan for the worst case."

Holystone

OAKEN STARED AT THE CEILING, NOT SEEING IT. SCATTERED ON HIS desk were books, sheafs of computer printouts, and dozens of pages of notes. His computer screen saver swirled in a multicolored waterfall.

He was wrestling with the same problem that had occupied him for the past two days: If in fact Syria was behind the bomb, what did it hope to gain? The most obvious answer didn't satisfy him. Whether it was the intelligence officer in him or the mile-wide stubborn streak Beverly complained about, Oaken was not sure, but he found it hard to accept anything at face value. There was a story behind everything, and a story behind every story.

So what was it here?

It all boiled down to ambition. A burglar steals to fulfill his desire for money. A terrorist kills to further his group's agenda. Nations do both, and more, to secure their national interests. What was Syria's greatest national interest? To have a nuclear device? No, that was too pat an answer. To blow Israel into the sea? Again, no. Bashar Assad was too savvy for that. Such a blatant attack would lead to his own destruction.

Suddenly, in an intuitive flash, two days' worth of rumination paid off. He bolted forward in his chair. "Gleiwitz," he whispered.

Aqrabah, Syria

THROUGHOUT THE DAY, THE SYRIAN ARMY EXERCISE GROUP, NOW under the direct command of General Issam al-Khatib, had been wrapping up its maneuvers. As dusk fell over the desert, the long column of tanks, APCs, and towed artillery began its journey north toward Damascus.

Trailing behind al-Khatib's jeep were the First Armored Division, elements of the Seventh and Ninth Mechanized, and the recently downsized but still lethal Golan Task Group, comprised of units from the Third Armored and the Tenth and Eleventh Mechanized. In all, the convoy consisted of 320 tanks, 510 APCs, 175 artillery guns, and some 16,000 soldiers.

The route took the convoy on a narrow and badly pocked secondary road. Before long, the column's pace slowed to a sedate five kilometers per hour, and as darkness fell, the lead elements were twelve miles from the border of the Golan Heights.

Tsumago

CAHIL WOKE UP TO A BLINDING PAIN IN HIS HEAD. FOR A LONG five minutes, he lay perfectly still until his senses returned, one by one. He felt himself lifting and falling and heard the *swoosh-hiss* of water.

He forced open his eyes and looked around. He was in a cramped room, lying beside a huge winch drum out of which rose several links of massive chain. He was still aboard *Tsumago*.

The previous night's memories came flooding back: the boarding and the firefight . . . he and Slud making a stand as the others went overboard . . . and then the sledgehammer blow to his chest. He remembered clawing at the passing hull and then being jerked to a stop. The snagline! He'd grabbed the snagline.

He explored his chest, searching for the wound, but instead, his fingers found a shattered steel D-ring on his vest. A millimeter to the right, and the bullet would have pierced his heart. He forced himself to a sitting position and probed the wound on his calf, a gash in the thick of the muscle. It was already bandaged. He didn't remember doing that, either.

Bad move, Bear, he thought. If he hadn't grabbed the line, he would be tucked in a cozy hospital bed in Rota instead of here, beat to hell and trapped aboard a ship with several dozen terrorists and a nuclear bomb.

What next? He could either go overboard and take his risks in the water, or he could make himself useful. It took him exactly one second to reach an answer. He was staying. Now the question was, what could he do? And where was Slud?

TWO DECKS BELOW CAHIL, SAUL AND BERNICE WEINMAN SAT huddled together under a blanket. All around them, other *Valverde* passengers were doing the same. Some were sobbing, others praying, others sleeping fitfully. They were all cold, hungry, and very frightened.

Their prison was barely big enough for each of them to lie down without crushing their neighbor. Dimly lit bulbs swung from the ceiling. At the back of the compartment was a single door with a peephole.

"Saul, what's going to happen?" Bernice whispered. "What do they want?"

He pulled her tighter. "I don't know, Bern. Try to sleep."

"I can't."

"Try." He pulled the blanket under her chin. "Everything will be fine."

SAUL HEARD THE *CLICK-CLICK* OF THE DOOR'S BOLT BEING THROWN.

The door swung open. Two Arabs marched inside, dragging a man in a black wet suit. His face was bruised and bloody; one eye was swollen shut. The guards dropped him in a corner and walked out, slamming the door behind them.

"Who is he?" whispered Bernice.

"I don't know," he replied. *Perhaps he had something to do with the shooting last night.* "He looks hurt." Saul began to stand.

"Saul . . ."

He patted her hand. "I'll be all right, Bern. I need to see if I can help him."

* * *

Beirut

TANNER RETURNED TO THE COMMODORE AND FOUND A SEAT AT the bar.

It was crowded with midafternoon drinkers, mostly journalists who had already faxed or phoned in their stories. For an hour he mingled, talking shop until he developed a rapport with several of the newsmen, including a Spanish writer for Reuters. Over their third round of beers, Tanner mentioned hearing something about a cruise liner in trouble near the Canaries. "Aren't the Canaries part of Spain?" he asked. The writer's curiosity was piqued. He told Tanner to wait, then left the bar.

He was back in twenty minutes. "I don't know where you got your information, but you were right. They were just about to put it on the wire. A liner was hijacked south of Fueraventura. It sounds like hostages were taken."

TANNER RETURNED TO HIS ROOM. SAFIR WAS WAITING FOR HIM.

"Are you all right, *effendi?*" he asked. "You do not look well."

Briggs sat down on the edge of the bed. *Bear* . . .

He now knew what had gone wrong aboard *Tsumago* but not what had happened to Cahil. Either he was dead, or he was still aboard. The latter was implausible, the former unthinkable. Briggs clenched his hands and stared at them.

"*Effendi?* Are you—"

"Is there anything happening at the warehouse?"

"No. I checked with Sadiq an hour ago. They changed guards early this morning, but nothing since then. Not to worry, though. They are patient boys."

"I know they are." Tanner took out his belly wallet and counted out six one thousand dollar bills.

"No, *effendi*—"

"Safir, you're a good friend, and you have a family to feed." He opened Safir's palm and stuffed the bills into it. "One is for Sadiq, one for Ahmed, and the rest is for you."

"Briggs, this too much—"

"It's not nearly enough. Take it."

Safir nodded solemnly and gripped Tanner on both shoulders. "Thank you."

"You're welcome. Tell Sadiq I'll relieve him after sunset."

SHORTLY BEFORE SIX, THERE WAS A KNOCK ON TANNER'S DOOR. He opened the door, and Camille stepped in, gave him a lingering kiss, then pulled away. She touched his face.

"You look pale," she said.

"Pardon?"

"Your face."

He ran his hands over it. His mind felt fuzzy. "Oh."

"Is everything okay?"

"Everything's fine. Are you hungry?"

"Famished."

THEY ATE AND WATCHED THE SUNSET. TANNER LIT A HURRICANE candle on the table and poured them another glass of wine. "If I try very hard," Camille whispered, "I can almost pretend we're here on vacation. You are a handsome and dashing stockbroker, and I am a housewife."

Tanner smiled. "Really. And where do we live?"

"Akron, Ohio."

"Why there?"

"It is Middle America, isn't it? Average, pleasant, routine." She sipped her wine. "As for our six children—"

"Six!"

"—we left them with your mother, who does not like me at all, but she tolerates me because I make you happy and her grandchildren are beautiful. . . ." She trailed off.

"Almost but not quite," said Tanner.

She stood up and walked over to him "Take me to bed, Briggs."

* * *

AFTERWARD, THEY LAY TOGETHER, HER HEAD ON HIS CHEST.

"What are we going to do, Briggs?"

What *could* they do? Looking back, Tanner had known the answer from the beginning. He had to find Azhar, and he couldn't do it like this. He could feel himself closing down, narrowing.

"I don't think we have a choice," he said. "We can't help one another, and we can't stay together. Not here, not now."

"And later? Somewhere else?"

"I don't know."

She sat up and hugged her knees. "How can this be so easy for you?"

"It's not, Camille." *If you only knew,* he wanted to say. "That's how it feels."

"I'm sorry."

"Are you? I don't know if I believe you."

"Don't do this, Camille. You know—"

"No, Briggs, I don't. That's the problem. I don't know how you feel, and I don't think you do, either. It's easier to let it go . . . to tell yourself it's too complicated."

Briggs felt his heart thud. *Jesus.* He felt transparent.

"Many things are complicated," she said. "It doesn't make them impossible."

"What, then?"

"I don't know."

He laughed softly. "I thought I just said that."

"I'm a woman. I'm allowed to be fickle."

"Okay. In another time and place, who knows, but right now, we both have jobs to do. We can't be together here, Camille. You know that."

"I know, but . . . I just wish it was different."

"So do I."

Tanner drew her back down beside him, and they lay quiet for a while.

Finally she said, "I should go." She dressed in silence. Tanner called the front desk and ordered her a cab. At the door, she said, "I know we agreed not to talk shop, but I have to ask . . ."

"Go ahead."

"This thing you're working on . . . I must tell them something. They know it's about more than a missing agent. Should I be worried? Should *we* be worried?"

Tanner was surprised how easily the lie came, and he hated himself for it. "No, it's nothing to worry about."

She stared into his eyes. "Okay."

"I'll walk you downstairs."

"Please don't."

They embraced for several moments, and then she looked up and smiled bravely. "Another time, then?" she whispered.

"Another time."

She kissed him and left.

TANNER FELT EMPTY. WHAT HAD HE JUST DONE? WHAT ELSE could he have done?

He splashed cold water over his face, stared into the mirror, then dressed and took the elevator downstairs.

The lobby was bustling with journalists and photographers hurrying about, shouting, and talking on the phone. A pair of policemen stood near the reception desk. Tanner spotted the Spanish writer. "What's going on?" he asked.

"You haven't heard?"

"What?"

"There's been two more assassinations! It looks like Amal made good on its threat of retaliation for the mullah's murder."

"Against who?"

"The Maronites."

At first Tanner didn't understand. The ALC was responsible for the mullah. Why attack the Maronites? Then he remembered: Iraq had a long history of supporting Lebanese Maronite factions. Unable to get to the ALC directly, Amal had attacked one of its clients.

"You said two. Who else?"

"Hezbollah. Someone ambushed the operations chief and his family. There's fighting all over the city!"

*   *   *

As Tanner was making his way east toward the waterfront, Camille was walking into her apartment in Mar Elias. She closed the door and leaned against it. Outside, she could hear the occasional shriek of falling Katyusha rockets.

In the darkness she saw the answering machine light blinking. She walked over and hit Play. There was a double burst of static, followed by three more.

"Damn it, not now," she muttered.

She removed the microcassette and laid it on the coffee table. Next she went through the apartment, retrieving various items: a cassette player, notepad and pen, and a half-dozen books, each of which she opened to a specific page. Pen in hand, she inserted the cassette into the player and hit Play.

This time what came out was not static but rather a decelerated version of the burst voice transmission that had created it. She copied down the forty-two character groups, rechecked it, then began decoding. The method was a simple book code, old-fashioned but reliable. It took ten minutes.

She stared at the message. "No," she murmured. "God no. . . ." Frantic now, her hands trembling, she replayed the message, decoded it again. The result was the same. "You bastards!"

60

SHERABI BARELY HAD A CHANCE TO ACT ON STUCKY'S INFORMA-
tion before he was summoned to the prime minister's res-
idence. Including himself, sitting at the conference table
were the director of Aman (military intelligence), the director of *Shin Bet*, the minster of defense, and the IDF's
chief of staff. They represented only a fraction of the full
cabinet, which was Sherabi's first clue the matter was
grave.

The prime minister poked at the logs in the fireplace until
coffee was served, then took his seat. He came to the point
immediately: "I've just received a call from the American
president. He informed me there's a ship in the Mediterranean we should be concerned about.

"This is what we know: This ship's name is *Tsumago;*
she is manned by approximately three dozen terrorists;
these terrorists have taken one hundred Israeli hostages; and
the ship is carrying a medium-yield nuclear device."

The table erupted. Shouted questions overlapped one another. Sherabi was stunned. *A bomb! Had Stucky known?*
he wondered. *Had the bastard known?*

The tumult was interrupted by the prime minister tapping
his spoon on his cup. "First and foremost, this information
does not leave this room. If it does, as God is my witness,
I will have that man's balls in my pocket. Understood?"

He got nods all around.

"I will be asking for full disclosure from the Americans,
but for now, we will concern ourselves with only one goal:
rescuing the hostages and seizing the device. To that end,
here is the background.

"The terrorists claim to belong to a pro-Iraq group called the Arab Liberation Command. The Americans believe this is either true or it is a Syrian ruse.

"The hostages were taken last night from a cruise liner named *Valverde*.

"Also last night the Americans—unaware of the hostages—attempted an assault of *Tsumago*; when the hostages were discovered, the operation was aborted.

"The CIA is currently running an operation in Beirut to penetrate the group responsible, but they gauge its chance of success as low.

"The nuclear device is estimated to have a yield of twenty to thirty kilotons. The Americans feel it will either be transported to Lebanon for delivery to Syria or Iraq, or it will be used against this country outright."

The prime minister looked around the table. "We have three days before the ship reaches our shores. Comments?"

"How much can we trust this information?" the defense minister asked.

"We can't afford not to. General, tell me about military options."

"Limited," said the chief of staff. "We have no idea where the bomb is or how it's set to detonate. Nor do we know the location of the hostages. Unless something changes, any boarding attempt would risk detonation."

"Which would pollute half the Mediterranean," muttered the defense minister. "As if we don't have enough enemies. We would be a pariah!"

"Better that than have Iraq or Syria get the damned thing," said the director of *Shin Bet*.

"Let's save the speculation and debate for another time," said the prime minister. "The Americans have promised their full cooperation, and I suggest we use it. The chairman of the Joint Chiefs and the CIA's operations director are awaiting your calls. Questions?"

"I have one," the director of Aman said and turned to Sherabi. "How is it you missed this, Hayem? The CIA is running this operation in our own backyard, for God's sake."

In for a penny, in for a pound, Sherabi thought. "I knew about it. In fact, we assisted the CIA with its preparations."

"What!"

"We knew about the operation but not its purpose. It was a favor for an ally."

"Good God, you simply sat there—"

"We did nothing of the kind. In fact, we've mounted our own counter-operation. The CIA's agent is under surveillance as we speak. If he manages to penetrate the group, we will know immediately."

"Little good that will do us now."

"Enough!" the prime minister shouted. "Stop your bickering and hear me clearly: We will not allow this ship to reach our shores. And we will not allow the device to fall into enemy hands. Hostages or not, environmental disaster or not, that ship will be stopped."

Tsumago

Twenty-four hundred miles west of Tel Aviv, *Tsumago* **had** just passed the Strait of Gibraltar and entered the Mediterranean. Inside the forepeak, Cahil sat against the bulkhead and considered his options.

He could not stop the ship, of that he was sure. The crew was on full alert, and every vital area would be guarded. In fact, since nightfall he'd heard the regular clump of sentrys' boots on the deck above.

His supplies were meager. He had his Glock and three spare magazines; two pencil detonators, one flashbang, a penlight, and his tactical radio with a range of three to four miles.

It could be worse, he decided.

"Could be dead," he whispered. It was an old bit of grim humor he and Briggs shared. No matter how bad it got, there was always an upside. Sometimes you had to look very hard to find it, but it was there.

He wondered about Tanner. Strange how it worked out, he thought. Tanner a couple thousand miles away, and him here, both of them working to stop this damned ship.

They'd come through tougher spots. But those were different, weren't they? If they failed this time, it would cost not just their lives but hundreds of thousands of others as well.

Okay, time to set priorities. He knew what he *couldn't* do. He had to decide what he could do. First, he needed to get a feel for the ship and its crew. Second, try to make contact with the outside world.

Beirut

IT WAS ALMOST MIDNIGHT BY THE TIME CAMILLE REACHED THE Commodore.

It had taken an hour to find a taxi driver willing to travel north of the Museum Crossing, where the heaviest fighting had broken out, then another hour to cover the five miles to the hotel. Many of the streets were blocked by various factions, each trying to secure their own fiefdom. Smoke filled the air, and the horizon glowed orange with fire. Rifle muzzles winked from darkened windows. With each passing mile, the driver's protests grew louder, and Camille kept throwing money over the seat. She had to reach Tanner. *God, what had they done?* In truth, she knew exactly what they had done.

To keep an eye on its volatile neighbor to the north, Mossad runs a vast network of informants, most of them in Beirut and its southern districts, but some in the Syrian-controlled Bekka Valley and the Iranian-dominated Baalbek. Known as *falach,* these stringer agents supply Mossad with thousands of bits of information every year.

It was into this network that Tanner's identity had been leaked. By now hundreds of *falachs* in Beirut were circulating the word: *This man is an American CIA agent. He is looking for a man named al-Baz. He will be taken. The* falach *who identifies his captors and their location will be rewarded.*

Though Lebanon is awash in rumors of superpower plots, all are taken seriously, and none are ignored. It would take only hours for the leak to reach the city's largest factions and groups. Patrols would be sent out, informants probed.

By morning, no place would be safe for Tanner.

The taxi—sporting a dozen new dents and scratches—screeched to a stop in front of the Commodore. "Get out!" cried the driver. "Out, out!"

She threw another wad of bills over the seat, ran into the lobby, and up the stairs to Tanner's door. "Briggs, it's me! Open the door!"

The door opened, revealing a man: not Tanner. He looked familiar, but . . . "You're his friend, aren't you?" she said. "Briggs's friend?"

"Yes. My name is Safir. What—"

Camille shoved past him. "Where is he?"

"I do not know."

"You must!"

"Tell me what has happened."

Camille paced the room. "I can't explain, but I have to reach him!"

Safir stared at her.

Damn it, damn it, damn it! "Okay, I know why Briggs is here, and I know who he works for. And now so does everyone else."

"What do you mean?"

"They burned him," Camille cried. "Don't you understand? Whoever he's hunting, is hunting him."

Safir's eyes widened and he went pale. "Oh merciful Allah . . ."

"We have to help him! Do you know how to reach him?"

Safir hesitated.

"Look, don't trust me, I don't care. But if you can reach him, do it!"

"Very well." Safir pulled out a cell phone, dialed, and handed it to her.

The line was full of static, but she could hear the ringing: Four . . . five . . . six . . . *Come on, Briggs, pick up!* Twelve rings . . . thirteen . . .

"Are you sure this is the right number?" she said.

"Yes."

She let it ring three dozen times, and still Tanner didn't answer.

*   *   *

OAKEN WALKED TO THE PODIUM AND ARRANGED HIS NOTES. HE took a deep breath and looked out at his audience. *You better be right about this,* he thought.

James Talbot said, "Mr. Oaken, Leland says you have some information for us. As you know, we're in the middle of a crisis, so if you don't mind . . ."

"Certainly, sir."

"Mr. President, gentlemen, I believe I know the purpose behind *Tsumago*'s voyage and the bomb she's carrying. Quite simply, the operation is designed to facilitate a full-scale Syrian invasion of Lebanon and possibly of Israel itself."

Half a dozen voices began shouting at once. Dutcher had warned Oaken to expect such a reaction, but he was taken aback as he heard the words "preposterous" and "idiotic" amid the clamber of voices.

"Gentlemen!" the president called. "Gentlemen!" The voices died down. "Let's hear Mr. Oaken out."

"Thank you, Mr. President," Oaken said. "First, let's look at some facts:

"Syria is a dictatorship . . . a well-run, even somewhat benevolent dictatorship, but a dictatorship nonetheless. It's controlled by Bashar Assad and his inner circle, most of whom are members of the minority Alawite sect . . . first loyal to Bashar's father and now to him. There are plenty of groups who'd love to see Assad fall, and he knows it. His power base depends on keeping the country militarized, remaining at odds with Israel, and projecting an image of strength to the rest of the Arab world. Combine these with Syria's centuries-old ambition of re-creating a Greater Syria—an area that once encompassed present-day Syria, Lebanon, Jordan, and Israel—and you have all the ingredients for an invasion.

"For decades, Syria has occupied portions of Lebanon, which it sees as a stepping-stone for a Greater Syria. There are some 30,000 troops in the Bekka and another 8,000 or so around Beirut ostensibly serving as peacekeepers. Their real purpose has always been to attempt to control the government. If they can't own Lebanon outright, the next best thing is to have a malleable government at their disposal.

"So the question is, why hasn't Syria made a serious play for Lebanon? It has, in fact, several times in the last two decades. Each of those invasions failed because of three reasons: one, afraid to leave its eastern half vulnerable to Iraq, Syria never fully committed itself to the attempts; two, its intrusion was unwanted by almost all the major factions in Lebanon . . . in other words, the watershed motivation wasn't there; and three, the Israeli IDF had always been too quick and too effective in its reaction."

Oaken paused. "I think if you look at the current situation, you'll find those conditions have either been remedied, or they soon will be."

"Explain," said Dick Mason.

"Condition one: The Iraqi threat. Iran is running a large exercise along its border with Iraq. This is not a coincidence. It was designed to draw a reaction from Saddam, and it's working. Iraq has shifted a good portion of its troops east, away from the Syrian border, thereby taking the pressure off the Syrian army.

"Condition two: No watershed. Before undertaking this operation, I suspect General Khatib brushed up on his history. Specifically, World War II history and a small Polish town named Gleiwitz."

"Gleiwitz?" said the secretary of state.

General Cathermeier answered. "In 1939, Gleiwitz was a German town on the Polish border. Hitler needed an excuse to invade Poland, so he dressed up a squad of SS in Polish uniforms, had them take over the town's radio transmitter, then broadcast a call for all Poles to rise up and attack Germany. It gave Hitler the excuse he needed. The next day, he unleashed the Blitzkrieg."

"So what are you saying, that Syria will create its own Gleiwitz?"

"It's happening as we speak," replied Oaken. "In the last

four days there have been four assassinations, starting with a Shiite mullah, which the ALC has taken credit for. This was followed by a Maronite leader, ostensibly a revenge killing by Amal, then a Hezbollah operations chief. And last, just hours ago, the deputy head of the Phalange. Beirut is on the the edge of full-scale civil war. This will be Syria's excuse. They'll probably call it a 'peacekeeping intervention,' but it'll be an invasion, plain and simple."

The president said, "You mentioned three conditions."

"Yes, sir. The third involves the Israeli response. Syria knows it can't beat Israel in a head-to-head fight. It's tried in the past and has gotten mauled each time. It can't afford that again. They need a trump card," Oaken said. "*Tsumago*'s bomb is that card."

"You're saying they plan to use the bomb as an extortion tool?" said Talbot. "To keep Israel from responding to the invasion? That's absurd."

Oaken shook his head. "No, sir, not extortion. Decapitation."

"What?"

"A thirty-kiloton blast in Tel Aviv Harbor would cripple Israel's ability to make war. The seat of government would be all but destroyed. Over half the city's population—almost 150,000 people—would be killed outright. The IDF's Central and Southern Commands would be temporarily cut off from the Northern Command, the one responding to the invasion. By the time they recovered enough to fight, the Syrian Army would be so entrenched that little or nothing could be done about it."

No one spoke.

Finally Talbot said, "Well, that's a tidy little story, but it's flawed. First of all, why in God's name would Iran cooperate with Syria? You said it yourself: Assad is an Alawite Muslim. Alawites are considered heretics by most of Islam's major sects. You think Iran would jump into bed with a leader it considers a heretic?"

"Strange bedfellows," replied Oaken. "Iran tolerates Syria because of their mutual hatred for Iraq."

Mason said, " 'The enemy of my enemy is my ally.' "

"Exactly," said Oaken. "Syria is a thorn in Saddam's side, which makes Iran perfectly happy. Plus, if Saddam gets blamed for the bomb, the West would either decimate Iraq or go in and remove him from power, leaving a void for Iran to exploit. Don't forget, Iraq has a huge Shiite population that's been persecuted by Saddam. And what's Iran's expense? A few weeks of border exercises? It's a small price to pay to eliminate your worst enemy."

"Okay, let's suppose your scenario is viable," said the president. "Could Syria pull it off?"

"I believe so," Oaken replied. "First of all, Israel would be hamstrung, if not crippled. That means you can count out the Southern Lebanese Army and any other Israeli-friendly combatants. Next, Syria knows how *not* to invade Lebanon. Namely, a piecemeal commitment of its forces. Of course, I'm not an expert, but if an invasion happens, I expect the exercise group will make a quick turnaround, race in, and drive a wedge north of the Litani River. Meanwhile, the Bekka Task Force will move to encircle Beirut. Right there, you're talking four divisions: almost eleven hundred tanks and thirty-five thousand men."

Cathermeier said, "Reconnaissance shows the Bekka quiet and dug in."

"I think once things get under way, they'll suddenly become very mobile."

"How about it, General?" asked the president. "Is this feasible?"

Cathermeier thought for a moment. "With Israel out of the equation and Iraq preoccupied with Iran, it's very feasible. The movement he's describing could be completed in sixteen to eighteen hours. And with Damascus only fifty miles from Beirut, Syria could pour another four or five divisions into the country within days."

"What about the *Independence* battle group? Anything they could—"

"They don't have enough firepower . . . not conventional, at least. We'd be able to stall them, but only for a few hours."

"I don't understand," said Talbot. "Doesn't *Indy* have a Marine Amphibious Unit attached? What about that?"

"A MAU consists of about two thousand men with minimal armor support. Putting them on the beach might buy us another day, maybe two, but the casualties would be very high.

"You see, the kind of front we're talking about would be only thirty miles wide. Into that space Syria would be packing four motor rifle divisions, six hundred artillery pieces, two thousand APCs, and almost a thousand antiair defense units. Well, you've got one tough nut to crack."

"What about the Lebanese Forces?" asked Talbot. "They wouldn't just roll over."

"They're no match for the Syrians," replied Oaken. "As for the Lebanese Army, two-thirds of it would either refuse to fight or simply switch sides. The remaining third would be bottled up within hours.

"But that brings up something that's nagged me," Oaken continued. "Syria might be able to take and hold the ground, but it would be fighting a guerilla war against various factions for years to come. Either they're willing to pay that price, or they believe they can quash the opposition."

Cathermeier turned to the president. "Sir, I'm not completely convinced Oaken is right, but I'll tell you this: It's plausible. The big problem is the exercise group. Their fuel and support units are back in their depots in Damascus. If they move an inch, we'll know. Without fuel, any strike force wouldn't get ten miles into Lebanon."

Oaken nodded. "I agree. That's the other thing that doesn't fit. Either I'm wrong about this—which, believe me, wouldn't bother me a bit—or Syria has already solved the problem, and we're not seeing it."

The president was quiet for a few moments. "Mr. Oaken, I hope you're wrong, too, but if you're not, what's your best guess? When would they move?"

Oaken paused. "Two days, sir. If it's going to happen, that's the window."

*   *   *

WHILE THE SUN WAS SETTING IN WASHINGTON, NIGHT HAD FULLY
enveloped Beirut. Tanner crouched in an alley beside Martyr's Square, waiting for a chance to cross.

The city was under siege. From his vantage point, he
could see three buildings burning. A few blocks south, near
the University of Saint Joseph, a pair of machine gun–
equipped pickup trucks were exchanging fire with a Lebanese Forces APC. Muzzles flashed from darkened windows.
The snipers were at work. He'd been fired on twice in the
last hour. He prayed Sadiq was safe and cursed himself for
leaving the boy.

To the right, he saw a figure dash across the square. A
rifle cracked. The figure fell, lay still for a moment, then
began crawling. The rifle cracked a second time, and the
figure lay still. Tanner watched the body, somehow hoping
it would move but also praying it did not.

It wasn't far now. Once across Martyr's Square, he would
cut north across the Weygand. The bait shack was only 100
yards beyond that. He and Sadiq could hunker down, wait till
morning, then make their way back to the hotel.

Across the square he saw another figure inching forward
from an alley. The figure rose to a crouch. This was a
perfect chance, Tanner realized. Two targets: a fifty-fifty
chance.

The figure stood up and sprinted into the square. The
sniper opened fire. Bullets sparked off the concrete. Tanner
took off, head down, eyes on the opposite alley. The rifle
cracked again, then again. Bullets sparked the ground at his
feet. He dove headfirst into the alley, crawled to the wall,
pressed against it. He peeked out. The other runner lay
sprawled near the fountain.

HE REACHED THE WEYGAND AND SLIPPED INTO THE DITCH. THE
road was empty. A quarter mile to the east, he could see

the Lebanese Forces compound; under the glare of spot-lights, troops hurried in and out of the barracks.

Once sure all was clear, he sprinted across the road, down the ditch, and into a clump of bushes, where he fell prone and crawled to the wall of the bait shack. He wriggled under the collapsed timber and dropped feetfirst into the basement.

At the other end of the basement, moonlight streamed through the window. Sitting beside it was Sadiq's hunched form. *Thank God.* Tanner started forward.

Then stopped.

Why hadn't Sadiq turned around when he came in? Tanner slipped the Glock from his waistband. He whispered, "Sadiq."

The figure turned. Tanner saw the outline of a beard. He dropped to one knee, took aim, and fired twice, dropping the man. He sensed movement to his left. He spun again. A second figure was charging out of the darkness. He fired twice more, both rounds striking center mass, then rolled sideways as the body crashed forward.

He clicked on his penlight and scanned the basement. It was empty. He checked each man to ensure he was dead, then picked up one of the AKs and checked the magazine. It was full.

He'd been ambushed. A thousand questions raced through his head, the foremost being, *How? Bad luck or design?* Perhaps a better question was, *Who? And what had they done with Sadiq?* He thrust all that aside. He had to get out.

Suddenly the basement was flooded with bright light. Tanner heard the static squelch of a bullhorn, followed by a voice shouting in Arabic.

It was a question, he realized. The voice wanted a status report.

Tanner hesitated, then shouted back in Arabic: *Everything's okay!*

It was the wrong answer. The voice began shouting orders. Tanner was able to understand only one word, but it was enough: *Grenades.*

He dove for the ground, pulled a stack of boards on top of him, and covered his head. As if seeing it in slow motion, he saw three soda can–sized objects arc through the window, bounce off the wall, and roll toward him.

Flashbangs, he thought. They wanted him alive.

In a blaze of blinding light and noise, all three grenades exploded at once.

61

Tsumago

IT TOOK ONLY A FEW HOURS' OBSERVATION BEFORE CAHIL REALIZED the roving sentries were on fixed schedules. It was the first good news he'd gotten since boarding *Tsumago*. He was surprised at the oversight but only too happy to take advantage of it.

At three A.M., he climbed the anchor chain into the locker above. Wind whistled through the hawse pipe. The air was cool and tasted of salt. He shimmied out the hawse pipe until he could reach the lowermost handrail, gripped it with both hands, took a deep breath, then pulled his legs free and let them swing.

Below, he could hear the *swoosh-hiss* of the water breaking on the bow. He looked down. The bow lifted and plunged, sending up a cascade of spray. *Don't watch it,* he commanded. *Just go.*

Hand over hand, he slid aft until he'd covered thirty feet. He stopped and listened. Thirty seconds passed. His arms began to tremble. Then it came: the click of footsteps. *Keep walking, buddy . . . just keep walking.* The footsteps went past him and continued forward.

Cahil began counting. He had thirty-five seconds.

He pulled himself level with the railing, looked right. The sentry was through the forward arch. *Twenty-one, twenty-two . . .* Cahil rolled onto the deck, dashed to the superstructure, and scaled the ladder. On the second level, he stopped in a crouch beside the boat davit. *Thirty four . . .* Below him, the guard walked past the davit and through the aft arch.

He crawled to the mainmast, a tower of crisscrossed girders jutting eighty feet into the darkened sky. He looked up but could see nothing of the top.

He slipped inside the latticework and began climbing.

AFTER AN ASCENT THAT SEEMED TO TAKE AN ETERNITY, HE PULLED himself onto the radar platform and lay flat. The wind was fierce now, whipping him from all sides. The platform was crowded with a short ladder that led up to the radar dish, the ESM dome, and the radio antennas. Aside from the hum of the spinning dish, it was eerily quiet, and every few seconds he felt an extra gust of wind as the giant bowl swept past him.

He pulled out his tactical radio, his combat tool, and two lengths of wire he'd stripped from the anchor windlass's power conduits.

Working from feel alone, he removed the back of his radio, exposing the battery leads, then unscrewed the antenna cap and removed the plug. Next he unscrewed the ship's antenna base plate. Beneath it he found four coaxial cables, two red and two blue. Which was which? Two had to be for the signal feed, the other two for power. He touched the red cables; they were warm to the touch. *Bingo.*

Using the spliced wire, he connected his radio's battery to the antenna's power feed, then connected its antenna plug to the main signal feeds.

What he had just done, he hoped, was boost the tactical radio's power and range enough to reach *Ford,* which he prayed was still out there somewhere.

He slipped the headset over his ears, cupped his hand over the mike, and keyed the transmit button. "Cowboy, this is Sierra Actual, over. Cowboy, Cowboy, this is Sierra Actual. . . ."

Langley

MASON'S CONFERENCE TABLE WAS LITTERED WITH COFFEE CUPS and scraps of paper. Mason, Dutcher, and George Coates stared numbly at the floor-to-ceiling white board, which was covered with notes, diagrams, and flowcharts. *Too many what-ifs,* Dutcher thought.

"You know the funny thing?" Coates said. "We know the damned thing's aboard, but the truth is, we haven't got a shred of proof."

If not for the hostages, Dutcher thought, Cahil and his team would have solved that question. Without the bomb, the whole affair turned into a straightforward hostage situation. But Coates was right: The bomb was there.

"It's all irrelevant now," said Mason. "Bomb, hostages, or both, the Israelis aren't going to sit still for it. They'll hit *Tsumago* the second she crosses the twelve-mile line. Christ, what a mess."

His intercom buzzed: "Director Mason, I have General Cathermeier."

"Patch it through."

"Dick?"

"Go ahead, General. I have Leland Dutcher and George Coates here."

"I think you ought to get over here. *Ford*'s got something you'll want to hear. Somebody's using Sierra's call sign."

"FORD'S TAO HAPPENED TO BE ON DUTY IN WHEN IT CAME IN," Cathermeier said when they arrived. "He recognized the call sign."

"Is he still transmitting?" asked Dutcher.

"Yes. He says he's only got a few more minutes."

"Has he authenticated?" asked Coates.

"Nope. Said he couldn't."

Dutcher said, "But he's using Sierra Actual?"

"Right."

"It's Cahil," Dutcher said to Mason.

"Dutch, he could be compromised. Hell, it might not even be him."

"I'll know."

Mason hesitated, frowning.

"Dick, this is the break we need. If it's him, it means we've got eyes aboard. It's worth the risk."

Mason nodded. Dutcher grabbed the headset and sat down at the console. He keyed the mike. "Sierra Actual, this is Coaldust, over."

Static. Then: "Roger, Coaldust, this is Sierra."

"Sierra, interrogative: Recognize transmitter?"

"Affirmative."

"Say initials."

"Lima Delta."

Dutcher nodded to Mason. *Thank God.* "Say status, Sierra."

"Feet dry and secure. Another Sierra aboard, status unknown. Options limited. Request instructions."

Cathermeier said, "Ask him if he can confirm the device."

"Sierra, say mission status."

"Negative confirmation on Kickstand. Will attempt to confirm and contact this time tomorrow."

"What the hell is Kickstand?" asked James Talbot.

Coates replied, "The code word we assigned the bomb. Dutch, tomorrow could be too damned late."

Dutcher nodded "Sierra, request you expedite."

There was a long pause. Dutcher tried to imagine Cahil's predicament. Trapped aboard a ship loaded with terrorists and a nuclear bomb, he must be feeling utterly alone.

"Understood, Coaldust," said Cahil. "Monitor this channel. Sierra out."

Dutcher took off the headset. "Well, he knows what we want."

Mason nodded. "Now the question is, can he do anything about it?"

MASON'S LIMOUSINE WAS PULLING THROUGH LANGLEY'S MAIN gate when Dutcher's cell phone buzzed. "Leland Dutcher."

There was a short pause, then a voice said, "Sunset."

"Pardon me?" Dutcher said.

"Sunset."

For several seconds Dutcher was too stunned to speak. Mason and Coates were staring at him. He forced a smile and said, "I'm in the middle of something right now." He pulled out his day planner, consulted it, and recited a number. "Call me there in two hours . . . collect, if you'd like."

The line clicked dead.

"Problem?" asked Mason.

"Family situation."

Once in the parking lot, Dutcher said his good-byes, got in his own car, and pulled out. Once clear of the gate, he hit the speed dial.

Oaken answered on the third ring. "What's up?"

"Meet me at the office in an hour."

"THOSE WERE HIS EXACT WORDS?" OAKEN SAID WHEN DUTCHER explained.

"Yep."

"How about the voice?"

"He sounded local."

Sunset was one of six code words Dutcher and Tanner had agreed upon before Briggs left. It was also the one word Dutcher least wanted to hear. It meant Tanner had either been compromised or was in imminent danger.

ALMOST EXACTLY TWO HOURS AFTER THE INITIAL CALL, THE PHONE rang. Oaken checked it. "Secure line," he said. "The recorder's running."

Dutcher picked it up and accepted the collect charges from the operator. "Hello."

"Hello. . . . You told me to call this number."

"Yes. First of all, where are you calling from?"

"A pay phone."

"Good. What's your name?"

"Safir. I am a friend of Briggs's. He said if there was trouble, I should call."

The man sounded scared but under control. He also sounded genuine. If Tanner had been compromised, he would have first worked through his covers and then, if pressed further, would have offered a duress code word.

"Tell me what's happened."

"Last night he went to a place near the Qarantina. He was watching a warehouse there. After he left, I found out a bounty had been put on him. I went to find him, but he was gone. Two people saw a man matching his description being taken from a building near the Weygand."

"Is that all? Have you talked to anyone else?"

The man hesitated for a moment. "No."

"Okay. For now, don't do anything. You understand? Nothing. Stay away from the hotel. Find another phone booth and call this number in four hours. Okay?"

"Yes."

The line clicked dead.

"What, Leland?" asked Oaken.

"Somebody burned Briggs. He's gone."

Syrian Desert

FOURTEEN MILES WEST OF DAMASCUS IN A *WADI*, A SYRIAN ARMY officer stepped from under a camouflaged tarpaulin and checked his watch in the moonlight. It was time. He glanced up at the sky and wondered which of the millions of specks of light was the satellite that had just passed overhead. It didn't matter, he decided. The infernal machine and its prying eyes were gone. They were free to move.

He keyed his radio and gave the command. Within moments, a dozen diesel engines roared to life, then a dozen more, then another dozen, until the ground shook beneath his feet and he felt it in his belly. One by one, tarpaulins began falling away as soldiers jerked them down. They were efficient and quick, having practiced this very operation hundreds of times.

The officer nodded with satisfaction. Barring any problems, they would be moving within the hour.

Beirut

TANNER SENSED THAT HE WAS MOVING BUT LITTLE ELSE. HIS HEAD throbbed and his ears felt stuffed with cotton. He forced open his eyes and found himself staring at a cobblestone floor. They were moving. Why was the floor moving? No, it was him. He was moving. He could feel hands gripping his arms.

A wooden door filled his vision. Thick wood . . . black iron hinges. *Like a dungeon,* he thought dully. With a squeak, the door opened. He was shoved inside. Rough hands jerked his arms behind his back, and he heard the *click-click* of handcuffs.

Something slammed into the back of his head, and everything went black.

TANNER FORCED HIS EYES OPEN. ABOVE HIS HEAD, A SQUARE OF pale light swam into focus until it became a small, barred window. The sky was dark. Was it the same night or the next? *Concentrate, Briggs!* This was how it started, he knew. First comes the shock of capture, then the sensation of lost time, each spiraling and feeding on one another until you start to crumble. *Think it through.* It had to be the same night.

The door squeaked open. Four men dressed in fatigues, their faces covered in kaffiyehs, marched inside. The last one was carrying a bucket. He barked a command in Arabic. Then again. Tanner realized it was meant for him.

No Arabic, he thought. *Don't give them anything.*

"You! Sit up! Sit up!"

Tanner sat up.

The man stepped forward and emptied the bucket over Tanner's head. Instinctively, thinking it was water, he opened his mouth. It was urine. He spat and coughed, felt bile rise in his throat. The trio roared with laughter.

"You like? Taste good? Plenty more!"

Let it go, Tanner told himself. He felt himself withdrawing, narrowing. This was just the start. It would get worse. Nothing mattered now but staying alive. *Keep it together and stay alive.*

The trio stopped laughing. "Bucket" and the other two guards leaned their rifles against the wall. The fourth guard remained in the doorway, AK-47 at the ready. They formed a semicircle around him.

As if on silent command, they began kicking him. Boots pounded into his thighs, his back, his stomach. He curled into a ball and covered his head. A steel toe struck his spine, and he involuntarily arched backward. One of the men saw the opening and stomped his solar plexus. Briggs felt himself retch. He could hear them grunting and panting with exertion, urging one another on with shouts. One of the boots found its way through his arms, and Tanner heard a *crunch* and felt his nose shatter.

Chests heaving, they stared down at him for a moment, then picked up their rifles and stalked out. The door slammed shut.

THE LIGHT CONTINUED TO BRIGHTEN UNTIL THE FIRST RAYS OF SUN-light sliced through the window. He heard a skittering sound and turned to see a rat scurry along the wall and disappear through a crack in the stone. Despite himself, Tanner chuckled softly. Could be dinner soon, he thought. He pictured himself scrabbling around the cell trying to catch the rat and found himself laughing even harder.

The door swung open, revealing the same four guards. Bucket walked in carrying two lengths of rope, one of which was tied in a noose. Two of the guards pulled Tanner to his feet and shoved him against the wall. Bucket tossed the rope over the ceiling beam, slipped the noose over Tanner's head, and cinched it tight. He secured the second length of rope to Tanner's handcuffs and tied it off to a bolt in the baseboard.

Bucket barked a command.

Briggs felt the noose tightening, lifting him until he was standing on his toes. The rope was tied off. Bucket plucked the rope with his fingertips and nodded. He smiled at Tanner. "Tiptoes," he said. "Tiptoes."

In tradecraft jargon, what they were doing was called *scarecrowing*.

Already Tanner could feel the noose cutting into his skin.

In a few minutes his calves would begin to cramp. In an hour they would be on fire, and his ankle joints would stiffen until they felt encased in molten cement. Breathing would become a moment-by-moment struggle.

From the corner of his eye he saw a figure standing in the doorway. The figure was dressed all in black except for a white flour sack hood. Two eyeholes had been cut in the material. Tanner felt his heart thumping.

"Out!" ordered Bucket. "Out!"

The rest of the guards left.

The hooded man walked over and stopped in front of Tanner. The eyes flicked over his face. Tanner stared back. The eyes were blank and emotionless. *Like he's watching a lab experiment,* Tanner thought. He studied Tanner for a few more seconds, then turned for the door.

Briggs lifted his head enough to ease the tension on his larynx. "The boy . . ."

The man stopped.

"The boy," Tanner croaked. "What happened to the boy?"

The man tilted his head, then looked to Bucket, who walked over and whispered something. "The boy is safe," the hooded man said. "We sent him home."

With that, he walked out. The door slammed shut.

Tanner felt sick to his stomach. He recognized the voice. It was Abu Azhar.

"THEY'VE MADE CONTACT," DICK MASON SAID, WALKING INTO THE Oval Office.

The president said, "How?"

"A goddamned cell phone call to the *Jerusalem Post*."

Mason slid a CD into the player on the coffee table and pressed Play. The voice spoke Arabic-accented English. "Attention government of Israel . . ."

"Interesting he chose English," said Talbot. "Who—"

"Audio says it's al-Baz," Mason replied.

". . . this is the Arab Liberation Command speaking. By now you know we are holding one hundred Israeli prisoners of war. Currently they are safe and unharmed aboard our ship, which is en route to your shores.

"Our demands are as follows: In exchange for the safe return of our prisoners, the government of Israel will fully and immediately cede the West Bank and Gaza Strip territories to Palestinian authority. Furthermore, these territories will be formally recognized by the government of Israel and the United Nations as states of a sovereign nation. These demands are not open to negotiation.

"Any attempt to attack, board, or otherwise molest this ship will be considered an act of aggression and will be responded to with maximum retribution. In addition, the passage of any military unit of any nation within twenty nautical miles of this ship will result in the execution of ten prisoners.

"Once this vessel is safely docked in Tel Aviv Harbor and Israeli forces—both political and military—have fully withdrawn from Palestine territories, and once the United

Nations has taken steps to ensure there will be no more interference by Israel or its allies in Palestinian concerns, the Arab Liberation Command will release unharmed its remaining prisoners.

"In conclusion, the Arab Liberation Command will offer a demonstration of its resolve. You will dispatch an unaccompanied, unarmed helicopter from Palermo to this vessel's position by no later than noon, Palermo time. This helicopter will contain one pilot and a two-person news crew with a video camera. If this demand is not met, we will execute ten prisoners.

"Make no attempt to contact this vessel. That is all."

Mason switched off the player. "The Israelis have managed to suppress it, but that won't last for long. They're handling the helicopter. We're monitoring the Iraqi response, but it could go either way. Even if this is a Syrian operation, Saddam might be inclined to go along for glory's sake."

"Interesting there was no mention of the bomb," said Cathermeier.

"They're holding it as a bargaining chip," replied Talbot.

"I disagree," said Dutcher. "If they plan to use it, why announce it? Why let the Israelis prepare? For all al-Baz knows, it's still a secret."

"Good point," said Mason. "That exclusion zone is a smart move."

"Why?" asked the secretary of state.

Cathermeier replied, "It guarantees the story will get out. To maintain that kind of zone, we're going to have to surround *Tsumago*. By morning, the whole world will know about this."

"Why only twenty miles, though? Why not farther out?"

"It'll let them keep an eye on the escorts, but it's far enough they'll have plenty of warning before an attack."

The president looked at Dutcher. "Dutch, what about your two men?"

"Cahil is trying to locate the bomb. As for Tanner . . ." He glanced at Mason and saw nothing on the DCI's face. There were only a few people who could have burned Tan-

ner, and Mason was one of them. Would Dick do such a
thing? Either way, he couldn't afford to tip his hand. "As
of his last transmission, no luck. Asseal's been taken, but
given the chaos in Beirut, tracking him is going to be
tough."

"We're just about out of options," said the president. "If
an invasion is coming, we've got no way to stop it, and we
sure as hell can't back out. The whole region would crumble."

No one spoke. Dutcher knew the president was facing a
terrible decision, and in this case there were no lesser evils
from which to choose. Whichever way he went, lots of
people were going to die.

"Gentlemen, I've been talking with the Israeli prime minister. We've reached an understanding. However unlikely,
if we manage to confirm the bomb is *not* aboard, this will
be treated as a hostage situation. It will be handled by the
Israelis.

"If there's any doubt about the bomb, or we get confirmation, *Tsumago* won't be allowed within Israel's twelve-
mile limit. Hostages or not, she will be sunk. If that
becomes necessary, I've decided that we will carry out the
attack."

Talbot blurted, "Mr. President, that would be political
suicide! With the election next year—"

"This isn't about politics, Jim. This is *our* mess. *Our*
responsibility. I won't ask the Israelis to kill a hundred of
its own citizens and cause the worst environment catastrophe in history. I won't do it."

Dutcher felt a wave of admiration for the president. He
was ignoring political considerations and simply doing the
right thing. At what price, though? Talbot was right: If the
worst came to pass, the president would be finished—as a
leader and as a man.

"This is my decision," the president continued. "There
will be no more discussion. I've asked General Cathermeier
to put together a plan. Go ahead, General."

"The unit we've chosen will be on station in three
hours," said Cathermeier. "The moment *Tsumago* crosses

Israeli's territorial boundary, we can put her on the bottom in less than two minutes."

Beirut

SAFIR WALKED INTO THE CAFÉ, SAW CAMILLE IN THE CORNER booth, and sat down.

"Did you reach Briggs's people?" she asked.

Safir nodded. "They asked me to try to find him."

"Do they know about me?"

"No. It is against my better judgment, but I said nothing." Camille had told Safir what she was; she suspected it was only his loyalty to Tanner that kept him from running.

"Safir, I know it's hard, but you have to believe me: I'm doing this for Briggs, not for my country. My people don't even know I've been in touch with him."

Safir considered this. "They may kill you for such a thing."

"I know."

"Do you love him?"

"Yes. Very much."

"As do I. He is a good friend. So what do we do?"

Tsumago

DEEP INSIDE THE SHIP, SAUL AND BERNICE SAT ON EITHER SIDE of Sludowski, who lay coughing and shivering. In addition to numerous cuts and bruises, the young man had been shot twice, once in the thigh and once in the lower back. This wound worried Saul most.

Bernice touched Slud's forehead. "He's burning up, Saul."

"I know. He's bleeding inside."

"Can't you do something?"

"He needs surgery, Bernice. There's nothing I can do here."

"He's so young."

"Yes." He was almost the same age as their own son.

Weinman felt a wave a sadness. Would they ever see their family again?

He stood up. "Wait here, Bernice."

He made his way to the door and pounded on it. "Hello! Hello out there! Please, we have a very sick man here!"

To Weinman's surprise, the bolt clicked back and the door swung open. A man with a handlebar mustache was standing in the doorway.

"Thank God," Saul said. "The man there, he is very ill. He needs help."

The man nodded to the guards, who put down their rifles and pushed past Weinman. They marched through the space, kicking and shouting at passengers too slow in moving. When they reached Bernice, they shoved her aside, lifted Sludowski, and began dragging him toward the door.

"Be careful, please," said Weinman. "He—"

"Do not concern yourself with him," said the man.

"He's very sick. He needs surgery."

"He will receive the appropriate treatment, old man. I suggest you concern yourself with your own safety."

WITH NOTHING TO DO DURING DAYLIGHT HOURS, CAHIL LISTENED to the waves pound the hull. In the distance he heard a faint thumping. He strained to hear. The sound increased until he recognized it: helicopter rotors. He climbed up the ladder, cracked the hatch, and peered out. A trio of men stood on the forecastle. At their head stood Mustafa al-Baz.

The beat of rotors grew louder until a white-and-blue-striped helicopter stopped in a hover off the port railing. Leaning from the door were two men, one holding a video camera, the second a microphone.

"What the hell . . ." Cahil whispered.

Al-Baz gestured at someone out of Cahil's view. Seconds later, two crewmen walked forward, dragging a man between them. *Slud!* He was badly beaten and barely conscious. They dropped him, then reached down and jerked him to his knees. Slud swayed from side to side, head lolling as he squinted up at the helicopter.

Then Cahil realized what was happening. *No, Christ, please don't. . . .* He drew the Glock from his holster. He counted targets: Five, all armed, the closest was forty feet away. He gripped the hatch and readied himself. Then stopped.

Even if he survived and managed to get Slud overboard, what then? What about the bomb? How many lives depended on his staying aboard and out of sight?

Even as all these thoughts raced through Cahil's brain, he watched al-Baz draw his pistol, step forward, and place it against Slud's temple.

No!

The *pop* sounded like a firecracker. Slud's head snapped sideways, and he toppled onto the deck.

63

Beirut

TANNER COULD ONLY GUESS AT THE TIME. SLIPPING IN AND OUT of consciousness, he watched the sun's rays shorten on the floor and draw up the wall. Noon or close to it. God, he hurt. . . .

The noose had already chafed his throat raw, and every time he moved, it felt as though the wound was being scraped with a wire brush. For the first two hours he had managed to remain on his toes without much problem, so breathing had been easy. At the end of the third hour, however, his calves began cramping, and he had to clench his jaw against the pain. His muscles began twitching violently. Halfway into the fourth hour, he began experimenting, taking a deep breath, then lowering himself for a few seconds at a time. It only made the pain worse when he raised himself up again. His head began to swell and pound. Blood rushed to his face. He felt like he was drowning.

Now, in what he guessed was the fifth hour, his body was almost numb, which scared him more than the pain. It was now that he could strangle himself without realizing it. But they wouldn't allow that, would they? The questioning hadn't started yet. Though he saw no one, he knew a guard was probably watching.

After a time, the numbness became almost soothing. The pain faded until it hovered at the edges of his consciousness. There was no contrast, no good against which he could measure the bad. It was then his mind suddenly cleared and the questions flooded in.

Who had burned him? What had happened to Bear? How far away was *Tsumago?* He tried to remember what day it was. By now, she was probably somewhere the Mediterranean, but where? Couldn't be more than two days away.

As for the first question, he had some ideas. Safir hadn't done it; he was too loyal. That left Stucky or Camille. As the old homicide rule went, both had motive and opportunity. The method seemed clear: Just as they had used Asseal, somebody was using him, probably tracking him through Mossad's network of stringer agents. How quickly would they find him? And how soon after that would the Israelis send in a team?

Outside, boots clumped down the corridor. *Time for round two,* he thought dully. He almost welcomed the pain; it would help him stay focused.

The bolt clicked back. The door swung inward. Two guards walked in, one carrying a square wooden table, the other a pair of chairs. They arranged the table and chairs, then withdrew to the corners.

Bucket walked in, followed by the hooded man Tanner believed to be Azhar. He sat down in the chair, folded his hands, and stared at the wall. Tanner could see the hood's mouth hole sucking in and out.

Bucket loosened the noose from around Tanner's neck and lifted it away. Tanner knew what was coming, tried to brace himself for it, but as his full weight came down, his knees buckled, and he collapsed. Pain shot up his legs and into his lower back. He felt his bladder start to go. He clenched his jaw against it. *No no no. . . .* The room swam around him.

Azhar's gaze remained fixed on the wall.

Bucket dragged Tanner to the opposite chair, plopped him down, and placed a glass of water before him. It was only then that Briggs noticed the leather wrist straps bolted to the tabletop. The wood beneath was scarred and flecked with brown stains.

"Drink," Azhar said.

Tanner didn't hesitate. As he drank, he could feel the scabs on his throat splitting open. When he was done, Bucket took the glass away. *They're very careful,* Tanner thought. No potential weapons, no missteps.

"How do you feel?" Azhar asked. "Are you in pain?"

Tanner saw no point in lying. "Yes."

"If you want it to end, you will answer my questions. Do you understand?"

"I understand."

"If you do not answer, things will go worse for you. Do you understand?"

Tanner nodded.

"Why are you here?"

Against all his training Tanner had already decided his course: If he had any chance to not only survive this but to also stop *Tsumago*, he had to go straight at Azhar. "I came to find you," Tanner said.

"Why?"

"Not with the others here. Order them out, and I'll tell you."

"You think I am stupid?" Azhar said. "They stay. What do you know of me?"

"Dismiss them, and I'll tell you," Tanner said.

Azhar half-bolted from his chair. "Answer me!"

"Once we're alone. Why does that frighten you? What can I do?"

Azhar sat back down. Through the hood's eyeholes, he could see Azhar's left eye twitching. He barked a command.

Bucket grabbed Tanner's hands, forced each of them under a leather strap on the tabletop, and tightened the wing nuts until his palms were pressed flat.

Azhar barked another command. The word sounded vaguely familiar to Tanner, and it took several moments to place it. *Oh, God* . . .

Bucket stepped forward. Clenched in his right hand was a hammer; the head was flecked with what looked like blood and matted hair.

"I order you again," said Azhar, "answer my questions."

Tanner took a deep breath. "When we're alone."

Azhar nodded to Bucket. With an evil grin, he splayed Tanner's left little finger apart from the others and pressed it to the wood. Tanner felt his stomach boil. He swallowed hard, and he kept his eyes locked on Azhar's.

"Well?" Azhar asked Tanner.

Tanner shook his head.

"Break it."

Tanner inhaled and set his jaw. As if seeing it in slow motion, he watched the hammer arcing downward. He heard a dull *crunch-pop*. White-hot pain exploded in his hand. He screamed and doubled over. Bile filled in his mouth. He swallowed it, tried to take a breath. In his ears he heard what sounded like distant cannon fire, and it took him a moment to realize it was his own heartbeat.

Bucket pushed him upright.

"You have an hour to decide," Azhar said. "After that I will break all your fingers, then move to your ankles, and then your knees."

Bucket released Tanner's hands, cuffed them behind his back, and shoved him against the wall. Tanner barely felt the noose slip back over his head. Black spots danced before his eyes. He heard the rope creaking, then felt the noose bite down.

Azhar looked up at him. "I will get what I want," he said. "I promise, before this day is over, you will answer my questions."

Tanner stared back into Azhar's eyes. As before, he saw nothing. *Like a doll's eyes,* Tanner thought. *Empty.*

Azhar turned and walked out.

THEY RETURNED AN HOUR LATER, BUT TO TANNER IT COULD HAVE been minutes or days. He felt fuzziness creeping back into his thought processes. His shattered finger throbbed in time with his heartbeat, and he could feel it pressing against his other hand, swollen and hot. Sights and sounds dimmed around him. A breeze blew through the window. It felt cool.

Stay alive! You'll either reach him, or you'll die. But talk only to him . . . no one else. If he managed to turn Azhar, there was no telling who in his group would stay loyal and who would rebel.

The door creaked open. He kept his eyes closed. The

noose slackened. Rough hands untied him, pushed him into the chair, and shoved his wrists under the straps. He opened his eyes and saw Azhar sitting across the table.

"Have you had a chance to reconsider?"

"I've been preoccupied."

Azhar said nothing; he gestured to Bucket.

Bucket stepped forward, splayed Tanner's ring finger apart from the others, and smashed it with the hammer. Briggs screamed and hunched over. Bucket shoved him upright.

They won't stop. They'll keep going until I die or I break. There had to be a way to reach him. Then he remembered. "My lugg—" The sound stuck in his throat; he coughed and tasted blood. "My luggage," he rasped.

"What?" asked Azhar.

"My luggage. Have you searched my room?"

Azhar looked at Bucket, who shook his head.

"The Commodore," Tanner whispered. "In the side pocket of my duffel, you'll find a black box. Bring it."

"I have no time for games—"

"No games. Get the box."

"If you're lying, you'll wish you were dead."

"I know."

Azhar was silent for several moments. The cloth sucked in and out, in and out. "Go to the hotel, bring the box. In the meantime, put him back on the wall."

For the next hour, perhaps two, Tanner stood against the wall gasping for breath, his ankles and legs burning. Azhar sat at the table and stared straight ahead, not even flinching as mortar rounds exploded outside.

Tanner could feel a knot of fear in his belly. *What if I'm wrong about him?* If this gambit failed, Azhar would surely kill him. He imagined Abu placing the gun against his skull and felt tears welling in his eyes.

THE DOOR SWUNG OPEN. BUCKET WALKED IN, WHISPERED TO Azhar, and placed a small black box on the table. "Get him down." Once Tanner was again secure in the chair, Azhar asked, "Is this it?"

"Yes. Open it."

Azhar looked at Bucket, who said, "It is safe."

Slowly, Azhar drew the box to him, unhooked the clasp, and lifted the lid. For a full thirty seconds he stared at the contents. His eyes blinked once.

Using both hands, Azhar lifted out the carved cedar camel. Across its hump was draped a square of turquoise cloth. The bit was made of a tiny gold nail, the bridle of gold chain. Azhar cradled it like a wounded bird.

"My name is Briggs," Tanner whispered. "Briggs Tanner. You gave that to me. It had been in your family for ten generations. You told me it was carved from the same cedar that was used to build your ancestral home in Afqa . . ."

Staring at the camel, Azhar shook his head.

"Yes, Abu! You know me."

"This is a trick! You are lying!"

"No!" Tanner said. "When you gave it to me you told me—"

"Shut up!"

"—that it had been given to you by your father, and to him by his father—"

"No!" Azhar pounded the table. He returned the camel to the box and closed the lid. "Put him back up."

The guards grabbed Tanner.

"No, Abu! You know me! My father's name is Henry. He taught at American University. My mother is Irene. We lived here, on the Corniche! You *know* me!"

"*Shut up!* Silence him!"

Bucket slammed his rifle butt into Tanner's groin. The air blasted from his lungs. He dropped to his knees. Another guard stuffed a rag in his mouth, pulled him upright, and slammed him against the wall. The noose was cinched tight.

Azhar turned in the doorway. "We've wasted enough time with him," he said. "Beat him. Beat him until he pisses blood."

64

FULL-SCALE BATTLES INVOLVING HUNDREDS OF FACTION SOLDIERS and militiamen had erupted across the Green Line. Artillery duels sparked fires in dozens of districts and they burned out of control as responding fire crews found nearly every street barricaded. Camille and Safir spent the day picking their way through the rubble-strewn neighborhoods, probing the few *falaches* in her network. No one had seen Tanner. Camille felt hope slipping away.

Late in the afternoon, she met Safir in the Atlas Hotel's coffee shop. As he sat down, she saw his clothes were torn and he was limping. "Are you all right?" Camille asked.

"Yes. I had trouble at the Museum Crossing. The fighting is very bad."

Just then the windows of the coffee shop rattled from a nearby explosion. Several people ran past on the sidewalk, several of them women clutching babies.

"Everyone is shooting at everyone. The PLO against the Maronites; the Phalange against the Shiites; the Shiites against the Lebanese Forces. I have never seen it like this."

"Worse than eighty-two?"

"Very much worse."

A smiling waitress came and took their orders.

My God, just another day in Beirut, Camille thought. Like the waitress, the shop's patrons seemed perfectly at ease, laughing and joking as they ate, oblivious to what was happening outside. She suddenly felt a surge of admiration for these people. What strength it must take to live here.

"I found someone who claims to know where Briggs is," Safir said.

"What? Where?"

"Karm el Zeitoun. The man claims he saw a gray Volvo pull up to a building and drag a man inside. The description sounds very close."

Karm el Zeitoun was a neighborhood in East Beirut near the Beirut River. And the gray Volvo . . . Was it the same one that followed her and Asseal? she wondered.

"There is a problem, however," said Safir.

"What?"

"He's already passed along the location to your people."

Oh God. "Do you know this neighborhood?"

"Yes."

"Take me there."

Tsumago

FOR A LONG TIME AFTER THE MURDER, CAHIL SAT IN THE LADDER shaft and stared out the hatch at Slud's body. It lay there for an hour before two of the crew appeared, lifted it between then, and heaved it over the side. One of them gave a comical wave as the surging water took it away. *Slud.* . . .

Finally, Cahil crawled back down the ladder and forced his mind back on track. Where was the bomb?

He closed his eyes and tried to recall what he knew about *Tsumago*. Certainly the cargo holds were the most likely hiding places, but then again, the bomb was probably no larger than a footlocker. It could be anywhere.

An image drifted into his mind. During his and Tanner's search, the forward hold had been half-covered with cables and scaffolding. Even so, Cahil distinctly remembered the layout: Six inset holds in a three by two pattern, all seated inside a larger hold. *Six inset holds . . .*

He scrambled up the ladder and peeked out the hatch. The main hold—whose hatch sat on a raised combing about ten inches off the deck—dominated the center of the forecastle, leaving only a small walkway around its edges.

"That's it," Bear whispered.

Instead of six inset hatches, there were only four. What had happened to the other two, and what were they doing with the space?

Tel Aviv

"WE HAVE A LOCATION," SHERABI TOLD STUCKY. "A BUILDING IN East Beirut near the river. We're moving tonight."

Stucky nodded solemnly; it was all he could do to keep from smiling. *Payback is a bitch, ain't it, Briggs?* His only regret was he wouldn't be there to see it. That would be the icing on the cake. Otherwise, things were working out perfectly. They would get Azhar and stop *Tsumago* . . . and Tanner would die in the fireworks.

"Who're you sending?" Stucky asked.

"It depends. The chief of staff may make that decision."

"Bullshit, Hayem. It's your op."

"We'll see. Who knows, with luck we may be able to even rescue your agent."

Asshole. The Jew was playing games. If an IDF unit such as Sayeret Golani or Flotilla 13 were sent instead of Mossad's own Unit 504, Sherabi would have no control over their orders.

"He may still be alive, you know," Sherabi said.

"Could be," Stucky replied. "Either way, I'm sure your people will do the right thing, just like I did the right thing when you needed help. You're not forgetting that, are you?"

"Nor have I forgotten you failed to warn us about the bomb."

"Jesus Christ, I told you: I didn't know!" Stucky put his palms on Sherabi's desk and leaned forward. "Let's stop fucking around. Do you know what'll happen to me if my government finds out I've cooperated with you?"

"It would be bad for you."

"No shit. But not just for me: For *us.* My getting nailed would put a real damper on our future relationship."

"I see what you mean."

"Glad to hear it. You just make sure it's your people who go tonight."

White House

THE PRESIDENT STRODE INTO THE ROOM. "LET'S SEE IT, DICK."

Mason aimed a remote at the wall-mounted TV, and the screen filled with an elevated view of *Tsumago*'s bow. In the background they could hear the beating of the helicopter's rotors. Two men walked onto the forecastle, followed by a second pair dragging Sludowski's inert figure.

"Al-Baz?" the president asked.

"Yes, sir."

In five seconds it was over. Mason clicked off the TV.

"Did he have a family?" the president whispered.

"A wife and a little boy," replied Cathermeier. "Four years old."

"Do they know yet?"

"The CNO is on his way to see them personally. Hopefully, he'll get there before the footage goes public. It's already getting a lot of play in Europe. By evening, the whole world will know what's going on."

"Where is *Tsumago* now?"

"Two hundred miles southeast of Sicily. Twenty-two hours from Tel Aviv."

"Is the exclusion zone in place?"

"I've ordered an SAG split from the battle group," Cathermeier replied. "Two frigates—including *Ford*—a cruiser, and a Burke destroyer. They'll be on station in a couple hours. If we need it, *Indy*'s Combat Air Patrol is only six minutes away."

"We can't have so much as a seagull getting inside that zone, General, or we'll be fishing corpses out of her wake."

"Yes, sir."

"Where's the *Indy* group now?" asked Dick Mason.

"Running racetracks twenty miles off Beirut. We're flying round-the-clock CAPs—Tomcats and Hornets—that can be over the beach in two minutes. As of an hour ago,

recon flights show the Syrian exercise group still moving
north toward Damascus."

"The Bekka?"

"Quiet."

"Good. Dutch, what about your man aboard *Tsumago*?"

"We expect him to make contact tonight, sir."

USS *Minneapolis*

AS CRYPTIC AS HE'D FOUND HIS NEW SAILING ORDERS, CAPTAIN
Jim Newman complied and turned *Minneapolis* from its
sector ahead of *Indy* and headed south. Best submerged
speed for his boat was thirty-plus knots, so the 130-mile
transit had taken just over four hours.

In his twelve years as a sub driver Newman had commanded plenty of attack boats, but none compared to this
688 Los Angeles boat, especially *Minneapolis*, which, as
luck had it, was named after his hometown.

Minneapolis was known as an improved 688, having
been refitted with vertical launch Tomahawk missiles to
complement her Harpoon antiship birds, SUBROCs (submarine rockets), and standard MK 50 torpedoes. The 688
boats were the most feared hunter submarines in the world;
they were fast, deadly, and so quiet they were known col-
loquially as "moving holes in the water."

Minneapolis's Tomahawks and Harpoons could destroy
land targets, sink ships, crater runways, and if the worst
came to pass, take out strategic targets. Of her fifteen Tomahawks, four were armed with tactical nuclear warheads, a
fact never far from Newman's mind.

After four hours of running a lazy ten-knot racetrack at
200 feet, Newman's executive officer, Lieutenant Randy
Stapes, walked over to the blue-lit tactical table.

"Flash traffic, Captain. Straight from the CNO."

"Pardon?"

"I checked, sir. It's legit."

For *Minneapolis* to receive orders directly from the chief
of naval operations, at least four separate commands had to
have been circumvented, including the commander of the

entire Sixth Fleet. Newman felt a sinking in his belly.

He took the message, scanned past the header, and read:

MINNEAPOLIS TO LOITER IN DESIGNATED SECTOR (REF A) UNTIL FURTHER NOTICE. USING COORDINATES IN REF B, ESTABLISH AND MAINTAIN TRACK ON CARGO VESSEL TSUMAGO AND BE PREPARED TO SINK SAME WITH MULTIPLE HARPOON ATTACK UPON ORDERS FROM THIS COMMAND. UPON EXECUTE ORDER, MINNEAPOLIS TO ENSURE TARGET DOES NOT ENTER TERRITORIAL WATERS OF NATION OF ISRAEL. TARGET EXPECTED TO ARRIVE MINNEAPOLIS RANGE IN TWENTY (20) HOURS.

"Holy cow," murmured Newman.

He handed the message to Stapes, who read it. "Sir, isn't this the ship that—"

"Yes, it is." Like the rest of the *Indy* group, *Minneapolis* had gotten the news about the hostages. "And now they want us to kill it."

Beirut

UNTIL THE MOMENT HE'D OPENED THE BOX, ABU AZHAR HAD LIVED two separate lives, one he hadn't let himself remember for fifteen years and another he wished was over. The end of his first life and the start of his second had happened on the same day: the day he learned his little girl—their miracle—was dead.

Whether from grief or hatred or the ache that seemed to squeeze his heart a little tighter every day, Azhar went insane. Every memory was forgotten. Every person he knew was dead to him. Friends saw the change in him nearly overnight. His hair turned white, and his face turned to stone. The warm and gregarious teacher who laughed often and easily was gone, and in his place was a husk of a man.

Azhar sat in his room—a spartan affair with a wooden table and a cot—and stared at the box. The figurine seemed so familiar, as did the American's name: Tanner . . . the ghost of a memory from another life. *"My father is Henry. . . . You gave that to me. . . . You know me!"*

"How can I know you?" Azhar whispered.

He'd approached but never crossed this threshold many times. He would see a familiar face on the streets of Beirut, and a distant voice would whisper a name or recount a party or a vacation. But he would dismiss it and walk on. Rarely did those former friends recognize him, further proof the whispering voice was wrong.

"My name is Briggs! You gave that to me. . . . It had been in your family for ten generations . . . carved from the same cedar. . . ."

"Afqa," he murmured. "Afqa."

How could the American have known his birthplace? If in fact he was CIA, they would have done their research. They are like that, the Americans, with their computers and spy networks and conspiracies. They found out about the ship, invented this fantasy, and sent this man to stop him.

Azhar reached out and touched the box. *A silly trinket, nothing more.* But the whispering voice was still talking to him: *"My name is Briggs Tanner. . . . My father is Henry. . . . You know me! You . . ."*

"No," Azhar said. He slid the box away from him. "No."

65

Beirut

DESPITE ALL HIS PREVIOUS SELF-ASSURANCES, TANNER NOW RE-
alized that, in his heart, he'd never been sure he could kill
Abu Azhar. But with each passing minute, as he stood half-
hung, gasping for every breath, his legs sticky with his own
urine, he realized he had no other choice. The Azhar he
knew was gone.

But would he get the chance to do it before they killed
him? They'd almost succeeded earlier. Four of them, each
armed with a sand-filled radiator hose, had taken turns on
his back and legs until he passed out.

He slowly flexed his body, searching for damage. His
breathing was wheezy, and with each breath he felt a stab
of pain in his side. They'd broken a couple of his ribs. He
felt a dripping sensation on his legs. He craned his neck
down. The stone beneath his feet was puddled with pink
urine.

They were killing him. With that thought, everything
snapped into focus.

He would gather his strength and watch and wait until
they got lazy. The moment would come, he knew, but it
would be very brief, and he would have to be very fast.
All he would need was a few seconds.

The door's bolt clicked back, and it swung open. From
the corner of his eye he saw a single figure standing on the
threshold. It was Azhar. The hood was gone.

Tanner hardly recognized him. Though the same age as
his father, Azhar looked twenty years older. His hair was
coarse and white, as was his mustache. He seemed shorter
as well, stooped like an old man. Tanner was most surprised

by his eyes. Seeing them through the hood's eyeholes had been deceptive; they were not merely emotionless, there was nothing there at all.

Then Tanner noticed the knife in Azhar's hand. He felt his heart stutter. This was it. He'd failed; Azhar was going to do it himself. He steeled himself for it.

Azhar walked forward and stopped in front of him. He studied Tanner's face. Without so much as the trace of an expression, he pressed his palm under Tanner's chin and pushed his head backward. The knife came up. Tanner felt the blade against his throat. He sucked in a breath, held it, closed his eyes. There would be little pain, he knew, just a sting and then a flood of warmth, and then—

Azhar's arm flashed forward. Tanner heard a *twang* and then he was falling. Azhar caught him and lowered him to the floor.

AZHAR LEFT AND RETURNED WITH A FIRST AID KIT, A TOWEL, A clean white *dish-dash* robe, and a basin filled with warm water. He sat at the table and stared at his hands while Briggs—still cuffed—stripped off his clothes, then washed and dried himself.

Tanner felt a dozen emotions at once: relief, confusion, sadness. He was too numb to sort them out, so he finished drying himself and slipped on the *dish-dash.*

Azhar gestured him to the chair. "Please sit."

Tanner hobbled over and sat down. Azhar opened the first aid kit and went to work, starting first with Briggs's two shattered fingers, which he splinted with stiff surgical tape, then moving to the cuts and abrasions on his face, legs, and back. There was nothing to do about the bruises or the swelling that had closed one of Tanner's eyes, so Azhar taped his broken nose and closed the kit.

"I think a couple of my ribs are broken," Tanner said.

"Lift your shirt."

Tanner did so, and Azhar wrapped a bandage around his chest. The relief was almost immediate. Briggs took a breath. The pain was bearable.

"I'll be back," Azhar said. "Please stay here."

He returned a few minutes later with a bowl of lentil soup, a loaf of bread, some pieces of cheese and fruit, and a pitcher of milk. He handed Tanner a pair of white tablets. "Aspirin. For the pain. It is all we have."

Tanner started eating and didn't stop until the tray was empty. Azhar took it and placed it on the floor. He sat down.

"I am sorry for what I have done to you," Azhar murmured, still not looking at him. "I didn't . . . I didn't realize . . ."

Tanner held up his cuffed hands. "What about these?"

"They stay on. After this is over, I will release you. You have my word."

"Once this is over? With the ship, you mean."

For the first time, Azhar looked him in the eye. "You know about the ship?"

"That's why I'm here. To stop it."

"By killing me?"

"If that had been my intention, I would have already done it."

Tanner was surprised to see a smile spread over Azhar's lips. It was a sad smile, but a smile nonetheless. *He's still in there somewhere,* he thought.

"Even as a boy you were very tactful, but that doesn't answer my question."

"You remember, then?" Tanner asked. "All of it? My father, our time here—"

"Those times are gone. But, yes, I remember you. You have not answered my question. If it had became necessary, you would have killed me. You still would, if you had no choice."

Tanner nodded. "Yes."

"Then we are enemies, you and I."

"It doesn't have to be that way."

Azhar shrugged. "It is what it is."

Tanner was torn. There was so much he wanted to ask, but time was short. "What happened to you, Abu?"

"How did I become a . . . terrorist? That's what you call

people like me, isn't it?" From the pocket of his *dish-dash* he pulled out the cedar camel and placed it on the table. "I gave this to you?"

Tanner nodded. "You told me it'd been given to you by your father. Because you and Elia couldn't have children, you . . ." Tanner trailed off. "It was one of my prize possessions."

Azhar slid it across the table. "It's still yours." He stood up and walked to the window. "Two years after I gave that to you, Elia found herself pregnant. The doctors said it was impossible, but the hand of Allah intervened. Nine months later, our little girl was born. We named her Amarah. She was healthy and happy. A joy.

"When she was two years old, the war was very bad, so I took her and Elia back to Afqa. I thought they would be safe there. The Israelis had other ideas.

"They got a tip that Afqa was a PLO haven. Early one morning, we heard helicopters. By the time I got outside, the soldiers were already on the ground, running from house to house, shooting and throwing grenades. I was knocked unconscious—I never remembered how—and when I awoke, the village was burned to the ground. Bodies lay in the streets. Elia had been shot in the back. Her spine was shattered."

"Is she—"

"She's still alive. She is paralyzed."

"I'm sorry, Abu," Tanner said. "What about Amarah?"

"For three days I looked for her. I thought she'd been killed. . . . There was so much fire, I thought perhaps . . .

"A year later, I found out she was alive. The soldiers had taken her back to Tel Aviv where a Jewish couple adopted her. My child. They kidnapped *my* child and gave her to someone else . . . to the same people who destroyed my village and crippled my wife."

"She's still there, in Tel Aviv?"

"Oh, no," Azhar replied. "You see, the authorities didn't bother to investigate the couple. A few months after they adopted her, she got colic, and as colicy children do, she cried a lot. One night the woman got tired of listening to it, so she put a pillow on Amarah's face and smothered her."

"Oh God," Tanner murmured. "Abu, I'm sorry."

"God has nothing to do with it, Briggs."

Tanner suddenly understood. They'd taken everything Abu had. His heart, his soul, his miracle. Grief had hardened into anger, which had boiled into rage. His revenge had been twenty years in the making, and now it was coming to an end.

"So now you see," Azhar said.

Tanner nodded. "I know there's nothing I can say to change what's happened, but what you're doing is—"

"Wrong? Do not dare lecture me about right and wrong."

"So what's it about? Revenge?"

"No, not revenge. Freedom, Briggs. If Lebanon had been the country it was supposed to be, none of this would have happened. Not then, not now."

"If you go through with this, lots of people are going to die—"

"If that is the price, then so be it—"

"—including tens of thousands of children—children just like Amarah."

"What are you talking about? None of the hostages are children. We were—"

"The bomb, damn it!" Tanner said. "We know about the hostages, we know about the ship, and we know about the bomb. We *know,* Abu!"

"There is no bomb."

Tanner felt like he'd been slapped in the face. Suddenly, as sure as he'd been about anything in his life, he realized Azhar believed what he was saying. What did that mean? *How could he not—* A thought came to him. *Could it be?* Maybe, just maybe, there was a way out.

Now he just had to stay alive long enough to make it work.

Tsumago

CAHIL'S HUNCH ABOUT THE CARGO HOLD MADE SENSE. EVERYTHING about *Tsumago* was designed to either resist siege or confuse prying eyes: The gas turbine engines; the Kevlar-reinforced superstructure; the powerful radar and ESM array; and a well-trained and well-armed crew. The bomb's location would be no different, he reasoned.

If he were right, the inset holds are camouflage. The forward two were probably linked, forming a single space inaccessible except through an opening he'd yet to discover. Such a compartment would not only thwart a cursory search, but it would also delay an attacking force, forcing them into a bottleneck that could be defended by only a few men.

Figuring out the secret had been the easy part. Now he had to find a way in.

Just after sunset, he climbed the ladder, cracked open the hatch, made himself comfortable, and started watching.

APPROACHING NINE O'CLOCK, THERE WAS STILL NO MOVEMENT aside from the roving sentry, so Cahil glanced out over the ocean. To port, far on the horizon, he could make out a faint black smudge. It was landfall, but where? He did a few mental calculations and decided it was probably Valletta, one of the Maltese Islands. If so, they were just passing Sicily, which put them not quite six hundred miles from Tel Aviv. At thirty knots, they'd be there in eighteen hours. *Midafternoon tomorrow.*

From the foredeck he heard a scraping sound. He turned in time to see a figure standing beside one of the capstans at the edge of the hold. As he watched, the figure leaned the capstan over and rolled it like a barrel to one side. Beneath it was a hatch. The figure spun the wheel and lifted. A faint red light shone through the opening.

"I'll be damned," Bear whispered.

The figure slipped feetfirst into the hatch and disappeared. Cahil looked aft. The sentry was walking onto the forecastle. *Come on, hurry it up. . . .* The sentry paused by the hatch, then turned and started aft.

Cahil began counting. He had ninety seconds.

He crawled out and sprinted across the forecastle, using

the pallets and winch drums to shield him until he reached the hatch. He looked down. A ladder dropped into darkness. Below, he could hear the murmur of voices.

Forty two . . . forty three . . .

He slipped into the hatch, descended until his feet were even with the end of the shaft, then turned himself on the ladder until he was hanging upside down.

The compartment measured twenty feet by twenty feet. Two crewmen stood talking together near the forward bulkhead. Between them, bolted to the floor was a square, waist-high cabinet made of crisscrossed pipes. Suspended in the center by spring-mounted cables was a stainless steel sphere about twice the size of a basketball. A bundle of wires ran from the top of the sphere, down the housing leg, to a black box, which one of the crewmen held.

On the face of the box was a single red-lighted button.

National Military Command Center

DUTCHER, OAKEN, AND OTHERS CAME AND WENT AS THEIR SCHEDules dictated, but as the hours passed and *Tsumago* edged ever closer to Tel Aviv, each found himself spending more time in the center, watching, listening, and hoping against hope.

Only hours before, as *Indy*'s Surface Action Group took up picket stations around *Tsumago*, the news broke of *Valverde*'s hijacking. Every network, newspaper, and wire service was running not only excerpts of the ALC's ultimatum, but also footage of Sludowski's execution.

With the exception of Iraq, which had remained quiet since the ALC had drawn the spotlight on itself, most of the world's interested nations—including Israel's Arab neighbors—released statements condemning the hijacking. Syria demanded action against Iraq's "obvious efforts to destroy the peace process." Syria's ambassador to the UN pointed to both *Tsumago* and the violence in Beirut as proof.

As *Tsumago* sailed southeast away from the Maltese Islands and approached the coast of Tunisia and Libya, scores of fishing boats came to greet her. Horns whooping and crews cheering, the boats were intercepted and turned away by the SAG's southern picket ships.

Through it all, *Tsumago* never deviated or slowed, moving forty miles closer to Israel with each passing hour.

"General Cathermeier, message coming in," reported the NMCC's comm chief.

"On speaker."

"Coaldust, this is Sierra, over."

Cathermeier keyed the handset. "Roger, Sierra, go ahead."

"Sitrep follows: Kickstand confirmed, area three, type two point one."

Mason murmured, "Oh, God."

"What?" asked Talbot. "What's all that about . . . type two?"

"Understood, Sierra," Cathermeier replied. "Say status."

"Operative but restricted."

"Stand by." Cathermeier turned to Dutcher. "Leland, he's your man. Do we order him out or leave him aboard?"

"Get him out. There's nothing more he can do. Can we send a rescue helo?"

"Damn right we can. The moment he's out of the exclusion zone, we'll pick him up." Cathermeier keyed the mike. "Sierra, you are ordered to exfiltrate. Angel is en route."

"Negative, Coaldust," replied Cahil. "I am still operative."

"Sierra, I say again, you are ordered to exfiltrate at once."

"Negative, negative. Will remain aboard as long as possible. Sierra out."

The speaker filled with static. Cathermeier removed the headset. "You think he knows we're going to sink her?"

"He's figured it out," said Dutcher. "Well, gentlemen, I'd say our problem has just gotten a whole lot worse."

Talbot blurted, "Would somebody tell me what the hell's going on?"

"We gave Cahil's team a list of words to use when referring to the bomb . . . its location, type, that sort of thing. The good news is, we know where the bomb is."

"And the bad news?"

"The type and trigger. We thought it would be a gun-barrel design. We were wrong: It's an imploder."

"So?"

"So, Mr. Talbot, instead of thirty kilotons, the yield is closer to fifty. If that thing goes off in Tel Aviv Harbor, the city will be flattened. And there's a man with his finger on the trigger as we speak."

66

Beirut

THE QUESTION ON TANNER'S MIND WAS NO LONGER WHETHER Azhar was behind the bomb but rather, now that he knew about it, what would he do? Would this Azhar he barely knew, armed with a weapon that could destroy the country that had destroyed his life, hesitate to use it? Tanner was gambling that he would not use it, but to find out, he first had to keep Azhar alive.

He'd shared with Azhar his suspicion about the Israeli commando team. It had taken more explanation than he wanted to give, but he had little choice. As it happened, Abu's paranoia worked in Tanner's favor. Within minutes of hearing Tanner's prediction, Azhar evacuated to a nearby abandoned apartment building.

Now Azhar and Tanner—still handcuffed and under the watchful eye of Bucket—sat beside a window and watched Azhar's old headquarters. Gunfire echoed in the distance, and every few minutes the skyline bloomed orange. In the brief intervals of silence, Tanner could hear screaming and the honking of horns.

"Where are your people?" Tanner asked.

"Nearby."

"They musn't interfere with the assault."

Azhar looked at him. "Why?"

Tanner hesitated and glanced at Bucket. Azhar ordered him out.

"It'll be Israeli commandos, Abu. Probably Unit five oh four . . . Mossad."

"What?" Azhar's eyes went wide and he reached for his radio.

"Abu, you have to let them go."

"Why?"

Because if they die, it'll be because I served them up, Briggs thought. "If you hit them, they'll pinpoint your location. You can be sure there's a couple F-16s orbiting up there just waiting to empty their racks."

"Why tell me this? Why not let them kill me? It would finish the job you came to do."

"Because in return for saving your life, you're going to listen to what I have to say."

"I made no such deal."

"Then make it now," Tanner said with a thin smile. "After I make my pitch, if you don't come around, then I'll just kill you."

Azhar hesitated, then chuckled. "Very well, I will listen."

"WE'VE SPOTTED TWO RUBBER RAFTS, ABU. THEY ARE PULLING onto shore. Ten men, all in black with assault weapons. Should we attack?"

Azhar paused, looked at Tanner. Briggs held his breath.

"No," Azhar called on the radio. "Leave them be."

"Abu, we can't just let them—"

"You have your orders."

Though only a mile lay between Azhar's old headquarters and the river, another thirty minutes passed before they spotted the team's scouts picking their way down the rubble-strewn alleyway.

"What took them so long?" Azhar muttered.

"It didn't," Tanner said. Thirty minutes to move undetected in a city at siege was fast work. He was unsurprised, though. He'd worked with 504 before. "If you hadn't been watching for them, they would've been on you before you knew what was happening."

"They are that good?"

"Yes."

"And how do you know so much?"

"I read a lot."

"Ah," Azhar said, returning to the scope.

He narrated what he saw as the commandos reconnoitered the building and slipped inside. Five minutes later, it was done. Having found nothing, the team exited the building as quietly as it had come and headed back toward the river.

"Can I see?" Tanner asked.

Azhar handed him the scope. Through the greenish glow Briggs watched the barely discernible figures slip in and out of the shadow until he lost sight of them. He was about to hand back the scope when Azhar's radio crackled.

"Abu, we have movement."

"Where and how many?"

"A hundred yards to your west. One. He slipped through the basement of the old shoe warehouse. He's watching from the east corner, second story."

Tanner trained the scope on the warehouse and scanned the windows until he reached the corner. There, hidden in shadow, a figure crouched below the pane.

With an eerie whistle, a stray Katyusha rocket flared above their heads and plunged to the street below, where it sparked briefly, then died. In that moment of illumination, the figure's face was visible.

Camille!

Though logically he'd known she could have been the one, he'd prayed against it. But here she was, watching the result of her handiwork—or what should have been her handiwork. He felt rage knotting in his chest. She'd used him. She'd used him from the start, and he'd fallen for it.

Azhar whispered, "Who is it?"

Tanner hesitated. One word, and she wouldn't get out alive.

Goddamn it.

"Nobody," he replied. "Just somebody looking for a place to hide."

Above Lebanon

"HOMEPLATE, THIS IS LOOKER FOUR-ZERO-FIVE, FEET WET."

Crossing the beach ten miles north of Beirut, Lieutenant

Tom "Grinder" Sterling put his F-14 into a gentle climb and glanced over his shoulder. Born and raised in Los Angeles, his first reaction was to compare Beirut to his memories of the L.A. riots, but the carnage here made those look like a rowdy church picnic.

Dozens of neighborhoods were burning, the flames casting orange light on surrounding buildings, many of which were half-collapsed, their remnants jutting toward the sky like skeletal fingers.

"Holy Moses," he muttered.

"Say what, Grinder?" said his RIO from the backseat.

"Just looking at that shit down there."

"Reminds me of that movie . . . y'know, *Escape from New York.*"

"Yeah. Give me a course home."

"Steer two-six-zero."

Two minutes later and sixteen miles from *Independence*, Sterling saw the ship's deck lights on the horizon, mere specks against the black ocean.

"Homeplate, Looker, I am on your one-six-zero radial for thirteen, angels eighteen."

"Rog, four-zero-five. Come on in."

Easing off the power, Sterling dropped through the clouds and lined up with *Indy*'s fresnal lens, or the ball, against which he could adjust his angle of approach and alignment.

Sterling radioed, "Four-zero-five Tomcat ball. State three point two."

Following calls by the LSO, or landing signal officer, Sterling flared out over *Indy*'s ramp and slammed down. He grunted against his harness as the 45,000-pound plane went from 150 knots to a dead stop in two seconds

"Three wire, Grinder," called the LSO. "Guess we'll let you eat tonight."

Sterling laughed. "I'd settle for a head call. I'm floating in here."

Sterling waited until the green-shirted arresting gear operators released the hook, then turned the nosewheel and began following a yellow-shirt to the elevator. Once stopped, he secured the cockpit, climbed out, and sucked in a lungful of air. Beneath the Tomcat, red-shirts were already detaching the TARPS reconnaissance pod from its hard point.

AN HOUR LATER, SHOWERED AND FED, STERLING HEADED DOWN TO the intell shack were the TARPS pictures would eventually end up. It was an old habit for Sterling. A recon mission wasn't over till he was sure he'd gotten the pics. He was constantly amazed at the behind-the-scenes efficiency of carriers ops. While he'd been stuffing his face with Salisbury steak, technicians had been extracting the TARPS's data, turning them into standard images and infrared line-scan pictures, then forwarding them to Intell where they were sequenced and matched to a map overlay.

Sterling pushed through the door, spotted one of the intell weenies leaning over the light table, and walked over. "Mine, Chic?"

"Yep."

"Did I remember to load the film this time?"

Chic nodded absently, staring at the photos. They looked like reverse-image negatives: IR shots.

"This is the Bekka, right?" asked Chic.

"Yep. Three passes."

"Anybody take any potshots at you?"

"No, why? Is there a problem?"

Chic picked up the phone and punched a number. "No shit there's a problem."

National Military Command Center

DUTCHER STARED AT THE THEATER'S MULTIPLE SCREENS. Displayed were radar and photo images from the SAG surrounding *Tsumago*; the *Independence* group off Lebanon; and a green-and-blue geographic display of *Tsumago*'s position in relation to the coast of Israel. Between the two, dead in the path of *Tsumago*, was the blue U representing *Minneapolis*.

The distances seemed vast, but Dutcher knew better. According to the scale at the edge of the screen, *Tsumago* was still 228 miles from Israel's territorial waters, but at her current speed, she would be within range of *Minneapolis*'s harpoons in six hours.

Again, he found himself wondering about Tanner and Cahil.

As much as he wanted to believe otherwise, he had to accept the fact they were either dead or soon would be. As if being in the hands of Azhar's people was not bad enough, Briggs was stuck in the middle of a city that was tearing itself apart. Ian was not much better off, riding a juggernaut that would either vaporize itself and ten miles of ocean around it or be sunk under a hail of missiles.

Oaken walked over. "Leland, I've never wanted to be wrong about something so much in my life."

"I know, Walt. There's still a chance."

One of the communication techs called: "We've got feed from *Indy*."

"What is it?" said Cathermeier.

"A recon pass over the Bekka. The captain thinks you should see it."

"Put it up."

The upper left screen went to static for a moment, then a black-and-white image appeared. Dutcher recognized the Bekka Valley's elongated horseshoe shape. Throughout the valley were hundreds of white dots: Tanks.

Three divisions, Dutcher thought. *Each dot a—*

"What the hell . . ." murmured Cathermeier.

"What are we seeing?" Talbot asked.

"Infrared pictures," replied Mason. "Four hours ago all we saw was a smooth, black background."

"So?"

"Each of those dots represents an engine heat bloom of a tank or an armored personnel carrier."

"*All* of them?"

"Yep. And they're moving."

Beirut

SEEING IT BUT NOT SEEING IT, TANNER WATCHED THE FIRST TINGE of pink appear on the horizon. Camille had betrayed him. No, it was worse than that. She smiled to his face, cried and pleaded, made love to him, and then ordered his death. He tried to muster some anger, but it wasn't there. It was his own fault. Had he not been so naive—

He stopped himself. What was he doing? Suddenly he felt everything falling away. None of it mattered. Forget her. He was alive, and there was still a chance.

"Briggs, did you hear me?" asked Azhar.

"What?"

"I said, how did you know they were coming?"

"Because I used the same method to track you," Tanner replied. "We burned Asseal, hoping you'd take him."

"And the Israelis turned around and did the same to you."

"Abu, what will you do with Asseal?"

Azhar waved his hand and chuckled. "He's a patsy. After this is over, we will release him."

"Thank you."

Azhar shrugged it off.

"Can you stop the ship?" Tanner asked.

"Why would I do that?"

"Why would you get involved with Iraq and the Arab Liberation Command?"

Azhar's eyes shifted ever so slightly, but Tanner caught it.

"Enough of this," Azhar said. "I told you I would listen. I did not agree to be interrogated."

"Okay, tell me about the bomb."

"Again with the bomb?" Azhar said. "There is no bomb."

Tanner decided it was time to go for broke. He started talking, beginning with Ohira's murder, then through his tracking of *Tsumago* to Parece Kito, then finally to his father's revelation about *Stonefish* and her cargo.

Azhar stared at him. "Fantasy."

"I was there from the start. It's all true."

"Briggs, we may have a history, but make no mistake: We are enemies. You come here, try to play on my memories, then expect me to pour my heart out to you?"

"No more than I believe you'd kill hundreds of thousands of people."

"For the last time, *there is no bomb!*" Azhar stood up and began pacing. "This is *not* about revenge! You understand *nothing*. How many years has your country ignored what's been going on here? You put Marines ashore for a few months, then leave. You sell Israel aircraft that bomb our villages! Your puppets in the UN make resolutions and pronouncements, and still our children die! You have the audacity to talk to me about death? What do you know about death? When was the last time tanks rolled through your village and burned your home to the ground? When was the last time your child was taken from you?"

Tanner didn't reply. There was nothing he could say.

"Answer me! Has it ever happened to you?"

"No."

"Then you know *nothing!*" Azhar walked to the door. "I promised I would listen, and I have. Ghassan!" Bucket appeared in the doorway. "Take him away."

"Abu," Tanner called.

Azhar turned. "What?"

"Do me one more favor: Think about it. What if I'm right? What if I'm not lying? Think about ten thousand children just like Amarah lying dead in the streets of Tel Aviv."

Azhar's eyes glazed over, then went cold. "Good-bye, Briggs."

National Military Command Center

THE PRESIDENT PUSHED THROUGH THE DOORS. "TALK TO ME, General."

"Syria's Bekka Group is gearing up," Cathermeier said. "We've got hundreds of heat signatures; everything they've got is running. I've ordered a visual pass. It should be en route now. That's first."

"And second?"

"It looks like Mr. Oaken's won the prize. We just got another feed from the Keyhole above Syria. Take a look."

The president leaned over the chart showing the Syria/Lebanon border.

"As of an hour ago, the exercise group was traveling northeast toward Damascus on this road . . . here. Near Qatana. As of ten minutes ago, the head of the column was here . . . eight miles to the northwest, near Raklah. By now, the spearhead is five miles inside Lebanon."

"How big is it?"

"The First Armored Division, parts of the Seventh and Ninth Mechanized, and a good chunk of the Golan Task Group. We're talking about almost six hundred tanks, seven hundred APCs, and almost sixteen thousand ground troops. We've got a recon flight headed in that direction, as do the Israelis."

"They know, then?" asked the president.

"I called their chief of staff immediately."

"Good. I'll be talking to the PM in a few minutes. What else?"

"The spearhead appears to be driving southwest toward the Litani River . . . which matches Oaken's prediction. Their most likely target is here . . . the high ground between the northwest corner of Dayr Mimas at the bend of the Litani. After that, we can expect the rest of the column to swing west along the river, digging in as it goes."

"How long?" asked the president.

"It's only twenty-five miles to Dayr Mimas and another twenty to the coast. The lead elements should be in position within two hours. They'll be followed by the antiair units and artillery. By noon, Tel Aviv time, the Litani will be a fortress."

"I don't understand this, General," said Talbot. "You told us the Syrians couldn't do this without support units, the same support units that were supposedly back in Damascus."

Mason answered, sliding a photograph across the table. "That's a supply column behind the spearhead. It turned up during the last Keyhole pass. We believe it was hidden somewhere along the border."

"That's absurd! That column is miles long. Where could they have hidden it?"

"Probably a wadi . . . a dry riverbed. Plenty of them are thirty or fifty feet deep and can stretch hundreds of miles."

Dutcher said, "Which would mean they've been planning this for some time. This kind of operation takes some real logistical finesse."

Cathermeier nodded. "More importantly, they've done it right this time. So far, the invasion has been textbook perfect. They're not going to make the same mistakes again."

"Speak English," said Talbot.

"Their plan is sound—even brilliant—all by itself. Add the bomb to the equation, and Syria is about four hours from owning Lebanon."

67

Beirut

TANNER HAD LITTLE TROUBLE IMAGINING ABU AS THE SCAPEGOAT: The mentally unbalanced zealot, his life destroyed, his daughter murdered by Israel, now exacting his revenge on the grandest scale imaginable. But there was the other possibility, one that terrified Tanner: Patsy or not, given the chance, Abu would gladly push the button.

The door swung open. Azhar stepped inside, followed by Ghassan. *Only two of them,* Tanner thought, gauging his chances.

"Stand up, Briggs."

Tanner heard the change in Azhar's voice and saw it in his eyes. What little animation he'd shown earlier was gone, replaced by the same expression he'd worn while ordering Briggs's finger broken.

Tanner stood up. He felt a wave of pain in his head. With each intake of breath he felt his ribs grating against one another. "Where are we going?" he asked.

"Never mind. Follow me."

Tanner stepped into the corridor. Five guards fell in behind him. Azhar led him down a stairway to a basement garage where an ancient Mercedes canvas-topped truck sat idling.

"Get in," Azhar said.

Tanner climbed in the back and was joined by four of the guards. Azhar, Ghassan, and the remaining guard climbed into the cab. The tailgate slammed shut, and the truck lurched forward.

*　　*　　*

THROUGH THE CANVAS HE COULD HEAR THE OCCASIONAL RATTLE of automatic weapons, but nothing else: no explosions, no honking of horns. It was eerily quiet.

"Has the fighting stopped?" Tanner asked one of the guards.

"For now."

"What's happened?"

The guard grinned broadly. "The liberation."

AFTER AN HOUR, THE TRUCK STOPPED AND THE GUARDS CLIMBED out, pulling Tanner after them. He blinked against the sunlight, stretched the cramps from his back and legs, and looked around. They were at the warehouse.

Across Tripoli Road, the skyline was dotted with fires, some still burning and some gushing clouds of black smoke. Of the remaining buildings in view, not one was unscathed, having either been holed by artillery fire or been reduced to rubble. Above it all, however, the sky was a pristine blue.

"We will rebuild," Azhar said. "We've done it before."

He led Tanner to the rear of the warehouse. There, tied to the pilings, was a thirty-two-foot fishing trawler, its engines growling at idle.

Azhar climbed down the ladder, followed by Ghassan, then Tanner, then the guard named Salim. Azhar gestured for Tanner to sit on the deck, then cuffed his hands to a cleat on the gunwale. Ghassan hurried to the bridge, and Salim began casting off the lines. As they pulled away from the pier, Azhar cast a salute to the guards on the dock. They raised their AKs and cheered.

"Where are we going?" Tanner asked.

Azhar looked down at him. "I thought you would have guessed. We have a ship to meet."

National Military Command Center

"THE BEKKA GROUP IS MOVING," CATHERMEIER ANNOUNCED, pointing to the chart. "Here, here, and . . . here are the lead elements. "Eight brigades of mechanized infantry moving east toward Beirut. They'll be at the outskirts in two hours. The rest will probably follow within a few hours."

"The rest? How much are we talking about?" asked the president.

"If they move it all, about twenty-five thousand men and nine hundred tanks. Only half that number will go for Beirut; the other half, including the AAA and artillery units, will probably form a second line between Beirut and the Litani."

"How about the southern group?" asked Dutcher.

"The lead elements are passing Hasbayya. We have a few scattered reports of skirmishes between the spearhead and the Southern Lebanese Army, half of which is pulling back to the border, waiting for support from Israel. The other half is scattering. By noon, the Syrians will be dug in from the coast to the Golan."

"That fast?" said Mason.

"Lebanon's only fifty miles at its widest point. With the spearhead moving at thirty miles an hour . . . You do the math."

The president turned to the secretary of state. "Are the Syrians talking?"

"The foreign minister is scheduled to give a news conference in forty minutes."

"They'll call it a police action," replied Oaken. "An intervention to protect Lebanon from falling into civil war."

The communications chief called, "Mr. President, I have the Israeli prime minister ready; he's on your button five."

The president turned to Cathermeier. "General, I want this room cleared of everyone except for the people at this table."

"Yes, sir."

Once the center was empty, the president hit the conference call button. "Mr. Prime Minister, can you hear me?"

"Yes, Mr. President."

"Good. You've received our latest recon updates?"

"Yes, we're looking at them now. The Syrian spearhead is moving quite quickly, it appears. At least now we know what they've been up to in the desert the past few weeks."

"Mr. Prime Minister, may I ask, what are your intentions?"

"We believe your scenario is the correct one. The bomb is intended to cripple us, to keep us from responding. Until the disposition of the device is decided, we are stuck between the proverbial rock and hard place. Tell me: Have you made the necessary arrangements?"

"I'll let General Cathermeier answer that."

"Mr. Prime Minister, the unit we've chosen for the attack is the *Minneapolis*, a Los Angeles–class attack submarine. When *Tsumago* crosses into your territorial waters, she'll be forty to forty-five miles north of Tel Aviv."

A new voice came over the line. "General, this is the chief of staff. What kind of weapon system have you chosen?"

"Harpoon missiles . . . four of them."

"Only four? Will that be enough?"

"Yes, sir. Standard allocation for a Russian Kirov cruiser is four; *Tsumago* displaces only a third as much as a Kirov and has no armor."

"I see. And their travel time from launch to impact?"

"Just shy of five minutes."

The line went silent as a murmured conversation took place in the background. The prime minister returned. "Mr. President, when the ship is fifteen miles from our coast, we are going to attempt a boarding to rescue the hostages."

The president looked to Cathermeier, who shook his head. "Sir, that would be inadvisable. You know what happened to our team."

"I do, but the decision has been made. Can we count on your cooperation?"

"Sir, I'm confused," said Cathermeier. "Are you asking us to delay launch until your assault is complete?"

"No, General. You will launch as scheduled. According to our calculations, from the time our team boards *Tsumago* until she crosses into our waters, we'll have six minutes. Add five minutes' flight time for the missiles, and that gives us eleven minutes to complete the rescue."

"That's a narrow window, sir."

"Desperate times, General."

Dutcher whispered to the president, "Ask them to wait a moment."

"Mr. Prime Minister, please stand by for a moment." The president muted the phone. "Leland?"

"We have to face facts. More likely than not, that bomb is going to detonate. There's no way we can damage *Tsumago* fast enough to prevent it, and there's no way a team can reach the trigger in time. It's *going* to happen, regardless of whether they rescue the hostages or not."

"What about that, General?"

"We might as well give them a chance. We owe them that much."

The president returned to the phone. "Mr. Prime Minister, you'll have whatever assistance you need. Good luck to you."

"To all of us, Mr. President."

Tsumago

SEVEN HOURS AND 180 MILES WEST OF TEL AVIV, CAHIL SAT LIStening to the wind whistle through the hawse pipe and wondering if he'd just made the biggest mistake of his life. What good could he do here? One way or another, *Tsumago* wouldn't survive to see another day. She would either be vaporized or sent to the bottom. Would his staying aboard change that? If he died here, he'd be leaving behind a widow and an orphan.

Decide, Bear, he thought. *Flip a coin if you have to, but decide.*

He checked his watch. There was still time. He would wait.

Off the Coast of Lebanon

TANNER SAT ALONE ON THE AFTERDECK, STARING OUT TO SEA AND thinking. The guard's comment in the truck had provided him the final piece of the puzzle.

It had been a Syrian operation from the beginning. The ALC and Iraq were the scapegoats, the excuse Syria needed to invade Lebanon and return it to the sphere of a Greater Syria. And Abu Azhar was the puppet behind it all.

The bomb would cripple Israel's ability to repel the invasion as well as weaken her should Syria decide to press its advance southward. The plan was chesslike in its brilliance. Syria takes a giant step toward reclaiming its empire; the peace process is derailed forever, thereby cementing Bashar Assad's power; and Israel, the eternal Arab nemesis, is decimated.

Whatever clinical appreciation he felt for the plan was immediately quashed as he imagined hundreds of thousands of charred bodies lining Tel Aviv's streets. And what about the environmental impact? How long would the Med be poisoned? Ten years? Twenty? Half a century?

Trying to ease the cramps in his legs, he shifted position. He felt the cleat move under his hand. With one eye fixed on the pilothouse, he studied the cleat. It was a butterfly type, palm-sized, and affixed to the gunwale by a single nail.

He began rocking it back and forth. Slowly, millimeter by millimeter, the nail began easing from the wood. A half inch appeared, then an inch.

After twenty minutes, his forearms ached with the exertion. He flexed his fingers for a few moments. Three inches of the nail was exposed. Would it be enough? he wondered. He would have to get very close.

He heard footsteps on the deck. He leaned over the gunwale, using his chest to press the nail back into place.

"Are you ill?" Azhar asked.

Briggs rolled back and wiped his chin on his shoulder. "No, I'm fine. How long until we're there?"

"Four hours." Azhar sat on the opposite gunwale and stared at the water.

"Tell me how it happened, Abu. How did you get involved with the Syrians?"

"Pardon me?"

"You used the ALC and Iraq as scapegoats. Don't get

me wrong, it's very smart. Given the world's opinion of Iraq, you could accuse Saddam of having assassinated Abe Lincoln and people would buy it. You kill a few leaders in Beirut to light the fuse, watch the city boil over into civil war, then point the finger at Iraq and wait for Syria to come the rescue. It was a good plan, but there was that one last hurdle, wasn't there?"

"What?"

"Israel. You and Khatib knew Israel wouldn't sit still while Syria took over Lebanon. You needed leverage. Without it, the rest of it wouldn't work. How am I doing?"

"Very well."

Tanner shook his head. "Do you really think hostages will be enough to convince Israel to sit on its hands? They used you. When this is over, Syria will point the finger at you and Iraq, then put a bullet in your head. Your life story, your hatred for Israel, your twenty-year war of revenge, your daughter . . . all of it will come out."

"Nonsense. They will negotiate. They will hesitate long enough to—"

"The only thing that'll stop Israel is the bomb *Tsumago* is carrying."

"Again with the bomb? There is no bomb!"

"Then there's only one possibility left."

"What?"

"You're so far gone you believe Israel will surrender Lebanon in exchange for a handful of hostages."

"That's enough! You don't know what you are talking about!"

"Answer me: Are you a mass murderer, or are you insane?"

In a flash, Azhar drew his pistol and pointed it at Tanner's head. "Not another word! I will kill you! On Amarah's soul, Briggs, I will kill you."

For a long five seconds, Tanner stared back. *Too far*, he thought.

Azhar holstered his pistol, turned, and stalked into the pilothouse.

68

AFTER ANOTHER TWO HOURS' INTERMITTENT WORK, TANNER MAN-
aged to lever the rest of the nail from the gunwale. It was
more a spike than a nail, he saw, six inches long and as
big around as his thumb. It would do, he decided. He slid
it back in place, then sat back and stared at the passing
coast.

The shore here was rocky and spotted with clumps of
brush. Earlier they'd passed a large harbor he assumed was
Haifa, so that put them just north of Tel Aviv. He leaned
his head over the gunwale until he could see forward.

In the distance, he could see six plumes of smoke on the
horizon. They were ships in convoy formation. He focused
on the lead vessel and could make out a five-inch gun on
the forecastle. Israeli or U.S.? Probably the former, heading
to meet *Tsumago*.

Azhar and Ghassan walked onto the deck. Ghassan unlocked Tanner's cuffs. "Stand up, Briggs," Azhar said.
"Into the pilothouse!"

As Ghassan shoved him inside, Tanner heard the thumping of helicopter rotors approaching. The sound increased
until it was poised directly overhead. The water swirled
from the downwash. Standing at the wheel, Salim glanced
nervously at Azhar.

"Keep going. We are in international waters."

*"Attention unidentified vessel, this is the United States
Navy. You are approaching a military exclusion zone. Turn
about. Acknowledge."*

Azhar walked onto the afterdeck and looked up, shielding
his eyes. He shrugged, tapped his ear, and shook his head.

*"Unidentified vessel, I say again: You are approaching
a military exclusion zone. Turn back at once."*

Azhar shrugged, waved, then ducked back into the pilothouse. After a few moments, the beat of the rotors increased, then faded into the distance.

"What do we do?" asked Salim.

"Keep going," said Azhar. "There is nothing they can do."

"They will attack us!"

Azhar shook his head. "By the time they realize we're not a stray fishing boat, it will be too late. We'll be inside the zone. They won't dare follow us."

Looker 405

"LOOKER FOUR-ZERO-FIVE, THIS IS HOMEPLATE, OVER."

"Looker," Sterling replied.

"Vector one-seven-five and switch to button four for Black Horse."

"Rog," said Sterling. He flipped open his call sign book and skimmed down until he found Black Horse: USS *Ford.* Sterling switched channels. "Black Horse, this is Looker, over."

"Looker, Black Horse. We have an unidentified and nonresponsive fishing vessel approaching our exclusion zone. Request you make a photo pass. Vessel is on your one-seven-seven for eight-zero nautical."

"Roger, Black Horse, I am en route."

ONCE THE HELICOPTER DISAPPEARED OVER THE HORIZON, AZHAR locked Tanner's handcuffs to the cleat and left Ghassan standing guard. In the midday heat, it took only a few minutes until the man's eyes began to droop.

In the distance Tanner heard a whine. He cocked his head, trying to localize the sound. He looked aft. A dot appeared on the horizon. It grew quickly, taking shape, until he realized it was a jet.

Tanner glanced back at Ghassan. The man's eyes flickered open, then closed again. In the pilothouse, Azhar and Salim were staring out the windscreen.

The dot grew larger until Tanner recognized it as an F-14. *Why a Tomcat?* he wondered. It had no antisurface weapons. . . . No, but it had TARPS.

The Tomcat was two miles out now, moving fast and low above the waves.

"Ghassan! You idiot!" Azhar yelled from the cabin. Boots pounded on the deck.

Tanner kept his eyes fixed on the Tomcat. It was nearly overhead, engines screaming. As the underbelly flashed past, he stared straight into the camera pod.

"Damn you, Briggs!"

Ghassan struggled to his feet and charged. Tanner sensed him coming but kept his face on the retreating Tomcat. *Come on . . . see me!* Ghassan jammed the AK's barrel under Tanner's chin.

"Stop, Ghassan!" Azhar called.

Panting, his face bloodred, Ghassan glared down at Tanner. He reversed his rifle and rammed the butt into Tanner's forehead. Light exploded behind his eyes, and everything went dark.

Independence

FIVE MINUTES AFTER STERLING LANDED, HE AND HIS RIO WERE standing in the CAG's (commander air group) office. "Which one of you saw it?"

"I did," said Chuck. "He was looking straight up at us."

"So he's a gawker."

"No, Skipper, this was different. It was like . . . like he wanted to be seen."

"Grinder?"

"I agree."

"Okay, what else?"

Chuck said, "Once we were past, some guy rushed out and stuck an AK in the guy's face . . . I mean hard, y'know. Like they were *not* friendly."

The CAG thought it over. "Where are your pics?"

*   *   *

National Military Command Center

"MORE IMAGES FROM *INDY*, GENERAL."

"How many?" asked Cathermeier.

"Put 'em up in sequence."

A black-and-white image of a fishing boat filled the screen. Sitting on the afterdeck was a single figure.

"Next."

Now the boat's afterdeck filled the screen. The figure was leaning backward, his face pointed upward. "What are we seeing, Chief?" said Cathermeier.

"A TARPS image from a Tomcat. According to *Ford*, this boat's approaching the exclusion zone. We warned them off, but they're still coming."

"How far from the zone?"

"Three miles from the outer ring."

"Next."

The next image was tightly focused, with the boat's gunwales nearly touching the photo's borders. The face was staring straight into the TARPS lens.

Dutcher bolted from his seat. "Good God."

"What?" said Cathermeier.

"It's him. It's Tanner."

Israeli Defense Forces Headquarters, Tel Aviv

CAMILLE PUSHED THROUGH THE DOORS OF THE ROOM AND LOOKED around. Like the pentagon's NMCC, the IDF's headquarters was filled with conference tables, communications consoles, and large-screen TVs. Technicians and messengers scurried from station to station, and the air hummed with radio chatter.

She spotted Sherabi standing beneath one of the monitors on which was projected a map of Tel Aviv's coast and the surrounding ocean. Beside Sherabi were the chief of staff, the prime minister, and another man she did not recognize; he had a crew cut and a slight paunch.

Sherabi saw her, hurried over, and embraced her. "Thank

God you're safe," he said. "I wasn't sure you had made the pickup."

When news of the invasion reached Sherabi, he arranged for a helicopter loaded with Sayeret Mat'kal commandos to slip through the SLA lines to Camille's emergency exfil point near Sayda.

"I have to talk to you," she said. "The assault—"

"I know. The building was empty."

"That's not what I mean. Why did you do it, Hayem?"

Sherabi took her by the elbow and walked her to the corner. "What?"

"You burned the American agent."

"I did no such thing."

"You're lying."

"Mind your tongue!"

"Tell me why you did it."

"I suggest you file your report, then go home and get some rest. When all of this is over, we will talk."

Sherabi started to turn away. Camille grabbed his arm. "I want an answer."

"Camille, do not test me. You can either leave voluntarily or—"

"Hayem," the chief of staff called, waving him over.

"Get out of here, Camille," Sherabi muttered.

Sherabi rejoined the group. Camille hesitated, then followed.

". . . word from the Americans," the chief of staff was saying. "They've spotted a fishing boat approaching *Tsumago*. It will enter the zone in a few minutes. According to them, it's carrying several men and an American . . . one of theirs."

Camille felt the room spinning around her. *Briggs! It had to be!* She saw Sherabi and the crew cut man exchange a glance.

"What's his status?" the crew cut man asked. Camille recognized his accent as American. *Briggs's controller,* she thought.

"He was handcuffed to the deck and under guard, it appeared."

Camille could no longer restrain herself. "But he was alive, General?"

The chief of staff turned. "Who is this, Hayem?"

"One of mine. She just returned from Beirut. She's on her way to debriefing."

"Let her stay," said the prime minister. "If she's been in Beirut, she may be able to lend some insight to what's going on."

Camille turned to the chief of staff. "General, was he alive?"

"Yes, he was alive. But if he stays on that boat, he won't be much longer."

CASTING A HARD STARE AT CAMILLE, SHERABI AND THE CREW CUT man walked past her into a nearby conference room. As the door swung shut, she heard the American say, "When those choppers lift off, I gotta be aboard. If he gets back . . ."

They're going to board ship. Camille knew her career—and perhaps her life—was teetering over a precipice. What she was contemplating was impossibly dangerous. Mossad had a long memory and an even longer reach. *The hell with it.* She took a deep breath and walked into the conference room.

"Camille, get out of here!"

"I will not!" she snapped. "You! Who are you?"

The American stuck out his hand. "Art Stucky."

"Well, you can go fuck yourself, Mr. Stucky. And you, too, Hayem."

"Camille!"

"You fed Briggs to the wolves, both of you. You *bastards!*"

Sherabi's eyes narrowed. "Tanner? The same man you—"

"Yes."

"You knew he was in Beirut? Good God, Camille, what have you done?"

"Don't dare lecture me! I may not understand why you did it, but when I figure it out, I'll make sure everyone knows."

Sherabi grabbed her arm. "Not another word! If you keep your mouth shut, you may—"

She jerked her arm free. "You have three choices, Hayem. Either you have me dragged out of here and put a bullet in my head; you get me on whatever chopper this *asshole* is talking about; or you get used to having the CIA as your enemy."

Stucky jabbed his finger in her chest. "Look, you cunt—"

"Stucky, shut up! Camille, for the sake of your father's memory, please—"

"My father would be sickened by what you're doing. Make your decision!"

For a long ten seconds, she and Sherabi stared at one another.

Stucky said, "Hayem, you can't actually be thinking—"

"Shut up, Art. All right, Camille, all right. You win."

Minneapolis

FORTY MILES NORTH OF TEL AVIV, NEWMAN ORDERED *MINNE-apolis* to periscope depth. "Sir, we are at PD, reading zero bubble."

"Very well. Sound general quarters."

The GQ claxon blared, and the conning tower's lights went red. Throughout the boat, watertight hatches slammed shut, and men raced to their stations.

"Captain, all stations manned and ready. All boards green."

"Very well."

Newman joined Speke and the fire control officer at the tactical table. Under their elbows lay a laminated chart of Israel's coastline.

"Radar, conn," Newman called. "How's our track?"

"Solid, sir."

"Read 'em off, starting with the target."

One by one, the operator recited the bearings and ranges

of *Tsumago* and the picket ships around her. Newman studied the plot. *Tsumago*, at the center of the ring, lay seventy miles to *Minneapolis*'s southwest and forty-five miles from Israeli territorial waters.

"Okay, we've got six friendlies to worry about, all within twenty-five miles of the target," Newman said. "It'll be tight shooting. Fred, we'll go RBL." Newman referred to a range and bearing launch. Its counterpart was a bearing only launch, which sent the Harpoons downrange, armed and looking for the first target to cross its path. An RBL, on the other hand, would direct the missiles to attack only those targets it found within a certain patch of ocean.

"Right," said the fire control officer.

"We're shooting four. All of them have to hit within ten seconds of one another, so make sure your way points are dead-on. Radar, conn, what's the target course and speed?"

"Course, one-one-zero, speed three-two knots."

"Conn, aye. Fred, start your track. Unless you hear otherwise, be ready to launch the minute she crosses the twelve-mile mark." Newman checked his watch. "Seventy-three minutes from now."

69

TRUE TO AZHAR'S PREDICTION, THEY SLIPPED THROUGH THE ZONE'S outer ring without incident, but twelve miles from *Tsumago*, they were met by a U.S. Navy frigate, which tried to hail them by loudspeaker. Azhar did his routine of waving and shrugging and then ordered Salim to sail on. The frigate broke off and turned for the coast, her bow slicing the waves and single screw spewing a rooster tail. As she faded in the distance, Salim and Ghassan began laughing with relief. Azhar stood at the window, staring ahead, his face blank.

Twenty minutes passed.

Tanner heard the whine of *Tsumago*'s gas turbines long before he saw her. Salim and Ghassan started pointing excitedly through the window. Azhar walked onto the afterdeck. "We're almost there,"

"I can hear it," said Tanner.

"I am sorry for this, you know. It was never supposed to be this way."

Tanner could feel the cleat loose under his hand. "I'm sorry, too."

A few minutes later, the boat turned to port, and Tanner caught his first glimpse of *Tsumago* since his and Cahil's penetration of the shipyard. She was a few hundred yards away and turning toward them. He found himself thinking of Bear. This is where it had happened. God, it didn't seem possible.

Let it go, he commanded himself. He forced it from his mind. He gripped the cleat until the head of the nail bit into his palm. *Have to be fast. . . . One, maybe two thrusts will be all you'll get. Wait for the right moment.*

Bullhorn in hand, Azhar left him and climbed onto the foredeck. On *Tsumago*'s bridge wing, a dozen rifle-armed men stared down at him.

Azhar called, "Attention captain of *Tsumago*. Permission to board."

A figure walked onto the bridge wing. Tanner immediately recognized the handlebar mustache: al-Baz. "Abu, is that you?"

"Yes!"

"Why . . . why are you here?"

"Do you think I would miss such a moment in history?" Azhar called, "After so much planning, my friend, did you think I would let you take all the glory? You have taken her this far, at least do me the honor of joining you the rest of the way."

Al-Baz hesitated a moment, then nodded. "You are welcome. Come aboard."

Tanner jerked the cleat free of the gunwale and tucked it into his waistband.

National Military Command Center

EVERYONE IN THE CENTER STOPPED WORKING AND STARED AS THE first images from the Orion loitering 10,000 feet above the Mediterranean came in. *Tsumago* lay at the center of the monitor with the SAG's picket ships at the edges, their wakes white against the blue water. Dutcher could just make out the single figure seated on the fishing boat's afterdeck. *God almighty, it's really him.*

"What's this from?" asked Talbot. "It looks like real-time."

"It is," said Mason. "A super zoom camera. Used for sub hunting."

"*Tsumago*'s slowing," said Cathermeier. They're going to board her. Chief, how far are they from the twelve-mile mark?"

"Ten miles, sir . . . twenty minutes if she resumes her same speed."

"When do the Israelis go?" asked the president.

"They should be lifting off now," said Cathermeier. "Chief, contact Tel Aviv, confirm that."

Thirty seconds later: "Confirm, General. Helos are en route. Eight minutes until they're over the deck."

Cathermeier turned to the president. "Time, Mr. President."

The president hesitated, then nodded. "Proceed."

"Chief, contact *Minneapolis*. I want secure voice-to-voice with the CO."

Minneapolis

"CONN, RADAR: TARGET IS SLOWING . . . NOW COMING TO A DEAD stop. Second vessel, designated unknown Bravo One, is merging."

"Conn, aye," Newman called.

"What's going on?" asked Speke.

"I don't know. Talk to me, Fred."

The fire control officer said, "Solid track, self-test complete on four birds." He flipped open a clear plastic cover on the console, inserted a key, and closed the cover. "We're ready to launch."

"Very well. Stand by. Radar?"

"Target still dead in the water, conn."

"Radio, conn: Skipper, we've got a secure voice-to-voice for you."

Newman and Speke walked to the radio room. The operator handed Newman the telephone handset. "Captain Newman here."

"Captain, this is General Cathermeier. Give me sit-rep."

"We're in position and ready to fire, General. The target has slowed—"

"We know. We expect her to resume course and speed shortly. She'll cross the twelve-mile mark in twenty minutes. The moment she does, you are authorized to launch. I say again: You are authorized to launch."

Tsumago

PRECEDED BY AZHAR AND FOLLOWED BY GHASSAN, TANNER climbed the cargo net and pulled himself over the rail onto the deck. He was immediately surrounded by half a dozen guards. Azhar and al-Baz embraced.

"Who is this?" al-Baz asked.

"A trophy. An American agent. He will give us extra leverage if we need it."

"Good. I must say, Abu, I am surprised to see you."

"Why is that?"

"The general said—" al-Baz broke off and glanced at Tanner.

"Whatever he hears will die with him," Azhar said.

"The general said you were . . . that you were not involved in the final phase."

"I know. Accept my apologies. For security reasons, some details were kept between only al-Khatib and myself. I'm sure you understand."

"Of course."

"So," Azhar said, "shall we get under way?"

"Yes, yes. Follow me."

IN THE WINDLASS ROOM, CAHIL HEARD THE CHUGGING OF THE trawler's engines, then the bullhorn exchange between Azhar and al-Baz. As the whine of *Tsumago*'s turbines died away and her momentum slowed, he climbed the ladder and peeked out.

Cahil almost didn't recognize Tanner's face. "Briggs . . ." he whispered. "Good, God . . . What did they do to you?"

To all outward appearances, Tanner looked beaten; his shoulders were hunched, his bruised face etched in pain. Then Cahil saw Tanner's eyes. Having seen the look a thousand times, he knew it instantly. *He's still there . . . looking for his chance.*

As the group moved off toward the pilothouse, Cahil

climbed down the ladder and began pacing. He had to do something. What, though? *Think!*

He felt the deck shudder beneath his feet. The whine of the turbines increased.

"Come on, come on. . . . Think—"

He stopped. He stared at his radio lying on the deck. Attached to it were the wire leads he'd canibilized from the anchor windlass.

A smile spread across his face. "That just might do it."

AFTER SETTING *TSUMAGO* BACK ON COURSE, AL-BAZ LED AZHAR and Tanner to his stateroom. Prodded by Ghassan, Tanner sat on the floor in the corner. Beneath his buttocks he felt the hum of the engines increase.

"You had some fun with him, I see," said al-Baz.

"It was necessary," said Azhar.

"Has he told you much?"

"Enough."

"Such as?"

"We can discuss that later. Is everything ready?"

"Yes, of course."

"The device?"

Tanner felt his heart skip. He kept his eyes on the deck.

"It's secure," al-Baz said softly. "Certainly you—"

"What kind of yield can we expect?"

"Pardon me?"

"The yield," Azhar repeated. "I understand it is large, but how large?"

"Fifty kilotons."

Fifty? Tanner thought. *How did—*

"And casualties?"

Al-Baz hesitated. "Have you not discussed this with General al-Khatib?"

"The general has been rather busy, Mustafa. How many casualties?"

"From the blast alone, one hundred fifty thousand. With radiation sickness, we expect another twenty thousand in three weeks."

Azhar nodded absently. "Very good," he whispered. "Let us go see it."

"What?"

"I will inspect the device. After it goes off, that won't be possible, will it?"

"Well, no, but—"

"Then lead the way, Mustafa. Time is short."

Tanner glanced up. Al-Baz remained seated, staring at Azhar.

"Is there a problem, Mustafa?"

"No, Abu, not at all." Al-Baz stood up and opened the door. "This way."

WORKING OVER THE WINDLASS'S CONTROL PANEL, CAHIL ALMOST missed hearing the rapid thumping in the distance. He looked up, cocked his ear. He climbed into the chain locker and peered through the hawse pipe. Dead on the bow, no more than a half mile away, a pair of helicopters skimmed over the waves.

"Too soon," he muttered. "Too soon . . ."

He scrambled back down, twisted the last wire into place, said a quick prayer, then threw the release lever. There was a two-second pause. First with a whine, then a thunderous rattle, the anchor's massive links began tumbling from the hawse pipe.

FLANKED BY A PAIR OF HIS OWN GUARDS, AL-BAZ LED THEM across the forecastle to the cargo hold. Al-Baz rolled the capstan aside, rapped twice on the hatch, then lifted it and called down. A voice called back. Al-Baz motioned one of the guards to enter, then gestured for Azhar to follow. Tanner, prodded by the other guard's rifle, went next.

Briggs took the rungs slowly. Near the bottom of the ladder, he felt a hand grab his boot and jerk hard. He slipped and crashed to the deck below. The cleat fell from his waistband and clattered to the deck. Azhar saw it, and his eyes narrowed. He kicked the cleat across the deck.

He grabbed Tanner's shirt and lifted him up. "Stand up!"

In that brief moment, Azhar's hand slipped into the waistband of Tanner's pants. When it withdrew, Tanner felt the unmistakable outline of a pistol against his belly.

"I'm sorry, Briggs," Azhar whispered. "I should have believed you. Wait for my move. We must be quick."

Stunned, it was all Tanner could do not to react.

"I said *move!*" Azhar barked, then shoved him forward. Tanner fell to his knees, and Azhar kicked him in the buttocks. "Stand up!"

The guards burst out laughing.

Al-Baz came down the ladder. "What happened?" asked al-Baz.

"Our guest has trouble with his balance," Azhar said.

"Put him over there."

One of the guards shoved Tanner against the bulkhead.

The space was small, perhaps twenty feet square, and featureless except for the lightbulbs hanging from the ceiling.

Bolted to the forward bulkhead was a rectangular scaffold and inside that, suspended by cables, a stainless steel sphere. One of al-Baz's men stood to one side, holding a black box in his hand. One of al-Baz's guards joined him, while the other posted himself nearer Tanner, his AK-47 trained on Briggs's stomach.

Staring at the bomb, Tanner realized something was wrong. Something about the design . . . There was no barrel for the uranium slug. . . . Takagi had built an implosion bomb! That explained the increased yield.

Tanner looked around, checking lines of fire. Once the shooting started, the compartment would become a death trap. Any bullet that didn't find a target would ricochet until it did.

Azhar stared at the bomb, transfixed. "So this is it?" he whispered.

Al-Baz nodded. "Beautiful, is it not?"

Azhar seemed not to hear. As though in a trance, he shuffled forward. The trigger man glanced nervously at al-Baz, who grabbed Azhar's arm.

"It would be best if you did not. He is under strict orders."

Tanner focused on the trigger man's forehead. *Have to take him first.*

"Of course," said Azhar. "Of course."

Abruptly, al-Baz cocked his head. "Do you hear that?"

"What?" asked Azhar.

Al-Baz pointed at the guard nearest Tanner. "Check!"

He scrambled up the ladder and returned a moment later. "Helicopters approaching from the bow!"

"Lock the hatch!"

From the corner of his eye, Tanner saw Azhar place his hand on his pistol. "It is best if we stay here," al-Baz said to Azhar. "Even if they manage to fight past my crew, we will trigger the device before they reach us."

"Why not now?"

"We are too far away. Don't worry, we have time."

Suddenly, the deck lurched beneath their feet. The engines whined. Tanner stumbled and fell. A shudder reverberated through the deck.

"What is it?" the trigger man called. "What are they doing?"

Al-Baz yelled, "The anchor's dropping!"

ONCE SURE THE CHAIN WAS RUNNING FREE, CAHIL CLIMBED THE ladder, popped the hatch, and climbed out. He glanced over his shoulder. Flying side by side, the helicopters were 200 yards from the bow. He sprinted toward the cargo hold. As he neared it, he saw a man rolling the capstan back into place.

"Hey!" Cahil yelled.

The man spun around. Bear shot him in the chest, barreled over him before he fell, and stopped beside the hatch. He cranked the wheel and heaved back. It didn't budge. He pulled again. Nothing.

He felt the downwash of rotors and looked over his shoulder.

One of the helicopters stopped in a hover over the forecastle. A dozen rope coils dropped from the doors, and commandos starting dropping to the deck.

Minneapolis

"TUBES ONE THROUGH FOUR ARE CLOSED AND FLOODED."

"Very well," replied Newman. "Weaps?"

"Ready to fly."

"Radar, conn: Talk to me."

"Target bears one-eight-zero, range four-zero nautical. Target coming up on the twelve-mile mark in five . . . four . . . three . . . two . . . one. Target has crossed."

Newman took a breath and nodded to the fire control officer. "Launch."

One following the next at ten-second intervals, each of the four Harpoons punched from their tubes and floated toward the surface. Encased in its watertight canister, the first missile broke the surface at a forty-five-degree angle, its nose jutting from the water. Inside the canister, the missile's computer fired the ignition solenoid, and the engines roared to life.

70

Tsumago

CROUCHED IN THE REAR THE LEAD HELICOPTER, CAMILLE WATCHED *Tsumago*'s bow flash past the open doorway. Beside her, Stucky cradled a Galil assault rifle. She watched his fingers flex on the stock and thought, *He's done this before.* He scared her, not only for her sake but for Tanner's as well. He had burned Briggs, and now he'd come to finish the job. Knowing that, she was in danger as well.

"Five seconds!" the pilot called. "Positions!"

As one, the ten commandos crouched over their rope packs. Camille flicked off her Beretta's safety and dried her palm on her vest.

"You piss your pants yet?" Stucky yelled over the rush.

"Go screw yourself."

"Maybe when this is done, sweetie."

Camille felt the helicopter jolt to a stop.

"Go, go, go!"

The commandos leapt from the door.

The PJ pointed at Camille and Stucky. "Go!"

Camille didn't think but grabbed the nearest rope and jumped. She hit the deck, rolled to her feet, and looked for Stucky. The CIA man was crouched a few feet away.

Above them, the helo turned broadside and accelerated away, the door gun firing. The pilothouse windows exploded. Glass peppered the deck. Muzzles flashed from the bridge wings. She felt something zip past her ear and dove flat.

"That's good!" Stucky shouted. "Stay here and get your ass shot off."

He got up and ran aft.

Camille struggled to her feet and ran after him.

TWENTY-FIVE MILES NORTH OF *TSUMAGO,* THE LEAD HARPOON skimmed over the waves at 500 miles per hour. A circuit in its computer brain instructed it to ascend, which it did, climbing to eighty feet, where the radar seeker clicked on. It swept out a pie-shaped section and spotted the target: slightly left of dead center. Another signal went to the fins, which responded by pivoting slightly and easing the missile a few degrees to the left. Once the maneuver was complete, the radar seeker clicked on again and scanned the pie. Now the target was dead center.

The Harpoon dove again, picking up speed as it went.

It was nineteen miles and two minutes from the target.

"FREEZE!"

Cahil looked up and found himself staring into a gun barrel. "I'm a friendly!"

One of the commandos, a captain, stepped forward. "Call sign!"

"Sierra."

"Right." The captain crouched beside him. "What's this?"

Bullets peppered the deck. They ducked. "The bomb's in this hold," Cahil replied. "Its locked from the inside."

"Do you know where the hostages are?"

"Gotta be on the third deck somewhere . . . midships is my guess."

The captain barked orders. Four of the commandos raced aft.

Art Stucky and a black-haired woman ran up and knelt beside the hatch. Cahil realized he recognized the woman and did a double take. "What . . . ?"

"Later," Camille said.

"Where's Tanner!" Stucky demanded.

"Down there."

"Open it!"

"It's locked—" Cahil broke off and stared up at the derrick. He turned to the Israeli captain. "Can you operate that?"

"Yes, why—"

"Get on the controls. We're gonna pry this thing open."

INSIDE THE CARGO HOLD, TANNER COULD HEAR THE MUFFLED CHATter of gunfire and boots pounding on the deck above. Al-Baz tore his gaze off the ceiling and glanced at his watch. "Four minutes," he said. "Four minutes, and we will be close enough. My men will give us time."

Tanner glanced at the trigger man. *One shot,* he thought. One shot was all he would get, and it would have to be the right kind of shot. *Bridge of the nose. . . .*

"You!" al-Baz yelled at Tanner. "What are you looking at?"

Azhar turned and backhanded Tanner across the face. Briggs stumbled into the bulkhead. Azhar drew his pistol, put the barrel against his forehead and hissed, "Do not even think about interfering!" Then, under his breath: "I will take the two guards, you take the trigger man. Wait for me."

Azhar turned and walked over to al-Baz. "Mustafa, a word in private?"

As al-Baz leaned forward to listen, Azhar lashed out with his elbow. It smashed into al-Baz's face, sending him crashing into the bulkhead. Azhar spun. Guard two turned toward him, his own rifle coming up. Azhar shot him twice, then spun toward the guard nearest the bomb. Tanner raised himself to one knee and drew his pistol. Azhar fired. His shot tore into the guard's chest, shoving him backward.

Tanner focused on the trigger man. *One shot. . . .* He fired.

The bullet found its mark, striking the man between the eyes. Like a puppet whose strings had been cut, he crumpled to the deck. The trigger box fell from his hand and clattered across the deck.

Movement. . . .

Briggs looked right and saw al-Baz reach for his AK. Tanner spun. *Too slow, too slow. . . .* Al-Baz raised himself to his knees, rifle turning. . . .

"Abu get down!"

Tanner fired. Even as his three rounds caught al-Baz in the side, flame burst from the AK's barrel. As if in slow motion, Briggs watched the flame lick outward and touch Azhar's chest. Azhar stumbled backward, crashed into the bomb housing, and slumped down the bulkhead.

Cordite smoke filled the air. Shell casings tinkled on the deck. Briggs stared at Azhar. Beneath him, blood was spreading across the deck like a pair of black wings. "Abu," he called. "Abu—"

"He's dead." A few feet away, al-Baz lay propped against the bulkhead. He grinned sleepily and rolled his head toward Tanner. "You're too late. It's done."

"What?"

"We've done it."

Briggs felt a chill. *What—?* He'd assumed if triggered, the bomb would detonate immediately. He cast his eyes around for the trigger box, saw it, scrambled over, and snatched it up.

On the faceplate, the LED read 04:52

71

TANNER WATCHED THE READOUT CHANGE TO 04:51 . . . 04:50. . . .
He looked at al-Baz; face bloody, his head lolled from side
to side. "How do I stop it?" Tanner asked.

"You don't. You can't."

"How do I stop it!" Briggs yelled. Teeth gritted against
the pain, he pushed himself to his knees and pointed the
gun at him. "Tell me!"

Al-Baz grinned, then his eyes fluttered, his chest heaved,
and he went still.

"There's got to be a—" Briggs stopped.

Someone was moaning.

AS THE FIREFIGHT BETWEEN THE ISRAELI COMMANDOS AND AL-
Baz's crew raged inside the ship, Cahil, Stucky, and Camille finished hooking the derrick's cable to the hatch, then
stood back. Hovering above them, the helicopters's gun
went silent. The pilothouse was destroyed, its windows
shattered and superstructure shredded. The helo crabbed aft
and stopped in a hover above the pilothouse; the door gun
began tracking back and forth, looking for targets.

Tsumago was still doing twenty knots but lurching
against the drag of the anchor chain trailing beneath her.
Gouts of black smoke spewed from the smokestack, and
the engines whined in protest.

"Okay, back away!" Cahil yelled, stepping off the hatch.
He signaled to the Israeli captain at the derrick's controls.
The cable went taut. The hatch's hydraulic arms groaned.
"Keep going! Go!"

The captain shoved the lever forward. Slowly, the cover
began lifting.

*   *   *

SIX MILES FROM *TSUMAGO* AND TWELVE SECONDS BEHIND THE lead Harpoon, the radar seekers inside Harpoons 3 and 4 had gone into continuous search mode, scanning their ever-contracting sectors for the target. Having no way of knowing *Tsumago* had slowed, both missiles were searching empty patches of ocean two miles ahead of the ship. They scanned without success for another twenty seconds and then, having reached the limit of their flight plan, shut down and plunged into the ocean.

Two miles ahead of them, Harpoons 1 and 2 were also in continuous search mode. However, having acquired the target early and made the necessary corrections, both showed *Tsumago* dead on their zero points. Satisfied they were on target, the computer brains in each missile sent two signals, one to the radar seeker, which switched to rapid pulse, and another to the 500-pound warhead, which armed itself.

TANNER HEARD THE WRENCHING OF STEEL ABOVE HIM. SUNLIGHT streamed into the compartment. He ignored it and kept crawling toward Azhar. Abu's eyes fluttered open and he saw Tanner. "Briggs. . . ."

"Hang on, Abu." Briggs felt tears fill his eyes. The AK's bullets had shredded Azhar's stomach; intestines jutted from his shirt. "Don't move."

With a shriek of steel, the hatch came free. Tanner looked up. Silhouetted by the sunlight, three figures stood on the combing. His vision cleared and he saw Cahil's grinning face. *Bear!*

Standing beside him were Stucky and Camille. *Doesn't make sense,* he thought dully. *Why are—*

"Briggs!" Cahil called.

Tanner raised his hand against the glare. Blackness crept into the edge of vision. God, he hurt. He levered himself to his knees and focused on Camille.

"It was you," he murmured. "It was you from the start."

*   *   *

As DESIGNED, BOTH HARPOONS' SEEKERS HOMED IN ON THE
strongest radar return, in this case, the corner where *Tsumago*'s superstructure met the forward arch, a confluence
of right angles that created an electromagnetic bull's-eye.
Also by design, each Harpoon's computer brain paused exactly $\frac{1}{100}$ of a second to let the nose cone burrow into the
ship, then detonated the warhead.

Tsumago rocked to starboard as though shoved by a giant, invisible hand. Flames and black smoke gushed from
the wound and rolled up the superstructure. A cloud of
shrapnel shot skyward. Fragments peppered the pilothouse
like hail.

On the main deck, Cahil was knocked to his knees. He
looked aft.

Hovering over the pilothouse, its rotors vainly clawing
at the air, the Israeli helicopter was rolling onto its side.
The blades slammed into the windows, sending shards of
glass and red-hot steel onto the foredeck. The helo flipped
onto its back and tumbled toward the forecastle.

Cahil shoved Camille toward the hatch, then he and
Stucky leapt after her.

THEY LANDED HARD INSIDE THE HOLD AND LAY STUNNED FOR A
moment.

Teetering on his knees, Tanner stared at them, his gun
dangling from his hand. He could feel the deck slanting
beneath him. "Bear," he muttered.

"Here, buddy." Bear crawled to him.

"Its running, Bear. They hit the button."

Cahil started toward the bomb but was stopped short.

"Don't move!"

Tanner and Cahil turned. Stucky was on his feet, rifle
pointed at them. To their left, Camille struggled to her feet.

"I said, *don't move!*" Stucky shouted again.

Tanner realized he was looking past them. Briggs turned.

Azhar sat propped against the bomb housing. In his left

hand he held the trigger. He stared at it, tears streaming down his face. He looked at Tanner.

"I'm sorry, Briggs. I'm sorry—"

"Don't . . . you . . . move!" Stucky bellowed.

Tanner said, "Art, he's not—"

"Shut up!"

To Stucky's right, Camille began edging toward an AK-47 lying on the deck. Tanner jerked his gun up. "Not another inch, Camille."

"Briggs, what—"

"Stay right where you are. Art, just relax. He isn't—"

"Bullshit!"

Camille said, "Briggs, what are you doing? I—"

"I saw you, Camille. I saw you at the warehouse. You led them there."

Another explosion rocked the ship. The deck canted beneath their feet. Shell casings began sliding toward the port bulkhead, clinking like broken glass. Tanner could hear the gurgle of seawater climbing the hull outside.

"No!" Camille said. "God, no! Briggs, I—"

"Bear, cover her," Tanner ordered.

Cahil raised his Glock. "Got her."

Tanner called over his shoulder, "Abu, how much time?"

"Four minutes," Azhar croaked.

Tanner turned back to Stucky. "He's not one of them, Art."

"You're one naive son of a bitch, you know that?"

"Don't do it, Art."

"Drop your gun."

"No."

"Drop it, or I'll shoot him right now!"

Cahil muttered, "Briggs?"

"Stay where you are, Bear. Okay, Art, just take it easy. . . ." Very carefully, Tanner leaned over and set the pistol on the deck. "There. We still have time—"

"Kick it away and step back."

Tanner kicked the gun across the deck and took a step to the right.

Stucky shook his head sadly and then chuckled.

In that instant, in Stucky's ugly grin, Briggs saw it all.
It was him.

Stucky said, "Payback's a bitch, ain't it?"

"Don't, Art."

"Fuck you."

"Don't!"

Stucky pulled the trigger. Tanner charged. As they collided, Briggs heard four rapid *pops*. Stucky grunted, they
fell backward together. As they hit the deck, Stucky rolled
sideways, trying to swing the rifle barrel into Tanner's
belly.

Tanner batted it away and heaved backward, pulling
them both to their feet. He wrenched the Galil from
Stucky's hands, reversed it, and slammed the butt into
Stucky's face. Blood exploded from his nose. He stumbled
backward, bounced off the bulkhead, and lurched forward.
Tanner was ready. He dropped his shoulder and swung with
everything he had. The Galil's butt caught Stucky under
the chin, snapping his head back. Stucky went down hard
and lay still.

Tanner stared down at him. The room was swimming.
He was the one, he thought. *Not Camille . . . him!* He took
a step forward and put the barrel to Stucky's temple.

"Briggs!"

One squeeze . . .

"Briggs, the *bomb!*"

The word hit Tanner like an electric charge. He turned.
Azhar lay faceup on the deck. He was dead. All four of
Stucky's shots had struck his face and neck. As the deck
continued to tilt, the body rolled onto its side and slid into
the corner.

Camille stepped forward and touched his arm. "Oh,
Briggs . . ."

He squeezed her hand. "I know. How much time, Bear?"

"Three minutes."

From above, they heard the sound of helicopter rotors
followed by shouts. A shadow passed over the hatch. More
shouts, then footsteps pounding on the deck.

"Can we stop it, Bear?"

Cahil crouched beside the housing. "It would take at least five minutes just to trace the wiring."

"It's an imploder?"

"Right."

"There might be a way, then."

Tanner explained what he had in mind.

"Risky," said Cahil.

"Is the alternative any worse?"

"No, I guess not."

They went to work. The deck was slanting badly now—fifty degrees at least—and they had to grip the housing to keep from sliding. Camille stood with one leg on the deck, the other braced against the bulkhead.

"Camille, you should leave," Tanner said.

"I'm staying."

"If you go now, you can get clear."

"I'm staying."

"Are your people getting the hostages?"

"Yes."

Fifty kilotons, Tanner thought. *What kind of blast radius?* If what he had in mind failed, they would soon find out.

"Give me your gun, Bear."

Cahil pulled out his Glock and handed it over.

Tanner removed the magazine and ejected a bullet. Using Cahil's multitool, he pried the slug from the cartridge and handed it to Bear. Next, careful not to spill the gunpowder, Briggs slid the cartridge into the Glock's chamber, closed the slide, and set the gun upright between his knees.

"Time?" he asked.

"Two minutes thirty."

The deck slanted past sixty degrees. Through the hatch, Tanner could see the sky tipping as *Tsumago* rolled onto her side. He lost his footing, slipped, and scrambled to pull himself back to the housing.

Using his index finger and thumb, Cahil pressed the slug against the deck. "Ready?"

Tanner nodded.

"Do it!"

Tanner reversed the multitool, took aim, and struck.

"Again," said Cahil.

Tanner struck again.

"Once more."

Cahil examined the bullet. The blows had flattened the hollow-point nose, but left the harder copper tail intact.

"It'll have to do," Tanner said.

Camille asked, "What are you doing?"

"Improvising," Tanner replied. "Time, Bear."

"Ninety seconds."

"Gimme al-Baz's kaffiyeh."

"I'll do it, Briggs. You—"

"Give it to me, Bear."

"Stubborn son of a bitch." Cahil grabbed the bloody scarf from around al-Baz's neck and wrapped it tightly around Tanner's hand and forearm. "Might not be enough, you know," he whispered. "Your hand will—"

"Ready?"

"Briggs, even if this works, there's enough C-4 inside to blow—"

"I know, Bear." Handling the Glock like fine china, Tanner pulled back the slide, peeked to make sure the cartridge was seated properly, then eased the slide closed. "Go ahead."

Cahil slipped the tail of the bullet into the barrel. It didn't fit. "Shit."

"Whittle it," Tanner said.

Cahil flicked open his knife, scraped a sliver from the bullet's tail, tried again.

Still too big.

He carved another sliver, tried again. This time it slid home. "Tight fit."

"Force it."

Using the multitool, Cahil screwed the bullet into the barrel until it could go no farther. The nose jutted from the barrel like a mushroom. "That's as good as it's gonna get, bud."

"Time?"

"Forty seconds."

Tanner turned to Cahil and smiled. "Look on the bright

side, Bear. If this doesn't work, we'll never know it."

"Always the optimist."

"You and Camille get topside."

"You—"

"I'll be there. Go, Bear."

Bear gave Tanner a final squeeze on the shoulder, then took Camille's arm and pushed her toward the ladder. She turned back. "Briggs . . ."

"Go on, Camille. I'll be right behind you."

Tanner watched them climb the ladder and disappear through the hatch.

Briggs turned back to the bomb. Beside his foot, the display clicked down to fifteen . . . fourteen . . .

He took a breath, pressed the Glock against the sphere, and pulled the trigger.

72

TANNER'S GAMBIT WAS BASED AS MUCH ON DESPERATION AS IT was on his marginal understanding of what was happening inside the bomb.

Of the two kinds of devices Takagi could have built, the gun-type bomb would have been the easiest to disarm. Prevent the uranium bullet from being shot into the pit, the weapon fails to reach critical mass, and there is no detonation.

The kind of weapon Tanner faced, however, was an implosion type.

Inside the steel sphere lay a pit of stable uranium, surrounded by a second sphere known as the soccer ball, which consists of seventy-two octagonal lenses of plastic explosive, each a flawlessly designed shaped charge. Upon detonation, these lenses explode inward with equal force, leaving the pit nowhere to go but deeper inside itself, an event similar to the process that takes place inside the sun's own internal furnace: Gravity (in a bomb's case, exterior force) compresses hydrogen atoms until they split into helium, which in turn generates thermonuclear fusion.

Powerful as an implosion bomb is, however, it has an Achilles' heel: If even one of the explosive lenses fails to detonate or detonates a split second later than its counterparts or directs its force a millimeter off center, the pit escapes the implosion and fails to reach critical mass.

WHEN TANNER PULLED THE GLOCK'S TRIGGER, TWO THINGS HAPpened simultaneously.

The impact of the slug against the sphere's shell sent a shock wave through the gun and up his arm, shattering bones and rupturing blood vessels as it went. Tanner was thrown backward.

Next, the flattened slug did not penetrate the sphere but rather created what is called the spawl effect as the tightly focused jolt broke loose a scab from the sphere's inner wall. Traveling at 2,500 feet per second, the BB-sized particle embedded itself in one of the lenses and tore it from the face of the soccer ball.

Two seconds later, the bomb detonated.

IN A FLASH OF ORANGE, THE SPHERE EXPLODED. NO LONGER FO-cused inward, the force found the weak spot in the sphere's wall and blasted through. With a *whoosh*, a ten-foot jet of white flame shot from the quarter-sized hole, passed over Tanner's head, and seared the aft bulkhead.

He felt the heat and concussion wash over him. He rolled into a ball, threw himself flat, and covered his face. The jet flared briefly, turned blue, then withdrew back into the sphere with a final *whoosh*.

Silence.

Tanner groaned and rolled onto his back. Blackness swirled in his eyes. He was tired, so tired. . . . He turned his head. Through the cargo hatch, he could see the ocean's surface and beyond that, a slice of blue sky. In the distance, ships and helicopters crisscrossed the water.

Water began pouring over the hatch combing. He watched absently as it rolled across the bulkhead, pushing debris and bodies before it. He reached out and touched the leading edge. The water felt cool. Soothing. God, he was tired. He would lie here for a while, he decided. *Just for a little while. . . .*

"BRIGGS! BRIGGS, DAMN IT!"

Tanner opened his eyes. The square of sky was smaller now and partially blocked by a blurred yellow shape. What was it? He squinted, then blinked until the shape resolved into a raft. The person in it was waving at him.

"Briggs! For God's sake, *move your ass!*"

Bear. . . .

Without thinking, moving on instinct alone, Tanner rolled onto his stomach, pointed himself toward the hatch, and began paddling with his one good arm. A wave broke over his head. Seawater poured into his throat and nose. He coughed, gulped again, sputtered. He paddled harder. He felt himself slipping, being drawn down. He reached for the surface, but it seemed so far away. *Too far. Just let it go.* The blackness began closing in.

And then a pair of hands appeared in the water and reached for him.

73

Ramstein Air Force Base, Germany

THE TIME FOLLOWING CAHIL'S PULLING HIM INTO THE RAFT WAS A blur to Tanner.

What he went through first in Beirut and then aboard *Tsumago* finally caught up with his body, and he shut down. He spent the next two days sleeping, never once stirring as he was first put aboard *Ford*, then helicoptered to Rota, then flown to Ramstein's hospital.

WHEN THE BOMB WENT OFF, ONLY HALF THE HOSTAGES HAD BEEN evacuated from *Tsumago*. The rest clung to the decks or jumped into the water as the ship sank beneath them. Unaware that Tanner and Cahil had defused the bomb, the U.S. and Israeli warships encircling *Tsumago* remained at the edges of the exclusion zone, not daring to enter. It was not until *Tsumago* finally capsized and slipped beneath the surface that the rescue effort began in earnest.

As Cahil was pulling Tanner from the water, dozens of helicopters, four destroyers, and a handful of civilian cargo ships swarmed the area.

After two hours, all the hostages had either been picked up or accounted for.

Of the one hundred, only three died. Saul and Bernice Weinman survived.

By nightfall, *Tsumago*'s last known position was cordoned off by U.S. Navy warships pending the arrival of salvage ships and environmental containment vessels.

*　　*　　*

WITH ITS TRUMP CARD GONE AND THE ISRAELI DEFENSE FORCES mobilizing, Syria immediately issued a statement that its intelligence services, having been similarly duped by Iraq, had misread the turmoil in Lebanon. Whatever tensions existed in Beirut appeared to be abating. Its intervention in Lebanon would be short-lived, the foreign secretary announced, and army units along the Litani river would be withdrawing by midafternoon the following day. Barring any unforeseen civil eruptions, the remainder of their forces would begin pulling out by week's end. To ensure this, the Israeli Air Force, supplemented by F/A-18 Hornets and A-6 Intruders from *Independence*, began overflights of southern Lebanon and Beirut.

The next day, as the units along the Litani began backtracking across the Syrian border, General Issam al-Khatib was recalled to Damascus and put under arrest pending court-martial. The next morning, he was found dead, hanging in his basement cell in *Mucharabat* headquarters.

ONE BY ONE, TANNER'S SENSES BEGAN FLICKERING TO LIFE. HE heard the hum of the air conditioner and caught the scent of disinfectant. The odor was unmistakable, and even before he opened his eyes, he knew he was in a hospital.

He cracked an eyelid and found himself staring at Cahil's grinning face.

"Good morning, Mr. Van Winkle."

Tanner groaned and tried to sit up.

"Uh-uh," Bear said, pushing him down.

Tanner opened his mouth to speak, but nothing came out. He tried again: "Water," he croaked.

ONE HOUR AND A QUART OF WATER LATER, HE FELT BETTER— beaten and battered and sore—but better. He saw the IV tube in one arm and the wrist-to-elbow cast on the other and asked, "Do I look as bad as I feel?"

"Worse," Cahil replied. "But it could be even worse."

Tanner smiled, then grimaced. "Could be dead."

"Leland and Walt are waiting outside. I'll get them."

"Bear, wait."

"What?"

"What about Camille?"

Cahil hesitated. "I don't know, Briggs. After *Ford* picked us up, I lost track of her. Last I heard, she was in Tel Aviv."

What will they do to her? Briggs wondered. Mossad was not known for its compassion.

"Briggs? What about Leland and Walt?"

Tanner shook himself. "Sure, I want to see them."

Dutcher and Oaken walked in.

"Good morning," said Dutcher.

"Awake at last," Oaken said with an ear-to-ear grin.

"All things being equal, I'd rather be back at the Starlight."

Cahil barked out a laugh.

"Pardon me?" said Dutcher.

"Nothing."

Oaken looked at Cahil. "Did you tell him?"

"What?" said Tanner.

Oaken hesitated for a moment. "Stucky's gone."

"I know that."

"No, I don't mean dead. He's missing. While you were aboard *Ford*, Bear saw him jump aboard an Israeli helo. That's the last anybody's seen of him."

"Mossad?"

"They claim they don't know where he is."

Tanner laid his head back. "Well, I'm sure he'll turn up. There's always somebody who needs a Stucky." He looked at Dutcher. "How long do I have to stay here?"

"The doctors say another week. In addition to cuts and bruises and burns numbering in the double digits, you've got that bad wing, plus some internal contusions." Dutcher paused. "They worked you over pretty good, son. It's a miracle you're not dead."

Tanner nodded. "He stopped it, you know."

"Azhar? Bear told me. Looks like he was the man you knew after all."

Tanner smiled. "Yes, he was."

*   *   *

AFTER A LUNCH OF JELL-O AND BEEF BOUILLON THAT TANNER
unsuccessfully tried to pawn off on his guests, Dutcher
checked his watch. "You feel up to some more company?"

Tanner didn't like the glimmer in Dutcher's eye. "Do I
have a choice?"

"Not really."

PRECEDED BY A TRIO OF SECRET SERVICE AGENTS, THE PRESIDENT
strode in. He walked to Tanner's bedside and shook Tanner's hand. "It's nice to finally meet you, Briggs."

"And you, Mr. President."

The president gestured to a chair. "Do you mind?"

"Please."

The president sat down and groaned. "Lord, traveling in
that damned overdecorated jumbo jet makes my joints ache.
What am I saying? How are *you* feeling?"

"Tired, but otherwise pretty good."

"Glad to hear it. Listen, Briggs, I thought about this all
the way over. I've always prided myself on knowing the
right thing to say at the right time. But I have to be honest,
I'm a bit stumped. What you did—"

"It wasn't just me, Mr. President."

"I know, I know. I read the report. A lot of people went
above and beyond the call of duty . . . including Leland, and
Walter, and Ian here. And Abu Azhar. But you put yourself
straight into the lion's mouth. I hope a simple thank-you
doesn't fall short."

Tanner smiled. "Not at all, sir."

"Good. No doubt you'll have some medals coming your
way from Mason and the Israelis, but I wanted to get to
you first." The president looked at his watch and stood up.
"Is there anything I can do for you?"

Tanner looked at him. "As a matter of fact, you can."

*   *   *

ONCE HE FINISHED TALKING, THE PRESIDENT SHOOK HIS HEAD AND chuckled. "Well, I'll say this for you, you don't do anything halfway. Have you got any idea what you're asking?"

"Yes."

"Briggs, she's an Israeli citizen and Mossad *katsa* to boot. I can't—"

"Sure you can."

"Okay, I can. Whether they go along is a whole different matter." The president paused. "I'll look into it. That's all I can do."

"I appreciate that. And my other request?"

"As luck has it, Mason has something similar in mind. I don't think it will take much to bring him around to your plan. I'll have a talk with him."

Falls Church, Virginia

"CAN HE SEE ME?" JUDITH SMITH ASKED, STARING INTO THE ONE-way mirror.

"No," said Paul Randal. "He knows somebody's in here—it's procedure—but he doesn't know it's you."

"It looks like a prison cell," she whispered.

"It is," said Randal. "Ms. Smith, you have to under-stand—"

"You don't need to explain it to me, Agent Randal. I know what he's done."

"Yes, ma'am. Sorry."

Judith stepped closer to the glass. She was torn. Anger and confusion and longing all fought for control of her mind, but underneath it all, her heart was saying only one thing.

IBRAHIM FAYYAD SAT ON HIS BED AND FOR THE HUNDREDTH TIME studied his room.

Room wasn't quite the right word, was it? Despite the comfortable bed and chairs and white walls and wonderful meals, it was a prison cell. His door was always locked, there were no windows, and every piece of furniture was

bolted to the floor. Not that it mattered, of course. Even if
he could escape, where would he go?

Latham had said the debriefing might take as long as a
year. After that, he would be sent to a maximum-security
federal penitentiary, most likely in Marion, Illinois. Would
he survive prison? he wondered. Real prison? He decided
it did not matter.

His life had come full circle. He'd lived the first fifty
years of it visiting evil unto others, and now he was seeing
the consequences. It was strange how prison changed one's
perspective; of course, the change had started with Judith,
but the truth was becoming clearer with each passing day.
Actions . . . consequences.

HE HEARD THE CLICK OF HIS DOOR'S BOLT BEING THROWN BACK.
The door opened, and in walked Judith Smith.

She stopped just inside the room. The door slammed
shut. She jumped, and looked over her shoulder.

She turned back. "Hello, Paol—I'm sorry. They told me.
Your real name is . . ."

He stood up. "Ibrahim."

She nodded absently. "Ibrahim."

"Judith, I'm so glad you came."

"I don't know why I did."

"Would you like to sit down?"

"No." Sticking close to the wall, she took a step forward
and looked around. "The FBI isn't much for decorating, are
they?"

"No. But the food is good, and all things considered, it
could be worse."

She looked up sharply; he saw a flash of anger on her
face.

"I'm sorry," he whispered. "Maybe it should be worse.
I'm sure you've thought the same thing."

Judith's expression softened. "When they first told me,
yes, I did."

"And now?"

"How can you ask me that?" Tears welled in her eyes, and Fayyad felt his heart lurch. He took a step toward her. She shook her head and crossed her arms over her chest. "Just tell me—and I want the truth—was it all a lie? All of it?"

"No, Judith. In the beginning it was, but before long, it wasn't. For a long time I've had these feelings. . . . I don't know how to explain. I was so frightened they were going to hurt you. You must understand: For twenty years, this is all I've—"

"*Twenty years?*" she whispered. "God. How many women?"

"Judith—"

"How many!"

"Too many."

"My God."

"You changed me, Judith."

"I wish I could believe that."

"You can. Why would I lie? There's nothing to gain from it. Judith, I'm going to die in prison—"

"Don't say that."

"I've come to peace with it. Besides, even if I were free, my former colleagues are not too happy with me." He paused. "Tell me: Are you and the senator still—"

"I've left him. I don't know what I'm going to do."

"You can do anything you want to do, Judith. Open a gallery." Fayyad smiled. "Take all of his money and open a gallery."

For the first time Judith smiled. "That's a thought." The smile faded. "I really wanted to come here and hate you."

"I know."

Abruptly, she stood up and walked to the door. "I have to go."

"Do you have to? We could sit and—"

"I have to go." She knocked on the door, and it opened.

"Judith?" Fayyad called. "Do me one favor?"

She turned. "What?"

"Be happy."

*   *   *

To the bittersweet surprise of Charlie Latham, the Vorsalov/Smith/Fayyad affair ended with a whimper.

Senator Herb Smith had announced his resignation on the senate floor the previous day. Rumor was he planned to move far from Washington and write his memoirs. In his secret heart, Latham hoped the son of a bitch died a lonely old man, which, of course was quite possible now that Judith had left him. In his secret heart, Charlie hoped she would move far from Washington, live another fifty years, and die a happy, happy woman.

Despite himself, Charlie had developed a soft spot for Ibrahim Fayyad. He hated what the man had done to not only Judith and the dozens of women before her, but also the countless people he'd helped kill, still . . . There was no mistaking the change that had come over the man. Too bad it came so late.

In the dozens of hours Latham had spent debriefing him, never once did the Jordanian complain or resist or defend his life. He owned it all. Latham had seen his share of criminals grow a jailhouse conscience, but in Fayyad it seemed genuine. Even so, his fate was sealed. Ibrahim Fayyad would spend the rest of his life in prison.

The biggest surprise was Vorsalov.

The Russian was cooperating but wasn't making it easy. Charlie decided it wasn't so much a case of evasion as it was one of character. Down to his marrow, Vorsalov was a cold-warrior, and it wasn't in his nature to give up the game.

Understanding that still didn't make what Latham had to do any easier.

He paused at the door to the interview room, took a deep breath, and walked inside. "Morning, Yuri."

Wearing his orange jumpsuit, Vorsalov sat at the table playing chess against himself. "Good morning, Charlie."

"Who's winning?" *Jesus, Charlie, you're supposed to*

hate this guy. What was that saying? "Revenge is a dish best eaten cold."

"No one, really, but I suppose that's the idea." Vorsalov slid the board aside and gestured to the chair. Latham sat down. "So, Charlie, more questions?"

"No, not today. I have some news."

"Judging by your face, it is not good."

"It isn't. Yuri, I was called over to Langley yesterday."

"Ah, the CIA. How is Mr. Mason and company—"

"Yuri, they made a deal."

Vorsalov stopped. "What kind of deal?"

"I didn't know about it. It happened when—"

"What is it, Charlie?"

"The FIS helped us track you in Cyprus, but there was a price tag. After five years, they get you."

Vorsalov stared at Latham for ten seconds. Finally, he nodded. "You knew nothing about it?"

"No. If I had, I wouldn't have—"

"Yes. I believe you, Charlie." Vorsalov chuckled. "We may be on opposite sides, but I always suspected you were a . . . What's the phrase? A stand-up guy." Vorsalov forced a smile and waved his hand in dismissal. "Oh, well. Politics. Who knows, much can happen in five years."

"Yuri, you won't get away."

"I know that."

"Once they get you back—"

"Charlie, I know exactly what they will do to me. You forget, I've done the same to others."

"Yeah, I guess you have. Still, I'm . . . I'm sorry, Yuri." Charlie stood and pushed in his chair. "I'll check in from time to time. Is there anything I can get you?"

Vorsalov thought for a moment, then smiled and slid the chessboard back into the center of the table. "Do you play?"

EPILOGUE

Atsumi Bay, Japan, Five Weeks Later

HIROMASA TAKAGI POURED HIMSELF A SNIFTER OF BRANDY AND walked to the window. Far below he could see the lights of the fishing boats on the bay. He stood for a while longer, finished his drink, then set it on the sideboard and walked into his adjoining office. A single desk lamp lit the blotter on his desk, leaving the corners of the room in shadow. He walked to the chair and sat down.

"Good evening, Mr. Takagi," a voice called from the darkness.

Takagi's head snapped up. "Who is that? Yamora?"

Briggs Tanner stepped forward into the light.

Takagi squinted. "You!" His hand shot toward the phone.

Tanner's hand came up holding a pistol. "Before you do that, I was hoping we could talk. After I'm done, if you still want to call your men, I won't stop you."

"I have no intention of talking to you." Takagi reached.

"Believe it or not," Tanner said, "I didn't come here to shoot you, but if you touch that phone, I will, I promise you."

"We have nothing to talk about."

"I think we do. But it's your choice: Either we talk or I shoot you." Tanner raised the pistol and centered it on Takagi's forehead. "You have five seconds."

"You're insane."

"Four seconds."

"You've made a mistake coming here."

"Three."

"Stop counting, damn it!"

"Two."

"All right! Fine! First, though: Where are my men?"

"I came right through the front door and didn't see a soul."

"You're lying."

"After we're done talking, you can check for yourself."

"I'll do that." Takagi leaned back in his chair. "You have my attention."

Tanner walked to the corner, clicked on the floor lamp, and settled into the leather wing chair. "For the past month I've been thinking about why you started all this. I don't know how you found *Stonefish*, and to be honest, I don't really care. What's been nagging is the *why* of it all. It couldn't have been money."

"Why not?" Takagi said. "What better reason?"

"For a lot of people there is no better reason, but for you . . . Somehow I didn't think so. Excluding money, that left one thing: power. For you, that's the real currency. Power to control, power to manipulate. Everything in life flows from power. How am I doing?"

"Go on."

"I have a friend who loves research. He's happiest when he's hunting for an answer that doesn't want to be found. Its an odd quirk of his, but I love him for it. In fact, he's the one that led me to Parece Kito."

"I wondered how you found it."

"That was him. He's been working on my unanswered questions about you."

"Which are?"

"One, what did you hope to get out of all this? And two, what could possibly be worth helping some madmen incinerate hundreds of thousands of people in a nuclear fireball?"

"You cannot prove that I had anything—"

"I'm not interested in proof. I know you did it, and that's enough for me."

Takagi waved his hand in dismissal. "How nice for you."

"Your greatest ambition is to rule Japan," Tanner said. "Not as prime minister, of course . . . that would come with too many built-in drawbacks. No, you wanted to be pulling the strings from behind the scenes.

"Of the hundreds of contracts you have in the Japanese government, one caught my friend's eye. Four years ago one of your subsidiaries—a security firm—signed a contract to guard and monitor all of Japan's nuclear power plants and disposal sites. It's your company, of course, but the citizenry doesn't know that. As far as they're concerned, the government runs the plants. The government handles pricing, regulation, safety—everything the average citizen is concerned about. And they *are* concerned. More than any nation on earth, Japan knows what nuclear energy can do if a tight rein is not kept on it."

Takagi was shaking his head. Tanner kept going.

"Here's how you saw it happening: Manned by a crew of fanatical Arab terrorists, *Tsumago* sails into Tel Aviv Harbor and vaporizes itself in a fireball. Israel—who you don't care much about—is decimated, and Syria—who you care even less about—rolls into Lebanon to keep the peace, and Iraq gets blamed for the whole thing. All this is fine with you. As far as you're concerned, it's all trivia.

"In the wake of the catastrophe, the world is outraged. Every nation on the planet is shouting for the head of whoever supplied the uranium to make the bomb. The actual construction of it isn't the issue; that's all mechanical know-how and rudimentary physics. The tricky part is getting the feedstock.

"Investigations begin. Intelligence agencies beat the bushes. You're not worried, though. You've insulated yourself. *Toshogu* is gone, Parece Kito is gone, all the people even remotely connected to the project are dead.

"Two months go by. The world still has no clue how it happened. All the investigations have turned up nothing. Of course, they know how big the bomb was and how much material it would have taken to build it, but not much else.

"Until one day," Tanner continued, "when an employee of your security firm happens to find an anomaly during a routine inspection of a plant's feedstock inventory. There's some uranium missing—just enough for the Tel Aviv bomb, in fact.

"The security company blows the whistle. The IAEA is called in. An investigation begins, and the world waits and watches. From there it snowballs, and before long the answer comes out: Through negligence or greed or simple stupidity, the Japanese government is at the root of the worst nuclear disaster in history.

"The Japanese people take to the streets. The ensuing scandal shakes the government to its foundations. Hundreds of heads roll, from the diet to the prime minister's cabinet. The voters demand change. A new party is formed that promises *this will never happen again*. The voters jump on the bandwagon, elections are held, and a new era of Japanese politics is ushered in."

Tanner paused and looked at Takagi, who had grown pale. "Care to guess who's secretly behind this new party?"

"This is all fantasy. You have no—"

"I told you, Mr. Takagi, I'm not interested in proof. The answer to the question is, the newly elected prime minister and his cabinet have been handpicked by you and the Black Ocean Society. In the space of a year, you've dismantled the current government, orchestrated a bloodless coup, and taken over. And now, instead of pulling the strings of your hundreds of companies, you're pulling the strings of an entire country."

Tanner sat back, looked at Takagi for a long ten seconds, then said, "Of course, I'm just guessing about all of this. I could be wrong, but somehow I don't think so."

"You're a wonderful storyteller, Mr. Tanner," said Takagi. "But that's all it is."

Tanner shrugged.

"What happens now?" asked Takagi. "What do you plan to do with this yarn?"

"Nothing. While I don't need proof, without it, none of this will stick."

"True."

"So tell me: How good was my story?"

Takagi paused, then tilted his head. "It was excellent."

"Thank you. You can make that call now."

Takagi reached for the phone. As his fingers touched the

handset, he jerked his hand back. "Ah! Something pricked me!" He stared at the tiny drop of blood on his fingertip.

Takagi's face went pale. His hand began curling itself into a claw. "What's happening?" he murmured. "What have you done to me?" He squealed and clutched his forearm. "Ahhh, God . . ."

"Don't worry," said Tanner. "It's just a mild paralytic agent."

"What!" Takagi croaked.

"It'll wear off in an hour or so."

Tanner's coat pocket trilled. He pulled out his cell phone, listened for a moment, then said, "Thanks, Sconi. You can head back. I'll be along shortly."

His facial muscles frozen and shoulders hunched around his ears, Takagi was sliding deeper into his chair. His eyes flicked up to Tanner. "What are you doing?"

"You and I, Mr. Takagi, are going on a boat trip."

TAKAGI FORCED OPEN HIS EYES AND FOUND HIMSELF STARING UP at the night sky. He felt a breeze blowing over his face. He heard the lapping of water and felt himself rocking. *A boat. Tanner had said something about a boat.* He lifted his hand and stared at it. He flexed his fingers. He felt a residual tingling sensation in them, but otherwise he felt fine.

He forced himself to a sitting position. He looked down at his feet and saw they were cuffed together.

"Feeling better?" Tanner asked, crouched a few feet away.

"Unlock me right now! Where am I?"

Takagi looked around and realized he was surrounded by water. To his left, perhaps five miles away, he could make out the shoreline of Atsumi Bay. He looked over Tanner's shoulder and saw the çonning tower.

"A submarine," he murmured.

Tanner nodded. "Ethan Allen-class. Old, but very quiet."

"What are you doing? You can't kidnap me!"

"I have no intention of kidnapping you."

"Then what?"

Tanner paused for a moment then said, "Let's just say I'm giving you an empirical lesson in the law of cause and effect . . . and irony. Can't forget irony."

"What the hell does that mean?"

In answer, Tanner stood up, walked to the conning tower, retrieved a large canvas rucksack, and returned. He dropped it at Takagi's feet with a *thunk*.

"What's that?" Takagi murmured, wide-eyed.

"A teaching aid."

Tanner stooped over the rucksack and reached inside. Before Takagi could react, Tanner snapped a padlock onto his leg cuffs. "What are you doing?" Takagi kicked wildly, smacking the padlock and chain against the steel deck. "Get this off me!"

Tanner unzipped the rucksack and lifted it away, revealing a fifty-pound cinder block. Takagi stared at the block, then looked up at Tanner. "You can't do this! Do you know who I am?"

Tanner stared down at him. "I know exactly who you are. You're a sociopath and a murderer. And it's going to end here."

"Goddamn it, Tanner, you can't just—"

"I am doing it."

"Please, God! I'm begging you, *please!*"

"Good-bye, Mr. Takagi."

Tanner turned and started walking toward the conning tower.

"Tanner! Damn you! You can't do this! *Tanner!*"

HE PULLED THE HATCH CLOSED, SPUN THE WHEEL, AND TOOK THE rungs to the deck below. Waiting for him was the sub's captain, who frowned, glanced up the ladder, then at Tanner.

"Something wrong, Captain?" Briggs asked.

"I thought . . . Where's our passenger?"

"He couldn't make it."

"Oh." The captain frowned again, then shrugged. "You're the boss. What now?"

Tanner smiled. "Take her down and head south," he replied. "I've got a date in Tahiti with a beautiful, recently retired Israeli secret agent."